Democracy's Missing Arsenal

VOLUME I: 1862-1900

A NATION SUNDERED — A WORLD ENGULFED

DEMOCRACY'S MISSING ARSENAL

Volume One
1862-1900

A NATION SUNDERED, A WORLD ENGULFED

MICHAEL B. KING & JOHN M. BREDEHOFT

Table of Contents

INTRODUCTION

"We must be the great Arsenal of Democracy."
Franklin D. Roosevelt,
Fireside Chat, December 29, 1940

A nd we were, and our world was saved——saved from what Winston Churchill warned would be "the abyss of a new Dark Age made more sinister, and perhaps more protracted, by the lights of perverted science." Moreover, America served as democracy's arsenal three times during the last century. First, we tipped the scales in the struggle with industrialized Prussian militarism. Next, we formed the linchpin of the alliance that vanquished Nazism in Europe and Japanese militarism in East Asia and the Pacific. Finally, we outwaited Soviet Communism in the twilight struggle of the Cold War (perhaps the most difficult of the three, because we also had to avoid the penalty for miscalculation of nuclear holocaust).

But what if there had been no United States of America to step in and revitalize the forces of freedom and democracy at these crucial moments? That is what our work explores: how the history of the twentieth century could have unfolded if the USA had not been able to serve, as FDR put it, as the "the great arsenal of Democracy."

It is our thesis that, as things stood late in the summer of 1862, the chances were no better than even that there would be a *United* States of America to play that role. Yes, there would have been a country by that name. But that country would have shared the North American continent with a second English-speaking union of states, the latter based on the principle that God had willed that white-skinned human beings should hold absolute dominion over black-skinned human beings. In the late summer of 1862, this other English-speaking union, a band of breakaway American states declaring itself the Confederate States of America, was just one battlefield victory away from prevailing in its struggle for independence. Although President Abraham Lincoln had come to recognize that the abolition of slavery must be made a chief war aim of the North's fight to subdue the secessionist South, if the North were to prevail in that fight, he also recognized that he dared not announce emancipation without a Union victory. And that victory had to be against what had become——in the eyes of the world——the Confederacy's chief instrument of war: Robert E. Lee's Army of Northern Virginia. The South was counting on "King Cotton" to compel England and France to intervene and force the North to lift its blockade, which as a practical matter would also force Northern acquiescence in Southern secession. By September of 1862, Paris was champing at the bit to do just that, holding back only because London, the paramount power of the day, had not yet decided to take the step. And the government of Lord Palmerston was awaiting only one more victory by "Bobbie" Lee to prove that the Confederacy was truly a nation worthy of recognition.

Of course, things turned out otherwise. Lee's thrust into the North in September 1862, with the nominal aim of breaking the vital railroad bridge across the Susquehanna at Chambersburg, Pennsylvania, was really designed to bring about a battle with the Army of the Potomac—a battle Lee felt confident he would win, and which Lee and Confederate President Jefferson Davis hoped would convince the British government to intervene. Lee's confidence reflected his belief that he had the measure of his opposite number, George McClellan (who had been recently restored to command of the Army of the Potomac). Hence, Lee's puzzlement when McClellan suddenly moved rapidly against Lee's temporarily divided forces, compelling Lee to pull back at the moment of his planned move into Pennsylvania and setting the stage for what we now know as the Battle of Antietam: still America's bloodiest single day of battle. For while the invigorating effect of perhaps one of the greatest intelligence coups in history had substantially worn off by the morning of that struggle, not even McClellan could manage to throw away completely the advantages his army had that day. McClellan *knew Lee's plan*. And although managing to fight to a tactical draw, Lee was compelled by heavy losses and far superior Union numbers to disengage and withdraw from Maryland, back across the Potomac into Virginia. An emboldened

Lincoln quickly followed up with an Emancipation Proclamation that, combined with Lee's battlefield reverse, caused Palmerston to shelve intervention. This—not Pickett's Charge or Sherman's March to the Sea or Sheridan's Ride—was the true turning point of the War. The South had never been so close to victory before and would never be so close again.

The Battle of Antietam illustrates what we believe to be the highly contingent nature of history: "For want of a nail"—or, in this case, for want of a copy of Lee's General Order No. 191, wrapped around a clutch of fine cigars stuffed into an envelope that apparently slipped from the saddlebag of a Confederate messenger, later to be found by two Union soldiers in a field near Frederick, Maryland. In point of fact, these two young men from Indiana acted promptly and appropriately, and the Lost Order made its way smartly up the chain of command to the Major General commanding. Even though some elements of the Lost Order had already been overtaken by events, its discovery still galvanized McClellan in a way nothing—not even Lincoln, who all but personally kicked McClellan in the pants—had done before or would do again.

But what if those Indiana boys had overlooked the packet, or, perhaps more plausibly, had smoked the cigars and thrown away the "wrapper"? (In point of fact, somebody between the troopers and McClellan *did* smoke the cigars, as only the copy of Lee's order reached McClellan.) No Lost Order recovered by Union troops…no sudden and wholly uncharacteristic quickening of the will of George McClellan; no quickening…no Antietam; no Antietam…and instead, a battle soon after somewhere to the north—and quite possibly with a far different outcome. Yet another Lee triumph, and….

That is our hypothesis, and what follows is our speculation as to the result. We readily acknowledge that others have done as much. What sets this work apart is our focus on the effect of a Confederate victory on international Great Power politics. Our narrative is designed to show that it is beyond American shores where a Southern victory would have had its most important, and—we will argue—most disastrous effect. Two unions based on antithetical social systems, whose relationship arises out of the nation-state equivalent of a bitterly contested divorce—this is a formula for a dramatic acceleration and exacerbation of the international politics of rivalry that brought on the awful bloodletting of the twentieth century. A divided America, fully integrated into the Great Power disputes of the last third of the nineteenth century, would have been a catalyst for war: war not only on the Western Front, but also on the Potomac Front—and the Ohio, Red River, and Rio Grande Fronts. Both American continents would have become battlefields instead of refuges, dooming any hope of the world breaking out of a cycle of Great Power violence, which instead would have ended only when those Powers, including the United States and the Confederacy, annihilated themselves in a final, nuclear war. We firmly believe that Abraham Lincoln was right when he called the United States of America the last—as well as the best—hope of the world. We also believe that this hope would likely have been extinguished in the fall of 1862, if not for the fortuity of a copy of Lee's order of battle falling into Union hands.

We acknowledge that the "what if..." topic of the American Civil War is ground that has been plowed and re-plowed and re-re-plowed again. We have read many of these efforts, and our work has been inspired by a handful among the many. Above all, we acknowledge Winston Churchill's great essay: "If Lee Had Not Won the Battle of Gettysburg." In that essay, the protean mind of Churchill wrote from the perspective of a 1931 in which a Lee *victory* at Gettysburg (on the traditional dates in July 1863) set in motion a series of events culminating in a peaceful resolution of the differences of the European Great Powers, thereby avoiding the catastrophe of our World War One. The importance of Churchill's essay to our work is two-fold. First, he recognized that a Confederate victory would have affected the course of global—not just American—history. Second, Churchill adopted the radically insightful point of view of writing from within the alternate history itself: his (never named) narrator is looking back from the 1931 in which the Confederacy *did* win its fight for independence and wondering how history might have turned out otherwise if the North had triumphed. We have adopted this approach, and we believe it will significantly assist our readers in coming to understand the truly *global* consequences of a failure of the North's effort to suppress the South's rebellion to preserve the institution of chattel slavery.

Democracy's Missing Arsenal is not a novel. It is not a work in which the reader follows fictional characters and through their lives is introduced to a world that might have been. It is a work of narrative history, albeit alternative, written by a historian who was born into a world in which the Confederacy won its fight for independence. Our narrator is trying to explain—to himself, as well as to future generations—how a Confederate victory led within a century to global catastrophe. Those we name are figures from our history, transported to a time in which they might also have lived and—as the reader will see—lived lives changed by the different course of that history. This first volume explores the global impact of a Confederate victory through the end of the nineteenth century; the next two will bring the story to its calamitous conclusion in the fall of 1962.

At this point, we wish to address a question of terminology in the alternate timeline that implicates the (still continuing) controversy in our timeline about how to refer to Americans descended from the black Africans held in slavery until the emancipation effected by Lincoln's Proclamation and the Thirteenth Amendment. The term "Negro" was sometimes used by Frederick Douglass and other liberated slaves during the run-up to the Civil War. But that term had troubling associations, being derived from the Latin languages of several of the European peoples who engaged in enslaving black Africans. By the end of the nineteenth century, the term "Afro–American" briefly eclipsed Negro as the term preferred by American blacks to describe themselves, to be replaced again by Negro by the 1930s. Afro–American enjoyed a brief revival in the 1960s, but it was ultimately displaced by *African*–American, which has come to be the predominant usage by the second decade of the twenty-first century. The narrator of *Democracy's Missing Arsenal*, a white American, will alternate between Afro–American and Negro, for reasons rooted in the development of race relations in the North following the South's victory in the War of Secession—a point we explore during the course of this work.

Which brings us to a still-sensitive issue for many Americans: one's point of view on the American Civil War. The sad truth is that the American Civil War remains unfinished business in America. This first volume of *Democracy's Missing Arsenal* is being published coincident with the Sesquicentennial of the Battle of Gettysburg. And as the opening of the Sesquicentennial of the Civil War so sadly confirmed, Americans are *still* divided over the moral and political lessons of our Civil War. It is literally *astonishing* to us to contemplate that the "leading" citizens of Charleston, South Carolina, would hold in December 2010 a *festive* period costume ball on the 150th anniversary of South Carolina's vote to secede from the

Union. What did these contemporary ball attendees think was the reason for South Carolina's vote to nullify the Union 150 years ago—to vindicate "states' rights"? If so, *what* state right do they think that vote vindicated, other than the claimed right of white-skinned human beings to hold as property their black-skinned fellows?

The reader should understand that we reject emphatically both the Lost Cause vision of the Civil War exemplified by *Gone with the Wind* as well as the "Reconciliationism" that came to define the historical understanding of the Civil War for white Americans—North and South—from the end of Reconstruction until the Civil Rights movement of the 1960s. We believe, with Abraham Lincoln, that America could not permanently endure half slave and half free. We believe that the tolerance of slavery embodied by our Constitution was a betrayal, however expedient, of the promise of equality embodied in the Declaration of Independence, and that the success of the American experiment in democracy required that, at *some* point, slavery had to be abolished in *every* state of the Union. We believe that a Southern triumph in its war for independence would have meant a re-empowerment of the idea that slavery was a morally acceptable form of social and economic organization at the very moment when the survival of slavery internationally was teetering in the balance. And we believe, most emphatically, that the *only* state "right" for which the leaders of the would-be Confederacy pitched the peoples of their states into bloody battle was the right to hold another human being in bondage. The six hundred thousand or more who died in the Civil War did not give their lives in a dispute over tariff reform.

We began crafting our narrative of this alternate—and grim—future in the fall of 1995, soon after returning from a college alumni tour of European sites recalling the fiftieth anniversary of the Allied victory in World War Two. Our stops included the recently reunited city of Berlin, where we took a (somewhat gloating) note of the embassy of the former Soviet Union on the *Unter der Linden*. It was a time when Americans still basked in the afterglow of the end of the Cold War and, looking back as the twentieth century began to wind down, felt great pride in the role our country had played in the tumultuous events of that century. We recognize that events since the tragedy of 9/11 have raised questions in many minds about whether the United States continues to be a force for progress in world affairs. But while we share many of the concerns about the choices the United States has made in the wake of 9/11, we certainly do not agree that Guantanamo or the invasion of Iraq somehow retrospectively prove that the United States *pre-9/11* was nothing more than just another amoral Great Power. We decline to ascribe moral equivalence to Dachau and drones. Whatever the international wrongs of the United States in the years preceding 9/11—and there were many—we believe emphatically that those wrongs pale when considered against the likely course of global events had the Confederate States of America won its independence in the fall of 1862: such that a *United* States of America could not have served, at *the* moment of crisis for human freedom, as the "Arsenal of Democracy."

The authors are both children of the Cold War and the aftermath of American victory in World War Two. One of us grew up in the Bronx: the eldest son of a German-American New York City cop and his second-generation Czech-American bride; his neighborhood resounded with spoken Italian and other dialects, and not a few of his older neighbors bore numbers tattooed on their arms. The other author grew up on the other side of our continent-spanning country: a child of parents whose people—Quaker, Moravian, Huguenot, Scots-Irish—came centuries before to the land that would become the United States of America, all seeking refuge from the tyranny of what used to be familiarly called the "Old World." Both of our lives exemplify the great, traditional vision of the American Dream in which the sons and daughters achieve success: the opportunity for which their parents worked hard to make possible. We believe deeply that our country has been and must remain a force for progress in world affairs.

And we believe perhaps even more deeply in the profoundly democratic notion that history is shaped by the actions of individuals, including many whose names have been lost to historians. The outcome of the American Civil War—and its effect on the course of global history—is a classic illustration of what we believe to be the truth of this idea: that the actions of individuals, and not just those of "great" men or women, can and do make a difference to the course of history. Alternate history, the speculation about how things might have been, is not simply a game for intellectual dilettantes. Asking what might have been is nothing less than asking how things could have turned out differently—for good or evil—had individual human beings made different decisions. It illuminates why citizens of a democracy, in the ever-present "here and now," should recognize that the choices they make as citizens—in conversations with fellow citizens about the issues of the day and in the votes they cast at the ballot box—can contribute to shaping the actions of this country, with very real consequences for human betterment or degradation.

Many, by their insights and indulgence, have contributed to the making of this alternate history. We take this moment to single out our wives, who have put up with the piles of books and the many late-hour drafting sessions over *so* many years. (And as this is only the first volume of a three volume work, and volume three is still very much a work-in-progress, we take this moment to apologize to them in advance for the fact those piles and late-hour sessions will continue for a bit longer.) We also thank the Hon. Danny Boggs, Judge of the United States Court of Appeals for the Sixth Circuit, who somehow found the time in his busy judicial schedule to review and comment on so many drafts. We thank, as well, the late Gary Andrews, who from 1995 through 2006 applied his masterly word processing skills to turn thousands of pages of paper drafts into working Word documents of excellent quality. And we thank one Mike Ralls, whom one of the authors encountered through the marvel of the Internet, and who for several years generously shared his insights and contributed materially to the final shape of our venture into what-might-have-been (most importantly as to the food supply implications of our vision of the Great Power Alliances that dominate the world of *DMA*). And we would be remiss if we did not also acknowledge the superb work of our graphics designer, John Engerman, whose cover powerfully captures the central theme of the book, and who took our rough-and-ready concepts for illustrations and made them look like they really *are* from another history.

Finally, we *dedicate* this book to the memory of our parents and to our children. We thank our parents for having imbued us both with what we believe to be true American values—a love of democracy, and a conviction that democracy fundamentally depends upon a recognition of the right of every human being within that democracy to the same rights and opportunities as are enjoyed by its wealthiest and most privileged members. And we thank our *children* for the chance to share in that unique opportunity that only a parent can have: that sense of responsibility for making every effort a parent can to pass along to their children a society that embodies those values of liberty and equality which *together* make human life worthwhile.

DEMOCRACY'S MISSING ARSENAL—A RETROSPECTIVE LOOK FROM THE VANTAGE POINT OF ANOTHER TIME

The following is a manuscript written by _____, President of the United States of America, 1953-1961. _____ had nearly completed a history of the period 1862-1962 at the time of his death from pneumonia in the third year of the Great Winter following the Final Alliance War. The manuscript is among those preserved in the library of the Society of Learning, located on the slopes of Mt. Washington in the former State of New Hampshire. The Society acknowledges the suzerainty of the Liberty League, which from its administrative locus in Montpelier, former Vermont, controls an area encompassing much of former Upper New England.

1

PORTLAND, MAINE, JANUARY 1963: INTRODUCTION

———

This history will be written by candlelight. Electric power is now reserved for vital defense and industrial installations, and the increasingly erratic availability of oil and coal means even they often go for days without. As for private citizens like myself, we have been plunged back into the world of the nineteenth century and are likely to remain there for the balance of the twentieth.

This history is an attempt to explain how we find ourselves in this predicament. Fortunately, at least assuming the ultimate value to posterity of this narrative, I had begun work on such an effort almost two years before, and the resulting outline, along with most of the primary and secondary source collection, had been left at my summer cottage near Portland when I returned to New York City last September. Had I shipped those materials home as I had originally intended, the present effort would have been rendered impossible by the loss of essential archival materials when New York was destroyed in the initial wave of German missile strikes. As for "we," I mean mankind, not just the denizens of Portland and the rest of Upper New England who have been spared at least the horrors of direct atomic bombardment. The last months have seen a breakdown in the world communications network, so when I write of mankind's present state, I confess I am engaging in extrapolatory speculation. Still, I have no reason to think that we in Upper New England are worse off than people living on the other fringes of the world's military and commercial centers. In fact, what news we receive over the shortwave suggests we may be among the fortunate—certainly better off than anyone in the vicinity of Buenos Aires and Rio de Janeiro, cities which may have the dubious distinction of being the last destroyed by thermonuclear bombardment. I say "last," because I do not think any of the major powers retains the technical capacity for nuclear warfare. Sadly, this development comes too late for my many colleagues and friends in New York City, most of whom undoubtedly died when the city was destroyed; my survival was the product of pure happenstance: a political and business trip to Maine that was scheduled only days before the outbreak of the fourth—but probably final—"World War."

The fact is that no country retains the capacity for conducting warfare based on advanced technology, because mankind has spent the better part of the last one hundred years first creating a magnificent technical civilization and then destroying it in a series of wars, culminating in the catastrophe of last October. Those wars now seem to have run their course, if only because the combatants have so ruined themselves that they lack the ability to continue their struggle—on a worldwide scale, at least. Earlier, I said we have been thrown back into the nineteenth century, but I fear the slide may not stop there. The fragmentary reports of famine and pestilence we receive from every corner of the globe make me think that this is how the Black Death years would have been reported—if there had been shortwave radio in the fourteenth century. (I would have added "and television," except there haven't been network radio or television broadcasts since last October; the destruction of global satellite systems by a series of ASAT strikes, combined with the disruptions caused by EMP throughout both the Northern and Southern Hemispheres, has seen to that.)

So, as we slip back into a life lived by "simpler" rhythms, those of us who had a hand in first creating and then destroying what once promised to be a better life for humanity owe it to the next century and beyond to explain where we went wrong so that this catastrophe is never repeated; for it could have been avoided. In fact, I believe the turning point that set the world on its rendezvous with disaster occurred almost exactly one hundred years ago on the fields of Maryland and Pennsylvania: site of the decisive battles of the American War of Secession. Had Robert E. Lee not triumphed over

George McClellan at Gettysburg in September of 1862, then the North might have (and I think probably *would have*) eventually crushed the South's rebellion. In turn, a Northern victory would have avoided the division of the North American continent between two well-armed, English-speaking confederacies. It was this development that ended the isolation of the Western Hemisphere from the currents of European Great Power politics and set in motion the creation of the global alliance system, whose rivalries plunged the world into the cycle of warfare that has so recently culminated with the destruction of technical civilization.

This is principally a political history. Given the violent nature of international politics over much of the last century, it thus may also qualify as a military history. I admit to lacking a certain facility for the "technical" side of military matters, notwithstanding the familiarity with such things required of any American president during the last several decades. I was too young to serve in World War Two, and my tour of duty in occupied Canada during the early 1920s was bereft of those intense experiences at arms that might have awakened any natural, if dormant, sense of such things. I must also apologize in advance to readers who seek detailed enlightenment about the social, economic, and cultural events of the past one hundred years. While I do address these matters, and in particular do give some detailed attention to the tragic impact of the Confederacy's victory on efforts to suppress the slave trade and extirpate slavery itself, it is the political and military context that forms the primary thread of my narrative. In any case, a social, economic, or cultural history of this century would offer only a grim chronicle of the steady militarization of every aspect of human affairs.

2

1862: LEE'S VICTORY AT GETTYSBURG AND THE ROAD TO DISUNION

Thoughtful readers may look askance at my insistence that the roots of our century's global travails can confidently be fixed in the outcome of one mid-nineteenth-century civil war. Surviving CSA partisans—should they ever have a chance to read this manuscript, which I doubt—undoubtedly will also bridle at the suggestion by a "Yankee" that their country could have lost its war of independence. But just as the British soldier who in 1778 had George Washington in his sights and held his fire may have changed the course of one American rebellion, equally small events could have changed the outcome of another. In fact, as leaders of the North *and* South recognized at the time, 1862 was the crucial year in a war whose outcome was far from assured. Contrary to confident Southern predictions in the winter of 1860, "King Cotton" did not command quick intervention by Great Britain and France. And while a true "cotton famine" had begun to devastate the British textile industries by mid-1862, still London hesitated to intervene. As USA President Abraham Lincoln recognized, slavery had always been the principal stumbling block to English recognition of the Southern Confederacy: Secession War records that survived the 1898 Sack of Washington indicate Lincoln intended to—indeed, had already decided to—issue an "emancipation proclamation" as soon as the Army of the Potomac managed a victory over Lee's Army of Northern Virginia. Had Lincoln done so, and even if the proclamation had been confined to the rebel states, I doubt Lord Palmerston's government would have taken the critical step it did and called for a peace conference to "reconcile" the warring American factions.

But the Army of the Potomac never did beat Lee. In September 1862, Lee launched his invasion of Maryland and Pennsylvania—in retrospect, a risky venture that could easily have produced exactly the Union triumph for which Lincoln waited. Once again, Lee divided his already smaller force, sending General Thomas "Stonewall" Jackson to capture the Union garrison at Harpers Ferry while moving the balance of his forces toward the Maryland–Pennsylvania border. Had McClellan shown the initiative to force the South Mountain passes of Turner's Gap and Crampton's Gap—which were held by only a small Confederate screening force—he would have threatened Lee with defeat in detail. Lee would have been forced to abandon his venture into Pennsylvania and to concentrate his forces for a pitched battle against a much larger Union host. Granted, any resulting contest (perhaps in the vicinity of Sharpsburg, Maryland) might still have seen another Confederate victory on the scale of Second Manassas only a month before—in which case, nothing would have changed. The Army of the Potomac would have been routed, yet again; emancipation would have been postponed; and foreign intervention probably would have proceeded as it actually did: with the same fatal consequences for the cause of reunion.

But a "Battle of Sharpsburg" in which McClellan managed to concentrate his forces and win, or at least force a bloody draw, would likely have compelled Lee to withdraw—indeed, anything but a "Third Manassas" would have compelled Lee to abandon his invasion, lest he forfeit his badly outnumbered army. Lee would have had his rear pinned to the Potomac, along a line running roughly from Harpers Ferry to Point of Rocks (in Maryland). Even in the event of a tactical draw, Lee's untenable position would have forced him to retreat, thereby leaving the field to McClellan. I am certain Lincoln would have seen in such an outcome enough of a "victory" to proclaim emancipation, at least as to the rebel states, which in turn would have put off the threat of foreign intervention until at least the 1863 campaign season. By then, the North would have been able to launch its planned campaign both up and down the Mississippi toward Vicksburg, and I doubt London and Paris would have come in on the side of slavery unless the South managed to maintain its communications with the Trans-Mississippi *and* regained the battlefield initiative against the Army of the Potomac. Considering how the North's undoubted economic edge would have begun to tell, I find it hard to believe the CSA could have managed to win on both fronts—not even Robert E. Lee, after all, could be in two places at once (although Lee might, in such a pinch, have agreed to detach Jackson or James Longstreet to command in the West).

Of course, none of this happened. As Lee recognized, George McClellan was incapable of taking risk. I confess to having developed a real contempt for McClellan. He may have been a brilliant drillmaster who also commanded the loyalty of his troops, but he was hopelessly mismatched in the field against the likes of "Bobbie" Lee. Frankly, I doubt that—short of Lee's plans falling into Union hands—McClellan would have done anything but what he did do: crawl to Frederick, Maryland, and then await news of developments lest he "endanger the army" by a "premature move." Indeed, a review of McClellan's papers from the period before the battle leaves the impression that he was preparing to do nothing so much as find an excuse for defeat. On September 10, 1862, McClellan wired to General-in-Chief Henry Halleck that "[a]ll the evidence …prove[s] most conclusively that almost the entire Rebel army in Virginia, amounting to not less than 120,000 men, is in the vicinity of Frederick City." Not only was McClellan badly outnumbered, he complained, but he was facing the Confederates' "oldest regiments…commanded by their best Generals," who, "with the prestige of their recent successes, will, without doubt, [be inspired] with a confidence which will cause them to fight well." Never one to put too fine a point on things, McClellan asked for more men, "at once"—"at the risk of being considered slow and overcautious."

Of course, McClellan *was* slow and overcautious—two qualities which Lee correctly counted upon. War Department records that survived the 1898 Sack of Washington contain at least two telegrams for each day in September, from McClellan to Lincoln, Stanton, or Halleck, all in one form or another "most respectfully, but strenuously [urging] the absolute necessity, at this critical juncture, of uniting all our disposable forces…. Every other consideration should yield to this[.]"

Unfortunately for his country, McClellan proved a better prophet than general. He at least had some sense that the ensuing campaign would resolve itself in Southern Pennsylvania. On September 10, he telegraphed to Andrew Curtin, the governor of Pennsylvania, "confirming" that 125,000 Confederates were at Frederick, Maryland, and cautioning the governor to concentrate his militia—"all the troops you can"—in the vicinity of Chambersburg and Gettysburg. And that same day he also told General Halleck, "[I]f we should be so unfortunate as to meet with defeat, our country is at their mercy." McClellan would prove disastrously correct on both counts.

The Union garrison at Harpers Ferry was the first to go. Harpers Ferry is surrounded on three sides by commanding heights which make a successful defense against any proper enemy improbable at best. Lee was careful to ensure that the corps commanded by Jackson was sufficiently augmented to constitute a proper enemy. Lee detached some twenty-six of his army's forty brigades to capture Harpers Ferry in order to secure the Army of Northern Virginia's lines of communication for the advance into Pennsylvania. In three wings, commanded by Generals McLaws, Walker, and Jackson himself, Confederate forces surrounded and then captured Harpers Ferry. They bagged—in addition to the garrison's entire complement of infantry and cavalry—some 2,500 Union soldiers who had fled to the supposed security of the town from nearby Martinsburg, hours ahead of Jackson's column. Confederate casualties were entirely negligible, and by September 19, the Army of Northern Virginia (less Brig. Gen. A.R. Lawton's Division, left to guard the aforementioned line of communications) had reunited at Hagerstown, Maryland.

In the meantime, McClellan's forces crawled into Frederick City well after Lee's forces had left; at all times, Lee—on the move—would stay at least a day's march ahead of the Union Army. As important as McClellan's caution was the fact that Lee's reunited forces were screened behind the 1,300-foot wall of South Mountain—the few negotiable gaps strongly defended by Stuart's cavalry. Having secured his line of communication, Lee now moved north, leaving the National Road at Hagerstown and heading toward the lush farmland and provender of the Cumberland Valley. It was not until McClellan received reports of the Army of Northern Virginia approaching Chambersburg, Pennsylvania—thereby threatening the vital

Pennsylvania Railroad Bridge across the Susquehanna at Harrisburg—that he was able to bestir himself, break camp, and order a belated pursuit.

Given McClellan's inexcusable but characteristic delay in responding to Lee's movements, Lee almost certainly would have beaten Union forces to the Susquehanna had Lee stuck to his original plan.

But Lee did not stick to his original plan. One element of Lee's command brilliance (learned courtesy of the USA government, of course) was his ability to abandon his planning: to seize opportunities and to take risks. Southern writers have suggested that the phlegmatic pragmatism of General James Longstreet was often a necessary counterweight to Lee's—and Jackson's—improvisational style; but in this final, decisive campaign of the war, it would be Lee's daring that first and foremost set the stage for the Confederacy's greatest victory. McClellan's forces, shadowing Lee, continued to lag well over a full day's march to the southeast. Moreover, McClellan remained convinced that Lee's forces outnumbered his by a substantial margin. The Union commander was almost paralyzed with apprehension for fear Lee would descend on his flank or on Washington City. "I am fully aware of the threat to east-west communications posed by the Rebels," McClellan telegraphed to an impatient Secretary of War Stanton, "but, as you must recognize, I cannot risk a strike by the enemy's superior forces against even more vital targets." In other words, McClellan's almost pathological fear of a chimerical Confederate superiority had convinced him that the "Republic's Savior"—i.e., himself—could prevent the fall of Washington only by acting with the greatest caution. At a time when daring might have led to victory, McClellan's timidity would instead sunder his country.

J. E. B. Stuart's reconnaissance reports, detailing the Army of the Potomac's glacial pace, prompted Lee to formulate his audacious plan to bring McClellan to battle. The plan was brilliant in its simplicity: a sharp turn to place the Army of Northern Virginia in a position that would force McClellan onto the tactical offensive. McClellan might reasonably assume that Lee would continue his movement due north from Chambersburg, foraging up the Cumberland Valley toward the military installations at Carlisle Barracks, or toward Harrisburg, the Susquehanna, and the strategic railroad facilities there. Lee confounded these "reasonable" assumptions by wheeling the bulk of his forces ninety degrees to the east: Jackson's entire Corps, together with elements of Longstreet's Corps and the lion's share of Stuart's cavalry, advanced from Chambersburg east along the Chambersburg Road. Transiting South Mountain at Cashtown Gap, this force made for the crossroads town of Gettysburg, Pennsylvania. At the center of a web of excellent roads, Lee's presence at Gettysburg allowed the Army of Northern Virginia simultaneously to threaten Philadelphia, Baltimore, and Washington. (Indeed, given McClellan's known penchant for seeing Rebels behind every tree, Lee might reasonably have expected McClellan to fear a simultaneous Confederate *move* on Philadelphia, Baltimore, *and* Washington.) Given the slow pace of McClellan's advance, the Confederates at Gettysburg would actually stand between McClellan and Baltimore as well as between McClellan and the more distant Philadelphia. Placing the Army of Northern Virginia at the Gettysburg road junction, therefore, would force McClellan to attack. Anything less would be politically unacceptable to McClellan's political superiors and could lead to his removal even at so desperate a moment—something of which McClellan would be all too aware and which the astute Lee could easily surmise.

Thus Lee intended to precipitate the battle he sought, to show the Union—and even more importantly, to show Great Britain and France: that the Confederacy could take the war into the North. Of course, Lee's plan involved substantial risk. In the face of a numerically superior force (although one whose commander believed to be numerically *inferior*), Lee divided his own. Yet, Lee remained justifiably confident of the outcome, principally because he believed McClellan to be constitutionally incapable of taking the sort of decisive action necessary to effect a defeat of the Confederates in detail.

In the event, Lee's judgment proved sound—from the Union perspective, disastrously so.

Once again, Jackson's men earned their sobriquet of "foot cavalry," gained earlier that year in the Shenandoah Valley campaigns. Stonewall Jackson's Corps of the Army of Northern Virginia made quick work of its return from Harpers Ferry, combining with the remainder of the Army of Northern Virginia and permitting Lee once again to exercise command over all of his forces. To replace Ewell's Division under A. R. Lawton, which

Jackson left at Harpers Ferry along the Confederate lines of communications, Lee detached D. R. Jones's division from Longstreet at Chambersburg and seconded it to Jackson. Thus, as he moved to occupy the strategic crossroads town of Gettysburg, Jackson disposed of four divisions of infantry: those commanded by D. R. Jones, by J. R. Jones, by D. H. Hill, and the "Light Division" under A. P. Hill. Jackson's men moved smartly to the town, making the forty-six miles from Hagerstown to Gettysburg in just thirty hours. Coming upon Gettysburg from the northwest and finding the advance still unopposed (even by local militia), Jackson pushed through the town proper and deployed his forces on the superb defensive ground immediately to the south. Grounded in the north on Culp's Hill, in the south on a granite spur now known as Little Round Top, and curving along an elevated ridge passing through and south of the town cemetery, this barb-shaped line offered Jackson—by disposition, biased to the offensive—an outstanding defensive position.

The rapidity with which Jackson redeployed these four divisions from Harpers Ferry and Chambersburg, arriving on the evening of the twenty-first and ready to greet the advance elements of the Army of the Potomac on the morning of the twenty-second of September, was *the* defining factor in the Confederate victory at Gettysburg. The presence of Jackson's troops before the Union column arrived and McClellan's continuing refusal to believe, for two critical days, that Jackson could have moved his Corps so rapidly, explain (if they do not excuse) McClellan's crushing defeat. Since that defeat was, I believe, the proximate cause of the dissolution of our Federal Union, it makes sense to examine in some detail McClellan's abject failure at the Battle of Gettysburg. We are fortunate indeed that the Official Records of the War of Secession were collected and printed prior to the Sack of Washington, for historians have available to them a wealth of primary source data on that campaign that, sadly, is denied to us for many subsequent chapters of the historical record. And the plethora of reports and correspondence, orders, and acknowledgements make it plain that George B. McClellan was simply not up to the task of commanding an army—much less the most important army in the nation—during the most critical battle in the struggle for the continuing life of that nation.

Jackson has been immortalized as the personification of the offensive: of sharp, slashing, unexpected attack. Yet he also possessed a keen eye for ground and a firm appreciation of the benefits to rifled musketry of fighting on the tactical defensive. Moreover, Lee, Longstreet, and Jackson thoroughly discussed, and agreed upon, the aim of forcing McClellan to attack during the next phase of the campaign. Each of these able commanders recognized that their forces were badly outnumbered, and each had seen first-hand the benefits accruing to men defending even the most modest of field entrenchments.

Lee's orders to his Corps commanders now reiterated the injunction to offer battle on the defensive, and no sooner had Jackson reached Gettysburg, than he decided the town itself was no place to fight a defensive battle. The town was flanked by open fields, and an enemy force attacking the town would operate on good exterior lines of communication. A Confederate force defending the town would be cut off from its lines of communication and retreat. In sum, Gettysburg itself was no place to fight a battle; but the high ground and wooded ridges south of the town itself offered *superb* defensive positions. Jackson ordered his troops through the town. Immediately south of the center of the town lies a steep hill crowned by a cemetery, and Jackson ordered A. P. Hill to occupy and fortify it. The vista to the south was dominated by two large hills or small mounts: the larger one, which we call today Big Round Top, was covered with dense forest and brush. The lower, and northernmost, of the two was the site of logging operations and, although not entirely cleared, offered a commanding position for artillery. This was Little Round Top, and Jackson placed the division of D. Harvey Hill upon it. Conscious of the strength of Little Round Top, Jackson assigned a fair portion of his Corps artillery reserve to support Harvey Hill and, in a move that would determine the opening course of the battle, detached J. L. Kemper's brigade from D. R. Jones and sent it to Harvey Hill. The remainder of D. R. Jones's brigades bivouacked in reserve; Jackson's old division—now under J. R. Jones—defended the middle of the Confederate position between Cemetery Hill and Little Round Top. (I have often daydreamed about how history might have unfolded had Jackson been less precise in his orders to these divisional commanders: the two generals Hill and the two generals Jones.)

Thus it came to pass that, late in the day of the twenty-first, Kemper's Brigade came south to support Harvey Hill. Harvey had no place to put Kemper's force. He suggested to J. L. Kemper that he find "some useful work" for his brigade. James Lawton Kemper was a young brigadier general: still shy of forty years old at the time of the battle. Notwithstanding his youth, he had already made his mark. A graduate of Washington College in Lexington, Virginia and a veteran of the adjoining drill fields at the Virginia Military Institute, Kemper had practiced as a lawyer in pre-war Virginia. Early on, he had turned his ambition to politics, winning five terms in the Virginia House of Delegates. Indeed, at the time of the battle of Gettysburg, Kemper was (albeit absentee) the Speaker of the Virginia House of Delegates. He had commanded the 7th Virginia Regiment at Williamsburg and First Manassas. On the Peninsula, A. P. Hill wrote that Kemper had been "conspicuous throughout for his daring and energy." At Second Manassas, he temporarily took command of the division. In short, when Harvey Hill suggested he find "some useful work," Kemper was not the kind of man inclined to seek a comfortable or conventional billet for his men.

Kemper now took his brigade of Virginians for a walk across the fields to the west of Little Round Top, toward the Emmitsburg Road. We do not know precisely how many men Kemper brought with him—he commanded five regiments of Virginia infantry, but the entire complement of D. R. Jones's Division in September 1862 was barely 2,400 men; perhaps seven or eight hundred rifles came with Kemper. He was a politician, yes, but Kemper could also read a map as well as anyone, and he knew that the Union Army's approach to Gettysburg would be northward up the Emmitsburg Road. That road ducks into the woods on Warfield Ridge, and emerges from the tree line in short order. Kemper discovered a slight depression in the ground (about 1,500 feet north of the place) where the road exits the wood. The declivity was too shallow even to be noticed from the road and not deep enough to shelter a standing man. But for a man lying on the ground—his rifle loaded and primed—it was another matter. Kemper made sure his men were emplaced on the morning of September 22.

Meanwhile, McClellan's forces reflected the slow and deliberate pace that characterized the thought processes of their generalissimo. McClellan had not only Corps and Divisional commands but had superimposed yet another level of organization on the ponderous beast he had birthed. Three "wings" of the Army of the Potomac had been declared. The Right Wing, comprising the First and Ninth Corps, was commanded by Major General Ambrose Burnside. The Left Wing, commanded by Major General Franklin, consisted of Franklin's own Sixth Corps and the one-division "Fourth Corps" of General Darius Couch. It fell to the Center Wing of the army to lead the advance northward, up the Emmitsburg Road, in plodding pursuit of Lee and his army.

The Center Wing created by McClellan was commanded by the superannuated Major General Edwin V. Sumner, a capable and intelligent officer whose best days were, unfortunately, well behind him. Sumner's Second Corps combined with the Twelfth Corps under Major General Joseph Mansfield to form the Center Wing. Sumner's friends and troops alike called him "Bull Head"—both for his booming voice and for the legend that a musket ball once had bounced off his skull. Born during the presidential administration of George Washington, Sumner was only eight years younger than the United States Constitution itself and the oldest officer to command a corps for any army during the war. During the battle at Williamsburg earlier in the year, and in McClellan's absence, Sumner exercised command over the Union troops—to no conclusive result and to McClellan's intense displeasure. With characteristic understanding and reserve, McClellan wrote to his wife that Sumner "was even a greater fool than I had supposed." It speaks volumes for McClellan's failure to anticipate battle that day that he nonetheless selected Sumner's Corps to march at the head of the Army of the Potomac as it entered the environs of Gettysburg late in the morning of September 22.

Sumner himself did not expect to do battle that day. He was, after all, marching on a well-maintained road through a pleasant rural community in Pennsylvania—not through the hostile territory of secessionist Virginia. Sumner had not been alerted that any threat lay ahead. McClellan had dispatched the Union cavalry to the southwest, in a vain attempt to probe through the South Mountain at Turner's Gap and locate Lee—Lee, whom McClellan still believed to be many miles and a mountain range away from Gettysburg. Sumner had not thrown out scouts, nor had he sent advance parties toward Gettysburg. He was re-deploying his forces through friendly territory. They passed in marching formation: in column and not in line abreast. It looked for all the world like a grand parade. Many men would pay for that insouciance with their lives.

At the very head of the entire Union force marched the 108th New York, followed by the 14th Connecticut, and then the men of the 130th Pennsylvania—most of them from York or Cumberland Counties, now back on the soil of their home state. They were raw troops, by and large: the Connecticut men had mustered in late in August; the Pennsylvania regiment, earlier that same month. And being new regiments, they comprised huge formations not yet winnowed by battle. The 14th Connecticut alone had over one thousand men on its roles that day; all had been civilians six weeks earlier. This was the Second Brigade of the Third Division of the Second Corps of the Center Wing of the Army of the Potomac. They were proud of their new-found skill of keeping formation as they marched. They marched up the Emmitsburg Road. They marched into the woods on Warfield Ridge. They marched out of the woods toward the shallow dip in the landscape where Kemper's men lay: five hundred yards...three hundred yards...one hundred yards.... Then came the shouted command: "Rise and fire!" Hundreds of Virginians leaped up as one, leveled their guns, and pulled their triggers. And the front ranks of the Second Brigade of the Third Division of the Second Corps dissolved into a thin red mist.

Confederate surprise was so complete—the astonishment of the Union troops so profound—that what had just happened simply did not register with the boys from Connecticut and New York and Pennsylvania. The blue-clad figures milled around in confusion while Kemper's officers urged their men to re-load. A second, albeit somewhat more ragged, volley tore into the Union ranks. Then, as if opposing poles on a pair of magnets, the forces parted. On the one side, and by pre-arrangement carefully communicated through the ranks, Kemper's Brigade, having loosed their second shot, withdrew entirely unscathed. They fell back into the Rose Woods, then across a wheat field, and finally toward the safety of Little Round Top. The Rose Woods also sheltered the Wise County (Virginia) artillery who, unmasked now and free to fire, poured canister rounds into the Union troops, literally blowing them backward as dried leaves before a storm. And from the teeth of that storm ran the northern men, in a well-deserved panic, running into the trailing formations to the south, infecting them with the same fear.

General William French, commanding the Third Division, had not yet passed out of the woods on Warfield Ridge and thus had not seen the square of land known thenceforward as the "Slaughter Pen." But he could see his Division dissolving before his eyes. His first and third brigades, men somewhat more experienced than those now bleeding in the fields before them, fell backward along the road, knocking their slower compatriots to the ground. Blind panic communicated itself down the ranks. It was some time before General French and his officers realized that neither the Devil nor the entire Confederate Army was on their tails. In the meanwhile, Major General John Sedgwick deployed the three brigades of his Second Division into the tree line, extending northwest and then southeast from the Emmitsburg Road, providing a secure base within which the Union troops might take stock.

McClellan's first fatal error was allowing Lee to get the Army of Northern Virginia athwart his communications with the north, forcing the Union commander to let his army be brought to battle at a time and place of his enemy's choosing. Now, McClellan compounded his error by frittering away the Union advantage in numbers, ordering repeated attacks by II Corps, the fraction of the army closest to Gettysburg. A bolder commander immediately would have risked exposing his left flank, slipping east to envelop Jackson's own left flank from the south. But McClellan was not a bolder commander, and this defining character would prove fatal to Union hopes.

The prompt disappearance of Kemper's Brigade from his front and the cession of firing convinced General Sumner that his men had stumbled across a raiding party or, at most, the rear guard of some small formation. He so reported to McClellan, and McClellan responded by ordering Sumner to press forward up the road, taking the high ground to his right and clearing his flanks. This order was the genesis of the movement which devolved into the repeated attacks on Little Round Top which comprised the remainder of the First Day's fighting. The army could not press up the Emmitsburg Road until the Confederate troops to the east of the road had been driven off. Yet, those troops were anchored firmly amid the rocky heights, and they now revealed their presence by a devastating bombardment from those heights. What began as a sweep to clear the eastern flank of the road became a series of increasingly bloody frontal attacks on what proved to be an impregnable Confederate position. The remnants of the Second Corps led the way. Sumner ordered in his First Division under General Israel Richardson, but Richardson's troops made it no farther than the jumble of boulders now called the Devil's Den. (A handful of them made it through the rocks to the small creek now known as Bloody Run—but not beyond the creek.) Richardson himself never realized the full extent of their failure, since his right arm was taken off by a shell at the shoulder, and he died on the field. His successor commanding the First Division, John Caldwell, had no more success in "clearing the flanks"; shot through the leg, Caldwell at least managed to survive the day. Piecemeal over the course of the next four hours, Sumner fed formation after formation into the meat-grinder at the foot of Little Round Top—to no avail. Twelfth Corps (the other unit making up the Center Wing) was no more successful than Second Corps in achieving their shared objective when it was thrown into the fight. Twelfth Corps commander Joseph Mansfield was felled by a sniper's bullet. He was replaced by Alpheus Williams from his First Division; General Williams's replacement, Samuel Crawford, commanded First Division for fifteen minutes before he was killed by a shell fragment. The Second Division of the Twelfth Corps lost two of its three brigade commanders in trying to ascend Little Round Top. The Union thrust failed.

That the Union attack on the First Day failed was due in equal measure, I think, to the initial disorientation effected by Kemper, and to the decision by Jackson to send his Corps-level artillery reserve to the summit of Little Round Top. Harvey Hill's infantry were never warmly pressed that day; the Reserve Artillery under Sandy Pendleton committed the slaughter almost on its own. Each Union advance was shattered as soon as it left cover. G. T. Anderson's Brigade, sent down from the reserve division commanded by D. R. Jones, picketed the thick brush of Big Round Top against the possibility of a flanking attack, but none materialized. It appears that the Union commanders conceptualized their repeated frontal assaults on Little Round Top as a flank attack—an attack to clear the flank of the Emmitsburg Road for further advance—and apparently it never crossed McClellan's nor Sumner's mind to swing south of Little Round Top. So heavy was the slaughter imposed by Pendleton's artillery, that Kemper was allowed to take his men—most of whom had never even worked up a sweat, and who had hardly been under fire all day even when they poured fire on the advancing units of Sumner's Corps—to rest east of the Round Tops at the Denner Farm.

The carnage on September 22 left Sumner a broken man. His "Center Wing" was more than decimated. Generals Mansfield, Crawford, and Richardson were dead. General Thomas Meagher, commander of the Irish Brigade, was dead. Indeed, eight of his fourteen brigade commanders had been killed or seriously wounded. Two entire batteries of the 1ˢᵗ Rhode Island Light Artillery had been captured intact while trying to gain a site to fire on the Confederates. Thousands of Union men lay dead, dying, or wounded along the road or in the waters of Bloody Run. Sumner resigned his commission that evening, leaving John Sedgwick to command the remnants of Second Corps. Sedgwick deployed the remainder of the Center Wing in a rough east–west defensive line, anchored on a refused flank by Big Round Top, and waited for the morning.

And what of McClellan in all this? For much of the day he was a dozen miles or more distant at Taneytown, ensuring that his orders to Fitz-John Porter's V Corps—to act as a "strategical reserve"—were carried out. They were: Porter's men saw no action that day or any other during the battle. Porter remained at his headquarters in the country house of Antrim, apparently meditating on the necessity of preserving "the last reserve of the last army of the Republic" from any damage. Late in the day, McClellan was miles to the south in Emmitsburg itself, presiding over a "Grand Council" of his commanders to plan his assault for the morrow.

What was that plan? Even after a full day of failed attacks against Little Round Top, McClellan refused to believe that he had encountered any substantial portion of Lee's army. His men had identified Kemper's Brigade at the ambuscade along the road—Kemper's Brigade, from D. R. Jones's Division, part of Longstreet's Corps. In reaching to the foot of Big Round Top, Union forces had identified G. T. Anderson's Brigade—again, from D. R. Jones's Division of Longstreet's Corps. McClellan had been informed of the surrender of Harpers Ferry to Jackson's men, and he was morally certain that Jackson—at any rate—was still far from Gettysburg. The evidence, he declared, pointed to only one conclusion: that Lee had committed the unthinkable military blunder of splitting his force. Only Longstreet was at Gettysburg—perhaps only a portion of Longstreet's Corps!—and here was the opportunity to smash Longstreet in detail, before Jackson could arrive from Harpers Ferry.

As the evening of the twenty-second gave way to full night, McClellan announced to his council of war that he had decided to obliterate Longstreet's men by re-enacting the Battle of Cannae. Like Hannibal in 219 BC, McClellan declared, he faced an enemy with more than twice as many men. Like Hannibal, he declaimed, he would execute a double-encirclement of the enemy, compensating for his lack of numbers by superior skill and strategy. There was no dissent. One wonders if, had the clear-thinking John Sedgwick been there instead of at the battle line, he would have reminded McClellan that, while the Romans were defeated at Cannae, Hannibal and Carthage eventually lost the Punic Wars, and the fields of ruined Carthage were sown with salt.

On the route of the march northward to Pennsylvania, Burnside's Right Wing had followed the Center Wing. Burnside had come up, and now McClellan ordered the Right Wing sent against the northern end of the Confederate line: the Confederate right. McClellan ordered his Left Wing, the last to reach the field, to hit the Confederate left. (Thus, the Left Wing would constitute the Union right, while equally confusingly, the Right Wing would attack from the Union left.) First and Ninth Corps, under the overall command of Ambrose Burnside, would move west behind the concealing ridges and tree lines, then north to the main Pike into town, and then back east through the town to exit southward and hit Cemetery Hill. Sixth and Fourth Corps, the Left Wing, had a simpler and far shorter route to cover: they would move due east from the Emmitsburg Road, slide to the south of Big Round Top, and attack up the road into the rear of the prior day's Confederate position. The two Union pincers were to meet in the rear of the center of the Confederate formation, while the battered remnants of II and XII Corps under Sedgwick held the Union center. It was not a fundamentally flawed plan—as plans by McClellan went. It was complex, but many complex plans have worked. It sought to take advantage of a perceived split in the enemy forces by ordering his own forces actually to split, but that could be borne. The forces holding the center were too weak, but every commander wishes to have more forces. McClellan's basic flaw—in this plan as all else—was hubris. He perceived himself as more accomplished than the enemy commander. He planned to act while neglecting to anticipate what actions his opponent might take in the meanwhile. And he simply did not believe that the enemy commander could have brought all of his forces together—did not believe that Jackson could have arrived from Harpers Ferry—since he, the "Young Napoleon," could not have made the trip so quickly.

McClellan's hopes for his grand encirclement did not survive the morning of September 23, the Second Day of the Battle of Gettysburg. The three divisions of the Left Wing smartly moved eastward into position and were ready to attack the approaches to Little Round Top from the southeast by an hour after dawn. They did so: Generals Slocum and Baldy Smith of Franklin's VI Corps sending their men in on a well-coordinated assault, with Couch's IV Corps division in reserve. But they could not break through. The main Union thrust consisted of ranks anchored on their extreme left by the forested tangle of Big Round Top—home to dispersed units of G. T. Anderson's Brigade, five regiments from Georgia, fighting independently by companies and squads. The dense woodland, steep slopes, and aggressive Georgians made it impossible to move any appreciable body of organized troops over Big Round Top. But neither could the Confederates mount a coordinated attack over that ground, and the prominence acted as a hinge to the Union lever of troops. Advancing over the cleared land of the Plank and Weikert homesteads, the Sixth Corps formations suffered as men were forced to avoid trees, splash through small streams, and forge onward across land sloping severely down and to their right. The closer the Union ranks came to Little Round Top, the clearer the line of sight for Confederate batteries concealed in the woods at the foot of the hill.

But the chief impediment to the progress of the Sixth Corps—and later to Darius Couch's reinforcement of those formations—was the presence of a substantial body of entrenched Southern infantry athwart their line of advance. Sixth Corps was not advancing into the undefended rear of a single division on Little Round Top. Rather, the defenses were manned by two full divisions deployed forward. By dint of battle flag and occasional close contact, Sixth Corps identified A. P. Hill's Division as well as Jackson's Division under J. R. Jones in strong defensive array—not just the expected rear guard from the force on Little Round Top. But these were *Jackson's* men—what were they doing *here*?

What, indeed? As we know, McClellan had been badly mistaken when he calculated that Jackson was still on his way from Harpers Ferry. Jackson's Corps, augmented by an additional division, had in fact beaten every Yankee unit to Gettysburg by almost a full day. Lee himself reached Gettysburg in the early evening of the First Day and established his head-quarters in a plain farm house to the east of Cemetery Ridge. As the major portion of Longstreet's Corps arrived during the evening and night, Lee and his two corps commanders personally oversaw the disposition of the troops. Perhaps the most important role was given to Stuart's cavalry, which was directed to range to the south of the field and to detect and pre-vent a possible flanking move by Union forces that might attempt a move-ment to the south and east. (No less than McClellan was Lee concerned with the ultimate disposition of his forces after the battle; the foreor-dained result of every raid is a withdrawal to friendly country, and Lee was acutely aware of the difference between his "raid" and an "invasion.") In point of fact, Stuart's men performed magnificently and during the Second Day actually screened McClellan from his own reserves, V Corps under Porter at Taneytown, Maryland (about ten miles from Emmitsburg and some eighteen road miles from Gettysburg). But to return to the action at hand: Walker's Division moved through the town and replaced A. P. Hill on Cemetery Hill, allowing Hill to redeploy south to protect the rear of the army. Hood's Division moved through the town in darkness and replaced Jackson's Division in the center, which similarly redeployed south. So when the Union attack began, on a front of two divisions with a third in reserve, it met entrenched veterans of equal number, supported by artillery as well as by Harvey Hill's Division higher up the slope.

The steady return of fire from the front, the sniping from the Georgia troops on their left, and the general downward slope of the land to the right, conspired to push the Northern attack at an angle—away from their objective of the rear of Lee's position immediately beyond Little Round Top. These same forces had the effect of drawing out and extending the exposed right flank of the attack in the direction of Denners' Farm—the same Denners' Farm at which Kemper's men had been relaxing since their encounter on the First Day. This well-organized unit formed, turned, and delivered repeated volleys into the extreme right flank of the Union lines.

The Sixth Corps did not crumble, and it did not run. General Franklin had entrusted his right flank to the brigade commanded by Brig. Gen. Winfield Scott Hancock, one of the outstanding officers of the war. Hancock was able to refuse his flank and retrieve the situation, avoiding panic and preventing Kemper from rolling up the line. But the Union assault had been blunted. Franklin tried again twice before sunset, hammering on the Confederate gate, but despite heavy Union casualties, the Southern line held.

At the extreme northern end of the battlefield, things had developed much more slowly—and even less successfully—for the Union. For this prong of his planned envelopment, McClellan had detailed much larger Union forces, totaling seven divisions. In addition, two brigades of cavalry had deployed, dismounted, in the trees across from the Confederate lines. These troopers screened the right flank of Burnside's huge column as it made its way northward along the banks of Willoughby Run and parallel farm tracks and roads. (The utter lack of sophistication in McClellan's thinking on the use of cavalry is revealed by his written order to Alfred Pleasanton, commanding the Cavalry Corps, in detaching these troops. McClellan warned Pleasanton not to "expose" his batteries of horse artillery lest they be attacked—and only in a *postscript* added, "P.S. Can you do any good by a cavalry charge?" McClellan's inability to utilize his cavalry effectively would prove a disaster on the Third Day.) Burnside aimed at Herr's Tavern, where a main north–south road entered the Chambersburg Pike. McClellan had ordered Burnside to move west out of sight of the Confederates and march north across the Confederate front, screened by trees and ridges. Burnside was to turn east on the Chambersburg Pike, enter the town of Gettysburg from the west, and then debouch on the Confederate rear behind the cemetery and across Culp's Hill. The plan had the benefit of coherence, but it was too ambitious by half. It would require

Hooker and Burnside to move their seven entire divisions the length and breadth of the field—secretly and largely in the dark—along farm tracks and a single badly paved road. The plan then assumed these seven divisions would pass silently through the town itself—without anyone raising an alarm—to fall upon the unsuspecting Confederates south of town, who would *still*, in any event, have been holding the high ground, which they would have had two days to fortify. It was perhaps well for the men of the I and IX Corps that they never got close to the town of Gettysburg, for while McClellan had been sitting in council, Longstreet and his men had been marching.

They arrived in the late evening of the twenty-second. As previously described, two of his four divisions—Walker and Hood—moved through the town to assume defensive positions, freeing Jackson's and A. P. Hill's Divisions to form their line south of Little Round Top, where they would stop the Left Wing on the Second Day. Longstreet's remaining two Divisions took up defensive positions along the Chambersburg Pike—the same road they had used to come in from the Cashtown Gap and the route Burnside intended to sneak along in the morning. Longstreet had not neglected his scouting.

In point of fact, when the lead elements of Burnside's forces finally reached toward the Chambersburg Pike in the mid-afternoon of September 23 (the Second Day), they found these two full divisions of Confederates barring the way. The four brigades of McLaws's Division were commanded by men of the highest caliber: Kershaw, Barksdale, Semmes, and Cobb. The central role of blocking the Pike itself devolved on Joseph Kershaw (a lawyer by trade), from South Carolina, together with over two thousand men of his brigade. These men had captured Maryland Heights at Harpers Ferry and were veterans. William Barksdale was a firebrand from Mississippi: a former US Congressman, commanding sixteen hundred riflemen. Howell Cobb, although commanding a mere brigade, possessed influence beyond his formal rank. He had already served as the Speaker of the House of Representatives of both the United States and the Confederate States, as Governor of Georgia, and as Secretary of the Treasury under US President Millard Fillmore. His command included Cobb's Georgia Legion, a force raised by his brother Thomas, an attorney and would-be historian. Paul Jones

Semmes was a plantation owner and banker, a graduate of the University of Virginia, and the former quartermaster for the state of Georgia. McLaws's Division was supported by the six brigades of Richard Anderson's Division, which included the Virginia brigade of Lewis Armistead. Longstreet had also detached a substantial portion of his Corps' artillery reserve, including the smartly turned-out and effective Washington Artillery from New Orleans—four companies under the command of Colonel J. B. Walton. This unit traced its heritage back to Spanish militia forces organized in Louisiana in 1730. Their battalion motto was "Try me."

When the First Division of the Ninth Corps, under General Orlando Wilcox, turned into the main road, they expected an unimpeded march into the town. They were rudely shocked to find themselves opposed by McLaws and Anderson, entrenched on McPherson's Ridge. Yet Burnside and, particularly, Hooker proved levelheaded and effective. The two Confederate divisions had the advantage of position and surprise. The seven Union divisions had the advantage of…well…seven divisions. The Confederates were pressed hard all through the afternoon and evening and into the night. Hooker's Corps, traveling slightly behind and to the east of Burnside, was able to launch a series of oblique attacks on the southern edge of the Confederate lines. These attacks managed to leverage McLaws out of successive defensive positions, slowly forcing the main Confederate line of resistance back toward the town of Gettysburg throughout the late afternoon and evening. The primary debility imposed upon the Northern forces during these attacks was the temporary incapacity of Hooker, who was shot through the shoulder late in the day. Hooker would recover completely but remained *hors d'combat* for the remainder of the battle, replaced in Corps command by his effective subordinate, George Meade. When the fighting petered out around nine o'clock, the Southern forces had been pushed back from McPherson's Ridge to Seminary Ridge, but they had barred the Union corps from entry to the town. Burnside's troops had moved too slowly and had needed to march too far to force the issue on the Second Day. Moreover, they confronted the Confederates on a relatively narrow front, where the Union numerical superiority could not be brought to bear effectively. Tactically, Burnside's flank attack was not a disaster for the Union—the Union, rather, had the better of it in the fighting along and between the ridgelines; nevertheless, it was a gross operational failure. The Northern forces never even reached the town—much less approached their ultimate target on Cemetery Hill. On McClellan's orders, Burnside's and Hooker's forces drew back. McLaws, who had been working feverishly to fortify the Seminary Ridge, withdrew to the town limits and, later, to Cemetery Hill. Lee moved Anderson's men, less used in the day's fighting, into reserve on Culp's Hill.

Two days of hard fighting had left the Confederates everywhere in possession of the field. Lee's calculations had been correct. By placing the Army of Northern Virginia between McClellan and Philadelphia or Baltimore, Lee forced McClellan to assume the tactical offensive. McClellan's mistaken but confident initial belief that he faced only a portion of Lee's forces led him to accept battle on Lee's terms. Moreover, Lee's casualties on the First Day had been negligible, while McClellan's were significant and everywhere obvious. The plain and apparent nature of the Union wounds pummeled morale. Kemper's men had fired and withdrawn almost without a shot returned in their direction. The carnage wrought on the remnants of II Corps had been done largely by artillery. On the Second Day, the battle was hard-fought on both sides, but again, it was the Confederates who fought from behind field fortifications and the Union troops who were forced to advance through fields and dells; the Northern casualties were, accordingly, disproportionately high. (In point of fact, despite his casualties, McClellan substantially outnumbered Lee at the start of the campaign, at the end of the campaign, and at every point in between.)

The failure of his planned Battle of Cannae left McClellan badly shaken; his comments to his commanders on the Third Day verged on the apocalyptic. McClellan was acutely aware of the extent of his casualties and his inability to dislodge the Confederates from their position astride his line of communications with Baltimore and Philadelphia. He had lost contact with Fitz-John Porter and his reserve. McClellan's continuing wild overestimation of Confederate numbers convinced him that Lee intended to leave ample forces to hold him here, at Gettysburg, while at the same time moving against Harrisburg and Philadelphia. Of McClellan's infantry corps commanders on the field, Mansfield was dead, Hooker wounded, Porter incommunicado, and Sumner debilitated and out of action. Burnside, who had been an effective divisional commander but who was a man acutely conscious of his own limitations, insisted to all who would listen that he would personally lead a charge against the Confederate entrenchments—perhaps hoping by this offer to be spared more expansive responsibilities on the day of battle he knew loomed ahead. More than a score of brigade or divisional commanders were dead or wounded. Thousands of dead and dying Union soldiers still littered the field. In the early afternoon of the Second Day, before it became clear that Burnside would not reach the town, McClellan telegraphed to General-in-Chief Henry Halleck that he was "in the midst of the most terrible battle of the war, perhaps of history—thus far it looks well, but I have great odds against me." McClellan concluded his missive with the thought, "It will be either a great defeat or a most glorious victory." Now, on the Third Day, it was clear a "most glorious victory" had not been achieved, and McClellan's focus had shifted to mitigating the "great defeat" he feared—indeed, perhaps already expected.

McClellan was certain that his attacks on the Confederate flanks during the Second Day had at least drawn the immediately available Confederate reserves to the ends of the line. Lee, McClellan reasoned, was strong in the north and strong in the south, but he could not be strong everywhere. An assault on Lee's center—however desperate—would surely break through, dividing Lee's supposedly enormous army and permitting McClellan, once again, to proceed against the separated parts in detail. Moreover, a successful thrust through Lee's center would allow McClellan to turn his forces and attack the Confederates at either end of the field from what would then be their rear, on interior lines. Finally, by attacking McClellan could fix Lee's attention on the Army of the Potomac and buy valuable time for the defense of Philadelphia and Baltimore. Perhaps it was the influence of Burnside's manic insistence that he lead a charge; or McClellan's misreading of the French military theorist Jomini, or his misinterpretation of successful French frontal attacks against the Austrians in Italy in 1859, *or* just an apparent lack of alternatives combined with a failure of imagination. Whatever the cause, McClellan re-assembled his counsel of war and ordered the attack known to history as Burnside's Charge.

Throughout September 24, the climactic Third Day, McClellan showed signs of ever-increasing desperation. He continued his dramatic overestimation of the size of Lee's force: in McClellan's mind, the estimate of 120,000 at Frederick City now gave way to Pinkerton's estimate of two hundred thousand—perhaps even more—made the prior month. McClellan was haunted by fears that Lee might detach some portion of this seemingly overwhelming host for a lightning strike against Philadelphia or Baltimore, for Lee, despite two days of Union effort, remained firmly established between the Army of the Potomac and these two vital metropolitan centers. Even more nightmarish a specter was the prospect of a raid by Stuart's cavalry—of whose location McClellan knew nothing—sweeping down upon Washington City from the north. Perhaps of greatest import for the events about to unfold, McClellan remained convinced that Lee was about to be joined by a reserve the equal of the force with which the Army of the Potomac had been grappling for two days. If Lee were to be driven from his position, it would have to be on the coming day—lest McClellan find his left flank overrun by the great host supposedly bearing down from the northwest. (In the midst of his planning for the grand assault on the Third Day, McClellan took time out to write to his wife, Mary Ellen. This letter reinforces the conclusion that McClellan had turned fatalistic. The issue of victory or defeat, he told her, was out of his hands. "I hope that God will give us a great success. It is all in his hands, where I am content to leave it.")

McClellan's fears had the paradoxical effect of giving him the courage to order an all-out assault against the Confederate line in the hope that Union forces could break through the center before Lee had effected a conjunction with his remaining forces moving in from the northwest along Chambersburg Road. In point of fact, these feared forces were merely a brigade of four North Carolina regiments under Brig. Gen. Robert Ransom, Jr., and the South Carolinians of Brig. Gen. Nathan C. Evans's Independent Brigade. These nine regiments of infantry plus the Macbeth South Carolina Artillery made this a force to be reckoned with—but not a force for McClellan to fear, and hardly the scores of thousands McClellan thought it to be. Indeed, after the failure of Burnside's men to attack the Confederate right on Cemetery Hill the morning of the Second Day, Lee had sent word that Ransom's and Evans's forces were to hold well to the northwest of Gettysburg and keep open the line of withdrawal which Lee fully intended to employ whatever the ultimate outcome of the ongoing battle. For unlike McClellan, Lee had the good sense to recognize that, even with a smashing victory, the Army of Northern Virginia would have to end what was only intended as a raid by returning whence it had come. But McClellan did not know of Lee's order directing Ransom and Evans to hold—and to the anxious commanding general of the Army of Potomac, Ransom's and Evans's Brigades had been transformed into the advance forces of entire Confederate corps, perhaps several corps, which "must" be bearing down onto the Union Army.

The ferocious attack McClellan ordered on the Third Day came heartbreakingly close to piercing through the Confederate center. But it did not succeed. It failed and, in the final analysis, failed spectacularly. The decisiveness of this failure gave Lee—and the Confederacy—the victory needed to impress the all-important English and French audiences.

McClellan mustered an impressive force for the attack. Although engaged for most of the Second Day, I Corps, now under a quickly brevetted Major General George Meade, and Burnside's IX Corps still represented a powerful if battered force of fourteen brigades of infantry. To these, McClellan added the Second Division of II Corps—having begun the battle under the command of John Sedgwick and having assumed largely defensive duties the first two days, Second Division was the only unit of II Corps which was still effective. With Sedgwick now in command of the Corps to replace Sumner, Second Division was led by Brig. General O. O. Howard, an ardent abolitionist. Finally, McClellan detached the Second Division of VI Corps, which had been least badly used on the Second Day. That division was now commanded by the effective Winfield Hancock, its nominal commanding general William Smith having been rendered insensible by a Confederate shell burst on the Second Day. Thus, the Army of the Potomac would attack with twenty brigades gathered from every corner of the Union: including regiments from New York, Indiana, Pennsylvania, Vermont, Wisconsin, Minnesota, Massachusetts, Connecticut, Rhode Island, New Hampshire, Ohio, Maine, Michigan, and even the border state of Maryland. (And although they did not participate in the assault, Simmond's Battery of the Kentucky Light Artillery supported their Ohio compatriots in the Kanawha Division of the Ninth Corps.) It was the largest single assault effected or even contemplated during the war. Burnside devolved operational command of his Corps on Major General Jesse Reno and assumed overall command of the grand assault.

Under the approving gaze of Burnside, resplendent in his immortal side-whiskers, the Union boys dressed their ranks in the cool shelter of the tree line, while supporting artillery sounded a cannonade said to be heard as far as Philadelphia and Baltimore. After two days of battle, no one knew exactly how many effectives mustered on the rolls for the assault, but it was certainly in excess of thirty thousand men and boys. At a slow march, then a quickstep, then on a dead run, they charged the center of the Confederate line. The Union forces emerged from the sheltering trees on Warfield's Ridge, aiming for the Confederate line on the opposing low ridge just to the north of the Round Tops. To get there, Burnside's men would have to cross the Emmitsburg Road, pass through a peach orchard, and then cross the same wheat field through which Kemper withdrew on the First Day. It was a long, exposed, and dangerous route to the center of the Confederate line.

The hour-long artillery barrage preceding the assault provided warning to the waiting Confederates, who used the time to bring up their reserves. Since the arrival of Longstreet at the end of the First Day, the center of the line had been held by John Bell Hood's Division. To this were now added the men of Richard Anderson's Division, which had escaped the bulk of the fighting against Burnside on Seminary Ridge during the Second Day, and two of the remaining four brigades of D. R. Jones's Division, which had been held in reserve since their arrival prior to the start of the battle. None of Hood's or Jones's men had yet been engaged, and the ten defending brigades were not grossly outnumbered by their attackers. In addition to the freshness of their troops, the Confederate commanders had enjoyed the luxury of two days to prepare their field defenses in the center, as McClellan probed at the ends of Lee's lines. And at various spots during the advance, Burnside's men fell under *enfilade* fire—not only from the defenders in their front but from the summit of Cemetery Hill and from the replenished artillery at the crest of untaken Little Round Top.

The men in blue died in rows as they fell. After two days of entrenchment and preparation, the thin gray line was almost unbreakable: *almost* unbreakable, because for a fleeting moment, it was broken. At the very center of the Confederate position—just to the north of the wheat field, by a copse of trees between the farms of John and George Weikert, boys from New York (the 59th and 42nd New York, most of them fighting under O. O. Howard for the first time) got in among the defenders, went over the entrenchments, and even laid hands on a Confederate cannon. The brave Virginians who faced them, under the command of Brig. Gen. Lewis Armistead, had been on the field yesterday, and they were tired. Now, the moment of crisis was at hand.

Sadly for the history of the next one hundred years, it was a crisis for which Lee proved all too well prepared. The South's last tactical reserve consisted of the remaining two brigades of D. R. Jones's division. Sheltered in a hollow behind the lines from the Union bombardment, Jenkins's Brigade from South Carolina (under the command of Col. Joseph Walker) and Pickett's Brigade of Virginians (under the temporary command of Brig. Gen. Richard B. Garnett) were rested. Hood called for reinforcements to plug the breakthrough, and Pickett's Brigade charged into the gap. The shock of the Virginians hitting the New Yorkers at full run blunted the attack—blunted, but not repulsed. It therefore fell to Hood's divisional artillery to provide the immediate, needed staunch to the wound in the Confederate line. The South Carolina Palmetto Artillery rolled forward with terrible effect. The artillerymen aimed at the seething mass of blue and gray, sweeping Union and Confederate alike before their blasts. "Double canister at ten yards" was ordered. But even with one breach repaired, others threatened. Notwithstanding thousands of Union troops dead or dying in agony before the Confederate line, the assaulting troops still outnumbered the defenders by thousands more; the line was in danger of being swept asunder through sheer weight of numbers. Lee and Longstreet rode up and down the line, allocating the last of the reserve regiments and encouraging the men. There is no question but that Lee exhibited great personal courage throughout this critical phase of the battle, exposing himself to Union fire as he directed his deployments.

Yet it was a younger, unrelated Lee who exhibited truly extraordinary daring, and his deeds could be said to have saved the day for the South—to the extent any one man can be credited for that victory. Stephen D. Lee was a twenty-eight-year-old colonel from Charleston, South Carolina. After a successful career, he graduated from West Point in 1854 and was commissioned into the 4th US Artillery. His pre-war career included service in Florida, Kansas, and the Dakota Territory. Despite his relative youth, he was an experienced artilleryman and had a fine appreciation for the force under his command. Sensing that a static defense of the entrenchment line was doomed to failure under the weight of the continuing Union attack, Colonel Lee (without orders) ordered his light artillery battalions to advance *outside* of the Confederate line: to the north of the point of greatest Union pressure. His men, mostly from Virginia (but including batteries from South Carolina and Louisiana as well), unlimbered, then fired canister, keeping up a withering series of enfilading blasts that decimated the men at the head of the Union charge.

General Lee later said that it was at this moment he changed his aim: from a battle seeking victory to one seeking annihilation. Lee had watched the development and now repulse of Burnside's Charge together with his three corps commanders: Longstreet, Jackson, and the exuberant Stuart. Jackson watched as Colonel Lee's artillery gouged huge holes in the left flank of the foremost Union forces, while those troops just a few yards to the rear continued to press onward—oblivious to the danger. As the Union mass compressed itself into an increasingly dense, increasingly immobile formation, Jackson advised Lee to send Stuart around the Confederate left to fall upon McClellan's other flank. Stuart seized upon the idea, exclaiming that he could thrust his troopers past the flanks directly into the Union rear and do so well before Burnside could disengage any substantial part of his forces. Amid Stuart's frenzied references to Napoleonic cavalry tactics, Jackson softly commented that, after all, the Cavalry Corps of the Army of Northern Virginia was the finest cavalry force in the world. Lee later related that he heard out Jackson and an increasingly excited Stuart and looked toward his "Old War Horse," General Longstreet. Longstreet said not a word, but locked eyes with Lee and nodded—a slight smile creasing his face. Lee unleashed Stuart.

Stuart's three brigades had not been engaged at any time in the battle and now would be completely unchecked by any Union cavalry force; McClellan had wasted his. As we have seen, two full brigades of Union cavalry were expended as a dismounted screening force for the Second Day's attack by the "Right Wing." On the Third Day, those troopers remained where they were—useless. Two other brigades remained many miles to the south of the cockpit of battle, for they had been sent to find Lee when McClellan thought Lee to be still over the mountains; they did not arrive on the field in time to matter. The remaining brigade under Col. John Farnsworth—for all intents and purposes, these four regiments comprised the entire cavalry arm of the Army of the Potomac—had been assigned to guard supplies at Emmitsburg, Maryland. These decisions and allocations now left the Confederate cavalry unchallenged at the decisive moment of the fight.

Stuart speedily rejoined his men in the fields to the east of Big Round Top and briefed his commanders. He led them south of the Round Tops, crossing Plum Run—Bloody Run—far south of the First Day's battle-field. He led his men into, and then out of, the woods east of the Currens House, where he captured the entire staff of the luckless II Corps. One brigade, under the aggressive Wade Hampton, drove north into the woods on Warfield's Ridge, and, with an unearthly yell, came to the far edge of those woods in the precise rear of the Union artillery. Hampton's sabers made short work of the few artillerymen who had resisted the understand-able impulse to flee when the rebel cavalry burst unexpectedly upon them. Hampton then brought up the horse artillerymen of Chew's Battery and bade them work the Union guns to fire directly into the backs of the tens of thousands of Union infantrymen. Burnside's forces now faced artillery fire from front, side, and rear. Meanwhile, Robertson's Brigade of cavalry struck to the northwest, ranging widely throughout the Union rear. His 2nd Virginia cavalry swept to the Biesecker house, where McClellan had been not ten minutes earlier, and bagged a haul of general officers. And just to the east, Stuart sent Fitzhugh Lee (Robert E. Lee's nephew and future President of the Confederate States of America) directly up the Emmitsburg Road through the rear of the remaining II Corps units, through the woods, and into the field where General Kemper had opened the battle days earlier.

The effect on the Union forces was electric and calamitous. At unimag-inable cost, they had marched across the open field against the entrenched Confederate center. They had pressed forward, even under canister and shot—even in the face of Colonel Lee's advanced artillery. Now they were under artillery fire from their *own* guns. They could not break and run whence they came; Confederate battle flags flew in those woods. The men who could, sought safety back down the Emmitsburg Road. Imagine their plight: fleeing southward on the road—when Confederate cavalry emerged in front of them from the woods astride the pike! The disarray was made complete by Stuart's horse artillery. Captain John Pelham unlimbered his batteries on either side of the road, unprotected by infantry and with nothing between his gunners and the Union troops but stands of autumn wheat. Pelham and his men stood their ground and poured round after round of solid and canister shot into Burnside's men.

It was all too much. At this point, the wavering in the Union ranks gave way to outright panic as the blue tide crested, broke, and recoiled rather than receded from the now-encircling Confederate lines. With nowhere left to run, hundreds and then thousands of blue-clad men threw their guns to the ground and raised their hands in surrender. "It is wonderful to see such courage in one so young," Lee remarked to Longstreet as he observed the twenty-four-year-old Pelham's exploit. The threat to the Confederate center was over: McClellan's bolt was shot; and the Army of the Potomac, shattered.

The repulse of "Burnside's Charge," as it has forever come to be known, broke the Army of the Potomac's will for further fighting. The Union left some ten thousand men on the field in front of the Confederate center—dead and wounded—including Burnside himself, mortally wounded by a Confederate shell as he tried to rally his men for one last effort. More than ten thousand others—*ten thousand*—would be captured. The remnant lost all semblance of unit cohesion; many ran alone or in small groups to the woods to rejoin the army days or weeks later—or never. And it all proved too much for the already frayed nerves of General McClellan. "Little Mac" went to pieces, collapsing into the arms of his *aide de camp* and crying, "Our country is lost! And it is my fault! It is all my fault!" (I doubt truer words have ever been spoken by the losing commander at the close of a battle.) Fortunately, by regular telegraph reports, President Lincoln and Secretary of War Stanton had been able to follow the progress of the struggle. Now, with the news of Burnside's apparent repulse, Stanton—with Lincoln's approval—

ordered McClellan relieved. George Meade of Pennsylvania, who had started the battle as a mere division commander, was appointed in his stead. (In his telegram to McClellan, Stanton made what would prove a prophetic rebuke: "Sir, I fear the country cannot survive the consequences of your command.") Stanton directed Meade "immediately to take all possible steps to prevent a Confederate move against Washington City or any other vital center of population now threatened by the Rebel raiders."

Of course, not even the telegraph could communicate to Washington the minute-by-minute details of the disintegration of the Army of the Potomac. Fortunately, General Meade kept his head about him and, gathering an *ad hoc* collection of units, managed to extricate himself from the field, with McClellan in tow (if not actually under arrest). Meade gathered what he could from the shattered Army of the Potomac, ordering forces of whatever size to rally in Emmitsburg, south of the Mason–Dixon Line. Hastily assembled screening forces (made up of militia from Eastern Pennsylvania and New Jersey) nervously sought to deter any strike toward Philadelphia or Baltimore.

Meade's re-constitutive efforts were made possible by the fact that V Corps, under the command of Maj. Gen. Fitz-John Porter, never saw action at Gettysburg. McClellan had insisted on holding Porter's three strong divisions (including an entire division of US Army Regulars) in "strategic reserve" at Taneytown—almost twenty miles from the battlefield—to meet the onslaught of the Confederate reserve that existed only in "Little Mac's" imagination. (In fact, there was no real risk of Lee making any move against any of Philadelphia, Baltimore, or Washington however vulnerable they appeared to worried Northerners contemplating a map showing the relative positions of the contending forces in the wake of the Union disaster at Gettysburg.) Now, Meade ordered Porter to place V Corps between Lee and any possible move by the triumphant Confederates on Washington.

Lee, of course, had no intention of moving anywhere other than back to Virginia via the crossing at Williamsport. The Army of Northern Virginia had been taxed to its limit by the three-day struggle. Although the Confederates' casualties paled in comparison to Union losses, they still represented a substantial portion of Lee's effective strength. Lee simply could not afford any other course but withdrawal back toward Virginia. A move farther east, against Philadelphia or Baltimore—much less southeast against the fortifications guarding Washington—was out of the question. Besides, Lee had never intended to occupy any of the great Northern cities. It had always been his intention to withdraw south of the Potomac after engaging McClellan. Lee's aim had been to show that the South could take the war into the North, and in this, he had succeeded brilliantly.

Equally brilliant was Lee's solution to his enormous haul of prisoners. Rather than assuming responsibility for ten thousand men, Lee corralled them in the open air for two days and then paroled every prisoner below the rank of colonel. In short, Lee released ten thousand ravenously hungry and utterly dispirited young men to fend for themselves in south-central Pennsylvania. Even if the Union possessed a force to chase Lee, it would never have made its way through the chaos that radiated from the Gettysburg fields for a score of miles in every direction.

Lee really required no persuading when Longstreet noted that the time had come for the army to retire back toward the Potomac. Lee ordered Stuart to detach a brigade of cavalry to carry a team of sappers on one last raid: to destroy the railroad bridge across the Susquehanna and sever the only rail link between the Union Northeast and Midwest. Stuart insisted on leading the raid, and the result was Stuart's famous Ride, as his forces dashed up the Cumberland Valley, covered the sappers as they planted their demolition charges, then dashed back to rejoin the main body of the Army of Northern Virginia as it made a deliberately destructive way through the rich farmlands of Southern Pennsylvania. Given the legendary status since acquired by Stuart's exploit, it bears repeating that the Confederate sappers failed to bring down the bridge's entire structure, and railroad traffic was restored within a week. The real significance of the raid was psychological; in combination with the devastation wrought by "Lee's March" back to the Pennsylvania–Maryland border, Stuart's Ride showed, as Lee had intended, that the South could take the war deep into the North. Moreover, Lee's decision to permit Longstreet to encamp strong detachments from his Corps both at the Potomac crossing at Point-of-Rocks and at Sharpsburg, Maryland—thus leaving troops on the ground north of the Potomac, in Maryland—reinforced the political verdict of Gettysburg: the South could take the war into the North, and it could even hold Union territory should it so desire.

Thus ended the campaign which brought on the Battle of Gettysburg. The collision of arms was characterized by a number of hard-fought clashes, and there were a number of occasions when one or another aspect of the battle might have turned out differently. But the overarching theme of the campaign—the one factor to which all others ultimately became subsidiary—was McClellan's failure of will. He was too timid to move his army quickly and too proud to believe his inaction would present his adversary with an insurmountable advantage. In the absence of any *deus ex machina* that would have motivated McClellan to effect a more vigorous pursuit of Lee, his profound failure might as well have been pre-ordained.

BATTLE OF GETTYSBURG – FIRST DAY

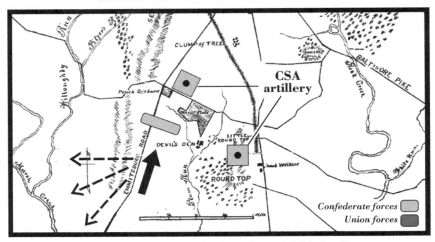

1st Phase: **Kemper's Brigade and CSA Artillery surprise and shatter French's Division.**

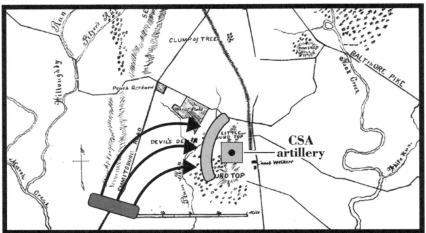

2nd Phase: **Unsuccessful Union attacks on D.H. Hill's Division and Jackson's Artillery Reserve on Little Round Top.**

BATTLE OF GETTYSBURG – SECOND DAY

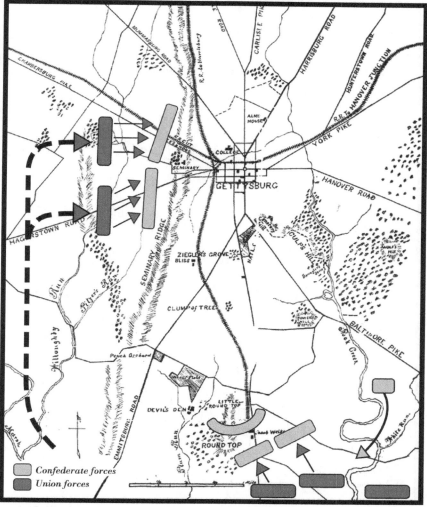

McClellan's attempted Cannae – the assault on the Confederate flanks

BATTLE OF GETTYSBURG – THIRD DAY

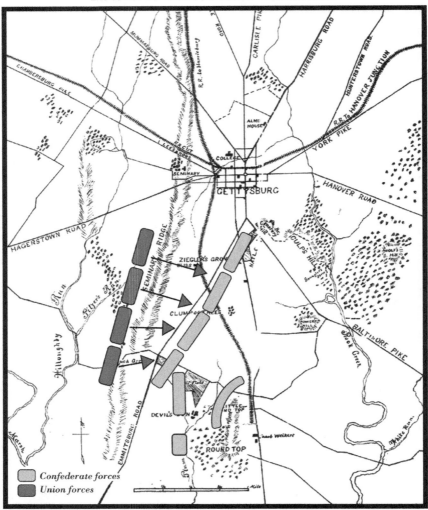

1st Phase: "Burnside's Charge"

BATTLE OF GETTYSBURG – THIRD DAY

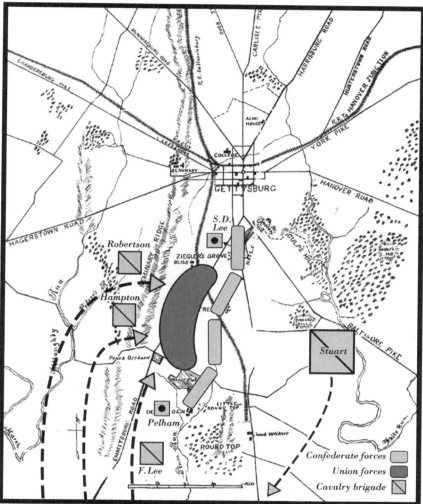

2nd Phase: "Lee's Cannae," as Stuart encircles the Union forces

(left) **George McClellan, whose crushing defeat at Gettysburg triggered the decisive diplomatic intervention of Great Britain and France, which ended the American War of Secession with the recognition of the Southern Confederacy's independence.**

(right) **Robert E. Lee, the victor of Gettysburg, rewarded by a grateful South five years later with election as President of the Confederacy.**

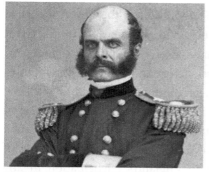

(left) **Union General Ambrose Burnside, who fell leading the final Union attack on the third day of the Battle of Gettysburg.**

(below) **Confederate General J.E.B. Stuart, whose cavalry delivered the decisive blow on the third day at Gettysburg.**

It took several days for the fact of Lee's withdrawal to become known. During the interim, only a dramatic personal appeal by Lincoln to crowds gathered outside the White House avoided a wholesale flight from the capital. Then events quickly moved out of Lincoln's control. First, the defeat at Gettysburg forced Lincoln to defer, now indefinitely, his proclamation of emancipation. Second, the news of Lee's latest triumph led directly to the call for "mediation," issued jointly on October 20 by the governments of Great Britain and France. Louis Napoleon had long been eager for the Great Powers to compel a North American peace based on Confederate independence, as he hoped to exploit a Southern victory to promote French ambitions in Mexico. London, however, had been more cautious. Although Prime Minister Palmerston concurred with his Foreign Secretary, Lord Russell, that the North's attempt to subjugate the Southern states was probably doomed to failure, Palmerston had resolved to await a "decisive" demonstration of Northern "impotence" before agreeing to England's participation in any call for mediation—a move that would carry with it implied recognition (at the very least) of the Confederacy's standing as an independent nation, and which therefore risked antagonizing the Union to the point of war. When Russell and Chancellor of the Exchequer (and future prime minister) William Gladstone, the leaders of the cabinet's pro-intervention faction, wondered how much more decisive a demonstration of Northern weakness there could be than the recent rout of the Army of the Potomac by Lee at Second Manassas, Palmerston—who also had to contend with a powerful anti-intervention group led by Secretary for War George Lewis—pointed out that the North still occupied substantial Southern territory in the West, while the Confederates had yet to show they could carry their war into the North.

For precisely that reason, Palmerston welcomed the news of Lee's move into Maryland. Should Lee administer yet another "drubbing" to Union forces—and this time on their home ground—Palmerston believed that Lincoln and his cabinet would have to recognize the futility of further bloodshed and accede to a European call for peace. Hoping that Lee was about to accomplish that drubbing, Palmerston scheduled a cabinet meeting for October 16. This was the state of affairs within the British government when word of Lee's victory reached London on October 9. Upon hearing the news from Russell, Palmerston declared that "the time for waiting has come to an end; our duty is clear: We must compel Mr. Lincoln to see the foolishness of further bloodshed." When the cabinet assembled as scheduled, it quickly became apparent that Her Majesty's government would respond affirmatively to the French Emperor's telegram urging a joint call for mediation. Gladstone repeated his recent Newcastle speech phrase about the South having "made a nation." Palmerston dryly responded that, "whatever the South may be, the North obviously cannot defeat it, and that is what really matters now." Palmerston, moreover, was seconded by Secretary for War Lewis, who announced that the Confederacy's triumphant Pennsylvania foray had convinced him Southern independence was "sufficiently an established fact" such that Great Britain should consider itself free to act to bring the "dangerously destructive" conflict to an end.

Having changed his view on the basic issue of intervention, Lewis characteristically became a vigorous advocate for the most decisive form of intervention. Rejecting a call limited to urging medication as a "dangerous half-measure," Lewis recommended that France's proposal be strengthened to include formal recognition of the Confederacy—with the added steel of a private communiqué to Lincoln, making clear that an Anglo-French squadron would be prepared to lift the Union blockade of Confederate ports should the North spurn Europe's peace initiative. Lewis also recommended the immediate acceleration of England's ironclad conversion program, as well as the prompt—and well-publicized—posting to Canada of several crack army regiments. Although Lewis believed the Great Powers now had a sound basis for intervention to end the war, he also recognized the substantial risk that the North might choose war with Great Britain and France rather than yield independence to the rebel states. With the issue of whether to intervene now resolved, and with Palmerston and the majority of the Cabinet agreeing to all of the Lewis proposals, the only real controversy was *when* to act. The remaining opponents of intervention urged no action until after the North's upcoming midterm elections in the hope that a victory for the "Peace" Democrats would force Lincoln to announce a unilateral armistice and thereby spare London the odium of intervention on the side of "the Slave Power." On this point, they received support from Lewis, who feared a pre-election intervention might infuriate Northern nationalists and return a reinvigorated "War Hawk" Republican majority.

Palmerston, however, shared Russell's concern that, if London held back, Louis Napoleon would try to force the British hand with a unilateral declaration that would fail—or (perhaps worse) succeed, and thereby allow France to claim the leadership role at the ensuing peace conference.

In fact, the news of the Anglo–French declaration, which reached the North a little more than a week before the midterm vote, arrived too late to have much of an impact either way. Although the Republicans' prompt rallying cry to reject any peace "imposed by European despotism" may have helped swing back a handful of congressional seats that would otherwise have been lost, a Democratic victory had been virtually assured by McClellan's disastrous battlefield performance in Pennsylvania. (McClellan considered himself a Democrat, but party leaders managed to convince the general to downplay his party affiliation until after the elections—thereby depriving the Republicans of a brush with which to tar the opposition with at least some share for the most recent drubbing at the hands of "Bobbie" Lee.) But the scale of the Democrats' victory proved narrower than the landslide so fervently hoped for by many in London and Paris. The Democrats took control of the House, but only because the Unionists (pro-war Democrats who had broken with their party over Secession) returned to the fold and gave Democrat Samuel Cox the votes he needed to be elected Speaker; the Republicans actually maintained control of the Senate—albeit with a reduced majority. And while the Democrats won several key gubernatorial contests, including in New York, the Republicans maintained control over a majority of state legislatures. In this regard, the Republicans were probably helped by the Union victories at Perryville and Harrodsburg in Kentucky and at Corinth in Mississippi, as the combination of Bragg's repulse from Kentucky and Van Dorn's failure failure to eject Grant's forces from Mississippi at least avoided the impression of a complete implosion of Northern arms.

The margin between Union victory and another Confederate triumph had been perilously thin, however, especially in Kentucky. There, the news from Gettysburg nearly resulted in a bloodless Confederate victory. Fear of an invasion of Ohio by Lee caused a panic, and the more irresponsible among the state's politicians implored General Don Carlos Buell—the commander of the "Army of the Ohio," which was about to march southeast from Louisville against the rebel forces of Bragg and Kirby Smith—to instead detach one-third of his force in order to protect Buell's "native state" from the "imminent danger" of invasion by the Army of Northern Virginia. Buell was an Ohioan and a cautious man averse to taking risks. He therefore wired Washington to inquire if the "more prudent course" might be to call off the planned advance and "await developments." Fortunately, Secretary of War Stanton had a firmer grasp of the political and military situation. Recognizing that the North would be demoralized if the government should acquiesce in the loss of Kentucky in the wake of Lee's rampage through Pennsylvania, Stanton wired back that same day with instructions dismissing the Ohio invasion fears as "rubbish" and directing Buell to advance "immediately...or I will find someone who will." Stung by this rebuke, Buell put his plans in motion, brought the Confederates to bay, and in the series of battles at Perrysville and Harrodsburg dealt Bragg and Smith sufficiently damaging blows to persuade them to abandon their Kentucky venture; although, it took the second defeat at Harrodsburg to finally convince the Confederate commanders to give up their dream of equaling the "glory" of Lee's Gettysburg victory by "liberating Kentucky on the battlefield of honor." (Buell's victories were greatly aided by the brilliant performance of Brigadier General Phillip Sheridan and his troops, as Sheridan's sound tactical sense and fierce determination to prevail each time allowed the Union forces to retain the initiative.)

Had Buell been allowed to call off his move against Bragg, the Confederacy could have claimed success in both bringing the war to the North in the East and in "liberating" Kentucky in the West. Indeed, only the sounds of Buell's guns broke up the installation ceremony of a Confederate administration in Frankfort. The Democrats then might have swept the midterm voting and taken control of the Senate as well as the House, which would undoubtedly have tempted them to interfere actively with the Lincoln Administration's conduct of peace negotiations. Moreover, had the South achieved the liberation of Kentucky by force of arms, that state would no longer have been available to the North as a bargaining chip to be yielded up in exchange for comparable Confederate concessions (e.g., concerning the status of the New Mexico Territory). These, however, were implications for a future in which the North had accepted that it must now yield up independence to the South. That decision had yet to be made, and on that point, counsel in Washington was badly divided. On the one hand, the military news from the West was good: The Confederates had been ejected from Kentucky, and Grant remained poised for an assault on Vicksburg that should succeed the following spring in severing the Trans-Mississippi's last link to the East. Balanced against these developments, however, was the disaster in Pennsylvania. Although Lee had withdrawn back across the Potomac, he had inflicted a devastating loss on the Army of the Potomac (thirty thousand casualties compared to under ten thousand for Lee's forces) and an even worse blow to Union morale—for who would stop the "invincible" Virginian when next he chose to move across the Mason–Dixon Line?

Far worse, Lee's victory had brought on intervention by Great Britain and France. Rejecting their offer of mediation would mean an expanded war in which the North would confront an Anglo-French–Confederate alliance. And while the North might fare reasonably well in such a conflict—Canada was probably indefensible against a determined assault—the Democrats' victory (however narrow and partial) in the midterm congressional elections raised serious doubts about whether the country would support a widened war. In fact, leading Democrats in the last days of the campaign had begun to counter Republican condemnations of "foreign despotism" with the pointed query, "Shall we now start a war to our North in order to win a war of compulsion against our brethren to the South? How will diverting Northern boys to Canada make Pennsylvania any more secure?" The divisions in Lincoln's cabinet reflected these countervailing considerations. Secretary of War Stanton favored a "war of no quarter" against the South and against any nation "dastardly enough to join in alliance with the slave power." Secretary of the Treasury Salmon Chase, on the other hand, recoiled at the financial implications of a "long, exhausting war" against Great Britain and France: "We are compelled by an undeniable turn of events at least to try and reach a peaceful resolution with our Southern compatriots, even though we may now have to let them depart in the process." And Secretary of State Seward, who had become perhaps Lincoln's closest counselor over the course of the war, was torn between the two. Seward agreed with Chase's ruthlessly gloomy assessment of the financial consequences of a war with England and France. But as one of the North's leading abolitionists, Seward was also appalled at the prospect of abandoning the South's four million slaves to continuing bondage. Lincoln took all counsel under advisement, knowing the responsibility for the decision ultimately was his to make (and also being shrewd enough to recognize that some in his cabinet thought him unqualified to make it).

The historic reluctance with which Lincoln finally accepted mediation is well known. His decision, at bottom, rested on his reading of God's will. As Lincoln told his cabinet, "By giving the Confederacy Lee's victory at Gettysburg and then the recognition of Great Britain and France, I can only conclude that His purpose in willing these outcomes must be, as sorrowful as it is to contemplate, something other than the preservation of our Union. I had hoped He would give us a victory to show He wished us to make of this war a fight for emancipation; instead, it would seem God has decided this question *against* the slaves. He has commanded us now to try and make a fair peace. And so we shall. For, as it is written, 'the judgments of the Lord are true and righteous altogether.'" On November 15, Lincoln sent word to Richmond, London, and Paris that the Union accepted the Anglo–French proposal for an armistice *en place*, and that the North's delegation to the peace conference—to be headed by Secretary of State Seward—would arrive in London by December 1.

Before I proceed with my narrative, I would pause and reflect on the question asked so often since then: Was Lincoln's decision the turning point? Did he err, and fatally so, for the future of a United States of America, in accepting mediation? Had Washington instead answered with defiance, would the British and French threat to lift the blockade proved a bluff? And even if war had ensued, would the outcome have been dissolution of the Union? Was the South's victory in the War of Secession the product of a loss of nerve by the Union's chief executive when he confronted the most challenging decision of his life? These are difficult questions, and a comprehensive treatment is beyond the scope of this work. Still, I will essay a few words on the subject—principally, because I believe the Union lost the War of Secession on the battlefields of Pennsylvania and the cabinet rooms of London and Paris—*not* in the mind of the last President of a *united* United States of America.

The "defiance alternative" instinctively desires a Lincoln shaped like Stanton, for whom ferocious combat was the essence of life. Lincoln was no such man. He did not shrink from struggle, but (as previously stated) he also believed deeply that the contest for the Union was shaped by God's will (although Lincoln's own view of God *was* highly abstract, at least as compared to the personal God of so many of his countrymen). Having come to believe that the war must be—perhaps always had been—about the future of slavery, Lincoln was on the verge of proclaiming emancipation of the slaves and awaited only the outcome of a battle he could fairly call a vital Union triumph—most preferably over Lee—to issue the proclamation and formally transform the nature of the conflict. Thus, when instead it was Lee who emerged victorious and the Great European Powers of England and France responded by taking the Confederate side and urging an end to the conflict, Lincoln saw God's work as a rebuke of Lincoln's plan to make war on slavery itself. As Lincoln made clear years later in his memoirs, he was overwhelmed at first by the—to him, physically sickening—idea that God might wish to preserve so hateful an institution. But as a deeply spiritual man, he did not feel *free* to defy what so clearly appeared to be God's will— at least for now. And given this man was charged with the responsibility to make the North's decision on whether to accept mediation, only Lincoln's sudden removal from office could have made possible any other outcome. But that is so not because Lincoln was weak or lost his nerve—to the contrary, it was Lincoln's strength of character and integrity that girded him to make the decision he made.

And if Lincoln had for some reason resigned or died before the fateful decision had been taken, what then? Vice President Hamlin was a nonentity and would presumably have accepted the recommendation of a cabinet filled with powerhouses such as Seward, Stanton, and Chase. Assuming that Seward came out firmly against mediation (as much to outmaneuver Stanton, whom he would have regarded as the greatest threat for the Republican presidential nomination in 1864—as Stanton actually proved to be) and that the North then threatened war if the British and French actually tried to break the blockade, what would have transpired? London and Paris had committed themselves to restoring "freedom of the seas" for the trade of a sovereign state they now both recognized—a recognition soon to be joined by Brazil and most of Latin America (with the possible exception of Colombia and the likely exception of Mexico) and also by the balance of the Great Powers of Europe, if not as quickly by Russia. British and French credibility could have been destroyed had they meekly acceded to "Yankee defiance." Great Britain had accepted war fifty years earlier to avoid just such a result. The fact is that Palmerston made the decision for intervention knowing full well that war might follow should the Union reject mediation, and he was fully prepared to take that risk. So the war between North and South would have continued, except now the North would have been fighting an alliance of the Confederacy, Great Britain, and France.

I do not believe the outcome of such a war a foregone conclusion. Unlike partisans of either the old Union or the CSA, I think the final result could have been either a Union or CSA victory, depending on the interplay of a wide variety of variables I do not intend to analyze in any detail here. (The "yestermorrow" literature has provided many detailed and thoughtful analyses of the course of a continued War of Secession had the North rejected mediation.) Still, I am compelled to comment, if only briefly, on the hypothesis that Lincoln erred so obviously and grievously in accepting mediation, because that particular possible history is directly at odds with my own. The idea that Lincoln erred assumes the North would have won in any case: either because Great Britain and France were bluffing or because those powers could not have brought force to bear in any way likely to affect the outcome. The "mere bluff" notion is quickly disposed of, because it is patently false. As for whether British and French intervention could have prevented a Union victory, I agree that Confederate partisans have tended to exaggerate the military benefits that the South would have accrued from their new allies. Certainly, Great Britain would have had its hands full if Washington had decided to make a concerted push for Canada; a single Union corps could probably have seized every principal city of that province—notwithstanding the reinforcements dispatched by Lewis from the British Isles. The British might also have discovered they had merely traded a cotton famine for a wheat famine—with the risk of serious urban unrest, as bread prices multiplied with the plunge in available flour stocks. On the other hand, Union partisans seem too inclined to minimize the tradeoffs that a continued and expanded war would have forced on the Union, especially in the short term. The Army of the Potomac was a wreck: what would prevent Lee from mounting another, even more devastating raid? Conversely, with the Union incapable of making any move against Richmond for several months to come, Davis might have detached Longstreet's or Jackson's Corps (possibly under Lee himself) and sent it West to raise havoc at any number of vital points. And as for Canada: While the North probably could have mounted an irresistible invasion, any such move before mid-1863 would have required diverting troops and material from other fronts (and this when the Army of the Potomac required substantial replenishment of every sort).

Finally, there is the matter of New Orleans and the French. Unlike Great Britain, France had no territory vulnerable to a Northern counterthrust and was not dependent on Union wheat. France, moreover, had an army already in place in Mexico, and was in the process of sending reinforcements even as Lee was launching his invasion of the North. Why wouldn't Louis Napoleon have seized the chance to earn the Confederacy's gratitude by postponing his Mexican adventure and instead offer his forces—supported by the French fleet—to aid Richmond in recapturing New Orleans? (This also would have been a natural assignment for a corps of the Army of Northern Virginia— say, under the command of the dynamic Jackson—to be detached for "temporary" duty out West.) I, for one, do not see how such an effort could have failed, save by incompetent execution of an extraordinary—and given the involvement of commanders like Jackson, unlikely—magnitude. With New Orleans and control of the Lower Mississippi from Vicksburg to the Gulf of Mexico safely back in Confederate hands, it is difficult to conceive how the North could force the rebel states back into the Union. The back of Winfield Scott's "Anaconda Plan" for strangling the South (by seizing control of the Mississippi, while blockading the balance of Southern ports) would have been broken with the restoration of New Orleans to Southern control. Moreover, the North could not expect to reprise its daring seaborne operation of April 1862. French and British squadrons would have quickly transformed the Caribbean into a *de facto* Confederate lake. And with Northern naval construction having shifted toward coastal ironclads (superb for defense of the littoral but utterly useless for contesting control of the open seas), it would have taken several years before the North would have had a blue-water navy capable of challenging the combined fleets of England and France.

Perhaps it still could have been done. By seizing Canada and holding it hostage to a British withdrawal, Washington might have driven Great Britain from the field. And without the support of the British Empire, France might also have given up the struggle, especially as Louis Napoleon's unsteady regime probably could not have withstood the strain of a prolonged war—much as the financial pressure of the growing Prussian challenge helped force France's withdrawal from Mexico by 1868. By that point, a fully mobilized Union probably could have worn down an isolated South by relentless attrition. But the end would have been a Carthaginian Peace—not the restoration of errant brothers to a restored Union. The Northern legions would have made a desert of the South, and such a "victory"—in 1870? 1875?—would have come at the cost of *millions* of casualties and billions of dollars: money, as Treasury Secretary Chase incessantly reminded Lincoln, which simply did not exist. The re-United States that emerged from such a struggle would have been economically exhausted and politically brutalized. In short, the fate that overtook all the great nations of the world in the twentieth century, even before the nuclear catastrophe of October 1962, would have overtaken America even before the beginning of our century. True, the USA–CSA rivalry would no longer have existed, and the absence of that dynamic might have slowed the development of a global alliance system involving the Great Powers of Europe. But once that system did emerge—and I believe the rivalries among Great Britain, France, Germany, and Russia would likely have resulted in the creation of rival alliances, notwithstanding—the end result for Europe would probably have been as bad as the fate suffered by the English-speaking peoples of North America.

My point is not that Lincoln's decision to accept mediation did not matter. It did matter, and I concede that history could have taken a materially different course, at least in certain respects, if mediation had been rejected. But before I resume my narrative of what was and leave the realm of what was theoretically possible, I must underscore that speculation about the possibilities for a rejection of mediation ignore the fundamental unlikelihood of that course. The decision to accept mediation was President Lincoln's, and to speculate about the likelihood of a history in which mediation was rejected requires one to ignore the fundamental character of Lincoln as he was in the fall of 1862. For that reason, Lee's victory at Gettysburg and the intervention by Great Britain and France which his victory produced—not Lincoln's decision to accept the offer to mediate of the intervenors—must be understood as the true turning point of the War of Secession. The relevant inquiry therefore must be whether the disaster of Gettysburg was avoidable.

Earlier, I commented that nothing short of McClellan being handed a copy of Lee's plan of campaign (disclosing Lee's decision to divide his forces at the outset) would have moved McClellan to strike at the Virginian's moment of greatest vulnerability. Incredibly, that might have been, because a copy of those orders *was* lost—a fact gleaned from the memoirs of Confederate General D. H. Hill, who commanded a division during the Gettysburg campaign. Hill reported receiving a copy from his commanding officer ("Stonewall" Jackson) rather than from Lee's headquarters—as should have been the case, given the way in which Lee's staff arranged for the distribution of that particular order. Hill speculated that the original sent from Lee's headquarters must have been dropped in transit. As for why Jackson's staff forwarded a copy, Hill could only wonder that Jackson took the initiative to have a copy of this vital directive made and sent to Hill, whose division had been temporarily detached from Jackson's Corps at the outset of the Maryland–Pennsylvania campaign. "Fortunate for the Cause that some Yankee trooper did not find the original lying in a field along our line of march—I shudder to think of the trouble even 'Little Mac' could have caused us with such a boon in hand." But as the hypothetical trooper did not find the lost copy—or if he did, failed to appreciate its significance—we are left to speculate about a different outcome upon the battlefield of Gettysburg, itself.

In this regard, I must register my dissent from the opinion of many Northerners who seem to see in every hour of that three-day struggle a chance for Union victory. If only Sumner's Corps had been supported by Hooker or Franklin on the First Day; if only Baldy Smith's Division had moved forward with Slocum's in the assault on Little Round Top on the Second Day; if only Pleasanton's cavalry had arrived in time to interfere with the deployment of Pelham's guns against Burnside's flank at the moment of crisis during the great charge up Cemetery Ridge on the Third Day—these are perhaps the most famous of the "what ifs" of Gettysburg. Yet, as fluid as any battle may be, I submit all these speculations ignore the limiting factor of the character of the opposing commanders. Hooker did not go to Sumner's support on the First Day, because McClellan's caution required he hold back I and VI Corps to meet a feared flanking attack from the northwest by what McClellan believed to be a Confederate army larger than his own. Baldy Smith's Division was late on the Second Day because of confusion over whether to concentrate all available forces against the left flank of the Confederate line—confusion directly attributable to McClellan's continuing concern for his own left flank. Pleasanton's cavalry arrived late, because, by the Third Day, McClellan had shifted the focus of his fears from the northwest to the southeast. Now he worried over a lightning strike by Stuart's cavalry toward Washington, and therefore held Pleasanton's six batteries of horse artillery so far from Burnside's planned assault that the Union cavalry was not available to disrupt Pelham's daring *enfilade* bombardment. In sum, the Union's failures to seize the chances for victory at Gettysburg reflect the character of its commander—a character no more changeable at that supreme moment of crisis and challenge than Lincoln's character was changeable when he confronted the awful choice of yielding to the Anglo-French proposal for a mediated peace.

At this point, I wish to take a moment to address a matter I suspect will by now be of concern to those of my readers who are also fellow Americans. If any of you read this work in years to come, you may be angered already by my tone, which seems to treat Lee and the Army of Northern Virginia with undue respect for their exploits. Such an attitude could be especially puzzling to those who know that the author served as President of the USA for two terms during the "Long Truce" that followed the Peace of Copenhagen ending the Third Alliance War in May 1945. I wish to respond to such likely reactions, because they bear directly on the whole point of this venture, which concerns the tragic consequences of American Disunion for our country and for the world.

Yes, I served as President during the hard and bitter years of the Long Truce. Moreover, as a child of the twentieth century (born one year after the Peace of Rio de Janeiro ending World War One), I have known little but the coarsening violence that has characterized the history of this benighted century—a coarsening that shaped me, as it shaped every American child "fortunate" enough to survive to adulthood during these terrible times. My first knowledge of the Confederacy was the story of their "barbaric" burning of the nation's capital at the outset of the First World War—told to me by my father. ("What can be said for a people who claim to honor George Washington as their hero, yet put the torch to the very city that bore his name?" I remember my father asking.) As an American Scout undergoing compulsory military training during World War Two, I confess to being as thrilled as the rest of my troop members by the news of the firebombing of Richmond and the death in that raid of former CSA President Woodrow Wilson. ("Serves 'em right for '98!" my troop leader exclaimed. "You betcha!" was our unanimous reply.) As an ROTC graduate on occupation duty in Canada in former Ontario Province, I enforced martial law with a vicious effectiveness that earned a commendation from Deputy Military Governor Douglas MacArthur. As US Attorney for Southern New York and then District Attorney for New York County, I employed the power of my office to suppress the last vestiges of the old Democratic Tammany Hall machine under the guise of busting the Irish Republican Brotherhood's terror gangs. (The fact that some members of the Tammany hierarchy were involved with the IRB should not obscure the domestic political goals of such "dual-purpose" operations.) As Governor of New York State and Military Commandant for the District of New York and immediate environs, I witnessed the damage wrought by the combined German–Confederate bombing raids of World War Three and also shared in the delight of Gothamites at the news of the devastating raids launched by Anglo–American forces against the cities of Germany and its allies. (Only now, as I contemplate such horrors as the destruction, in one terrible week in October 1939, of the great cathedrals of London, Paris, and Cologne, do I recognize how twisted my thinking had become—twisted by decades of war and unremitting brutality.) When Winston Churchill was assassinated by Congress Party agents in 1946 in retaliation for the summary execution of Nehru and scores of other Congress leaders after the abortive Indian Army Mutiny during World War Three, I heartily endorsed the responsive "administrative massacres" that took tens of thousands of Hindu lives. As President of the USA from January 1953 until January 1961, I was responsible for ordering numerous "black operations" that killed and wounded thousands more—deaths and injuries never publicly acknowledged as an American responsibility, since we were (at least formally) no longer in a state of war. And I must also acknowledge the "disappearance" of hundreds of Americans, done at my direction, without the benefit of any process of law beyond my signature on a "kill" order—*murders* that reduced our country to the level of the Star Chamber and Charles I, making a mockery of any vestige of a credible claim we might have to be the standard-bearer for respect for human rights and the rule of law.

Finally, I was among those "elder statesmen" who urged a young President John F. Kennedy to use the German missile emplacements in Confederate Cuba as the excuse to launch our long-planned war to destroy the Confederacy and thereby deprive Germany of a platform from which to stage attacks during the "Final War" between Germany and the United States, which the leaders of both countries had come to view as inevitable. This course of action may have been fully justified as a matter of legal right—given the stationing of those missiles clearly violated the Peace of Copenhagen—but the awful fact remains that our attack set in motion an escalation that only ended with the nuclear wreck of all industrialized civilization. In sum, it is precisely because I have played so central a part in the history of our times and because I still consider myself an American patriot (although I fear that notion has been rendered an anachronism by recent events) that I must now insist on casting aside the tone of hatred and contempt with which we in the USA have spoken for so long of our former brethren in the Confederacy. To be sure, I do not subscribe to any of the notions of moral equivalency that were the recent fashion of the underground press. I remain firmly convinced that chattel slavery was, and is, a terrible evil, and for that reason the Southern cause was the side of wrong in the War of Secession. But I also believe that the greatest tragedy of the Confederacy's victory was the sundering of what Lincoln aptly described in his memoirs as "the last, best hope of earth."

Had Lee not won at Gettysburg; had the high tide of Confederate good fortune not washed away the last barriers to British and French recognition and intervention—the Union would surely have emerged victorious. Then, men like Lee, Davis, Benjamin, Longstreet and so many others would once again have been our countrymen. The process of reconciliation would undoubtedly have been difficult, and the inevitable compromises could very well have meant fewer freedoms for many (most notably, the Afro–Americans of the North, whose social integration could very well have been stymied for years if they came to be seen by white Americans as merely a part of a greater mass of liberated slaves whom Southern whites would likely have attempted to keep as close to a state of bondage as the formal abolition of chattel slavery might allow). But a united America, and especially one freed at last of the incubus of chattel slavery, could also have been a powerful force for progress in the world—indeed, a veritable arsenal for the forces of democracy. The sundering of the American Union into rival nations, however, had the very opposite effect for the peace and well-being of all mankind.

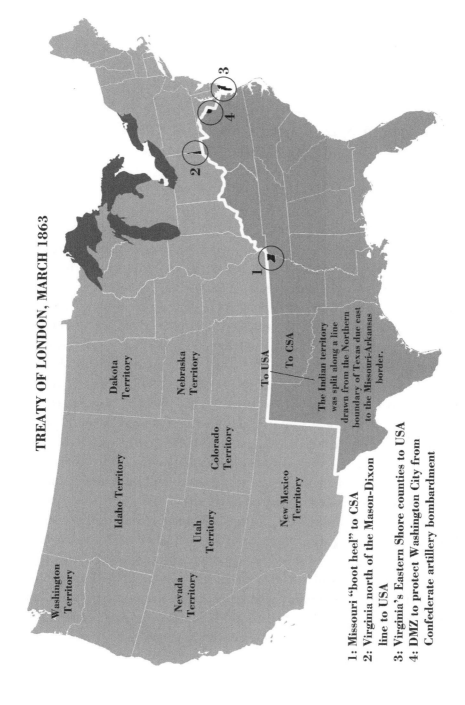

TREATY OF LONDON, MARCH 1863

Washington Territory

Idaho Territory

Dakota Territory

Nebraska Territory

Utah Territory

Colorado Territory

Nevada Territory

New Mexico Territory

To USA

To CSA

The Indian territory was split along a line drawn from the Northern boundary of Texas due east to the Missouri-Arkansas border.

1: Missouri "boot heel" to CSA
2: Virginia north of the Mason-Dixon line to USA
3: Virginia's Eastern Shore counties to USA
4: DMZ to protect Washington City from Confederate artillery bombardment

3

MEXICO, RUNAWAYS, AND THE FAILURE OF RECONCILIATION

So, the world started down the path which has placed us in our present terrible state. The North's acceptance of the armistice pending the outcome of the peace conference meant *de facto*, if not yet *de jure*, acceptance of Southern independence. The Treaty of London, signed by the conference delegates in March of 1863, formally ended the War of Secession—but just barely so. Southern fire-eaters almost torpedoed the treaty and reignited the war when the news reached Richmond of the terms agreed to by the Confederacy's delegation (led, like the North's, by the country's Secretary of State, Judah Benjamin). Of the four so-called "Border" slave states, the South would receive only Kentucky, and it was the "surrender" of Missouri which particularly rankled—never mind that the Confederacy had never managed to exercise control over any substantial portion of the state from the outset of war. Southern expansionists (whose ranks included President Davis) were also keenly disappointed by the disposition of disputed territories west of the Mississippi. The North would retain the entire New Mexico Territory (confirming the verdict of the Battle of Glorietta Pass a half-year before Gettysburg, where an *ad hoc* collection of Union forces rebuffed a Confederate invasion) and all of the Indian Territory north of a line running due east from the northernmost point of the border of Texas. Matters were not helped by the treaty provisions relating to Virginia's western and easternmost counties. The western counties had been on the verge of admission into the Union as the state of "West Virginia." While the balance were restored to the Old Dominion, the North successfully insisted that the portion north of the

Mason–Dixon Line be detached and awarded to Pennsylvania (to eliminate what would have been a Confederate "finger" pointing directly at Pittsburgh). The North was also awarded Accomack and Northampton Counties on the eastern shore of Chesapeake Bay to prevent the Confederacy from controlling access to Baltimore Harbor. The disposition of the "Virginia Counties" issue constituted quite the introduction to the territorial principles of international *realpolitik* for North and South; in both cases, the overwhelming majority of the affected populations were bitterly opposed to their fate. And in the case of Western Virginia, Richmond confronted violent guerilla resistance in the remoter hill country which was not fully suppressed until well into the 1870s. (The much smaller, less concentrated population of the pro-slavery Eastern Shore of Virginia, along with a geography far less suited to guerilla warfare, spared the North a similar experience there.)

Touchiest of all were the terms requiring the Confederacy to keep its forces stationed more than ten miles beyond siege gun range of Washington. Early in the Secession War, the Union had moved promptly to occupy and fortify the high ground in Virginia, directly across the Potomac River from Washington, D.C. This area had originally been ceded by Virginia to form part of the District of Columbia; the land south of the river was retroceded back to Virginia in the 1840s. The most prominent point in this County of Alexandria was Robert E. Lee's wife's home—built by her father (Martha Washington's grandson)—named Arlington House. Confederate artillery placed at Arlington could dominate the Union capital: emplacements at Arlington House were a mere three miles from the Capitol; under two miles to the USA War Department, Treasury, White House, and Georgetown College; and less than a mile-and-a-half from the vital Long Bridge.

Arlington House and the rest of Alexandria County were simply too close to the nerve center of the Union to permit its fortification by the Confederates. Development of the City of Alexandria itself into a fortified port across the river from the District of Columbia also would pose intolerable risks. Even regular field artillery—such as the ubiquitous twelve-pound smoothbore Napoleon, with a usual range of about a mile—could bombard the White House from the heights of Arlington and command the river. Range increases sharply with elevation and height: a twelve-pound rifled Whitworth gun firing at a thirty-five-degree elevation could reach ten thousand yards, and from Arlington Heights, even these relatively small Confederate pieces could rain down destruction on the Capitol. The thought of larger CSA pieces—Tredegar had been producing seven-inch Brooke rifles, of the type used on CSS Virginia, since the start of the war, and the ten-inch Confederate Columbiad could have battered the Capitol Building into ruin in short order—was simply impossible to bear.

As part of the general settlement, therefore, the North demanded—and the South acceded to—a "De-Militarized Zone," or "DMZ," to insulate the Union Capital. Confederate artillery was forbidden within the confines of the County or City of Alexandria, the retroceded portion of the District of Columbia. (President Lincoln actually convinced the Union Congress to repeal the Act of Retrocession of 1846: a bit of legislative legerdemain that made no impression on Richmond.) In addition—since the retroceded territory narrowed to the north and south (for, after all, it had made up about a third of the ten-mile square or diamond originally given to the federal government)—the DMZ also extended into Virginia in a ten-mile radius from each of the Long Bridge and Chain Bridge, below and above the federal District. Thus, the Confederates were forbidden to emplace artillery on the Virginia side of the river southward past the former Union Fort Hunt, although Mount Vernon itself was outside the DMZ—as was the Virginia territory immediately across the river from Union Fort Washington. The zone extended west into Fairfax County, well past the venerable Falls Church, and upstream along the Potomac to a point about parallel to Dranesville Tavern (where J. E. B. Stuart had exercised his first independent command in a skirmish with Union foragers early in the war). Given current and then-anticipated advances in artillery technology and the demilitarization of the Heights themselves, Union negotiators felt they had scored a major victory in establishing both the DMZ and a regime of periodic neutral inspection; and indeed, they had.

The acceptance of this affront to Virginian pride was only assured when General Lee urged the CSA Senate to accept the treaty in his open letter, "Let Us Have Peace" (in which Lee wryly noted that his restored Arlington home would remain under the threat of "Yankee cannonade"). In the end, cooler heads, aided by the flow of badly needed specie from cotton sales (which had resumed with the North's "suspension" of its blockade as part of the armistice during the pendency of peace talks), managed to steer the treaty through the Confederate Senate. "Do not take the criticisms to heart," Jefferson Davis advised Judah Benjamin, upon his return from London. "Although even I might like to change this or that portion of the arrangement you have struck, Confederate men of vision acknowledge that our cause has been well served by your efforts." Most importantly, the North's acceptance of the Treaty confirmed the Confederacy's freedom from a Union that the South's slaveholding elite felt could no longer be trusted to leave slavery alone, following the victory of the overtly anti-slavery Republican Party in the presidential election of 1860. The War of Secession had been fought to secure the future of slavery, and the Treaty of London confirmed the South's victory in that fight.

By the summer of 1863, the more hopeful predicted that the division between USA and CSA would now allow two different social systems to live in peace: the "impossible" demand that they remain under one political roof having been eliminated by the South's successful bid for independence. These prophets of peaceful coexistence, however, ignored two vital facts. The first was the end of a common American diplomatic front. The division of the American union into two countries at the behest of Europe's two leading powers dealt a death blow to the Monroe Doctrine, and the enduring entry of the European powers into Western Hemispheric affairs would keep the USA and CSA at odds, starting with the French intervention in Mexico. When the War of Secession erupted, Spain, Great Britain, and France were preparing to send a military expedition to Mexico to compel payment of substantial debts. Shortly after the expedition landed at Veracruz in December 1861, the three powers fell out over France's obvious plan to use its troops to intervene in Mexico's turbulent internal politics. Louis Napoleon believed it his manifest destiny to restore France's New World Empire—lost on the Plains of Abraham in 1759—with a new one based on Mexico. To that end, he planned to overthrow the republican government led by President Benito Juarez and replace it with an aristocratic administration controlled by France. When Madrid and London withdrew their forces in early 1862, France's stayed. French imperial troops marched on Mexico City, only to be checked by republican forces at Puebla that May.

This is how things stood when the Confederate delegation arrived in London in December for the opening of peace negotiations. The French made clear that one part of the price for their support at the negotiating table would be CSA support for France's plan to crush Juarez and install a regime beholden to Paris. President Davis's administration agreed— although not without extracting a French promise to look sympathetically on Confederate ambitions to acquire Cuba from Spain. Thus, when the French drove Juarez from Mexico City in the spring of 1863 and installed the Habsburg Archduke Ferdinand Maximilian as Emperor of Mexico, the CSA promptly recognized the new Imperial Mexican government. And when Juarez refused to go into exile and Republican resistance continued, the Confederacy permitted—indeed, encouraged—thousands of former Confederate troops to volunteer for service with Maximilian's army; supplied arms to the nascent Imperial forces from the rapidly expanding Tredegar armament works; and "assisted" the new Imperial government by sending forces to effect a "friendly" occupation of a substantial stretch of Mexican territory immediately south of the Rio Grande (territory the pro-slavery Polk Administration had tried—but failed—to acquire from Mexico in 1848).

The North was outraged by these developments and quickly moved to support Juarez and the Republican resistance. The New Mexico territory throughout its southern length was converted into a sanctuary for Republican forces, and the transfer of twenty thousand Union troops and a rapid buildup of fortifications served to deter possible incursions by CSA, French, or Imperial Mexican forces. (Plans to divide New Mexico into separate New Mexico and Arizona territories, which had progressed to the point that a bill effecting that division had passed the House of Representatives in March of 1862 but had then been delayed pending the outcome of the London peace negotiations, were now shelved due to concern that a division of the territory would complicate any military response to a Confederate or French incursion; a separate Arizona territory would not be created until after the suppression of the Apaches, at the end of the 1870s.) The North also moved to match CSA arms shipments which, along with maintaining a substantial force in New Mexico, had the ancillary benefit of providing business for Northern arms manufacturers, who had committed to a massive expansion in capacity and had been worried that the end of the War of Secession would require cutbacks that could have bankrupted many firms. Union officers, commissioned and non-commissioned and largely drawn from the Secession War's western theaters, provided training for *Juarista* recruits at camps based in New Mexico and Southern California.

The result might very well have been renewed war between the USA and the CSA (this time including France and its Imperial Mexican protégé) had not the growing Prussian threat, following Berlin's defeat of the Austrian Empire in the Seven Weeks War of 1866, forced Napoleon III to abandon his Mexican adventure. All French forces had been withdrawn by the end of 1868, and the CSA (its attention focused on an imminent war with Spain over Cuba) followed suit by January 1870. Left to fend for themselves, Maximilian's indigenous supporters were quickly routed; Maximilian surrendered himself to Republican forces that May. Juarez returned in triumph to Mexico City, where he ordered Maximilian to be tried by a court-martial in which the government demanded the death penalty. Found guilty, and his only appeal promptly rejected by Juarez, Maximilian was executed by firing squad on June 18, 1870.

The French intervention in Mexico perfectly illustrates the destructive consequences of the Confederacy's victory in the War of Secession. Had Lee been repulsed in the fall of 1862, I doubt Louis Napoleon would have continued his Mexican escapade. His army having been defeated at Puebla that May, he then paused to see whether the course of the American civil war would produce an opportunity to resume the conflict on more favorable terms. Absent that opportunity, Louis probably would have withdrawn his forces by the following spring. And even if Louis had resumed the drive on Mexico City in 1863 without the benefit of CSA support, *and* his army had managed to oust Juarez and install Maximilian, a restored American Union would certainly have moved promptly and decisively to compel French withdrawal. Faced with crack Union troops arrayed along the Rio Grande and a squadron of Union ironclads loaded with Marines *en route* to Veracruz, there could be no other imaginable outcome except a quick skedaddle. Literally hundreds of thousands of lives would have been saved, including that of the erstwhile Emperor Maximilian—it being inconceivable he would have tried to hold a throne to which he had no time to develop any strong sense of attachment.

But Lee did win, the British and French did intervene, and Louis Napoleon therefore was able to resume his pursuit of a Second New France. The cost to Mexico of the resulting long and bitter struggle to restore its independence was terrible, including the virtual destruction of Mexico City, as the CSA-trained artillerists of Maximilian's forces turned the capital, including its great cathedral, into a rubble-choked wasteland before finally relinquishing it to advancing *Juaristas*. Of more immediate relevance was the poisonous effect that Confederate support for the French intervention had on nascent relations between the two American unions. Northerners were appalled by what they saw as the Confederacy's betrayal of "fundamental American traditions" (to wit, the Monroe Doctrine) by allowing a European power to place a European prince— a Catholic Habsburg, no less—on a throne from which to rule over a Hemispheric people. Worse, the Confederacy had not merely acquiesced in France's move but had diplomatically and militarily supported the overthrow of Mexico's lawful republican government and its replacement with a European royal house. Of course, viewed realistically, the CSA's actions were eminently justifiable: French support had been essential to achieving Southern independence and gave rise to a debt that Richmond was obliged to repay (and in the only sort of currency honored by Great Powers). The Northern public, however, was in no mood to hear such *realpolitik* justifications of Confederate behavior. What they perceived was a Southern betrayal of shared American ideals—within months of the signing of a treaty in which the South had pledged to honor "basic principles held in common by the peoples of the Union and the Confederacy." To Northerners, one of the most basic of those principles was the Monroe Doctrine exclusion of intermeddling in New World affairs by the Great Powers of the Old; in the eyes of the North, the South had defaulted on their treaty obligation to uphold this fundamental American tradition. (It hardly mattered to Northern public opinion that the primary prop of the Monroe Doctrine had, all along, been the Royal Navy.)

My point is not that the USA was right, and the CSA wrong, in this particular quarrel. From their respective points of view, both were right: The

CSA had no realistic alternative to honoring its agreement with France, and the USA had good cause to be incensed at the CSA aiding and abetting a gross breach of the Monroe Doctrine. Rather, my point is that the division of the former United States of America into two countries left those countries with interests irremediably intertwined with European Great Powers—interests that were immediately at odds.

This brings me to the second factor that put paid to any hopes of peaceful reconciliation between North and South: the divergent paths of social development triggered by Southern independence, rooted in the institution of slavery. Had Lee somehow been prevented from winning his decisive victory at Gettysburg and had the North gone on to win the War of Secession, black slavery as a juridical institution undoubtedly would have ended throughout a still-unified USA. A relatively quick Northern victory by the summer of 1863—unlikely but not impossible—would probably have led to compensated or gradual abolition (at least in the non-seceding slave states and quite possibly in the seceding states as well, notwithstanding any presidential emancipation proclamation presuming to liberate slaves in those states). A longer war, with the North victorious in 1865 or 1866—only after having to overrun the Southern heartland—would likely have seen immediate, unconditional abolition, certainly as to the slaves in the seceding states (although slave owners in the non-seceding "loyal" states might still have received compensation). But a Northern victory of any type would doubtless have ended American chattel slavery by 1870, at the very latest. Notwithstanding a legal emancipation, however, Southern whites would almost certainly have tried to maintain the effective subservience of their former slaves, who (in turn) would presumably have demanded federal intervention to protect their newly won rights. This could well have created a political crisis in the North, given deeply felt anti-Negro racial prejudice in some areas combined with a probably powerful and universal sense of war weariness. For unless the North were prepared to reconstruct Southern social institutions from the ground up, Southern resistance would eventually have compelled some form of compromise whereby the white South would cease resistance to Northern authority, while the North averted its eyes as Southerners reconstructed their antebellum social order. A not-unlikely result would have seen the former slaves forced back into servitude in substance if not in form. Such a defeat for racial equalitarianism would have rendered the rest of the country susceptible to a self-justificatory racism, a necessary excuse for the abandonment of ex-slaves to the tender mercies of their former owners. In turn, this may have licensed the spread of racially discriminatory practices through the country as a whole. The end result might well have been a united America in which black Africans were condemned on *both* sides of the Mason–Dixon Line as racial inferiors and where the War of Secession was viewed as a wholly unnecessary conflict brought on by an irresponsible alliance of starry-eyed abolitionists and tariff-seeking industrialists. In short, in a unified American republic, prevailing nationalism and American exceptionalism would have been strengthened—at the cost of decades of racial repression.

But the North did not crush Secession, and Southern slavery was not abolished *de jure*. On the contrary, the newly independent South immediately set about to strengthen slavery's social and economic foundations. And rather than promoting a white racialism as a unifying factor across the formerly sectional—now international—divide, this "Southern values" campaign soon produced a social and economic backlash in the North.

The immediate trigger was the "runaway slave" issue. Under the Treaty of London, the South had agreed not to demand repatriation of slaves who reached Northern territory before February 22, 1861, the date Jefferson Davis was inaugurated as President of the Confederacy. The North agreed to recognize the legal claim of owners to slaves who had been able to escape only "as the result of military occupation by armed forces of the United States of America seeking to prevent the secession of the Confederate States of America from the prior existing Union." In other words, the parties compromised: Southerners yielded their claim to slaves who fled before the Confederacy was a functioning political entity, and the North agreed to return fugitive slaves if the owner could prove the slave had been able to escape only because of the effect of occupation by Northern forces during the War of Secession. Nothing, however, was said about slaves who escaped to the USA after the war (or, more precisely, after the withdrawal of Northern forces from Confederate territory pursuant to the terms of the Treaty of London). The omission was deliberate, as both sides recognized during the course of negotiations that any attempt to resolve the issue of future runaway slaves risked torpedoing talks and restarting the war. The South likely would have balked at any express waiver of its right to seek the return of future runaways, while the North certainly would have refused to countenance the express internationalization of Fugitive Slave Act principles. Yet, while silence on the issue of future runaways probably was a necessary price for avoiding a recommencement of hostilities, it soon became clear that Northerners and Southerners held irreconcilable views about what that silence implied.

If the Confederacy had taken the path of "gradual emancipation," the runaway issue should have proved a passing nuisance at most. Moderate Northern voices could have held out to their more militantly anti-servitude compatriots the credible assurance that the slavery that generated the runaways would itself soon come to an end (hence, the militants should exercise restraint in the name of future good relations with a slave-free Confederacy). But the South did not take the path of gradual emancipation. To the contrary, the newly independent Confederate states set about vigorously to restore and strengthen the foundations of their "peculiar institution."

In retrospect, it seems obvious there was little chance that the CSA would have taken any other course. Confederates of every political stripe have forthrightly admitted—nay, proudly proclaimed!—that their rebellion was made to preserve slavery. In the event, hostilities were suspended at a fortunate moment for slavery's future. Although much of Tennessee and Louisiana (including New Orleans) were under Northern occupation and federal forces held enclaves along the Atlantic Coast from Virginia to Florida, the North had yet to penetrate deep into the heartland of Southern slavery—the "Black Belt" cotton country stretching from South Carolina in the east to Mississippi in the west. And Lincoln's unwillingness, in the wake of Lee's victory at Gettysburg, to adopt emancipation as a war policy meant far less disruption to the slave-based economy in areas subject to Union occupation than might otherwise have been the case. Had the war dragged and the North driven deep into the Black Belt yet the South had somehow still managed to win independence, one can imagine at least a close debate in Confederate councils about whether to try and put back together what would then have been a much-ravaged institution. (Some have even imagined a CSA, *in extremis*, trading emancipation for Negro Confederate regiments—a speculation that, at least for me, stretches the boundaries of counterfactualism beyond the reasonably plausible.) But the North failed to make the necessary inroads, and influential Southern leaders who might in such circumstances have supported some program of gradual emancipation kept silent when the cry went up for the full restoration of Southern "traditions" in those areas where slavery had been disrupted by the war.

What seems obvious in retrospect, however, is often far from so at the time, and many Northerners grasped at the South's failure to insist on extending *ante-bellum* fugitive-slave-law principles beyond the immediate postwar period as proof that the South would move toward some form of gradual emancipation—if only after a "decent interval" to satisfy domestic political imperatives. Then, Southern authorities pressed ahead with brutal energy to reestablish slavery in the territories being evacuated by USA forces. The vast majority of slaves liberated by the Northern military were still within the Confederacy's boundary when the armistice was declared. Many began a desperate journey north, pursued by slave trackers operating openly behind what were still technically Union lines as Union forces confined themselves to captured towns and hastily erected fortifications to await the outcome of the London negotiations. Thousands of slaves committed suicide rather than fall back into the hands of their former masters—sometimes in full view of withdrawing Northern forces. Many thousands more were chained into coffles and marched back to their owners along the same roads Northern forces trod out of the victorious South. Summary executions of entire fleeing slave families, many carried out by the flying squadrons of the "Kuklux Knights" under Nathan Bedford Forrest, added to the horror felt by the retreating Northerners. Forrest's punitive massacre of over two hundred slaves (including dozens of women and their children) in full view of Union forces withdrawing by gunboats from Fort Pillow, Tennessee, after some of the slaves were said to have opened fire on Forrest's men, was only one of dozens of atrocities widely publicized throughout the North. The horrifying spectacle convinced many Northerners (above all, the overwhelming majority of returning Northern troops) that the North could never reconcile with a people who would commit such terrible wrongs. These feelings were only compounded by the spectacle of thousands of slave owners sending agents across the new USA–CSA border to track down runaway slaves and initiate the legal proceedings authorized by the Treaty of London to effect the return of runaways expressly subject to repatriation under the treaty's terms. The treaty's neat distinctions quickly broke down as slave owners pressed claims to blacks who either insisted they had fled prior to Davis's Inaugural or admitted they had fled during the war but insisted their flight had not been facilitated by Northern military occupation. The evidentiary difficulties inherent in resolving such claims quickly produced an inconsistent patchwork of adjudications, which in turn triggered protests by the Davis Administration accusing USA authorities of undermining slave owner claims by unofficial assistance to those helping accused runaways in repatriation proceedings.

To this explosive mixture was soon added the incendiary question of runaways who had fled the Confederacy after war's end and, therefore, were not expressly subject to—or protected from—repatriation under the Treaty of London's terms. It quickly became apparent that North and South held irreconcilable views on whether the North was obligated to repatriate these runaways. The CSA insisted that the general "mutual recognition" provisions of the treaty, under which the two countries agreed to enforce obligations arising under their "mutual statutory and common law inheritance," meant the USA must continue to enforce the pre-war Fugitive Slave Act laws unless the Treaty of London expressly negated those obligations. The pre-war Fugitive Slave Act, although effectively suspended by a USA Congress War Act in March 1862, had never been formally repealed, and the Confederacy now insisted that the peace had superseded the War Acts and thereby reactivated slave-owner rights under the pre-war law. The Lincoln Administration would have none of this Southern legal legerdemain, insisting that the treaty's failure to institutionalize the repatriation obligation beyond the narrow period called for by the exigencies of reconstruction meant slave owners had no right of repatriation for slaves who ran away after war's end. The Administration's firmness on this issue was undoubtedly reinforced by Lincoln's desire to see his able and trusted Secretary of State win the Republican nomination for the presidency.

Lincoln knew he had no chance of winning a second term, and he did everything he could to protect Seward from the charge of his Republican rivals that Seward had betrayed the Abolitionist cause at London by making a very public show of no concessions to the South in the implementation of the terms of the peace negotiated by Seward. Nor was the Supreme Court about to step in and try to "solve" the problem, as its Southern majority had tried to solve the pre-Secession slavery controversy with the politically disastrous *Dred Scott* decision. Although three fugitive slave cases had reached the Court by the summer of 1864, the Justices declined to set any of them for a hearing. The result was to make slavery a central issue in the 1864 Northern Presidential and Congressional elections—as it had been in the elections preceding Secession. The issue was framed by the Republicans principally as a matter of national pride: Republicans asked whether the USA would allow the Confederacy to export its slave system by force of legal process when the Confederates had supposedly seceded so they could be "left alone" to pursue "their way of life. Nor should the force of this argument be underestimated, for the Confederacy, by the systematic brutality of its postwar campaign to reconstruct slavery, had made clear its rejection of Northern "Free Soil" ideology as the "enemy" of a Southern "way of life" based on the right of whites to hold black Africans in bondage.

The Republicans were also able to exploit the broader issue of Northern development. The Democrats—after managing to take effective control of the House of Representatives in the 1862 midterm elections by capitalizing on Republican disarray in the wake of Lee's triumph at Gettysburg—had badly misjudged the temper of the electorate. Although the Democratic leadership wisely tabled backbench demands for repeal of the Homestead Act and the transcontinental railroad charter, the leadership blocked funding of some measures (for example, refusing appropriations for any of the land-grant colleges authorized by the Morrill Act passed the previous year). The Democratic leadership also prevented the adoption of other initiatives: most notably, the proposed acts calling for federal land grants to support the construction of a railroad across Kansas in the direction of Santa Fe in the New Mexico Territory and another across the Upper Midwest and Great Plains with a proposed terminus on Puget Sound. When combined with the Democratic call for a policy of "open economic borders" (the Treaty of

London having left the economic relationship between North and South to future negotiations), the result raised fears that the Democrats wished to restore the pre-war economic relationship under which the South's planter aristocracy and its cotton economy had held political sway. Even though the South's agrarian economy had been losing ground to the North's burgeoning industrialism during the 1850s, the fact that measures such as the Homestead Act and the initial transcontinental-railroad charter were only passed once the South's *de facto* political veto ended with the onset of Secession gave credibility to fears that a policy of open economic borders (i.e., no tariffs between the two unions) was a "nefarious Southern scheme" to dominate the North by blocking vital economic and social reforms.

Overall, the Democrats simply failed to grasp the degree to which Northern opinion had hardened against the South since the fall of 1862. The decision to pair New York Governor Horatio Seymour with the anti-war firebrand Clement Vallandigham further reflected this failure of judgment, as Democratic leaders should have recognized that Vallandigham's stridently pro-Southern rhetoric had once again fallen into disrepute. But they did not, and the Democrats' 1864 platform of "national reconciliation" with "our Southern brethren" proved a gift to the Republicans (who still might very well have lost without Lincoln's shrewd decision not to seek a second term and instead work for the election of the widely respected Seward). Seymour and Vallandigham carried the three slave states of Delaware, Maryland, and Missouri, but to these expected victories could add only Connecticut, New Jersey, and Pennsylvania among the Union's free states; the Republicans also swept back into control of both Houses of Congress. Over the next two years, slaves in the Border States that remained with the USA under the Treaty of London were emancipated (their owners receiving token compensation), and the Thirteenth Amendment was adopted, forbidding slavery and indentured servitude. Congress also declared its "understanding" that the runaway-slave repatriation clause of the Treaty of London did not apply to slaves who fled after the end of the War of Secession, and they underscored this action by repealing the pre-war Fugitive Slave Act. The Supreme Court then used these actions as the basis for summarily vacating the judgment in the one case before it in favor of a Southern slave owner seeking to recover a slave who had fled after the effective date of the Treaty of London and declaring the entire issue to be a non-justiciable "political question." The stalled Southwestern and Northern Pacific Railway Acts were now passed, and statehood was granted to Nevada. (These last measures also reflected a response to fears that only the fullest integration of the undeveloped territories of the West could assure that California would not attempt to follow the South's example and establish a "Pacific Republic" that might also encompass the state of Oregon, Washington Territory, and what had been California's *de facto* colony of Nevada.)

Calls, however, for more comprehensive measures to integrate the North's Negroes more fully into Northern society—by constitutional amendments guaranteeing them the vote (specifically) and equal protection of the laws (generally)—were tabled. As President Seward explained to Afro–American spokesman Frederick Douglass, "The time is not yet ripe for the Free Union of American States to take these steps. Rest assured, the time will come when the justice of such acts will impel their adoption—but now is not that time." In fact, Seward proved prophetic, as Douglass himself later acknowledged. Northern Negroes would, by the close of the 1880s, secure (as a matter of constitutional guarantee and Congressional enactments enforcing that guarantee) such basic rights as the right to vote, own property, make contracts, and sit on juries. Northern courts would reverse pre-Secession decisions and declare that Negro children could not be excluded from the rapidly expanding public school system. Northern Negroes would bring the process of integration into the political and social mainstream, winning election to public office and taking a leading role in certain areas of social life (perhaps most notably in the law, and as professional baseball players as the major leagues began to organize in the 1880s). The resulting divergence between Northern and Southern society would only reinforce the increasing tendency of each country to assume the worst about the other's conduct and intentions.

Of course, there was nothing "inevitable" about the course of USA politics and social policy during the years immediately following the Secession War's end. If the Democrats had proved less ham-handed or if Lincoln had insisted on standing for a second term, there might well have been a Democratic victory in 1864. But while a Democratic administration would have at least initially pursued reconciliation with the South, a President Seymour would not have been likely to accede fully to Confederate demands on the status of future runaways. And whatever accord a Democratic administration might have reached on such "inter-Union" matters, there would also have remained the growing problem of Southern ambitions in the Caribbean and Latin America. Ultimately, the two American unions were fated to move further and further apart because of their fundamentally different visions of what constitutes a just society and because of their increasingly conflicting interests as competing nation states. The South's slavery-driven vision would all too soon have a powerful—and sinister—impact on societies elsewhere in the Western Hemisphere and, in doing so, increase the stakes of the competition between the USA and the Confederacy.

(left) **Benito Juarez, President of Mexico, whose forces, with USA support, defeated the French-backed Emperor Maximillian and restored Mexican independence.**

(below) **The Ft. Pillow Massacre, one of dozens of Confederate atrocities committed against slaves seeking to escape the victorious South.**

4

"MAKING THE HEMISPHERE SAFE FOR SLAVERY": THE CONFEDERACY, BRAZIL, AND CUBA AND THE FIRST UNFOLDING OF THE BALEFUL CONSEQUENCES FOR THE HEMISPHERE, AND EVENTUALLY THE GLOBE, OF THE CONFEDERATE CONQUEST OF CUBA IN THE SPANISH–CONFEDERATE WAR OF 1870

———

While the Confederacy's recognition and subsequent support of Maximilian's regime had put North and South initially at odds, the more fundamental problem was the reason *why* the Davis Administration had chosen to repudiate the Monroe Doctrine and support Louis Napoleon's Mexican escapades—the Confederacy's desire to revitalize slavery. Despite the bluster of Southern "fire-eaters" in the years before the outbreak of the War of Secession, most of the South's political and social elite recognized that slavery faced a crisis rooted in demography: the number of slaves was diminishing—at least in the "Outer Southern" states (most notably, Virginia). Unless the breadth of slavery's population base was somehow replenished, its political base would be fatally compromised. The War of Secession had been fought precisely to avoid that result. Although the William Lloyd Garrisons were useful bogeymen who inspired fear of Northern abolitionism, most Southern leaders recognized that the truly dangerous "Yankees" were those prepared to let the slave states keep their peculiar institution while barring slavery's extension into the territories. For if slavery were so confined, the institution would continue to weaken in the outer slave states (Missouri, Kentucky, Virginia, Maryland, and Delaware) until it reached the point where these jurisdictions would emancipate their remaining slaves. And once these states abandoned slavery, the Southern slave heartland would be isolated: its Senate veto lost and facing the increasing likelihood of some form of compulsory emancipation by Congressional enactment.

It was precisely for this reason that Lincoln's election was a *casus belli*. Lincoln was believed to be an opponent of slavery who could—and would—implement the dreaded "confinement" solution. Secession thus eliminated the danger to slavery posed by remaining within a union dominated by the Lincolns, who favored ending slavery through a policy of slow strangulation. Of course, separating the South from the Union also ended any chance—however slim—of solving the demographic problem by extending slavery to the Union's remaining territories. On the other hand, secession left Richmond free to pursue a *foreign* policy dedicated to promoting the growth of slavery by acquiring new territories outside the boundaries of the former union to which slavery could be extended, and also by encouraging the preservation of slavery in those other countries and territories of the Western Hemisphere in which the practice was still allowed. As for acquiring new territories, the Confederacy's leadership already had its eye on the Spanish island of Cuba, where four hundred thousand black African slaves toiled on plantations dedicated to sugar and other crops. (As I will discuss more fully in the narrative of the Spanish-Confederate War of 1870, Cuba had long been a target of Southern slaveholder ambitions; Confederate President Davis himself vigorously championed annexation while serving his home state of Mississippi in the USA Senate before the outbreak of the War of Secession.) Cuba's acquisition would give an immediate boost to the "Mainland" slave economy and also promised opportunities for further exploitation by slave-based agriculture. For precisely this reason, the Confederacy's founders had carefully crafted the country's constitution to allow for the expansion of slavery by territorial expansion. Although Article I, Section 9 forbade the importation of slaves from "any foreign country other than the slaveholding States or Territories of the United States of America[,]" Article 4, Section 3 provided that the Confederacy could acquire new territory, and that "in all such territory, the institution of Negro slavery, as it now exists in the Confederate States, shall be recognized and protected by [the Confederate] Congress and by the Territorial Government." In short, while the Confederacy promised to observe the international ban on the African slave trade, that ban would not apply to slaves from a territory acquired by the Confederacy. (And as I will later demonstrate, the promise to honor the slave-trade ban would prove much less than quick scrutiny would suggest, when applied by pro-slavery Southern authorities to evasive devices such as "joint ownership" of plantations by Confederate and Brazilian interests.) Indeed, it was to advance the goal of acquiring Cuba for which Richmond proved most willing to abandon the Monroe Doctrine in exchange for French support of Southern efforts to gain "the Pearl of the Antilles."

CSA ambitions, moreover, were not limited to acquiring territory in the Caribbean. Richmond's goal was nothing less than to make the entire Western Hemisphere "safe for the Southern way of life" (i.e., slavery). To do that, the Davis Administration immediately set about to win the friendship of the Hemisphere's only other independent slave power. The relationship between the Confederacy and the Brazilian Empire illustrates, in perhaps its earliest manifestation, the insidious consequences of the South's successful secession for the internal development of other countries. Brazil, like the American South, confronted a crisis over the future of slavery. Brazil had only reluctantly acceded in 1851 to the British-promoted ban on the slave trade. And although the adverse effect of the ban on the Brazilian slave economy soon strengthened the hand of those urging the institution's abolition—a course already favored by Emperor Dom Pedro II, who had emancipated his own slaves years before—the Brazilian plantation owners who dominated the country's political life remained opposed to emancipation. Precisely because the fate of Brazilian slavery still hung in the political balance, Brazilians of every political stripe took a keen interest in the outcome of the attempt by the North American Union's slaveholding states to break free and establish the Hemisphere's second "great nation" with a slave-based economy. And from the war's outset, the country's slaveholders exerted their influence to assure as much Brazilian support as possible to the Confederate cause.

Although Brazil did not take the risk of granting the CSA diplomatic recognition until after an armistice had been declared, Brazil had early gone out on what at the time seemed a bit of a diplomatic limb by recognizing the

South's status as a "belligerent." Moreover, Rio de Janeiro promptly recognized the Confederacy following the news that London and Paris had taken that step, and Richmond moved just as quickly to exploit these good feelings. Thus, President Davis made quite a show of appointing the CSA's first Minister to Brazil before filling the same posts for any of the European powers (save, of course, the ministerships to England and France). Moreover, Davis made an inspired choice in selecting Commodore of the Confederate Navy Matthew Fontaine Maury, as Maury proved to combine diplomatic talents with genuine recognition and popularity in Brazil (stemming from Maury's authorship of the widely read pre-Secession work, *The Amazon and the Atlantic*, in which Maury had taken a highly positive view of Brazil). Nor did Richmond limit itself to contacts at the government level—also encouraging less formal interchanges in order to develop friendships between the slave owners of each country. Confederate representatives let key members of the planter class and their allies in the Brazilian government know of Confederate ambitions toward Cuba and of plans to strengthen the CSA's slave economy by intensive development of Cuba's existing (but neglected) slave-based agriculture. These informal conversations are known to have included broad hints that Brazilian participation in various Cuban "joint ventures" would be welcomed—once the Confederacy had somehow managed to oust the Spanish and thereby end any chance of the abolition of Cuban slavery by Madrid. The CSA's Brazilian policy thus appealed to a variety of Brazilian prejudices and interests, with an emphasis on: tradition (the historic hostility toward Spain); culture (a common experience with slavery); and economic interest (the prospect of mutual gain by the joint development of slave-based enterprises).

Emperor Dom Pedro II remained a quiet supporter of emancipation notwithstanding the Confederacy's victory in the War of Secession; although, the political resurgence of emancipation opponents in the wake of that victory did cause the Emperor to "temporarily" shelve his plan to call publicly for gradual emancipation. Had Confederate–Brazilian relations simply proceeded along the course marked out immediately following the Treaty of London—at least until the CSA's seizure of Cuba from Spain in 1870—the fate of Brazilian slavery might have continued to hang in the balance for several years more. The emancipationists might even have regained the upper hand: at least to the extent that Dom Pedro would have run the risk of confronting slave owners with a public call for emancipation in some form. Such a possible course of events, however, would be cut off by the War of the Triple Alliance, which pitted Paraguay against the three-party alliance of Brazil, Argentina, and Uruguay.

The War of the Triple Alliance began in November 1864, when Paraguay's megalomaniacal dictator, "Field Marshal President" Francisco Solano Lopez, closed the Paraguay River—a vital branch of the Plata network—to Brazilian traffic, then ordered Paraguayan gunboats to capture an imperial steamer carrying the president of Mato Grosso province. (Only after that did Solano Lopez notify Brazil's minister that Paraguay was breaking diplomatic relations!) The immediate cause of this conflict was political strife in Uruguay—between the mercantile *Colorado* faction based in Montevideo and the federalist *Blanco* faction representing hinterland cattle interests. Brazil and Argentina had clashed repeatedly over the territory of the "East Platine" until the compromise that created Uruguay, thereby assuring that *neither* country would possess the area. Having removed rivalry over control of the East Platine as a source of conflict, Brazil and Argentina then found themselves aligned in support of the *Colorado* but unwilling to impose a "*Colorado* solution."

So it came to pass that a *Blanco* Uruguayan president, Atanasio Cruz Aguirre, confronted a Brazilian ultimatum in the spring of 1864: Pay for damage to Brazilian property allegedly caused by Uruguayan bandits raiding across the border, or Brazil would seek satisfaction through military means. It was this ultimatum that triggered the War of the Triple Alliance. To the north, Paraguay had lived in friendless isolation for almost fifty years. Its government of military dictators, fearing absorption by either Argentina or Brazil, had built up South America's strongest army (a standing force of twenty-eight thousand with another forty thousand in reserve troops), along with a powerful riverine navy and an impressive supporting infrastructure of fortifications and interior lines of communication (including the continent's longest rail and telegraph lines). Then in 1862, Paraguay's ruler, Carlos Antonio Lopez, was succeeded by his son, Solano Lopez, a genuine megalomaniac whose neo-Napoleonic ambitions included establishing Paraguayan control over the entire Plata River network. Solano Lopez seized on the

Brazil–Uruguayan crisis as the chance to realize his dream of an "Empire of Paraguay." When Solano Lopez learned of Brazil's ultimatum to Uruguayan President Aguirre, Lopez urged Aguirre to spurn Brazilian demands and promised Paraguayan support in the event Brazil made good its threat of intervention. Emboldened by these promises, Aguirre did just that; when Brazil responded with a blockade and an invasion, Aguirre fled north into the Uruguayan interior toward Paraguay.

Aguirre's *Colorado* successor promptly agreed to meet Brazil's indemnification demand, and there the matter might have ended had not Solano Lopez—believing the Uruguayan crisis had opened the door to the creation of a Paraguayan empire by force of arms—decided to keep Paraguay's promise to Aguirre and move against Brazil. The Paraguayan army first invaded the Brazilian province of Mato Grosso, planning to link up with Aguirre's forces in northern Uruguay. But to do that, Solano Lopez needed permission to cross Argentine territory—which Buenos Aires refused to give. Paraguay responded by seizing Argentine vessels on the inland waterways and invading the Argentine province of Corrientes. Thus, by the spring of 1865, Brazil and Argentina (along with the Uruguayan government in control of Montevideo) found themselves at war with Paraguay. The resulting War of the Triple Alliance would prove the bloodiest international conflict fought prior to the First World War: At its end in 1869, Paraguay's population had been cut in *half* (with *nine-tenths* of Paraguayan males slain in battle and related massacres); total deaths on both sides exceeded three hundred thousand. (By contrast, total dead during the War of Secession numbered 150,000.) Paraguay was crushed: its army and navy annihilated, its capital city of Asuncion destroyed, its rail and telegraph system wrecked, and its surviving population forced to eke out a subsistence existence. (Solano Lopez himself did not survive. Escaping the destruction of Asuncion in January of 1868, he fell in battle at the head of a ragtag guerilla band in March of the following year.) Only the mutual suspicion between Brazil and Argentina saved Paraguay from political annihilation; unable to agree on a division of the spoils, the two powers settled for a "mutual guarantee" of Paraguay's "territorial integrity," thereby maintaining the country as a buffer state.

But in the spring of 1865, that Alliance triumph lay four years in the future. And while Brazil and Argentina possessed a tremendous advantage in military-age male population, the pre-war disparity in ready, armed forces so lopsidedly favored Paraguay that most neutral observers gave Solano Lopez a decent chance of seizing large chunks of Brazilian and Argentinean territory, which he could then hold hostage to the negotiation of favorable peace terms. If this disparity helps to explain Solano Lopez's decision for war, then the ensuing catastrophe perhaps may best be explained as a consequence of Paraguay's decades-long and self-imposed isolation. For a more cosmopolitan leader might have recognized what Solano Lopez did not see: war pitting Paraguay against Brazil and Argentina would quickly draw in the two North American unions, as the CSA and the USA competed to curry favor with South America's two largest countries. And that is exactly what happened—with the Confederacy leading the way in Brazil and the North struggling to keep up through counterbalancing aid to Argentina.

Not that what the North Americans did was essential if the Alliance were to defeat Paraguay, for the Alliance's most important victory—the destruction of Paraguay's river navy in the Battle of Riachuelo on June 11, 1865—was won before the receipt of any significant aid from either the Confederacy or the USA. North American aid, however, was essential to effecting the rapid transformation of the Alliance armies and navies into professional forces able to meet the well-trained Paraguayans on equal terms. In this effort, Confederate aid to Brazil played the decisive role. Naval assistance to Brazil was coordinated by James Toombs, Chief of the Confederacy's Naval Ordnance Bureau. Toombs, who pioneered many innovations in mine (then called "torpedo") technology, organized Brazil's effective response to the mines with which Paraguay sought to deny river passage to the Brazilian and Argentine navies. Equally crucial was Confederate assistance in equipping and training the Brazilian army, and particularly its new artillery corps (the latter effort headed up by Major General John Pelham, the hero of Gettysburg and deputy chief of the CSA Army Ordnance Bureau). But perhaps most important was the sheer size and spirit of the Southern effort: By the spring of 1866, the CSA had dispatched over one thousand advisers, and Brazil had contracted with Tredegar for the delivery of over 250 artillery pieces of the latest Confederate designs. (Brazil's ironclad needs were being met—like the Confederacy's at this early date—through contracts with British shipyards.) The result was an army and navy that soon proved more than a match for Paraguay, as Brazilian forces began to employ an aggressive style learned from their Confederate tutors. Thus, Brazilian Admiral Joaquim Marques Lisboa (Marquis of Tamandare), seizing on reports from Confederate advisers of the Paraguayan failure to mount sufficient batteries at a key point, ordered an early attack on the stronghold of Curupayti by the combined Brazilian–Argentine force under his command. On September 3, 1866, Curupayti fell to an assault that cost the Alliance fewer than one thousand casualties. This victory opened the door to an early investment of the fortress of Hamaita, whose fall at the end of 1867 opened the way to Asuncion and sealed Paraguay's doom.

The War of the Triple Alliance transformed Brazilian society and drew the country much closer to the Confederacy—both politically and socially. The war left Brazil with an army of seventy-five thousand regular troops and a navy of ten seagoing ironclads (along with dozens of other vessels of a wide variety of types). Brazil's riverine forces were modern and effective, incorporating lessons learned by the CSA in Hampton Roads and on the Mississippi. The officer corps of this new military had spent four years in the field with their Confederate advisers, creating a social institution with an anti-emancipationist outlook acquired from its slave-owning mentors. The importance of personal relationships to the course of politics in Brazil should not be underestimated, and the war produced literally thousands of personal ties—many later reinforced by intermarriage—between Confederate and Brazilian officers. The emergence of this powerful new voice against emancipation broke the back of what was already a waning political force. Reluctantly, Emperor Dom Pedro abandoned his hopes for the adoption of a "Law of the Womb," which would have doomed Brazilian slavery demographically by freeing children of slaves born after a certain date. (The hundreds of USA advisors who spent the same years working with Argentina's armed forces similarly brought home affection for their Argentine *compadres*, along with vivid tales of the Pampas as a beef-growing region to rival lost Texas; in the long-run, however, the establishment of Tredegar affiliates in Salvador and Sao Paulo would prove more enduring than displaced Nebraskans raising calves.)

Brazil's emancipation proponents might yet have seized back the political initiative had it not been for the successful and near-simultaneous culmination of the Confederacy's drive to acquire Cuba. Without Cuba, Confederate slavery would have remained in a state of crisis, and Brazilian emancipationists could have exploited this fact to win back those in Brazil's political and social leadership who had abandoned emancipation in response to Confederate blandishments. But with the acquisition of Cuba, the South breathed new demographic life into its own slave economy *and* created opportunities for joint Confederate–Brazilian ventures in the development of slave-based agriculture (while greatly enhancing the two countries' ability to circumvent the anti-slave trade conventions to which both were parties).

The island of Cuba had been an object of Southern ambition long before the moment the first Confederate administration had been organized at Montgomery. In fact, acquiring Cuba had been a goal of American statesmen from the North as well as the South, dating back at least as far as then-Secretary of State John Quincy Adams's observation in 1823 that Cuba was a "natural appendage" to the North American continent, whose annexation was "indispensable to the continuance and integrity of the Union itself." But the desire to acquire Cuba always burned brightest below the Mason–Dixon Line, and future Confederate President Jefferson Davis had been one of annexation's chief proponents—for the express purpose of "increasing the number of slaveholding constituencies." Davis was so determined to see Cuba's four hundred thousand slaves joined to the Mainland's that he openly encouraged the *filibustero* invasion efforts of the early 1850s; although Davis declined the invitation of Narciso Lopez to lead the first of Lopez's—ultimately unsuccessful—expeditions, Davis made clear his support for the endeavors. By the eve of Secession, there remained virtually no support for annexation outside the slave states, as most Northerners had become determined to block the incorporation of a territory they feared could tip the country's political balance decisively in the "Slave Power's" favor. The desire to acquire Cuba thus became for some Southerners an additional reason (albeit nowhere a decisive one) for electing secession.

But if President Davis and his able Secretary of State, Judah Benjamin, believed that only "Yankee abolitionism" had prevented the former Union from acquiring Cuba, they were quickly disabused of that notion. Cuba was ruled by Spain, and Spain did not want to part with what was now its principal New World territory. During the Ostend Manifesto imbroglio of

1854, the Spanish government had vehemently rejected suggestions that Spain should yield Cuba to the United States. A decade later, when the newly appointed Confederate Minister to Madrid opened his ministry with a proposal for the Confederacy to purchase Cuba, Queen Isabella and her ministers reacted with such hostility that Davis concluded there was little chance of the South gaining Cuba by purely peaceful means. Benjamin, however, remained reluctant to give up on the diplomatic avenue and tried to enlist Louis Napoleon as an intermediary. But while there had been some initial sympathy in Spain for a monarchical restoration in Mexico, Spanish opinion by 1865 had turned decisively against what most now condemned as "Bonapartist adventurism." Madrid spurned French feelers on the Confederacy's behalf, and Benjamin now concurred with Davis that Spain would not yield Cuba without a preceding clash of arms. The Confederacy therefore began to lay the diplomatic foundations for such an effort. Thus, when Spain confronted Chile in 1866 over a debt dispute (leading to the bombardment of Valparaiso by a Spanish naval squadron), the CSA protested Madrid's actions in the strongest possible terms—part of Richmond's policy of driving a wedge between Spain and its former South American colonies to assure Madrid's isolation during a Spanish–Confederate war over Cuba. In the Chilean case, CSA Secretary of State Benjamin shrewdly exploited the failure of a nearby USA naval squadron to intervene and prevent the Spanish bombardment of Valparaiso, thereby encouraging hostility toward Washington as well as friendship with Richmond.

Still, matters might not have come so swiftly to a head had not rebellion broken out on Cuba in 1868. The rebels were led by Creole planters who feared that Madrid intended to emancipate their slaves. In fact, Queen Isabella and her ministers—in the wake of the Confederacy's successful war for independence and the revitalization of slaveholding interests in Brazil—had concluded that prudence dictated delay in any emancipation of Cuban slaves. The Spanish government, however, failed to clearly communicate this change of heart to key Cuban slave holders. Then, when revolution in Spain saw the deposition of the monarchy and the establishment of a republic in September 1868, the island's slave owners feared that the worst was about to come to pass. Egged on by promises of arms from Confederate agents, a coalition of Creole landowners declared Cuba's independence.

For nearly two years, the insurrection raged: Richmond aided the rebels; Madrid accused Richmond of doing so; and Richmond piously denied the charges while continuing to pour in arms. Robert E. Lee's accession to the Confederate presidency in 1867 produced no change in CSA policy, especially as Lee retained Benjamin as his Secretary of State. By February 1870, when Richmond dispatched the cruiser CSS *Alabama* to Havana for a "friendly visit," matters had reached a flash point. Whether the subsequent burning of the *Alabama* in Havana Harbor on the night of February 15 was an accident or sabotage will probably never be known, primarily because the relevant Confederate records probably did not survive the 1918 Richmond firestorm raid—and certainly not the USA's nuclear strike this past October. While I doubt the Lee Administration countenanced the destruction of a warship that the South might need to confront Madrid's not-insubstantial navy, Richmond undeniably seized with alacrity on the loss as a *casus belli*—even though Confederate agents were reporting that the local Spanish authorities likely had nothing to do with the fire.

Secretary of State Benjamin recognized that the Spanish government would reject as a point of honor his demand for an "independent Confederate" investigation of the *Alabama*'s burning, after Benjamin insinuated that the local Spanish authorities should be considered "persons of interest." Benjamin proceeded over the next several weeks to orchestrate an escalating crisis which culminated at the end of March with Madrid's recall of its minister from Richmond, following the finding by a—probably rigged—CSA Navy Court of Inquiry that the *Alabama* had been deliberately burned by "persons unknown though of undoubted local origin." There quickly followed a stage-managed plea by the "Cuban forces of liberty," asking their Confederate "brothers in liberty" to intervene and "lift off the yoke of Spanish oppression," and a responsive resolution by the CSA Congress adopted on April 19 which authorized President Lee to take all necessary measures—including "use of the land and naval forces of the Confederacy"—to "carry into effect the wishes of the Cuban people." By this time, of course, the Confederacy was ready to strike—swiftly and boldly. Upon his accession to the presidency, Robert E. Lee had selected James Longstreet to be Secretary of War. Lee and Longstreet now managed to persuade the third member of the Army of Northern Virginia's "Gray Triumvirate" (Thomas

"Stonewall" Jackson) that he should come out of retirement to his beloved Shenandoah Valley farm and lead the Confederacy's Cuban Expeditionary Force. The Confederate navy imposed a blockade of the island, while Jackson's forces effected landings near Havana and Santiago. Havana quickly fell, but Spanish forces near Santiago fell back on well-prepared siege lines, awaiting relief from Spain.

The military climax came in June: on land and at sea. In a brilliantly executed charge up San Juan and Kettle Hills—led by Major General George Pickett—the Confederates gained the heights surrounding Santiago, thereby exposing the city to devastating artillery bombardment. (Pickett, a dashing figure who had expressed frustration over "missing all the fun" at Gettysburg, did not survive his troops' exploits, falling mortally wounded by a Spanish sniper at the threshold of victory.) The day after, in a sharp engagement off Guantanamo Bay, the CSA's ironclads dealt the Spanish relief squadron a serious reverse, forcing the Spanish to retreat to their anchorage at San Juan, Puerto Rico. The Confederate squadron sank three Spanish broadside ironclads—*Arapiles*, *Tetuan*, and the flagship *Numancia*—and suffered only minor damage to its British-built flagship, CSS *Biloxi*. The Spanish ships' smoothbore shot—only *Arapiles* carried a handful of rifled guns—failed to penetrate the armor of the three strongest Confederate ships: *Biloxi* and her sisters *Mobile Bay* and *Shreveport*. In contrast, the Confederates' nine-inch rifles made short work of the lightly armored Spanish fleet. (One political beneficiary of the battle was Secretary Benjamin, who had been a strong proponent of acquiring the modified *Audacious*-class warships from Great Britain.)

When news of these Southern victories reached Madrid and Washington, a crisis ensued that nearly brought the USA into the war on Spain's side. The Spanish government of Juan Prim was still reeling from an abortive attempt to put a Hohenzollern prince on the Spanish throne—restored under the country's new constitution adopted after the overthrow of Queen Isabella in 1868. (A momentous side effect of this kingship controversy was the outbreak of war between France and Prussia, as Prussia's chancellor Otto von Bismarck manipulated the ensuing diplomatic *contretemps* to bring about a war by which Bismarck intended to—and would—effect the establishment of a united German Reich as the premier power on the European continent.) Prim recognized that Cuba was lost but, faced with Confederate demands for Puerto Rico as well as Cuba, Prim also was prepared to carry on the war—if only because he knew his government would be overthrown if it countenanced the loss of both islands. Washington also recognized that the Confederates had made good their campaign for Cuba, but President Seward and the Republican congressional leadership were ready to fight rather than allow the CSA to acquire a virtual stranglehold on the Caribbean—which would result from Richmond's acquisition of Puerto Rico as well as Cuba. In the meantime, Richmond echoed to the cries of "On to San Juan!" Many Southerners believed that Seward was bluffing, and that the North would never go to war for "Catholic Spain"—a fair point, considering the strident anti-Catholicism of key areas of Northern opinion, typified by Thomas Nast's cartoon in *Harpers Weekly* lampooning "Prim's Second Inquisition." Yet, Seward's firmness communicated itself to Richmond: both in words and in the somewhat less articulate, but nonetheless unmistakable, message conveyed by the dispatch of a squadron of Northern seagoing ironclads to San Juan. Lee agreed with Longstreet and Benjamin that Puerto Rico itself was not worth a war with the North—especially as Great Britain had made clear it would not intervene to prevent a Northern blockade of Southern ports.

Through the good offices of Argentina and Brazil, the Spanish–Confederate War was brought to a formal close at the end of 1870. Spain acknowledged the Confederacy's conquest of Cuba, while the Confederacy agreed to "respect" Spain's ownership of Puerto Rico and to "acknowledge" that Spain would still occupy a "special position" toward its former Cuban territory. The ink was barely dry on the treaty, however, when the Confederacy's triumph had set in motion in the alliance-building dynamic that would eventually draw in the Great Powers of Europe—with such tragic consequences for the course of world history.

The first concrete manifestation of this process saw Spain and the USA move swiftly to form an alliance in order to check the CSA's growing power in the Caribbean. The USA agreed to finance the development of major naval and army installations on Puerto Rico, and Spain agreed to give the USA basing rights for its navy (with the added intention that a Spanish squadron would be based permanently at San Juan). The USA also entered into an alliance with the black-ruled nation of Haiti, which had been thrown into a panic by the prospect of the slaveholding Confederacy now less than one hundred miles to the west. Talks had been ongoing since 1866 over the establishment of a USA naval base at the deep harbor Môle St. Nicholas, but Seward had been reluctant to offend Spain by entering into such an agreement (Spain's military reoccupation of Santo Domingo in 1861 having caused a rift in Haitian–Spanish relations). The Confederate conquest of Cuba, however, swept away this one obstacle to a USA–Haitian base deal: Haiti now welcomed a continuing Spanish presence in Santo Domingo as a check against CSA designs on that territory, while the Spanish saw a major US naval presence at the Môle as a useful counter to Richmond's expected development of Guantanamo Bay to the west as a Southern naval base. The Greater Antilles were thus turned into a series of bristling fortresses from which rival warships would weigh anchor to prowl the surrounding waters.

The destabilizing effects soon spread south. At the outbreak of the Spanish–Confederate War, Colombia had been engaged in talks with the USA about the possibility of a USA-led consortium building a canal across the Colombian-controlled Isthmus of Panama. Although the Clayton–Bulwer Treaty of 1850 had defused tension between the United States, Great Britain, and Colombia (then New Granada) by guaranteeing the "neutral" development of an Isthmian canal, civil unrest in New Granada had discouraged anything beyond the most preliminary of survey work. Then, in 1856, riots in Panama caused extensive loss of life and destruction of property, and disputes over American reimbursement demands embittered relations between the two countries. These bad matters went to even worse with the outbreak of civil war in New Grenada at virtually the same moment that the South seceded from the Union: Dealings between Washington and Bogota were paralyzed for over two years, as contending New Granadan factions sent rival ministers to Washington clamoring for recognition.

New Granada's civil war ended shortly after the Confederacy's victory in the War of Secession, and the liberal Tomás C. Mosquera was inaugurated in July 1863 as president of the new United States of Colombia. The triumphant Colombian liberals identified with the dynamic capitalism of the North, had openly hoped for a Southern defeat, and were appalled by the Confederacy's success. The Colombians also blamed the pre-Secession tensions between the former American and New Granadine unions on the ambitions of Southern slaveholders, whom the Colombians suspected (quite rightly) of desiring to dominate the whole of the Caribbean basin. Colombia therefore moved quickly to repair ties with the USA by resolving the outstanding Panama Riots claims. In early 1864, a new convention establishing a claims commission was agreed to—with the Danish minister to the United States serving as umpire. Colombia and the USA also cooperated in opposing France's intervention in Mexico (Colombia rejecting Louis Napoleon's claim that a French presence in Mexico would provide a "Latin" barrier against Anglo–Saxon advances). Both these issues, moreover, contributed to a simultaneous souring of Colombian–Confederate relations: The Confederacy rejected the mixed claims commission as a forum to resolve "its share" of the Panama Riots claims, and Bogota was infuriated by Richmond's open support of Mexico's putative Emperor Maximilian. Colombia also was disturbed by the CSA's support for slavery in Brazil and for the slaveholding Cuban insurrectionists in their fight against Spain. (Colombians were virtually unanimous in their view—a prescient one—that the Confederacy was positioning itself for an attempted seizure of Cuba.) Thus, by the end of the 1860s, the time was ripe for the USA and Colombia to reach agreement on a treaty providing for the construction of a canal across the Isthmus of Panama. There remained differences, however, over such details as the extent of the territory to be dedicated to the project, the degree of USA responsibility for the canal's defense, and the amount of USA financing of construction and ancillary defense costs. These issues had delayed Colombian approval of a proposed treaty until 1869 and then stalled action on the part of the American Senate. The outbreak of the Spanish–Confederate War, however, galvanized the Senate into action, and the treaty was ratified only days after news had reached Washington of the Confederacy's decisive Cuban victories on land and sea.

There ensued a period of preliminary work: which included identifying the individuals to whom the task of building the canal would fall. After Ferdinand De Lesseps's triumph at Suez in 1869, he became the popular candidate to head the venture—a popularity reinforced by the resurgence of French Republicanism following the fall of the Second Empire in 1870. USA interests, however, were loath to surrender their presumed position of leadership. Then, at the New York "Canal Congress" convened by the USA and Colombian governments in 1873 (and to which "The Great Frenchman" had been specially invited and for which his expenses had been paid), De Lesseps announced he favored a canal *à niveau* and *sans écludes*—at sea level and without locks. The Americans had just finished a comprehensive survey (through a series of government-sponsored expeditions) which showed a sea-level canal à la Suez could not be built across the Isthmus. They therefore balked at placing De Lesseps in charge. Ultimately, the matter was resolved by having De Lesseps chair the effort (his prestige after Suez made exclusion politically impossible) while leaving the engineering decisions to a committee dominated by the Americans who favored a locks design. The project would be administered by a special company chartered by the Colombian government, but finances would be guaranteed by the USA, thus assuring ultimate American control. A massive undertaking, the canal took over ten years to complete: opening on October 28, 1886, in a grand ceremony presided over by De Lesseps, USA President Grover Cleveland, and Colombian President Rafael Nunez. Nunez was a liberal who had been overwhelmingly reelected the year before, as Colombians expressed their approval of the economic benefits flowing from the canal's construction and ever closer economic ties to the USA. But the completion of the canal also represented the effective cementing of Colombia on one side of an emerging alliance system that could put it in the front lines—along with Spain—should war erupt between the USA and the Confederacy and the fighting spread to the Caribbean Basin. (In fact, as I shall later relate, the Colombians would find themselves the target of a Confederate assault even before the project's completion: during the final stage of the Western War of 1882–84, between the USA, Mexico, and the Confederacy.)

(left) **William Seward, President of the USA, whose diplomatic and military policies checked Confederate ambitions in Mexico, established the American alliance with Spain, and set in motion the construction of the Panama Canal.**

(right) **Mathew Fontaine Maury, Confederate Minister to Brazil, who out-dueled Seward for the heart and soul of the Brazilian Empire during the War of the Triple Alliance, and thereby "saved" Brazil for slavery.**

5

SECESSION, DISUNION, AND THE EMERGING SOCIO-ECONOMIC DIVISION BETWEEN NORTH AND SOUTH

———

Before I continue my chronicle of how the international political and military consequences of Secession eventually engulfed the Hemisphere from the Yukon to Tierra Del Fuego, I want to pause and comment on the effect of Secession on the course of economic and social change within the two American unions. The transforming effects wrought on Colombia by the Panama Canal venture were paralleled by comparable and even greater effects on the USA and the Confederacy during the first two decades following Secession, and these changes only served to widen the gap between the two American unions.

Consider, for example, the effect of Secession on the development of the Northern railway network—with its implications for Northern economic development. The reader will recall that during the French and Confederate intervention in Mexico, the USA provided substantial aid to the *Juaristas* fighting to overthrow Maximilian. As part of that effort, the New Mexico Territory became a "safe haven" where Republican forces received arms and training, under the "protective umbrella" of over twenty thousand USA federal troops stationed in the area to deter incursions by Imperial Mexican, French, or Confederate forces. The Southwestern USA, however, was unprepared to support such an effort, lacking—among other things—any rail connection to the outside world. The reader will also recall that, following the midterm vote of 1862,

Democrats used their newly-won control of the House of Representatives to block passage of a second Pacific Railroad Act that would have provided for the development of a railroad line from Atchison, Kansas to the New Mexico Territory boundary. The Republican election victory of 1864 eliminated this impediment to congressional action, but the growing needs of the effort to support the *Juaristas* now required a much more ambitious undertaking. The Southwestern Railroad Act passed in early 1866 therefore called for establishment of a second transcontinental rail link—to be formed by joining the planned Atchison, Topeka & Santa Fe line to be built from the east, with a comparable expansion of the Southern Pacific out of Los Angeles from the west—a truly aggressive plan, considering the SP had yet to approach (much less cross over) the San Gabriel Mountains into the Los Angeles basin.

The push to complete a transcontinental railway through the Southwest proved much more difficult than the more northerly effort by the Central Pacific and Union Pacific railroads, and the Southwest link was not completed until 1877—seven years *after* Maximilian's defeat and Juarez's restoration. But the link was made, and the effort soon transformed Southern California and the Southwestern territories. The Southern Pacific had moved aggressively to establish its network in California, laying track down the west side of the San Joaquin Valley in the mid-1860s and arriving in Los Angeles by 1869. As the SP then pushed east into the Mojave Desert to link up with the Atchison, Topeka & Santa Fe, the California-based railroad began to "ballyhoo" the joys of the Golden State in an intensive advertising campaign. The effort succeeded in boosting the population of Los Angeles to over twenty thousand by the time of the Southwestern Linkup at Winslow, Arizona, in 1877. At that point, the combination of perceived economic opportunity, coupled with new inducements—principally a drastic cut in rates, coordinated between the SP and its AT&SF "Southwest partner"—triggered a flood of settlers. Over two hundred thousand people moved into the Greater Los Angeles Basin in the next five years, and although the Western War would interrupt the Southwestern rail connection to the Eastern USA, this disruption was more than made up for by a local "war boom" in armaments and related industries. (Among other things, the necessities of the war effort produced the transformation of the great mudflat of San Pedro Bay into a modern harbor, with the completion by 1884 of the necessary system of breakwaters.) By 1890, the city of Los Angeles boasted a population in excess of five hundred thousand. Moreover, the 1877 linkup of the Southern Pacific and AT&SF also unleashed a stream of settlement into the Southwestern Territories of Arizona and New Mexico (the former New Mexico territory having finally been divided—at the end of the 1870s—into the separate territories of New Mexico and Arizona). The flow of settlers into these desert regions triggered a major investment in irrigation systems, in turn creating agricultural opportunities that drew still more immigrants, and leading to the admission in 1889 of Arizona and New Mexico as the Union's twenty-seventh and twenty-eighth states.

The rapid development of the southwestern railway network reflected the high priority placed on completion of the transcontinental railroads as a means of binding the Pacific coast states and territories (above all, California) to the eastern remainder of the former Union. In fact, the North had reason to fear a secession attempt: if not by California as a whole, then certainly by its southern counties. In 1859, the California Legislature had adopted and forwarded a resolution to the federal Congress, calling for the division of California into two states—the latter to consist of the southern six counties and to be named "Colorado." In 1860, Lincoln only carried the state because the rival Stephen Douglas and Breckinridge tickets split the Democratic vote—and Lincoln received virtually no support south of the Tehachapi Mountains. Although the overwhelming majority of Californians rallied to the Union during the crisis months that followed Lincoln's election victory, North and South recognized the Union's political vulnerability in sparsely populated southern California—hence, the Confederacy's abortive attempts to launch a "liberating invasion" of the Southwest, which came a cropper in the Battle of Glorieta Pass east of Santa Fe in March of 1862. Although the award of the New Mexico Territory to the North in the Treaty of London somewhat calmed concerns about a California secession, the Republican leadership (including Lincoln and his eventual successor Seward) agreed that every practicable step should be taken to "bind the Golden Commonwealth to the Northern Union." This goal helped tip the national government to favor the "Dual Solution" to the question of where to locate the western terminus of the transcontinental railway. Until Lee's triumph at Gettysburg triggered the decisive intervention by Great Britain and France, Northern discussions seemed fairly well resolved that only one terminus should be built, and that it should be located on San Francisco Bay. Had Lee not won at Gettysburg and had the South's bid for independence been crushed, I suspect the restored Union would have proceeded to build just one initial transcontinental rail link and would have located the western terminus in the vicinity of the financial capital of the reunited country's Pacific coast holdings. But with Lee's triumph and the Confederacy's resulting departure, concern for preventing a "Second Secession" tipped the scales decisively in favor of simultaneous development of two transcontinental lines, with termini in Northern *and* Southern California. The likely rejection of a Southern California terminus, pre-Secession, had contributed to pro-Confederate sentiment in that portion of the state, and the North's national political leadership was not about to take further risks based on notions of prudent economy which had so clearly been overtaken by events. (A not-incidental byproduct of building the Southern transcontinental route would, of course, be an enhanced ability to redeploy troops and other military assets toward the Confederate border.)

In sum, the Confederacy's successful secession bid had a substantial effect on the development of the North's railroad network by tipping the balance in favor of simultaneous development of multiple transcontinental links. This effect was not limited to the Southwestern USA; although American administrations worked assiduously in the years immediately after Secession to stay on good terms with the British Empire, the developers of the Northern Pacific nonetheless were also able to capitalize on the desire to bind the surviving elements of the Union more closely together and to help bring about the completion of their system only one year after the southwestern link: in 1878. Moreover, it seems fair to conclude that what would later come to be called "security concerns" contributed to the pace at which the railroad effort went forward. Nothing better illustrates this effect than the scandal that erupted at the outset of 1865, over the lagging pace of the Union Pacific's efforts. Documents (apparently purloined) from the Union Pacific's Omaha office disclosed that its general manager was deliberately delaying construction in an effort to manipulate the Omaha real estate market for his personal profit. The documents were apparently provided by frustrated railroad employees to members of the incoming 39th Congress in the hope that the new, "pro-railroad" Republican majority might be willing to take action. If that was the calculation behind the "Omaha Disclosures," it proved right on target. A special investigating committee, co-chaired by Representative (and future USA President) James G. Blaine, uncovered a wealth of evidence showing how personal greed—possibly combined with Confederate economic sabotage—had for nearly two years stalled the progress of the Union Pacific portion of the premier transcontinental link.

As a result of the "Omaha Investigation," the Republican congressional leadership and the Seward Administration concluded that the national government would have to take a more active role in the development of the transcontinental railroad system. In 1866, the Railroad Development Act provided for a system of direct federal subsidies (in the form of loan guarantees) for the construction of railroads "contributing vitally to the economic health of the nation as a whole"—i.e., to the three transcontinental rail ventures then underway. In exchange for this financial support, recipient railroads agreed to a degree of oversight of their internal financial affairs unprecedented in American history, in order to prevent the sort of "insider" dealings which had held up progress on the UP line for nearly two years. This pledge of national financial support was also directly responsible for the adoption, three years later, of the National Banking Act of 1869. This measure effectively undid Andrew Jackson's anti-National Bank policy by authorizing the federal government to charter national banks permitted to issue notes secured by government bonds. (A 10 percent tax on state-issued bank notes—all such notes being "deemed" to be instruments of interstate commerce, and therefore subject to tax—provided the necessary spur to force conversion to the federal system.) And since the demands of subsidizing the construction of the intercontinental railroad system had substantially contributed to a financial crisis—demanding quicker action than could be provided under the complex procedures for establishing a new banking system—Congress also authorized the issuance of up to $250 million in additional Treasury notes. These notes, legal tender receivable for all debts public and private, represented the first "greenback" authorization since the adoption of the Legal Tender Act in February of 1862.

Finally, both to supplement the "fiat money" provisions of the Banking Act and to emulate the anti-inflationary policy of the Secession War period, Congress increased several of the taxes imposed by the Internal Revenue Act of 1862, including an increase in the tax (from three to six percent) on annual incomes over eight hundred dollars.

It is difficult to understate the long-term significance of these measures—both for public finance and the development of the Northern economy. The Banking Act represented the extension to peacetime of measures that previously had only been politically acceptable during war. The Democratic-controlled House of the 38th Congress had tried to repeal the Internal Revenue Act of 1862, ostensibly on the grounds that the December 1862 Armistice rendered these taxes no longer "necessary" as wartime measures and therefore "improper" under the Constitution's "necessary and proper" clause. Although repeal was blocked by the GOP-controlled Senate, the Democrats managed to table consideration of Treasury Secretary Chase's proposal for national banking reform—the same reform that constituted the centerpiece of the 1869 banking act. The Democrats had wrapped their positions in a mantle of constitutional tradition, but their real motives reflected a combination of Jacksonian opposition to anything that promoted central financial power and the desire of certain Northern economic interests to dismantle the wartime economic structure that could prevent the reintegration of the Northern and Southern economies on terms favorable to the South and those interests.

By the presidential campaign year of 1868, the strain of the transcontinental railroad effort, an ambitious national defense program (about which, I will say more later), and related internal improvements had, as indicated, created a public finance crisis. President Seward and the congressional Republicans made this issue a centerpiece of the campaign, urging replacement of the country's "jury rigged, house of cards" system of public finance and raising the specter of economic collapse—and Confederate invasion—as the alternative. "Do not think for a moment that Jefferson Davis, Robert E. Lee, and the rest of the Slave Power gang will just stand idly by if they see railroad construction come to a halt, our shipyards fall silent, and the dread quietus of economic stagnation spread across the land," Seward warned in a speech to the leading banking and business leaders of Chicago in May of 1868. Of course, Seward was too sophisticated a man to take his own words at face value. He realized (as, I suspect, did the majority of his Chicago audience) that the South was then too deeply engaged in Northwestern Mexico to seriously contemplate a military assault on the North. On the other hand, Seward's real point was not that the Confederate Army lay just across the border, waiting to pounce at the earliest sign of Northern financial weakness. Rather, Seward and his fellow Republicans believed that the failure to reform Northern public finance at the national level would force the USA to abandon either the transcontinental railroad effort or the national defense program, and that either step would cripple the country's long-term ability to check the growth of Confederate power.

With this point, a clear majority of the electorate were inclined to agree. Moreover, the Republican sponsorship of the east–west railroad network, combined with other internal improvement efforts (e.g., a program of port and harbor modernization on both coasts to provide adequate facilities for new ironclad squadrons), had helped accelerate the growth of a variety of commerce, most notably: iron and steel and the ancillary resource industries (timber, coal, and the like). Voters whose livelihoods depended on continued growth in these sectors were very receptive to the Republicans' argument that the Democrats' opposition to financial reform would "cut off the flow of specie, necessary to maintain the vigor of our commerce"— in other words, create a money crunch that would trigger a panic in which tens of thousands would lose their jobs, and many more would see their wages slashed. Effectively playing on these fears, Seward was returned to the White House and the Republican hold on the Congress—somewhat weakened by the normal swing against the incumbent party during the 1866 midterm elections—reached two-to-one in both Houses.

I previously mentioned the national-defense effort, launched by the Republicans after Seward's successful campaign to succeed Lincoln. Initial hopes for a major reduction in military spending had been dashed by France's intervention in Mexico. After winning back the House in 1864, the Republicans pushed through a package of national-defense measures that included authorization of a fleet of twenty "oceangoing" ironclads and a permanent draft to assure a standing regular army of 250,000. The draft proved politically impossible to implement. Registration efforts in the late spring of 1866 touched off violent protest in some working-class wards of New York City, and although these were quickly contained by local constabulary already mobilized to deal with a cholera epidemic, federal authorities quietly decided not to press ahead with outright conscription—an accommodation of short-term political realities which would create grave manpower difficulties sixteen years later at the outbreak of the Western War. The expansion of the navy, however, proved popular. Initially slow to start, by 1870, the USA Navy was adding two to three "capital ships" to its inventory each year. Of course, the technological ferment of those years made the definition of a capital ship itself somewhat of a moving target; even so, the Union Navy sought and achieved a fleet of more than a score of oceangoing ironclads, armed with high-powered, often rifled guns. When the Secession War ended, the Navy was in the process of commissioning a number of *Passaiac*-class monitors; they were larger and more stable than the original *Monitor* (which itself foundered in a storm off Cape May, New Jersey, on New Year's Eve, December 31, 1862). But they remained underpowered (with a maximum speed of no more than a very brisk walk), and their light draft made them generally unsuitable for blue-water operations. These monitors were soon followed by the somewhat more effective *Canonicus*-class ships—longer, better armored, more stable, and capable of at least a limited non-littoral role.

By late 1864, the lead ships of each of two classes of oceangoing monitors had been commissioned: the *Dictator* and the *Monadnock*. Much of *Dictator*'s 4,400-ton displacement was taken up by armor—up to fifteen inches of iron on her single turret, which contained two fifteen-inch smoothbores powerful enough to pierce eight inches of contemporary armor. *Monadnock* (slightly smaller at 3,300 tons) mounted four fifteen-inch guns in two turrets. Lighter armor and greater freeboard made her more seaworthy, and she made the trip from New York to San Francisco around the Cape without incident. By 1870, the middle of Seward's second term, squadrons of improved *Dictators* and *Monadnocks* were undertaking fleet exercises in open water, and the *Monadnock*-class *Adamenticus* caused quite a stir on a "good-will" visit to London. Admiral Baldwin Wake-Walker, who had overseen construction of the Royal Navy's first iron-hulled ship, HMS *Warrior*, reportedly blanched when informed that, in tests, the guns *Adamenticus* carried routinely pierced the six-inch iron—backed by wood—that protected contemporary Confederate vessels: *Warrior's* armor nowhere exceeded four-and-one-half inches. The Navy was seen as a point of national pride, and the tens of thousands of jobs it generated in shipbuilding, chemical manufacturing, iron and steel making, and the like, did nothing to hurt its popularity. The steady expansion of Northern shipbuilding and munitions also gave the USA the ability to provide material assistance abroad. It allowed the North to respond to the Confederacy's generous aid to Brazil with its own program of assistance to Argentina, which gave a further boost to Northern armaments and related industries and also laid the foundation for closer ties to Buenos Aires.

On the whole, the majority of Northerners had come to come to perceive the ambitions of their former Southern compatriots with sufficient concern that Northern opinion was prepared to accept what opposition Democrats hyperbolically condemned as the transformation of the USA into an "armed encampment." (Sadly, what was hyperbole in the late 1860s would become established fact by the middle of the next century.) Moreover, this public resolution hardened as the North watched a Confederacy determined to strengthen slavery throughout the Hemisphere: first by wooing Brazil with a flood of arms and other assistance during the War of the Triple Alliance and then by the wresting of Cuba from Spain. The additional factor of a substantial Confederate Army, numbering nearly 150,000, and a fast-growing Confederate Navy underscored the apparent threat. (Although the CSA had suspended draft calls after the armistice, Richmond had quietly left its Secession War draft law on the books, even while loudly protesting the North's adoption of its own draft law three years later.)

It was the Spanish–Confederate War, however, that truly united Northern opinion behind the belief that the CSA sought "Hemispheric Hegemony," and that only a powerful navy and army could deter future Southern "aggression"—although outright conscription call-ups remained politically off-limits. The financial reforms adopted in 1869 proved vital to the continuing military effort and also created a monetary cushion that permitted the Northern economy to escape the worst effects of a general international economic contraction brought on by an increase in British interest rates in 1873. As the City of London was the principal international source of finance capital during this period, a rise in domestic British interest rates threatened the prosperity of foreign economies, because British capital tended to withdraw from foreign ventures whenever "safer" domestic investments offered improved rates of return. The 1873 interest-rate increase had precisely this effect, and if the USA had not implemented its 1869 reforms, the effect could have been immediate and calamitous. Of course, improved domestic banking efficiency and the authorization of additional "fiat" money did not change the underlying economic facts of life: The USA was a debtor nation, and an outflow of British capital, sustained over time, would have a deleterious effect on the American economy. But the 1869 reforms could, and did, substantially cushion the immediate effect of British capital outflow, turning what could have been a disastrous panic into a milder economic retrenchment.

Still, the Northern economy did experience a substantial slowdown, and although an outright panic was avoided (e.g., no principal banking houses—such as those involved in the ongoing transcontinental railroad projects—were forced to close their doors), the economic reverses were serious enough to trigger a crisis in labor–management relations. Capital interests moved to cut wages. When nascent labor unions announced their intention to resist by strikes and other disruptive measures, management in key industries responded by seeking—and winning—injunctions ordering labor back to work. Capitalizing on understandable voter discontent, the Democrats made substantial gains in the 1874 midterm elections (although failing to win control of either house of Congress) and seemed poised to make their first competitive run for the White House in twenty years. But again, they blundered: this time by nominating New York Governor Samuel Tilden, whose calls for drastic economies (cancellation of the Panama Canal project, a 50 percent reduction in navy shipbuilding) proved unpopular among key voting blocks (notably factory workers in the iron and steel industry, already hard hit by firings and wage cuts). In the end, Republican incumbent James G. Blaine won a comfortable victory (and the party's pre-1874 margins in both houses of Congress were restored) on the platform of the "New Social Covenant." This package of reform measures, centered around the Donnelly–Schurz National Labor Relations Act, embodied a recognition of labor's right to collective bargaining in exchange for increased tariff protection. The principal political losers were traditional agricultural interests, whose influence had been drastically diminished with the loss of their southern Jeffersonian allies.

Following the adoption of the Covenant program in 1877, opponents challenged its constitutionality on several grounds, including the traditional Jeffersonian basis of a narrow reading of the Necessary and Proper Clause as well as a new interpretation of the Due Process Clause of the Fifth Amendment, under which Congress would be constrained to respect the "fundamental" right of "liberty of contract." (Ironically, the latter concept was intended to favor the unfettered development of the very private economic interests that had benefited so greatly from the national government's support for the transcontinental railroad links—and related measures.) As the *Dred Scott* case so aptly illustrated, those in the political minority have traditionally been the quickest to resort to the courts, and the challenge to the Covenant was no exception. But the challengers had already suffered a preemptive body blow when the Supreme Court in 1870 upheld the Legal Tender Act of 1862. (Seward reportedly promised Treasury Secretary Chase the Chief Justiceship in exchange for Chase's support against Stanton at the 1864 Republican convention; if so, Seward's choice proved a wise one, as Chase voted to uphold the Act.) The opinion in the *Legal Tender* case took an expansive view of congressional power over the currency—a fairly obvious response to the public finance crisis of the late 1860s, with its national defense overtones. Moreover, the *Legal Tender* case provided the precedential authority for the upholding three years later of the validity of the tax on state bank notes—a central element of the banking system reform embodied in the Banking Act of 1869.

Hence, by the time the Supreme Court heard the challenge to Covenant measures requiring key firms engaged in interstate commerce to bargain in good faith with *bona fide* unions, the result was a virtual certainty. The Court unreservedly rejected both the traditional "necessary and proper" and more innovative "liberty of contract" challenges, in a 7–2 opinion authored by Chief Justice Stephen Field (who had succeeded Chase upon the latter's death in 1873) which affirmed the broad power of Congress to legislate on matters "affecting interstate commerce, directly or indirectly, in order to achieve ends that the Congress deems vital to the safeguarding of our

National Union." Field, a Californian and a Democrat, had been appointed an Associate Justice by President Lincoln; when Chief Justice Chase died in 1873, newly elected President Blaine chose Field to succeed Chase. The outcome of the War of Secession had convinced Field of the need to combine a strong central government with a "social union" to meet the challenge of "slave power despotism." Gifted with extraordinary analytical skills and a forceful personality, he came to dominate the Supreme Court in a fashion reminiscent of John Marshall and must be considered one of the country's truly great chief magistrates. (Unfortunately, Field's last years were marred by a physical decline that left him increasingly incapable of carrying out his duties; his death in the CSA bombardment of Washington at the outset of World War One in October of 1898 spared the country the spectacle of a forced removal on dubious constitutional grounds.)

In sum, by the close of the 1870s, the North had become a nation with a strong central government (at the least, one greatly strengthened compared to the pre-Secession regime), a dynamic industrial sector increasingly dependent on defense and defense-related business for its rate of growth (and profitability), and with the right of labor to organize and bargain collectively recognized and federally protected. In the meantime, the South had become increasingly committed to a militarized industrialization based on slavery. Tredegar's growing complex of facilities—which included special compounds housing thousands of slaves who received special exemption from the illiteracy rules so they could be trained in the operation of the increasingly sophisticated manufacturing technology—constituted the apotheosis of this "New South." Industrialized slave labor had been a hallmark of Tredegar since 1847, when its managers dismissed its striking, free workforce and bought themselves a new one. European investment and incessant military orders now enabled Tredegar, under the management of Joseph Anderson, to absorb the foundry and rolling mill at Selma, Alabama, and to establish what would eventually become the massive Tredegar–Krupp Works at Birmingham (about which, more later). The entrenchment of a slave-based industrial society further reinforced the social—as well as economic—differences between North and South and made any hope for a reconciliation between the two unions grow ever fainter.

While hostility between the two American unions certainly was not "inevitable"—after all, what in history ever is?—the circumstances of their creation made the chances for a reconciliation a matter of long odds, at best. If Louis Napoleon had abandoned his Mexican adventure after the French reverse at Puebla in 1862; if Dom Pedro had pushed earlier and harder for the emancipation of Brazil's slaves—perhaps if one, and certainly if both, of these "what ifs" had occurred, then the Confederacy's foreign *and* domestic policies might have taken a different course (principally because the South might not have yielded to the tempting vision of a Western Hemisphere "made safe for slavery"), and North and South might then have worked out a *modus vivendi*. But France continued to pursue intervention in Mexico; Brazil did not emancipate its slaves; the Confederacy sought to make the hemisphere safe for slavery—and by the mid-1870s, the American unions had become fierce rivals. That rivalry, moreover, was powerfully reinforced by the increasingly different paths each union's socioeconomic development now took.

(left) **Representative (and later Senator) Ignatius Donnelly, co-sponsor of the Donnelly-Schurz National Labor Relations Act, centerpiece of the "New Social Covenant" that transformed Labor-Capital relations in the USA for the balance of the 19th century.**

(right) **Joseph Anderson, general manager of the Tredegar munitions works in Richmond, who helped lead the Confederacy's slavery-based industrial revolution.**

(above) **The Tredegar-Krupp Steelworks in Birmingham, Alabama, circa 1890.**

(below) **The Port of Los Angeles at San Pedro, circa 1890.**

The USA and the Confederacy both experienced industrial booms in the decades after Secession, based on dramatically different labor systems and driven by their rivalry as well as their involvement in the Great Power Alliance system that had taken firm hold by the 1890s.

6

GROWTH OF THE GLOBAL ALLIANCE SYSTEM: THE USA'S LINKS WITH SPAIN, FRANCE, AND MEXICO AND THE CONFEDERACY'S RESPONSIVE SEARCH FOR A COUNTERWEIGHT TO "YANKEE ENCIRCLEMENT"

———

The USA–CSA rivalry had begun to systematically draw in the European powers by the end of the 1870s. Although Spain was no longer accounted a power of the first rank, its surviving holdings in the Americas, East Asia, and the Pacific gave it standing to claim the status of a country of importance. Indeed, the issue of who would sit on the reconstituted Spanish throne was the immediate *casus belli* of the Franco–Prussian War of 1870–1871. Admittedly, when the Confederacy made war on Spain, the Great Powers of Europe did not intervene—even when it became apparent that a former member of their club was about to lose a prized overseas possession to a New World upstart. The prospect of renewed war between the USA and the Confederacy prompted Great Britain to make clear, however, that Richmond could not count on London's support if such a war broke out due to Confederate overreaching in the Caribbean. But such an ability of European Powers to maintain their distance from the developing differences among the nations of the Western Hemisphere would begin to rapidly diminish when France followed Spain into the Northern orbit, and the Confederacy moved to cultivate German and British counterweights.

The Franco–Prussian War overthrew Louis Napoleon and, with him, the Second French Empire. Although the Third Republic would not be

formally constituted until 1875, the resurgent republicans who dominated the provisional government between the end of the Second Empire
and the Third Republic's formal establishment moved swiftly to reverse
the New World policy of their imperial predecessor. Even out of power,
French Republicans remained a contentious lot; they were angered by the
CSA's support for Napoleon III's anti-republican adventurism in Mexico,
offended by the close ties that had developed between the Confederacy and
the slaveholding Empire of Brazil, and said as much in a torrent of pam-
phlets and articles which the Empire's rather languid secret police made
only desultory efforts to suppress. French Republicans also admired the
United States for its support for Mexican Republicanism—and even more
for its move to emancipate those slaves left within its boundaries. Although
Northern sympathies were overwhelmingly pro-Prussian at the outbreak
of the Franco–Prussian War, Napoleon III's swift defeat and abdication,
followed by the heroic resistance of a revitalized Republican France during
the siege of Paris, caused a sea-change in American sentiments (which the
crushing of the radical Commune did little to affect). President Seward
shared his countrymen's general delight at the revitalization of French
Republicanism; of even greater practical import was the collapse of a regime
that had made possible the success of the South's rebellion and which then
attempted—with the newly independent Confederacy's assistance—to
bring Central America back under the control of Old World despotism.
Seward saw an opportunity to replace an enemy of the USA (and ally of
the Confederacy) with a Republican *confrère* of "Free America." Despite
his own declining health, Seward moved swiftly and decisively to seize
the opportunity by communicating American support for the reestablishment of a republican French government. Of even greater immediate consequence was Seward's offer to sponsor a "reconciliation" of France with
Latin America, under which the French would pledge their support for the
restored Mexican Republic and contribute their engineering abilities to the
construction of a canal across the Isthmus of Panama in Colombia.

The reconciliation plan proved a stroke of genius. It gave French
Republicans a way to "make amends" for Louis Napoleon's misdeeds in
Mexico and appealed to French vanity as well as the French love of the
grand gesture: pride over the construction of the Suez Canal by Ferdinand

De Lesseps and the chance to offer the services of "the Great Frenchman" for the further benefit "of all mankind." Even more important, staunch USA support for the provisional republican government helped it to survive the "crisis years" of 1871 to 1875, when it was very much an open question whether the republic—which avoided constitutional extinguishment by margins as close as a single vote as late as January 1875—would prove only a transitional regime to yet another monarchical or imperial restoration.

The resulting sense of solidarity between the two countries was reinforced by the triumphant Philadelphia Exposition of 1876. The French participated enthusiastically in what proved a near-militant celebration of the anti-aristocratic and equalitarian values of the USA and the new French Republic, culminating in the announcement at the Exposition's conclusion of the French government's decision to help finance the construction in New York Harbor of Gustave Eiffel's titanic "Statue of Liberty." (At the opening ceremony, President Patrice de Mac-Mahon of France joined USA President Blaine and Mexican President Porfirio Diaz in starting up the great Corliss steam engine, celebrated in Henry Adams' famous essay, "The Virgin and the Dynamo"; suggestions that the Emperor of Brazil be invited were rejected in favor of the democratic symbolism of having only republican heads of state participate.) Franco–American economic and cultural *rapprochement*, moreover, had already begun the transformation into a political alliance as early as the Spanish crisis of 1874, when the constitutional monarchy established after the revolution of 1868 was threatened by a military *pronunciamento*. The intervention of the USA in Spain's war with the Confederacy had permitted Madrid to save Puerto Rico and the semblance of an honorable peace. The dynamic Juan Prim, Prime Minister and leading figure of the revolution, then seized on the opportunity created by the trauma of the loss of Cuba and the necessity for an alliance with the United States to force through a long-needed program of political and military reforms, including modernization of the army and navy. Prim was given vital support in this effort by the new King, Amadeo of the House of Savoy, who had accepted the offer of the Spanish crown in October 1870. Prim's energetic leadership, however, had earned him many enemies (only the quick action of his security detail, a wartime measure prudently continued following the end of hostilities with Richmond, saved Prim from assassination in December 1870), and when the third series of military professionalization measures caused several thousand (incompetent) army officers to be cashiered in the fall of 1874, a coalition of the regime's conservative opponents raised the banner of revolt in several cities.

The rebellion was well timed, coming at a low point in the government's political and economic fortunes. The reader will recall the global economic contraction set in motion by a rise in British domestic interest rates in 1873, which hit Spain especially hard. The rebels might well have succeeded (or plunged the country into civil war) had not Paris and Washington made clear their strong support for Prim and his constitutional government. The actions of the USA in particular deprived the rebels of crucial support within the expanded and reformed military—a reflection of the growing ties between the Spanish and American armed forces, based on their program of joint defense in the Caribbean. Indeed, due to logistical constraints in the Western Hemisphere, it is not too much to say the Spanish Army was beholden to the Americans for support. The French and American ministers brilliantly coordinated their efforts to rally political support in Madrid and other key metropolitan centers for the embattled Prim, and Franco–American political cooperation was soon being duplicated in the military sphere. Often overlooked is the fact that the USA and France shared the common, bitter experience of recent defeat in a major war, resulting in significant loss of territory and irredentist aspirations. Both powers also had a common interest in effective military modernization (the USA to at least keep Confederate ambitions in check; France, to rearm for the day of *revanche* and the restoration of Alsace and Lorraine). It was only to be expected that the blossoming of diplomatic relations between the two would lead to expanded contacts at the military level; by the end of the 1870s, initial exchanges of staff officers had led to visits by naval squadrons and participation by guest regiments in each country's annual maneuvers.

USA efforts to cultivate Spain and France were paralleled by Washington's forging of close ties with Mexico. Upon the restoration of his government to Mexico City, the democratic and anti-slavery Juarez promptly entered into negotiations for a treaty of friendship with the USA. The Confederacy's hesitance to withdraw from portions of the Mexican states along the Rio Grande—which Southern troops had occupied as part of Richmond's support of Maximilian's ill-fated empire—only confirmed *Juarista* suspicions of Richmond's imperial ambitions south of the Rio Grande, and the concomitant need to develop close ties with Washington. The resulting treaty of friendship and cooperation between Mexico and the USA (with its references to "mutual assistance in times of a threat to either's vital interest") was signed and ratified in 1871. Juarez promptly initiated staff talks between his country and the USA. Central to these discussions were plans for the extension of the Atchison, Topeka & Santa Fe railway line (which then terminated just above the border, near Deming), along a line running southeast and paralleling the south bank of the Rio Grande to the Gulf of Mexico. This strategic extension would permit the rapid shuttling of USA and Mexican troops in response to any Confederate move against Mexico's northeastern states as well as allow the expansion of Matamoros into a naval station to monitor the construction of the CSA Navy's logistics facility at Port Isabel. Although Juarez died of a heart attack in 1872, the election of General Porfirio Diaz as his successor assured no change in Mexican policy toward the Confederacy. If anything, Diaz (Mexico's leading general in the war against "the Intervention," and the victor of First Puebla in 1862 as well as the Oaxaca campaigns of 1865–66) was even more convinced than Juarez that the CSA was Mexico's mortal enemy, which could only be deterred by a policy of maximum military strength based on an "iron link" with the American North.

But while Mexico and the USA saw the construction of a Rio Grande rail network as a defensive measure, the Confederacy saw an encircling chain that could choke off the Trans-Mississippi. The line included links to Mexico City and via the capital to Mexican Pacific Coast ports through which Northern arms—and more troops—could pass in the event of war. To this chain was added a strong Colombian link, when the USA and Colombia agreed on the construction of a canal across the Isthmus of Panama. Although the terms of the Clayton–Bulwer Treaty of 1850 required that any canal not be fortified, Richmond did not credit the long-term value of that "mere paper constraint." Moreover, the USA arguably did not need to fortify the canal itself, given the imposing USA naval facilities under construction on Haiti and Puerto Rico—an ironic consequence of the Confederacy's successful effort to wrench Cuba away from Madrid. While Spanish squadrons stationed in the Caribbean almost certainly could not tip the naval balance in any future war with the North, the possible addition of the French Navy to Northern blockade efforts was another matter altogether. Of course, what Richmond condemned as "aggressive enrichment" was only the natural reaction to its own policies of expansionism (first supporting the French in Mexico; then, seizing Cuba from Spain). But the Confederacy's leaders did not see things that way, and they reacted by seeking the friendship of the new German Empire established by Bismarck after Prussia's crushing defeat of France in 1871, as well as stronger links with Great Britain.

Germany was a natural relationship to cultivate—for several reasons. There was the affinity between the military values of the self-styled "Southern Cavalier" and the Prussian Junker. And both elites nurtured a strong agrarian ethos (although neither Junker nor Cavalier would actually sully hands working the land). Prussian observers were impressed by the performance of the Confederate Expeditionary Forces against Spain, and the CSA observers accompanying Von Moltke's victorious armies in France (led by none other than J. E. B. Stuart) returned the compliment. This reinforced the boost Confederate–Prussian relations had already received from the friendships that Prussian officers had developed with the Confederate observers attached to Prussian forces during the Austro–Prussian War in 1866. Favorable reports about Confederate artillery were followed by contacts between representatives of Tredegar and Krupp which would lead to joint ventures for the development of advanced field pieces and long-range siege artillery. That the Confederacy and Germany were drawn to one another really should have come as no surprise to anyone. Besides the affinity in values reinforced by the mutual experience of victory in wars of national aggrandizement, the countries enjoyed complementary economies: The Confederacy's cotton exports did not compete with the Prussian Junker's agricultural base, and the decision of the South's leading arms manufacturer to join forces with Prussia's Krupp would eliminate what could have proven an alienating competition. But while Paris was soon expressing nervous concern about as already being described as the Confederate–Prussian "axis," Prince Bismarck's German Empire of the 1870s neither could, nor would, provide the South with support in the event of a war between the Confederacy, the North, and the North's European allies. Bismarck simply saw no benefit whatsoever from entangling Germany in disputes over Haiti or New Mexico—more remote by far than the Balkans, which Bismarck at one point opined were "not worth the bones of a single Pomeranian Grenadier."

At least in the short term, that left Great Britain—the country of Wilberforce and the continuing campaign against the slave trade but also the birthplace of the Industrial Revolution and whose textile mills continued to depend on the South's cotton. In the decision to intervene in favor of Southern secession after Lee's triumph at Gettysburg, qualms about supporting slavery had been overcome by a combination of economics and a peculiarly Victorian idealistic desire to "do something" to prevent further bloodshed. But the CSA's subsequent moves to strengthen slavery at home and abroad put a chill on London's relationship with Richmond, and the Confederate seizure of Cuba put CSA–British relations in a virtual deep freeze for the balance of the 1870s. Indeed, Great Britain nearly went to war with the CSA in 1878, when a British frigate cruising off the West African coast seized the "rogue" slave trader *Beauregard* and discovered documents directly implicating the Confederate government in the scheme to circumvent the slave trade ban via Cuban-based "joint ventures" between Confederate and Brazilian planters. Perhaps only because the British were already on the verge of war with Russia—due to its attempt to impose crippling peace terms on the Ottoman Empire following St. Petersburg's successful military intervention on the side of the rebellious Bulgars—and because former CSA Secretary of State Judah Benjamin was an able diplomat widely admired by English society (Liberal as well as Conservative) did Richmond manage to emerge from the *Beauregard* fiasco without a complete rupture in Confederate–British relations. Yet even without such a rupture, the *Beauregard* affair still did the Confederacy no good.

Notwithstanding the *Beauregard* Affair and other slavery-related difficulties, the South doggedly continued its efforts to persuade the British that they should align themselves with the Confederacy against the USA. Nor did the Confederates lack substantial arguments for such an alliance. Quite to the contrary: by the 1880s London had grown increasingly concerned about the USA—and especially about its close relationship with France and its outright alliance with Spain. At first, post-Secession relations between the USA and Great Britain had developed along fairly amicable lines. Although most Northerners resented London's role in securing Southern independence, the political and economic leadership on both sides of the Atlantic recognized that good relations were in both countries' best interests. Well into the 1870s, these attitudes assured there was no fatal break along any of the potential fault lines. Thus, when the Fenian Brotherhood—the North American support organization for the Irish Republican Brotherhood (an organization that will feature prominently during the course of this history)—organized raids into Canada in 1866 and again in 1870, the Seward administration took pains to reassure Canadian and British authorities that the USA's government condemned the raids and was prepared to cooperate fully in assuring the suppression of the Fenian "threat." Likewise, when Northern nationalists agitated for the "annexation" of Canada following the impoundment by Canadian patrol ships of American fishing vessels for violations of the restrictive fishing convention of 1818 (the later reciprocity agreement having been allowed to lapse in 1866), President Seward instead invited Canadian and British representatives to a conference for the purpose of resolving this and other outstanding disputes. (The Americans initially suggested Washington as the conference site, but Ottawa and London demurred out of concern for Confederate sensibilities, and the parties met instead in New York.)

The result was broad agreement on virtually all issues: ten-year access to Canadian fisheries for American vessels; Canadian fish admitted duty free into the USA; *and* settlement by arbitration of the boundary line between British Columbia and Washington Territory. Yet, not even the genuine good feelings engendered by the Treaty of New York could entirely dispel the continuing fears of American ambitions to incorporate their "northern cousins"—which were exacerbated by suspicion of some sort of American involvement in the First Riel Uprising during the winter of 1869–70 (about which, more later). Gladstone's government therefore acceded to Ottawa's request that British regulars be maintained at Fort Garry in Manitoba as well as at the Royal Navy's Halifax naval station to underscore Great Britain's continuing commitment to its North American holdings. This decision not to withdraw British army forces from Canada reflected the deeper stresses underlying USA–British relations—stresses that fishing agreements and arbitration accords could at best paper over. The fundamental problem was longstanding American sentiment to acquire Canada and Canadian fear of that prospect. The abortive invasion during the War of 1812 was a living memory for the Scots-Irish settlers of Ontario, and recurring calls by American editorialists and politicians for the "acquisition" of Canada as a "counterbalance" to CSA ambitions south of the Rio Grande did nothing to put these ancestral fears to rest. The USA's purchase of Alaska from Russia in 1867 had also engendered concern—and for precisely this reason—although the removal of the traditional Russian foe from the border of British North America ultimately was seen as outweighing any worsening of the nascent Yankee threat.

Still, as long as London remained confident that the leadership in Washington was firmly committed to respect Canadian sovereignty, British governments continued to resist calls for wide-ranging changes in either foreign or defense policy based on concerns for Canadian security. Thus, during the naval scare that briefly convulsed London in 1868, Benjamin Disraeli (then Conservative leader in the House of Commons under the premiership of the ailing Lord Derby) ridiculed the suggestion that the USA's oceangoing ironclad fleet should be added to the estimated strength of traditional rivals France and Russia—a step that would have strengthened the Admiralty's case for increasing the naval estimates. "If the USA's ships are to be counted as against us, then with equally compelling logic, we should treat the Confederacy's squadron as our own," Disraeli dryly pronounced to an amused House during the course of reaffirming the government's commitment to "prudent naval economy." At the time, the number of genuine blue-water USA ironclads (no more than eight, albeit with two more under construction or in refit) was still small enough that Disraelian sarcasm proved sufficient to quell demands for an increased British effort to counter the "Yankee" naval threat. Yet, the fact remained that British preference for a policy of "splendid isolation" to secure vital interests could only work if the British fleet maintained a decisive advantage over the combined forces of potential enemies. And by the end of the 1870s, the regional naval arms race between the USA and the CSA had produced a Northern ironclad fleet at least theoretically capable of cutting off Canada from the

British Isles—particularly if the USA coordinated such an effort with a simultaneous French operation against British Mediterranean interests. Admiralty fears could no longer be so easily dismissed as they had been in 1868. Only the fact that the Anglo–French *detente*, established between London and Paris during the early days of Louis Napoleon's "Second Empire," had continued to hold despite the replacement of an Imperial with a Republican regime permitted Gladstone—viscerally opposed as he was to any increase in military expenditures—to beat back demands for a major expansion in the Royal Navy's ironclad fleet to meet what an ever increasing number of British leaders saw as a growing American threat to Canada.

(above) **USA President James G. Blaine and French President *Le Marechal* Patrice Maurice de MacMahon engage the "Corliss Engine" in the Hall of Machinery of the American Centennial Exhibition at Philadelphia, July 1876.**

(left) **Juan Prim, Prime Minister of Spain, who seized the opportunity of an alliance with the USA after the loss of Cuba to the Confederacy, and whose government survived the would-be *pronunciamento* of 1873 with the help of France and the USA.**

7

THE WESTERN WAR AND THE CREATION OF THE ANGLO-CONFEDERATE ENTENTE: (1) THE PRE-WAR SOURCES OF A DESTRUCTIVE DYNAMIC

———

Then came the Western War of 1882–84. For the reader fully to apprehend the baleful effect of this conflict on the future course of Great Power relations, one must examine the pre-war sources of the dynamic that—once fully unleashed by the Western War—produced what a confidential State Department paper of the 1950s aptly described as "the Fatal Alliance" between London and Richmond. I therefore must set a double stage: one located in the Western Hemisphere and centered on Mexico; the second, located across the Atlantic and centered on Ireland.

First: Mexico. The reader will recall that the French intervention in Mexico ended with the withdrawal of French forces, the defeat and subsequent execution of the unfortunate Maximilian, and the restoration of Benito Juarez as President of the Mexican Republic. The war had been a devastating and bitter experience, leaving over one hundred thousand Mexicans dead; the country's capital city in ruins; and the public treasury bankrupted and the economy in a shambles. The restoration of constitutional authority, moreover, did not mean the establishment of true peace. Not only was the country wracked by brigandage, but the withdrawal of the French still left the Confederacy to contend with. And while the CSA did eventually withdraw its forces from Mexican territory along the Rio Grande border with Texas, Mexico's republican leaders were unanimous in their fear that the Confederacy would someday try to subjugate Mexico and extend the South's slave code to encompass the country's poor Indian majority. Mexico therefore could not afford to let down its guard and would have to orient its policies of reconstruction toward assuring it had the ability to defeat the expected Confederate attempt at conquest.

The implications of these policies were several. First, Mexico would have to maintain a large and modern standing army on a scale that would dwarf anything previously seen in Central America—the stated goal was at least seventy-five thousand regular troops plus an equal number of trained reservists (almost doubling the forces raised to oust the French and overthrow Maximilian). Of necessity, these troops would be drawn substantially from the country's Indian population, which until now had felt little connection to the idea of "Mexico" (regarding it as the province of the "whites," the Spanish-descended elite). And Indian soldiers could not be counted on to put up a fight in the defense of Mexico unless the population from which they came believed it had a stake in preserving Mexico from the Confederate threat. This meant there would have to be real reform of the *hacienda* land tenure system—a step that Juarez, who had encouraged *de facto* land reforms as a device for recruiting local Indian populations to fight the French during the later stages of the war, was quite willing to take. Second, the country would have to raise sufficient capital to pay for the creation of a transportation and communication infrastructure sufficient to sustain the army in the field against the Confederates—specifically: a network of railroads and telegraph lines that would permit the government in Mexico City to concentrate forces quickly in any area threatened by the CSA and then to sustain that force in the field by a regular flow of arms and other supplies.

To a degree perhaps unforeseeable at the time, these two programs— the creation of peasant loyalty by assuring security of land tenure and the development of an extensive rail network by attracting private foreign capital—would set up a grave tension, as the protection of peasant landholdings would come to clash with the demands of the railroad developers. These, however, would prove problems for the next generation of Mexico's leaders. For in the aftermath of the ouster of the French (and their Confederate allies), President Juarez and his cabinet, supported by the Congress and the overwhelming majority of state governors and other men of influence, plunged enthusiastically ahead with their double program for securing Mexican security. Among their immediate decisions was the cancellation of Maximilian's project to construct a rail line from Mexico City to Veracruz and the redirection of available resources to the creation of a railroad network between Mexico City and the Pacific Coast ports of Mazatlan, Manzanillo, and Salina Cruz (all of whose harbor facilities benefited from a parallel program of improvements). Without the CSA threat, Veracruz might have emerged as Mexico's preeminent port; the Confederacy's conquest of Cuba, however, meant that traffic into Veracruz could be throttled by Richmond at will. Moreover, as Veracruz had twice within living memory proven the gateway of invasion—by the USA in 1847 and by France in 1861—it was thought better to reorient Mexico's external commerce toward the Pacific and transform Veracruz into the first of a line of fortifications designed to prevent a Confederate reprise of past aggression. (The announced plans for a Panama Canal, to be completed by the mid-1880s, also meant that shifting from Caribbean to Pacific ports would have little or no adverse impact on Mexico's European trade.)

The extent to which Mexico had become institutionally committed to the policy of "armed reconstruction" was demonstrated in 1872, when President Juarez (overwhelmingly elected to a third term the previous year) suddenly died of a heart attack. In the election called to select his successor, General Porfirio Diaz easily defeated Sabastian Lerdo de Tajeda (the Chief Justice of the Mexican Supreme Court). While Lerdo was a man of obvious ability, Diaz spoke with the authority of a military man who would carry out Juarez's plans and who could not be intimidated by Richmond; this was a claim that the victor of Puebla, Oaxaca, and Mexico City could make with a persuasive power that Lerdo could not match. Diaz, moreover, had developed a close relationship with the Northern military—particularly with General Sheridan, the commander of the substantial American forces now permanently stationed in the New Mexico Territory—and pressed ahead with the military staff talks to which Juarez and Seward had agreed shortly before Juarez's death. These talks quickly resulted in a treaty of alliance and mutual aid, which committed the USA to come to Mexico's aid in the event it was attacked by "any foreign power"—i.e., the Confederacy. (Seward did not long outlive Juarez, succumbing in October 1872 to the debilitating nervous system disease that now bears his name. Speaker of the House James G. Blaine, the Republican nominee for President who easily triumphed in the elections held just weeks after Seward's death, shared his predecessor's commitment to an American–Mexican alliance and moved swiftly to secure Senate ratification of the agreement the following year.)

The Confederates did not take kindly to these developments. First, as the Mexicans suspected, many Confederates (and not just those living in the Trans-Mississippi states) desired to acquire, if not the whole of Mexico, at least its states bordering the Rio Grande. Although Texans were undoubtedly the most vociferous about the "unfinished business of 1848," they had powerful supporters in Richmond, most notably Jefferson Davis, himself a veteran of the Mexican War. For precisely that reason, when the withdrawal of French forces beginning in 1868 brought on the final crisis for Maximilian, the CSA had continued its occupation of the border territory even after Maximilian's defeat had become inevitable, and agreed to withdraw only when the demands of the impending war with Spain and the threat of war with Mexico and the USA convinced Richmond that it was not yet time to fight over "the Trans-Rio Grande." Second, while the Mexicans pursued an alliance with the USA in order to check Confederate ambitions, the Confederacy claimed to see in the USA–Mexican military alliance and railroad building program—particularly the linking up of the North's Atchison, Topeka & Santa Fe line with Mexico's new Ferrocarril Mexicano system—an attempt to encircle the Trans-Mississippi in a "noose of iron" that the "Yankees" would pull tight at the first opportunity.

The South therefore undertook, albeit surreptitiously, the momentous step of encouraging Indian resistance in the USA's New Mexico Territory in the hope that the Apache tribes would so disrupt the railroad construction efforts that they might never be completed. Of course, Richmond recognized that Indian raids alone could not prevent the eventual completion of the USA's Southwestern railway system. But, if the system were delayed long enough, the Confederacy might be able to effect a change in Mexican policy by a combination of measures—cultivating links to the traditional conservative opponents of the *Juarista* liberals, with promises to respect Mexican sovereignty and "territorial integrity"—that could (perhaps with the help of a well-timed *coup d'etat*) decouple Mexico City from Washington.

These were the foreign origins of the bloody "Apache War" of the 1870s, which ultimately produced the virtual annihilation of the Apache peoples (with the singular exception of the Navajo, who refused to join the campaign against the railroad and white settlements). The Confederacy (and Texas in particular) had only recently finished its own war against the Comanche—perhaps the most powerful Indian people to be found west of the Mississippi. Into the 1850s, the various Comanche tribes had controlled a territory—"Comancheria"—centered on the Texas Panhandle Country and extending north to the Arkansas River in the Kansas Territory, south as far as the Guadalupe River, west to the Pecos River in Texas and the New Mexico Territory, and as far east as the middle of Southeastern Indian Country. But that decade saw a brutal campaign by Texas authorities, led by the paramilitary Texas "Rangers," sometimes with support from the federal army, which by the outbreak of the War of Secession had nearly broken Comanche power. The War of Secession temporarily arrested the progress of the Texan campaign; the Comanche, supported by their ally the Kiowa, managed to regain control of a portion of the territory from which they had been driven over the past ten years. If the War of Secession had continued for several years more—and especially if the tide of that war had, as likely, gone against the Confederacy—resurgent Comanche power might have been carried as far east as the Gulf Coast; at the very least, Texas would have faced a daunting task to reestablish the control they had wrested from the Comanche only by many years of fighting that saw savage atrocities committed by both sides and the name "Comanche" become a byword for terror.

But the War of Secession ended barely halfway into its second year, and the seasoned troops of General John Bell Hood returned by the spring of 1863 to resume the campaign with redoubled determination and even greater force. Hood took the war to the heart of Comancheria in the Texas Panhandle. In a series of engagements culminating in the Battle of North Fork (along the North Fork of the Red River on September 28, 1866), the leading Comanche war bands were destroyed, and the survivors (mostly women and children) marched off to reservations established in western

Confederate Indian Country. More decisive than pitched battles, however, was Hood's ruthless policy of slaughtering the buffalo herds around which the Comanche way of life was organized. The ensuing starvation, even more than superior Texan firepower, broke the Comanche will to resist.

In deciding to stir up the Apaches of the USA's New Mexico Territory, the Confederates recognized that the North was bound to apply the same ruthless tactics against the Apaches which had worked so well for the Texans against the Comanche. In fact, Richmond had no illusions that the Apaches could permanently block the completion of the USA–Mexican railroad link. As stated, the goal was to disrupt progress long enough until a change of government in Mexico City could be effected that would end the USA–Mexico alliance. And for the first few years, the Apaches, sustained in the field by a steady flow of arms orchestrated by Richmond, managed to slow progress on the completion of the rail link. But after the Apache destruction (on June 25, 1876) of a column of the Seventh Cavalry under the command of the dashing but fatally reckless Lieutenant Colonel George Armstrong Custer, General Phillip Sheridan stepped in to take personal command of the anti-Apache war effort. The ruthless Sheridan quickly instituted what would prove the deadly but effective policy of "Concentration." Seizing on the newly available fencing device of barbed wire, Sheridan's columns rooted out Indian communities and forced women, children and the elderly into armed camps ringed by the new wire. The death toll in these poorly supplied "Concentration Camps" was appalling (and something for which Sheridan offered no apology). Moreover, with the approval of the Diaz administration, Sheridan carried out Concentration on both sides of the border, receiving extensive assistance from several thousand Mexican army troops. Concentration would prove brutally effective: Apache raids had ceased by the end of the 1870s.

The Apache War did not prevent the completion of either the Southwestern prong of the USA transcontinental railroad or the link-up of that system with the Ferrocarril Mexicano, although the war did slow the rate of settlement of the New Mexico Territory. Meanwhile, in Mexico, the Confederacy was able to establish contacts with those interests that were increasingly disenchanted with the direction of Mexican economic and social development—particularly *hacienda* owners who resented the government's new constraints on their ability to evict farmers in order to develop sugar and other cash crops. The Confederates also maintained their links with some of the local political bosses in Mexico's Rio Grande border states and gave covert aid to the bandit gangs that still infested the Northeastern Mexican countryside—with an eye toward eventual acquisition of these territories by interfering with Mexico City's ability to maintain control while developing "shadow" state governments willing to serve under the Confederacy "when the time came."

Although the Confederacy's actions in the American Southwest and Mexican Northeast were tantamount to an undeclared war against the USA and Mexico, neither was prepared to go to war to end Confederate depredations, particularly when the Confederacy proved adept at keeping its fingerprints off the flow of guns and ammunition that sustained Apache war bands. And by the beginning of the 1880s, it was becoming increasingly apparent that the CSA's policies had failed to achieve any of the Confederacy's primary goals. The "encircling" railroad network was completed and operating; the Apaches in the American Southwest and the brigand bands in the Mexican Northeast had been effectively suppressed; and the promise of USA government support for irrigation measures was attracting a flood of settlers to New Mexico (now divided into the separate territories of "Arizona" and "New Mexico" as a prelude to their admission as separate states).

The Confederacy saw perhaps its last opportunity to reverse this unfavorable tide when Mexican President Diaz agreed to step down after two terms, to be succeeded by his Secretary of War, Manuel Gonzalez. Diaz initially resisted suggestions that he not pursue a third term, but he was eventually persuaded that he could exercise effective control behind the scenes and that pursuing a third consecutive term would probably trigger a revolt by opponents itching for an excuse to undo the social reforms of the last several years. (Even worse, the rebels might then "request" Confederate aid, leading to Richmond's reoccupation of Northeastern Mexico.) Gonzalez was dedicated to continuing Diaz's policies, but he overextended the regime financially. Unwilling to neglect foreign debts or military modernization, Gonzalez stopped the salaries of many government officials. The resulting outcry made clear that Gonzalez could not be reelected, opening the door to Diaz's return to the presidency. But this was "unacceptable" to the Confederacy and its Mexican political allies, for Diaz was both a capable executive and an unwavering opponent of the American South.

I will not rehash the controversy over the South's alleged role in the ensuing attempt to assassinate Diaz. I tend to agree with those who argue that President Breckinridge did not directly authorize CSA involvement in the plot to kill the Mexican president. It is nonetheless an established fact that the Mexican federal police uncovered conclusive proof that the Office of Confederate Special Services had a hand in the events of May 5, 1882. It should also be remembered that OCSS Director John Singleton Mosby was reckless enough to initiate such a plan without informing the Gray House. Be all that as it may, the fact remains that once the CSA role had been uncovered, war between Mexico and the Confederacy—and therefore between the Confederacy and the USA—was virtually assured.

But before reviewing the course of the conflict itself, I must set the second, and more distant, stage necessary for an understanding of the consequences which flowed from the outbreak of the Western War—Ireland. The reader will recall mention of the Fenian raids across the USA border with Canada in 1866 and 1870. As indicated, those raids were organized by the Fenian Brotherhood, the support organization among Irish immigrants in the USA for the Irish Republican Brotherhood. The "IRB" and the Fenian Brotherhood represented the principal institutional manifestations of "Fenianism," an Irish political and cultural movement calling for the establishment of an independent Irish Republic. The Fenians looked to the USA as a source of financial and political support: the former directly from the large Irish emigrant community centered in the Northeast, and the latter indirectly through a hoped-for war between the USA and England that would create the conditions for a nationalist uprising.

When the Canadian raids did not produce a war between the USA and Great Britain, the IRB turned its attention to promoting Irish nationalism at its base. By that time, the "Irish Question" had become a central feature of British politics, as Fenian violence on *both* sides of the Atlantic had made leading English politicians (notably Liberal leader William Gladstone) take heightened notice of the troubled state of Irish politics. The conflict between landlord and tenant in the Irish countryside had defined the fundamental contours of Irish politics for centuries, and the suffering induced by the Great Potato Famine of the 1840s only made already bad conditions that much worse. Yet, at the very moment Fenian violence thrust Irish matters onto the center stage of English politics, land controversies were entering a period of (relative) quietude. Starting in the mid-1860s, Ireland experienced a period of good harvests that took the sharp edge off land tenure disputes for much of the next decade. Irish Question debates therefore initially focused on the constitutional relationship between Ireland and England. Many Irish—Conservative as well as Liberal—had become convinced that only some form of "Home Government" (or "Home Rule," as it came to be called) would allow Ireland effectively to address its social ills. Discussions in the House of Commons saw an ever increasing number of the "Irish members" pronounce in favor of Home Rule—especially after the appearance on the parliamentary scene of that charismatic figure, Charles Stewart Parnell.

The IRB reorganized in the early 1870s, and its new leadership agreed to allow Ireland's parliamentary representatives an opportunity to make good on their Home Rule demand. The IRB still wanted an independent republic, but the failure of their violent campaign of the previous decade persuaded the leadership not to oppose a measure that would at least weaken the constitutional tie to England. Then the land question revived with the agricultural crisis of 1879. In fact, agricultural production and profits had begun to slide after 1876, and the next two years saw disastrous harvests followed by inadequate recovery. But 1879 saw poor conditions turn universally disastrous: potato production plummeted, credit dried up for small farmers, and outright starvation returned to the western counties for the first time since the 1840s. Moreover, this crisis came at a time when some of the tenantry had become accustomed to making a good living—at least when compared to the terrible destitution of past decades. The extent of the collapse thus threatened shopkeepers, large tenant farmers, small merchants, and traders with the loss of this (comparative) good life, creating a broad social front in favor of some kind of ameliorative action, which had not existed during the Great Famine of a generation ago. To this was added a local political leadership that had been purged of its most corrupt "feudalistic" features over the previous decade by a series of electoral reforms and which therefore was ready to respond positively to demands for action to alleviate the tenancy's dire circumstances.

Parnell quickly seized the public initiative with the formation of the National Land League and his accompanying calls for tenants to pay only rents that were "according to the times." Parnell also worked in alliance with the Fenian IRB, which received several—publicly unacknowledged—positions on the Land League executive committee. Within a year, the tactic of rent withholding had spread throughout Ireland, accompanied by outbursts of rural violence that deeply worried the landlord class. Parnell's campaign had plunged Ireland into the crisis that he and his followers hoped would at last force "genuine reform" out of Westminster. In the fall of 1880, Parnell traveled to the USA to raise funds from "Ireland Abroad." He was received everywhere by wildly enthusiastic crowds that seemingly confirmed his right to claim the status of leader of the "Irish nation." (It was while visiting Cincinnati, just across the Ohio River from Kentucky, that Parnell reportedly called for an independent Irish republic. In response, the Breckinridge Administration revoked Parnell's permission to extend his tour into the Confederacy—a gesture of goodwill that did not go unnoticed, or unappreciated, by London.) Parnell returned to an Ireland still roiled by clashes between landlord and tenant, where matters reached a head in October 1881: Gladstone's government banned the Land League; Parnell was arrested and imprisoned in Dublin's Kilmainham jail; and there followed a descent into near anarchy in much of the countryside.

Gladstone—now doubting the wisdom of combining land tenure reform with coercive measures such as the suppression of the Land League and Parnell's jailing—opened clandestine negotiations with Parnell. In fact, Parnell had concluded even before his arrest that Gladstone's land tenure reforms (embodied in the Land Act passed that summer) were—notwithstanding Parnell's contrary public statements—achieving real relief for the tenantry, and that the violence must end. (This, unfortunately, was a position not shared by Parnell's IRB allies.) For Parnell, the one outstanding issue concerned holdings on which considerable arrears of rent had accumulated; if Parnell and Gladstone's government could reach agreement on this point, Parnell was prepared to cut his ties to the IRB, call off any further "agitation," and urge cooperation with the Land Act's newly established system of "Land Courts" for resolving rent disputes. An agreement along these lines (dubbed the "Treaty of Kilmainham") was reached, and Parnell was released on May 2, 1882. Then on May 7, the newly appointed Chief Secretary and Under Secretary for Ireland were found murdered in Dublin's Phoenix Park. (They had been stabbed to death with surgical scissors.) The IRB denied responsibility and blamed a "renegade" group called the "Invincibles," but it is now generally accepted that the IRB's leadership knew in advance of the Invincibles' plans and also let it be known that no steps would be taken to alert the authorities.

Perhaps if Gladstone and Parnell had been given a chance to build on the good feelings created by Parnell's release and the parallel improvement of conditions in the countryside, matters might have turned out differently for Anglo–Irish relations. Parnell was able to turn even the horror of Dublin Park to some advantage by the strength of his (undeniably) sincere condemnation of the murders, which was very well received in England and echoed by all quarters of Irish opinion—*except* for the IRB. But the Dublin Park killings also demonstrated the vulnerability of reform hopes to violence. For Gladstone was compelled by English opinion to respond with coercive measures; Parnell was compelled by Irish opinion to condemn those measures; and the resulting public acrimony forced a suspension of cooperation on the issue of "Home Rule." Still, given just a few months of peace, Gladstone and Parnell could have dropped the pose of confrontation and resumed their common effort to find a Home Rule solution acceptable to the majority of English and Irish opinion. But history now dealt these two men of goodwill a second (and far more grievous) blow than Dublin Park: the outbreak of the Western War on the other side of the Atlantic.

(left) **Porfirio Diaz, President of Mexico, who built the Mexican army into a force ready and able to defend Mexico against a Confederate bid for conquest.**

(below) **The Narodnik assassination of Tsar Alexander II in 1881, which agents of the OCSS failed to duplicate against Diaz one year later; the discovery of their role in the attempt led to the outbreak of the Western War.**

8

THE WESTERN WAR AND THE CREATION OF THE ANGLO-CONFEDERATE ENTENTE: (2) THE RESOLUTION OF THE FIRST INTERNATIONAL CRISIS AND THE CONFLICT'S ENSUING COURSE

The reader will recall that the proximate trigger of hostilities was the discovery that the OCSS had a hand in the attempted assassination of former President Diaz during the Cinco de Mayo celebrations of 1882. Taking their cue from the *Narodniki* murder of Russia's Tsar Alexander II the year before, the would-be killers threw bombs at the former president's carriage while he was on his way to the principal celebrations in Mexico City. Fortunately for Diaz, his attackers bungled the job: only one bomb exploded—and that, a safe distance from Diaz's carriage. Diaz's bodyguards captured two of the attempted assassins, who after fairly minimal "persuasion" confessed to their membership in a conspiracy that the Mexican authorities soon traced across the border to the Confederacy. President Gonzalez initially temporized over whether to confront Richmond with evidence of the OCSS's involvement, concerned over Mexico's readiness for war. But when word of the OCSS link leaked to the press, Gonzalez's hand was forced: Mexico demanded Richmond agree to a "full accounting" for the Confederacy's "gross violation" of Mexican sovereignty. When the Breckinridge Administration responded in what Gonzalez (and, perhaps more to the point, Diaz) considered an "insolent" manner, Mexico declared war on August 1, 1882.

But it was the Confederacy that struck the first blows—and against both Mexico and the USA. Confederate President John C. Breckinridge and his Cabinet were convinced that the USA would stand by its Mexican ally, and nothing in Washington's conduct as the crisis escalated through the spring and into the summer gave the Confederate leadership reason to believe otherwise. Accordingly, when news of Mexico's declaration of war reached Richmond, Breckinridge immediately put in motion war plans that included preemptive attacks against the rail network on both sides of the Mexican–USA border. The Confederacy had been given the chance to break the "Yankee–Mexican" encirclement and perhaps in the process acquire the Trans-Rio Grande territory that Richmond had reluctantly yielded up after the fall of Maximilian, and Richmond now proceeded to seize that chance with both hands. Within two weeks, a pair of Confederate columns was on the move against Santa Fe and Rincon, New Mexico; a third struck south from El Paso aiming for Chihuahua; and a fourth crossed the Rio Grande heading toward Monterrey. In the meantime, the largest Confederate force prepared to embark from Havana for Veracruz, which was, in a deliberate echo of the Mexican–American War of a generation ago, to be seized preparatory to a march on Mexico City.

Simultaneous with the issuance of the orders for these attacks, Breckinridge dispatched to Washington an ultimatum timed to expire shortly before the scheduled initiation of Confederate operations. Only then—and supposedly because President James A. Garfield had failed to give a "satisfactory" response—would Breckinridge request a declaration of war upon Mexico and the USA. Except for the fact that New Mexico was now USA territory, the Confederacy's war plans represented a virtual duplicate of the successful American campaign against Mexico in 1846. But the fact that New Mexico was USA territory underscores the dangerous game that Richmond had chosen to play—especially dangerous in light of the frayed state of Anglo–Confederate relations, which had yet to recover from the *Beauregard* incident and the difficulties of which were now compounded by the identity of the occupant of 10 Downing Street. William Gladstone had been profoundly alienated by the South's employment of Cuba for slavery joint ventures with Brazilian planters. He vigorously attacked the "abject failure" of Disraeli's government to administer a "sufficient rebuke" to the "slave powers" at the time of the *Beauregard* seizure, comparing the continuing practice of slavery by the Confederacy and Brazil to the recent depredations of the Turks against the Bulgars. But Gladstone also had come to view Anglo–Irish reconciliation as his personal mission and was increasingly irritated by the North's failure to curb IRB fund-raising activities (to which the Confederacy's highly public rebuke of Parnell, at the height of his "Land War" agitation in America, stood in marked contrast). English textile mills, moreover, still depended on Southern cotton, notwithstanding the (halting) development of alternative supplies from Egypt and India.

Richmond therefore surmised that the North would at least hesitate before attempting a blockade of Southern ports—a hesitation reinforced by the South's potent, if substantially smaller, ironclad squadron. To exploit these uncertainties and to keep any conflict with the USA limited to a Trans-Mississippi theater of operations, President Breckinridge now sent his famous "Limited War" letter to USA President Garfield. Breckinridge urged that the "American Unions" exercise "restraint" in this "unfortunate clash of arms," lest the war spread and consume "the entire continent and even beyond": To that end, Breckinridge pledged to maintain the peace "as if there were no war" east of the Trans-Mississippi—including the continuation of normal traffic along the Mississippi River, which at this time remained a vital artery for Northern commerce. (The permanent closure of the Mississippi following the end of World War Two in 1918 will be addressed at a later point in this history.) Breckinridge combined this proposal with a stroke of genius in the field of international statecraft, disclosing that he had sent a copy of his letter to Prime Minister Gladstone in the hopes that the "three great Anglo–Saxon powers" would find a way to avoid this "unfortunate episode" becoming transformed into a "global maelstrom." (Former Confederate Secretary of State Judah Benjamin is generally credited with the inspiration for involving Gladstone in this fashion.)

Breckinridge's letter came at a crucial point in Northern deliberations over steps that would have transformed the Western War into a continental struggle that would almost certainly have drawn in Great Britain. Advocates of a blockade realized such a move risked war with Great Britain; yet, instead of shrinking from the prospect, those calling for a blockade instead urged a preemptive move against Canada. In fact, when Breckinridge's "limited war" proposal reached Washington, President Garfield and his cabinet were on the verge of approving mobilization of forces along the Canadian border preparatory to a possible invasion. Cooler heads now prevailed, and the resulting delay also gave time for Gladstone's government to receive and respond to Breckinridge's communication.

In fact, Breckinridge's missive was received with something approaching rapture by Gladstone, for the North American situation was not the only international crisis requiring attention—and possible military action—by the British Empire. In Egypt, that June, rampaging mobs in Alexandria had killed dozens of Europeans. The ensuing crisis moved even the pacific Gladstone to acknowledge the need for military intervention to restore order—a precondition to sorting out the chaos left in the wake of the overthrow the previous September of the Ottoman "Khedive." (The Khedive was the nominal Turkish ruler of Egypt, still technically an Ottoman province; real power, however, was exercised behind the scenes by the British and French, under a complicated arrangement dominated by London.) The demands of an adequate military effort in Egypt, however, would create grave difficulties for London's ability to deter any assault by the USA against Canada; while she undoubtedly ruled the waves, Britannia's land forces remained miniscule in 1882. Worse, the Egyptian Crisis had strained Great Britain's heretofore still good, if fraying, relations with France at the same time that the North American crisis threatened war with France's (albeit informal) American ally. Leon Gambetta, the vociferous nationalist who had only recently lost the premiership, had already begun haranguing his cautious successor, Charles de Freycinet, on the need for "free Republican solidarity with the United States against the perfidious English and the slavery despots of *Richmonde*."

Gladstone therefore lost no time in dispatching a reply to Washington and Richmond in which he congratulated Breckinridge on his "vision" in seeking to contain "the misfortune of war." As at the moment of crisis over Spain in 1870, London's "good offices" were offered to resolve the conflict. Conspicuously absent, however, was any statement to the effect that Great Britain would take no sides in the "tragic breakdown" of the American peace—to counterbalance Gladstone's express warning that London would view with the "gravest concern" any action that might "widen the threatened conflict's apparent intended scope." Although things had gone too far this time for war to be avoided, Washington got the message: A blockade of the South risked war with the British Empire, which was also prepared to fight to defend its Canadian holdings. (The well-publicized dispatch of broadside ironclad reinforcements for the Royal Navy's North American and West Indies Stations underscored Gladstone's point.)

Thus passed the first international crisis engendered by the Western War. As I will describe, the second would come two years later, when the Confederacy's bold—some would say desperate—attempt to break the military stalemate once again nearly brought on war between the North and the British Empire. But first, I must chronicle the course of the Western War itself.

Charitably put, the conflict was not the finest military hour for either North or South (whereas Mexico's new peasant regular army acquitted itself quite well—much to the surprise of virtually every foreign observer sent from Europe, although not those from South America). And as even Confederate historians—the more objective ones, at any rate—later admitted, the South's armies came off the worse in this first clash since Secession with those of their Northern rival.

Of the many reasons offered for what then seemed so shockingly poor a performance by "the Gray Legions" who had won the battle for Southern independence and then wrested Cuba from Spain, I believe the hubris of champions best explains the Confederacy's failure in the Western War. The men who had triumphed at Gettysburg and Santiago—A. P. Hill, Hood, Armistead—still commanded in New Mexico, along the Rio Grande, and at Veracruz. Two victorious campaigns had left them confident that their third war need only be fought like their last two. Far too little attention had been paid to technological developments such as the Gatling gun and barbed wire. Equally important was the related fact that these "aging lions" for the first time were fighting without the benefit of guidance from Lee, Longstreet, or Jackson. Lee had died in 1878. (The outpouring of grief that convulsed the Confederacy did not extend across the border; whereas Lincoln's passing in 1875 evoked many generous tributes from Southerners who praised Lincoln's "statesmanship" in yielding to the "justice of the Confederate cause"; Northerners remembered with bitterness the destructive course of

"Lee's March" through the Pennsylvania countryside, following his triumph at Gettysburg.) In 1879, Longstreet joined the ranks of the Confederacy's leading elder statesmen upon completing his term as CSA President. Jackson, the last member of the "Gray Triumvirate," had then insisted on resigning his post as Confederate Army Chief of Staff and returning to his beloved Shenandoah. Without the genius of Lee, the prudent caution of Longstreet, or the boldness of Jackson, their successors—brilliant regimental, brigade, and divisional commanders—proved woefully deficient in the far more demanding arts of full army command.

Not that the North's field commanders markedly out-generaled their Southern counterparts. In Sheridan, the USA had a truly able commander, and he got the clear better of A. P. Hill in New Mexico. But "Baldy" Smith and William Rosecrans proved to be as much past their prime as their former Secession War opponents—and their "primes" had not been as good in the first place. The Northern generals, however, at least commanded forces whose armaments had kept reasonable pace with technological change: as the case of the Gatling gun well illustrates.

Richard Gatling patented his "cranked" machine gun in November 1862, just as the Lincoln Administration acceded to the Anglo–French calls for an armistice and negotiated peace. The armistice being *en place*, USA military authorities continued to prepare for a resumption of hostilities well into 1863; only after the ratification of the Treaty of London did the withdrawal process get underway. Gatling, who had given his gun a successful public demonstration in Indianapolis several months before patenting the device, was able that January to persuade the War Department to place an initial order for two hundred guns. Secretary of War Stanton was Gatling's prime advocate. Stanton doubted that the London negotiations would produce an acceptable peace and had also been convinced by the string of Union defeats at Lee's hands the previous year that the North could only redress the "deficit of command" through technological superiority. Gatling's prospects temporarily waned when the Democratic-controlled House in the 38th Congress cut army funding, but the Republican victory of 1864 soon combined with the crisis over French intervention in Mexico to assure a steady flow of orders from Washington, and the Cooper Firearms factory in Philadelphia (with which Gatling had formed a joint venture to meet the Union army's first order) soon had to double the capacity of its facilities to meet demand. Although the War Department prohibited sales to the Confederacy, samples soon came into the South's possession—first by capture from *Juarista* forces in Mexico and later as a result of aid provided to Argentina in the Triple Alliance's war against Paraguay. (War Department objections to providing Gatlings to the Alliance armies—out of concern that the Brazilians would acquire the guns from the Argentines and pass them along to their Confederate advisers—were overruled by President Seward after vehement protests from Buenos Aires at the prospect of being deprived access to this "new and vital instrument of war.") Yet, while the South subsequently employed a number of Tredegar's model of the Gatling during the Cuban campaign—they played an important, if subsidiary, role during Pickett's famous uphill charge at the Siege of Santiago—the Confederates failed to appreciate the devastating implications of machine gun technology for the South's favored tactic of the attack. Never mind that the Confederacy's victory at Gettysburg had been won when Lee's maneuvers compelled the Union forces to *attack* the Army of Virginia after it had occupied the superior *defensive* positions of Cemetery Ridge and Little Round Top—this fact seemed to have been forgotten by all of Lee's lieutenants still in active service at the time of the Western War's outbreak.

Moreover, the South's victorious war record bred a rather bad case of victory disease, which reinforced the tendency to overlook the revolutionary implications of new technology. Not so for the North, where the trauma of losing the War of Secession produced an upheaval in the USA army command, ultimately bringing to power three men of talent and determination who would transform the former Union army into a modern military machine the equal of any foreign force. As indicated, despite the armistice announcement of November 1862, Secretary of War Stanton doubted an acceptable peace could be achieved in London. Stanton also believed the Union must plan for a war that would quickly widen upon renewal to encompass Great Britain and France as enemies ranged on the side of the Confederacy. Army General-in-Chief Henry Halleck concurred, and he and Stanton also agreed on the need for a comprehensive reorganization of the various army commands: to place in key posts those officers capable of conducting a wider—and more ferocious—form of war. With Lincoln's support, Stanton and Halleck began the work to identify this new group of commanders; although that process was not completed before it became apparent that Secretary of State Seward had managed to negotiate an acceptable peace, the Secretary of War and the Army Chief of Staff (again with Lincoln's support and active participation) continued their efforts even after peace had been agreed.

Out of that process, three men (the North's own "Blue Triumvirate") emerged: Ulysses S. Grant, William T. Sherman, and Phillip Sheridan. Grant and Sherman had enjoyed widely acknowledged success in the war's Western theater of operations, where the armistice had found them planning an assault against the vital Mississippi River fortress city of Vicksburg. Sheridan was a less prominent figure at war's end, but he had early on caught the eye of Halleck and had then cut a particularly dynamic figure at the Kentucky battles that had forced Bragg and Kirby Smith to withdraw just prior to the Armistice. Halleck, with Stanton's approval, chose Sheridan to command the twenty thousand troops sent to the New Mexico Territory as part of the USA's support for Juarez against France and the Confederacy. In that capacity, Sheridan served under Sherman, who had overall responsibility for the operation as commander of the Army's newly formed Southwestern Department. (In the meantime, Grant was supervising the establishment of defenses along the new international boundaries of the Ohio and Potomac Rivers.) Sheridan again performed brilliantly, and when Grant succeeded Halleck as General-in-Chief and recalled Sherman to Washington, Sheridan became Southwestern commander—a post he would hold through the Apache and Western Wars until appointed to succeed Sherman in 1886 as the USA's Chief of General Staff. (That post was held first by Grant upon its creation, and then it was held by Sherman upon Grant's retirement—fatally ill with throat cancer—in 1881.) These three men shared a vision of war as a "total enterprise" that required the full mobilization of the North's great material and technological resources. All were also very impressed by the Prussian performance against France in 1870–71, where Sherman headed up the USA's substantial observer corps; Sherman's detailed report led directly to the establishment of an American General Staff as well as a permanent Bureau of Military Railroad Operations.

Besides instituting a general staff system along German lines, the Triumvirate promoted reforms of the army's ordnance and supply bureaus, transforming hidebound agencies debilitated by patronage appointments into offices with at least the promise of efficient and professional performance (although as the Western War would show, a substantial gap remained to be closed between actual and potential capacity). In all these efforts, moreover, the Triumvirate was aided by the most basic of military circumstances—necessity. For while the South had twelve years of peace after the conquest of Cuba, the North (along with its ally, Mexico) was engaged in a ferocious, ongoing conflict with the Apache—superb light cavalry, armed abundantly with modern Confederate weapons supplied, albeit clandestinely, by the Confederacy. The Triumvirate used that war to compel the institution of reforms that the military bureaucracy might successfully have resisted in peacetime. Thus, when investigators learned that Custer had left behind half a dozen Gatling guns before his fatal foray, Sheridan—backed by Grant and Sherman—forced through a reform of Army tactics that integrated Gatling guns down to the company level, while also working to disabuse the notion of many officers that the "machined gun" was just another kind of artillery. ("I refuse to slow down my horsemen by dragging along those damn crank-operated cannon!"—so Custer is supposed to have exclaimed before setting off without the Seventh Cavalry's complement of Gatlings for that ill-fated encounter with Geronimo.) These changes—along with Sheridan's decision to pursue what proved to amount to the virtual extermination of the Indian enemy—made a major contribution to the USA's and Mexico's triumph in the Apache War. They also helped transform the USA's army into a tested fighting force able to employ the latest in weapons technology—a process that would also prove of great benefit to the new Mexican army, whose regiments trained closely with their American allies.

With this background in mind, I shall resume my narrative of the Western War's course. Almost immediately, the Confederacy's multi-pronged assault ran into grave difficulties. Armistead put three divisions ashore at Veracruz, seized the port, and commenced investment of the Mexican fortifications inland that guarded the invasion route to Mexico City, but several costly attacks failed to break through these imposing defenses. In the north, Hill managed to break the Atchison, Topeka & Santa Fe rail line north and south of Santa Fe—which effectively put that city under a state of siege, while cavalry raids organized by J. E. B. Stuart, combining Confederate regular cavalry with allied Indian "light horse" from the Confederate Indian Country tribes, disrupted Northern efforts to re-supply the New Mexico Territory from the east. (The Indian light horse served under William P. Ross, a lieutenant colonel of a Confederate Cherokee regiment during the War of Secession; Ross went with the Cherokee who chose to emigrate from the Cherokee area of Indian country when it was awarded to the North under the Treaty of London.) Hill's forces, however, suffered a repulse well outside of Rincon, while along the Rio Grande the attacks toward Chihuahua and Monterey under General Hood ran into severe difficulties against well prepared Mexican defense lines (including very effective use of Gatling guns and barbed wire, a combination that everywhere would cost the Confederates thousands of casualties). The onset of winter found the Confederacy's principal forces stymied on all lines of advance, and for the next several months, Southern soldiers endured miserable conditions in hastily dug entrenchments, which the Confederate offense-minded commissary department proved woefully unprepared to supply them with the most basic of goods.

Northern and Mexican forces, however, also suffered from a failure of provisioning. The Confederacy's success in severing the Southwestern transcontinental rail link effectively reduced the USA to reliance on the transcontinental line operated by the Central and Union Pacific Railroads. (The Northern Pacific's terminus at Tacoma on the Puget Sound in Washington Territory was too far north to be able to make any substantial contribution to supply of theaters of operation centered on the Southwest and Mexico.) Unfortunately, the UP line was bottlenecked by a ramshackle facility in Omaha, Nebraska, which could not cope with the volume of traffic forced to re-route by the Confederacy's investment of Santa Fe. The resulting disruption was compounded by an even more basic problem: the failure to adopt a standardized time system for scheduling trains. The outbreak of the war found the USA's railroad system still operating under a *laissez faire* time system, under which each railroad set its own "clock" while honoring innumerable "sun times" established by communities along individual lines. (One station in Buffalo displayed three clocks, each showing different times; the State of Wisconsin reported thirty-eight different times based on local "sun time" determinations.) By October, rail traffic in the USA was in chaos, as the Byzantine pre-war scheduling system collapsed under the double strain of the Omaha backlog and the volume of military transport demands. (Santa Fe came within a whisker of falling when misrouting of a train reduced the stock of Gatling ammunition to just a single day's supply.)

A hastily convened "railroad summit" met that December in Chicago, where representatives of the railways agreed to adopt the General Time convention and put into effect four standard time zones governing the continental USA. Although no law required the rail companies—privately held rather than state-owned, as in Prussia—to conform to the directives of the Bureau of Military Railroad Operations, the owners realized that their continued economic independence would have been at risk if they had refused to bring order to what had become intolerable chaos. When the newly elected 48th Congress convened in an extraordinary wartime session called by President Garfield the following July, both Houses quickly passed the "National Defense Time Standardization Act," making permanent the GTC adopted at the Chicago Rail Summit. Yet, even the rapid implementation of standard time could only do so much to untangle the rail traffic snarl, as the "Omaha problem" could not be effectively resolved without also expanding the Missouri River rail crossing at Council Bluffs, Iowa. There, all traffic was routed across a single-track bridge built in 1872; the bridge's iron post connections had begun to show fatigue, and local railroad officials feared the structure had been pushed to the point of collapse by the strain of war traffic. Railroad representatives at the Chicago Summit agreed to pool their resources and embark on a "crash" program to replace the bridge with a double-track steel structure. The threat of nationalizations of operations under Army control, called for by several bills introduced in the waning days of the 47th Congress, and whose sponsors promised would be pursued with redoubled vigor when the new Congress convened the following year, helped spur the owners to act. Before its final adjournment in March of 1883, the 47th Congress did appropriate funds for the Army Corps of Engineers to assist in the Council Bluffs bridge project, and Chief of Staff

Sherman appointed Herman Haupt, an outstanding railroad engineer, to coordinate the Corps' efforts with that of the Union Pacific (the owner of the existing bridge). The program's estimated minimum six-month completion date, however, forced the North to route an increasing percentage of war tonnage across the Isthmus of Panama, using the canal company's extensive railroad network. (The inability to pass a needed second appropriation until the new Congress convened in the special wartime session in July also contributed to the delay, and was the direct cause of the swift adoption of the Fourteenth Amendment, which provided for a January convening of Congress after each election—for good measure, the presidential inauguration date was also moved up from March to January.)

USA–Mexican forces thus became dependent on a lifeline running through the distant—and vulnerable—choke point of the Panama Canal Zone. As we shall see, that vulnerability would eventually prove too much of a temptation to a Confederacy frustrated by another year of stalemate on the Trans-Mississippi and Mexican battlefields of its own choosing. But such an expansion of the war beyond the limits defined by President Breckinridge's letter—which would bring on the second and decisive international crisis of the conflict—lay in the future. In the meantime, the spring of 1883 saw a renewal of the Confederate offensive, now concentrated along the two most distant axes of the South's initial abortive advance. After the abysmal failure of the attacks across the Rio Grande against Chihuahua and Monterrey, President Breckinridge decided to concentrate the Confederate offensive effort at the two "ends," while leaving enough strength in the center to tie down as many Mexican troops as possible. So, to the south, Armistead's forces received new heavy guns—the first fruits of the Tredegar–Krupp joint venture. After a devastating bombardment lasting a week, the Confederates launched an assault from three sides. The exhausted Mexican defenders could not hold the line, and by June, Armistead was preparing for the advance toward Puebla—and Mexico City. Meanwhile, across the border in the New Mexico Territory, Hill renewed his attack on Santa Fe and Rincon.

On the New Mexico front, there now ensued two individual events that juxtaposed the tragic end of one heroic career with the beginning of another of far greater consequence to the course of this history. J. E. B.

Stuart, the "Cavalier" beloved of every Southerner for his dashing performance under Lee, had showed flashes of his old brilliance during the opening phases of the Western War. Given command of both Hill's cavalry and a special "horse reserve" designated to operate out of Northwestern Texas and Confederate "Indian Country," Stuart had organized—in concert with the South's Indian allies—a wide ranging series of raids that, as previously indicated, played havoc with Northern rail traffic all along the AT&SF line. When Hill began planning his spring offensive, he recalled Stuart, directing him to prepare the cavalry aspects of the upcoming campaign. When the assault was renewed on Santa Fe that April, Stuart placed himself at the front to observe—and to participate in the fighting, should a "legitimate chance" to evade the confines of high command come his way. There, on May 12, 1883, Stuart was killed by counter-battery fire from the Northern lines. (Stuart's fatal wound, from shrapnel that sliced through his stomach and exited just an inch to the right of his spine, was actually inflicted on May 11; Stuart lingered, in terrible pain but ever insouciant, until the following morning.) Stuart's death plunged the Confederacy into mourning; his shattered body was returned by special train to Richmond, where he lay in state before a funeral presided over by President Breckinridge and attended by former comrades Longstreet and Jackson.

Stuart's death also became intertwined with the Western War record of future USA President Theodore Roosevelt. In the spring of 1882, Roosevelt was in the New York State Assembly, leading a group of young legislators— at twenty-three, "TR" was the youngest member of either the Assembly or the New York State Senate—in a vigorous assault on corruption in high places. Influence-peddling and other abuses of power were rife due to the explosion in railroad construction and the emergence of the "military-industrial axis"—TR himself coined the phrase—and Roosevelt rocketed to prominence as a freshman Assemblyman by compelling an official investigation into the shady connections between a member of the New York City trial bench and a hotly disputed railway takeover effort. When the Assembly adjourned that June, state political observers were predicting that Roosevelt could become the youngest speaker in Assembly history—should the Republicans retain their majority in the upcoming midterm elections. But by then, Roosevelt was giving little thought to such matters: Shocked by the attempted murder of former Mexican President Diaz, TR joined enthusiastically in the call for a "war of punishment" against Richmond when the news broke of a Confederate hand in the "dastardly deed." And after the South declared war, Roosevelt promptly resigned his Assembly seat and began campaigning for permission to organize a volunteer regiment to fight "the damn Johnnies."

Despite the adoption of a permanent draft in 1865, the North had failed to maintain adequate army manpower levels—principally because no administration had been willing to implement actual call-ups after the New York City draft registration riots of the following year. Chief of Staff Sherman had therefore been compelled to use the Secession War system of raising new volunteer regiments by state to fill the gap. (Sherman insisted that the new units be commanded by a regular army colonel and leavened with a core of veteran noncommissioned officers.) So it was that in the fall of 1882, with Santa Fe under siege, Roosevelt got his wish: He would be a lieutenant colonel and second in command of the brand new 29th New York. Charged with organizing the recruiting of the regiment's members, Roosevelt plunged into his responsibilities with enthusiasm and effectiveness. The result was a regiment raised in record time—and also top-heavy with Ivy Leaguers drawn from the same privileged milieu as their lieutenant colonel. The 29th New York departed in December for field training at Fort Leavenworth in Kansas and was then hurried into the line to help meet the renewed Confederate assault on Santa Fe that April. The future governor, cabinet member, and president quickly proved he was a man of physical courage as well as administrative ability. An accident of timing then placed the 29th New York at the point in the line where—and on the same day when—J. E. B. Stuart was killed. The Confederate press became convinced that Roosevelt had ordered his regiment's gunners to aim for "the Great Cavalier," and the Roosevelt name became a veritable expletive in the Southern vocabulary. In fact, Roosevelt gave no such order, although he did loudly cheer Stuart's fall. Like other members of the North's "New Generation," Roosevelt felt no affection for any of the Confederacy's leading military figures; in turn, such bitter hatreds as the South's for Theodore Roosevelt would now serve to reinforce the sense of separation and mutual hostility dividing the former halves of the old Union.

TR's valiant efforts, along with those of innumerable other defenders, combined to repulse Hill's second attempt to take Santa Fe. In Roosevelt's case, heroism meant leading a counterattack under heavy fire to retake a hill and silence a Confederate battery. Another hero of Santa Fe was future Chief of Staff Arthur MacArthur, who won the Congressional Medal of Honor while leading a charge that drove the Confederates from a key position. By June, it was apparent that Santa Fe would not fall, and also that the North had repulsed Hill's second try for Rincon (which was one of Hill's mistakes; had he concentrated his effort against Santa Fe, he might very well have captured the city that April). Meanwhile, beyond Veracruz, Armistead had been stopped by the deadly nest of forts built by the Mexicans at the mountain pass at Cerro Gordo. This time, there would be no successful flanking maneuver by the attackers, as the Mexicans—recalling how Winfield Scott had come down upon Santa Anna's troops from the rear—had carefully extended their Gatling-gun and barbed-wire defenses to either side of the pass. For six months, the Confederates beat their head against this "Juarez Line" and were rewarded only with steadily increasing casualties for their efforts. Finally, when their numbers had been so reduced that they risked being cut off by a Mexican counteroffensive, Armistead's remaining forces retired to their Veracruz lodgment, where, for all practical purposes, they were placed under siege by the Mexicans. (The Mexican decision of a decade before—to concentrate on Pacific Ocean harbors and bases, combined with local Confederate naval predominance—at least meant Armistead's men could look forward to adequate re-supply.)

Besides creating the opportunity for Theodore Roosevelt to become a war hero, the Northern manpower crisis also produced a peaceful resolution of the long-simmering "Mormon Question." The Mormon leadership quietly approached Chief of Staff Sherman and proposed the raising of several "Mormon regiments"; in exchange, the government would agree, if the Mormons did their duty, to admit the Utah Territory as the State of "Deseret" at war's end. The Mormons, moreover, agreed to abandon polygamy as a formal tenet of their faith—if the government would agree to repeal the recently passed Edmonds Act banning polygamy in federal territory and instead leave the matter to state authorities. In need of the troops, the Garfield Administration accepted the Mormon offer; the Mormons met their battlefield obligations with distinction; and Deseret entered the Union as its twenty-sixth state, in 1886. Given the proximity of Utah to New Mexico, one wonders what might have happened if Washington had spurned the Mormon offer. A Mormon revolt would not have been entirely out of the question, especially given the passage of the hated Edmonds Act just that spring, and the resulting additional strain could have meant the fall of Santa Fe, leading to a widening of the war which would eventually have involved Great Britain and perhaps other European Powers. Indeed, as the reader will now see, such a widening and ensuing internationalization, albeit due to different specific causes, would only just be avoided.

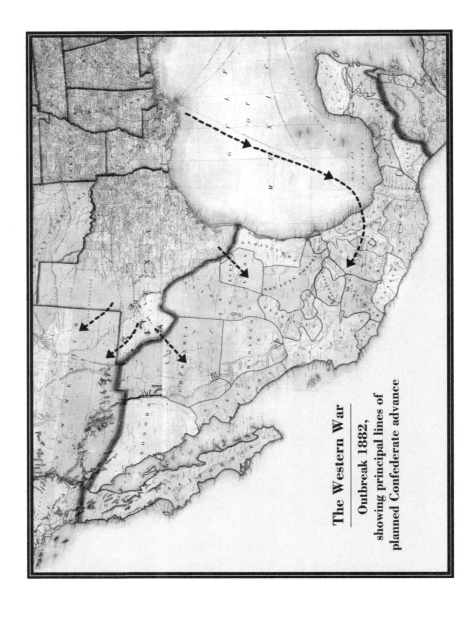

The Western War

Outbreak 1882,
showing principal lines of
planned Confederate advance

9

THE WESTERN WAR AND THE CREATION OF THE ANGLO-CONFEDERATE ENTENTE: (3) THE SECOND INTERNATIONAL CRISIS AND THE CONFLICT'S RESOLUTION

A ll the belligerents recognized that a crisis point had now been reached. The Confederacy's attempt to reprise the Mexican campaigns of 1846–47 had failed. Armistead's exhausted forces in Veracruz, while well-fed, were nonetheless suffering the ravages of that malarial country for the second Winter in a row, while Santa Fe and Rincon still held out against Hill. As for the Rio Grande, a renewal by the Confederacy along the war's dormant "central front" would require stripping defenses east of the Mississippi of troops needed to meet any sudden Northern move. The harsh truth was that the Confederacy had plunged precipitately into war, and by the terms of its own plan of campaign had been defeated—unless Richmond was prepared to risk a wider war, in the hope of shifting the battlefield balance back in its favor.

In fact, this was precisely what Breckinridge and his cabinet were preparing to do. The reader will recall that the Confederacy had managed to disrupt Northern rail traffic so as to force Washington to divert the critical margin of supplies for the New Mexico and Juarez line defenders on a roundabout journey through the Panama Canal Zone. Breckinridge believed that if the Panama supply route could be rendered inoperative for as little as thirty days, a sustained assault against either Santa Fe or the Juarez Line would succeed. Of the two choices for an attack, Breckinridge believed the Juarez Line to be the more inviting target. A breakthrough at Cerro Gordo would expose Mexico City itself, and Breckinridge believed that the Mexican government could be persuaded to accept a "sensible resolution" of the conflict if the alternative was the capture—and devastation—of the country's capital city for the second time in a generation.

Of course, the Mexicans had responded to the loss of Mexico City to the French by taking the fight to the hinterlands, and Breckinridge recognized they might very well do so again. But Breckinridge was also counting on a Panama raid to be treated by the North as a breach of the limited area of engagement—as established by the Confederate President's own letter. If Washington responded by imposing a blockade, Breckinridge was confident that the result would be war between the North and the British Empire.

In reaching this conclusion, the Confederate leadership counted on the worsening state of USA–British relations, which was directly traceable to the disastrous impact of the Western War on the course of Anglo–*Irish* relations. The reader will recall that the IRB had given up the immediate pursuit of an Anglo–American war and opted to support those like Parnell whose program of "Home Rule" at least offered the chance to weaken the ties to London. But the "new IRB" had not foresworn the ultimate goal of an independent Ireland or even the desirability of an Anglo–American War—only the immediate utility of the pursuit of such a conflict as the primary aim of IRB policy. The IRB leadership therefore watched with increasing excitement as the American unions and Mexico moved ever closer to war during the summer of 1882. And when war exploded that August and Gladstone seized on CSA President Breckinridge's letter as an excuse to stay out, the IRB resolved to take "all steps necessary" to bring Great Britain in on the Confederacy's side. Within weeks, a series of bombings hit targets in Ireland and England. Moreover, a carefully publicized support effort for the IRB in the USA—reviving the network from the Fenian days—made sure that London would suspect a connection between the bombings and "Ireland Abroad." Just to be sure that British authorities drew that conclusion, the IRB organized marches in New York City, Boston, and other Northern cities with substantial Irish–American communities, in which British "oppression" was loudly condemned, and "the brave boys of the brotherhood" lustily cheered (and money openly collected for "the cause").

The IRB's campaign rapidly produced its intended effect. A frustrated Gladstone was forced to reinstitute the police-power measures only just suspended. In turn, that move compelled Parnell loudly to condemn the government for its "disgraceful disregard of the natural rights of a free people." As the IRB's campaign of "outrages" continued unabated into 1883, Parnell began to come under attack from Liberals who until now had gone along with their leader's insistence that Parnell must be allowed to "vent" against the government, lest he lose credibility with the "responsible" center of Irish opinion. To these Liberals—who looked increasingly to the dynamic Joseph Chamberlain as *their* leader, in spirit if not in name—the notion of a responsible center of Irish opinion seemed exposed as a mirage; the ostensibly responsible Irish had proven incapable of containing or even confronting the IRB. They now joined a Conservative chorus demanding the government "do something" to "make the Yankees curb *their* Irish," whose monies were financing IRB bombings.

Gladstone found his room for maneuver increasingly circumscribed, as the Liberal party showed signs of cracking over the contentious issue of "Irish appeasement." And because the Government's majority rested on ever more fragile foundations, Gladstone also was compelled to abandon other cherished reform plans: such as an overhaul of the electoral system, which would have substantially expanded the eligible electorate beyond the bounds set by the Second Reform Bill of 1867. As for Parnell, he was unwilling by conviction to embrace the IRB yet unable to condemn them without risking alienating the increasing portion of Irish opinion—especially among the young—that instinctively backed "the brotherhood" in response to British coercion.

This was the state of affairs that Breckinridge and the rest of the Confederate leadership sought to exploit by deliberately courting a widening of the war. On February 22, 1884, a CSA squadron weighed anchor from Havana and set course for the Panama coast of Colombia. During the early morning hours of February 24, the residents of Colon awoke to the sound of shells crashing into the city and harbor dockworks. Six CSA ironclads, led by the Confederate flagship *Old Dominion*, were blasting away with their ten-inch guns. By a stroke of good fortune for the South—aided by an inexcusable failure of intelligence by the North—no

Northern or Colombian warships were within one hundred miles of the city. Given the accelerated pace of naval technological change at the end of the 1870s and the start of the 1880s, these Confederate ironclads, although fairly new, were already obsolescent. The immediate future would belong to steel cruisers and barbetted battleships. But that was of no matter for the here and now, as the ten-inch Tredegar smoothbores and Armstrong rifles made short work of the masonry coastal defenses; only one ship, CSS *Albermarle*, was even hit by the defenders. After one hour, the bombardment ceased, and over 1,500 crack CSA Marines swarmed ashore from the accompanying transports.

The mission was not occupation—but destruction. The Confederate force swept aside USA and Colombian army quartermaster units and made their way to the railroad line. Ignoring the neighboring, but still incomplete, locks, the first company of sappers placed their charges to do maximum damage to the tracks. A series of terrific explosions split the air; when the dust settled, the Panama Canal Railway had been reduced to a twisted wreck for several miles. Throughout the day, a second team of sappers was doing equally great damage to the Colon docks. By the next morning, the Confederate raiders had made good their escape; they left behind a burning city, several hundred civilian and military dead and wounded, and a transportation system that would be unable to carry a single shipment of supplies across the Isthmus for at least six weeks.

News of the Panama raid reached Washington, Mexico City, and Bogota within forty-eight hours. Colombia promptly declared war—a result expected by Richmond, and also believed to be of no military consequence. It would certainly not matter, Breckinridge reasoned, to the outcome of the imminent renewal of the assault against the Juarez Line (a judgment that would prove very much in error). Of greater interest to the Confederacy was the reaction of the USA. Breckinridge hoped for the imposition of a blockade, and the Panama raid touched off an outcry in which many leading editorialists and politicians demanded just that. Moreover, with the demand for a blockade came renewed calls for a preemptive "occupation" of Canada. President Garfield and his cabinet, however, were divided over how to respond to what the public considered a clear breach of Breckinridge's pledge to limit the war to the Trans-Mississippi. In fact, Breckinridge's pledge had carefully not mentioned territory outside the continental USA proper, and the Canal Zone was Colombian territory, to boot.

Ultimately, Garfield decided on a grab-bag of measures that did not include a blockade but still raised the alarm in Ottawa and London. One hundred thousand new troops would be called up. In the meantime, a force of twenty-five thousand would be moved to northern Minnesota and the Dakota Territory and placed within a day's quick march of the Canadian Pacific transcontinental railway (then still under construction). The draft itself was in full swing, the political constraints on its operation having been swept away by the necessities of war; nor would it ever again be reduced to the inactivity of the period between the New York Registration Riots of 1866 and the outbreak of the Western War sixteen years later. Moreover, given Parnell's anti-British maneuvering, the draft was now supported by urban Irish–Americans, who had previously provided the mass of street-level opposition to registration. And while a blockade would not be imposed, the USA Navy would launch retaliatory raids against Confederate bases on Cuba and Confederate ports on the CSA mainland.

The crisis came in April 1884, as events merged to form a dizzying political kaleidoscope whose vertiginous effects nearly resulted in the wider war the CSA so desperately sought. Within a week of the Panama Raid, the Confederate army had gone back over to the offensive. A reinforced Armistead swept smartly out of Veracruz and renewed his assault on the Juarez line. The Mexicans again fought courageously, but the ensuing exhaustion of supplies in the wake of the Panama Raid proved too much; the Mexican defenses broke, and Armistead was threatening Puebla (and from there, Mexico City) by the end of March.

In the meantime, the USA Navy had commenced its raids on Confederate ports. The Americans managed to sink a blockship—an obsolescent steam frigate chained to rubble-filled coal barges—in the main channel approaching New Orleans. Given New Orleans's site over sixty miles from the Gulf, it was not deemed practicable to sail upriver and bombard what was still the South's largest city. The American navy, therefore, had to be satisfied with disrupting the flow of commerce from New Orleans and the developing bulk-carrier depots across the river that would later become the enormous Port of South Louisiana. To that end, four old

Casco-class monitors—*Modoc, Suncook, Yazoo,* and *Yuma*—lurked off the Mississippi Delta, but their take was limited to a handful of small trawlers and a single inbound Confederate transport riding in ballast, and they were soon driven off by a relief squadron steaming from Mobile.

When the monitors withdrew, the channel was promptly cleared, and the North's "punitive expedition" against the Crescent City proved of little lasting effect. Far more consequential was the Northern effort against Charleston, South Carolina, targeted at least as much for emotional as economic reasons. The flagship of the USA fleet was the oceangoing monitor *Dictator*, accompanied by the *Kalamazoo*-class monitors *Shakamaxon* and *Passaconoway*. Each vessel's armor scheme had been augmented during an 1880–81 refit, and they were powerful (if somewhat dated). These three ships together mounted ten fifteen-inch smoothbores and sufficient armor to close with the Confederate shore batteries. They reduced the northern shore defenses of Charleston—Forts Beauregard and Moultrie—to rubble and dismounted all of the defending guns of Fort Gregg and Battery Wagner on the southern harbor entrances. The attackers then spent a leisurely full day steaming back and forth between Fort Sumter and the city itself, doing substantial damage to ships tied up at the city's many docks—as well as to the city itself.

One specific Northern aim was frustrated. Commander Charles Clark aboard *Shakamaxon* had written his family back in Vermont before departing, waxing eloquent about his intention to destroy Institute Hall (also known to Charlestonians as Agricultural Hall), the meeting place where South Carolina officially signed the very first Ordinance of Secession on December 20, 1860. Little did the good captain realize that a small cooking fire in December 1861 had spread into a conflagration that consumed Agricultural Hall as well as a full quarter of the city.

Although Agricultural Hall was no longer available as a target, the USA Navy proceeded to prove that "New Charleston" burned as readily as had the old city. Southern sentiments were most enraged by the participation of the *Dictator*'s "half-sister" ship, the five-thousand-ton *Puritan*. Her two massive twenty-inch Dahlgren smoothbores were able to loft enormous explosive shells into the city of Charleston itself, while the monitor stayed outside the effective range of any inner harbor defenses. Given her fifteen-inch-thick iron armor plating, newly covered with a two-inch steel plate, even point-blank range would probably have proven ineffective against her. *Puritan's* first shells burst just north of the city market: near the corner of Pickney and Church Streets. *Puritan* scored direct hits on Castle Pickney and Battery Point, set the Cooper River wharves afire, and demolished both the old Courthouse and the Customs Building. Civilian casualties—largely among those who had gathered harbor side to picnic and watch the defenders drive off the impudent Yankees—ran to the thousands, with over six hundred civilian dead. Southern opinion was outraged by the "Rape of Charleston." A correspondent for the *Illustrated London News* happened to be present during the punitive expedition, and his sympathetic treatment of the civilian victims (including many women and children) helped enrage British opinion—although that outrage was not directed entirely against the attackers. One of *Puritan's* shells scored a direct hit on a slave market, and engraved illustrations of the mangled bodies of young slaves—albeit dismembered by American fire—generated what one observer in London called "intensely ambivalent" feelings.

Another result of the "Great Raid" was a prolonged campaign of vilification of the "Damnyankees" by the Mayor of Charleston—which even Richmond ultimately would find excessive. Mayor William Ashmead Courtenay had enlisted in the Secession War as a private, had seen combat at First Manassas, and had risen through the ranks to a captaincy. Courtenay had then devoted his postwar life to the rebuilding, expansion, and modernization of Charleston. The North's punitive expedition against his beloved city—his home on Ashley Avenue was burned to the ground during the bombardment—provided Courtenay the lachrymose theme of a well-publicized address, delivered each year on the anniversary of the raid until his death in 1908.

The sole substantial Northern reverse came off Santiago de Cuba. At Charleston, as at the other bombardment sites, accompanying USA warships were able to keep CSA spar torpedo boats well away from the bombarding monitors. In Charleston Harbor, the Confederate navy lost the *New David*-class spar torpedo boats CSS *Lamar* and CSS *St. Patrick*, and elsewhere, the spar torpedo vessels declined to challenge the invaders. However, at Santiago a new element burst upon the Northern fleet.

The Luppis–Whitehead company at Fiume, in Austria–Hungary, had been manufacturing self-propelled submersible torpedoes since 1870. Although the torpedoes' range was short and their payload limited, the Royal Navy had been conducting detailed experiments with self-propelled torpedoes for over a decade by the time of the Western War. In 1878, two Russian torpedo boats attacked and sank a Turkish revenue cutter in the Black Sea. So, it should have come as no real surprise that the Confederate navy might have some similar craft defending its harbors.

In point of fact, the CSA navy had two British-built torpedo boats at Santiago de Cuba in 1884, both undergoing trials. The first was the CSS *George E. Dixon*; the second, CSS *John A. Payne. Dixon* was, in essence, an *Avvoltoio*-class torpedo boat, built at Yarrow from designs prepared for the Italian Navy. She was launched in 1882 and commissioned late in 1883. *Dixon* was fast (with a top speed of almost 22 knots) and armed with two tube-mounted fourteen-inch Whitehead torpedoes. *Payne* was a somewhat older model, built at the Thames Ironworks in London and modeled on the successful *Zieten* torpedo gunboat built for the German Imperial Navy in 1876. At 1,200 tons and 260 feet, *Payne* was much slower than *Dixon* and could make little more than 16 knots. *Payne* boasted, however, a full clipper rig of sail and an astonishing ten re-loads for her two fifteen-inch torpedo tubes (one each, fore and aft). Although the CSA naval base at Santiago had been tasked to determine which type to purchase from the British—or to manufacture at Tredegar under license—*Dixon* and *Payne* were truly complementary rather than competitive: *Dixon's* speed and small size (her crew of twenty were crammed into a twenty-five-ton displacement) made her ideal for harbor defense, while *Payne* was suited for long patrols.

The USA fleet approaching Santiago de Cuba was sighted by the *Antilles Pearl*, a Confederate patrol ketch operating out of Guantanamo Bay, as the fleet positioned itself for a dawn attack. Alerted to the presence of the Northern vessels, both *Dixon* and *Payne* made steam and left Santiago under cover of darkness. As dawn broke, *Dixon's* miniscule silhouette was less than three hundred yards from the ancient *Passaic*-class monitor USS *Patapsco*. Both of *Dixon's* torpedoes hit the twenty-year-old *Patapsco*, and she promptly turned turtle, taking her entire crew of eighty men and officers to the bottom. *Payne* engaged the *Improved Canonicus*-class monitor

USS *Tippecanoe*. Although *Payne* lacked the speed of *Dixon*, she was still twice as fast as *Tippicanoe* and managed to fire four torpedoes before the fifteen-inch guns of the Northern monitor blew her in half. One of *Payne's* four torpedoes scored a hit, jamming *Tippecanoe's* steering; her captain beached her, and her crew was taken into captivity by the Confederate forces. *Dixon*, too, did not survive the attack, although the near miss that swamped her still allowed most of the crew to swim to safety. The torpedo boats did not stop the bombardment of Santiago; the surviving monitors pounded the harbor defenses, aided by the eight-inch rifled Parrott guns of the old converted ironclad USS *Quinnipiac* (formerly USS *Roanoke*). The Santiago expedition also included a shallow-draft *Casco*-class vessel, USS *Napa*, brought along expressly to navigate the narrow channel into the harbor of Santiago itself. This she did, and her eleven-inch smooth-bore and eight-inch rifle (co-located in a single turret) took a full measure of revenge on the dockworks and warehouses. Still, the loss of two large, albeit elderly, monitors in exchange for two flimsy torpedo boats made the Santiago punitive expedition largely ashes in the mouth of the USA navy. (To this victory by the Confederate torpedo arm at Santiago should be added the results of a running battle off Cape Hatteras in which a squadron of Confederate ironclads drove off a substantially larger Northern force, sinking the superannuated USS *Carondolet* and crippling another ironclad without suffering the loss of a single ship.)

The attacks on New Orleans, Charleston, and Santiago, along with others against Wilmington, Savannah, Tampa, Mobile, Galveston, and Havana, were on the whole sufficiently ruthless in their execution and indiscriminate in their violence that Southern cotton and armaments exports had been cut by over half by the end of March. Most foreign ships ceased to be willing to carry Southern products when the Underwriters at Lloyds suspended writing coverage for voyages from CSA ports, and Confederate-flagged vessels were too few to make up the difference. And while the CSA's small but still formidable navy managed to disrupt some of the raids, as long as the Confederates had to face the American navy alone, the damage to Confederate commerce would only worsen. But the slashing reduction in Confederate exports also meant a severe cut in the cotton needed to keep British mills running at full capacity. Hoping for an incident that would force a still-reluctant Gladstone to send the Royal Navy into action against USA "pirates," and trigger an all-out war between England and the North, CSA President Breckinridge issued a call for an additional fifty thousand troops and began shifting forces from the quiet New Mexico and Rio Grande fronts to key points along the Ohio and Potomac Rivers.

As Breckinridge girded the CSA for a widened war, an equally hopeful IRB stepped up its terror campaign. Attacks on British targets now were launched on both sides of the Atlantic in the hope that the British would convict the Americans of complicity, given widespread Northern sympathy with Irish nationalism. And that is exactly what happened: On March 25, the head of the British consular office in New York City was critically wounded, and members of the House of Commons from both parties were soon condemning the (admittedly) lethargic response of the Irish-dominated city police. Worse, and just as Breckinridge and other Confederate leaders had hoped, the North's naval raids had finally gone beyond inflicting incidental damage to British shipping in Southern harbors, to the killing of British seamen: On April 5, the freighter *Liverpool Lady* was lost with several hands when two Union steam frigates opened fire as the ship was leaving Charleston Harbor. The Union captains insisted they only fired because they had mistaken the freighter for an armored Confederate sloop, but this defense was drowned out by the shouts of "jingo" marchers taking to the streets to reprise their famous ditty of the Anglo–Russian crisis of six years before—only now directing their ire at the USA.

Gladstone's government was badly divided over whether to issue an ultimatum to Washington demanding the cessation of "interference" with neutral shipping. Chamberlain was strongly in favor, but the Prime Minister still hesitated. Gladstone feared that war with the USA—the heartland of "Ireland Abroad"—might cause the IRB to attempt to make good the famous but failed rebellion of 1798, with forces recruited from the Irish American diaspora. In this regard, Gladstone likely was aware of the widely publicized exploits of the "San Patricio" regiment: a force of Irish expatriates, Northern First-Generation Irish immigrants, and even the odd Irish-heritage Confederate deserter, which was already in action alongside Mexican forces, defending their Catholic Mexican co-religionists against the "Bloody Anglo-Saxon Prods." (As the reader will see, Gladstone was right to fear the IRB might attempt, with American support, a reprise of 1798; in the event, the attempt would come on the 101st anniversary of that rebellion, in the midst of the First Alliance War.)

It might have comforted the British leaders to know that their American counterparts were just as badly divided, as the pressure mounted on President Garfield to launch a preemptive assault against Canada. The President's decision was not made any easier when New York Governor Cleveland (Garfield's expected Democratic challenger in the upcoming presidential vote) while addressing a cheering crowd of thousands of Irish-Americans gathered outside the Governor's Mansion in Albany, made headlines across the country when he warned Garfield against "kowtowing to English oppression." Had Armistead managed to overrun Puebla and reach Mexico City, the result probably would have been war between the USA and Great Britain—if only because so serious a reverse in Mexican-American fortunes likely would have forced Garfield to move against Canada. But Armistead's drive stalled forty miles east of Puebla, giving the Mexicans time to establish a defensive line in depth; and the North time to shift forces—including several thousand fresh Colombian troops—in behind the Mexican positions and stiffen their resistance, sufficient to beat back Armistead's assault. (During the fighting, future USA President John M. Schofield distinguished himself by an adroit employment of his forces, blunting a Confederate attack that threatened to break through the center of the Allied line.)

It soon became apparent that Armistead would never reach Puebla that year—which also meant that the Confederacy could not win the war. Breckinridge's hope had been that Armistead's capture of Mexico City, combined with the outbreak of war between the North and Great Britain, would have led to the collapse of the USA–Mexico alliance: As Washington rushed forces north for a campaign to conquer Canada, the resulting perception by Mexico that it had been "abandoned" by its ally would have triggered a constitutional crisis in which Gonzalez (and Diaz) would have been overthrown. The South would have broken the encir-clement of the Trans-Mississippi created by the USA–Mexican alliance and would also have had a renewed chance to acquire the long-sought

Trans-Rio Grande territories should Mexico disintegrate into civil war. But with Armistead checked, these fond hopes now foundered on the harsh reality of Confederate finances. The Confederate treasury had been drained by the cost of eighteen months of war, and with the North's port raids cutting in half the flow of trade revenue from abroad, Breckinridge—as well as Confederate elder statesmen such as Davis and Longstreet—recognized that the South simply could not afford to persevere for another year in the hopes Puebla and Mexico City would fall "next time." If there were to be a "next time," Breckinridge ruefully acknowledged to his Cabinet, it would have to be during the "next war."

Albeit with great reluctance, the Confederacy at the end of April approached the governments of Argentina and Brazil, requesting their "mutual intercession" to bring the conflict to a halt. Breckinridge also sent Gladstone a personal letter, urging London to do "whatever was felt within the power of Her Majesty's Government to restore peace to North America." By June, an armistice had been declared, and representatives of the warring states as well as all "interested parties"—including Great Britain—had convened in Buenos Aires to negotiate peace terms.

The negotiations, however, threatened to founder over the act that had triggered the war: the attempted assassination of former Mexican President Diaz (a matter made even more difficult by the impending return of Diaz to the Mexican Presidency). The Mexicans insisted that the Confederacy acknowledge responsibility for the attack, and Richmond just as adamantly refused. But when Mexico (backed by Columbia and the USA) threatened to walk out, the British announced they would view a resumption of hostilities as "the most grave and disturbing of developments." For the second time in six months, Great Britain and the USA stood on the brink, as jingoes on both sides of the Atlantic worked to whip their respective publics into war frenzy. Gladstone, however, remained determined to avoid such an "unqualified calamity." (His conviction had been reinforced by the outbreak of a crisis over sudden German demands for a colonial position in Africa and the even more urgent matter of relieving the siege of Khartoum in the Sudan by the forces of the "Mahdi.") Now was not the time, Gladstone told his cabinet, for the British Empire to risk a war with the powerful "Yankee Union." The British delegates at the Buenos Aires

Conference therefore were instructed to approach the American representatives in an effort to ease tensions and find a solution to the diplomatic impasse. The British made clear to their American counterparts—in private—that Mexico could not "sensibly" expect the South to acknowledge responsibility for the attack on Diaz. The Mexicans lacked "concrete" proof tying participation by OCSS operatives to orders from Richmond, and Washington therefore had to make its "hot-tempered" ally "see reason." In other words: Diaz had proven all he needed when his army had turned back the South's vaunted forces; insisting on more would be to indulge a personal grudge which would only show Mexico could not yet be considered a "mature power."

To ease the way for Mexico, the British proposed a series of international investigations, charged with responsibility for disposing of all claims arising out of the war. Under London's plan, a special commission would have jurisdiction broadly and flexibly enough defined so as to give Mexico a public forum for pursuing the determination of "responsibility" for the attack on Diaz. The commission would also have jurisdiction over such other thorny matters as the USA's damages claims for Stuart's raids on the AT&SF railway system, Colombia's and the North's claims arising out of the Panama Raid, and the South's—and Great Britain's—claims for the USA's attacks on Southern ports. London didn't really intend for Mexico to use the claims commission to put the Confederacy on trial for the attempted murder of a neighbor's former head of state; the British expected something akin to an international arbitration to assess money damages. Had Diaz proved so foolish as to seek the satisfaction of a trial in which the Confederacy was arrayed in the dock like some outlaw state, the British would have made sure the effort foundered on a variety of procedural obstacles. Rather, Gladstone was counting on Diaz to be "realistic," to seize upon the commission proposal as a face-saving way to end the war, and then let the issue of the attack die from neglect as a source of continuing public controversy between Mexico and the Confederacy. (Whether Mexico's leaders would continue to hold the matter against the South in private was something the British recognized as beyond their control.) In the end, Mexico agreed precisely because Diaz was a realist: Mexico had proven itself on the battlefield—and Mexico also could not afford to prolong the war on a point of personal honor.

(above) **The original Union Pacific Missouri River Bridge at Blair, Nebraska, built in 1872, the inability of which to support wartime traffic triggered a crisis in USA-Mexican logistics.**

(below) **The Panama Canal Railway, the increasing importance of which to supplying USA-Mexican forces made it an irresistible Confederate target.**

(left) **General Lewis Armistead, commander of the Confederate forces charged with driving on Mexico City, whose second attempt in 1884 would come within a hairsbreadth of success.**

(right) **General (and future USA President) John Schofield, whose troops played a key role in preventing Armistead from breaking through to Mexico City when the Confederate was on the very threshold of victory.**

10

THE WESTERN WAR AND THE CREATION OF THE ANGLO-CONFEDERATE ENTENTE: (4) THE CONFLICT'S BALEFUL CONSEQUENCES

The Treaty of Buenos Aires was signed in September 1884, providing for a peace on the basis of the territorial status quo *ante bellum*. As for the *Cinco de Mayo* attack, Mexico chose not to press the issue with any vigor before the claims commission (which itself fell victim to the increasing polarization of international politics). It had yet to issue a definitive ruling on any claim when the First World War broke out in the fall of 1898, and the commission then suspended its work to await the "cessation of hostilities"—it never met again. The Peace of Buenos Aires was in turn the prelude to the final international crisis spawned by the Western War, which would play a vital part in the emergence of the Anglo–Confederate entente. I refer to the Anglo–American confrontation of 1885, which centered on Canada and the second uprising led by Louis Riel.

The reader will recall my earlier discussion of the post-Secession efforts by the USA and Great Britain to maintain cordial relations, and how Canada was at the center of those efforts. The country eventually called "Canada" had itself undergone a tremendous transformation shortly after the Secession of the Southern States from the American Union when the British North America Act of 1867 established the Canadian Confederation (a subject to which I will return in greater detail later in this narrative). Prior to that time, the name "Canada" actually referred only to a portion of the varying jurisdictions constituting what was comprehensively referred to as British North America. Nominally a "confederation," the new Canada's charter actually was designed to avoid the danger of an American-style secession by giving the central government "all the great subjects of legislation" as well as any unnamed or residual powers. The provinces were granted jurisdiction only over a specific list of subjects; the grant of jurisdiction over education would prove the opening wedge for the fatal Quebec Uprising of 1916.

The Canadian Confederation initially consisted only of Ontario and Quebec (the former Province of Canada), along with the Maritime Provinces farther east. The Hudson's Bay Company still had title to its vast holdings pursuant to a charter issued by Charles II in 1670, and British Columbia on the Pacific coast also remained outside the new confederation as a separate crown colony. By 1871, "Canada" had expanded from its eastern base to reach across the continent: The Hudson Bay lands were purchased in 1869, and British Columbia agreed to join in 1871. British Columbia's entry, however, came with an express condition: The central government in Ottawa must bring about the construction of a transcontinental railroad, and the construction of this "Canadian Pacific" railway became the central focus for Canadian politics and economics over the next fifteen years and also proved a source of rising tension with the USA—which culminated with the crisis of 1885.

Construction of the railroad languished after the conservative leader Sir John McDonald was driven from office by scandal in 1873. McDonald had masterminded the creation of the Canadian confederation; he was an avowed Canadian nationalist who disdained the "imperial democracy" of the USA and believed that all of Canada west of Ontario would be absorbed by the "Yankees" unless the whole country was bound together by a Canadian railroad. When serving as Prime Minister of the Province of Canada, McDonald had flirted with the idea of an alliance between Great Britain and the Confederacy to protect British North America against "Yankee ambition," but London's evident determination to stay on good terms with Washington in the wake of Southern Secession put an end to such hopes, and McDonald redoubled his efforts to create a continental union to deter USA aggression. McDonald's liberal opponents, however, did not share his belief in the necessity of a transcontinental railroad to assuring Canada's security, and they neglected the project during their five-year tenure in Ottawa.

McDonald returned to power in 1878, and the financial wherewithal to restart the CPR project would—rather ironically—come from the USA and a syndicate (including Canadians) who had made a fortune creating what eventually became the Great Northern Railway based out of St. Paul, Minnesota. In 1880, the Canadian government contracted with the syndicate's newly formed Canadian Pacific Railway company for the completion of a transcontinental line connecting Ontario through to the British Colombia coast. The Canadian parliament approved the measure in early 1881, and construction began in earnest. (Passage was made easier by quiet but definite word from London that Gladstone's government wanted to "nip American temptation in the bud" by completion of this "vital imperial project.") Then came the outbreak of the Western War and the first of what Canadians called the "War Scares." McDonald now determined that nothing must delay the railroad's completion as soon as physically possible; without a completed railroad, any re-supply of Canada west of the formidable barrier of the Great Shield—the granite wilderness running from Western Ontario to Winnipeg and extending from the Great Lakes to Hudson's Bay—would be a fool's errand, and those western territories would assuredly be lost to an American invasion. Meeting McDonald's accelerated construction goals, however, would require substantial additional funds. Unfortunately, the cost of construction had been drastically underestimated from the start, and well before the outbreak of the Western War, the CPR's initial government subsidy of twenty-file million Canadian dollars ("C$") had been exhausted.

So began the company's effort to raise the additional funds necessary to complete the railroad—which would lead to a series of financial maneuverings that would explode into an international scandal in the aftermath of the Western War and contribute mightily to the formation of the Anglo–Confederate alliance. Although the British government had let City of London financial circles know of the government's support of the Canadian Pacific project, the company still got a lukewarm response when it increased its authorized capital stock from twenty-five million to one hundred million shares and then sought assistance with underwriting the new issue. The problem was that a completed CPR threatened the established eastern Canadian railway system known as the "Grand Trunk," and the—mostly British—owners of the Grand Trunk (the "GT") were determined to use any means at their disposal to prevent that from happening. What few guessed was that the GT would be willing to go beyond such conventional tactics as engineering a defamatory press campaign and enlist the aid of USA financial interests in a bid to take over the CPR (technically, a privately held company) and kill the project by internal manipulation of the construction itself—at the very time when Canada and the British Empire had been brought to the brink of war with America. Thus, when the CPR increased its authorized capital stock from twenty-five million to one hundred million, the GT worked with certain New York financial circles—whose identity remains unknown, and after October 1962 probably will never be known—to buy up enough of the new issue to be able to take control at the next general shareholders meeting. The GT's lines served American Midwestern markets, and the GT's owners cared not a whit about the success of Canada's "national project"—despite the fact that the GT's general manager was a Canadian and a previous supporter of McDonald and the Conservatives.

The takeover effort failed when Canadian management supporters narrowly outvoted the Americans at the general shareholders meeting held in March 1884. It would be two years more before Canada—and Great Britain—learned of this "Yankee conspiracy" to "sabotage" the completion of Canada's national railway (and of the "treasonable role" played by the Grand Trunk line). In the meantime, the Canadian Pacific was to play a vital role in the suppression of the second prairie uprising led by Louis Riel. Riel was a member of the "Metis," a term employed to describe a French-speaking Roman Catholic of mixed race. The Metis—less politely called "Half-Breeds" by other Canadians—were the product of intermarriage between French–Canadian trappers and the Indians who dwelt along the rivers where the trappers plied their trade. Metis settlements stretched in an arc from the Red River ("Riviere Rouge") in the east to the middle reaches of the North Saskatchewan River in the west. Riel's first rebellion (1869–70) had originated in the Metis'—quite justified—fear that the impending sale of Hudson Bay Company lands to the new Confederation would doom their culture (a society centered on the buffalo hunt and whose members lacked title to their traditional settlement grounds). The rebellion was put down by a force including British regulars. But because this force had to cross the Shield by foot, the geographic center of the country was effectively lost to insurrection for several months—a vulnerability that the Metis exploited to wring from Ottawa the promise to establish the Province of Manitoba. Precisely for this reason, McDonald resolved that construction of a transcontinental railroad must be the new country's first priority. McDonald was also certain that Riel had received encouragement—including arms—from the USA, where nationalists hoped to exploit the Red River Crisis to acquire the whole of Metis-dominated territory; McDonald was right on both counts.

Riel himself went into exile in Montana—a fact of which McDonald would later make much, even though he had countenanced the move at the time. By 1884, Manitoba and the North Saskatchewan River territory were in turmoil, as continuing Metis resentment combined with Indian and white settler frustrations. The Saskatchewan Metis wanted title to their settlement lands; the Indians faced starvation with the collapse of the buffalo hunt; and white grain farmers already resented the CPR's discriminatory pricing practices on completed portions of the railway. Riel was visited in Montana by a Metis deputation, and in June of 1884 agreed to return to Canada and lead the fight for all the grievants in the Saskatchewan country. After a period of several months, during which Riel limited himself to making demands while Ottawa attempted to fob him off with vague promises, the situation boiled over. In March of 1885, Riel set up a provisional Metis government; armed clashes in the central Saskatchewan country forced a withdrawal by badly outnumbered Royal Canadian Mounted Police units; and into the vacuum poured Riel's Indian allies—who perpetrated several massacres. Moreover, all but a handful of British regular forces had been withdrawn from Canada once it was clear that the Buenos Aires negotiations would peacefully resolve the Western War, and London was not prepared to risk another embarrassing defeat like Isandlwana or Majuba Hill by yet again arrogantly underestimating a "native" opponent. The remaining regiments at

Winnipeg (formerly Ft. Garry) would only move against the Metis once they had been "suitably reinforced," and those reinforcements would have to come from Canadian ranks.

McDonald's government and the CPR management now sprang into action: By the first week of April, a force of over eight thousand troops—two-thirds Canadian militia—were entrained and heading west. In fact, the railroad across the Shield was not complete, and the soldiers had to cross the gaps on foot in appalling conditions. But the railroad proved its worth: A crossing that took months in 1870 now took exactly one week. By May, the rebellion had been crushed; and Riel, captured. This time, there would be no American exile; despite serious doubts concerning his sanity, Riel was put on trial for treason, found guilty, and executed by hanging at Regina on November 16, 1885.

Many of Riel's Metis and Indian associates escaped across the USA border—much to the fury of Conservative and Liberal Canadians. McDonald was also convinced that Washington had arranged for Riel's return to Canada in hopes of exploiting the Prairie Country crisis by disrupting completion of the CPR and thereby discouraging further settlement—which had blossomed in the railroad's wake. Had Riel's second rebellion occurred in isolation, British opinion might not have given much weight to such concerns; McDonald might also have decided to set his suspicions to one side rather than make them the inspiration for a Canadian approach to Westminster on the issue of Imperial Security in the Western Hemisphere. But the 1885 insurrection came on the heels of the Western War crises, which at one point saw tens of thousands of USA troops mobilizing along the Canadian border, while American editorialists and politicians were in full cry for a "preemptive war" to fulfill America's "northern manifest destiny." Moreover, McDonald had more than suspicions engendered by difficult times to fuel his belief that Riel was a "Yankee tool." Some Americans *did* seek to exploit Riel's return by providing arms to the Metis and their Indian allies, and those arms were later traced back across the border. Although Washington vigorously denied that the arms shipments were done with the approval or knowledge of the national government (and what records I have seen show that newly elected President Cleveland was as surprised—and nearly as infuriated—as McDonald when the shipments were uncovered), no denial was likely to have altered McDonald's judgment about the need for a drastic change in Empire policy toward North America.

McDonald traveled to London in December 1885. Convinced that the only hope of deterring a "Yankee grab" for Canada lay in an Anglo–Confederate alliance, McDonald, upon arrival, immediately set about to make his case to both the government and the opposition. Thus, the issue of Canadian security was injected into a British political scene already highly charged with tension over what every observer of any insight knew was going to be a tremendous clash over the "Irish Question." Although Gladstone's government had received a boost from its deft handling of the Buenos Aires negotiation to end the Western War, it suffered what proved a fatal blow in February of 1885 with the news that Khartoum had fallen to the Mahdi, and that General Charles "Chinese" Gordon had been slain in the city's defense. Khartoum, with Gordon in command, had been besieged for months, and the story had captivated the British imagination. When the city fell and Gordon (a romantic figure to many) was killed, Gladstone was blamed for the bumbling relief efforts that failed to effect a rescue. The Conservative leader Lord Salisbury formed a caretaker government, and both sides prepared for the inevitable general election. The Liberals managed to win a plurality over the Conservatives, but the results were very close: 307 to 284, with the balance—seventy-nine—held by Parnell's Irish Nationalist Party. The seemingly indestructible Parnell had remained the dominant force in Irish politics despite the IRB's "war campaign," and he now demonstrated a renewed ability to make the Irish Question the central issue in English politics: first by voting with the Conservatives to bring down Gladstone, and then by continuing to flirt with Salisbury to ensure that "Home Rule" remained in the forefront of the ensuing campaign.

The election thus gave Parnell the power to make either a Liberal or a Conservative government, and Parnell was determined to use this chance to compel "England" to grant Ireland "justice through Home Rule." During the campaign, Gladstone had kept his council about what he was prepared to do about either Ireland or "the damn Yankees." While the Irish Question and Home Rule dominated the election, what to do about the "American threat" had also become a substantial concern. The British Empire had come to the brink of war with the North three times in as many years. Moreover,

"America," as an issue, was intertwined with Ireland, as Washington's "indulgence" of "Ireland Abroad" during the IRB crisis was blamed by many for preventing a resolution of the Irish Question. Gladstone was among those who saw an "Atlantic Connection" between Great Britain and its Irish troubles. And while he chose not to reveal his thinking during the campaign, Gladstone had actually already resolved on what he believed England must do if its United Kingdom was to be preserved.

Months out of office in the summer and fall had given Gladstone the time to make a deep study of the history of Anglo–Irish relations, and from this effort, Gladstone had drawn the conclusion that England's error lay in the Act of Union adopted as a response to the Rebellion of 1798 (when Irish rebels tried to throw over English rule, with assistance from Napoleonic France). In Gladstone's view, the Act had forced too close a relationship with England upon Ireland, crippling the ability of the Irish to develop healthy indigenous political institutions capable of responding effectively to the island's all too acute, but distinctive, social and economic afflictions. The result was a buildup of suffering and political frustration, which finally erupted in the violence of the "Land War" of 1879–82 and had continued with the IRB's campaign of murderous provocation during the Western War crises. Gladstone feared, most of all, the consequences for England's liberal traditions if the Irish Question could not be positively resolved. He felt deeply the symbolism of being the first Prime Minister since the post-Napoleonic Wars unrest to have a police bodyguard. Although he had successfully resisted calls for the extension of coercion measures to the whole of the British Isles, Gladstone was convinced that a failure to effect reconciliation now through a fundamental reordering of the Irish–English relationship would mean the eventual death of "Free England." Gladstone initially hoped the Conservatives would decide to pursue Home Rule in coalition with Parnell; although this would mean yielding up the fruits of a victory in the election just past, Gladstone was prepared to do so in order to assure the passage of what he had concluded was an essential measure for the country's well-being. Conservative sponsorship would have transformed the measure from a party program into a true constitutional reform, thereby increasing the power of the bill as a symbol of reconciliation between England and Ireland.

The Conservatives under Lord Salisbury, however, decided against Home Rule for reasons heavily influenced by their growing conviction that the root of the Irish "problem" now lay across the Atlantic and therefore must be dealt with as a matter of international politics and imperial military grand strategy. Once the unwillingness of the Conservatives to pursue Home Rule was manifest, Gladstone seized upon the first opportunity to bring down Salisbury's government. In the event, yet another Irish coercion measure provided the symbolically appropriate grounds for compelling Salisbury's resignation. On February 1, 1886, Gladstone—for the third, and last, time—returned as head of Her Majesty's Government. He immediately set about constructing a cabinet with the single-minded goal of carrying through the adoption of some form of Home Rule. I shall not detain the reader with a detailed elucidation of the course of the ensuing debate on such points as whether Ireland would retain a right to representation in the Westminster Parliament or how such a franchise would be limited (e.g., whether Irish representation would be limited to "Imperial" questions of interest to the Empire as a whole). Although the importance of these issues to the eventual outcome should not be underestimated, it is the international aspect of the debate that is my concern. For by the spring of 1886, the issue of Home Rule had become entangled in an intensifying debate over what many (Conservatives *and* Liberals) had come to see as the "Imperiled Empire."

A series of shocks, in addition to the jolts felt from North America, had called into question the foundations of British imperial security. In the summer of 1884, German gunboats had appeared off the coast of Cameroon, and London quickly discovered that German Chancellor Bismarck had done a *volte face* on the question of African colonies. Berlin now declared it had a "duty"—as well as a right—to found a German colonial empire. The disruption caused by Germany's "rough shoulder" tactics ultimately were resolved peaceably by a conference of the participants in the ongoing European "Scramble for Africa" held later that year in Berlin. Still, the saber rattling of the intervening months had been particularly unsettling in London, coming as it did when Great Britain stood on the brink of war with the USA. For as the more astute observers in London (and elsewhere) took note, Great Britain was not prepared to fight a war with the Americans while simultaneously confronting Germany in Africa.

As bad as the *contretemps* with Germany over African colonies had been, the Central Asian crisis of the following spring proved much worse. For decades, Great Britain and Russia had been engaged in a "Great Game" in Central Asia. As the British consolidated their hold on India, the Russians absorbed—usually by brute force of arms—the Muslim kingdoms and city-states along the ancient "Silk Road" between China and the Near East. Although England and Russia had been allies against Napoleon, their strategic interests had drifted apart and then become directly at odds as Russian expansionism eastward along its southern frontier came to be viewed by London as a threat to vital British interests in the Near East and in India. By the 1850s, the differences driven by these developments had become sufficiently acute as to contribute materially to the decision to join the French in an assault on the Russian Crimea—in an effort to reinforce the Ottoman Empire as a check on Russia's Asian ambitions.

It was in Afghanistan, positioned uneasily between Russia to the North and British India to the South, that the conflicting interests of the two powers nearly brought on war in the spring of 1885 (and as the reader shall see, would contribute thirteen years later to the outbreak of World War One). The flash point was the remote and little known oasis of Pandjeh, lying halfway between Merv and Herat. For some time following their annexation of Merv, the Russians had been eyeing Pandjeh, insisting during the correspondence leading to the establishment of the Anglo–Russian Boundary Commission that Pandjeh belonged to Russia by virtue of its acquisition of Merv. The Afghans disagreed, and so did the British. (Pandjeh lay astride the approach to Herat, which explained both Russia's interest and Anglo–Afghani determination to resist.) In early March 1885, the Russians looked to be about to occupy the town. In response, the Afghans—partly due to British prompting—sent troops to strengthen the oasis's defenses, while the Imperial British Government of India mobilized two corps of the British Indian Army to be ready to intervene in support. The Russians, knowing that Gladstone's Home Government was distracted by the Sudan crisis (Khartoum had just fallen) and that British troops were not yet in a position to intervene, connived to provoke the Afghan force in Pandjeh into firing first. Claiming "self-defense," the Russians attacked and overwhelmed the outnumbered and outgunned Afghan defenders.

The Russians had miscalculated. Gladstone was horrified by what he considered an act of wanton slaughter and also furious at what he considered deception on the part of the Tsar's government. Moreover, precisely because of the Sudan mess (as well as the Riel uprising in Canada, which was then reaching its military climax and also raising concerns about a possible "Yankee" role), Gladstone could not risk taking anything but a very hard line with St. Petersburg. Parliament voted the largest credits since the Crimean War; the Royal Navy was put on alert with orders to occupy Port Hamilton on the Korean peninsula as a base for operations against Vladivostok; plans were drawn up for a strike against the Caucasus with Turkish assistance; and for much of April, the general expectation throughout the "civilized world"—a term I can no longer employ without irony—was of war between the Russian and British Empires. Fortunately, the Emir of Afghanistan took the fall of Pandjeh with great forbearance, and this restraint gave London and St. Petersburg the essential breathing space within which to find a solution short of war. (The British had fought in Afghanistan only five years before, and the Emir feared for himself and for his country's independence should another war erupt so soon after the restoration of a badly needed peace.) Ultimately, the Russians agreed to withdraw from Pandjeh, which would be neutralized until all three powers reached agreement on its fate. (They never did, and the fate of Pandjeh—along with that of the rest of Afghanistan—would be resolved by force of arms during World War One.)

For the sake of global peace in the 1880s, it was probably fortunate that Russia's advance did not reach Pandjeh one year earlier. With the Western War at its height and Great Britain and the USA poised on the brink of war, St. Petersburg might have gambled on holding Pandjeh and perhaps even moved against Herat. Such a gamble could have caused similar miscalculations by one or more Western War participants and could have ended up plunging Great Britain and Canada into a war on the side of the Confederacy—with Russia, the USA, and several other countries arrayed in loose coalition on the other. Although that sort of calamity was averted in the spring of 1885, observers in London (and elsewhere) recognized just how close-run a thing the issue had been. And for many of those in London, the lesson learned from the recent crises was that the policy of "splendid isolation" represented a luxury the British Empire could no longer afford. The naval scare debate of 1868 was now repeated—but in a drastically different, and far more disturbing context. A comparison of naval strengths arrived at by adding up the modern forces of the USA, Russian, and French navies could no longer be ridiculed as the conjurings of a paranoid Admiralty. The Canadians feared the USA; the Government of India feared the Russians; and both joined together in fear of a Russo–American axis to which would probably be added a hostile France. To Ottawa and Calcutta, the obvious—and only—solution was some form of countervailing alliance with the Confederate States of America. And the ensuing demands for a London–Richmond *entente*, to guarantee "Empire Security," quickly became intertwined with the debate over Irish Home Rule.

Gladstone recognized that the Irish Question had an international element, and his pursuit of Home Rule was intended in part to disarm the growing clamor for an "end to isolation" and entry into some form of alliance with the Confederacy. The reader will recall Gladstone's turn against the Confederacy following the slave trade revelations of the *Beauregard* incident. Gladstone remained adamant against London in any way associating with the "slave power" and hoped that Home Rule would reconcile "Ireland Abroad" sufficiently that the USA's Irish–Americans would become a force for Anglo–American reconciliation. With the bitter benefit of hindsight, Gladstone's hopes seem willfully naive. Among other things, Gladstone was ignoring the strong push for an Anglo–Confederate relationship coming from Richmond in the person of former CSA Secretary of State Judah Benjamin. The reader will recall that Benjamin led the Confederate delegation to the London peace talks, which ratified the South's *de facto* achievement of independence following Gettysburg and the Anglo–French intervention. During his several months stay in London, Benjamin charmed British society, befriending leading members of the Palmerston government and the Tory opposition and getting on particularly well with Disraeli. Following the signing of the Treaty of London, Benjamin returned to Richmond and continued to serve as Secretary of State under Presidents Davis and Lee—masterminding the "special relationship" between the Confederacy and the Brazilian Empire and the South's acquisition of Cuba from Spain.

When Longstreet was elected in 1873 to succeed Lee as Confederate President, Benjamin asked to be relieved of the burdens of the office he had held for eleven years. Benjamin also declined Longstreet's offer of the Chief Justiceship of the Supreme Court: As Benjamin explained to the incoming President, as well as Longstreet's predecessors (especially Benjamin's mentor Jefferson Davis), "I am not as young as I used to be, and I will be able to do our Confederacy greater service if I can take a reinvigorating interlude as a private citizen and member of the Bar." Although Benjamin now returned to his adoptive New Orleans, he intended to remain a political force and was prepared to serve as the Confederacy's "ambassador at large" as the need arose. The first such opportunity came in 1878 with the Anglo–Confederate crisis created by the seizure of the slaver *Beauregard*, which Benjamin defused with consummate skill. British Prime Minister Disraeli was then in Berlin at the congress called to resolve the Russo–Turkish dispute over Bulgaria. Benjamin traveled directly to the German capital to confer with Disraeli; he managed not only to defuse the *Beauregard* incident but also to make a favorable impression on Bismarck, who is said to have admiringly remarked of both Disraeli and Benjamin, "*Der Konfederat und der Englander Juden, sie sind Menchen!*" In 1882, Benjamin suffered a mild heart attack but quickly recovered; two years later, he again answered the call of public duty by leading the Confederate delegation to the Buenos Aires peace negotiations. His rapport with the British once more made a vital contribution, as Benjamin persuaded Great Britain to face down the USA over Mexico's insistence that Richmond apologize for the Diaz attack. The following year, Benjamin agreed to accept appointment as the Confederacy's first full Ambassador to the Court of St. James, where his task would be to persuade Great Britain to abandon its policy of "splendid isolation" and enter into a political and military alliance with the Confederacy.

President Breckinridge, in consultation with his surviving predecessors (especially former President Davis), had come to the conclusion, in the wake of the Western War fiasco, that the Confederacy required an alliance with the British Empire in order to check the growing threat posed by the North. The South had made great strides toward the establishment of an industrial economy, capable of supporting a modern war machine. Birmingham had become a major metals center and Tredegar had established substantial facilities in Alabama as well as expanding its Richmond plants. The Norfolk shipyards rivaled any single Northern facility for the ability to build and launch ironclads of the most advanced design; the continent's largest dry dock was on the Elizabeth River in Norfolk. A determined railroad building effort had produced a tenfold increase in the South's pre-war rail mileage, and the primitive pre-Secession system had—for the most part—been replaced with standard-gauge track of modern design. Still, the wealth of the South remained concentrated in the land, and it could not hope to match the North's rate of industrial growth. The implications of the growing imbalance were grave—and not just for the long term. USA President Garfield had announced in the fall of 1884 that the North would embark on a massive naval expansion effort for the express purpose of assuring naval "mastery" of "American waters." And while the Confederate leadership had been pleased by the victory of New York's Democratic Governor Grover Cleveland in the 1884 USA presidential vote, no one was prepared to bet on the first Democratic Administration in Washington since Secession reversing a policy decision that, among other things, reflected the increasing importance of the armaments industry to "Yankee" prosperity. This was especially so, because Cleveland had (shrewdly) not campaigned in opposition to naval expansion—but only on a promise to clean up the corruption in military contracting, which the stresses of the Western War had revealed to a shocked Northern public.

Breckinridge knew the South could not match the North's planned buildup of naval strength, and that a Northern navy capable of taking on the British would readily be able to impose its will on the Confederacy. But if the navies of the Confederacy and Great Britain were to be "joined as one" in alliance, Washington would confront a strategic challenge of quite a different sort. Moreover, while Richmond's fears of a Northern war of pre-emptive aggression may fairly be dismissed as self-justificatory fantasies, a Northern bid for Canada must be acknowledged to have again become a realistic concern for Ottawa and London, after the experience of the Western War had soured the good relations with Washington which had been so carefully cultivated in Secession's wake. And although Washington disclaimed any intent to employ an enlarged American fleet against British interests, a Northern navy capable of preventing the Royal

Navy from breaking a blockade of Southern ports could just as easily prevent London from coming to Canada's rescue—should it be invaded by its neighbor to the south. In sum, the existence of *any* other power capable of challenging the Royal Navy was of vital concern to the Empire. A *Yankee* navy capable of such a challenge, especially if joined with the naval forces of France and Russia, could prove *fatal*. This starkest of *realpolitik* calculations constrained Whitehall to react to Northern naval capabilities—and not to expressions of intention that could prove all too transitory.

Not that an alliance with London would be a guarantee of security for Richmond. British Conservatives as well as Liberals viewed the Confederacy as the aggressor in the Western War, and even the proponents of an *entente* with Richmond believed it should be limited to one of mutual defense—if the Confederates got into trouble on their own accord, the British Empire should be under no obligation to rescue them. In turn, the Confederate leadership recognized that London would insist on such formal limits to any Anglo–Confederate undertaking. But Breckinridge and his advisers (especially the masterfully calculating Benjamin) also knew that the dividing line between a war of defense and a war of aggression is always blurry and indistinct at its vital edge. The Confederate leadership further counted on Northern perceptions of strategic necessity in the next crisis to compel a move against Canada, thereby bringing the British into a future North–South war. (In this, they would prove all-too-realistic judges of the future.)

Still, the decision to enter into an alliance with one of the Great Powers of Europe was a momentous one for the South, and the "open secret" that the Confederacy's leaders were pursuing an Anglo–Confederate alliance triggered what would prove the country's last meaningful debate over the course it had charted—socially, economically, and politically—since Secession. And although a comprehensive treatment of Confederate social and economic development is beyond the scope of my narrative, I will pause to briefly review several developments that bear on how the two American unions set out on the different paths that contributed materially to their deep and bitter rivalry.

Upon the declaration of the Armistice in December 1862, the South stood at a social and economic crossroad. It had beaten an economically superior foe by a brilliant performance of arms in the most politically sensitive theater of the war. But as President Davis and other farseeing Confederate leaders recognized, the war had shown the new nation to be dangerously weak in areas vital to the emerging art of industrialized war. Davis and others of like mind therefore resolved to institutionalize many of the economic measures instituted by the government during the War, which had been designed to counter the North's initial advantage in manufacturing and technical capacity by dint of better organization and coordination of available resources.

These measures—government promotion of arms and related manufactures; government support for a program of railroad construction and related internal improvements (such as harbor expansion and fortifications); and the maintenance of a substantial army as well as the development of a proper ironclad fleet and a merchant marine—were opposed by many Southerners, who felt they had fought the War of Secession to be "left alone." The *last* thing these Southerners wanted to see was centralized industrial intrusions on what they believed to be an idyllic agrarian society. Admittedly, few carried their opposition to central government to such lengths as Georgia's Governor Joseph E. Brown, who claimed that Georgia had a "sovereign right" to maintain an independent army and navy. But critics of the "Big South" policies of Davis and his allies did not need to threaten armed resistance in order to erect powerful roadblocks to implementation of the "Strong Confederacy" program. For the Confederate Constitution itself, crafted in the flush of states'-rights enthusiasm that characterized much of the Southern mood at the outset of Secession, constituted a formidable obstacle to realizing the Davis plan. The central government was barred from appropriating funds for internal improvements "intended to facilitate commerce" (except for coastal navigation); barred from using tariff duties to "promote or foster any branch of industry"; *and* expressly barred from levying an income tax. Moreover, this Jeffersonian hostility to national initiatives of virtually any sort was joined to the attitudes of some members of Davis's own planter class, who saw in proposals for Southern industrialism a threat to the plantation way of life which many of them (buoyed by the boom in cotton prices in the years just before Secession) had embraced as superior to the "wage slavery" of Northern urban society.

Ultimately, the Jeffersonian and Agrarian objections were overcome by a combination of three factors. First, the eyes of a vital portion of the planter class had been opened by the War of Secession to the military necessity of a Southern industrial capacity that would at least substantially offset the advantage held by the North. Second, the very cotton famine that the South hoped would compel Great Britain and France to intervene and force Northern acceptance of secession had also triggered a move in Lancaster away from Southern cotton and toward supplies from Egypt and India. Although intervention came in time to restore access to Southern markets before a major shift to these alternative markets could be effected, shrewder Southern planters could see that the "Great Boom" could not be sustained as Egypt and India developed as rival sources of almost limitless supply.

Finally, and most importantly, there was slavery itself. The South had fought the War of Secession to preserve slavery, and President Davis and his allies were determined to pursue a policy of strengthening slavery by (among other things) acquiring Cuba and the Trans-Rio Grande. That policy, in turn, required a military strong enough to seize the desired territory if the opportunity arose, and to prevent the USA from frustrating the Confederacy's ambition to make the Hemisphere safe for the country's "peculiar institution." All this meant the South simply *had* to embark on a policy of government support for the economic elements (armaments, railroads, and related infrastructure) necessary to achieving such goals— which brings one back to the military origins of the Davis postwar program of Southern industrialization. The preservation of slavery demanded independence for which a war had to be fought and won. Upon achieving independence, the preservation of slavery now demanded continued government intervention in the economy to sustain the military strength to assure the ability to fight and win future wars to continue to preserve that principal fruit of the War of Secession. The chance of effective political opposition in the face of these powerful imperatives was not enhanced by the fact that Davis was succeeded as president by Lee, then Longstreet, and then Breckinridge—all men committed to the military rationale for government intervention to promote Southern industry, even at the expense of the agrarian ideal with which all of them claimed to sympathize. And because the Strong Confederacy program *was* tied to the preservation of slavery, the South's traditional intolerance of public opposition to slavery began to affect the willingness of its leaders to tolerate opposition to an economic program considered so vital to the future of that institution.

What soon emerged is what Northern historians caustically dubbed, and not without cause, the "Culture of Southern Lawlessness." As noted, the Confederate Constitution presented grave obstacles to a policy of central government-sponsored industrial development. Confronted with this difficulty, Davis and his successors resolved to flout the Constitution in the name of what came to be called the South's "Paramount Law"—the preservation of slavery. Of course, the Confederate Constitution, like the original USA Constitution on which it was modeled, had been crafted in fairly broad strokes. At least some areas permitted an interpretation sufficiently elastic to allow for government support of industrialization. There was, for example, no express prohibition on chartering railroads or supporting their development through loan guarantees. On the other hand, the prohibition on the use of tariff duties to "promote or foster any branch of industry" meant the central government could not employ such duties to make good on those guarantees. Moreover, the prohibition on a national income tax crippled Richmond's ability to provide an equivalent revenue source to offer as credible support for its own guarantee of loans made to railroads by third parties. As a result, Southern railroad development sponsored by the central government represented a much riskier investment than the North's rival transcontinental systems. To the surprise of no one with a basic understanding of the working of international capital markets, City of London investors proved quite slow to purchase the bond offerings of the "Confederate Central" and "Confederate Trans-Mississippi." By 1870, neither system had made a fraction of the progress hoped for when plans for both were announced in 1865. Of course, the failure of the Central and Trans-Mississippi lines did not mean the stagnation of Southern railway development; with what support Richmond could offer, individual states sponsored railroad construction within their boundaries. The major industrial enterprises—such as Tredegar and the Birmingham Iron Works—also developed trunk lines to serve their needs. Such lines could draw on foreign sources of capital ancillary to investments in industrial plant itself. Thus, for example, much of Alabama's track was ultimately paid for in bonds redeemed by

Krupp. But the result was a patchwork: affected by inconsistencies in gauge and leaving gaps at key points—the most troublesome being the Mississippi River, where by 1875, only one line crossed below Vicksburg and above New Orleans.

The uneven development of the Confederacy's railroad network epitomized the state of Southern infrastructure at the outbreak of the Spanish–Confederate War. The parlous state of supply routes into northeastern Mexico had contributed to Richmond's decision to withdraw from those territories following the restoration of the Mexican Republic. As President Lee pointed out to a delegation of Texans, who had traveled to Richmond to meet with Lee and urge him to stay put—even at the risk of war with the USA, as well as the victorious *Juaristas*—the single railroad track which ran to Laredo along the Rio Grande could not support the necessary force. "Gentlemen, I fully concur in the goal of acquiring the Trans-Rio Grande," Lee told the disappointed Texans. "But to acquire the Trans-Rio Grande, we must first develop the Trans-Mississippi, and this we have yet to do." (The question of the Trans-Mississippi represented a political, as well as an economic, concern for the Confederacy's leadership; Texas was bound only by tenuous links to the balance of the Southern union, and for precisely that reason, Davis and his successors saw the completion of a Confederate railway network as vital to strengthening the Trans-Mississippi link—an echo of Northern concerns about California.) The deficiencies of the country's cobbled-together transportation network became manifest during the early stages of the Spanish War. Moving troops and supplies to the embarkation points for the CEF proved a laborious process: with vital supplies arriving days, sometimes weeks, behind schedule, due to traffic snarls at chokepoints created by incomplete connection lines and mismatched gauges. "If the Yankees could see this mess, it would just confirm their lowest opinions of Southern efficiency," Secretary of War Longstreet complained at the height of the transport imbroglio. "We are fighting a war to fulfill our destiny, and constitutional obligation, to preserve and strengthen the institution of slavery, and yet that same constitution has repeatedly been invoked to frustrate measures essential to achieving this end," former President Davis told a gathering of congressional leaders in Richmond, as the fighting in Cuba approached its climax that June. "We must not allow legalisms and pettifoggery to prevent our Confederacy from fulfilling its sacred duty, to advance our most vital interest—the Southern way of life."

The Spanish War and its logistical fiascoes (which, unfortunately, never interfered sufficiently with the sterling field performance of Jackson's CEF to prevent the Confederates from overrunning Cuba) proved the decisive event that pushed the central government onto the path of constitutional circumvention. When Lee completed his term as Confederate president, Longstreet was elected to succeed him—on a "Confederate Party" platform calling for "constitutionally essential development of commerce and industry, vital to the preservation of fundamental Southern values." The 1873 campaign for CSA president was the first true "party contest" in the South. Davis had been selected under the extraordinary circumstances of effecting Secession, while Lee was the unanimous choice of every state in balloting that reflected his revered status. By 1873, however, two principal factions had emerged, and their differences could no longer be obscured by asking the country to elevate a national icon to the presidency. (Besides, the South only had one Robert E. Lee, and he could not serve for more than a single six-year term.) By selecting "Old Pete," Lee's most trusted lieutenant, the party of Davis and his fellow proponents of a "Big South" shrewdly chose a man who could assume Lee's heroic battlefield mantle, while simultaneously speaking as a representative of "One South." Longstreet had no defined association with a single state; he also believed deeply in the legitimacy of the Davis Strong Confederacy program of industrialization as a necessary measure to preserve Confederate independence. Even more fundamentally, Longstreet believed in the overriding claim of the sword against other forms of authority. "It is fair to assume that the strongest laws are those established by the sword," he declared in a speech given shortly before his nomination as Confederate Party candidate for CSA President. "The fundamental right to own slaves, which I will call the law of slavery, was confirmed on the battlefield, at Gettysburg, eleven years ago; I do not see how the just demands of slavery for its preservation and promotion may now be frustrated, at least not in the name of any law of our Confederacy."

Longstreet overwhelmed Louis Wigfall, the choleric Texan nominated by the newly formed "Liberty Party," losing only Tennessee and North Carolina. (Wigfall could not even carry his home state, which preferred

Longstreet's promise to build the railroads necessary to end the isolation of the Confederate Trans-Mississippi.) Longstreet, backed by strong Confederate Party majorities in both houses of Congress, pushed through a series of measures providing for railroad modernization and harbor developments on the mainland and the promotion (by subsidization) of joint ventures based in Cuba between Confederate and Brazilian plantation owners. On their face, these measures flouted a number of constitutional prohibitions. Longstreet and his supporters, however, now invoked the principle of "Paramountcy": So long as a central government measure was taken to preserve or promote slavery, then that measure was shielded from constitutional challenge by the "paramount principle" that anything done to preserve or promote slavery could not be prohibited under "fundamental Confederate law." In other words, if the central government said something was being done to preserve or promote slavery, that measure could not be invalidated on any constitutional ground. The inevitable legal challenge, argued for the government by Benjamin himself, saw Paramountcy validated by the Confederate Supreme Court. Moreover, the Court went so far as to hold that it was not competent to look behind a claim that a challenged action did, in fact, serve to preserve or promote slavery. "Such a determination," wrote Chief Justice Lucius Q. C. Lamar for the Court in the case of *Confederate States of America ex rel. Charleston Harbor Improvements Association v. Johnson,* "is beyond the competence of the judiciary, which is compelled by the nature of that question to accept the legislature's express determination of such a purpose as *bona fide* and conclusive."

With the central government thus untrammeled, the South now experienced a surge in its rate of industrialization. The government worked closely with the emerging "Great Enterprises" of the Confederacy—Tredegar, the Birmingham Metal Works (later Tredegar-Krupp), and the Powder Works of Augusta, Georgia—to eliminate logistical bottlenecks and create an integrated economy. By the 1880s, the South had taken great strides toward establishing itself as an industrial power that, while not a competitive threat to the USA in peacetime pursuits, had the ability to compete effectively with the North in the field of "industrialized war." Thus, the tiny hamlet of Birmingham had been transformed into a city of over 150,000 that served as the center of a network of iron and coal towns. By 1880, Confederate pig-iron production had outstripped the pre-Secession output of all of the former United States, and Confederate finished-steel products (e.g., railway rails) were beginning to displace imports. Industrialization was also accompanied by increasing urbanization. Southern census figures show the percentage of urban population had reached between 15–30 percent in virtually every southern state by 1890, and several cities boasted populations in excess of one hundred thousand. (Richmond, the capital and home to Tredegar, had over 350,000 free residents and some 150,000 registered slaves—many of the later laboring in factories or shipping.)

Moreover, although the Confederacy needed foreign capital—principally British—to finance the military-industrial boom of the first two decades following Secession, a change in slave economics meant increasing indigenous capital to finance the country's industrial enterprises. The late 1850s had witnessed record high prices for raw cotton, but planters found their profits were almost entirely consumed by the increasing cost of slaves. The problem was the shrinking supply of slaves due to the abolition of the international slave trade and the effective confinement of the institution to the existing slave states. Secession removed both these limitations. Although the Confederacy's constitution piously outlawed the slave trade with any "foreign country" and Richmond also pledged to honor the Union's signature to international anti-slave trade conventions, the South soon set about the systematic evasion of both these restrictions. The conquest of Cuba proved invaluable to these efforts. Cuba being part of the Confederacy, any transfer of slaves between Cuba and the Confederate mainland did not come within the prohibitions on the international trade. Cuba also became the center for various Confederate Brazilian "joint ventures" in slave-based agriculture and industry (a practice soon reciprocated by the Brazilians). These arrangements provided fertile ground for a variety of subterfuges, behind which a substantial Confederate–Brazilian slave trade developed. (The physical isolation of Cuba also provided security for the first Confederate–Brazilian "slave-breeding" enterprises.) Thus, by the 1880s, the South (and Brazil) had effectively eliminated the problem of the "capital trap" faced by the pre-Secession slave states (as well as

Brazilian plantation owners). The real price of slaves had begun to decline, and slave-based enterprises no longer suffered from a competitive disadvantage due to the high price of replacements. This also meant that slavery became even more attractive as a source of mass labor in enterprises other than the cotton field. Most important for this narrative, the elimination of the capital trap meant the slave economy could also contribute capital to the development of the industrial enterprises essential to the South's ability to maintain the military force required for Richmond to play the role of a Great Power on the international stage.

But the achievement of this New South social order, even if based on the most fundamental Old South principle of chattel slavery, had come at a significant cost to other Southern traditions. Jeffersonian Democracy in the former Union, which opposed the Hamiltonian government activism of its Whig rivals, had drawn its primary political support from the slave states. And while slavery was the cause of Secession, Southern support for Secession was often expressed in Jeffersonian terms—the right to be "left alone," free of government interference with one's chosen "way of life." Nor should one underestimate the political power of such convictions—especially when the leaders who had called on Southerners to fight to protect the right to be left alone now proceeded, in the wake of victory, to repudiate that right. Add to this the fact that many who had been socially prominent and financially secure *grandees* of the old Southern social order now lost position and security in the tumultuous process of change unleashed by the push to close the industrial gap with the North, and one has a potent formula for social conflict. These tensions were already simmering when Longstreet stepped down as President to be succeeded by John C. Breckinridge of Kentucky. Breckinridge, also the nominee of the Confederate Party, might have had a difficult run for the office had not good economic times combined with the Liberty Party's foolish decision to nominate Joseph Brown of Georgia—a man of extreme states'-rights views who alienated swing voters in key states such as Virginia and Louisiana.

The fiasco of the Western War, however, brought underlying social tensions to a full boil. The Confederacy had suffered over one hundred thousand casualties; its ports had been raided; its treasury drained—and the country had nothing to show for its sacrifice. A coalition of disaffected elements announced their opposition to any "entangling foreign alliances," hoping to use the proposed Anglo–Confederate alliance as a rallying point. The Liberty Party opposition saw in the upcoming Confederate presidential election their best chance yet to capture the presidency and engineer a "constitutional restoration" that would undo over a decade of central government economic intervention. The anti-alliance coalition, however, had no intention of repudiating the Confederacy's commitment to slavery. Yet, it was that commitment, as coalition critics pointedly observed, which required the South to pursue policies (the acquisition of Cuba; the "special relationship" with Brazil) that put the Confederacy at odds with the North and which in turn demanded that the South organize its institutions and invest its resources so that it could field a military sufficient to deter Northern aggression. Of course, this characterization of North–South relations bordered on the lunatic—it was Southern, slave-driven expansionism, not Northern "aggression" that threatened the peace of the Hemisphere. But the fact that Southern perceptions may have inverted objective reality does not change the fact that Southerners acted on their perceptions as if they reflected objective reality. Hence, the anti-alliance coalition was placed in a politically untenable position. According to the accepted axioms of Confederate politics, (1) slavery was the defining Southern institution, (2) slavery therefore must be preserved, and (3) the North would destroy slavery if it could, which was the reason for Secession and the establishment of the Confederacy. Moreover, the proponents of an Anglo–Confederate alliance were correct that the North, notwithstanding Southern industrialization efforts, had the *capacity* to commit resources the South could not match and create a fleet capable of swiftly destroying the Confederate navy and imposing a crippling blockade. Only an alliance with London would guarantee that war by the North on the South would also require war between the USA and the British Empire. The South's agrarian plantation economy was based on slavery; preserving slavery required Southern independence; preserving independence required deterrence of the North; and deterrence required an Anglo–Confederate alliance. *Quod erat demonstrandum.*

Alliance proponents, however, proved unwilling to rely merely on the persuasive power of their arguments—even in combination with the usual pork barrel inducements for the electorate's support. The slave states before Secession had developed a political culture of utter intolerance toward anything remotely suggestive of abolitionism. This ingrained intolerance represented a temptation to the politically unscrupulous *and* the politically righteous, both of whom were prepared—albeit for different reasons—to tar their opponents with the "abolitionist" brush and to urge "appropriate" measures against them. And that is exactly what transpired during the Confederacy's alliance debate: With President Breckinridge—supported by former Presidents Davis and Longstreet—taking the lead, the Southern political establishment thundered against those "agents of abolitionism" whose real motive in opposing an Anglo–Confederate alliance was to undermine the country's "defining and sacred institutions." Nor were these condemnations limited to mere rhetorical denunciations: State criminal sedition prosecutions were initiated against several alliance leaders, and these efforts crippled the opposition by effectively closing off their access to the press and other public fora. Thus, the practice of constitutional circumvention was joined with a revival of the sort of pre-Secession Southern political practices that had made the Slave Power so odious to so many Northerners, cementing in place the culture of lawlessness that would henceforth dominate, and characterize, the government of the Confederacy. The anti-alliance forces were crushed at the polls; Confederate Party nominee Fitzhugh Lee (Governor of Virginia, hero of the War of Secession, and—most importantly—the nephew of the sainted Robert) won an overwhelming victory over Zebulon Vance of North Carolina, who could not even carry his home state.

By the spring of 1886, the Confederacy's domestic political crisis—such as it was—had passed. There could be no doubt that, if agreement could be reached with London, the Confederate Senate would ratify the measure. (Breckinridge, however, would not live to see the treaty signed; prone to bronchial difficulties, the Kentuckian had been worn out by his exhausting term of office and died of a pneumonia contracted that winter.) The defeat of the treaty opposition also effectively constituted the last gasp of the anti-industrial and agrarian Southern political tradition. Henceforth, the Confederacy was firmly committed—as a matter of "enforced consensus"—to the Military–Industrial state forged by Davis and his successors to give the Confederacy the ability to make the Western Hemisphere safe for slavery. This would prove a tragedy: not only for the Confederacy but for the world at large. For the Confederacy, it would mean that any opportunity created by the passing of the "Secession Generation" of leadership to rethink the nature of Southern society and the country's relationship to the North had been lost. For the world, the triumph of the military-industrial slave state would set the stage for Richmond's decision to seek new territories far from North America in which to further develop what by now had become the South's *sacred* institution—a decision that would contribute to the outbreak of the First World War and cast slavery's shadow over the Far East.

Having diverted from my path so the reader might better understand the roots of the Confederacy's decision to seek an alliance with Great Britain, I will resume my narrative at the point where the various British parties girded in the spring of 1886 for their own "Great Debate" over Home Rule. The turning point of the debate proved to be the defection of Joseph Chamberlain to the ranks of the opposition. Chamberlain's decision to oppose Home Rule was grounded in his belief that the Irish Question was bound up in a connected set of issues he referred to as the matter of "Empire Security." Chamberlain might have opposed Home Rule even without the complications of the various "North American" issues (Canada and the proposal for an Anglo-Confederate *entente*) if the forcefulness of his attack on many of the particulars of Gladstone's Home Rule proposal is any indication. Be that as it might have been, the fact is that Chamberlain expressly linked his opposition to Home Rule to what he described as the government's unwillingness to address the "real danger" to British security, which he identified as the "Atlantic Connection"—the IRB's determination to foment a war between Great Britain and the USA and what Chamberlain saw as "the inability of supposedly responsible Irish opinion to behave responsibly in the face of continued IRB depredations."

Chamberlain had concluded that an acceptable form of Home Rule could never be adopted until the IRB saw the futility of their campaign to provoke an Anglo–American war. But Chamberlain also believed the IRB would never draw that conclusion as long as the USA was tempted to make war on Great Britain. In Chamberlain's view, only an Anglo–Confederate alliance would deter Washington from thinking it could profit from such a war by acquiring Canada by force of arms. Moreover, Chamberlain saw a direct connection between the North American crises and Britain's recent confrontations with Germany in Africa and Russia in Central Asia. "The whole world is watching," Chamberlain told a crowd of thousands in Birmingham, "to see if the leadership of the British Empire has the nerve to say 'no' to the forces that disturb the peace at home, and if certain powers conclude we do not have the forthright courage to enter into those proper engagements necessary to strike a blow at the forces of lawlessness who disrupt life here in these islands, they will draw the inevitable conclusions, and we will pay a terrible price for our present appeasements." Chamberlain was now firmly allied with the Conservative leader Lord Salisbury and just as firmly at odds with Gladstone—the leader of Chamberlain's own party, for while Gladstone shared Chamberlain's belief in an Atlantic connection, Gladstone was determined not to allow "our fears" to "stampede us into an alliance with the forces of immorality"—i.e., with the slave-owning Confederacy.

Gladstone believed that his Home Rule measure represented the "last chance" for England and Ireland to reconcile. He urged the House of Commons—in his final speech in favor of the measure—not to let "the ephemeral concerns of the day distract the members from recognizing that the roots of the Irish Question remain in Ireland, have not passed beyond the shores of these Isles, and must be dealt with here." (Gladstone the humanitarian and anti-imperialist also feared the consequences of an alliance which, he believed, would only increase what he called the "destructive influence" of the "military cast of mind.") Chamberlain's and Salisbury's arguments, however, proved the more powerful: the Commons rejected Home Rule; Queen Victoria granted Gladstone's request for dissolution; and the country experienced its second general election in less than a year. Although Gladstone's Home Rule Liberals probably would have lost in any case, the shocking revelations of what came to be known as the "Grand Trunk Affair" now helped push many wavering electors into either the Conservative or Anti-Home Rule Liberal camp.

The reader will recall that the British owners of the Canadian Grand Trunk Railway had conspired—not to put too fine a word on it—with certain American financial interests, during the height of the Western War crises, to take control of the Canadian Pacific Railway corporation and derail the project. Just as the British general election campaign got underway, the London *Times* came into possession (how, has never been clear) of private correspondence between the Canadian manager of the Grand Trunk, several British members of the company's board, and certain American banking representatives. This correspondence made plain that the parties to the takeover effort were pursuing their financial interests—even if the result made British North America more vulnerable to a "Yankee" invasion. Of course, there was no evidence that either Gladstone or anyone in his government had known of, much less in any way supported, the conduct of the GT conspirators. Moreover, both Chamberlain for the Liberal "Unionists" (as they were coming to be called) and Lord Salisbury for the Conservatives made clear they did not believe the government had been so derelict in its duty. But the leaders of the emerging "Unionist" alignment did seize on the fact of the scandal as further evidence of the need for a new policy—in Chamberlain's words—"based on hardheaded realism and not softhearted idealism."

The election was a stunning defeat for Gladstone, whose Home Rule Liberals were reduced to only 159 seats. Salisbury was called upon to form the new Conservative government. Although Chamberlain remained outside (he was still technically a Liberal), Salisbury asked him to lead a British delegation to Richmond to "sound out" the possibility of an "*entente*" between Great Britain and the Confederacy. Salisbury remained committed to the notion that Great Britain should not enter into a treaty of "alliance" as such, but he also was convinced—like Chamberlain—that a relationship akin to an alliance would put a needed check on Northern ambitions toward Canada.

Chamberlain accepted the appointment, departing for Richmond in December after a series of talks with CSA Ambassador Benjamin. Chamberlain's mission proved an easy one, principally because Benjamin had the confidence of his government and was able to reach agreement with Chamberlain on the essential terms before Chamberlain left for Richmond. By April 1887, the Anglo–Confederate Alliance was a fact (whatever name the parties chose to call it).

Certainly, the outcome on the battlefield of Gettysburg in late September 1862 did not preordain that the Confederacy and the British Empire would become allies in the spring of 1887. The reader could probably identify half a dozen points in time, chronicled in this narrative, which would have meant no such alliance would have emerged in April 1887 (or perhaps for many years thereafter). But what should be plain—from the history so far recounted in these pages—is the baleful effect of Secession on Great Power relations. Perhaps the point can best be made by asking whether Great Britain and the United States of America would have become warring enemies before the end of the nineteenth century had Great Britain and France not intervened in the War of Secession and the Southern states bid for independence instead been crushed. It is difficult to imagine how an Anglo–American war could have come to pass if the European powers had stayed out and the Union had been preserved. But the European powers did not stay out; the Union was not preserved; and by the spring of 1887, there had emerged two powerful alliances whose point of contact lay along the armed and hostile border of the two American Unions.

(above) **The Phoenix Park murders of Lord Cavendish and his personal secretary by the IRB, May 1882.**

(left) **Canadian troops passing through Winnipeg, Manitoba, on the Canadian Pacific Railway, to take on Louis Riel's Second Uprising, April 1885.**

The Western War placed what proved a fatal stress along the Irish and Canadian fault lines of Great Britain's relationship with the USA.

(left) **Charles Parnell, leader of the Irish Nationalist cause until brought down by the O'Shea scandal in 1890.**

(right) **William Gladstone, Prime Minister of Great Britain, 1868–1874, 1880–1886.**

Gladstone's and Parnell's efforts to resolve the Irish Question peacefully by granting Ireland "Home Rule" within the British Empire were undone by the Liberal Party crack-up brought on by Gladstone's resistance to a naval alliance with the Confederacy.

(left) **Judah Benjamin, who served the Confederacy's first two presidents as Secretary of State and who later, as the CSA's "Special Ambassador" to the Court of St. James, was responsible, as much as any single man, for the formation of the Anglo-Confederate alliance.**

(right) **Joseph Chamberlain, Liberal Party leader (and future Prime Minster), whose split with Gladstone over the issue of "Imperial Security" opened the door to the formation of the Anglo-Confederate Naval Understanding of 1887 — the "Fatal Alliance" that would lead to the Great Power Alliance System and the ensuing Alliance Wars, which would end only with the catastrophe of the Final War of October 1962.**

11

THE CONFEDERACY, SLAVERY, AND THE SLAVE TRADE: A PAUSE FOR REFLECTION AND COMPARISON

I said that Chamberlain's mission to Richmond proved "easy." In this regard, I confess to having overstated the smoothness with which Great Britain and the Confederacy reached agreement on the terms of their "defensive entente" (to use the phrase that Lord Salisbury employed to describe the relationship that marked the abandonment by England of its prized policy of "splendid isolation"). For one issue roiled even the calm diplomatic waters that marked Chamberlain's passage: slavery. And before I proceed to recount the next phase of the development of the alliance system that would bring such misery to humanity, it would be appropriate to pause and review the course of slavery's "progress" during the nearly quarter of a century that intervened between the South's triumph on the battlefields of the War of Secession and its triumph at the green baize tables of diplomacy with the formation of the Anglo–Confederate alliance. Moreover, it would also be useful to compare the development of slavery under the protective jurisdiction of the Confederacy and the Brazilian Empire with the course of race relations in the USA. For the separation of North and South at least freed the North of the demands by the "Slave Power" that the rights of slave owners be recognized and protected throughout the Union. And this result of Secession must be acknowledged to have had positive consequences for the social and political future of the Northern Negro—at least for the short term and when viewed in isolation from the broader and far more destructive forces that Secession also unleashed.

The reader will recall that the Confederacy embarked upon a policy of reinforcing slavery both at home and abroad, and that by the 1870s, Richmond had made great strides in both fields—most notably in the creation of a "special relationship" with the Brazilian Empire and the conquest of Cuba. But this undoubted revival of the fortunes of slavery in the Western Hemisphere also gave rise to significant tensions between Richmond and London, as the *Beauregard* incident so clearly illustrates. To be sure, the Royal Navy's anti-slave trade patrols never fully suppressed the flow of African slaves to the Western Hemisphere, even before the establishment of the Confederacy. As USA Supreme Court Chief Justice W. E. B. DuBois later demonstrated in his magisterial study, *Failure of the Suppression of the Slave Trade* (published the year before his elevation to the Chief Justiceship in 1924), the period of the Union saw the successful illegal importation of tens of thousands of slaves through a network that functioned even in the face of central government suppression efforts (and the unwillingness of Southern officialdom to—at least openly—defy such efforts). But with the dissolution of the Union, planter interests in the Confederate "Black Belt" began to organize openly for the full restoration of slave imports from Africa, while agitating for the repudiation of the Confederacy's formal constitutional commitment to the slave trade ban. And while neither Richmond nor state and local Confederate authorities could openly support these efforts, all could turn a blind eye in a way that had not been possible before Secession. By 1870, an illicit slave trade had sprung up of sufficient magnitude to contribute to the first real decline in slave prices in decades; the percentage of slave ownership among the Confederacy's white population also began to inch upward after dropping to a record low of just over ten percent prior to the outbreak of the War of Secession.

It was the acquisition of Cuba, however, that marked the decisive turning point for reviving the economic fortunes of slavery. Despite British efforts, antebellum Cuban slave owners had continued to replenish their supply of labor with smuggled African imports: Out of a slave population numbering over four hundred thousand in 1868, an estimated 40 percent were African-born slaves. Although the Cuban slave economy suffered during the two-year insurrection preceding the Confederate conquest (Spanish authorities retaliated against the slave-owning rebel leadership by instituting case-by-case emancipation, and the Cortes was considering the adoption of a partial general emancipation program when war broke out between the CSA and Spain), these disruptions were quickly overcome by the merger of the Cuban and Confederate slave systems. Most important, the barrier to slave sales represented by the international boundary between Cuba and the CSA was dissolved, and Cuban and mainland Southern slave owners could now trade in a market to which four hundred thousand new slaves had been added to the existing supply. Confederate owners saw the overall cost of slaves fall even as Cuban owners saw the relative value of their slaves rise, and many Cuban owners chose to sell their holdings to eager Confederate buyers and pocket the increase rather than invest the resources to rebuild estates disrupted by the anti-slavery war measures of the Spanish government. Moreover, the legal legerdemain of treating slaves owned by Confederate–Brazilian joint ventures as part of the Confederate slave market—no matter where those slaves were located—further expanded the pool of slaves available for sale and thereby further reduced the labor cost of slave-based enterprises.

The reader will recall my prior description of how Confederate and Brazilian slave interests proceeded to exploit Cuba together, transforming the island into a center for the "modernization" of slave-based enterprise. Part of this "joint-venture" effort involved the incorporation of the island's illicit African slave trade. Nominally, such operations violated the Confederacy's constitution. But Southern slaveholding interests managed to effectively nullify that ban through a variety of devices: the most important of which was the special legal status of Cuba. Designated a "national territory" after the conquest, Cuba was administered directly from Richmond. This allowed the Confederate central government to erect a maze of procedural obstacles that crippled efforts by the British to interfere with the flow of slaves into Cuba. Of particular significance was the resulting ability of Brazilian slave owners to replenish their own supply. Richmond encouraged the Brazilians to acquire ownership interests in Cuban (and even CSA mainland) plantations and other slave-based enterprises and then took the position that the transfer of slaves by their Brazilian "co-owners" to the owners' Brazilian facilities did not violate prohibitions against the international slave trade. The slave had been bound to its Brazilian owner, the argument went, and the owner's movement of his property from Alabama or Santiago to Sao Paulo therefore was not "trade" at all.

Although the British government protested these transfers, the uncomfortable truth was that they probably did *not* violate the slave trade ban. The various anti-slave trade measures had been crafted when the trade was conducted with slave societies—but not between them. Consequently, the prohibitions did not account for the possibility that a slave trade would develop from one slave society to another. Moreover, the plain language of the prohibitory measures did not forbid transfers that were insulated by the "intra-venture assignment" and similar devices. Of course, the anti-slavery movement in Britain vehemently disputed this interpretation of the anti-trade legal regime, and their "broad view" was endorsed by Gladstone's first government (1868–1874). But protests against violations of the intended scope of slave trade prohibitions simply brought the (rather smug) reply by the Confederate and Brazilian governments that no one (including the British government) had a legal right to interfere with a practice that was not expressly prohibited under international law.

This response also illustrates a truth that is painful for anyone committed to the principle of the rule of law to acknowledge: In matters of international relations, the law has never been anything but a weak force in shaping human conduct. For a brief period in the mid-nineteenth century, it appeared that "the rule of law" might acquire a truly independent impact on interstate relations and the conduct of nation states—principally because the dominant power of the time, the British Empire, was a country where the law counted for much: both in ordering conduct within British society and as an ideal to be promoted as a guiding rule for interstate relations. Moreover, at least until the Confederacy's victory in the War of Secession, it appeared that international law, embodied in a number of anti-slave trade agreements (and backed by the power of the Royal Navy), would prove an effective means of suppressing the slave trade (and thereby, perhaps, slavery itself).

But within a decade of the Confederacy's victorious war for independence, the power of law against both the slave trade and slavery had been shown to be illusory. Before the South's victory, slavery had been on the decline—principally because of the internal weaknesses of the major slave economies to which the suppression of the legal slave trade contributed but was not the principal cause. (As stated, the ban was never close to 100 percent effective; as Chief Justice DuBois pointed out, in the former United States the illegal trade operated under the very noses of Federal authorities in the harbor of New York City.) With the Confederacy's victory, there soon came the realization that existing legal constraints on the slave trade could not prevent a slavery revival in the Western Hemisphere. To extend the anti-slave trade legal regime, so as to expressly encompass what became known as the "secondary" slave commerce between the Confederacy and Brazil, would require an act of political will on the part of the Great Powers. But as the British election of 1874 made clear, that will was lacking even at the very center of the international movement to curtail slavery. Although Gladstone attempted to make "the infamous circumvention" a central issue in the campaign, his decisive rebuke at the electorate's hands—Disraeli's Conservatives won 340 seats against 255 for Gladstone's Liberals (along with fifty-seven for the self-proclaimed Irish Home Rulers, making their first election appearance)—showed that, even if a clear majority of the British electorate agreed with Gladstone on the slave trade issue (which they undoubtedly did), the voters did not consider the matter of decisive importance.

Not that the British public had become indifferent to the slave trade—on the contrary. As the ferocious reaction across the political spectrum to the seizure of the *Beauregard* clearly demonstrated, there remained certain bounds beyond which British opinion would not tolerate the Confederacy and Brazil to cross. Still, it would exaggerate the danger of war created by the *Beauregard* incident if one were to assert as a virtual certainty that, had Gladstone rather than Disraeli been Prime Minister, the British Empire would have come to blows with the South and Brazil over violation of slave trade prohibitions. Granted, the documents found on board the *Beauregard* (itself not actually a slave carrier) fairly conclusively implicated the two slave powers in violations of the internationally recognized African slave trade ban. Nor would I presume to suggest that the Confederacy was *not* fortunate to have as British Prime Minister a man perhaps uniquely able, among British statesmen of that time, to set aside considerations of "sentimentality." (Disraeli's rebuke of Gladstone's famous philippic against the atrocities just then perpetrated by the Turks against the Bulgars—"of all the Bulgarian horrors, this is the most horrible"—aptly captures Disraeli's ability to distance himself from the sympathetic reactions typical of Victorian Englishmen.) Yet by the same token, the humanitarianism that caused Gladstone to thunder at Turkish misdeeds and then condemn as "execrable infamy" the Confederate and Brazilian involvement in the African slave trade established by the *Beauregard* papers also caused Gladstone, *when in power,* to blanch at the prospect of employing force and instead to seek whenever possible the peaceful resolution of every conflict—however much a will-o'-the-wisp that goal might prove to be.

Moreover, by 1878, British financial interests had become heavily engaged in both the Confederacy and the Brazilian Empire—and that engagement extended to the expanding slave-based enterprises in both countries. The City of London was well represented on the boards of Tredegar and the Birmingham Metal Works and also held substantial shares in the growing Brazilian coffee plantations, all of which extensively employed slave labor. I am not suggesting that Whitehall was the puppet of finance capital. But the fact that financial concerns did not dictate the course of British foreign policy hardly proves the converse—that financial and economic matters were of *no* concern to government decision makers. Such interests were of concern, and during the height of the *contretemps* over the *Beauregard*, it mattered that the City of London, through the various channels available to it, made clear to the government the City's desire that war with the Confederacy and Brazil be avoided lest substantial British (i.e., City) investments be endangered. To the City's concerns were added those of Manchester and the textile interests, for British mills remained dependent on Southern cotton—Egyptian and Indian alternatives notwithstanding. Disraeli probably did not need to give significant weight to the economic factor to decide against a war over violations of the African slave trade ban. Besides Disraeli's disdain for Gladstonian sentimentalism, there were—and not just in the Prime Minister's view—far more vital matters to be resolved, involving Russian threats to British interests in the Near East and Central Asia. But the fact the British financial and textile communities were openly opposed to war—despite evidence of clear violations of slave trade prohibitions by two countries signatory to treaties embodying those prohibitions—was nonetheless important, because it demonstrated a decided erosion in the material foundations for Great Britain's commitment to the slave trade ban as a matter of national policy.

By "material," I mean the alliance between the moral and mercantile interests that had made possible the original transformation of humanitarian outrage against slavery into a concrete government program backed by the will to employ force in the form of ships of the Royal Navy. Yet, while that alliance had been seriously weakened by the 1880s, it had not been altogether disrupted. Thus, when the idea of an Anglo–Confederate *entente* became a part of the political program of the coalition of Conservatives and "Unionist" Liberals led by Salisbury and Chamberlain, their opponents turned to the slave trade issue as the hoped-for political ace of trumps. Nor were the opponents of an Anglo–Confederate alliance (whose ranks included virtually the whole of Gladstonian Liberalism) mistaken in their assumption that a substantial portion of British opinion still instinctively recoiled at the notion of a military alliance with a "slave power." For precisely that reason, Chamberlain felt compelled in his London talks with CSA Ambassador Benjamin to insist that Richmond take "concrete steps" to "reassure the British people" that the Confederacy would maintain its commitment—reaffirmed in the wake of the *Beauregard* affair—to the "eradication" of the slave trade.

Benjamin, of course, was only too happy to give such reassurances and was secretly delighted when news of his pledge caused an uproar in Richmond (and Rio de Janeiro). For Benjamin, along with CSA President Fitzhugh Lee and like-minded Brazilian leaders, recognized that the giving of such commitments, even if accompanied by a demonstrative crackdown on illicit slave trading, would not impose a substantial burden on the burgeoning slave-based sectors of the Confederate and Brazilian economies— and that any burden would undoubtedly prove only a temporary one to be cast off once British defense policy had become fully dependent on the "Confederate connection." By 1887, the combined Confederate–Brazilian slave "pool" had grown to nearly ten million, and the real price of slaves in both countries had been cut by two-thirds from where it stood in 1870. Both slave economies therefore could be expected to weather a temporary interruption of external supply with a minimum of disruption (especially in light of the "breeding" centers that had been established in Cuba in the prior decade and which had already begun to make inroads into their African "competition"). As for the duration of the disruption of the African supply, the Confederate and Brazilian leadership were confident that, once Great Britain had become dependent on its alliance with the Confederacy to assure "Imperial Security" in the Western Hemisphere, no British government—Conservative or Liberal—could afford to sever the country's ties to the CSA, even if proofs of a resumption of the Confederate–Brazilian slave trade operations as damning as the "*Beauregard* papers" should again fall into Royal Navy hands. Moreover, while Richmond and Rio de Janeiro did proceed to make a fairly good show of cracking down on the African slave traders, what London did not know—and would not learn until the violent course of future events rendered the point quite moot—was that the CSA and the Brazilian Empire had quietly exempted from the crackdown their mutual efforts to develop a new source of supply through the Congo Free State controlled by King Leopold II of Belgium.

By the 1880s, the African slave trade system was rapidly approaching a crisis point for reasons unrelated to the decades-old suppression efforts of the Royal Navy. As shown, trade had managed to flourish despite those efforts. But a key to that survival had been the rudimentary political development of the African coast. The principal native kingdoms were located many miles inland, and the European presence was limited to isolated coastal trading posts, producing a vacuum of authority in which the slave traders could carry on their centuries-old activities with a substantial degree of security—despite the Royal Navy's patrols. Then came the European "Scramble for Africa." At the Scramble's start in the mid-1870s, European powers controlled much less than half of the coastline of Western Africa south of Senegal, and a substantial portion of that was under Portuguese rule—a country stubbornly resistant to British insistence that it suppress the slave traders operating out of its territory. Within ten years, essentially all of this region had come under European control. In and of itself, this development need not have threatened the continued viability of the slave trade. The real problem was *which* European powers were in the vanguard of the Scramble. In this regard, the slavers (and their Confederate and Brazilian clients) could be said to have drawn a very poor hand—Great Britain and France were, far and away, the leaders in the move to occupy the sub-Saharan Coast, and both of these powers were committed to suppressing the slave trade. In France's case, its commitment represented a return to historic French policy after the fall of the Second Empire; France had joined the Royal Navy's anti-slave trade patrols starting in the 1830's only to see Louis Napoleon de-emphasize these efforts during the *de facto* Franco–Confederate alliance in Mexico—although in a classic example of "fence straddling," Louis also allowed a major international anti-slavery conference to meet in Paris in 1867.

The adverse effect of the Scramble was seemingly exacerbated by the outcome of the Berlin West Africa Conference (which met from November 1884 through February 1885) to resolve the "colony crisis" triggered by Bismarck's sudden demand that Germany share in the African colonial spoils. The apparent problem for the slave powers was the anti-slave trade theme of the Conference, centered on the "humanitarian" pledge of the participants to "help in suppressing slavery." The trailblazing efforts of the missionary David Livingstone, the journalist Richard Stanley, and several others had uncovered the existence of a booming trading network that moved slaves from the African interior to the East African coast and from there to the markets of Turkey and Arabia; the desire to suppress this trade had fired the imagination of a good portion of European opinion in a way that Conference participants could not ignore. But the careful reader will note my employment of the terms "seemingly" and "apparent"; in fact, the Berlin Conference marked the beginnings of the collaboration between King Leopold II of Belgium and the Western Hemisphere's slave powers— which would decisively undermine the effort to suppress the West African slave trade.

Leopold was a skilled diplomat, a tremendously wealthy man, and a "visionary" who believed passionately that Belgium needed a colony to realize its potential for greatness. After casting about in out-of-the-way places such as New Guinea for a venue in which to locate such a colony, Leopold's imagination was captured by the reports of the great undeveloped wealth of Central Africa—and particularly that portion located along the Congo River. Starting in the late 1870s, Leopold financed a series of expeditions to the mouth of the Congo to develop the area as the site of a future Belgian colony. Leopold's ambitions, however, were quickly caught up in the Great Power "Scramble," and Leopold soon faced a challenge from France, spearheaded by that country's energetic explorer, Pierre de Brazza. The Berlin Conference therefore came at an opportune moment for Leopold, as he would be able to lobby for the recognition of his planned "Congo Free State"—a nominally independent country with no direct constitutional link to Belgium except that both would share Leopold as head of state. Leopold realized, however, that he would be opposed in his efforts by at least two Conference participants: (1) France, which sought control of the North bank of the Congo (to form the boundary of its own "French Congo" colony); and (2) Portugal, which would view the Congo Free State as an encroachment on Portugal's venerable (if decrepit) colonial holdings of Angola, immediately to the south. Leopold therefore needed to recruit sufficient support from other Conference participants to isolate France and Portugal and persuade them to yield.

Enter the Confederacy and the Brazilian Empire, both of which had been invited to participate as "observers" (as had the USA, the two Great European Powers—Russia and Austria-Hungary—with no African colonial holdings or ambitions, and a host of smaller countries). Although the Confederate and Brazilian delegates recognized the need to tread lightly at a conference that would likely conclude with a formal pledge to seek the end of slavery, they still came ready to seize any opportunity to ensure the continuation of their African supply. Sadly for the future of millions of black Africans, Leopold now concluded that his dream of a Belgian African "empire" would best be achieved by collaboration with the Western Hemisphere's slave powers. Brazil could disarm Portuguese resistance by promising financial and other assistance in reviving the moribund Angola colony by developing the interior in tandem with the exploitation of the Congo basin, while the Confederacy could promise a variety of expertise that would assist in the development of the Congo interior. In exchange, Leopold would allow Confederate and Brazilian plantation ventures to operate in that interior. In other words, Leopold's Congo Free State would tolerate a continuation of the Central African slave trade—at least, that portion which provided "supply" for Confederate and Brazilian slave enterprises, "harvested" by Confederate and Brazilian slavers operating in the heart of the Congo and then "washed" (much like stolen money is laundered) through a chain of "legitimate" Confederate and Brazilian ventures stretching across the Atlantic.

Had Leopold truly been the humanitarian he claimed to be (and which many believed him to be), this proposal would have been a nonstarter. But Leopold was not the humanitarian of public myth. Neither was he a personally cruel man nor a believer in the propriety of slavery, as such. Rather, Leopold was driven by ambition for himself and his country and capable of the utmost ruthlessness in the achievement of those aims. Portugal was a rival for the mouth of the Congo. Brazil and the Confederacy could persuade Portugal it was in its best interests to abandon a claim to territory it could not hope to develop on its own. France sought control of the right bank of the Congo—a result that would cripple the development of any Congo Free State. But France was also a rival of Great Britain in Africa, and by accepting the Confederate–Brazilian offer of support, Leopold would create a Conference alignment in which the British would receive the support of the CSA at a time when many in Britain wished to reach out and establish an alliance with Richmond. Leopold could also offer London the promise that the Congo Free State would be a tariff-free zone open to goods from everywhere—as contrasted with France's commitment to extend the country's restrictive tariffs should the area of the proposed Free State fall to her.

Of course, allowing an illicit slave trade to continue by which slaves would be funneled out of the Congo, across Angola, and from there to Brazil and the Confederacy, while solemnly pledging to aid in the suppression of slavery, risked a disaster if the ruse were later unmasked. But Leopold had confidence that the ruse would not be unmasked, especially as he was prepared to make a great show of cooperating to suppress the flow of slaves from the Congo Basin east to Zanzibar. Moreover, Leopold was a realist about relations among nation-states and also had the foresight to see the emerging alliance system that was well on its way to dividing the world into two hostile camps. Leopold recognized that Africa would likely be a battleground between these two groupings, and that the survival of his cherished "Belgian African Empire" therefore would depend on picking the winning side. Great Britain was the greatest power in Africa, and Leopold believed it was only a matter of time before London and Richmond joined forces against the USA (and thereby against America's ally, France). "If the British are prepared to make an alliance with the world's greatest slave power, which I am convinced they are," Leopold is reputed to have told his astonished advisers upon explaining the terms of his agreement with the Confederacy and Brazil, "Great Britain will forgive our little arrangement with so valued an ally of theirs, assuming the fact of that arrangement should ever become a matter of public knowledge." As the reader will see, in this, the calculating Belgian King proved right on the money.

So it came to pass that the Confederate–Brazilian slave economies weathered the slave trade crisis triggered by the "Scramble for Africa." And because the "arrangement" with Leopold's Congo Free State was in place by 1886, it became all the easier for the Confederacy and Brazil to make the show against the illicit slave trade required by the terms of Richmond's *entente* with London. (Rio de Janeiro, of course, was not bound by the Anglo–Confederate agreements in this regard, but the Brazilian leadership recognized the wisdom of "voluntary cooperation" with the Confederacy's efforts.) By the mid-1890s, the volume of "illicit" slaves flowing into the Confederate–Brazilian slave economies from Africa was double the level of the 1870s. True, Leopold did overestimate the ability of the Free State administration and its Confederate and Brazilian collaborators to keep the secret of the flow of slaves to the Slave Powers. As early as July 1888, the trade had become the target of the international anti-slavery movement—after Cardinal Lavigerie (Archbishop of Algiers and Primate of Africa) thundered against the "Congo horrors" from the pulpit of Sainte Sulpice in Paris. With breathtaking cynicism, Leopold met the charges by convening an international anti-slavery conference in Brussels the following year. There, denying any involvement on the part of Free State officialdom or Confederate and Brazilian agents operating under Free State auspices (a bald-faced double lie), Leopold blamed Arab traders operating under the banner of the Sultan of Zanzibar. Promising to "stamp out this infamy within one year," Leopold then pled poverty and asked for permission to levy up to a 50 percent duty on all Free State imports to finance a "decisive campaign." (In fact, the Free State "take" from the Confederate–Brazilian slave trade had already put the country's finances in the black, but

Leopold was not about to open up his fiefdom's books to an independent inspection.)

Leopold's maneuver succeeded brilliantly. Anti-slavery sentiment swung round and praised him for his "bold humanitarianism." Leopold's request for the authority to levy duties on Free State imports, however, foundered on the opposition of several conference attendees—which was precisely the result Leopold had hoped for, because it allowed the Free State to shift the blame to the "Berlin Powers" (i.e., the signatories of the 1885 Conference Agreement) for the inevitable reports of continuing Congo-based slave trading. (One wonders how the course of history would have been affected had either the American or French governments had the wit to call Leopold's bluff by offering to foot the bill for Leopold's promised "final crusade"; at the very least, Leopold would have had to scramble to escape a trap of his own making to avoid making good on his own pledge.) Of course, by the mid-1900s, the existence of the Congo Free State's slave trade with the Confederacy and Brazil would be an open secret, and neither Leopold nor the Free State government would bother to issue more than the most perfunctory denials. But as Leopold had shrewdly foreseen, by then, the iron laws of state interest were operating in an environment so changed by recent violence and the resumption of war that "humanitarian" concerns received only the most cursory of hearings from the leaders of nations who—just a few years before—had made the suppression of the slave trade a matter of high importance and international policy.

It bears emphasizing that the African slave trade probably was not essential, in any economically meaningful way, to the preservation, or even expansion, of the slavery-based sectors of either the Confederate or Brazilian economies. Perhaps, if Leopold had elected a different course and managed to acquire his desired Congo-based colonial empire without Slave Power assistance, the Belgian King might have proven a powerful force in the campaign to suppress the African slave trade. But given the murderous methods employed by Leopold's agents in the ivory and rubber trade, I have my doubts; indeed, only with the introduction into the Congo of open Confederate and Brazilian plantation operations in the 1900s—once Leopold was confident that the British were no longer in a position to throttle the by-then Belgian Congo, merely on a point of "humanitarian" principle—did the terrible death rate among native Congolese finally drop. The value of the African slave trade to the CSA and Brazil was less economic than political. The survival of the trade represented the decisive strategic defeat of the political movement against chattel slavery, which had experienced an unbroken series of international triumphs that appeared, by the mid-nineteenth century, to promise the impending suppression of the vile institution. The Confederacy's victorious war for independence represented the first in what would prove a connected chain of setbacks for the anti-slavery cause, culminating with the collapse of the anti-African slave trade efforts, which opened the political door to the reintroduction of slavery in Europe itself (e.g., by Germany and Austria–Hungary in the territories those two Powers acquired from Russia under the Treaty of Brest–Litovsk, which ended a defeated Russia's participation in World War Two).

The North took a very different path following the South's departure from the Union. The reader will recall my brief sketch of the way in which Northern Negroes became integrated into the country's political and social life. Secession by the Union's principal slaveholding states took the great majority of the country's black African population, leaving only a small percentage of Negroes in the North: 1.5 percent in the Northeast, just over 2 percent in the old Northwest, and no measurable presence farther west. Moreover, aside from Delaware, Maryland, and Missouri (the "border" slave states remaining with the North), no state except Rhode Island had a Negro percentage over 2 percent. Admittedly, these pre-Secession populations experienced some increase during the war and its immediate aftermath—due to the flood of slaves fleeing from the re-establishment of Confederate authority in those areas occupied by Union forces. But the Northern Negro population re-stabilized when the Seward Administration honored the "Unwritten Compromise" of 1865 and suppressed the revived Underground Railroad. Although the North had categorically rejected the Confederacy's demand for the return of fugitive slaves who managed to cross the border (the reader will recall the previous discussion of this aspect of the fugitive slave dispute), Washington did, albeit quietly, agree to "discourage" slave flight by rooting out the Underground Railroad ("UR") system, without which few slaves could manage to make good their escape.

The suppression of the Underground Railroad triggered an outcry from the strong abolitionist wing of the Republican Party. New England, in particular, was in an uproar, and leading Republicans employed the harshest of language to condemn "the vile betrayal of the principles that distinguish our nation from Slave Power tyranny." "If our own government is prepared to put our courts and policy at the service of slavery," thundered Massachusetts Senator Charles Sumner to twenty-five thousand Bostonians who gathered to hear him speak on the Boston Common in May of 1865, "then we must ask ourselves whether duty compels the men of New England to cease their association with such corruption." But threats of a "counter-secession" quickly dissipated in the face of a triple political reality. First, there was only minority support for such a move even among "strong abolitionist" New England Republicans, which made secession even regionally untenable. Second, the Seward Administration could safely turn a blind eye to UR activities in New England, precisely because those operations could not be sustained on their own; the "logistical heart" of the UR was in Illinois, Indiana, Ohio, and Western Pennsylvania, and resistance to suppression in those areas proved spotty and quick to fade.

Finally, Seward deftly outflanked Sumner and other vocal suppression opponents by reaching an accord with Frederick Douglass, the acknowledged leader of the Northern Negro community. When one thinks about the Frederick Douglass of history—US Senator from Massachusetts and a towering figure in Republican Party politics—it is difficult to grasp that this man nearly abandoned the USA for the black Africa of Liberia. In fact, despondent over the news that Lincoln had accepted an armistice and knowing this meant the Confederacy had won its fight for freedom (which would mean continued enslavement for nearly four million of his fellows—Douglass himself having escaped from bondage), the future senator had to be talked out of emigrating by leading members of the New England abolitionist community. But once having resolved to remain in America, Douglass steeled himself to the task of assuring for every Negro in the North "equality of legal and social position with our white brothers." Settling permanently in Boston, Douglass threw himself into the campaign to elect Seward and a majority Republican Congress. For Douglass and his fellow Negro Republicans, the immediate issue was the status of slavery in the three border states—Missouri, Maryland, and Delaware—retained by the North. The Republican platform declared the party's intent to "drive the scourge of slavery from American soil," but such grandiloquence neatly sidestepped the issue of how—or when—slavery would be abolished in the Border States. Seward had refused to commit to a precise course of action out of concern he would thereby tip vital swing states to his Democratic opponent, New York Governor Horatio Seymour. Seward was not concerned about losing the Border States themselves, considering them beyond the Republican reach. Seward was concerned, and rightly so, that his open endorsement of "compulsory abolition" could cost him the votes of those who supported Stephen Douglas in 1860. Without them, Seward could not win a two-man race, as he would almost certainly lose the swing states of Illinois, Indiana, and Pennsylvania. (In the event, Seward did lose Pennsylvania, but he held Illinois and Indiana.)

The reader will recall that the Republican victory included recovering control of the Congress. (By most estimates, the Republicans held 90 percent of their 1860 support while winning two of every five voters who supported Douglas.) Now, Seward had the breathing room to move decisively against Border State slavery. In fact, the Underground Railroad issue forced Seward to act even more quickly than even he had intended. As a pre-Secession abolitionist, Seward had denounced slavery in the most unqualified terms, but the responsibilities of administration (first as Lincoln's Secretary of State and now as President) brought the New Yorker's more cautious side to the fore. Seward feared an overly aggressive approach could ignite an insurrection, especially in Missouri. "If that happens," Seward worried in conversation with some political intimates shortly before his inauguration in March of 1865, "I fear the South will not resist the opportunity to make a grab, and we will be right back into it before summer." For precisely that reason, Seward had put off meeting with a Negro Republican delegation led by Douglass, who had asked to address the "pressing issue" of "bringing a prompt end to the continuing enslavement of our African brethren on Northern soil." Seward remained in close touch by personal correspondence with Douglass and at one point offered the position of US Marshal—a post Douglass declined, out of concern acceptance would compromise his ability to continue the fight for Border State emancipation.

Douglass proved to have made a shrewd choice. Having avoided placing himself in Seward's debt, Douglass was well positioned to extract the
concession he wanted most when Seward approached him that fall with
the Underground Railroad controversy at its height. To be sure, Douglass
shocked and alienated many in both the Northern Negro and abolitionist
communities when he emerged from a meeting with President Seward and
announced his "reluctant" support for "reasonable measures" necessary to
"bring an orderly end" to the activities of the UR. But Douglass's standing was restored, and more, when Seward quickly honored his promise
to Douglass and declared "my administration's determination to see the
abolition of slavery in this country, by the securest of constitutional measures, and within my term of office." The Thirteenth Amendment, abolish-
ing slavery and indentured servitude, passed both Houses of Congress the
following spring (although the measure did have to be modified to provide
for government compensation in cases of "genuine economic hardship," in
order to win over the Democratic votes necessary to achieve a two-thirds
majority in the House of Representatives). The amendment then moved
quickly through the state legislatures, as the Republicans held the majority in the necessary three-quarters following their victory in 1864. (The
moderate swing to the Democrats in the midterm vote of 1866 cost the
Republicans a sufficient number of state legislative seats to have endangered the ratification of the "Emancipation Amendment," but those losses
turned out to be concentrated in states whose legislatures had already
voted to ratify, and so slavery was abolished in the North.)

Emancipation was the vital first step along the road to political and
social integration of the Northern Negro. Without emancipation, a majority would have remained in servitude, reproducing in miniature the relative
position of free and slave Negroes in the former Union. The continuation
of slavery would also have been a powerful validation of the anti-African
prejudices of what must be acknowledged to have been a majority of white
Northerners, even in the immediate wake of Secession. If anything, those
prejudices were reinforced by the Confederacy's departure, as some whites,
especially among the urban working class, blamed "the Naygur" for the
Union's fracture. But with emancipation, especially when embodied in the
potent symbolism of a constitutional amendment, social prejudice could no

longer receive the powerful reinforcement of lawful slavery. Emancipation did leave untouched a wide range of social and political intercourse (contracts, jury service, and—above all—the vote) in which the white majority could still give free expression to its prejudices. Douglass and his supporters knew this; Douglass, in particular, held a harshly realistic view of the capacity of his white countrymen to seize every available chance to deprive his Negro compatriots of full legal and social equality. Precisely because he was a realist, however, Douglass had been willing to endure the condemnations of many of his friends in the pre-Secession abolition movement and accept the suppression of the Underground Railroad in exchange for the essential first step of the emancipation of Northern Negro slaves. "We must face facts," Douglass wrote in the November 1866 issue of *North American Review*. "The fate of the Negroes of the South is a tragedy. But, with the division of the former Union, it is no longer our tragedy, any more than is the enslavement of a Black African tribesman by the Sultan of Zanzibar. We are citizens of the United States—not subjects of the Confederate States, thank God! Our duty, and responsibility, is to our fellow Americans. We must first assure equality for the Negroes of our country; endangering that achievement, in the name of the Negroes of the Confederacy, the denizens of what is now a *foreign* land, would constitute a breach of that sacred trust. Now, we must look ahead to building upon the foundation of emancipation, to the achievement of *full* equality for the Negro in America."

Douglass, of course, was right—certainly, as a matter of realistic politics, but also as a matter of an ethical conscience sensitive to consequences and not only ideal conduct. Moreover, the obvious correctness of his argument, as well as the undeniable success of the Thirteenth Amendment, eventually healed the breach between Douglass and most of his abolitionist compatriots who had split with him over the issue of UR suppression. (But not all: Harriet Tubman had defiantly continued her UR work, eventually being arrested and convicted for "unlawful resistance to the authority of a federal marshal"; choosing to emigrate to France rather than stay in the USA, she bitterly attacked Douglass as "worse than Judas, who has sold the freedom of the people for the sake of petty favors from the American Pharaoh.") By the 1870s, Douglass had become a power in the Republican Party; when Senator Sumner died in 1874, Douglass succeeded him—partly on the strength of Sumner's oft-expressed hope that he and Douglass would some-day together represent Massachusetts in the United States Senate. Yet, this personal success did not blind Douglass from the fact that the emancipation of the Border State slaves did not constitute a guarantee that Northern Negroes would be allowed equality of legal rights—much less social standing—with white Americans. Although some states adopted programs granting Negroes legal equality (e.g., the right to vote; to serve on juries) and a measure of social equality (e.g., the right to make contracts and acquire real property; the right to have children attend the new public school system with white children), other states—notably the former slave Border States—adopted new disabling measures designed (in the words of one Missouri legislator) to "keep the Nigrahs in their place," even if they could no longer be held as the property of white men.

Douglass now pressed for what he called the "Fulfillment Amendments"—constitutional amendments that would guarantee Afro–Americans (a term Douglass popularized, to replace the ambiguous circumlocution, "Northern Negro") the right to vote and "equal protection of the laws." Although the Republican Party platforms of 1876 and 1880 endorsed such measures, neither the second Blaine nor the Garfield Administration took action to push the proposals through Congress, where they languished in committee.

Then came the Western War and the crisis over Chinese immigration. The war revitalized the Northern sense of equalitarian identity, and the courageous service of thousands of African–American troops—perhaps most notably that of the 54th Massachusetts, whose successful defense of an isolated outpost during the siege of Santa Fe, against a Confederate attacking force ten times the regiment's number, led to the award of *eleven* Congressional Medals of Honor (four posthumously) and a presidential citation for bravery for the entire unit—provided powerful ammunition for Douglass's Fulfillment Amendments campaign. The serendipitous timing of the Chinese exclusion issue gave Douglass the opportunity to make yet another artful political concession to advance the cause of Afro–American equality. The controversy over Chinese immigration had been building to a head in California, and the railroad logistics crisis of the Western War caused the issue to boil over. In the fall of 1882, a rumor swept San Francisco and Los Angeles that the "railroad interests" planned to import "25,000 Chinese" to construct a track parallel to the Union Pacific–Central Pacific line to relieve the congestion caused by the CSA's interruption of the SP–AT&SF link. Of course, a moment's considered thought would have demonstrated the foolishness of this fear: one *million* Chinese laborers could not have built a transcontinental link parallel to the UP–CP line in time to relieve the North's immediate logistical crisis. But in matters of strongly felt prejudice and fear, considered thoughts rarely can make a difference. Moreover, the railroads' demonstrated preference for "docile" Chinese labor, during the height of the transcontinental construction process, gave at least a patina of plausibility to the notion that the railroads—increasingly on the defensive in recent union contract negotiations—might use the war as an excuse to try to break the railroad unions (thereby accomplishing indirectly what the New Social Covenant's Schurz–Donnelly National Labor Relations Act was designed to forbid directly).

Be that as it might have been, the effect of the "Chinese Importation" rumor on California politics was electric: the Democratic candidate for governor, expected to lose handily, won a stunning two-to-one victory, and the Democrats also captured the State Assembly (although not the Senate). Combined with the victory of Democrat Grover Cleveland in the New York gubernatorial race, the California vote sent shock waves through the American political establishment. The specter of an independent "Pacific Republic," revived by the California vote in the midst of renewed war with the Confederacy, now merged with the (more concrete) reelection concerns of President Garfield to create irresistible pressure to "do something" about Chinese immigration. California Democrats were calling for a ban on future immigration, and the expulsion of all Chinese residents in the USA—a measure unacceptable to a wide variety of interests, and not only the railroads (who *were* still employing Chinese laborers in great numbers to complete a number of key feeder lines on the western railway network). At this point, Frederick Douglass quietly proposed that African–Americans would not oppose a "Chinese Exclusion Act" that barred *future* Chinese immigration if the Garfield Administration committed itself to push vigorously for immediate Congressional approval of the Fulfillment Amendments. This offer represented a change in position by African–American political associations, which had opposed any anti-Chinese proposals as aimed at perpetuating

"Slave Power" attitudes. Douglass's offer represented precisely the sort of *realpolitik* offer that the party leadership could not refuse—especially with President Garfield facing a tough reelection fight, should the Democrats have the wit to nominate Cleveland (which, in fact, they did).

Once again, Douglass had struck a bargain that could advance the cause of Afro–American equality. In his 1883 State of the Union message, President Garfield announced his administration would support a bill to bar future Chinese immigration, effective January 1, 1884. But Garfield also declared that congressional passage of the Fulfillment Amendments would be a priority for his administration, "exceeded only by our determination to repel the Confederate aggression against the American West and our valiant Mexican ally." In the event, congressional passage of the Fulfillment Amendments was secured with the votes of western Democrats who could not otherwise achieve adoption of any anti-Chinese immigration measures—which they had made the touchstone of their program. Ratification of the amendments, however, would have to await the "Great State Making" of 1889. Despite the best efforts of Douglass and other GOP panjandrums, Garfield was defeated for reelection, as Cleveland rode the issue of corruption in government war contracts to a narrow victory. And once in office, Cleveland proved a party stalwart at least on the issue of admitting new states from the West, vetoing a bill passed by the still GOP-controlled Congress to admit the two Dakotas, Montana, Wyoming, Idaho, Washington, Arizona, and New Mexico, along with the Mormons' promised Deseret. (Cleveland later signed a separate bill for the admission of Deseret alone, acknowledging that the Mormons had earned their state through "blood spilled on the field of battle.") But after Cleveland's defeat by General John Schofield in 1888, the logjam was broken, and the overwhelmingly Republican legislatures of the new states provided the needed votes to ratify the Fulfillment Amendments. (As an aside, I note that the positive resolution of the Mormon Question during the Western War had one other effect on the Great State Making, besides the admission of the State of Deseret; concern about a Mormon-dominated state of Idaho had sufficiently eased that proponents of a measure to detach the Idaho Territory's northern "panhandle" and restore the area to the Washington Territory were able to effect that change as a part of the 1889 act admitting those territories as states.)

With the adoption of amendments guaranteeing African–Americans the franchise (the Fifteenth Amendment) and "equal protection of the laws" (the Sixteenth Amendment)—and the subsequent passage by Congress in 1891 of a civil rights act authorizing suits in federal court to enforce those guarantees—the last legal barriers to Negro integration into the political and social mainstream had been removed. The ensuing contrast with the contemporaneous (and successful) effort by the Confederacy and the Brazilian Empire to frustrate the suppression of the African slave trade perfectly illustrates the degree to which the two American Unions had grown apart since the Confederacy's victory in the War of Secession. While the Southern Union was successfully converting its economy to an industrialization based on slavery, the North—in less than a generation— had elevated black Africans to a position of political and economic equality that vindicated the wildest fulminations of Southern, pre-Secession slavery ideologues.

Whether a still-united United States would have taken the same path is a question whose likely answer troubles me still. Douglass had the tremendous advantage of being freed of the difficult task of integrating the great balance of Negro Americans held in bondage at the time of the Southern rebellion. Frankly, I consider it highly unlikely that the majority of whites in a preserved Union—even one in which the enslavement of Negroes had been abolished—would have granted a comparable degree of equality to so much larger a population of freedmen, at least not to the same degree and certainly not as rapidly as these rights were granted by a Union shorn of the slaveholding South. Even so, I would hope that, given a choice, one as wise and realistic an American as Frederick Douglass would have elected the course of delayed freedom for Negroes in a united America rather than the terrible future that has since befallen Yankee and Johnny, white and black, free and slave, in our benighted century.

(left) **Frederick Douglass, an escaped slave who transformed himself into the political spokesman for the Afro-American community of the USA, and who as U.S. Senator from Massachusetts worked unstintingly and successfully to achieve political and social equality for Northern blacks.**

(right) **King Leopold of Belgium, the founder and owner of the Congo "Free State," whose ambitions led him to align with the Confederacy and the Brazilian Empire, making possible the final destruction of Great Britain's efforts to suppress the global slave trade.**

12

GERMANY, RUSSIA, AND
THE CONSOLIDATION OF
THE GLOBAL ALLIANCE SYSTEM

———

H aving chronicled the effective collapse by the end of the nineteenth century of the anti-slave trade campaign and contrasted those events with the North's integration of black Africans into the country's political and social fabric, I will resume my narrative of the development of the Global Alliance System with a discussion of the Great Power consequences that now flowed from the formation of the Anglo–Confederate *entente* in the spring of 1887.

Ironically, at least from the perspective of certain decision makers in London, the short-term effect was a deterioration in British Empire security because of the ensuing response by the USA and France. The reader will recall that, from the mid-nineteenth century, France and Great Britain had enjoyed an extended *detente* that survived the fall of the Second Empire and the establishment of the Third Republic. In the 1880s, however, Franco–British relations began to sour for two primary reasons.

The first was rooted in the historic enmity of the two peoples, which in France had become institutionalized in the "person" of the French Navy and which reemerged—as the navy seized upon the mission of promoting a French colonial empire in Africa—to revive the Anglo–French rivalry. The French took the first steps to expand their African holdings by moving up the Senegal River in 1879 and then against the independent authority of the Bey of Tunis in 1881. The promoters of these moves in the *Ministre de Marine* (which by an unfortunate accident of history also had jurisdiction over France's colonies) looked forward to the expected British counter-move with the relish of an old fighter about to renew combat with a hated foe. And to their delight, the Gladstone government proceeded to behave in a fashion seemingly intended to convince a fair-minded observer that the French Navy and its allies in the Quai d'Orsay were perhaps justified in their mistrust of perfidious Albion. London condemned the Tunisian intervention—even though both Bismarck *and* Disraeli, only three years earlier at the Berlin Conference called to settle the Russo–Turkish crisis over the Balkans, had urged France to do in Tunisia exactly what it was now proceeding to do. Although an objective observer would probably blame this British about-face on Gladstone's incorrigible moralistic naiveté in international matters, the Anglophobes in the French government chose to credit Gladstone with greater sophistication and therefore condemned him for trying to deny France its rightful share of *"la gloire colonielle."*

Tunisia might have proven only a temporary hiccup had it not been followed by the Egypt Crisis of the very next year. The reader will recall how Great Britain found itself confronting simultaneous crises in the summer of 1882: with the outbreak of the Western War in North America and the explosion of nationalist violence in Egypt. In the latter case, Gladstone responded with unusual forcefulness, authorizing an intervention to safeguard the Suez Canal and restore order in Alexandria and Cairo by force of arms. The intervention succeeded brilliantly, as British forces smashed the Egyptian nationalists at the Battle of Tel el-Kebir and restored the symbolic authority of the Khedive (who had fled when the Nationalists seized power). The French, who shared the real power with the British in Egypt under an agreement reached in 1878, failed to contribute to the expedition against the Nationalists (for reasons having more to do with the Byzantine politics of the Third Republic than anything remotely resembling a considered policy toward the Egyptian crisis). But somehow, the fact that France had funked its share of responsibility for assuring order in Egypt was forgotten by the Anglophobes of the *Marine* and the Quai d'Orsay, who began to condemn the 1882 intervention as a British attempt to shoulder France aside and take sole charge in Egypt. Nor should the symbolic importance of Egypt to France be underestimated, for Egypt was the site of one of the French Navy's worst defeats (Aboukir Bay, at the hands of Nelson himself) as well as of France's greatest technical achievement (the construction of the Suez Canal by Ferdinand De Lesseps). (I also recall the New Louvre exhibiting a painting of Napoleon astride his charger at the Pyramids of Giza, but I suspect that work is now only a memory—lost when Paris was blasted off the face of the globe by American or British H-bombs.)

By the opening of the Berlin Conference in November of 1884, the Anglo–French *entente*—a vital buttress to the peace of Europe since the days of King Louis-Phillipe of France—had been substantially undermined. The course of events at Berlin would now bring the tottering edifice down in ruins, as Great Britain joined with Germany, Portugal, the Confederacy, and Brazil to block French ambitions to occupy the North Bank of the Congo in favor of Leopold's plan for a "Congo Free State" to control the entire Congo basin. Still, the collapse of an *entente* did not necessarily mean the restoration of an enmity bound to explode into conflict at the earliest opportunity. Although these events might on their own have set France and Great Britain on the road to Fashoda and to war, the possibility of such an outcome would have been substantially reduced had there not also been a rivalry between the two American unions, which introduced an additional—and decisive—strain on Anglo–French relations.

The reader will recall that, by the beginning of the 1880s, there had blossomed a close working relationship between the USA and Republican France, which had come to be characterized in the cabinet rooms of other interested powers (especially Great Britain) as an "alliance." In fact, while the USA did have a formalized relationship with Spain (the result of the intersection of the two countries' very concrete and mutual interest in deterring Confederate power in the Caribbean Basin), Washington lacked a comparable relationship with Paris. And although the two Republics had established a series of cooperative military arrangements in the 1870s, the genuine sense of affinity that developed in the decade since the establishment of the Third Republic had not produced a relationship of formal cooperation and mutual commitment on matters of grand strategy, which is the fundamental characteristic of an alliance.

From the French point of view, there were two reasons why Franco–American relations had not developed along such lines before the mid-1880s. First, France did not perceive that it had Western Hemisphere strategic interests comparable to Spain's surviving Caribbean holdings, whose security would benefit from a formal military alliance with the USA. Second, and far the more important, as long as the "quasi-alliance" of the Anglo-French *detente* lasted, France did not feel the need to further develop its "close friendship" with America. But with the collapse of *détente* with England, Paris now felt compelled to look upon London as a source of danger—especially to France's burgeoning colonial empire in Africa. (Of course, France didn't *have* to consider London a threat just because French relations with the British had soured; but it seems to be a sad truth of international relations that whomsoever cannot be assuredly accounted a friend must then be treated as at least a potential enemy.) And if Great Britain were now to be accounted at least a potential enemy, the threat it posed must also be recognized as maritime—specifically, the severing of the lifeline between Metropolitan France and its growing colonial holdings: in Africa and Southeast Asia. Although the French fleet was respectable (and whenever combined in accounting exercises with the Russians and the Americans, gave the willies to members of the British Admiralty), the blunt truth was that France could not hope to hold its own in a fleet conflict with Great Britain, whose Mediterranean Fleet was the most powerful element (and most prestigious posting) of the Royal Navy.

Under such circumstances, it was only natural that Paris would turn to Washington. But if the more powerful USA fleet were to be added to the balance on France's side—as a matter of an actual alliance and not just an Admiralty war game scenario—the British truly would have their hands full with maintaining North Atlantic communications with Canada, while simultaneously neutralizing the French. Sufficient British forces might be siphoned off from the Mediterranean, the South Atlantic, and the Indian Ocean to give France a fighting chance at holding its own in those vital theaters—and, in combination with Spain, perhaps even a shot at seizing Gibraltar and turning the tables on *Les Anglais*. And in the USA, France found a receptive audience to the suggestion that the two countries should expand and formalize their already cooperative relationship. The Cleveland Administration had quickly condemned the Anglo-Confederate *entente*; far more surprising for a Democratic Administration was the subsequent announcement of plans to redouble *again* the expansion of the American fleet—which had already been underway since the end of the Western War. And given the rapid pace of technological evolution at sea characteristic of the period, this new construction would prove disproportionately power-ful, on a per-unit basis, when compared with existing Royal Navy ships. Washington also unveiled a series of additional measures intended to fur-ther complicate the task of Anglo–Confederate forces in the event of war. Along the USA–Canada border, fortifications and railheads would be built that would give American ground forces the ability to launch an invasion of Canada at the outset of any war with Great Britain (although the American government insisted the program was "purely defensive"). To the south, the USA and Mexico announced a program to expand and upgrade the system of Mexican fortifications along the Rio Grande, the railway network to support these defenses, and the Pacific Coast harbors that would serve as disembarkation points for supplies and reinforcements in the event of war. Finally, Washington and Bogota declared that the establishment of an alliance with the "Confederate raiders" constituted a waiver by Great Britain of the constraints on fortifying any Panama Canal imposed by the Clayton–Bulwer Treaty; the Americans and Colombians would now pro-ceed with a massive fortification effort, including the construction of naval bases at Colon and Panama City.

All these measures were a not entirely unexpected reaction by the North to the establishment of Anglo–Confederate ties, and London and Richmond (along with Ottawa) were already preparing a program of countermeasures. But the newly formalized alliance between the USA and France announced in May of 1889, along with a parallel agreement between Paris and Madrid, presented additional and more difficult chal-lenges. For one, the program of Franco–Spanish naval expansion and cooperation in the Mediterranean would be on a much greater scale and would proceed more quickly than London had anticipated, as the new Schofield Administration had pledged financial support greater than either Salisbury or Chamberlain had thought likely. (Schofield's ascendancy to the Presidency owed much to the death of Phillip Sheridan, Sherman's suc-cessor as Chief of the General Staff; Sheridan, despite his Irish Catholic heritage, had been widely regarded as the favorite for the GOP nomination in 1888, but a precipitate decline in Sheridan's health in the fall of 1887, due to heart disease that would kill him by the following summer, caused the nervous Republican leaders to scramble for another heroic general of the kind thought necessary to unseat President Cleveland. They eventually settled on Schofield, who promptly resigned as Chief of the General Staff, a position to which Cleveland had appointed him in the hope of sidelining the popular general for the upcoming campaign.) London also failed to anticipate the Franco–American decision to commence the construction of substantial naval fortifications on the Lesser Antilles islands of Guadeloupe and Martinique, both held by France. Finally, there was the wholly unexpected decision of the new alliance to develop a joint naval presence in the South China Sea, with the French transforming Haiphong Harbor in French Indochina on the Asian mainland into a major naval base, and the USA stationing a new naval squadron in the Philippines, where it would join Spain's "Pacific Fleet"—thereby threatening to cut the lifeline for Great Britain's Chinese holdings, while also endangering the British position on the Malay peninsula (Singapore), as well as communications with the Australian states and New Zealand. Thus, by the start of the 1890s, Gladstone and other critics of the Anglo–Confederate *entente* could say, with some force, that the alliance had at best made no appreciable contribution to "imperial security" and, if anything, had only made London's task all the more complex.

All these developments set the stage for the consolidation of the Global Alliance System, with the adherence of Germany, and then Russia, to opposite sides of the emerging divide. For Germany, the crucial period proved to be the first five years of the reign of Kaiser Wilhelm II, by the end of which Bismarck's eastward-looking policy of a neutralizing reinsurance *entente* with Russia had been overthrown in favor of an alliance with Great Britain, to be based on the power of a new "blue water" German navy.

It would probably be claiming too much to say that world history was changed by one book and the effect it had on a young and mercurial head of state. Still, it is a fact that USA Navy Rear Admiral Alfred Mahan's *The Influence of Sea Power Upon History* struck Wilhelm II with epiphanic force, convincing him that Germany could not be a world power (instead of merely a European one) unless it possessed a powerful navy. Had Wilhelm developed his belief in the necessity of a German navy to German greatness under different circumstances, one can imagine that German naval expansionism might have produced the opposite effect on Anglo–German relations than it actually had—perhaps even making rivals of the British and German Empires, given how jealously the British sought to preserve their naval supremacy. But as matters actually transpired, Wilhelm developed his desire for a "blue water" German navy at a time when the British government was coming to the painful realization that Great Britain could not maintain its naval supremacy alone in the face of the challenge being laid down by the USA and its allies. Hence, when Germany indicated its desire to develop a navy in concert with Great Britain (with the understanding that the new German squadrons would act as a counterweight to the growing Franco–American threat), Salisbury's government found it had been made an offer that could not responsibly be refused.

This description, however, could be read as implying that the Anglo–German alliance was purely the product of one man's sudden fascination with making his country a world naval power. In fact, the emergence of the Anglo–German alliance was the product of several influences, including a powerful constituency in Germany that favored an alliance with Great Britain because it would *also* mean an alliance with the Confederacy. Important elements in the new Imperial German state had come to favor some form of cooperative relationship with the Confederacy years before the Anglo–American naval arms race that precipitated the establishment of the Anglo–German–Confederate *entente*. One important influence was the rural landholding worldviews common to both the Junker and the Confederate plantation aristocrat, each of whom held disproportionate influence in the military and the halls of government. Another decidedly non-agrarian advocate for the Confederacy was centered on the great armaments firm of Krupp, and its development sprang from a most ironic source: the pig-headed refusal of the Prussian General Staff to acknowledge the essential contribution made by Krupp's innovative cast-steel artillery to Prussia's victory over France in the crucial frontier battles of the Franco–Prussian War of 1870–71. No sooner had Krupp's cannon smashed one empire and heralded the foundation of a second than the (new) Reich's Ministry of War urged (now) Kaiser Wilhelm I to scrap his cast-steel Krupp barrels and reintroduce all-bronze guns. Alfred Krupp responded by urging comparative trials pitting Krupp's latest designs against the War Ministry's preferred bronze cannon—only to be told that now was not the time to directly challenge the authority of War Minister General Emil Von Roon, who, despite the patent silliness of his campaign to restore all-bronze guns (more a reflection of Roon's personal dislike for Alfred Krupp than the War Minister's considered judgment about artillery technology), deserved credit for a brilliant logistics effort that had contributed vitally to Prussia's victory over France. (Krupp was also assured that no decision would be taken on Roon's proposal to scrap Germany's steel cannon.)

Enter the Confederacy, in the form of the Tredegar Iron Works. The reader will recall that Confederate observers had been warmly received by Prussian forces during the 1866 war with Austria and the climactic encounter with France four years later. Likewise, Prussian observers had been enthusiastically received during the Confederacy's conquest of Cuba. The German contingent in Cuba had included a team from Krupp, and they approvingly noted how Tredegar had already moved away from all-bronze guns by adopting Sir Joseph Whitworth's innovation of wrought iron barrels strengthened by exterior coils and also how the Confederate artillerists employed these guns with devastating effect against the Spanish (whose forces employed the traditional all-bronze barrel). But the German admiration for Confederate artillery paled in comparison to the effusive reaction of the Tredegar representatives attached to the Confederacy's observer corps, who witnessed the devastation wrought by Krupp's steel cannon upon a French army that most neutral observers had expected to carry the war deep into the territory of upstart Prussia. So it came to pass that in the fall of 1871, Tredegar proposed to Krupp that the two firms enter into a joint venture for the development of a wide array of artillery. Tredegar sweetened the deal by offering access to the coal and iron ore center—the future "Confederate Ruhr"—then under development in Birmingham, Alabama.

Initially, Alfred Krupp demurred, preferring to concentrate his energies on his battle with the War Ministry. But when the request for a gunnery competition was refused, Krupp reconsidered, and in the spring of 1872 decided to accept the Tredegar offer. This may seem incomprehensible to readers familiar with the state paranoia of the mid-twentieth century, which by then had made unthinkable the notion of a country's principal armament specialist sharing the secrets of advanced weapons technology with another country (even if that country is a close ally). Krupp's decision, however, was taken before the terrible events that would make secrecy a veritable and universal "state religion." In fact, Krupp felt free to sell his cannon to virtually anyone, and in the wake of the German victory over France, his firm signed contracts to provide guns to governments as distant as Siam and China. (Even the tiny principality of Andorra purchased a Krupp field piece, only to discover the gun's range meant it could not be test-fired without hitting French soil.) This is not to say that Krupp felt free to sell anything to anybody: as the controversy over his contract to deliver five hundred guns to St. Petersburg well illustrated. (Krupp neatly handled pointed inquiries from the German government by directing that the guns—whose specifics had been left to Krupp's discretion—should be built so heavy as to be less maneuverable than those being provided to the German army.) But in the case of the Tredegar offer, Krupp was under no such constraints. The Confederacy was far away, the Germans admired the South's "martial virtues," and—to the extent the relevant officialdom gave any thought to it—a joint venture with the capable Tredegar firm could be of benefit to the German armed forces. In fact, the Tredegar–Krupp joint venture would prove a tremendous success. The two firms' research and development teams worked very well in tandem, and the combined resources of the two companies (particularly Krupp's access to European capital markets) were employed to develop advanced facilities "from scratch" outside of Birmingham. It was here, not in Germany, that Krupp—with Tredegar—first employed the new Gilchrist Thomas steel-making process, which allowed for the absorption of phosphorus from pig iron.

But of greatest significance for this point in my narrative are the political and personal connections that developed between the Confederacy and Germany as a result of the Tredegar–Krupp collaboration. Most important of these was the warm feeling that the Krupp family itself developed toward the South—and particularly the conviction on the part of Friedrich Alfred Krupp (son of Alfred and successor to leadership of the firm) that Germany should make an alliance with the "dynamic militarists" of the Confederacy. "The Confederates are the Prussians of the New World," Friedrich told a group of associates in 1887, "and a combination with the Prussians of the Old World would make Prussianism the master of both." Friedrich had quickly gained the confidence of Wilhelm II upon the new Kaiser's ascension, and when Wilhelm began to contemplate an alliance with Great Britain, Friedrich became a forceful advocate for such a move because it would also bring Germany into close association with the Confederacy. Friedrich and his like-minded colleagues, however, only gained full access to the young Kaiser after the fall from power of Chancellor Otto von Bismarck. To be sure, Bismarck himself had occasionally leaned toward an alliance with Great Britain and had actually proposed such an arrangement to Disraeli in September 1879 (one month after yet another Anglo–Russian crisis that had nearly plunged the two powers into war—a result that could not be avoided indefinitely, as the fall of 1898 would conclusively demonstrate). Disraeli, however, declined the proposal, principally because he recognized that an Anglo–German alliance would almost certainly bring an end to the British *entente* with France which had well served British interests for decades (and which was of particular concern at the time, as French aid was essential to resolving a financial crisis that was then threatening to bring down the Khedive of Egypt).

The Confederacy was another matter. The reader will recall Bismarck's acerbic comment about the CSA being more distant than the Balkans, and that comment perfectly captures Bismarck's view of what he often called the "damn fool" distraction of the New World. For Bismarck, the vital issue was always maintaining Germany's position of advantage in Europe, and Bismarck recognized that the rivalry between the American North and South represented a force in international politics that increasingly threatened to affect relations among the European Powers, thereby immensely complicating Bismarck's task. Bismarck therefore sought to discourage any notion that Germany should enter into any sort of association (however informal) with the Confederacy. And as the crises of the 1880s drove Great Britain toward an alliance with the Confederacy, Bismarck grew cool to the idea he had once pursued of an alliance with England, recognizing that such a commitment would effectively mean an alliance with Richmond and therefore would put Germany on a potential collision course with the USA and its European allies—a circumstance that could plunge Germany into a war because of distant events that Berlin could neither reasonably anticipate nor hope to control. Thus, in November 1887, shortly after concluding the secret Reinsurance Treaty with Russia, Bismarck rejected yet another call by the "Anglo–Confederate" lobby to seek an alliance with Great Britain. "While the preservation of Anglo–German goodwill is a most important thing," he informed a small group including Friedrich Krupp, "we have no alliance with England, nor do we need to seek such an alliance, for no differences exist between England and Germany."

Of course, Bismarck's resistance to an Anglo–German alliance at that time was also influenced by his desire to isolate Crown Prince Frederick, whose liberalism (and liberal English wife) Bismarck saw as a threat to the autocratic order of the Second Reich. But even after Frederick's brief reign was cut short by throat cancer and his son became Kaiser Wilhelm II, Bismarck continued to resist any "English entanglements" and took every opportunity to forcefully remind the young emperor of the need to maintain Germany's relationship with St. Petersburg while staying out of "foolish adventures in the New World." It was not disagreement over these issues that forced Bismarck from office, however; a dispute over social welfare policy brought on the final confrontation between the Kaiser and his venerable Chancellor. Moreover, the fundamental problem was neither foreign nor domestic policy, but personality—Wilhelm II was not willing to be a figurehead Kaiser subservient to the brilliant Chancellor the way his grandfather Wilhelm I had been, and Bismarck failed to recognize this until it was too late to avoid resignation. Bismarck's departure in March of 1890 thus opened the door to an Anglo–German alliance, and Wilhelm was instinctively predisposed to favor such a relationship by heritage and avocation. Although Wilhelm began his reign with an embarrassing social misstep involving his uncle, the Prince of Wales, good feelings were restored by the new Kaiser's first state visit to Great Britain in the summer of 1889. Among other things, Victoria made Wilhelm an honorary Admiral of the Fleet, and the delighted Kaiser—who had developed a boyhood fascination with, and affection for, the Royal Navy—thanked his grandmother for the commission in words that would prove all too prophetic: "I now am able to feel and take interest in your fleet as if it were my own, and with keenest sympathy shall I watch every phase of its further development, knowing that the British ironclads, coupled with mine and my army, are the strongest guarantees of peace.... Should, however, the will of Providence lay the heavy burden on us of fighting for our homes and destinies, then may the British fleet be seen forging ahead side by side with the German, and the 'redcoat' marching to victory with the 'Pomeranian Grenadier'!!"

It seems incredible that Germany's momentous decision to pursue a "blue water" navy could have been so much the product of its Kaiser's personal impulses—Wilhelm's childhood affinity for the Royal Navy, combined with his desire as Kaiser for Germany to imitate that exalted fleet in order to achieve *Weltmacht* for Germany. Keep in mind, however, that parliamentary government in Germany was gravely weakened by the structure of Bismarck's constitution, which concentrated great power in the hands of the Kaiser and therefore made national policy vulnerable to a monarch's personal whim. Bismarck's force of personality had reduced the monarchy's power to mere formality during the reign of Wilhelm I, but with Bismarck gone, there was no one with the ability to disabuse the young Wilhelm II of the idea that (as he once put the point early in his reign), "The King's will is the highest law." In fact, Wilhelm II's will was weak: he blew hot and cold on issues and also exhibited a tendency to lose his nerve at moments of crisis. Perhaps Wilhelm discharged Bismarck precisely because the young Kaiser sensed his own vulnerability to the venerable Chancellor's stronger will. Be that as it may, the Kaiser did find the nerve to see his way through the extremely difficult task of evicting Bismarck from the office he had held since the founding of the Second Reich. But that effort also proved the last time that Wilhelm, over the course of his fifty-three year reign, summoned the strength of character necessary to resist either the blandishments of those with the ability to master the art of manipulation by flattery or the pressing demands of those who combined a powerful personality with a vision that the Kaiser at least fitfully shared.

Alfred von Tirpitz was no flatterer. But when it came to the future of the new German navy, Tirpitz would not need to employ flattery and guile to achieve his aims. In a regime vulnerable to powerful personalities, Tirpitz (like Bismarck before him) would prove a singularly effective proponent of a particular vision for Germany's future—in Tirpitz's case, of a great German battleship fleet and its political corollary of an alliance with the British Empire. Although Wilhelm's instinctive desire for *some* form of a strong German navy asserted itself in the first month of his reign (when he insisted on canceling plans for building torpedo boats and approved the construction of four ten-thousand-ton battleships—the first new capital ships added to the German navy in five years), the Kaiser had no clear notion of what sort of navy Germany should develop. In particular, Wilhelm vacillated between those who urged a fleet based on fast (but lightly armored) cruisers, and the advocates of a true "battle fleet" of slower but more powerful capital vessels. The cruiser champions grounded their case on the need to protect the sea-lane connections to Germany's African colonies; the battle fleet proponents argued for a force that would make "even the greatest sea state in Europe more conciliatory toward Germany's world aspirations." The battle fleet proponents, however, did not seek a confrontation with England for its own sake; to the contrary, they could see the strain being placed upon Europe's greatest sea power by the USA challenge, and the fleet proponents hoped the construction of such force would make Germany an irresistible candidate for England's ally. (The Krupp interests threw their support to the battle fleet proponents because Krupp would profit from such a course *and* because an alliance with Great Britain would bring Germany that much closer to one with the Confederacy.)

Tirpitz intervened decisively in this debate. Seizing the opportunity of a dinner with the Kaiser at Kiel Castle in the fall of 1890, Tirpitz argued the case for a battleship fleet with such vigor that Wilhelm appointed him chief of the naval staff and also personally commissioned Tirpitz to develop a strategy for a high seas battle fleet. Within a year, Tirpitz had readied a plan for a seventeen-ship force, based on two lines of eight battleships plus a fleet flagship. Tirpitz set forth his proposal in a memorandum titled: "General Considerations on the Constitution of Our Fleet According to Ship Classes and Designs," in which he demonstrated how the construction of his fleet would achieve world power for Germany. In essence, Tirpitz sought to force England to embrace Germany as an ally. If England did so, Germany would achieve equality of status in the vital North Atlantic theater of operations in a war with the Franco–American alliance; if England hesitated, it risked having the German fleet operating as a hostile force in the North Sea. Tirpitz realized that the British could not risk the latter, because they could not afford to build a fleet capable of neutralizing the new German threat while having a realistic prospect of maintaining control in the Mediterranean (against the French and Spanish) and in the Atlantic (against the Americans). London, therefore, would have to respond favorably when Berlin followed up the announcement of its new naval ambitions with an offer of an alliance.

Tirpitz's reasoning won over Wilhelm, who stood firm as Tirpitz's opponents tried to undermine the Kaiser's support for this "radical venture." To neutralize parliamentary opposition, Tirpitz had proposed the Reichstag bind itself by the extraordinary step of a naval bill establishing an "unalterable" seven-year program for building the new fleet. When the Naval State Secretary balked at the naval bill scheme as "politically untenable," Wilhelm replaced him with Tirpitz. But unlike most of the leadership of Wilhelmine Germany, with their open contempt for the "parliamentary rabble," Tirpitz proved himself a master of the Reichstag precisely because he was willing to treat the members with respect. Tirpitz also had a genuine sense for the seamier aspects of mass politics, and from the point when the bill was proposed on November 30, 1892, he did not hesitate to identify and exploit the interests and connections vital to key members and organize a national campaign to overcome the predictable opposition of mossback conservatives (who could not imagine any other useful expenditure than on the army) and the Social Democrats (who—quite correctly—feared the fleet would be used to put Germany on a collision course with the USA and its allies: France and Spain). On March 26, 1893, the Navy Bill passed. Under its terms, Germany would begin construction of a fleet that, upon its scheduled completion in 1900, would catapult the nation into the first rank of sea powers. But on whose side would the new German fleet steam? That question was resolved with remarkable speed and in favor of an alliance with Great Britain and the Confederacy—but only at the price of driving Russia into the arms of France and the USA.

In the wake of Bismarck's fall from power, Germany did not renew the secret Reinsurance Treaty with Russia. The Reinsurance Treaty was the linchpin of Bismarck's system of alliances: providing for German neutrality if Austria attacked Russia and Russian neutrality if France attacked Germany, the treaty certainly violated the intent—if not the literal wording—of Germany's alliance with Austria, but also insured that Germany would not face the danger of a two-front war against Russia and France. The decision to cancel the treaty had little to do with carefully considered grand strategy and everything to do with personal ambition and bureaucratic empire-building. Friedrich von Holstein, First Counselor of the Political Department of the Foreign Ministry, had long resented Bismarck's disregard of his advice against entanglements with Russia; with Bismarck gone, Holstein seized the chance to engineer the cancellation of the Reinsurance Treaty on the grounds that disclosure of the secret agreement's terms would alienate Austria–Hungary. Bismarck's successor, General George Leo von Caprivi, also persuaded Wilhelm that the treaty conflicted with Germany's alliance with Austria–Hungary. Because the Reinsurance Treaty had been secret, its cancellation was only known initially to Berlin and St. Petersburg. But the effect on Russia was immediate and eventually profound—deprived of any assurance of German neutrality in the event of a war with Austria–Hungary (a very real prospect, given Vienna's rivalry with St. Petersburg for influence in the turbulent Balkans), Russia was bound to go in search of allies. And the logical place for Russia to turn was precisely the place Bismarck worried the Russians might someday go and for that reason had taken the step of enmeshing them in the "reinsurance relationship"—France.

Nor did that move take very long to develop. In the first place, and as Bismarck had feared even prior to his departure from office, Russian military opinion was already souring on the Russo–German understanding (even if it was only defensive), while warming to the French and also to the USA. The Anglo–Russian competition in central Asia continued apace after the "near miss" of the Pandjeh Crisis of 1885. The Germans could render no assistance to Russian policy in this sphere, while the French (with their growing fleet and their position in Africa and the Mediterranean) and the Americans (with their even more powerful fleet and common border with Canada) would directly threaten the British ability to wage war against Russia in Afghanistan and Persia, forcing the British to draw off forces there to protect other vital holdings.

Russia was remarkably far from inimical in principle to the idea of some sort of formal relationship with the USA. Immediately after the

Battle of Gettysburg, with Britain and France providing the whetstone for carving up the North American continent, Russia had conspicuously declined to join in. Russian Foreign Minister Gorchakov told USA Charge d'Affaires Bayard Taylor that Russia desired "above all things" the continuation of the Union. Tsar Alexander II saw in the anti-slavery forces in the North a reflection of his 1861 decree intended to effect the emancipation of the serfs. (The actual effectiveness of that decree and the ultimate fate of Russia's "bound" peasantry will be addressed later in this narrative.) Port visits to San Francisco by the Russian Far East Fleet and to New York by the Russian Baltic Fleet, both in 1863—although admittedly driven primarily by Russian operational concerns in case of war over the latest crisis involving Congress Poland—had received almost riotously favorable receptions. But it was an alliance with France that would be the key.

When Russia received the news that the Reinsurance Treaty—which its ambassador to Germany, Count Paul Shuvalov, had returned to Berlin fully expecting to renew—was instead being allowed to lapse, Tsar Alexander III and his closest ministers began to move (with remarkable alacrity for the Russian Bear) to open a dialogue with Paris and Washington. Although Russia's foreign minister, Nikolai Karlovich Giers, tried over the next few months to repair the damage to Russo–German relations done by the Reinsurance Treaty's lapse (among other things, Giers feared a Russo–German fracture exposed Russia to the risk of a war with Germany, which Giers—presciently—believed would be a calamity for his country), others in the Russian government were already putting in motion events that would soon create an irresistible pressure to establish a Russo–Franco–American alliance. The War Ministry contrived at the invitation of the Chiefs of the General Staff of France (General Raoul Le Mouton be Boisdeffre) and of the USA (General Nelson A. Miles, Schofield's successor) to attend the annual grand maneuvers to be held in the vicinity of Narva on the shores of the Gulf of Finland in August of 1890. Although Kaiser Wilhelm, Chancellor Caprivi, and several high-ranking German offices also attended, it was readily apparent that the political climate in Russia had shifted—a point confirmed by the reports of Generals Boisdeffre and Miles to their respective governments.

Still, the "Narva Talks" (as they came to be known) were only that: preliminary talks, which indicated the interest of both sides in reaching some sort of understanding but which did not reach anything remotely approaching an outline of what the terms of the relationship might be. In this regard, one must not underestimate the difficulty created in Russia by the symbolism of the Tsar—the personification of a patrimonial state—entering into an alliance with a republic that symbolized *the* revolution against which Russia stood in announced opposition. Only the year before, Alexander had refused to allow Russian participation in the great Paris Exposition celebrating the centennial of that revolution—in which, Alexander pointedly reminded his ministers, the King and Queen of France met their deaths. Nonetheless, the Narva Talks had been constructive, and the next year, they were followed by two events—one symbolic, the other political—which accelerated the move toward an alliance. The symbolic event was the reception of a French naval squadron at the Russian naval base of Kronstadt, immediately outside of St. Petersburg. For a two-week period in July 1891, the French officers and crew were feted in a virtual delirium of celebration, the likes of which St. Petersburg had not seen in decades (in part because public demonstrations in the city had been discouraged following the abortive Decembrist Uprising of 1825). The high point, which also captured the attention of world leaders, came when Alexander III stood bare-headed while the "Marseillaise" was played; although the French national anthem and therefore entitled to respect from another country's head of state, the piece was also the musical symbol of the Revolution of 1789, and its performance had long been banned by edicts issued in the name of the very Tsar who now bowed his head as its strains rang out within the heart of Imperial Russia.

Even as Alexander III removed his hat to the tune of the hymn of Republican France, another moment of high drama in the "Great Game" between Russia and the British Empire was unfolding in the remote and uncharted mountain kingdoms and principalities that lay between the Russian Empire and British India. In August, a force of four hundred Cossacks entered the Pamir Gap from the North, where they encountered none other than Lieutenant (later Field Marshal) Sir Francis Younghusband. Younghusband enjoyed a fairly convivial meeting with the Russians, but as the British party was outnumbered several dozen times over, Younghusband had little choice but to withdraw when the Russian officer in charge produced a map purporting to show the entire area as belonging to the Tsar. Worse: before departing for India, Younghusband learned that the Russians had also conducted a "mapping raid" into Chitral—an area that the Government of India regarded as lying strictly within its defense perimeter and sphere of influence. When news of the incident reached London, it triggered a storm of protest from both sides of the political aisle. While the Indian army mobilized a division of troops in case the Russian "seizure" of the Pamirs led to war, Lord Salisbury's government delivered a strong protest that challenged Russia's claims and demanded a formal apology for Younghusband's expulsion. As Russia was in no shape for a war with Great Britain (a terrible famine held much of the countryside in its grip, while the country's finances had yet to recover from the collapse of a major refinancing package in March), it backed down in public: Russian troops withdrew from the Pamirs pending a "final" reso- lution of the disputed border, and the colonel in charge received a public reprimand for expelling Younghusband.

The Pamir fiasco prompted Alexander III to urge an acceleration of efforts to reach an accord with France and the USA, with initial efforts to focus on the French. Military staff talks with the French were begun in ear- nest in St. Petersburg the following spring, but they soon bogged down over the structure of any alliance. Since the Franco–Prussian War and the loss of Alsace–Lorraine, the *summum bonum* of French foreign policy had been the recovery of the Lost Provinces. Although France had a close relation- ship with the USA, and the Anglo–French *entente* had foundered on African rocks several years before, France did not regard England as an enemy the way it regarded Germany as *the* enemy. For Russia, on the other hand, the British Empire was its principal rival, with which (counting Pamir) it had nearly gone to war three times in the previous thirteen years. And while Russo–German relations had cooled since Berlin's decision not to renew the Reinsurance Treaty, St. Petersburg's goal in entering into an alliance with France was to acquire an ally in the event of a war with England. So when General Boisdeffre submitted France's proposal for an alliance directed against Germany and its Triple Alliance with Austria–Hungary and Italy (which would require the Russians to commit "the totality of their forces not absolutely indispensable to further commitments on other fronts" against

Germany, should France be attacked by the Triple Alliance or by Germany alone), the Russians could hardly fail to take notice that the French proposal said nothing about Great Britain. Nor did the proposal address how France's obligations to Russia would be coordinated with France's obligations under its naval conventions with the USA and with Spain.

The combination of these silences could be taken to imply that France sought only a Russian "insurance policy" to protect France against the danger of a German attack—in the event France went to war with Great Britain. An Anglo–French war (even if it did not include the USA or Spain as cobelligerents on the French side) would be primarily a naval struggle, concentrated in the Western Mediterranean, the Central and South Atlantic, and the waters along the African coastline of the two powers' burgeoning colonial holdings on that continent. For decades, the *Jejeune Ecole* had held sway in French naval circles. Adherents believed that control of the Channel could be contested by swarms of small boats; the French therefore had not attempted to match the capital shipbuilding program of Great Britain. Further afield, French naval presence had depended largely on cruisers to fight a commerce war against British shipping. Not until the Plan of 1889 did the French propose building a fleet of true blue-water battleships. Yet, the French did not propose any mutual obligation related to a war involving either party and Great Britain. While this omission meant Russia would be under no obligation to go to war with Great Britain (i.e., in Central Asia) should the British attack the French in some remote part of Africa, likewise the French would be under no obligation to take action against Great Britain should it attack Russia (e.g., in the Pamirs, the site of the most recent Central Asian affair). From this the Russians inferred—correctly—that the confidential military conventions that supplemented the publicly disclosed terms of the Franco–American Naval Convention of 1889 effectively assured the USA's support of France in any conflict with the British *except* when the French were obviously the aggressor. In that case, Washington would feel free to sit the conflict out unless vital American interests were best served by supporting the North's bellicose ally. (This was an "escape clause" common to all the alliances of the period, which were invariably cast in terms of aiding an ally who was the object of an attack but without defining with any precision what it meant to be the object of an attack.)

Not surprisingly, the French proposal proved a nonstarter in St. Petersburg. The Russians insisted that Great Britain must be added to the list of powers whose aggressions would trigger the obligation of mutual support. Moreover, the Russians also insisted that the talks be adjourned until a representative of the USA could join the discussions. The Russians were determined to insure that any alliance with France stood on equal footing with France's engagements with the Americans; if that meant entering into an alliance that included the USA, St. Petersburg was prepared to do just that. Boisdeffre therefore returned to Paris at the end of August and reported that the Russians had rejected France's proposal for a *petite entente*, but they had also indicated they were prepared to try and reach agreement on a *grande alliance* that would join Russia, France, the USA, and possibly Spain. Although the Russians had incorporated the mutual support provisions of the French memorandum in their counterproposal, they added an equivalent obligation in the event of an attack by Great Britain ("alone or in concert with any other power") on any alliance member. By these changes, St. Petersburg effectively proposed to shift the strategic focus from Germany to Great Britain. Yet, while each of the proposed members had interests in conflict with the British, none of those interests overlapped as did Russian and French interests in the case of Germany, a neighbor with whom each shared a border. As the veteran statesman Charles de Freycinet, then serving as Minister of War, put the matter, "If Russia has its way, we will all end up at war with the British Empire because of some godforsaken Afghani watering hole!" (One wonders if Freycinet gave any thought to this remark in October 1898, when—once again at the head of the French government—he made the decision to go to war over the outpost of Fashoda, surely as "godforsaken" a Sudanese outpost as any Afghan oasis.)

Despite their concerns, the French agreed that the parties should continue their dialogue, and that the USA should join the discussions as a potential participant in a Franco–Russian *entente*. Because General Miles, the USA's Chief of General Staff, had been in attendance at the Narva Talks, Premier Emile Loubet (at the urging of Freycinet) addressed a personal request to USA President Schofield that Miles be appointed to represent American interests when the talks next resumed. Schofield, who was in the final stages of a successful reelection campaign, referred the matter to Secretary of State John Hay and Secretary of War Robert Gould Shaw. Schofield requested that they, in consultation with Miles and the heads of the individual services, analyze the question of whether the USA should consider joining in a Franco–Russian alliance that would commit the North to war in the event of attacks by either Great Britain, Germany, or a member of the Triple Alliance of which Germany was a part, on either France or Russia. But before Hay and Shaw could do more than develop a timeline for the completion of so vital a study, the strategic picture was dramatically altered by the introduction in the German Reichstag of Tirpitz's proposed Naval Law (which the reader will recall was unveiled on November 30, 1892). The news that Germany intended to become a major naval power—and before the end of the century—broke upon the governments of all the major powers in Europe and the Americas like a thunderclap from a clear blue sky. Every cabinet room heard the same questions debated: Why did Germany seek a "blue water" battle fleet? Would the Reichstag even go along? And if it did, against whom would the new fleet be directed?

The answers to these questions were not long in coming. The Naval Law passed the Reichstag in March of 1893. But even before then, word leaked that Count Paul von Hatzfeldt, Germany's Ambassador to the Court of St. James, had been engaged in a series of talks with Prime Minister Salisbury and Colonial Secretary Joseph Chamberlain. (When the Conservatives won reelection in 1892 in alliance with the Liberal Unionists, Chamberlain accepted Salisbury's invitation to enter the new "Unionist" government and specifically requested the Colonial Office instead of the more prestigious Treasury; the choice created the "working partnership" on foreign policy between Salisbury and Chamberlain which would cement their relationship and position Chamberlain to succeed Salisbury as Prime Minister in 1901.) In these discussions, the Germans were remarkably frank—a reflection of the fact that all of the key actors in the German government (the Kaiser, Chancellor Caprivi, Tirpitz, and the influential Holstein) were united in their goal. On the one hand, the German leadership was seized by the notion of *Weltmacht*—Germany must have it, and the new battle fleet was essential if Germany were to have it. If the pursuit of *Weltmacht* by means of a "blue water" navy put Germany on a collision course with

England (the world's greatest sea power since Abukir Bay and Trafalgar, and still so even in the face of the USA's challenge), then Germany's leaders—especially Tirpitz—seemed willing to say, "So be it." But while these men declared themselves ready to "take on the English," they actually wanted the English to join them in an alliance that would merge German and English power. "We must have the Anglo–German Alliance," the Kaiser told Chancellor Caprivi in the winter of 1893, "because if Germany and England stand together, no power on earth would dare to challenge us."

As events would show, Wilhelm's estimate of the deterrent power of an Anglo–German alliance was too optimistic. But on the fundamental question of whether London and Berlin should join forces, Ambassador Hatzfeldt found a receptive audience—especially in his talks with Chamberlain. The reader will recall that Chamberlain had championed the Anglo–Confederate *entente*, and that he was instrumental in bringing about the signing of that engagement in April 1887. But Chamberlain became alarmed by the next few years' developments, which seemed to negate much of the benefit to "Imperial Security" that the relationship with the Confederacy had promised to achieve. The USA announced it would increase its already tremendous naval expansion program in order to nullify the effect of Anglo–Confederate naval cooperation; Chamberlain realized that the USA's industrial dynamism meant it could probably make good on its threat. Even worse was the Franco–American Naval Convention of 1889; although the public terms could be interpreted by the hopeful as limited and defensive, Chamberlain was convinced (correctly) that the inevitable secret military protocols probably meant the Royal Navy would have to deal with the French fleet in any war with the North Americans. Given the remarkable French military revival of the 1880s (which had benefited from the close, if informal, Franco–American military relationship dating back to the 1870s) and the announcement by the French Ministry of the Marine in 1890 that France would increase its oceangoing fleet by 50 percent within the next ten years, Chamberlain believed the Royal Navy would have grave difficulty in maintaining communications with Canada, while also preserving control of the Mediterranean and the sea passage along the African coasts, in the event of war with the USA and France. The parallel threat of an isolated India standing alone against Russia was equally chilling.

To those worries had then been added the cooling in Russo–German relations and the open secret of ensuing Russo–French military talks in the wake of such symbolically dramatic events as Tsar Alexander III's bare-headed *homage* to "Le Marseillaise." When the ever-troublesome Central Asian "fault-line" between Russia and the British Empire nearly triggered a break in relations and war over the Pamirs, Chamberlain became convinced that the Empire was moving into ever more threatening waters and that something must be done to reverse the trend—but what? Fundamentally, England needed a *naval* ally: one whose power on the high seas, when added to that of the Royal and Confederate navies, should deter the USA and its allies from any aggression. Going into 1892, neither Chamberlain nor Salisbury could see any candidate who might play the role. The Triple Alliance powers (Germany, Austria–Hungary, and Italy) each possessed naval power, but not even in combination could such a force be counted on to restore Great Britain's needed margin over the USA and France. Then came the November 1892 announcement of Germany's ambitious naval program, and suddenly Chamberlain saw the solution: an alliance with Germany, whose planned battle fleet of seventeen powerful battleships, of the latest design, should be sufficient to restore Britain's margin of safety well into the next century. It was Salisbury who asked the difficult follow-on question: "I quite agree with you that, under the circumstances, a closer relation with Germany would be very desirable. But how can we get it?" Almost too terrible to contemplate was the possibility that Germany would refuse to entertain such an alliance, because it wished to use its newfound naval power *against* England. If so, London would face an awful choice: acquiesce in the construction of a German Navy that upon completion would deprive Great Britain of security for the British Isles themselves or launch a preemptive strike against the new German force before it became a threat. ("I blanch at the idea of a second Copenhagen," Chamberlain wrote to Salisbury in December of 1892, "but I see no way to avoid that course if the Germans refuse to treat with us.")

It therefore came as a great relief when Ambassador Hatzfeldt arrived shortly after the New Year, carrying a memorandum from Chancellor Caprivi declaring that Germany wished its new navy to be a "complement" to British power and proposing the two countries enter into discussions on the question of Great Britain adhering to the Triple Alliance. Kaiser

Wilhelm simultaneously wrote to his "dear Grandma," Queen Victoria, declaring (in the Kaiser's typically effusive style) that it was Germany's "fervent wish—as I have expressed to you so many times before—to re-forge the iron links that bound German and Englishman together, as in the great days of Wellington and Blucher." Chamberlain seized upon the German proposals with an enthusiasm bordering on ferocity and urged Salisbury to proceed immediately to issue an "acceptance in principle" of the goal of an Anglo–German naval *entente*. While Salisbury felt compelled to rein in his more impulsive colleague ("We really ought to find out if this alliance will bind us to make war because of some ridiculous sideshow"), the Prime Minister agreed that Berlin should be given a positive response. "We welcome the invitation to a productive dialogue," Salisbury wrote to Chancellor Caprivi, in proposing the two countries appoint a working group of civilian and military representatives who would initiate a series of discussions, starting in London that February with meetings alternating thereafter between the German and British capital cities. Salisbury also suggested that a representative of the Confederacy be invited, "in view of the maritime focus of the discussions and our existing naval arrangements with that power"; the Prime Minister's failure to mention any representation of Austria–Hungary or Italy was intended as a veiled hint that Great Britain was not prepared to become a member of the "Triplice."

The narrative has now reached one of those points in history, where sorting out cause and effect becomes a well-nigh hopeless task, because the participants are acting parallel to one another, and each move on one side of the divide influences the actions of those on the other side. This was precisely what now ensued among the interested Great Powers—France, Russia, and the USA on the one hand, and Germany, Great Britain, and the Confederacy on the other. By the spring of 1893, Germany had announced its determination to become a "Blue Water" naval power of the first rank; the Germans and British (along with the Confederacy) were known to be engaged in discussions, believed by most observers to concern a possible Anglo–German–Confederate naval alliance (and perhaps even a British association with the Triple Alliance); *and* France and Russia were also engaged in military talks of an undisclosed nature, but at a time when Russo–German relations had markedly cooled while Russo–French relations had (remarkably) warmed.

To each of these actors, their own conduct was seen as primarily reactive to the threatening actions of other powers with whom they had come to be in conflict over vital interests. In fact, these powers' interests were in conflict—and over matters that were vital to each. But that fundamental fact notwith-standing, it would be futile to try to extract a single moving cause among the tangled interplay that ensued, beginning in the spring of 1893. Instead, I will try and identify the various events that constituted the material and interac-tive elements, beginning with two developments in Germany.

One is already familiar: the passage by the Reichstag of Tirpitz's Naval law in March of 1893. Although themselves quickly rendered obsolete by the relentless march of naval technological advance, the battleships built pursuant to this law, starting with the *Brandenburg* class, were as far advanced from Secession War-era monitors and ironclads as the origi-nal USS *Monitor* was from HMS *Victory*. Compound nickel-steel armor replaced wrought iron; rifled eleven-inch breach-loading guns replaced smoothbore muzzle-loaders; and speeds of 15 knots all made these ships notable and, above all, *destabilizing*. The second development was also a military measure—an Army Bill that passed the Reichstag that July 16 over the opposition of the Social Democrats (who condemned what they called the "double militarism" of the government in the wake of the earlier pas-sage of Tirpitz's naval program). Under the bill, the army's peacetime size would increase by seventy-two thousand, and a new system of reserve rein-forcements would make it possible for Germany to mobilize on very short order a force of 520,000 men. The adoption of these measures alarmed the French—just as the USA delegation headed by Chief of General Staff Miles arrived for consultations prior to the first scheduled meeting of the two allies with Russian representatives. The announcement of Tirpitz's Naval Law, its subsequent passage in March, and the reports of high-level dis-cussions ensuing between Germany and Great Britain had persuaded Hay and Shaw of the need at least to respond affirmatively to the Russo–French invitation; that April, they recommended (and President Schofield agreed) that the USA would send a delegation, to be headed by the Chief of the General Staff. The French, especially distressed by the Army Bill with its disturbing implications for the course of any future battles in Alsace and Lorraine and therefore all the more eager to finalize a deal, now proposed to the American delegation that France and the USA be prepared to accede to Russian demands for a commitment to intervention in the event of a British attack on Russia (in other words, that the allies be prepared to support Russian interests in Central Asia).

The Americans initially were wary—their instructions were to avoid committing the USA to supporting Russia in Central Asia, unless the Russians would commit to reciprocal action in the event of British intervention in support of the Confederacy in a conflict between North and South. But when the French warned that the combination of an Anglo–German naval accord, plus an increase in the initial striking power of the German Army, would (certainly by the time of the completion of the German battle fleet) force the French on the maritime defensive in any war because of the need to commit substantial forces for Atlantic coast defense to guard against Anglo–German raids and to retain a larger Mediterranean fleet to cope with a British force that would no longer be depleted by Canadian supply line defense due to German assistance in the North Atlantic, Chief of Staff Miles cabled the War Department, urging authorization to endorse the proposed French approach to St. Petersburg. Although Secretary of State Hay was still wary (noting that an Anglo–German agreement remained only hypothetical), Secretary of War Shaw concurred in Miles's recommendation. Shaw also received the enthusiastic support of Theodore Roosevelt, who had been appointed Assistant Secretary of the Navy that January. "An alliance with the Russians will, at a stroke, transform the Kaiser's planned fleet from a weapon of attack aimed at our coast to one of defense, forced to stand guard against a Baltic Fleet breakout. Our vital interests compel us to seize this opportunity," Roosevelt wrote to Shaw in a memorandum which the War Secretary endorsed and passed along to President Schofield. On September 15, Miles received his new instructions: "Proceed in accordance with General Boisdeffre's proposal for a joint Franco–American approach to St. Petersburg."

Of course, Secretary of State Hay was correct: Great Britain and Germany had not announced the formation of an Anglo–German *entente*. Moreover, Anglo–German discussions had become entangled in the scope of any association, with the Germans pressing for, and the British resisting,

Great Britain's full entry into the Triple Alliance. This dispute had been exacerbated by the participation of the Confederacy, which welcomed the idea of an Anglo–German–Confederate naval alliance but had no desire to risk a war over some Austro–Russian Balkan *contretemps*. But events in two widely separated locations, both far from Europe, now helped to break this impasse. First, in Central Asia, the British again confronted the Russians— and yet again in the Pamirs. Russian forces had occupied Botai Gumbat, a flash point in the Pamir crisis of two years before. Worse, the Russian move came as the strategic kingdom of Chitral was plunged into chaos by the death of its aged ruler. Although the Russian Foreign Ministry uttered soothing words, the St. Petersburg press (known to serve as a mouthpiece for the War Ministry) urged Chitral be taken under the Tsar's "protection." Given the Russian tendency to promise one thing and then do another, this latest episode persuaded Salisbury that another effort must be made to reach an agreement with Germany—although Salisbury still insisted, supported by the Confederacy, that membership in the Triple Alliance was out of the question. The issue thus became whether Germany would yield on this point. In fact, none of the key actors in the German leadership were strongly committed to requiring any Anglo–German–Confederate *entente* be conducted within the structure of the Triple Alliance; it was principally pressure from Vienna that had caused Berlin to take that position. Now, developments in the mid-Pacific convinced Kaiser Wilhelm II and Tirpitz that Austria's desires would have to be subordinated to the pursuit of German *Weltmacht*.

I refer to the annexation of Hawaii by the USA, which unfolded beginning with the coup that overthrew the Hawaiian monarchy that January and ended with the ratification of the annexation treaty by the USA Senate in June. For several years, the Pacific had been a source of tension between the USA, Great Britain, and Germany, as each country sought to establish coaling stations for merchant and navy vessels; to this had been added increasing Confederate interest in the Philippines, exemplified by attempts to develop a presence through commercial penetration. Both Confederate and Brazilian entrepreneurs saw the still-Spanish Philippines as an ideal place to which to extend their "joint venture" slave economy, and the Brazilians were active participants in the effort to develop a foothold in the local economy. In March of 1889, the competition for coaling stations nearly triggered a war between the USA and Germany over the Samoan islands (which both powers claimed, as did Great Britain). Only the timely fortuity of a typhoon, which compelled the would-be combatants to join forces in a struggle against the violence of nature, avoided a battle between the American and German squadrons. Although the Samoan Crisis was then defused by a treaty that divided up the islands among the three powers, the competition for Pacific advantage continued as each country staked its claim. Central to the American position was the Kingdom of Hawaii. American missionaries came to the Hawaiian Islands in the early nineteenth century; they were followed by other Americans who developed the sugar plantations that boomed when the War of Secession cut off Southern supplies to the North.

The development of the American cultural and economic presence was paralleled in the diplomatic and military sphere. In 1842, President Tyler presumed to extend the Monroe Doctrine to Hawaii. In 1867, the USA acquired Midway Island (one thousand miles to the west) and began developing the interest in Samoa which would lead to the clash with Germany in 1889. Neither Midway nor Samoa, however, proved suitable for a major naval anchorage; on the other hand, Pearl Harbor on the Hawaiian island of Oahu was ideally suited for a navy base, and the Americans employed their political and economic dominance to acquire the site (by lease) in 1880. With the formation of the Anglo–Confederate alliance in 1887 and the growing Confederate interest in the Philippines, Pearl Harbor began to assume immediate strategic significance as a forward base to support the USA's ally, Spain, in its Far Eastern possessions (which included the Marianas Island chain, lying to the east of the Philippines). In 1889, Washington announced the posting to Cavite Bay in the Philippines of an "Asiatic Fleet" (of two battleships and four armored cruisers) and a program to transform Pearl Harbor into a first-class base capable of supporting a "Pacific fleet" several times that size. The posting to the Philippines was at the express invitation of the Spanish government; the Hawaiian government, however, learned of the planned expansion of Pearl Harbor after it had been announced in the American press. King Kalakaua made no public response; the King had been stripped of most authority by a veritable "planters' coup" in 1887, which had left him psychologically and politically defeated. (Although devoted to the cause of Hawaiian nationalism, Kalakaua considered further resistance to American power a useless gesture.) But Kalakaua's sister, Liliuokalani, issued a vehement protest against the Pearl Harbor decision, and its strident condemnation of "American arrogance" coupled with a call to "force a reconsideration of the Hawaiian–American relationship," alarmed Washington—which, quite rightly, feared the King might abdicate in favor of his sister.

In 1891, those fears were realized: Kalakaua abdicated, and Liliuokalani became queen. The planter community, led by Sanford Dole, was ruthlessly dedicated to their collective interest, and they reacted to Liliuokalani's ascension to the throne with a virtual fit of apoplexy. The planters supported the American military presence because that was the price Hawaii had paid under the Reciprocity Treaty to assure duty-free access to the USA for Hawaiian sugar. Now, Dole and the other leading planters feared the new queen was willing to sacrifice their interests, if necessary, to serve the cause of Hawaiian nationalism; they therefore began to conspire at the overthrow of the monarchy and the annexation of the Kingdom by the USA. Discreet contacts with the Schofield Administration confirmed the planters' beliefs that Washington shared their concerns about Liliuokalani and also suggested that the American government would react positively to a call by "the Hawaiian people" for annexation to the USA. The Queen soon provided the excuse for a "revolution" when the planters learned she was secretly preparing a new constitution that would restrict the vote to "true" (i.e., Polynesian) Hawaiians. On January 17, 1893, the planters' "Committee of Safety"— with the assistance of the American minister and several companies of USA Marines—overthrew the royal government. Expecting such a move (although uncertain of the precise timing), the Schofield Administration welcomed the Committee's call for the "joinder" of Hawaii to the USA. A treaty of annexation (secretly drafted several months before) was submitted to the Senate; a Democratic filibuster caused only a few weeks' delay, and the treaty was ratified in June.

This news proved to be what the British needed to persuade the Germans to decouple the proposed Anglo–German–Confederate naval convention from Germany's Triple Alliance with Austria–Hungary and Italy. The Germans had established contacts with Queen Liliuokalani, and the German minister's wildly optimistic reports had caused Berlin to hope that the Americans might soon be forced to withdraw from their Pearl Harbor anchorage—with German Navy ships invited to take their place. Consequently, the Queen's fall and the USA's annexation of the Islands proved a double blow: German naval planning for the Far East and the Pacific would now have to account for an American Hawaiian presence, which might even be supplemented by basing ships on outlying islands (e.g., off Lahaina on Maui). Tirpitz was particularly disturbed by this news, as he believed a strong German naval presence in the Pacific was vital to the establishment of Germany as a world power. The German Naval and Army ministries were also concerned about the potential threat a strengthened American naval presence in the Pacific might pose to Germany's developing ties with Chile—about which, more later. Tirpitz therefore urged the Kaiser to abandon linkage between the Triple Alliance and an Anglo–German naval convention and "meet England halfway: She needs us in the Atlantic, and we need her in the Pacific—and as for the Austrians and Italians, they need us everywhere." (As the reader will see, Tirpitz would be proven right in every respect, although Italy would learn that lesson the brutal hard way. Angered by Germany's failure to gain British adherence to the Triplice, Rome would repudiate its obligations and sit out World War One as a neutral, then switch sides and join the Franco–American alliance in a bid for a Mediterranean empire—choices that would have disastrous consequences for the Italian people.)

The Kaiser agreed with Tirpitz, and once the issue of the "Triplice" had been removed from the table, the negotiations proceeded rapidly to their conclusion. On September 7, 1893, representatives of Germany, the British Empire, and the Confederacy issued a joint communiqué in London, announcing that the three powers had entered into a "cooperative agreement" to secure "the freedom of the seas in time of war." And with the public declaration of the Anglo–German–Confederate alliance, events now moved swiftly to resolution on the opposite side of the emerging international political divide. For the Tsar, the Anglo–German announcement was the final blow that convinced him that Russia's relations with Germany had been so utterly smashed they could not possibly be repaired. The adoption of the Army Bill by the Reichstag would also now be given the most sinister interpretation; the USA's annexation of Hawaii, on the other hand, now demonstrated a welcome ruthlessness on the part of a prospective ally. Alexander's decision in favor of a Russo–Franco–American alliance was reinforced by the enthusiastic receptions recently given Russian naval squadrons on separate visits to San Francisco and Toulon—the latter: the French Navy's principal Mediterranean anchorage—as well as the genuine enthusiasm with which the Tsar was received on board the flagship of a French flotilla that paid a special call at Copenhagen during the Tsar's annual summer vacation with his relations, the King and Queen of Denmark. And as Alexander was finally resolving in favor of an alliance with France and the USA, the Schofield Administration had concluded that the Anglo–German–Confederate alliance required the USA to enter into a "responsive association" (in Secretary of State Hay's words) with France and Russia.

As for France, although its leaders had expressed doubts about going to war over some remote contested outpost in Central Asia, the passage of the German Army Bill in July had convinced the doubters that France's vital interest required entry into an alliance with Russia and the USA. Moreover, the civilian leadership of the Third Republic had already seen how aggressive international "alliance politics," with its attendant increased flow of resources to the military, helped strengthen the ties between the republic and the officer corps. The entry into force of the Franco–American alliance (in January 1889) had helped defuse the threat then posed by the populist former General Ernest Boulanger by demonstrating the Republic's militarist *bona fides* to the army and navy leadership and thereby neutralizing the danger of support for a Boulangist *coup d'etat*. Thus, Premier Emile Loubet and his cabinet enthusiastically greeted the messages from Washington and St. Petersburg indicating that each now concurred in the scope of the alliance as previously had been under discussion when the Paris talks last adjourned. On January 4, 1894, representatives of France, the USA, and the Russian Empire issued a joint communiqué in Paris, announcing to the world the formation of an "association" for the "preservation of the peace of the world and the protection of the vital interests" of the signatories. The agreement was ratified by the USA Senate that spring—albeit over the vigorous opposition of some members of the Democratic minority.

And so, two hostile groupings of the great nations of the world now stood confronting each other. Each was publicly a creation of its members to assure the common defense while preserving world peace. Both abjured any intimation that their respective formation was the product of anything but the most understandable and defensive of motives—but also implied that the same could not be said of their counterpart. Whatever the truth of these pious pronouncements (and as a former American President, I know how men of power can convince themselves that they act only out of the best motives), what would matter to the future of humanity was the way in which these alliances would affect the behavior of their members. Henceforth, the act of each member of one grouping would be scrutinized by every member of the other grouping on the assumption that, whatever the act, it must be aimed at undermining some vital interest of the opposing alliance. And within a little more than four years, and for precisely such reasons, the members of these two alliances—publicly formed to preserve the peace—would be at each other's throats in a world war that would bring death and destruction to millions.

Could the choices of 1893 and 1894 have been avoided? Could the consequences of those choices have been avoided? If by these questions one asks if the formation of the Great Alliances in 1893 could have been avoided and thereby the outbreak of World War One in 1898 have been avoided, my answer would be—yes, but only by postponing what was rapidly becoming, by the convergence of a series of events (some small, but many large) the closest thing there is to a historical inevitability. If Kaiser Frederick III, Wilhelm's father and a very different man, had not been afflicted with cancer; or if then-Captain Alfred Tirpitz had been killed while on a torpedo boat patrol in a North Sea storm—the odds of Germany choosing in 1893 to pursue *Weltmacht* on the bridge of a "blue water" battle fleet could have been decisively reduced. In turn, had Germany not decided to put to sea—then, Great Britain likely would not have entered into the discussions that produced the Anglo–German–Confederate naval convention. Or, to choose another path, had Wilhelm II and Bismarck managed to establish a positive working relationship, Germany would have renewed the Reinsurance Treaty with Russia, and Tsar Alexander III would almost certainly have rejected the advice of those in his military who favored a break with Germany and an alliance with France—and perhaps the USA as well.

In short, the outcome of the events that culminated in the creation of the Alliance System by the mid-1890s—like all particular historical outcomes—was partly the result of a conjunction of personalities and accidents that, if altered in any material particular, could have happened otherwise. And if the Alliances had not come together by 1894, then the Crisis Year of 1898 might have seen a different outcome: with different choices made over the Yukon, Central Asia, and the Sudan, and a world war thereby avoided—but for how long?

By the 1890s, the fundamental problem was rooted in the structure of interstate relations, which had placed the vital interests of two Great Powers—the USA and Great Britain—on a collision course. The conflict between the USA and the Confederacy was genuine, profound, and enduring; that conflict, in turn, eroded the foundation upon which any peaceful relationship between the USA and the British Empire had to rest. Once those foundations were recognized to have been fatally compromised, both parties were bound to seek to protect their affected interests by military means. The effects of those choices, however, could not be confined to the Western Hemisphere—not in the age of oceangoing, steam-powered steel warships. The result was the Anglo–Confederate *entente*, which produced the Franco–American naval convention in response. And once this political and military dynamic was set in motion, I submit it was only a question of how and when—not whether—the other Great Powers would be drawn in, with disastrous consequences for the well-being of the world.

(left) USA Navy Rear Admiral Alfred Mahan, whose book "The Influence of Sea Power Upon History" made the young and impressionable German Kaiser Wilhelm II determined to transform Germany into a world naval power, if possible in alliance with the Royal Navy he had admired from childhood.

(right) Grand Admiral of the *Kaiserliche Marine* Alfred von Tirpitz, who carried out Wilhelm II's plan to build a German bluewater fleet, and also agreed that Germany make Great Britain the offer of a naval alliance which he knew London could not refuse in the face of the growing Franco-American naval threat.

13

THE RUSSO-JAPANESE CRISIS OF 1895: EXPANSION OF THE GLOBAL ALLIANCE SYSTEM IN THE FAR EAST

The confrontation between Japan and Russia in the wake of Japan's crushing victory over Imperial Manchu China in the Sino–Japanese War of 1894–95, illustrates how the critics of the decisions taken in the summer and fall of 1893 err in describing those choices as the root cause of our century's tragic history. For if different voices had been heeded and the formation of the two Great Alliances postponed, the events of 1894–95 in the Far East could easily (and, I submit, probably would) have proved a sufficient, substitute catalyst.

In the event, the decisions had already been taken by the time Russia and Japan confronted each other, as Russia sought to deny Japan the fruits of its battlefield victory over the tottering Manchu Dynasty. Thus, instead of providing the catalyst for the formation of the two Great Alliances, the Russo–Japanese confrontation would prove significant for other reasons. First, at its end, the Alliance System would be extended to Northeast Asia by the alignment of Japan along the Anglo–German–Confederate axis. Second, the events of 1895 would also show how dangerous a place the Alliance System had made the world: although world war was avoided, peace was preserved by the barest of margins and only at the cost of an increase in the antagonism felt by each bloc toward the other and in an acceleration of the preparations for war already well under way on both sides—thereby helping to set the stage for the Crisis Year of 1898 and the outbreak of World War One.

By the 1890s, Russia and Japan were on a collision course due to their irreconcilable ambitions in China and over China's traditional vassal, the

Kingdom of Korea. Russian ambitions in the territory ruled by the Manchu centered on their homeland of Manchuria and dated back to the mid-1600s (virtually contemporaneous with the Manchus' overthrow of the Ming and conquest of Han China in 1644). In 1658, the newly established Manchu court in Peking dispatched a force to oust Cossack bands that had recently appeared in the Amur River Basin separating Siberia from Manchuria. The Russians were routed—only to return in 1685—prompting the Emperor K'ang-hsi to send an army of fifteen thousand men (equipped with over two hundred cannon) to deal with the intruders. The Manchu were again victorious, but the Russians promptly regrouped and returned, necessitating yet another expedition to drive them away. This bloody cycle might have gone on for many years except that neither Russia nor the Manchu could afford the luxury of a border war. Peter the Great faced a deadly challenge from Sweden in the Baltic, while the Manchus were still in the process of consolidating their rule over all China (and particularly feared that the Russians might ally with the nomadic Zunghar tribesmen, who had seized control of much of Outer Mongolia). In 1689, the two empires entered into the Treaty of Nerchinsk: The Amur River would define the border between Russia and the Manchu home province of Manchuria, and trade would be permitted to those merchants granted licenses by Peking. Most notably, the Manchus granted Russia the singular honor of treatment as a coequal sovereign state; dealings with the Russians were conducted through a special bureau—rather than through the Ministry of Rituals which handled the so-called tributary relations with countries such as Holland, Spain, and Portugal.

With the signing of the Treaty of Nerchinsk, Sino–Russian relations were established on terms that would remain fairly stable until the mid-nineteenth century. Sino–Japanese relations enjoyed an even longer period of stability, although for very different reasons. In 1592, the great peasant general Toyotomi Hideyoshi, after vanquishing his opponents and unifying the country's warring samurai clans, led his superbly trained and equipped army in a campaign to conquer China (then ruled by the Ming). Landing at Pusan in southeastern Korea, Hideyoshi's army of over one hundred thousand men surged up the Korean peninsula, capturing Seoul within three weeks of the Pusan landings. But when the Japanese took

Pyongyang, and stood only eighty miles from the China–Korea border, they were met by a Ming army of over two hundred thousand. Although the Chinese lacked muskets, they still forced an exhausted (and depleted) Japanese army to withdraw to the south. For the next six years, the war raged over the peninsula,until Hideyoshi—his attempts to reinforce frustrated by Korea's ironclad "turtleboats," which Japan's wooden warships could not match—acknowledged he could not break the resulting stalemate. In 1598, the Japanese withdrew, leaving a devastated Korea and a Ming China so drained by the war that it would soon become easy prey for the rapacious Manchus.

The Japanese, however, would not attempt to take advantage of the final crisis of the Ming Dynasty. For at the very moment that the Ming entered the last stages of decay—with the rebellions led by Li Tzu-ch'eng and Chang Hsien-chung in the 1630s—Hideyoshi's successor, the "Shogun" Ieyasu Tokugawa, had reached the decision to close Japan off to the outside world. For the next two hundred years (until the arrival in 1853 of the "Black Ships" of the United States commanded by Commodore Matthew C. Perry), Japan took no interest in the rest of the world, including China. Perry's arrival, however, brought on a *crise de regime* for Tokugawa Japan, which resolved itself in dramatic fashion by 1868: the Shogunate was overthrown, the reactionary Emperor Komei was poisoned, and the new Emperor Meiji agreed to preside over a dramatic program of modernization aimed at giving Japan the means of avoiding the fate of Asia's other ancient cultures at the hands of the "barbarian" West. Above all, the new Japanese leadership had been spurred to action by the dreadful example of China; by 1868, the Manchu Empire was in an advanced state of decay, and the Great Powers of Europe had already begun the process of piecemeal dismemberment which would end within just a few decades with the overthrow of the Manchus and the outright partition of the Middle Kingdom. Japan had determined to avoid such a fate—but, true to the aggressive tradition of Hideyoshi, Japan was also determined to share in the spoils when the tottering Manchu edifice finally collapsed.

It was this ambition that put Russia and Japan on a collision course. For as Japan revived its dream of overlordship over China (at the very least, over the Korean peninsula and the Northeastern provinces as far south as the Shantung Peninsula), Russia revived its ambitions to control Manchuria, including an ice-free port located on either the Korean or Liaotung peninsula. Thus, each country came to covet territory sought by the other; only if one elected to abandon its ambitions could a collision be avoided, and by the 1890s, there was no chance of either nation doing that. The stage therefore was set for a Russo–Japanese clash, which awaited only the inevitable triggering event.

That event proved to be a war between Manchu China and Japan which broke out in July of 1894. Korea lay at the center of the conflict—as it had the last time China and Japan had gone to war, three hundred years earlier. From the start of Japan's modernization program under the Emperor Meiji, Korea was an object of revived expansionist ambition and a spur to reformist efforts aimed at giving Japan the capacity to achieve that ambition. In the early 1870s, the Korean government had repeatedly refused to recognize the Restoration regime of the Emperor Meiji, but the Japanese government quashed calls for a retaliatory armed assault: Japan's armed forces were woefully unprepared to attempt the subjugation of Korea, and failure could expose Japan and Korea to intervention by the European powers. But after the suppression of the last samurai rebellion in 1877, the Japanese could forge ahead with an ambitious program of military modernization, designed to give the country an army (and navy) capable of projecting Japanese power onto the Asian mainland—i.e., into Korea; and after Korea, into Manchu China.

Although the Japanese initially hired French advisors for their new army, the Confederate victory over Spain in 1870, coupled with the Prussians' triumph in the decisive frontier battles of the Franco–Prussian War later that year, prompted Japan's army leadership to switch to the victors. The Japanese adopted the Prussian General Staff model and a combination of Prussian and Confederate artillery and infantry tactics (the Japanese found the offensive sensibility of the Confederates, inculcated by Jackson and Pelham, culturally apt). In the meanwhile, the nascent Japanese Navy had hired British advisors, which led to the Japanese naval hierarchy developing close ties to the Royal Navy and Great Britain, just as the Army developed a sense of identity with Germany and the Confederacy. While this modernization program proceeded, Japan signed a treaty with

Korea under which Korea recognized the post-Tokugawa Meiji regime and granted Japan access to several Korean ports. This seemingly constructive resolution of the initial post-Tokugawa crisis in Japanese–Korean relations, however, was marred by the Japanese method of choice to "persuade" the Koreans to enter into normal diplomatic relations with Japan: the dispatch of an over-awing naval force. In fact, a majority of Korean society opposed the treaty, and it was probably accepted only because King Kojong and Queen Min could see no other way to acquire access to Western technology without running the additional risk of opening up the country to the Western powers themselves.

Young Koreans now flocked to Japan for education, and upon returning to Korea, they agitated for modernization. Although the King and Queen favored some reform, they were opposed by the traditionalist upper classes whose leader, the "Taewon-gun," had served several years as regent and still retained great influence behind the scenes. In July 1882, the Taewon-gun organized riots in which Japanese nationals were murdered, and the Japanese minister was forced to flee Seoul. The resort to mob violence backfired. The Manchus intervened to restore order, several rebel leaders were executed, the Taewon-gun was forced into exile, and the Japanese returned with a substantially reinforced military presence. Peking now resolved to check the growing Japanese (and European) influence in Korea by formally re-subordinating the country as a tributary vassal. In response, Japan encouraged a *coup d'etat* by pro-Japanese "reformers." In December 1884, this group attacked the palace, captured King Kojong, and announced their intention to implement a program of internal reforms—in "close cooperation" with Japan. The Chinese forces in Seoul, however, recaptured the palace; riots ensued, Chinese and Japanese forces in Korea confronted each other, and war would probably have been the result had not both powers realized that a war over Korea was not (yet) in either of their interests. Japan knew its armed forces were not ready to sustain operations on the Korean peninsula, while China could not risk war with Japan because of a crisis with France over French claims to Annam, which the Manchus also claimed as a tributary vassal. (While Peking and Tokyo managed to reach a negotiated solution to their Korean dispute, China and France ended up fighting a short, if undeclared, war, in which the French destroyed the Manchus' southern naval forces while they rode at anchor in Foochow harbor; in the end, the Manchus had to acknowledge, at least *de facto*, their loss of suzerainty over Annam.)

Under the terms of the Treaty of Tientsin, entered into by China and Japan in 1885, both countries agreed to withdraw their forces, give advance notice of any intention to send troops back into Korea, and affirmed their support of Korean "independence." China, by retaining its prerogative to appoint a Manchu regent (the commander of the local Chinese forces, Yüan Shih-kai), gained the political upper hand—an advantage conceded by Tokyo only because surveys carried out by the General Staff showed the Imperial Army was not yet strong enough to oust the Manchus by force. For precisely that reason, Japan's military was able to persuade the government to increase even further the flow of resources to the country's army and navy. Moreover, the military and their civilian supporters could also legitimately invoke a growing "Russian threat" to Japan's interests in Korea (and Japanese long-range ambitions in Manchuria and the balance of northeastern China). When defeat by the British in the Opium War (followed by near-overthrow at the hands of the Taiping) confirmed the Manchus to be in a state of advanced decay, Russia had moved quickly to resume its seventeenth-century ambitions toward Manchuria and its adjacent territories. Taking advantage of the punitive expedition by the Western Powers against Peking in 1860, Russia compelled the vulnerable Manchus to yield all the territory east of the Ussuri to the Pacific Coast (including the site for Russia's future Far East naval center, Vladivostok). This acquisition extended Russian rule to the northern border of Korea, and soon, voices were being raised in St. Petersburg urging the acquisition of an ice-free port: either in Korea or at the southern tip of the Liaotung peninsula, in Manchurian territory immediately to the west. Vladivostok might claim the title of "Ruler of the East," but its reign was limited by the ice packs that isolated it from the open sea during the depths of the Siberian Winter.

In 1883, Russia made a bid for a port in Korea. During the Sino–Japanese struggle for control, the Russians seized on an ostensible Korean invitation to become advisors to the Korean Army. In exchange for these services, Russia would receive an ice-free port to be named "Port Lazarev." This provoked immediate opposition from Great Britain, whose naval forces promptly occupied Port Hamilton (at the entrance to the Gulf of Korea), to compel Seoul to abrogate its agreement with St. Petersburg. Russia, recognizing it could not sustain its forces in a war with the British in the Far East, abandoned the Korean offer of "Port Lazarev." The British then withdrew from Port Hamilton. Russia, however, did not abandon its goal of an ice-free port in the Far East, and a new stage in the pursuit of this objective opened with the decision, in March of 1891, to build a railway across Siberia: from European Russia to Vladivostok. The brainchild of the future Minister of Finance and Prime Minister, Sergei Witte, the railway represented the means by which Russia would make possible its systematic economic penetration of Siberia and Manchuria, while providing the ability to reinforce that position militarily with forces from European Russia. Japan's military leaders had used the Russian bid for "Port Lazarev" in 1883 as a buttress for their case in favor of accelerated modernization of the Japanese armed forces. The announcement, eight years later, that Russia intended to build a railway linking its European heartland with the Far East, reinforced the determination of the Japanese military to give Japan the means to seize the very next opportunity to bring Korea firmly into the Japanese orbit—lest the Russians beat them to the prize.

By the 1890s, Japan's Army and Navy had made remarkable strides and would soon be ready to demonstrate that Japan had graduated into the first rank of the modern, industrialized military powers. The Army, in particular, had benefited from a program combining rigorous training and technical modernization under the tutelage of a brilliant Prussian Staff College instructor, Major Jacob Meckel, as well as a series of Confederate military missions, including one under Pelham himself. By 1890, its leaders—including General Aritomo Yamagata, the "father" of the modern Japanese army, who at various times served as Chief of Staff, Home Minister, and Prime Minister—believed the country's military was on the verge of being able to assert Japan's claim to its "line of advantage." The concept of the "line of advantage" originated with Yamagata, who that year publicly presumed to distinguish Japan's "line of sovereignty" (the border of territories it actually possessed) from the country's "line of advantage," which Yamagata defined as nearby territories whose fate could have a material effect on Japanese strength and safety. According to Yamagata, Japan's line of advantage embraced Korea. Friendly, the Korean peninsula was a buffer against invasion from the continent; in hostile hands, Korea became a dagger to Japan's heart. Yamagata feared that either China or Russia might seize the dagger's hilt. "In order to defend oneself by remaining stationary," Yamagata warned, "one must have enough strength to launch an attack." In other words, Yamagata believed Japan should launch an attack at the earliest opportunity to secure its line of advantage in Korea. And Yamagata believed the Japanese Army (and Navy) would soon be ready to do just that—as they had not been, in the confrontations with the Manchus in 1882 and 1884.

Given that China had acquired the upper hand in Korea under the 1885 Treaty of Tientsin, Yamagata's reasoning necessarily implied that it would be the Manchus, not Russia, whom Japan would have to fight to acquire control over Korea. In the event, the crisis came less than four years after Yamagata had proclaimed securing the Korean line of advantage as the goal of Japanese policy. An anti-foreign religious sect, the Tonghaks, had risen in revolt; although they sought the expulsion of all foreigners from Korea, they received the secret backing of Japanese ultra-nationalists who hoped the rebellion would bring China and Japan into armed conflict over the future of the peninsula. The Tonghaks were defeated by indigenous Korean forces, but their Japanese supporters had calculated correctly. Before its victory over the rebels, the Korean government had issued a call for help from Peking, which promised to send troops; in response, Japan invoked its right under the Treaty of Tientsin to send a corresponding force. Both forces arrived after the Tonghaks had been suppressed; therefore, each should have been withdrawn. The Japanese, however, saw this as the opportunity to seize the "line of advantage"—for it turned out that the Manchus had sent 1,200 men, while Japan had sent nearly six times that number. Included with the Japanese contingent was a battalion of field artillery manned by Japanese gunners but suffused with Confederate advisers. This unit was equipped with Tredegar–Krupp versions of the Krupp 9 cm C/73 *Feldkanone*, an 88 mm breach-loading weapon incorporating the lessons of the Franco–Prussian War. The increase in rate of fire made possible by breach-loading, combined with advanced metallurgy (reducing barrel failures) and contact fusing to greatly overmatch the Secession War-era artillery of the Chinese forces.

Thus fortified, instead of withdrawing, the Japanese demanded that the Korean government immediately agree to implement a program of reforms, including the express right of Japan (but not China) to maintain troops on Korean soil. When the Koreans rejected these proposals, Japanese troops—on July 23, 1894—seized the royal palace, and King Kojong was compelled to sign a decree expelling the Chinese and establishing a new cabinet favorable to the Japanese reform program.

The Manchus, anticipating this move, had already begun to reinforce their forces in Korea by sea, including the charter of a British registered ship, *Kowshing*. On July 24, *Kowshing* was intercepted by the British-built Japanese-protected cruiser *Naniwa*, under the command of Captain Heihachiro Togo. Four years later, Admiral Togo would be the victor over the Spanish–American squadrons at the Battles of Manila Bay and Cape Bolinao and would subsequently receive the enthusiastic cheers of Londoners at a postwar reception hosted by the Anglo–Japanese Friendship Society at the Royal Albert Hall. (Togo had been invited as a special guest to be honored during the centennial celebrations of the Battle of Trafalgar.) But on July 24, 1894, Togo nearly rendered himself *persona non grata* in the British Isles and also almost put paid the hopes of those in London and Tokyo who were already urging the establishment of an Anglo–Japanese naval alliance.

Togo signaled the (unarmed) *Kowshing* to follow him; the British captain agreed, but Chinese officers on board ordered the ship to sail on, threatening to kill the captain if he disobeyed. After several hours of negotiation, and fearing a Chinese naval flotilla might appear at any moment, Togo ordered the ship evacuated. When the order was ignored, the Japanese opened fire at point-blank range—over one thousand Chinese soldiers and sailors were lost. Togo did rescue the British captain and a few other Europeans—including a German artillery adviser to the Chinese!—all of whom reported that the Japanese had ruthlessly machine-gunned the Chinese who managed to make it into lifeboats, although some of these witnesses also stated that the Chinese still on the sinking ship had fired first. Besides giving China a first taste of the brutal violence about to descend upon—and all too soon rend—the Middle Kingdom, the *Kowshing* incident is also emblematic of the internationalization of the arms industry at the end of the last century. The Japanese cruiser, built at Newcastle-upon-Tyne by Armstrong, was armed with ten-inch Krupp naval guns. The hapless *Kowshing* had been escorted by Chinese warships built at Stettiner AG Vulcan (in Imperial Germany) but modeled after the British cruiser *Hotspur*. The *Kowshing* herself was owned by the Indochina Steam Navigation Company, a London-based subsidiary of Hong Kong's Jardine, Matheson & Co.

Eventually, a Japanese offer to have the matter adjudicated by a British court, as well as compelling *raison d'etat*—the impending entry of Japan into the Anglo–German–Confederate naval *entente*—would push this dubious action into the shadowed background of what would prove the career of Japan's greatest admiral. All that, however, lay in the future on July 24, 1894. Of more immediate significance, Togo's decisive action helped to prevent the Manchus from reinforcing their desperately weak position on the Korean peninsula. Four days later, Japanese troops attacked and dispersed Chinese forces guarding the entrance to Inchon Harbor. On August 1, Japan belatedly declared war on China. In fact, the Japanese leadership in Tokyo had hesitated out of concern that Japan might lose. Historians of the Sino–Japanese War of 1894–95 have often overlooked the fact that the Manchus had embarked on their own program of military modernization, parallel to Japan's. Under the vigorous leadership of Li Huang Chang, China had armed several hundred thousand troops with modern weapons. Ironically, in view of the close relationship between the Japanese army and Germany, Krupp was China's principal supplier of artillery. China had also purchased (largely from Germany) a navy *twice* as large as Japan's. Although the ensuing abysmal performance by Manchu land and naval forces would demonstrate the foolishness of equating mechanical measures of military strength with ability in battle, the Japanese could not be certain that would prove the case. To the contrary, Li's modernization efforts, on paper, were every bit as impressive as Japan's. Perhaps for that very reason, Yamagata himself had recently become pessimistic about Japan's chances in a head-on clash with China. But Yamagata's concerns were overridden by a combination of younger generals allied with Foreign Minister Munemitsu Mutsu (who also believed a victory over China would increase Japan's chances of becoming a "full partner" in any alliance with Great Britain, Germany, and the Confederacy).

In fact, China's modernization, however impressive on paper, proved woefully incomplete in the vital intangibles of training and command—as the key battles on land and sea soon demonstrated. Japan achieved mastery of Korea in just two days: On September 16, the Japanese captured the walled fortress city of Pyongyang; then on September 17, a Japanese squadron smashed China's northern fleet in the Battle of the Yalu River. In the latter engagement, fought near Port Arthur at the southern tip of the Liaotung peninsula, the Japanese used superior seamanship and gunnery to defeat a larger Chinese force of better armored vessels equipped with heavier caliber guns. The Chinese proved deficient in the quality of their crews and officers, losing six battleships while damaging only one Japanese cruiser. By October 9, the last Chinese troops had withdrawn from Korea. On October 24, the Japanese crossed the Yalu River and began their assault on Manchuria, concentrating on the Liaotung peninsula and its key port cities of Dairen and Port Arthur. Landing a force directly on the peninsula, the Japanese captured Dairen on November 6, then moved against Port Arthur. Although "Arthur" was defended by seventy heavy Krupp guns located in a network of concrete and steel forts, the Chinese defense collapsed in the face of a determined Japanese frontal assault, and the city fell on November 20.

The way to Peking itself now lay open, and the Japanese Army commanders (including Yamagata, who had insisted on a field command at the outbreak of the war and had rediscovered his enthusiasm for the venture in the process) wanted to march on the city through the Shanhaikuan Pass— the route the Manchus had taken to overthrow the Ming in 1644. But the civilian leadership in Tokyo feared the international political consequences of so aggressive a move and directed the military to instead invade the Shantung peninsula (lying southwest, across the Chilhi Strait from the Liaotung territory captured that November). In January 1895, a force of twenty thousand Japanese troops landed on the Shantung and moved against the fortified port of Weihaiwei, to which the balance of the Chinese fleet had retired after the disaster off Port Arthur the previous September. Seizing the fortifications from the landward side, the Japanese turned the guns on the Chinese fleet, sinking several capital ships. The Manchu court in Peking finally realized that China had been utterly defeated and sent

Li Huang-chang to Japan to sue for peace. Talks ensued in the port city of Shimonoseki that March, and Japan's terms proved harsh. Under the Treaty of Shimonoseki signed that April, China was to cede Formosa, the Pescadores Islands, and the Liaotung Peninsula; recognize the "autonomy and independence" of Korea; *and* pay an indemnity of $35 million. Moreover, Japan would be entitled to occupy the port of Weihaiwei until the indemnity was paid, thus giving it at least temporary control of the Chilhi Strait and the sea approaches to Tientsin, the gateway to Peking.

At this point, a regional war became transformed into an international flash point. Russia was appalled at the prospect of Japanese control over Korea, and the cession to Japan of the Liaotung. The specter of Japanese accession to the Anglo–Confederate–German alliance system confronted St. Petersburg with the prospect of hostile forces both in Austria–Prussia *and* along the Pacific Coast. Russian fears of encirclement by an alliance reaching from Lemberg through Louisiana to the Laiotung were given concrete form by the threat to the Tsar's plans for an ice-free outlet to the Pacific. The Russians had been on the verge of completing a treaty entitling them to extend the Trans-Siberian railroad's Manchurian spur down the Liaotung to Port Arthur, which the Russians also anticipated leasing from Peking; now, Russia faced the loss of any chance for an ice-free port in the Far East—either in Korea or Manchuria. Russia sought to enlist the support of the other Great Powers for an ultimatum that would compel Japan at least to give up the Liaotung Peninsula. The Russians discovered, however, that they could only count on the support of their fellow alliance members. Great Britain, Germany, and the Confederacy refused to countenance a major power intervention to deprive the Japanese of the fruits of their victory. For London, Berlin, and Richmond all saw in Japan a new power who could check Russian ambitions in the Far East and, in doing so, facilitate the advancement of their own. The Confederate Navy, already contemplating the possibilities of a Confederate Far East empire based on the Philippines, strongly supported preventing Russia's navy from extended Pacific operations. And the British Admiralty was especially keen to keep the Russian fleet out of either Dairen or Port Arthur, and the Sea Lords received Joseph Chamberlain's powerful support on this point; as Colonial Secretary with responsibility for safeguarding Britain's Chinese holdings, Chamberlain believed the decaying Manchu would eventually yield the Liaotung to Russia. "It is better to have a potential ally than a decided foe in possession of so strategic a point," Chamberlain advised Lord Salisbury, who also agreed that London and Berlin should respond positively to a Japanese proposal for talks among the three powers about "matters of mutual interest." Not even the attempted assassination of Manchu peace envoy Li, by a gun-wielding Japanese assailant, could budge the British, Confederates, and Germans from their refusal to intervene on Peking's behalf—although the Japanese avoided the possibility of real damage by quickly apologizing for what its Foreign Minister denounced as the act of an "obvious lunatic." (Worried that further actions by "loose-cannon" fanatics could prejudice impending negotiations with London and Berlin, Foreign Minister Mutsu and the Japanese commanders in Korea coordinated the implementation of extra security measures; these proved a wise precaution, as ultranationalists that October tried to murder Queen Min, whom they considered an implacable opponent of Japanese influence. The attack was foiled by a joint Japanese–Confederate special honor guard detail posted outside the royal palace pursuant to Mutsu's security directive.)

Once St. Petersburg recognized that it could not organize a "Quadruple Intervention" against Japan by the four European powers with the most substantial interests in China (France was the fourth, and Paris supported its Russian ally), the new Tsar Nicholas II and his advisors had to settle for condemning what they called a "brutal and unjust peace." They did so not without first engaging in some naval "saber-rattling" that produced an international war scare: At one point the Russians put their Far Eastern fleet on twenty-four-hours' notice to be prepared to steam south, but the Japanese coolly refused to respond when news of the move leaked out— and when the British and Germans then put their Far East forces on alert (joined by a squadron of Confederate cruisers paying a call to Singapore), St. Petersburg backed down, realizing it was still in no position to wage war against Japan, notwithstanding the initiation of the Trans-Siberian railway project. Russia persuaded France, the USA, and Spain to join it in condemning "Japanese aggression." Just what the "Condemning Powers"—as they came to be known in Japan—hoped to achieve by this remonstration is unclear. In fact, all they accomplished was to hasten Japan's alignment along the Anglo–German–Confederate axis (and thereby extend Global Alliance System politics into Northeast Asia). The Japanese were furious at what they considered a clear case of "Western hypocrisy," orchestrated by a Russian leadership whose real regret was having been beaten to the punch by "upstart Orientals."

Japan's anger at the Condemning Powers, however, was soon replaced by concern about Russian plans. In May 1896, Li Huang Chang visited Moscow for the traditional Kremlin coronation of the new Tsar and signed a treaty of alliance with Russia. Under the Treaty of Moscow, Russia committed to defend China against Japan, Chinese ports would be open to Russian warships, and Russian troops would be allowed passage across Chinese territory in the event of a Japanese attack on Russia's Far Eastern territories. Moreover, to facilitate communication between Russia and China, a new railway would be built across Manchuria, cutting off the Amur Salient and linking Vladivostok by a substantially shortened route to Siberia. In addition, the planned railway to the Liaotung Peninsula would still be built; only now, the Chinese would establish a major arsenal and other supply centers at its southern terminus. Given that both railways would match Russia's wide-gauge railroad network, the import of these projects was plain to see: China had ceded Liaotung and its vital ports at gunpoint, and it was determined (with Russian help) to regain the territory at the first opportunity. And Russia's contemporaneous announcement of plans to speed up the Trans-Siberian project confirmed St. Petersburg's determination to be in a position to provide such "assistance" as soon as practicable.

If Japan needed any additional incentive to complete its talks with Great Britain, the CSA, and Germany, the Manchu–Russian alliance certainly sufficed. In September 1896, Tokyo and London announced that the Japanese and British Empires had established an association to "maintain peace and security" in "areas of mutual interest" and that this association would be "coordinated" with the obligations of the signatories to the Anglo––German–Confederate agreements. And so, by the end of 1896, the Global Alliance System had been fully extended into what was rapidly becoming the tinderbox of Northeast Asia. Since the 1860s, the European Great Powers had exploited the terminal weaknesses of the Manchu Dynasty to seize bits and pieces of China for themselves and to extend their influence from the "Treaty Ports" along the coast well into the interior—except for Russia, which approached by land, exploiting its long-established border with the Manchu home territory of Manchuria. The Japanese victory in the Sino–Japanese war exposed the hollowness of Manchu reform efforts and would almost certainly have spurred an acceleration of Western encroachment—even without the additional incentive of the rivalry between the two great alliances. Perhaps, if the alliance dynamic had not arisen at all, the European powers with interests in China would have responded differently to Japan's victory. After all, the Japanese were "Asiatics," and the doctrine of race, which would play so powerful a role in shaping twentieth century history, was already influential enough to shape at least the visceral reaction of many Western leaders to Far Eastern political questions. Thus, Kaiser Wilhelm initially thought favorably of Russia's call for support against the Japanese acquisition of the Liaotung peninsula, invoking "solidarity" against "the Yellow Peril". Navy Secretary Tirpitz had to remind Wilhelm that, skin color aside, the imperatives of Germany's drive for *Weltmacht* required that it ally with the Japanese to prevent the Russian fleet from acquiring Port Arthur. Only after this corrective lecture in geostrategy did Wilhelm agree that Germany would follow the British and Confederate lead and refuse to support a Western intervention to deprive Japan of the fruits of its victory over the Manchus.

Without the imperatives created by the Alliance System, it seems quite likely that Russia would have persuaded the rest of the Great Powers with substantial Chinese interests to participate in a "Quadruple Intervention" and compel Japan to at least give back the Liaotung and Port Arthur. The alliance dynamic, however, had arisen; and if events in the summer and fall of 1893 had failed to produce German and Russian adhesion to the existing alliance structure, the crisis over the Treaty of Shimonoseki would probably have provided the needed, final catalyst. Great Britain likely would have seen the Russian challenge as an attempt eventually to acquire Port Arthur as a base for an expanded Russian Far East fleet (a concern that Tirpitz, along with the Confederate naval staff at Semmes House, certainly shared). Moreover, London would also have feared that Russia could have been able to pose as the "Protector of China," since St. Petersburg would be able to claim credit as the moving force behind a Western intervention that saved the Liaotung from the Japanese. The Russians would then have been able to draw Peking into an even closer orbit, paving the way for further Russian penetration of Manchuria and also Chinese Turkestan (thereby increasing the threat to India by giving Russia easier access to Tibet).

All these concerns should have been sufficient to convince Salisbury and Chamberlain that Great Britain should bridge whatever gap then still remained between London and Berlin (perhaps a continuing argument over whether an alliance should include British adherence to the Triplice). And once the establishment of the Anglo–Confederate–German alliance was a public fact, it would only have been a matter of time before Russia, France, and the USA responded with a more formal association of their own. The end result would therefore have been virtually identical to events as they actually unfolded: The Russian intervention call would have been spurned; Japan would have joined the Anglo–German–Confederate alliance; and Northeast Asia would have become a prospective theater of operations in—and potential source of the trigger for—a global war. In either case (history as it happened—or history as it probably would have transpired), the reader can see the insidious consequences of an international politics based on hostile power blocks. As the great powers align on either side of a divide defined by suspicion, every place where interests come into contact becomes a potential flash point. By 1897, this was the sad and dangerous reality of interstate relations on virtually every continent.

ALLIES

"Oh, East is East, and West is West . . .
But there is neither East nor West, Border, nor Breed, nor Birth,
When two strong men stand face to face, tho' they come from the ends of the earth!"
Rudyard Kipling.

(above) **An episode during the naval Battle of the Yalu River, in which a smaller but far more skilled Japanese squadron destroyed China's principal battle fleet, assuring Japan's victory in the Sino-Japanese War.**

(right) **A cartoon hailing the formation of the Anglo-Japanese naval alliance, which followed the refusal of Great Britain to support Russian demands that Japan relinquish Port Arthur and other key gains from her victory over China.**

14

WORLD WAR I: (1) PRELUDE TO THE CRISIS YEAR OF 1898—WHY SOME PARTS OF THE GLOBE ESCAPED THE VIOLENCE OF GLOBAL WAR

———

I have now reached the point in my narrative where the structure of interstate relations among the powers (defined by their division into two hostile blocs) had created the conditions that would constitute the "staging grounds" for the First World War. But before I set forth the course of events that proved the immediate trigger for that war, I want to discuss two places on the globe which would be spared the violence and destruction of World War One—and why that proved to be so.

I refer to the "Southern Cone" region of South America and to British South Africa, and I will begin with the former. The reader will recall the Confederacy's enthusiastic intervention in the War of the Triple Alliance on the side of Brazil and its allies against Paraguay and also Richmond's attempt to curry favor with Chile as part of Judah Benjamin's policy to isolate Madrid prior to the South's bid for Cuba. In the latter case, Benjamin's condemnation of the 1866 Spanish attack on the Chilean port of Valparaiso gained the CSA credit with Santiago—at the expense of the Spanish and the USA. Spain and Chile were in a state of war following Spain's seizure of the guano-rich Chincha Islands off the coast of Peru. Initial Chilean attempts to stay neutral in the ensuing Spanish–Peruvian conflict had infuriated the local Spanish navy commander, who demanded symbolic redress for Chile's refusal to provide coaling facilities to his squadron; the "insulting" nature of these demands caused the Chileans to declare war—even though Chile's tiny navy should have been no match for the Spanish.

In fact, the Chilean and Peruvian navies actually got the better of the Spanish in a couple of encounters, and it was in retaliation for these embarrassing reverses that the Spanish decided to bombard Valparaiso. Although British and USA naval squadrons were in port, both withdrew to avoid involvement in the conflict—a move that proved especially damaging to the Americans, principally because it confirmed the view of many Chileans that the USA was a "cowardly" country whose recent defeat at the hands of its rebellious southern states had demonstrated that Washington was unfit to wear the mantle of Hemispheric leadership. Remarkable as it may seem to those familiar with Chile's catastrophic defeat at the hands of the USA and its South American allies at the outset of World War Two in the fall of 1914, the fact is that, during the nineteenth century, Santiago considered itself a legitimate rival of Washington (even before the War of Secession) for the role of preeminent Hemispheric power. Hence, CSA President Davis and his Secretary of State knew they were sowing fertile ground when they moved swiftly in the wake of Spain's attack on Valparaiso to condemn Spanish aggression *and* "Northern pusillanimity" in the face of that aggression. (Richmond somehow managed to overlook the failure of the Royal Navy to come to the Chileans' aid.) But it would be another thirteen years before the Confederacy would have the chance to build on that gesture. That opportunity came with the outbreak of the "War of the Pacific"— between Chile, on the one hand; and Peru and Bolivia, on the other.

The War of the Pacific originated in the resistance by Peru and Bolivia to the expansionist ambitions of Chile. Chile's traditional heartland consisted of the central valley between Santiago and the Bío Bío River; in the 1830s, its effective national territory extended to encompass a zone bounded by Copiapó in the north and Concepción in the south. (I will discuss Chilean expansion south of Concepción when I take up the collision between Chile and Argentina; it was Chile's expansion to the north which brought it into conflict with Peru and Bolivia.) Copiapó lay on the southern edge of the desolation of the Atacama Desert. By the 1870s, Chilean miners had moved north from Copiapó into the heart of the Atacama. What had once been scrubland (that evoked only indifference on the part of either country) had been transformed by the discovery of silver, guano, and nitrates into an extremely valuable territory. In 1874, the resulting border wrangling (which almost degenerated into war) was resolved by fixing the border at the line 24°S: Chile abandoned its claim to a portion of the Atacama, while Bolivia pledged not to raise taxes on the *Compañía de Salitres y Ferrocarril de Antofagasta*, the Chilean nitrate combine operating in the Atacama. This arrangement, however, could only paper over differences rooted in the inability of Bolivia's government to exercise effective control over such an economically important—but geographically distant—province, which had been capitalized and peopled by foreigners. La Paz possessed neither the bureaucracy nor the military strength to control a territory separated from the Bolivian heartland by the Andes mountains and whose majority population identified itself overwhelmingly as Chilean.

As I said, the root cause of the War of the Pacific was Chilean imperialism. The Chilean elite considered Chile a worthy rival to the former United States for the role of principal power in the Western Hemisphere, and such notions (however extravagant they make strike readers familiar with twentieth century history) help to explain Chile's expansionism during the nineteenth century. Although the valiant efforts of USA Minister Thomas Nelson actually swung Chilean opinion behind the Union at the outset of the War of Secession, the South's victory at Gettysburg, followed by Lincoln's acceptance of the Anglo–French intervention, convinced many Chileans that the breakup of the United States would create new opportunities for Chile to become the preeminent Hemispheric power. But Chileans were also disturbed by France's intervention in Mexico— and even more so by what many saw as the contemporaneous revival of Spanish imperial designs on its former Latin American colonies. As a consequence, Santiago's policy toward the two North American "Anglo-Saxon" Unions bordered on the schizophrenic in the years immediately after the Confederacy's victory. Most Chileans saw in the USA the true successor to the "vulgar, commercial" United States that Chile had traditionally seen as its rival for hemispheric hegemony; Chile, however, also condemned Richmond's support for France's Mexican adventure. This confusion only began to resolve itself with the bombardment of Valparaiso by the Spanish. Then, four years later, after France had abandoned its pursuit of the Mexican empire, the Confederacy won its war with Spain—a result enthusiastically greeted by Chileans, who technically remained at war with

Spain and saw the Confederate victory as effectively eliminating the threat posed by the Spanish navy to Chile and its coastal neighbors.

And yet, the 1870s did not see a Chilean move to resume its territorial expansion in the wake of the reduction of Spanish power by the Confederacy and of American power by the loss of its Southern states. To the contrary, as indicated, the Chileans chose to resolve their border dispute with Bolivia by agreement in 1874. Chile, whose foreign trade was principally with Western Europe, suffered from the contraction of those economies which ensued in 1873; the resulting financial difficulties reinforced the perceived need to achieve government economy and spurred Chilean willingness to compromise their quarrel with Bolivia. Moreover, Chile also reached a peaceful settlement with Argentina. There, Chilean settlers had prompted Santiago to assert a claim to at least a portion of Patagonia. In the meantime, the Argentine government, having overcome rebellious provincial bosses (*caudillos*), had embarked on a campaign to suppress the Indian tribes of Patagonia—who, as late as 1876, penetrated to within one hundred miles of Buenos Aires on a raid in which they seized upward of three hundred thousand head of cattle and five hundred white captives. The anti-Indian campaigns brought Argentine forces into contact with the Chilean settlers, causing Buenos Aires to insist on their withdrawal from Patagonia; to this was added a demand for exclusive Argentine control of the Straits of Magellan. War was only averted when Chile agreed to confirm Patagonia as Argentina's and to share control of the Straits. But it *was* averted—and principally for the same reason that Chile had compromised with Bolivia: a Chilean economy still weakened by declining trade that had yet to recover from the continuing European economic slump.

The agreement with Argentina, however, proved ill-timed for Chile's relations with Bolivia. There, a barely literate sergeant named Hilarión Daza had shot his way into the presidency in December of 1878. Believing Chile would now "strike its flag as it did with Argentina," Daza moved to increase taxes on the *Compañía de Salitres*; moreover, Daza was bolstered by the knowledge that Lima—with its not insubstantial fleet and under the terms of a "secret" treaty between Bolivia and Peru (which actually was no secret to Santiago)—would support La Paz in the event of war with Chile. Daza, however, overestimated the political room for maneuver of the Chilean government. Convinced they would be the victims of mob violence if they yielded to Bolivia's (undeniably clear) breach of the 1874 accords, Chilean President Pinton and his Cabinet felt compelled to order the army to seize the Bolivian port of Antofagasta. Chile's leaders were gambling that Daza would revoke the tax increase on the *Compañia de Salitres*, in which case Chilean forces could be withdrawn to the 1874 border; instead, Bolivia declared war, and when Peru indicated it would honor the treaty with La Paz, Chile responded by declaring war on Bolivia and Peru.

The first phase of the war was naval. Bolivia had no navy, but both Peru and Chile had invested in foreign-built ironclads. Peru had obtained three *Canonicus*-class monitors from the USA: the *Manco Capac* (formerly *Oneota*), *Pachauti* (formerly *Saugus*), and *Atahualpa* (formerly *Catawba*). These were products of the Union's frenzy for monitor building at the end of and immediately after the Secession War; however, Peru and the USA had not followed up their purchase with any agreement for maintenance, parts, or advisors. Their shallow draft made them unsuited for open-water operations, and their general decline into desuetude over the preceding decade limited their usefulness; all three took limited part in the war (without signal success), and all three eventually were scuttled. Peru also boasted two more effective units. *Huascar* was a square-rigged ironclad ram built by Laird in Liverpool and launched in 1865. She was built to Peruvian specifications and had two ten-inch Armstrong guns. The Peruvian broadside ironclad *Independencia*, also built in the United Kingdom, carried two seven-inch and a dozen six-inch rifled guns; she was the most powerful ship in the navy.

The Chilean navy was built around two powerful, modern ironclad frigates designed and constructed in the United Kingdom—*Almirante Cochrane* and *Blanco Encalada*—each of which was armed with a half-dozen nine-inch rifles. These ships, acting in concert, eventually ran down and captured *Huascar* at the Battle of Angamos in October 1879. But Chilean popular imagination was captured by the events of the Battle of Iquique in May of that year. *Huascar* and *Independencia* were detached from the rest of the Peruvian fleet to raise the Chilean blockade of the Peruvian port of Iquique. Believing that the Peruvian fleet was concentrating around the northern port of Callo, the Chileans had entrusted their blockade to weak and obsolescent units, including the unarmored corvette *Esmeralda* and the schooner *Covadonga*. The Chilean blockading forces were no match for the *Huascar* and *Independencia*; *Esmeralda* sank after attempting to ram the Peruvian ships, and *Covadonga* made smartly for the open seas, pursued by *Independencia*. Carlos Condell, captain of the *Covadonga*, knew he could not outrun *Independencia*, and that the loss of the race would mean the destruction of his command. Condell daringly sailed his ship inshore, drawing *Independencia* over a reef and grounding her on the rocks. At this point, serendipity reared its head in the form of Irvine Stephens Bulloch of the Confederate States Navy, commanding two armored corvettes. In the late 1860s, Sir Edward James Reed, chief engineer for the Royal Navy, had designed a relatively inexpensive bark-rigged ironclad for the burgeoning export market. The ships were exported to Japan—armed with Krupp 170 mm and 150 mm breach-loading rifles (as the *Kongo* class)—and to other friendly powers. The Confederacy saw the wisdom of experimenting with the type as well as an opportunity to enhance its domestic arms-manufacturing industry. Eight corvettes were built in the United Kingdom and brought to Charleston for fitting out in the CSA with Tredegar–Krupp versions of the same breach loaders. As tensions in South America grew, Chile contracted with the CSA for two of the ships to be named *del Pozo* and *de la Sotta*. Bulloch was on *del Pozo*, delivering the vessels, when he came upon the battle. Upon the appearance of the newcomers, the *Huascar* beat a hasty retreat; Bulloch positioned his ships around the immobile *Independencia*, allowing Captain Condell to board and capture her. In a stroke, the most powerful vessel of the Peruvian navy had become Chilean; Condell became a national hero, and Bulloch (whose ships never fired a shot) was feted throughout Chile. (Bulloch's career itself presents a noteworthy story. He was a patriotic Confederate—a son of Georgia. He was the youngest-ranking officer on the Secession War raider CSS *Alabama*, which terrorized the Eastern Atlantic for several months in 1862. His sister Mary, however, married a Yankee before the Secession War and moved to New York City—where she would become the mother of Theodore Roosevelt. Bulloch—Confederate hero, Chilean idol, and a living link between the CSA and Chile—was the uncle of TR.)

The correlation of naval forces now overwhelmingly favored Chile and allowed the landing of troops at will on the Peruvian coast. In November 1879, Chilean forces landed at Pisagua, in the Peruvian province of Tarapacá. The Peruvian plan was to destroy the invaders by combining forces with their Bolivian allies. But the Bolivians, after a disastrously mismanaged march from La Paz to the coast, turned back without notifying their allies. The Peruvians then attempted to oust the Chileans on their own, but after a series of engagements in which neither side gained a decisive advantage, the Peruvians abandoned Tarapacá, enabling Chile to occupy the vital port of Iquique. Thus, by February 1880, Chile had seized Bolivia's sole port (Antofagasta) and Peru's chief source of revenue (its nitrate exports, via Iquique), and Chilean forces were preparing to invade the Peruvian province of Tacna.

At this point, the War of the Pacific began its transformation from regional conflict into potential Hemispheric *casus belli*. At the outbreak of war, both the USA and CSA reacted cautiously. The Confederacy had established friendly relations with Chile as the Southern factories of Tredegar–Krupp became a principal source of arms for the Chilean military, and Richmond and Santiago were drawn even closer together by common opposition to Northern initiatives: such as the construction of the Panama Canal. This reflexive "anti-Yankee" policy, however, was opposed by important sectors of Chilean society; in the case of the Panama Canal, the nitrate interests argued that Chile would benefit from the shortening of the trade routes to the country's European export markets and urged a more "nuanced" approach to Chile's relationship with the North American unions. And although the Longstreet Administration expressed initial sympathy for Chile's position, doubts about easy analogies being drawn between the War of the Triple Alliance and this latest South American conflict caused the Confederate leadership to await the initial outcome of events and thereby avoid antagonizing Peru and Bolivia by what might prove a wholly unnecessary intervention on the Chilean side.

In fact (and setting aside Chile's Anglo–Confederate arms purchases), it was the USA that took the first step toward a North American intervention. The Blaine Administration viewed Chile as aligned with Richmond in a "concert of action" antagonistic to American interests. When Chilean forces conquered Peru's province of Tarapacá and followed up with an invasion of Tacna, Washington became alarmed at the possibility that Chile would eventually occupy Lima in a bid to annex the whole of Peru. Such a move would bring Chile (seen as a virtual ally of the Confederacy) to the border of Colombia and thus threaten the American position in Panama. At the same time, Washington was disturbed to learn that British and French interests with holdings in Peru were urging their governments to impose a settlement. While the Blaine Administration shared this concern for Peru, the USA also opposed a European settlement as a violation of the Monroe Doctrine (a principle that Washington still valued, not least because excluding the European powers from Hemispheric affairs also would inhibit the Confederacy from utilizing those powers as formal allies in Hemispheric matters). Making clear its preference for "an American solution to an American dispute," in July of 1880, the USA offered its good offices to mediate a settlement of the war.

This effort, however, quickly foundered on the gap between the stances of the warring parties—a gap reinforced, on the Chilean side, by a clever Confederate campaign to frustrate the North's peacemaking initiative. Bolivia demanded a return to the territorial status quo *ante bellum* before even considering other issues. Peru adopted a more flexible attitude but also insisted that Chile should be willing to enter into talks with no territorial preconditions. Chile, on the other hand, had come to believe that it must, at the least, occupy the Bolivian littoral and the Peruvian province of Tarapacá until La Paz and Lima reimbursed Chile for the cost of the war. Moreover, the longer the war continued, the less confident the Chilean leadership became in the ability of Bolivia and Peru to pay significant reparations; as the possibility of reparations became remote, the Chilean government felt politically compelled to insist on territorial compensation—precisely the kind of concession that neither La Paz nor Lima was prepared to make. (These political constraints were exacerbated by Confederate efforts to frustrate Washington's peace initiative by encouraging the belief that Chile could not feel secure against the danger of Bolivian and Peruvian *revanche* except by depriving those countries of their access to the nitrate-rich territory of the Atacama— even though neither La Paz nor Lima was presumptively likely to accept a peace based on a loss of territory to Santiago). When representatives of the belligerents met on the new steel cruiser USS *Pennsylvania* in October 1880, the Confederacy's efforts bore fruit. The Chilean envoys demanded: the cession of the Atacama and Tarapacá, the payment of a substantial indemnity, the abrogation of the Peruvian–Bolivian alliance, *and* Chile's right to occupy the Peruvian provinces of Tacna and Arica until Lima fulfilled its treaty obligations. The Peruvians refused to negotiate over such draconian terms, and the Chileans—angry over Lima's "intransigence"—quit the meeting.

The USA mediation effort having collapsed, the Chileans resumed their Peruvian campaign. By January 1881, Chilean forces were poised to attack Lima. After short but sharp engagements outside the city—in which several thousand Chileans and Peruvians were killed or wounded—the Peruvian government fled the capital, which was occupied by the Chilean army on January 15, 1881. There now ensued the most dangerous period of the war: when the combination of military stalemate and increasing Confederate and American support for the opposing sides threatened to trigger a Hemisphere-wide conflict. Although Chile had taken Lima, this success did not end Peruvian resistance. Peru's President Nicolás Piérola, invoking the example of Benito Juarez, promised to wage a war of attrition to expel the Chilean occupiers. Moreover, Piérola now lost control of much of the Peruvian interior, where leading military men (General André Cáceras and Admiral Lizardo Montero) repudiated Piérola, while also pledging unceasing resistance until Chile withdrew from all Peruvian territory captured since the war's outset. Since Santiago was now insisting on the cession of Tarapacá, Tacna, and Arica provinces as the minimum condition for peace, Chile confronted the need to extend its control over the whole of Peru as a precondition to achieving peace on Chilean terms. This gloomy prospect was underscored when Santiago's attempt to install a new, pliant Peruvian government backfired. Shortly after capturing Lima, the Chileans orchestrated the election of García Calderón as Peru's president by the rump of the Peruvian Congress that had remained in the capital; Calderón, however, *also* refused to consider ceding any of the provinces claimed by Santiago.

As bands of Peruvian irregulars (*montoneros*) began to harass the occupying army, the Chilean government ordered a punitive expedition dispatched into the Peruvian interior. In the meantime, after the failure of the October 1880 mediation effort, Washington had kept an increasingly anxious eye on developments. During his two terms as USA President, James G. Blaine had sought to check Confederate expansionism (and rehabilitate the Monroe Doctrine's exclusion of the European powers from Hemispheric affairs) by developing close economic and political ties with as many Latin American countries as practicable. For precisely that reason, Blaine resented what he (correctly) viewed as Chile's policy of frustrating the USA's Inter-American initiatives. Blaine was also concerned by Santiago's increasingly close ties to Richmond, and when the news of the outbreak of war between Chile, Peru, and Bolivia first reached Washington, Blaine immediately suspected "a Confederate war on Peru, with Chile as the instrument, and Colombia—and the Panama Canal—as the ultimate goal." Blaine's worst fears appeared to have been realized when Chile occupied Lima, and he urged incoming USA President James Garfield to be "prepared to take whatever action is necessary to compel a Chilean evacuation of Peru." But while Garfield agreed with Blaine's strategic assessment, the new President did not share his predecessor's personal investment in the outcome of the war. Perhaps for that reason, when the crisis came in November of 1881, Garfield did not issue the ultimatum that Blaine almost certainly would have and thereby probably avoided embroiling the United States in a South American war that would have been raging when the *Cinco de Mayo* escapades of Mosby's OCSS agents triggered the Western War. One wonders whether the ensuing "War of the Western Hemisphere" could have been contained, given how the much smaller Western War came so close to involving Great Britain on the Southern side.

Prior to the crisis of November 1881, however, Garfield's policy proceeded on the course laid down by Blaine. The USA had recognized the Calderón government and then encouraged its resistance to territorial concessions while attempting to persuade Chile that it should accept a substantial monetary indemnity in lieu of territory. Given that Peru had a terrible credit rating and Chile occupied the country's richest province, Peru's ability to finance an indemnity appeared highly doubtful. But then the Credit Industriel et Commercial, a French banking firm with ties to French president Jules Grevy and some powerful American contacts, offered to service Peru's international obligations, liquidate any indemnity that Chile might levy, and provide Lima an annual income; in return, the company would receive the right, under USA protection, to develop Tarapacá's mineral resources. Emboldened by the Credit Industriel proposal (and by a similar plan—advanced by a newly formed Peruvian company—headed by a speculator with Washington political connections), President Calderón stiffened his refusal to cede Tarapacá to Chile. In response, the Chileans confiscated Calderón's treasury and denied him control over his (largely ceremonial) army. Calderón answered by requesting that his legislature approve Admiral Montero as his successor and by reiterating his opposition to territorial concessions. Infuriated, the local Chilean commander had Calderón arrested that November, exiling him to Chile's far south.

Had Blaine still been President, he would probably have responded by threatening to break diplomatic relations with Santiago unless Calderón was immediately restored to power. (At least, that is what Blaine said in his memoirs that he would have done, and there is no reason I know of to doubt his word on this point.) Garfield was more cautious—principally because he wanted to avoid a war unless there was no other way to preserve Peru's territorial integrity (which was the vital concern from the point of view of the USA's Colombian ally as well). Moreover, while Calderón's arrest removed one Peruvian opponent of territorial concessions, Chile now had no single authority which it could credibly treat as the legitimate government of Peru. Pierola, Admiral Montero, and General Cáceres were all at large and—like the deposed Calderón—opposed territorial concessions. Furthermore, it was becoming increasingly apparent that Chile's attempt to suppress the *montoneros* had failed. Peruvian guerillas were ambushing Chilean units with ever-increasing frequency and even killing its soldiers on the streets of Lima. Thus, the Garfield administration settled for a strong (but not incendiary) protest of Calderón's dismissal—while also arranging, with Colombian support, to provide arms to all three of the principal *montoneros* groups.

This dangerously unstable situation might very well have led to the widening of the war which Garfield had earlier avoided had not the *Cinco de Mayo* crisis of the following year caused both the USA and the Confederacy to concentrate their attention and energies much closer to home. In early 1882, the Chileans had sent another punitive expedition into the Peruvian highlands which completely failed to pacify the interior. After months of fruitless effort, the troops were ordered to withdraw; as they retreated, General Cáceres struck his most devastating blow of the war: annihilating a Chilean detachment at the Battle of La Concepcion. The battle occurred on July 9, 1882. By that time, Washington and Richmond were caught up in the diplomatic and military dance that would culminate with the outbreak of the Western War that August. Had there been no such crisis to the north, the battle (more accurately, the massacre) at La Concepcion might have triggered politically irresistible demands in Santiago for war with the USA, as many Chileans would have blamed "Yankee arms" for the disaster and demanded retaliation. In fact, there were such calls, but cooler heads could see that with the USA and the Confederacy on the verge of war, the combination of the bloody disaster of La Concepcion and the impending cutoff of American arms to the *montoneros* (for soon the Yankees would obviously need every gun and bullet to deal with the Confederacy's "Gray Legions") meant Chile, Peru, and Bolivia might now be able to bring their conflict to a close—and on terms favorable to Chile.

In fact, that is precisely what transpired. A number of prominent Peruvians had come to a similar conclusion, and one of these, General Miguel Iglesias, had also managed to establish a government at Cajamarca. Iglesias indicated a willingness to cede Tarapacá but balked at yielding Tacna and Arica. Santiago, under pressure from an increasingly war-weary population, was also willing to compromise: Chile would receive Tarapacá but would only occupy Tacna and Arica for ten years—at the end of which a plebiscite would determine final ownership. Iglesias agreed, as did all of the principal *montonero* leaders—except General Cáceres, who had to be subdued by one last Chilean expedition, which defeated the rebellious general at the Battle of Huamachucho in July 1883. With Cáceres defeated, the way was cleared for Chile and Peru to sign the Treaty of Ancón in October 1883. Chile and Bolivia then signed an "indefinite truce" in April 1884, under which Chile was granted the "temporary" right to occupy the Bolivian littoral. During this final period of the War of the Pacific, both Washington and Richmond played virtually no role, being caught up in their own Western War struggle. But with the resolution of the Western War, the Confederacy moved quickly to resume the development of close ties with Chile and discovered that Santiago was eager to do likewise. The War of the Pacific had convinced the overwhelming majority of the Chilean elite that the USA was truly the successor to the despised "Yanqui," and that Washington was determined to frustrate Chile's legitimate claim to "equality of primacy" in the Western Hemisphere. Moreover, although most Chileans had come to disapprove of slavery by the 1860s and therefore tended to look askance at the Southern States when they rebelled to preserve so dubious a "peculiar institution," many Chileans had reconciled themselves to the country's close friendship with one of the Hemisphere's two slave powers. This change in outlook was made easier by the Chileans' embrace of an "Andean racialism" to explain Chile's victory in the War of the Pacific and its entitlement to the territorial fruits of that conflict. (Although the Chilean masses—like those of Peru and Bolivia—were Indian, the white Chilean elite claimed that the country's "heroic" Araucanian Indians were racially superior to the "savage" populations of Peru and Bolivia.)

These attitudes helped to rationalize Chile's conquests in the War of the Pacific by casting the country in the role of the benevolent imperialist, bringing the benefits of civilization to "savages bereft of the spirit of European civilization." And racialist prejudice also made it easier for Chile to draw closer to the Confederacy as a counterweight to "Yankee power." For although some Chileans crowed that their country was now "Empress of the Pacific," most recognized that Chile, alone, would be no match for the USA—and especially no match for the American fleet (which by 1884 was second only to the Royal Navy in number of capital ships). To be sure, having added the wealth of the Bolivian and Peruvian nitrate to its own, thereby acquiring an effective monopoly over this increasingly vital commodity (a position that would ironically prove the country's undoing in World War Two), Chile could now afford to embark on a substantial expansion of its navy. By the 1890s, the Chilean navy had quintupled in size, including the addition of four battleships as powerful as anything in the USA fleet—spurring a responsive effort by Chile's wary neighbor Argentina, which would ultimately have fatal consequences for the peace of the region and for Chile itself. But while a formidably augmented navy might give the USA pause, the government of President Santa Maria, which made the decision to embark on a program of naval expansion, also recognized that the planned additions to Chilean sea power could not prevent defeat should the USA bring to bear the full might of its navy. "We must," Santa Maria told his cabinet in December of 1885, "marry Chile's power on land and sea to an ally with whom, in combination, we can inflict so great a wound on the Yankees that they will be persuaded never to chance such an encounter in the first place."

The Confederacy was the obvious candidate for such a combination, and had Richmond been able to make the decision in isolation, it seems very likely that it would have entered into a military alliance with Santiago shortly after the end of the War of the Pacific. But the Confederacy could not make such a decision in isolation. Richmond's first priority—in the Western War's wake—was the establishment of an Anglo–Confederate alliance. CSA President Breckinridge had dispatched Judah Benjamin to London to achieve the formation of that alliance, and Benjamin soon had to apprise Breckinridge's successor, Fitzhugh Lee, that those in Great Britain who supported an alliance with the Confederacy also opposed London taking sides in Latin American disputes. "We enjoy good relations with all the principal powers of South America," Lord Salisbury reminded Joseph Chamberlain as the latter prepared to enter into his "informal communications" with CSA Ambassador Benjamin. "The Confederates simply must understand that we will not allow them to entangle us in some conflict between countries, such as Chile and Argentina, with both of whom we have long had peaceful and profitable intercourse." In other words, while the South remained free to develop a "close friendship" with Chile, Great Britain would view the formation of a formal Confederate alliance with the "Prussia of South America" as a breach of the understandings that preceded the establishment of an Anglo–Confederate *entente*.

Richmond got the message. Following the announcement of the Anglo–Confederate alliance in April 1887, the Lee Administration broke the disappointing news to President José Manuel Balmaceda and his Cabinet: Although the Confederacy wished to maintain "intimate" ties with Chile and to cooperate "as closely as practicable in all areas of common interest" (cooperation that would extend to matters "touching on the two countries' shared security concerns"), the South did not believe that a "public formalization" of this relationship was "presently" in either of their mutual interests. Although some Chileans resented what they declared to be a Southern "jilting" of Chile in favor of Great Britain, most (including President Balmaceda and the chiefs of the country's armed services) recognized that Chile would actually gain, informally, virtually everything it would receive through a public alliance with the South. Moreover, the more far-sighted among this group also saw that, should the Confederacy and Great Britain go to war with the USA, the allies would want to assure that Chile—with its potent fleet and its near-monopoly control over the nitrates essential to the production of modern high explosives—was friendly to their cause. "When the time comes," President Balmaceda told the country's military leaders, "Chile will be able to demand the privileges of an ally, and the Confederates and the English know this—even if the English do not wish to admit this publicly, out of concern for their Argentine investments."

By "Argentine investments," Balmaceda was referring to Great Britain's role as chief financier of the Argentine economy—a position which the British had acquired by the middle of the 1870s. In fact, the Argentine economy and state had become heavily dependent on British capital. But merely because Chile and Argentina shared a common source for vital investment needs did not prevent relations between the two countries from deteriorating due to a combination of historic rivalry—a long and disputed border—and Chile's decision to embark on a major naval buildup following its victory in the War of the Pacific. The reader will recall how the two countries nearly went to war over Chile's incursions into Patagonia and its assertion of the right to the entirety of the territories guarding the inter-ocean passage through the Straits of Magellan. Chile and Argentina seemed to have substantially resolved these issues by the treaty agreements of 1878 and 1881. The agreed frontier was to follow the line of the highest Andean peaks as well as the Atlantic and Pacific watersheds; there would be "joint control" over the Straits; and Patagonia was acknowledged to be Argentine. These agreements, however, left several key points unresolved. Worse, the two lines chosen as benchmarks for fixing the border proved not always to coincide. Moreover, Chile's naval buildup soon prompted Argentina's naval chiefs to press for a responsive expansion of the Argentine fleet.

By the beginning of the 1890s, a full-blown naval arms race was under-way which, in turn, set off alarms in Rio de Janeiro. At this point, one might have expected the Brazilian Empire to respond with its own naval buildup, to "answer the challenge" from Buenos Aires. Although Brazil and Argentina had fought as allies in the war of the Triple Alliance, this association com-pelled by immediate necessity had been preceded by decades of rivalry—punctuated by war over the border territory that became Uruguay precisely because Brazil and Argentina could see no other way to resolve their con-flict than by mutual denial. Moreover, following the victory over Paraguay in 1869, the two countries' relationship quickly reverted to the traditional pattern of mutual suspicion—a hostility that would be reinforced as paths of development diverged: with Brazil's decision to reject emancipation and modernize its slave-based economy in concert with the Confederacy, while Argentina opted for the free-labor export path under a limited franchise regime established after the defeat of regionalist *caudillos* in 1870. Although both countries initially experienced comparable rates of economic growth and each country's export sectors proved equally vulnerable to the "boom and bust" business cycles of the period, Brazil became increasingly con-cerned by the divergence in immigration patterns that emerged by the mid-1880s. While Brazilian immigration remained fairly constant between 1860 and 1885 (15,774 free immigrants in the former year, contrasted with 25,440 in the latter), Argentine immigration soared, reaching an annual rate of well over one hundred thousand by the end of the same period.

Although the overwhelming majority of the Brazilian elite denied any connection, there is little doubt that Brazil's inability to increase its immi-gration rate was rooted in the decision to reinforce, rather than abolish, slavery—a conclusion underscored by the Confederacy's similar inability to attract free immigration compared to the influx achieved by its American rival. By 1890, Argentina's population had risen to four million; Brazil's, on the other hand, stood at 12,750,000 (and slaves accounted for 25 percent of the latter). Although Brazil still held a clear edge, its military leaders fretted that—at established growth rates—Argentina's population would surpass Brazil's within a generation. And while the two countries had resolved the "East Platine" question by the creation of Uruguay, there remained points of contention: most notably, the Misiōnes Territories (an area of over fourteen thousand square miles, southeast of Paraguay). By the early 1890s, influential voices could increasingly be heard, urging a "preemptive war" to "strangle Argentine power in its cradle" and encouraging the formation of an alliance with Chile and the Confederacy to assure that "overwhelming force" would be brought to bear to assure the success of such a "sacred mission." Nor did such talk (and its encouraging reception in certain Chilean and Confederate quarters) escape the notice of Buenos Aires. In response, many leading Argentines began to encourage an approach to the USA and its Colombian ally—as well as Peru and Bolivia—in order to create a defensive "American *Entente*" that would discourage Brazilian (and Chilean) adventurism.

I now come to one of those moments in history which illustrates the importance of the individual in the course of human events. Although Brazil and Argentina were poised to take the first step that would have unleashed in South America the same destructive alliance dynamic that was already well advanced in the Northern Hemisphere, the majority of the Brazilian and Argentine elites, in fact, shrank from the prospect of open antagonism (with its attendant cost in arms and risk of much worse). Encouraged by discreet contacts with Buenos Aires, Brazil's Foreign Ministry proposed that the two countries seek to ease tensions by resolving the issue of the Misiōnes by equal division of the territory. When the Brazilian Congress, at the urging of the more vocal anti-Argentine faction in the military, refused to approve such a treaty, the Foreign Ministry sidestepped the opposition by proposing the submission of the dispute to an impartial arbiter. Argentina agreed, and the two countries selected the president of Switzerland as mediator. To present Brazil's case, the government of Empress Isabel chose José Maria da Silva Paranhos Júnior, the Baron of Rio-Branco. Rio-Branco was Brazil's leading historian of the Rio da Prata (the Plata River system). In preparing his country's case, Rio-Branco based his arguments on eighteenth century documents as well as on Brazilian settlement of the area. Rio-Branco's presentation was masterful, turning the best Argentine arguments to his advantage. When the Swiss Federal Council delivered its award on February 6, 1895, Rio-Branco won an overwhelming victory for Brazil.

Rio-Branco, however, accomplished much more than a signal success in resolving a longstanding border dispute with a powerful neighbor. The

Baron was an accomplished diplomat who also saw the war clouds gathering to the north and was determined to exercise Brazilian leadership to keep South America out of any conflict between the "Northern Power Blocs." Having lanced the boil of the Misiōnes, Rio-Branco (who assumed the post of Foreign Minister in 1896 and would become Prime Minister in February 1898) now turned his attention to disarming the increasing tensions between Chile and Argentina by offering Brazil's "friendly assistance" in resolving the festering border dispute between the two countries. It was Rio-Branco who was able, by dint of perseverance and personal diplomacy, to bring the presidents of Chile and Argentina together at the height of the "Border Crisis" of 1898. With Rio-Branco presiding, the two heads of state met that fall at Punta Arenas; there, at the very moment that French and British forces were marching toward their fateful encounter at Fashoda, the leaders of Chile and Argentina performed the much-celebrated *Abrazo del Estrecho* (the "Embrace of the Straits") with which they agreed to submit their countries' dispute over the Puna de Atacama to a neutral mediator. In fact, this mediation never came to pass (the outbreak of World War One prompted a "temporary postponement" of the selection of the arbiter, and that temporary delay proved permanent). But the good feeling engendered by the *Abrazo* helped to keep the Southern Cone powers out of *La Guerra del Norte*. As the reader will see, the conflicting associations of these powers with the two warring blocks would later come perilously close to bringing all three into the war, notwithstanding Rio-Branco's continuing efforts to maintain the peace; had it not been for the Peking Legation Massacre and the suspension of hostilities engendered by the need for concerted Great Power action to deal with the Boxers, I suspect the First World War would have engulfed virtually the whole of South America by the end of 1900. Be that as it might have been, the fact remains that Rio-Branco's efforts were instrumental in sparing virtually the whole of South America the death and destruction of the first of the Alliance Wars.

Turning to British Southern Africa, this may be the one part of the world which was, at least initially, spared a war because of the creation of the Alliance System. I refer to the simmering dispute between the Boers and the British Empire which had boiled over several times already during the 1800s and seemed on track to do so again when Kaiser Wilhelm II intervened with his dramatic mediation offer of January 1896 in the wake of the Jameson Raid. The Boers were the descendants of Dutch settlers who had come to the southern tip of Africa and founded Cape Town in 1652. Great Britain took this "Cape Colony" from the Dutch during the Napoleonic Wars in order to establish a naval base at nearby Simonstown and thereby secure the passage to British India. Relations between the Boers and their new English overlords were rocky at best, but when Parliament decreed an end to slavery throughout the Empire, matters rapidly deteriorated. The Boers despised black Africans and made slavery an integral part of the Boer agricultural economy (as well as a means of assuring control over people from whom the Boers had wrested the land). When the promised compensation for the value of their emancipated laborers proved (in the Boer view) too little and very late, some six thousand Boers left the Cape Colony, crossed the Orange and Vaal Rivers, and proclaimed the new Boer republics of the Orange Free State, Transvaal, and Natal.

At first, the "Great Trek" and its political offspring were both condemned as illegal by the British government. Natal was actually reabsorbed by Great Britain (as a colony separate from the Cape). But Natal had a useful harbor at Durban. The Free State and Transvaal did not, and this fact, combined with another period of Liberal lethargy, allowed the latter two Boer republics instead to wrangle guarantees of "independence" from London. The ensuing "mellowing" of British–Boer relations ended abruptly in 1867 with the discovery of diamonds in West Griqualand, along the border of the Orange Free State. Within five years, the Colesberg *kopje* (hill) had become the "Big Hole" of the Kimberly mines—the largest manmade hole in the world. The Cape Colony had gone from rags to near-riches as its revenues multiplied several-fold, and this newfound economic promise opened the door to Dominion status in 1872 (putting the Cape on a political par with Canada, some of the Australian states, and New Zealand). The Boers of the Orange Free State, however, bitterly resented the new wealth of their English-ruled rival, claiming West Griqualand (and Kimberly) was theirs. But when the diggers instead invited the British to annex the mine country, there was little the Free State could do except protest. Moreover, the Boers were soon in desperate need of British assistance, as Transvaal got itself into a nasty fight with the Pedi tribe. Battlefield reverses and an empty treasury forced Pretoria to call for help. The British responded with the promise of troops—but on the condition that Transvaal "accept the authority of Her Majesty's authority and rule." The Transvaal Boers were badly divided over the offer, and the visiting British High Commissioner seized upon the acceptance of his terms by the republic's English-speakers to proclaim annexation in a ceremony in Pretoria held in April of 1877.

But no sooner had the British presumed to absorb Transvaal than they found themselves thrown on the defensive: first by the neighboring Zulus and then by the resurgent Boers. In 1878, the British managed to provoke the Zulus into war, and although the conflict ultimately ended with the suppression of the independent Zulu kingdom, British prestige suffered a severe reverse with the annihilation of a one-thousand-man force at the Battle of Isandlwana on January 22, 1879. Then in 1881, the reunited Transvaal Boers, infuriated by what they perceived as Gladstone's "betrayal" of his 1880 campaign promise to restore their republic and emboldened by the example of the Zulu success (albeit fleeting) two years before, rose in rebellion. Once again, British blundering produced a military disaster. At the Battle of Majuba, on February 27, 1881, a force of Boer farmers stormed a rocky ridge and overwhelmed six hundred regular army troops. This time, however, there would be no devastating counterblow, because Gladstone's Liberals had no stomach for a bloody fight to hold Transvaal. Under the "Convention of Pretoria" entered into later that year, Great Britain restored the Transvaal Republic, retaining only a formal "suzerainty" that permitted London an (ill-defined) authority in matters of foreign and defense policy. This arrangement might have proved fairly durable—given the insular Boers' general lack of interest in matters beyond their borders—had gold not been discovered in the Transvaal hills of the Witwatersrand (the Rand) in 1886. Before the decade's end, the impoverished republic of Boer farmers had been transformed into a wealthy nation flooded by a rush of immigrants seeking their fortunes in the gold mines of the booming city of Johannesburg. The Boers welcomed the wealth, but they did not welcome the newcomers (the "Uitlanders") and denied them the vote to assure continued Boer political supremacy.

The Uitlanders included men of great wealth and ambition—two of whom were partners with Cecil Rhodes. The future "Father of British

South Africa," Rhodes made his first fortune in diamonds, his second in gold, and then used his wealth to finance a British "Great Trek" north into Mashonaland, establishing a new colony ("Rhodesia") under the authority of a royal charter granted to the British South Africa Company—which Rhodes controlled. Rhodes had grand dreams of British rule in Africa, and at the center of those dreams was a Union of Southern Africa, which would rival the Canadian confederation in size while outstripping the wealth of all of England's other imperial holdings due to the diamonds of Kimberly and the gold of the Rand. But the Rand lay within the boundaries of Transvaal, and as the Uitlander population swelled, the Transvaal Boers moved to assure their continued control by increasing the franchise residency period from five to fourteen years. To Rhodes, this action demonstrated the congenital obstinacy of the Boers—which could only be remedied by the overthrow of their administration and its replacement by a government representative of the whole Transvaal. And since the Uitlanders already outnumbered the Boers and also controlled the gold production of the Rand, a "representative" government would be an Uitlander government—dominated, of course, by its wealthy elite, who just happened to be the partners of Cecil Rhodes.

In this way, Rhodes would gather into his hands all the strands necessary to bring about the creation of a South African Union. Rhodes was a resident of Cape Town, a citizen of the Cape Colony, and a member of the Cape Parliament (and, at times, the Cape's Prime Minister). He controlled the British South Africa Company, which held the charter to "Rhodesia." With Transvaal in hand, the isolated Orange Free State could not hold out but must yield to the demand for a merger of the patchwork of Great Britain's varied southern African holdings into a single federal Union, organized along Canadian lines. "But unlike Canada," Rhodes wrote to Colonial Secretary Joseph Chamberlain in 1894, "a South African Union will be blessed with great wealth and a location that places it about as far from the Americans as a British dominion could wish to be. Thus, South Africa will be able to make a positive contribution to Imperial security rather than constitute a drain on vital resources."

That Chamberlain was persuaded by these arguments there can be little doubt. Whether he authorized what became known as the "Jameson

Raid" is less certain. (The telegrams that were mysteriously leaked from the "closed" files of the Rhodes Archives and published in the Boer press during the deterioration of Boer–British relations in the 1920s strongly suggest that Chamberlain had advance notice, but they do not prove—contrary to Boer claims—that Chamberlain was involved in planning the uprising.) A rather motley collection of some five hundred men armed with a handful of machine guns and artillery, accompanied by three Regular Army colonels conveniently on leave (who "volunteered" to "assist"), and led by Dr. Leander Starr Jameson, Rhodes's closest retainer (who also commanded the force that in 1893 had conquered neighboring Matabeleland for the new colony of Rhodesia), had been secretly assembled on the Rhodesian-Transvaal border during the fall of 1895. Jameson's mission was to cross into Transvaal and ride to the relief of a "spontaneous" Uitlander uprising. Should Jameson and his men prove unable—in combination with Uitlanders armed with guns smuggled across the Rhodesian border over the preceding months—to subdue the Boer government, Rhodes counted on Chamberlain persuading Salisbury to authorize intervention by Regular Army units stationed in Natal.

By December 1895, everything was in readiness on the Rhodesian side of the border; Jameson only awaited the signal that the Uitlanders had rebelled as scheduled (the rising having been set for December 28). But December 28 came and went without any signal; in fact, the Uitlander leadership had been seized by doubts almost literally at the eleventh hour and had let the moment pass. Jameson, however, was not about to do the same. Fearing that the Boers would soon uncover the conspiracy—but confident that he could take Transvaal "with half a dozen revolvers"—Jameson and his troopers set off across the border on December 29. The result was a fiasco and might very well have triggered a Boer–British war had it not been for the benevolent impulses of Kaiser Wilhelm II. Although Jameson's force got within fourteen miles of Johannesburg, by then they were outnumbered six to one. With nearly one-quarter of his men dead, wounded, or missing, and with no sign of either Uitlander or British Army support, Jameson realized his mission had failed. On January 2, 1896, he surrendered himself and his men; his men were disarmed and immediately released, but Jameson and his officers (including the three British

Regulars) were handed over to the Cape government on the Transvaal-Natal border with the expectation that they would be sent back to England for trial. Undoubtedly, they would have been had not "fate," in the form of the German Kaiser, now intervened.

The Transvaal Republic had developed strong ties with Germany following the discovery of the Rand gold field in 1886. Fifteen thousand Germans moved to Transvaal; German businesses established branches in Pretoria; a railroad from Pretoria to the Indian Ocean, through the Portuguese colony of Mozambique, was built with German engineering and capital; and the railway's terminus of Lourenco Marques became a steamship terminus for the North German Lloyd and Hamburg–America Lines. Moreover, even the establishment of the Anglo–German naval alliance in 1893 had not entirely eliminated Africa as a source of tension between London and Berlin. Ever since Bismarck's sudden colonialist initiative in 1884, Great Britain and Germany had found themselves at odds whenever Germany's African colonial ambitions were rekindled—most notably over the competition for Uganda and the headwaters of the Nile in Lake Victoria. (This complicated scramble, at one point involving England, Germany, France, *and* Leopold's Congo Free State, extended over several years before being resolved by a territorial trade between the British and the Germans. London relinquished the island of Heligoland in the North Sea, a rocky bit of land which threatened the passage from Hamburg and other key German ports; in exchange, Berlin gave up its pursuit of Uganda and also effectively ceded to the British the ability to establish a line of control literally running "from Cairo to Cape Town.") The Boers of Transvaal, under their implacably anti-British leader Paul Kruger, had (rather unsubtly) attempted to exploit the Anglo–German African rivalry from the moment Bismarck suddenly announced his (seeming) conversion to colonialism in 1884. That year, Kruger visited Berlin on his way home from signing a convention forbidding Transvaal from signing treaties without British approval. In clear derogation of the spirit—if not the letter—of the agreement he had just signed, Kruger, in a personal audience with Bismarck, urged Germany to come to the aid of the Boers (comparing his country to a "child" in aid of adult protection).

Bismarck wisely demurred, but the subsequent onset of the Rand gold rush brought thousands of Germans and millions of Deutschemarks to

Transvaal—which transformed the territory in the eyes of the German public. What had been an obscure corner of distant Africa was now a redoubtable little republic ruled by a *Brudervölker* with whom Germans shared a common *Kultur*, whose economic well-being was also increasingly intertwined with Germany's. Moreover, the Boers were especially fortunate in the appointment of the German consul, Herr von Herff, a man of great energy who never missed a chance to further develop and reinforce Germany's growing ties to Transvaal. Herff, who had developed into an aggressive Anglophobe due to his extended residence among the Boers, openly criticized the Anglo–German alliance in conversations with Boer leaders, including President Kruger. But fortunately for the peace of Southern Africa during the crisis in Boer–British relations triggered by the Jameson Raid, von Herff would also prove a realist about German vital interests, and therefore willing to employ his personal credibility with the Boer leadership to persuade them to accept the terms of what would become known as the "Wilhelm Mediation."

That "happy" outcome, however, lay in the future when, at the very end of 1895, London and Berlin first learned that Jameson and his force had invaded Transvaal. On the night of December 30, Chamberlain was preparing to host a ball at his house in Birmingham when a messenger brought the news; publicly vowing to "crush" Jameson's adventure, the Colonial Secretary left shortly after midnight on the first train to London. In fact, Chamberlain's display of shocked surprise was genuine—but not for the reasons he led his immediate audience to believe animated his display of righteous indignation. As we now know from the disclosure of the "Rhodes Telegrams," Chamberlain would not have been surprised by the fact of *a* raid. What caught Chamberlain unawares was that Jameson had jumped in before any word of an Uitlander rising. Chamberlain now feared (correctly) that the Uitlanders had gotten cold feet. Under such circumstances, Jameson was bound to fail. Much worse (in Chamberlain's view), this result would likely reinforce the influence of those Boers (led by Kruger) who opposed any move toward a political union with British South Africa. "Battling Joe" was a political realist as well as an aggressive imperialist; he knew that a hostile Boer nation in the British rear could be a damaging drain on Empire resources in what Chamberlain already called the "coming war" with the

USA, France, and Russia. Chamberlain therefore had to move quickly to distance himself, the Salisbury government, and Great Britain from Jameson's failed escapade. Yet, even as Chamberlain arrived at the Colonial Office and proceeded to coordinate a veritable barrage of telegrams and other actions, he could not help but feel that there was nothing anyone in England might do that would, fundamentally, repair the damage to British interests in Southern Africa which would result from "this perfect piece of imbecility."

Chamberlain was almost certainly right: there was essentially nothing anyone in England could do to undo the damage done by Jameson and his fellow raiders. Yet, within less than a week, someone outside of England, moved by impulse more than anything else, would do something that would not only repair the damage, but also bring about the very "British South Africa" (or close to it) that Jameson's adventure had been intended to achieve. The deteriorating situation in the Transvaal had introduced some strain into Anglo–German relations during the course of 1895. Notwithstanding the creation of the Anglo–German–Confederate naval convention less than two years before, many Germans were instinctively inclined to take the side of their "cousins," the Boers, as the dispute over Uitlander status continued to fester. When Transvaal President Kruger used the occasion of a party held at the German Club of Pretoria in honor of the Kaiser's birthday to proclaim the Boers' belief that Germany "would stop England from kicking our child republic," Great Britain's ambassador to Berlin protested the language to the German Secretary of State. That Autumn, the ambassador repeated what he described as London's concern about German "encouragement" of Boer "aspirations." These admonishments did not go down well with the Kaiser, who publicly expressed his exasperation with England "threatening its one true friend, the German Empire, over the fate of a few square miles of palm trees peopled by savages." But when von Herff telegraphed on December 30 with news of Jameson's raid, the Kaiser excitedly seized upon what he called "a God-sent chance for Germany to help bring about the reconciliation of our great friend, England, and our little cousin, Transvaal." Rejecting von Herff's suggestion that a naval landing force be brought into Johannesburg by rail from Delagoa Bay ("to protect German citizens and property," the consul urged), Wilhelm instead insisted on offering his services to mediate between Great Britain and the Boers.

On January 3, 1896, Wilhelm sent simultaneous telegrams to President Kruger and to Queen Victoria (his grandmother and counterpart—as Great Britain's Head of State). Decrying the "sad breakdown in effective communications between the British and Boer peoples," and expressing his "sincere desire to bring about a permanent reconciliation that will be the best assurance against further outbreaks of the most recent sort," the Kaiser offered his "personal services" as mediator and invited Pretoria and London to send representatives to Berlin to begin discussions "as soon as practicable." Chamberlain seized upon the invitation—much as a drowning man clutches at a life preserver. Chamberlain (and Salisbury) knew that Cecil Rhodes had been behind the raid. Chamberlain alone knew the degree to which he, personally, had been at least a silent "party of interest" to Rhodes's planning of the whole Uitlander uprising device for overthrowing Boer power and bringing about the long-sought "Union of South Africa" under British rule. When news of Jameson's capture reached London, Chamberlain also knew that any ensuing court proceedings would become the focal point for criticism of the government's African policy and would probably lead to the discovery of his own role in what many Englishmen were already calling a "nasty piece of freebootery." In one stroke, the Kaiser's telegrams had altered the landscape. Here was a chance perhaps to bring about the very Union whose fortunes seemed only days before to have been hopelessly blasted by Jameson's blunder. "By God, thanks to Willie, we may get a British South Africa yet, never mind that bungler Jameson," Chamberlain exulted to Salisbury, who had to agree that (in the Prime Minister's drier style), "For once, the Kaiser has ended one of his impulsive leaps on both feet—and without trampling any valued flora at that."

President Kruger, on the other hand, was stymied by the call for mediation. A *tête-à-tête* with the despised British was the last thing the seventy-year-old Kruger wanted—no matter how presumably sympathetic the host for such a function. Kruger, however, recognized that he could not say "no" to the German Emperor. First, Kruger had made too much, too recently, of Germany as the Boers' protector. Now that Germany seemed to be offering a helping hand (even while extending a second one to the hated British), Transvaal could not respond by slapping that hand away—not if Pretoria ever hoped to receive more decisive German assistance at some future and more desperate time. Second, Kruger's domestic political position was actually far more vulnerable than many outsiders appreciated. Younger Transvaal Boers chafed under Kruger's leadership, blaming his generation's anti-British attitudes for having (somehow) let control of the Rand gold fall into non-Boer hands. Should Kruger insist on spurning the Kaiser's offer (perhaps at the cost of war with Great Britain) Kruger knew he would have a difficult time holding on to power—especially if an ensuing war with the British Empire took its all-too-likely course.

And so, by March of 1896, Transvaal and Great Britain had accepted the Kaiser's offer. Negotiations opened in Berlin that spring and lasted some six months, at the end of which the "Convention of Southern African Unity" was entered into between the Cape Colony, Natal, Transvaal, the Orange Free State, and Rhodesia. The conference was "attended" by a representative of Her Majesty's government; for different reasons, Pretoria and London found it useful to have the gathering structured so as to obscure the political reality that Germany was mediating between the British Empire and one particularly obstreperous subordinate. The outcome was by no means assured: principally because Kruger and his Transvaal Boer faction were determined to resist any material concession on either the issue of Uitlander rights or on the broader question of "subordination"—the relinquishment of sovereignty necessary to effectuate the creation of a meaningful union out of a disparate collection of polities with no connection other than their (sharply divergent) relationships with the British crown. Moreover, Kruger was able, at least at the conference's outset, to forge a Boer "united front" with the Boers of the Orange Free State—who had enjoyed fairly good relations with Great Britain for decades and usually looked askance at the "pigheadedness" of Kruger and his followers. Kruger was able for a while to overcome these longstanding divisions by invoking the specter of "that criminal Rhodes." "He will elevate the *Kaffir* over us," Kruger warned Transvaal and Free State Boers alike, "and we will be as downtrodden as the Chosen People who labored in the mud pits of Egypt."

The Free Staters, and probably even most of Kruger's Transvaal compatriots, undoubtedly took the old man's jeremiads with more than a grain of salt. But the overwhelming majority of Boers from both of the "Trek States" were also unwilling, in the wake of the Jameson Raid, to enter into a general union along Canadian lines as long as Cecil Rhodes would continue to play a powerful political role in such a confederation. The Boers no longer trusted Rhodes (assuming a majority of them ever did—which is doubtful), and for that reason it soon became apparent to conference participants that a South African Union along Canadian lines was no longer a possibility. ("An African Canada, I fear, is no longer in the cards," Rhodes acknowledged to a close friend when the Berlin conference was only a few weeks along. "When Jameson raised the white flag at Doornkop"—the hill near Johannesburg, where Jameson surrendered to Transvaal forces—"he also gave up any chance that a British confederal flag might one day wave over Pretoria as well as Cape Town.") But while Kruger could block a Canadian–style confederation by using Rhodes as a bogeyman, Kruger could not avoid, try as he might, the corollary fact that Rhodes was the most powerful man in Southern Africa. Rhodes was determined to seize the opportunity of the Kaiser's intervention to compel the creation of *some* form of British South African union. In this regard, Rhodes now received the timely assistance of Chamberlain and Salisbury. Chamberlain persuaded Salisbury that any judicial action against Jameson (and the three Regular Army officers who joined the raid) should be postponed—pending the outcome of the conference. "It is not proper," Chamberlain informed the House of Commons, "for Great Britain to presume to treat this as a routine matter for English Law Courts and thereby possibly prevent a new South African Union from meting out the justice, or mercy, which that government, whose interests would be far more concerned by these events than our own, might choose to impose or grant."

In short, Her Majesty's Government would allow nothing—either in the form of a criminal action against Jameson, army disciplinary proceedings against his three Regular Army confederates, or (of greatest personal significance to Chamberlain) a parliamentary inquiry—to interfere with the course of the conference unfolding in Berlin. Jameson would remain under house arrest in Cape Town, and the officers likewise confined to barracks nearby (ostensibly to keep them "readily accessible" to the new Union authorities but also making them effectively—and for Chamberlain, conveniently—inaccessible to those interested members of the press and Parliament in England who also might be hostile to the government). Rhodes was thereby assured that his enemies—whether Boer or English—would be stymied in their efforts to uncover proof linking him to the Jameson Raid. Of course, Kruger already had the damning documents found on the site of Jameson's surrender, but the shock value of that evidence had long since worn off. Moreover, Rhodes and Kruger both knew that, as matters of *realpolitik* and economic interest took center stage at Berlin, Kruger needed to produce something "new," if he were to reinforce Boer distrust of Rhodes sufficient to stiffen Boer resistance to any form of union.

Kruger now proved unable to produce that "something," and when Rhodes, through allies, introduced what came to be called the "Swiss solution," the Boer front cracked wide open. Under the so-called "Swiss Plan" for South African union, the Cape Colony, Rhodesia, Transvaal, and the Orange Free State would be joined in a confederacy linked by a council executive—a structure resembling the Swiss Confederation with its plural executive; hence, the name attached to it by proponents and opponents alike. Each "state" would retain its Parliament, which would be supreme in certain "domestic" matters. The union executive council would have primary jurisdiction over certain "security" matters, and by unanimous vote, it could veto a state enactment if it were found to violate "fundamental" union interests. But each state would still retain daily control of its police and armed forces, although the latter would be subject to call in the event the British Empire was at war with a foreign power. The Crown would be the Head of State of the union and, by this method, the chief (if indirect) executive of each state (including the two Boer republics). As for the union council, its members would be chosen by whatever method was selected by that member's particular state, and a union "president" would be chosen from among the four: the position to rotate by an order fixed initially by a draw done by Kaiser Wilhelm himself.

These were the general provisions establishing the structure of the new union, and they went a long way to meeting the desire of an undoubted Boer majority in both Transvaal and the Orange Free State to preserving a substantial degree of autonomy as part of any sort of "British South Africa." ("After all," as one Cape Town delegate is said to have told his Free State counterpart, "you Boers will still have your own army—something the Irish and Quebeckers are unlikely ever to get!") Indeed, some of Rhodes's long-time supporters now openly criticized him for "abject surrender" to the Boers, and Rhodes himself acknowledged that even if he became

"President" of the new union (a virtual certainty, since he was bound to be selected by the Cape Parliament as the Cape's first representative on the executive council), he would preside over a much looser confederation than he and like-minded imperialists (including Chamberlain) would undoubtedly have preferred. Nonetheless, Rhodes was now convinced that the Swiss approach was the best—perhaps only—chance of bringing about any form of British South Africa, and he threw himself into the effort to persuade the doubters, both among English-speakers in the Cape Colony and among influential members of the British Parliament (who could scuttle the plan by blocking enabling legislation), that Imperial interests were best served by its acceptance. In this regard, Rhodes could invoke the personal financial sacrifice he would make, since the British South Africa Company, which he controlled, would have to surrender its interest in "Rhodesia"—although more cynical observers could, and did, retort that company shareholders, Rhodes included, would undoubtedly do quite well in Rhodesia's purchase of the lands that would constitute the new state.

As for Kruger and the other Transvaal "irreconcilables" (as they came to be known), the unveiling of the Swiss solution signaled their impending defeat. There remained, of course, the issue of Uitlander rights in Transvaal. (This was not an issue in the Orange Free State, which had never imposed a discriminatory residence requirement—but also had never experienced a great influx of outsiders, not being blessed with gold like its cousin republic.) On this point, Kruger dug in his heels, and for a while it looked like the conference might founder on the issue, until the Kaiser himself suggested a compromise: Each state would be entitled to maintain a residence requirement of up to seven years. Although Kruger wanted to reject this proposal as well (rightfully fearing he would lose the Transvaal presidency in an election in which tens of thousands of Uitlanders would suddenly be eligible to vote), Kruger was stymied when the Kaiser played his last card— an emotional speech at one of the many banquets at which the conference attendees were feted. In this speech, Wilhelm "pledged the honor of the German people to preserve the integrity of all the peoples of the glorious new Union of South Africa." "I would be remiss, and less than honest," he went on, "if I did not acknowledge the special bond we Germans feel for our *Brudervölker*, the Boers of Transvaal and the Orange Free State: I took the extraordinary step of calling this conference because we Germans feel a special obligation to this people, and I now assure them that we Germans shall never waver in our devotion to their well-being." The Boer representatives, including Kruger, were overcome with emotion by this remarkable declaration. Perhaps needless to say, many of the British in attendance were less taken, and the Wilhemstrasse hurried to reassure Whitehall that the Kaiser "did not intend, by his words, to suggest that Germany considered either Transvaal or the Orange Free State to be, in any way, a protectorate of the Reich." But even as the German Foreign Ministry was reassuring London, others were—very privately—telling the Boers that Wilhelm's words *did* constitute a "guarantee" by Germany of the terms of the union convention "intended to insure the integrity of the Boer nation."

These words would eventually come back to haunt Germans, Boers, and the British. But for now, the Kaiser's public—and private—assurances proved sufficient to force Kruger to accept the "Swiss solution." On September 3, 1896, an ecstatic Kaiser Wilhelm II announced that agreement had been reached on the formation of a "great new union that will unite the peoples of Southern Africa and help bring the blessings of peace and Christian civilization to that continent." (By "the blessings of …Christian civilization," the Kaiser certainly did not intend to include any possibility of equality of rights for the black African populations of the Transvaal or the Orange Free State; the new union left those matters, by implication, to each of the member states, thereby allowing the Boers to continue their policy of ruthless subjugation of the black denizens of the two republics.) Kruger was right to fear enfranchising the Uitlanders. In 1897, he lost his bid for reelection to the Transvaal presidency (and therefore his seat on the Union Council) to Piet Joubert, and it was the new Uitlander voters who gave Joubert his margin of victory. Rhodes, on the other hand, returned to Cape Town a hero and was promptly selected by the Cape Parliament the Cape representative on the Union Council. It was neither Kruger nor Rhodes, however, but the Orange Free State's President, Marthinus Steyn, who, in the drawing of lots conducted by Kaiser Wilhelm, received the honor of serving as the first Union President.

As for Jameson, he received a pardon from the Cape authorities—which was ratified by the Union Council. He then returned to Rhodesia, where he went into politics and ultimately achieved the Union Presidency. (Rhodes did not live to see that triumph for his trusted retainer and friend; he died of a heart attack just after the century's turn: the result of a life of great stress imposed on a fundamentally fragile constitution; Rhodes's early death also deprived him of the honor of serving as President of the South African Union that he had done so much to bring into being.) There was no investigation of Jameson's raid—either through court action or by the British Parliament; to the contrary, Salisbury and Chamberlain invoked the "triumph" of "British South Africa" in the Conservative–Unionist coalition's successful reelection campaign the following year. As the reader will see, while the new union carried within itself the seeds of its own destruction, the immediate conse-quence of the formation of "British South Africa" was almost certainly the avoidance of a war between the Boers and Great Britain—a war that the British undoubtedly would have won, but only at a terrible price in loss of life and the probable devastation of Transvaal and perhaps also the Orange Free State. Moreover, it is difficult to imagine the Kaiser acting as he did in the wake of the Jameson Raid had his worldview not been shaped by the overarching fact of the Anglo–German alliance (entered into less than three years before). Indeed, without the incentive for such an alliance (created by the Anglo–American rivalry rooted in the division of the American Union into Northern and Southern wings), one can imagine the Kaiser sending a very different sort of telegram and only to President Kruger: one that might have led to war between Great Britain and Germany as well as the British and the Boers. In sum, Southern Africa may well be the one place where the events set in motion by the Confederacy's victory actually preserved the peace rather than setting the stage for war. But as the reader will see, this effect would prove all too short-lived. And when war did come to Southern Africa, it would come with a vengeance and reap a terrible price.

(left) Parnahos José Maria da Silvar Junior, the Baron de Rio Blanco, Brazil's able and far-sighted statesman who managed to keep the Great Powers of southern South America out of the Alliance system he foresaw would lead to global war.

(right) The "Embrace of the Straits," the culmination of Rio Branco's efforts, which would spare South America's "Southern Cone" the destruction of the First Alliance War.

(left) **Cecil Rhodes, the brilliant and bold English transplant to Southern Africa, and the "founding father" of the South African Union.**

(right) **The Boer leader Paul Kruger, Rhodes' principal antagonist, whose determined opposition to a merger of the Afrikaner Republics into a greater Southern African union was overcome by Kaiser Wilhelm II at the Berlin Conference of 1896.**

15

WORLD WAR I: (2) THE CRISIS YEAR OF 1898—IMMEDIATE CAUSES OF THE WAR AND ITS OUTBREAK

Having reviewed why two key areas of the globe—the Southern Cone of South America and the British South African Union—were spared the destruction caused by World War One (perhaps more familiarly known as the First Alliance War), I now turn to the events that proved the immediate precipitating causes of that conflict. Although the dynamic of the Global Alliance System was the root cause, one must look more closely to identify the specific reasons why world war erupted in October of 1898—as opposed to March of the previous year or five years after that. Although historians have never reached a consensus on this point, I believe the evidence implicates three crises that came together in such a fashion as to trigger war between the Alliances in the fall of that fateful year. Because the Franco–British collision at Fashoda in the Southern Sudan is the most familiar, and also because it is regarded as the immediate cause of the conflict, I will save that discussion for the end. The first crisis I will address is the tension between the USA and Great Britain over Canada, set in motion by the Yukon Gold Rush of 1897. But to understand the dynamic of the Yukon–Alaska Crisis of March 1898, once must return to the immediate aftermath of Secession and its effect on Canadian–USA relations.

The South's victory in the War of Secession had a profound impact upon what was then known as "British North America," of which Canada was only one part. At that time, Canada consisted only of "Canada West" and "Canada East," corresponding to the later confederal provinces of Ontario and Quebec and which together formed the Province of Canada—also called the "United Canadas." British North America was little more than a name applied to a patchwork of territories with no constitutional connection other than a common allegiance to the Crown of England. Its greatest area was an immense land owned by the Hudson's Bay Company under a royal charter, stretching from Canada West (Ontario) to the independent crown colonies of British Columbia and Vancouver Island—but virtually devoid of white settlement. British Columbia and Vancouver Island, on the Pacific Coast, felt virtually no link to the distant Canadas, which in turn sensed little binding them to the separate Maritime Provinces of New Brunswick, Nova Scotia, Newfoundland, and Prince Edward's Island. The Canadas themselves were united in little more than name. Canada West (Ontario) was dominated by Protestant settlers from England and Scotland, while Canada East (Quebec) was split between an English-speaking economic elite and an impoverished French–Catholic majority (who as recently as 1837 had risen in rebellion against British rule). This division effectively paralyzed the provincial legislature and prevented what should have been British North America's most influential province from exercising any leadership.

Perhaps these squabbling and disparate interests would have managed to come together without the spur of the breakup of the American Union to the south. The fact remains, however, that the War of Secession produced an upheaval in BNA politics, leading to the establishment of the Canadian Confederation in 1867. Beginning with the *Trent* crisis in the fall of 1861 and continuing through the crucial weeks of October and November 1862 (when the issue of peace—or war—between the USA and the British Empire hung on President Lincoln's answer to Lord Palmerston's offer to "mediate" an end to the secessionist struggle), those who had previously seemed to cry out in the political wilderness for a British political union stretching from the Atlantic to the Pacific suddenly found in the Canadas as well as the Maritimes a newly receptive audience for their proposals. During the *Trent* crisis (I refer to the seizure of two Confederate representatives bound for England, taken forcibly from the British steamship *Trent* by a Northern man-o-war in November 1861), Great Britain managed to dispatch ten thousand troops across the Atlantic. Yet the notion that this force alone could have prevented a Northern invasion of the Canadas was so patently ludicrous, and the state of the Canadian militia that would have had to support them so painfully insufficient, that union proponents were able to seize upon the issue as proof that the existing patchwork of British North America could not protect its citizens against the "Yankee" threat to the south. Then, in May of 1862, the Parliament of the Canadas rejected a militia bill designed to address the deficiencies disclosed by the *Trent* affair. Although London managed to rush an additional ten thousand men to North America during the height of the "Recognition Crisis" later that year, those with eyes to see knew that had war come between the USA and Great Britain, both "Upper" (Ontario) and "Lower" (Quebec) Canada would probably have been overrun by superior "Yankee" forces.

In other words, although the "Imperial Connection" could be counted upon, it could not substitute for a strong "Canadian" effort. And as the militia bill fiasco had shown, the existing political structure could not assure that effort would be made in time—if at all—to defeat an American invasion. Only a union joining (at the very least) the Province of Canada to the Maritimes offered any realistic hope of breaking the Protestant–Catholic deadlock within the Canadas, thereby eliminating the chief political obstacle to an effective Canadian defense effort. To be sure, the push for confederation also benefited from factors having little or nothing to do with events south of the USA–Canada border. But the War of Secession remains the central defining moment that galvanized support for a Canadian Confederation. "I have often wondered where Canada would be today," Conservative leader and Prime Minister John McDonald is said to have mused in the early 1880s, "had the Americans not obliged by offering up the example of their fissiparous conduct. I would like to think we could have resisted the inevitable pressure to become a part of 'the American enterprise' had Richmond lost its valiant struggle for independence. Yet what I would like to think and what would likely have been might very well have proven different things."

But if Secession played a vital role in the creation of the Canadian Confederation, the new confederal government proved almost as reluctant as its provincial predecessors to make the major investments necessary to transform the Canada–USA border into a bristling chain of fortifications. First, Ottawa quickly recognized that any such effort would have to be made without assistance from London. Neither Palmerston's government nor its Conservative successor proved willing to spend the millions of pounds sterling required to fortify the Canada–USA frontier. To the contrary, in the wake of the signing of the Treaty of London in the spring of 1863, the British went out of their way to smooth over relations with Washington, including— over sharp Canadian protest—the withdrawal of the bulk of the regiments sent during the *Trent* affair and the Recognition Crisis. These withdrawals were coupled with a clear message that there would be no funds forthcoming from London either to fortify the land border or to establish naval flotillas on the Great Lakes. (London's unwillingness to pursue a policy that might in any way jeopardize the cultivation of an Anglo–American *detente* in the late 1860s also put an end to speculation on the part of some Canadian leaders— most notably John McDonald—that a new British American confederation could achieve security against a "Yankee" invasion by an alliance between the "Mother Country" and the South.)

The result was a defense policy that made no realistic effort to address how the Canadian Confederation should defend itself in a war with the USA. Although Ottawa managed to persuade Gladstone's government to retain a Regular Army presence at Fort Garry in the new Province of Manitoba after the suppression of the First Riel Uprising in 1870, Disraeli's cabinet ordered these units reduced to a single regiment in the midst of the Anglo–Russian Crisis of 1878. In the meantime, the Canadian government, whether made up of McDonald's Conservatives or Alexander McKenzie's "Grit" Liberals, failed to make any but token investments in the sort of defenses that Canada would require even to slow an American attack. Washington had calmed Canadian fears by embracing London's invitation to maintain "peaceful and open relations" with Great Britain and British North America. Although short term political calculation caused the Seward Administration to allow the ten-year trade reciprocity agreement to lapse in 1866, Washington resisted calls by Northern expansionists to develop an "advanced" military presence along the Canadian border, and both the Seward and Blaine Administrations took care to honor the "Spirit of New York" established by the tripartite agreement of 1871. (The reader will recall my earlier discussion of the negotiations leading to—and the resulting terms of—the Treaty of New York.) Moreover, Canada was anything but a cash-flush country.

It had committed to a unifying, but expensive, transcontinental railway project. With the onset of the economic slump of the mid-1870s (which hit Canadians much harder than their American neighbors), starvation rations for Confederation defenses became a politically irresistible policy—especially to the Grit–Liberal government that held power from 1872 to 1878. Indeed, it was not the Americans but the Russians who spurred the first political crisis over neglect of Canadian defenses. During the Anglo–Russian Crisis of 1878, the sudden specter of war between the British and Russian Empires caused a hue and cry when a hurried inventory revealed what everyone in Ottawa had known for years: Canada was utterly unprepared to defend itself against attack—whether by distant Russians or neighboring Americans.

The Anglo–Russian war scare quickly passed, and despite the appalling state of Canadian defenses disclosed during the weeks when a clash with St. Petersburg seemed imminent, little was done to rectify the situation. Although McDonald was a visceral opponent of "Yankee" power (the reader will recall how McDonald toyed with the notion of a British–Canadian–CSA alliance even before the establishment of the Canadian confederation), he was also committed upon returning to power in 1878 to completing the transcontinental rail link between British Columbia and Ontario, which had languished under MacKenzie. For precisely that reason, McDonald was prepared to continue the Liberals' neglect of Canada's defenses—if only because McDonald realized that the country could not afford both a concerted drive to complete the transcontinental railway and even the beginnings of a defensive buildup. In McDonald's view, the railroad was the essential "national project." If left undone much longer, British Columbia, as well as the former Hudson Bay Company lands, would be lost to the Americans—and not because of military conquest: BC (into which Vancouver Island had been merged in 1866) would quit on the grounds that the Canadas and the Maritimes had broken the promise of a railroad which was the condition for BC joining the Confederation, while the "great empty space" would be settled by Americans (brought west on the Northern Pacific and St. Paul lines) who were virtually certain then to demand they be allowed to make "their" lands a part of "Greater America."

To be sure, McDonald did insist that Canada must begin to reverse the consequences of years of neglecting the country's defenses. But when the Liberal opposition raised a hue and cry over the cost of new fortifications and McDonald's French–speaking Quebec allies warned against a *Canadien* backlash over any attempt to convert the existing fragmented militia system into a true regular army controlled from Ottawa, McDonald—immersed in the battle for passage of the Canadian Pacific Railroad Bill—made clear that defense reform would only be pursued with all "deliberate" speed. It took the Western War crises of 1882 and 1884, and the Second Riel Uprising the following year, to shake Canadians out of their complacency and give McDonald and his allies the political maneuvering room necessary to force through a program of military reforms. Even then, what McDonald's government was initially willing to do proved far too little in the view of those in Great Britain (Conservatives and Liberals) who agreed with McDonald that the "Yankee threat" could only be dealt with by an alliance with the CSA. Essentially, all McDonald offered was a Canadian promise to "modernize" the country's hapless militia. Beyond that, it was apparent to Joseph Chamberlin and other proponents of an Anglo–CSA Alliance that the Canadians expected the "Mother Country" to assume the entire financial burden of developing the extensive series of fortifications and Great Lakes flotillas essential if Canada were to have any chance of repelling an American assault. As McDonald quickly learned, this was unacceptable to the British supporters of the very alliance whose establishment McDonald had come to London to urge—Canada would have to accept a "fair" (i.e., substantial) share of the costs of a truly effective defense. The Imperial Lion would bear the lion's share—but no more than that.

McDonald returned to Canada in March of 1886—just as the debate over Gladstone's Irish Home Rule Bill was gathering steam. Although McDonald could report the good news that a coalition of leaders capable of commanding a parliamentary majority (Salisbury for the Conservatives and Chamberlin for the "Unionist" Liberals) were committed to a policy of an alliance with the American Confederacy, McDonald also had to temper this report with the firm word that Canada would be expected to shoulder a much greater share of the ensuing costs than it would prefer to assume.

The result would be Canada's second political crisis over defense. Arguably, the Great Defense Debate of 1886 was only a continuation of the "national argument" that began with the First Western War Scare of August 1882. The response that summer had been quintessentially British in its improvisionality and Canadian in its substantive evasiveness. A reluctant Gladstone had authorized the dispatch of (once again) ten thousand British regulars as well as an additional squadron of ships to the Royal Navy's Halifax station, but by the time these forces arrived, the immediate threat had passed (disarmed, the reader will recall, by Breckinridge's brilliant diplomatic stroke of offering to "limit" the war to west of the Mississippi). In the meantime, seemingly faced with imminent invasion by upward of one hundred thousand USA troops, McDonald's government ordered mobilization of the militia. The result was a fiasco: although the militia on paper represented a "front-line" force of sixty-five thousand (nominally increased by twenty-five thousand since 1878), mobilization proved these numbers a fraud. By mid-September 1882, weeks after any real danger of an American invasion had passed, only twenty thousand widely scattered militia had reported as "ready" to repel the expected invader.

McDonald, for one, recognized the mortal danger this performance represented. But with the Canadian Pacific Railway financial crisis rapidly approaching its peak, and with the immediate threat of invasion receding, McDonald had no practical political choice but to fob off demands by outraged citizens (even including many Grit–Liberals) that Canada's defenses be strengthened. This only postponed the need to address the issue; when the Second Western War Crisis flared in 1884, Ottawa confronted the appalling prospect of a repetition of the embarrassing performance of two years earlier. The ensuing armistice avoided a public demonstration of the complete extent of Canada's failure to address the fundamental deficiencies in the country's defenses disclosed by the fiasco of 1882, but the crisis of the Second Riel Uprising the following spring forced thoughtful Canadians—Liberal as well as Conservative—to acknowledge that the country could not hope to repel an American attack without a total overhaul of the country's existing military force. Although the militia (with the vital assistance of the British regulars yet to be withdrawn when the news of Riel's uprising reached Ottawa) performed well in meeting and defeating Riel's *Metis* and his Indian allies, the dangerously close-run nature of several of the ensuing battles provided all the proof that should have been necessary that the militia could not provide a sound foundation for Canadian defense against any sophisticated foe. I say "should have been," because the hydraulic pressures of politics can crush even the most incontrovertible-seeming of "objective" facts. As McDonald quickly discovered, the realities of Canadian politics proved stubbornly resistant to the objective reality of the country's defense needs.

The fundamental political problem reflected the old dividing line between English- and French-speaking Canada. McDonald had returned to power in 1878, in part because he mastered the class-based divisions of Quebec *Canadien* society—exploiting the antagonism between the elite *bleus* of Montreal and the impoverished *rouges* of the countryside to build a majority Anglo–French coalition. But when the *Canadien* elements of that coalition learned McDonald had committed, during his London visit, to replacing the militia with a true regular army controlled by Ottawa, the resulting political explosion threatened to bring down his government. Fortunately for McDonald, the pace of political developments in England relieved him of the need to force an up-or-down vote on the proposed "militia reform." Had the vote been taken that year, McDonald's government probably would have fallen, and the "anti-army" Liberals would have swept into power—with possibly severe ramifications for the ability of the new Unionist government in London to complete an alliance with Richmond. But precisely because England was in the throes of its own election, McDonald was able to avoid a vote by the Canadian Parliament. Once the Anglo–Confederate "understanding" was an established fact the following year, McDonald was prepared to go to the country and demand a "mandate" to carry out Canada's "sacred obligation to the cause of Imperial defense." Even so, the defection of many of McDonald's *Canadien* supporters made the election a very close-run thing; the Conservatives were returned to power—but with a substantially reduced majority.

At this point, events outside Canada began to play a decisive role. One reason McDonald was able to overcome the defection of many formerly Conservative *Québeçois* was the belligerent response of the Garfield Administration to the formation of the Anglo–Confederate alliance. The announcement by Washington of an expanded naval building program, coupled with the expressed intention to develop railheads along the USA–Canadian border (necessary to assure American forces of the ability to make a fast attack), convinced many Canadians (including numerous formerly Grit–Liberal voters) that the "Yankee threat" was now a reality. In response, the new Parliament approved McDonald's army reform measure (designed to establish a standing Canadian regular army of 125,000 by 1893) as well as a program of fortification and Great Lakes flotilla development. The implementation of the army reforms then produced exactly the political uproar over the end of the militia system which McDonald's Quebec allies had warned against almost a decade before. Moreover, this controversy was exacerbated by the growing fear among *Canadiens—bleus* as well as *rouges*—that the alliance with the CSA would inevitably lead to a war between Canada and France. Still, McDonald pressed ahead, and his incomparable political skills managed to carry the Conservatives to one more general election victory (in 1891). McDonald, however, did not survive the terrible physical toll of the effort, dying within a few months of this last triumph. The Conservatives, deprived of his leadership, lost the next general election to the resurgent Liberals. But by then, the militarization of Canada was too far gone to be reversed—and the new Liberal Prime Minister Wilfred Laurier had no intention of reversing it, in any case.

Laurier had been convinced by the great broadening of the Global Alliance System in 1893 and 1894 that Canada was almost certain to find itself under an American assault—in a world war that could now break out at virtually any time. Under such circumstances, Laurier believed he would be guilty of "criminal negligence" to follow the advice of his more radical supporters and adopt a policy of demilitarization. Laurier's fear was that war with America might destroy Canada from within, unless Quebec was sufficiently reassured that Canada's English–speaking majority was prepared to respect the rights of *Canadiens* to their distinctive French culture. In fact, Laurier's fears would ultimately prove justified; as the events of 1916 would definitively confirm, an utterly alienated French Canada was the Achilles heel of the Canadian Confederation. But in 1896, *Canadiens* had only started down the path that would culminate in the 1916 uprising—with its fatal, final consequences for Canadian independence. As of

1896, Canada, and Laurier as the country's leader, faced a different kind of threat to national independence: the stark reality that the USA, in the wake of the collapse of the policy of peaceful coexistence exemplified by "the Spirit of New York," was now evidently committed to achieving the conquest of Canada in the event of war with the Anglo–German–Confederate Alliance. And the harsh truth confronting Canadians was the obvious ability of America, given its vastly greater population and wealth, to accomplish a Canadian conquest even in the face of vigorous Canadian resistance. For this reason, Laurier was determined to avoid giving Washington any excuse to start a war.

Given this policy of "nonprovocation," it is ironic that a Canadian–American dispute would prove one of the triggers for World War One. Unfortunately for Laurier, the discovery of gold in the Canadian Yukon in 1896 made acute the need to resolve the uncertain border between Alaska and the Yukon—and under circumstances ill-suited to the peaceful resolution of such a controversy. British North America and the USA had been able to resolve prior border disputes without resort to war. The Webster–Ashburton Treaty of 1842 settled the border between Maine and New Brunswick. In 1846, the Oregon country dispute was handled by extending the Forty-Ninth Parallel line from the Rockies to the Pacific Ocean. In 1871, Kaiser Wilhelm I of the new German Empire arbitrated a resolution of the San Juan Islands question on the Washington Territory–British Columbia border. Had Canadian–American relations been able to take a more peaceful course, one can imagine a similar resolution of the Alaska–Yukon boundary issue (especially as this was the only portion of the lengthy boundary between the two countries that remained in controversy). But by the time the discovery of gold in the Canadian Yukon set off a "gold rush" that rivaled California's in intensity, Canada and the USA had become opposed parts in a global alliance system. Even worse, traditional American annexationist sentiment had become virtual government policy—even if William McKinley had been elected President in 1896 in part because he seemed to promise a cooling of the "war fever" in Washington. Although the vigorous and youthful Democratic nominee, William Jennings Bryan, had skillfully exploited the growing fear of war engendered by Republican "bellicosity," McKinley was able to turn back

Bryan's challenge in part because the voters sensed the Ohioan's genuine desire to avoid war.

McKinley's personal commitment to peace grew out of his Secession War service. As a supply sergeant with the Army of the Potomac, McKinley earned accolades for his cool bravery at the Battle of Gettysburg but also took away an abiding horror of the slaughter he witnessed. McKinley's views, however, were rare among the Republican leadership. Far more typical were the sentiments expressed on Memorial Day of 1895 by Massachusetts Chief Justice (and future US Supreme Court Chief Justice) Oliver Wendell Holmes, Jr. Holmes, like McKinley, had served in the Army of the Potomac. Shot through the neck at Gettysburg, Holmes survived, and his battlefield experiences were immortalized by his father's essay, "My Hunt after the Captain." (Holmes, Sr., was a prominent Boston physician who achieved national renown through his *Atlantic Monthly* column, "The Autocrat of the Breakfast Table"; his essay about traveling through the wreck of Union defeat to find his elder son touched a deep chord among Northerners in the dark days that followed the disaster of Gettysburg.) Even before appointment to the US Supreme Court bench, Justice Holmes had become known for his literary style and his fierce dedication to the cause of a "fighting America." In the famous 1895 Memorial Day address titled "The Soldier's Faith," Holmes reminisced about his Secession War experience and then urged his Harvard College audience to prepare for "the next chapter of the struggle":

> [P]erhaps as long as man dwells upon the globe, his destiny is battle, and he has to take the chances of war.... [I]n the midst of doubt, in the collapse of creeds, there is one thing I do not doubt, that no man who lives in the world with most of us can doubt, and that is that the faith is true and adorable which leads a soldier to throw away his life in obedience to a blindly accepted duty, in a cause which he little understands, in a plan of campaign of which he has no notion, under tactics of which he does not see the use.... It is the more necessary to learn the lesson afresh from perils newly sought.... ("The Soldier's Faith," reprinted in *The Mind and Faith of Chief Justice Holmes*, Max Lerner, ed. (Boston, Little, Brown & Co., 1943))

Holmes could not fairly be called a member of the Republican politi-cal leadership, but his Memorial Day address became a sensation, receiv-ing praise from Assistant Secretary of the Navy Roosevelt and numerous other "war hawks." That then-Governor of Ohio William McKinley kept silent indicated his very different conviction: that, as he repeatedly articu-lated during the next year's presidential campaign, "every reasonable and prudent effort must be made to avoid the calamity of a third war between North and South in less than a generation."

The Yukon would contribute mightily to the frustration of these hopes. Gold had become an international obsession by the 1890s, as the break-neck speed of industrialization (fueled, in important part, by the demands of a burgeoning armaments industry) placed increasingly severe strains on the international monetary system and its "gold standard." The gap between demand for gold and available supplies had contributed to the economic instability of the period, which had been marked by recurrent financial panics. Although the USA had not been seriously affected by the first of these contractions which began in 1873 and ran nearly five years in much of the rest of the industrializing world (America benefited from a combination of substantial public investments in railroads and defense as well as the banking and monetary reforms of the late 1860s), the country could not avoid the full force of the economic downturn that began in 1893 and came to be called the "Great Depression."

It was the suffering of the Great Depression that brought the Democrats within a whisker of winning the presidency in 1896. Bryan trailed McKinley by only twenty thousand popular votes, although the Electoral College contest did not prove quite so close. In fact, the causes of the economic difficulties of the last quarter of the nineteenth century were manifold, and the "gold drought" was more a manifestation than a contributing cause. The public perception, however, was that too little gold was "the" source of economic travail; accordingly, "the" solution must come through the expansion of the gold supply. For precisely this reason, the public in North America and Europe developed a "refined sensitivity" to any suggestion that prospectors had found the "real thing"—a gold field that could, over-night, bring an end to the crippling effects of the international specie short-age. And for that reason alone, the news of a vast-seeming gold discovery in the Canadian Yukon would have triggered excitement. But that news, which in July of 1897 burst upon the outside world with the arrival in San Francisco and Seattle of ships, only days apart and each carrying dozens of ragged men loaded with gold, came at a time peculiarly suited to set off a veritable international stampede. Although the establishment of the basic contours of the Alliance System had quickly been followed by a war scare in 1895 (over the denouement of the Sino–Japanese War), by the summer of 1897, jangled nerves had settled sufficiently that full attention could be devoted to the exciting news from remotest Canada.

Moreover, the Pacific Northwest region of the USA was peculiarly vulnerable to the stimulating effect of the Yukon news. Although the completion of the Union Pacific Railroad's transcontinental link (with its Puget Sound terminus at Tacoma) had brought a measure of prosperity, the area with its high debt load had suffered particularly hard during the economic downturn of the early 1890s. For precisely this reason, the announcement of gold in the Yukon could not help but fire the local economic imagination: not only of those who would set out for the goldfields but also of those who would see in the business of supplying would-be prospectors a way out of the economic doldrums. By the fall of 1897, a flood of thousands making their way north was pouring through the port of Seattle, and the resulting boom's beneficent effects were soon felt in the surrounding area. The chaos of this "stampede," however, quickly gave rise to tension along the ill-defined border between the Alaska panhandle and British Columbia. The first wave of would-be "sourdoughs" had arrived in Alaska, only to discover that the principal pass route to the "Klondike"—as the gold-bearing territory in the Canadian Yukon now came to be known—was closed for the winter. Although several thousand nonetheless tried the "White Trail" pass that fall, only a handful made it; the balance fell back on Skagway, which seemingly overnight was transformed into a teeming city—and just as rapidly degenerated into a center of lawlessness.

USA President McKinley and Canadian Prime Minister Laurier both desired to handle the gold rush in (as McKinley put the matter to his cabinet) "a measured, calm fashion." Despite the common border with Canada, the USA had never maintained a substantial regular army presence in Alaska—beyond a single outpost at Sitka. Now, in response to the news of the gold strike in the Yukon, the McKinley Administration elected only to send a team of undercover intelligence agents (whose members included the future war hero and author Jack London, for whom this would be his first major assignment). When the news of the gold strikes reached Ottawa, the Laurier government had dispatched two companies of Royal Canadian Mounted Police from the RCMP outpost at Fort Nelson in British Columbia to Dawson (the locus of the Klondike mining area). Like McKinley, Laurier rejected sending regular army troops lest such a move provoke Washington to do likewise. But "the Mounties" (as the RCMP were popularly known) had served as Canada's *de facto* "Army of the West" during the militia period, and their commander was now a member of the Canadian Army General Staff. These heavily armed troops might be called "police," but news of their dispatch still triggered a call by American war hawks for "commensurate measures." Laurier, however, had calculated correctly that sending only the Mounties would give McKinley sufficient "cover" to resist pressure for a regular army response. "We do not need to invite trouble in this distant corner of the globe," McKinley said in rejecting war hawk calls for the dispatch of several army regiments, "and we can best avoid that trouble by showing confidence in the local authorities on both sides of the border to maintain good order."

The problem for this theory was the absence of local authority on the American side. The official vacuum had quickly been filled by a gang of criminals led by the notorious Richard "Soapy" Smith, and the depredations of the Smith gang triggered a vigorous response by Canadian authorities. The RCMP had taken quick charge upon their arrival in Dawson and almost immediately began to institute measures along the Alaska–BC border that were bound to offend even moderate American sensibilities. The initial problem, however, was not Skagway's lawlessness, but the appalling spectacle of desperate men—and women—trying to force their way up from Skagway through White Pass to Lake Bennett (and from there by water to Dawson and the Klondike). Fearing a human catastrophe, the RCMP quickly implemented measures that undoubtedly prevented hundreds of deaths—but also initiated a cycle of action and reaction in far-off Washington and Ottawa which would bring the two countries (and their allies) to the brink of war by the following spring. To begin, the Mounties initiated inspections of pack animals to prevent diseased animals cross-ing into Canada. This was no minor matter. Conditions on the White and neighboring Chilkoot passes were exceedingly harsh, and most of the eager "Klondikers" had little or no experience with handling horses or mules. By September, the pass trails were littered with the rotting carcasses of hun-dreds of animals, while the brutalized survivors were usually so weakened as to be very easy prey to—and carriers of—disease. Next, the Canadians announced that no one could enter the Yukon Territory without a year's supply of food: some 1,150 pounds. This second measure was a response to conditions in the Klondike itself, where the tenuous supply lines between Dawson and the "outside world" literally threatened to bring on a famine that fall.

The supply restrictions did not apply until someone sought entry into the Yukon. An American could pass freely from Alaska into British Columbia without having to satisfy the rule. Yet the demands of public necessity, however reasonable when considered from the point of view of an RCMP commandant in Dawson, could not look the same to American political leaders in Washington. They only understood that Canada—in the person of the RCMP forces on the spot—was seeking to bar American access to the wealth of the Klondike. The reader may find it puzzling that the USA government should presume to take offense over a Canadian attempt to limit access to a valuable national resource. But the guarded point of view of the mid-twentieth century was not that of the late nine-teenth: when it was generally believed that nations should allow anyone—not just their nationals—a "fair chance" to extract a country's mineral wealth. Still, suspicion that Canada might be trying to exclude Americans from their "rightful opportunity" to share in the Klondike's riches probably would not have been sufficient to bring Canada and the USA to the brink of war. It was the combination of this perception with the vagaries of the Alaska–British Columbia border that proved decisive. The RCMP estab-lished checkpoints on the White and Chilkoot passes—initially to enforce the "healthy pack animal" requirement and then to prevent the Smith gang from gaining access to the interior (and also, if possible, to prevent the suspected American intelligence agents from slipping across the border). The Mounties established these checkpoints on what they considered to be the Canadian side of the border. These locations, however, encroached on American understanding of the border's location—a fact made clear to Washington in the reports of Jack London and his colleagues.

When these reports reached Washington, McKinley was compelled to respond to what appeared to be a clear infringement of USA territorial sovereignty. In February, the first USA regular army units reached Skagway and neighboring Dyea with orders to move up the White and Chilkoot trails and "establish control over all national territory—up to the point of the international border." The commander of the American forces, however, elected a cautious approach, sending a probing patrol only up the Chilkoot (the one open pass) to "investigate and assess." (USA forces had their hands full just establishing law and order in Skagway—a process that was not completed until March, when "Soapy" Smith and his gang were sent packing under armed guard back to Seattle to face federal charges of "interfering with the exercise of lawful military authority.") But by spring of 1898, Washington would brook no further delay. American control over the international boundary at the point of the passes from Alaska into British Columbia had to be reestablished "with every means at your disposal"—so read the directive from Secretary of War Robert Lincoln. The Canadian government, fearful of just such a move, had already dispatched regular army troops to reinforce the RCMP. These forces, however, could not hope to reach the area of the disputed passes until April, and the Americans knew it. On March 10, 1898, two American columns, each proceeding up a different trail, approached RCMP positions. The Mounties' orders were clear: they were not to put up a fight absent "sufficient assurance of holding their ground," and without reinforcements, there was no reasonable prospect of that (at least, not in the view of the RCMP commanders on the scene). On the morning of March 12, the Canadians began an orderly withdrawal, yielding up the passes and establishing new positions some ten miles farther inland.

The news of America's "victory" reached Washington before Ottawa, but the Laurier government was still swift to react, demanding the "immediate" end to what it termed an "American incursion onto Canadian soil." It was now May, and President McKinley realized that, with Canadian army troops pouring into Dawson, several thousand American citizens, who had either reached the Klondike or were on the way there, risked being taken hostage in the event of war. (One of the human tragedies of the world war that would break out in less than half a year was the fate of the thousands of Klondikers and would-be Klondikers; the war completely disrupted both the flow of supplies into the Klondike and the routes leading to the outside, with the result that hundreds, perhaps thousands, died—many by starvation—in the ensuing panic to escape.) Fortunately, both McKinley and Laurier remained determined to avoid a war, and it is almost entirely to their credit that Canada, the USA, and their respective allies avoided a world war that spring. Overcoming the resistance of Republican war hawks who saw an opportunity to acquire gold resources rivaling the great South African fields, McKinley negotiated a mutual withdrawal that established a ten-mile "disarmed zone" at key disputed border crossing points. McKinley was aided in his efforts by the timely arrival of Jack London's latest report, demonstrating the wholly local and quite sensible reasons for the various Canadian measures that had so agitated official Washington. Despite the Mounties' best efforts, London had managed to get to Dawson, where he was able to confirm how desperate the supply situation had been which triggered the imposition of the minimum supply rule.

By June, it appeared that the "Yukon Crisis," like the Far East Crisis of 1895 and the less acute Eastern Mediterranean Crisis of the previous year, had passed. (It is an irony of the Yukon Crisis that the gold strike proved only a fraction of the value of the South African fields, to which comparison was so frequently made—a fact only learned after World War One when miners were allowed to resume their efforts in what was by then the American Yukon.) Unfortunately for the cause of continuing peace, the badly frayed nerves of the Chancelleries of the Alliance Powers could not be much settled because of yet another confrontation in Central Asia between the British and Russian Empires—a confrontation exacerbated by the Yukon–induced "war scare" but also with independent sources found in the continuing "Great Game" being played with ever deadlier earnestness over the border lands lying between Russian Central Asia and British India. The reader will recall that Central Asia (and particularly Afghanistan and its immediate environs) had been the locus of a series of Anglo–Russian confrontations during the 1880s and 1890s. The last of these—the Chitral

Succession Crisis of 1893—occurred immediately prior to the formation of the Grand Alliances and directly contributed to breaking the diplomatic impasse between Great Britain and Germany over the scope of an Anglo–German naval alliance. When the aged Aman-Ul-Mulk died in August of 1892, his son Afzul attempted to seize power—only to be ambushed and murdered by Aman-Ul-Mulk's brother, Sher, who then proclaimed himself ruler. In the meantime, the dead king's older son and rightful heir, Nizam, had escaped to British–controlled Gilgit; organizing an expedition under approving British eyes, Nizam marched back into Chitral. Sher, sensing defeat, fled to Afghanistan. (It was during this time that calls by the St. Petersburg press for a Russian "protectorate" over Chitral persuaded Salisbury to redouble British efforts to reach an accord with Germany.)

Nizam's triumph proved short-lived. The following year (1894), he was murdered by his teenage half-brother Amir, who proclaimed himself king—the country's fourth ruler in less than three years. The British authorities were appalled by this development, as they had supported Nizam against Sher and in any case considered Amir utterly unsuited to the demanding task of ruling Chitral. Fortunately, Amir did not turn to the Russians for help: instead seeking the support of Umra Khan, ruler of the neighboring "Kingdom" of Swat. Despite relief that Amir had not turned to the Russians, the Government of India still feared a possible move by St. Petersburg and quickly marshaled forces to advance into Chitral and overthrow Nizam's murderer. A dramatic series of operations culminated in April 1895 with the arrival in Chitral of a powerful British force that quickly took control. (Amir had actually been deposed months before, but the advance British guard that accomplished that *coup de main* was then placed under siege by a returning Sher; only the extraordinary exertions of a relief column, braving the terrible wintry conditions of the Shandur Pass, avoided an awful massacre.) The issue then became what to do with the previously independent kingdom of Chitral; despite the vociferous objections of the St. Petersburg press, London concurred with Calcutta that Chitral must be annexed outright.

An important reason for this decision was the failure the year before of talks between the British and the Russians, aimed at resolving the status of the Pamirs, the mountainous region that constituted a political "no-man's land" east of Afghanistan and west of Chinese Turkestan. A British proposal to extend Afghanistan eastward—and thereby create a "buffer zone" between the Russian Empire and British India—had fallen on deaf ears. (This should have come as no surprise, given the culmination that same year of the talks producing the establishment of the Great Alliances; a less polarized diplomatic context might have meant a different resolution of Anglo–Russian differences in Central Asia, but with the decision of London and St. Petersburg to enter opposing coalitions, the effort to achieve a peaceful resolution of the "Central Asia Question" was effectively foredoomed.) Advocates of the "forward school," led by George Curzon (then Undersecretary of State for Foreign Affairs and soon to be appointed Viceroy of India), persuaded Lord Salisbury's government that Chitral was needed to guard against a Russian move against India through the Pamirs—particularly in view of the evident absence of any diplomatic alternative to secure India against Russian ambitions. Curzon was strongly supported by Francis Youngblood, who had accompanied the principal relief column into Chitral while on detached service as a special correspondent for the London *Times* and whose dispatches helped whip up public enthusiasm for annexation.

As indicated, the incorporation of Chitral into British India provoked a storm of protest by the St. Petersburg chauvinist press. Moreover, as that press often served as a mouthpiece for the Russian military, it now looked to be only a matter of time before the Russians tried some countervailing move—either in the Pamirs or some other Central Asian "hot spot." In the event, the crisis came in the spring of 1898, and once again, the flash point proved to be the Pamirs as well as Chitral. Matters could easily have come to a head the year before when the Government of India was faced with a virtual insurrection by the fierce Pathan tribesmen in the portion of the newly created Northwest Frontier Province immediately south of the former independent kingdom of Chitral. Fifty thousand British troops were dispatched to deal with the uprising, and this "Malakand Field Force" had its hands full for several weeks during the fall of 1897. (Among the participants in the campaign was twenty-two-year-old Winston Churchill, then a young cavalry officer who distinguished himself by courageous service and subsequently captured the attention of the British public with *The Story of the Malakand Field Force*, a frank critique of the campaign that offended much of the army bureaucracy but also impressed many leading Conservative politicians—among them the new viceroy, George Curzon, who had arrived in India only a few months before but had immediately set about a comprehensive program of reform, including establishment of the Northwest Frontier territory.) The Russians, however, made no move to exploit the Pathan rebellion—principally because St. Petersburg was focusing on points much farther to the east.

The reader will recall that Russia had been frustrated in its attempt to force Japan to disgorge some of the fruits of Japan's victory over China (principally the Liaotung Peninsula and Port Arthur). Faced with accepting a diplomatic setback or going to war with Japan, the new Tsar, Nicholas II, heeded the advice of his more moderate ministers (in particular, Minister of Finance Sergei Witte), who urged that Russia was utterly unprepared to fight a major war in the Far East—much less a conflict in which its armies were simultaneously engaged in Europe and Central Asia. (Although Japan was not yet a member of the Anglo–German alliance, London and Berlin had made clear they would view a Russian attack on Japan as a "serious development" with "grave consequences"—a veiled threat of war that Nicholas was persuaded could not safely be treated as a bluff to be called.) Witte, who had already persuaded Alexander III to commit to building the Trans-Siberian Railroad, now convinced Nicholas II that the key to "putting the Japanese in their place" was an acceleration of the pace of work on the ambitious cross-country project combined with an alliance with a Manchu Court eager for revenge against Japan. But this ambitious program represented a long-term strategy that also mandated St. Petersburg exercise caution for the present, lest the country blunder into war before it was truly ready. For precisely that reason, Witte and his allies sought to have the new Tsar put a restraining leash on Russia's forces in Central Asia, fearful that yet another provocative move—like the near-kidnapping of Youngblood's party in the Pamirs in 1891—could trigger a war before Russia was ready to move against the Japanese positions on the Liaotung and in Korea. Hence, when the Pathans brought chaos to the Northwest Frontier, the Tsar rejected calls for a move to annex the whole of the Pamirs while the British were distracted reasserting control to the southwest.

To placate his War Ministry, Nicholas authorized the preparation of contingency plans for a move into both the southern Pamir and Chitral, "in the event an opportunity presented itself." Unfortunately, the Russian military on the spot (exercising the sense for discretion that so frequently characterized the behavior of Russian officialdom during the days of the Tsar) allowed word—and documentary confirmation—of these intentions to come to British attention in April of 1898. By this time, Curzon (Viceroy for just under two years) had already set in motion a program designed not only to strengthen Indian defenses against a Russian invasion but to make possible a British move into Afghanistan, the Pamirs, and even Tibet in the event of war. Plans drawn up by the Indian Army General Staff, which had called for a slow mobilization based on the existing Indian railroad network, were rejected in favor of rapid concentration of powerful corps at predetermined "jumping off" points, at which armories would be maintained to assure adequate supply for an offensive campaign on the shortest possible notice. The implementation of Curzon's plan had been slowed by a terrible famine which had the country in its grips after the failure of the monsoon in 1896–97. Although Curzon was able to use the disastrous inability of the subcontinent's rudimentary railroad system to get relief supplies to those in need as an additional justification for an ambitious railway expansion effort, Curzon's plan for establishment of railheads in northwestern and north central India promised little improvement in the effectiveness of relief efforts: for the obvious reason that these new lines would do nothing for the rate of grain shipments to regions such as the Deccan that had been worst affected by the recent crop failures.

Curzon's militarization program also required a substantial increase in the tax burden levied by the government of India at a time when the declining value of the rupee in relation to the pound (due to the world slump in silver prices while the pound remained on the gold standard) and previously depressed world economic conditions (which caused a drastic fall-off in demand for Indian cotton and other produce) had placed much of India's peasant population on the knife edge of survival. Despite these difficulties, Curzon insisted that India must be prepared to "bear any burden and pay any price" (as he put the matter in a February 1897 report to Colonial Secretary Joseph Chamberlain) in the cause of Imperial defense. Nonetheless,

Curzon recognized that the disastrous economic conditions attendant to his appointment as Viceroy placed some real constraints on India's ability to effect implementation of the new "forward policy." Accordingly, Curzon (if reluctantly) accepted the failure to meet his initial goals for railroad expansion as principally the product of "extreme circumstances, beyond the power of human institutions to affect." Still, Curzon was able to effect a sufficiently significant expansion in Indian rail capacity so that, by the spring of 1898, the Indian Army was ready to put double the previously estimated forces into the field against the Russians—within thirty days of the outbreak of war. Thus, when news of the Yukon Crisis reached Calcutta that spring, Curzon was able to order twice the expected number of divisions forward to the Afghanistan and Pamir zones.

Absent more, British forces likely would have been withdrawn that summer when it was clear there would be no war over the Yukon. But the news of American–Canadian border tensions arrived in Calcutta almost simultaneously with the discovery by British agents of a cache of documents, appearing to evidence Russian intentions to move across the Pamirs and against Chitral—as well as into Afghanistan—if war between the British and Russian Empires "appeared imminent." "Imminence," as a standard, seemingly implied the Russians now intended to launch a "preventive war" in Central Asia to prevent the increasingly mobile and ever more powerful Indian Army from beating Russian forces to the punch. Even without the spur of the Yukon Crisis, Curzon would almost certainly have responded by announcing implementation of the first stage of his "forward deployment" plan, moving some twenty-five thousand troops to new advanced bases within a few days march of Kabul and the Pamirs as well as a move into Tibet (the latter being a personal goal of the new Viceroy). As it was, Curzon responded to the Yukon Crisis by a full-scale mobilization; but when the crisis had ebbed by June of 1898, Curzon refused to "stand down," instead leaving a substantial portion of the Indian Army on alert and ready to move across the border within a few days' notice of hostilities. Curzon's reason (excuse) was the apparent Russian plan to move into Afghanistan and through the Pamirs combined with the news that the Russians had concentrated several divisions in the vicinity of the Russian–Afghan border when the Yukon Crisis reached its international peak in March and

April—only to leave them in place even after it became apparent that the determined diplomacy of McKinley and Laurier had avoided an outbreak of war over the precise location of the Alaska–British Columbia border.

Curzon claimed that the Russians had delayed their withdrawal because they intended to make a sudden move against the increasingly unsteady regime of Great Britain's ally, Abdur Rahman, the Emir of Afghanistan. In fact, St. Petersburg had no such plans. The Yukon Crisis had caused near panic in the ranks of the Tsar's advisers, who believed Russia needed at least two more years before it would be ready to fight offensive operations in the Far East, while simultaneously checking expected German and Austrian moves against Russian Poland. As for Central Asia, the Russians actually had no plans to do anything other than prevent the British from occupying Afghanistan or the disputed territory of the Pamirs. To be sure, the Russians would have preferred to acquire both for themselves; but given the state of Russia's military, St. Petersburg recognized it could do no more than attempt to deter or prevent a similar British move. Curzon was too brilliant *and* well informed not to have recognized the fundamental weakness in Russia's strategic position in Eurasia. For precisely that reason, I find it difficult to take seriously his claim that Russia was "on the verge of attempting a *coup de main* against all Afghanistan that would make the affairs of Pandjeh and Botai Gumbat look like trifles in comparison." On the other hand, Curzon was a visionary (determined to make Great Britain the preeminent power in Asia) who had concluded from personal field studies of Russian advance into Central Asia that Russia represented the greatest threat to establishing a British Asian hegemony.

Perhaps Curzon simply could not take seriously the more mundane reasons offered for the continuing presence of substantial Russian forces just north of Afghanistan (e.g., the still woefully inadequate state of the Russian railway network east of the Urals), because he had too much respect for his foe. "If I were in General Amilakhvari's shoes, I cannot imagine letting such a glittering opportunity slip through my fingers," Curzon stated in a letter to Chamberlain (referring to the Georgian general detailed from the Caucasus to command the Afghan front in 1897). "Only the stoutest show of force by the British would deter me. Well, I am determined to provide such a show as will persuade the Georgian Bear to stay in his Bokharan lair." Curzon's show, however, had the opposite effect. Confronted with the very public news that the British would maintain at least a portion of the recently deployed forces in their positions close to the Bholan, Khyber and Shimshal Passes, Nicholas II yielded to the insistence of his Central Asian military chiefs that the scheduled withdrawal of Russian forces be postponed—to prevent precisely the sort of British surprise move against Afghanistan which Curzon's deployments were intended to prevent the Russians from attempting. Thus, although the Yukon Crisis itself was weathered, powerful figures distant from the Yukon seized upon events to advance the pursuit of what they deemed their nation's vital interests. As a consequence, the British and Russian Empires entered the fall of 1898 in an unprecedented state of war readiness in Central Asia.

It was into this tinderbox that the Fashoda confrontation was now tossed—with an affect akin to a burning brand. Fashoda represented the culmination of a series of episodes in the Great Scramble for Africa; like Fashoda itself, the political crisis to which that Nile River island gave its name stood at the confluence of what began as unconnected streams in the Scramble's earlier course. The first of these was Great Britain's long-delayed move against the Mahdists, the indigenous Moslem power that had defeated the British at Khartoum in 1885 (the struggle in which "Chinese" Gordon lost his life) and who since had controlled the Sudan and the Upper Nile region. Although embarrassed by Gordon's defeat at Khartoum, the British quickly discovered that the Mahdists had their uses—principally, as a barrier to French efforts to penetrate the Sudan from the southwest. London had no intention of leaving the Mahdists indefinitely in control of the Upper Nile, because that clashed with the strategic goal of British control of Eastern Africa extending in an unbroken line from "Cairo to the Cape." Lord Salisbury, however, favored rolling up the Mahdist kingdom from the south by sending British troops down the Nile out of British East Africa. To do that required building an eight-hundred-mile railway from Mombasa to Lake Victoria, and the project did not look to be completed before the turn of the century.

This leisurely pace, along with the whole strategy of a southern approach, was suddenly thrust aside in March of 1896 by a desperate Italian call for help in the Horn of Africa. Italy, under the leadership of the autocratic and vainglorious Francesco Crispi, had entered the Scramble late; with prime coastal territory already spoken for, Italy had to make do with such poor prospects as Massawa, a malaria-ridden outpost (on the Red Sea) that the Egyptians had abandoned in 1885. The Italians were barely able to establish a foothold for their new colony of "Eritrea" when they faced destruction at the hands of the Ethiopian Emperor Yohannes. But Yohannes was killed in 1889 in a battle with the Mahdists, and the Italians were able to sign a treaty with Yohannes's successor, Menelik II, under which Italy claimed a "protectorate" over Menelik's kingdom. Menelik never accepted this claim to effective suzerainty, and it was only a matter of time before the Italians and Ethiopians were bound to clash. In the event, it was the Ethiopians who forced the issue, mobilizing an army of seventy thousand warriors and advancing on Eritrea in late 1895. The Ethiopian army won some early victories on the fringes, but their overextended supply lines would probably have forced a withdrawal had not Crispi recklessly ordered the Italian forces to humble Menelik on the battlefield. Instead, it was the Italians who were embarrassed on March 1, 1896, at Adowa, when the Ethiopians routed the Italian army sent to drive the Ethiopians back into the highlands.

It was this disaster that produced an Italian cry for help which forced Great Britain's hand. Crispi had already asked the British to assist in the campaign against Menelik by advancing up the Nile to Dangola and thereby deterring a Mahdist advance against Eritrea from the west—a move that would secure the Italian flank and permit the entirety of their African army to be committed to the invasion of Ethiopia. Salisbury had declined, still planning on crushing the Mahdists from the south. But Adowa altered the calculus. Italy was the "weak link" in the Triple Alliance, and even though Great Britain had assiduously avoided joining that grouping (London's alliance with Germany was carefully separated from any duty to the Triplice), the British were concerned lest Rome should switch sides and go over to the Franco-Americans—a decision that would immediately complicate the strategic situation in the Mediterranean. And this concern was quite justified. Although some Italian leaders, notably Crispi, fancied France an enemy, most Italians considered Austria-Hungary—a fellow Triple Alliance member—their chief foe because of Italian irredentist claims to much of the Austrian Tyrol. Indeed, Italy had joined Prussia in its attack on Austria in 1866—only to receive a bloody nose on land *and* at sea, including the defeat of the Italian fleet in history's first "all ironclad" battle, fought at Lissa in the Adriatic; the Italians made substantial territorial gains in Venezia, but only because of their association with triumphant Prussia. Salisbury, with Chamberlin's enthusiastic backing, now authorized General Kitchener to advance to Dangola—which would place British forces in a position to assault the Mahdist strongholds of the Sudan.

The move, however, enraged the powerful Anglophobes of France. It may strike the reader as odd to speak of French "Anglophobes," as if they were by this time only one faction of French politics. Yet, when it came to Africa and matters of French colonial policy, despite France's decision to enter into a formal alliance with Russia and the USA, many influential Frenchmen still hoped for a *rapprochement* with Great Britain—a sentiment shared by key English statesmen: most notably, Lord Salisbury. Thus, in 1890, the British and French were able to enter into an agreement whereby France received a "sphere of influence" over a generous-looking chunk of Western Africa. But this apparent resolution of Anglo–French disputes over their mutual colonial efforts in West Africa left unresolved which of the powers would control the stretch of territory that embraced the Mahdist domains along the Upper Nile. By 1893, the more ambitious elements in the newly formed French Colonial Department had decided to launch an expedition from Brazzaville northeast to the Bahr al-Gazhal and Fashoda; not until the spring of 1896, however, did a small but well-organized force under the command of Jean-Baptiste Marchand actually begin the arduous journey to the southern Sudan. By June 1898, Marchand's force had reached Fort Desair and launched a flotilla of small sail boats into the waters of the River Sueh, at the western extreme of the Upper Nile system.

By then, the efforts at an Anglo–French African *rapprochement* that seemed so promising in 1890 had completely broken down, and the race for Fashoda and control of the Upper Nile was on in earnest. The forces engaged in the contest were decidedly unequal—at least insofar as they presumed to represent the military force that one country was prepared to commit to buttress its own claim against that of its rival. Marchand's group consisted of one company of black *tirailleurs* commanded by a handful of French NCOs and officers. Of course, the French had planned to reach Fashoda with no less than three expeditions—not just Marchand's from the Congo.

Moreover, these groups were expected to link up with the Mahdists and somehow convert the Dervishes' unruly thousands into a modern army that would force Kitchener to withdraw into Egypt. But this half-baked scheme quickly unraveled when the other two expeditions—separate columns heading west from the Horn of Africa (under a vague association with the Ethiopian King Menelik)—were forced to withdraw well short of their goal. Not that the success of the Ethiopian efforts would have made much difference. For bearing down from Egypt toward Khartoum and the Mahdist heartland was a force of twenty-five thousand crack troops, commanded by Sir Herbert Kitchener, the "Sirdar" of this nominally Egyptian—but in actuality, British—army.

By September 1, 1898, Kitchener faced the main Mahdist force at Omdurman, just north of Khartoum. The next day, the Mahdists were crushed in a battle that saw a medieval army attempt to brave modern firepower and end up slaughtered by the thousands without laying so much as a chain-mail glove on its foe. (Most of the comparatively few British casualties were suffered by the 21st Lancers, who while on mid-battle reconnaissance charged a Dervish position and used only their swords and sidearms, losing nearly a quarter of their number in the process and giving a vivid lesson in war to the neigh-ubiquitous Winston Churchill, who through his family political connections had wrangled a transfer from the Afghan Frontier to the lancers so he could accompany Kitchener's expedition.) Kitchener then occupied Khartoum, having fulfilled a vow made over a decade before to avenge the Mahdist "murder" of Gordon. But Kitchener could take no time to rest on his newly won laurels. Having taken back Khartoum and ended Mahdist power, Kitchener was instructed to continue south and take "appropriate steps" to evict any representatives of any foreign power who presumed to challenge British authority over the Nile.

In fact, Kitchener had already received word from Dervish sources that unknown "foreigners" had attacked a Mahdist gunboat at Fashoda. On September 10, a flotilla of five Anglo–Egyptian gunboats, carrying one hundred Cameron Highlanders, two battalions of Sudanese troops, and a gun battery, steamed south under Kitchener's direct command to confront the unidentified foe. The foreigners were, of course, Marchand's band of ten Frenchmen and 140 blacks, who a few weeks before had driven off an attack by over one thousand Dervishes. (It was this fight—in which the devastating effect of superior French firepower served as a prelude for Omdurman—that the defeated Mahdists unblushingly transformed into an attack on their gunboats, in their report to Kitchener about the foreigner at Fashoda.)

On September 17, Kitchener's flotilla reached Fashoda, and Kitchener, meeting face-to-face with Marchand, informed the Frenchman that his group had to vacate the mud fort they had just reinforced and withdraw from the Sudan. Although the ensuing exchange has been reproduced in numerous histories of the First World War, in view of the destruction of so many library and other records wrought last fall, I shall reproduce it here:

> Kitchener: My instructions are to regain possession of Fashoda in the name of the sublime Porte and His Highness the Khedive.
>
> Marchand: My orders are to occupy Fashoda and other parts of the Upper Nile abandoned by Egypt and therefore without a legal owner.... Until we receive orders to retire, we shall not haul down our flag but are ready to die at our posts.
>
> Kitchener: But this situation could lead to war.

Marchand did not respond, save to incline his head, as if to confirm that this was indeed the case. Given an overwhelming superiority in firepower (among other things, the French had no artillery to match against the British five-gun battery), Kitchener could have started the First World War right then by annihilating Marchand's little band. But Salisbury had warned Kitchener that, if possible, there were to be "no corpses" made in effecting the recovery of the Sudan south of Khartoum. Kitchener therefore decided not to take decisive action—Marchand's force would be left in control of Fashoda's mud fort (although the British would raise the Union Jack a short distance away), and a report detailing the situation and requesting further instructions would be sent to London. Leaving a portion of his force to watch Marchand, Kitchener steamed south to where the Sobat joined the White Nile to establish another British outpost—thereby blocking Marchand's line of retreat up the river—then returned to Khartoum, from whence a report to London could be telegraphed.

On September 26, a copy of that report (in which Kitchener declared Marchand's position to be "as impossible as it was absurd") was delivered by Great Britain's ambassador to France to France's Foreign Minister, Theophile Delcassé, along with a note from Her Majesty's government making quite plain that Great Britain insisted on Marchand's prompt withdrawal from Fashoda and the Sudan. Under different circumstances, France and Great Britain might have peacefully resolved what we now call the Fashoda Crisis. Fashoda itself was a small island possessing a single, crumbling mud hut (to which "fort" was really far too grandiose a term to apply). Moreover, the Sudan had been Egyptian territory for decades before the Mahdi's defeat of Gordon, and Kitchener had merely reestablished that control. It bordered on the absurd for France to claim the right to Fashoda in such circumstances. (An *opéra bouffe*, as the French, in less dramatic circumstances, would almost certainly, and all to aptly, have described it.) Such an analysis, however, was made impossible by the context in which London and Paris had to deal with the issue of Marchand's intrepid band— an increasingly tense and belligerent international atmosphere directly attributable to the suspicious and competitive dynamic of Alliance rivalry. The Alliance Powers had already stood to arms earlier that year, and only the determination of McKinley and Laurier to avoid a war had kept the peace. Now, a different and more volatile chemistry would be created by the interplay between the leadership of the two countries—Great Britain and France—whose interests were most immediately affected by the latest flash point.

To be sure, Salisbury was no jingo—as his private caution to Kitchener about "no corpses" makes clear. But Salisbury also had no instinctive aversion to war comparable to that felt by USA President McKinley. Moreover, establishing British control over all of Eastern Africa ("from Cairo to the Cape") had been at the heart of Salisbury's personal foreign policy for decades. Marchand's presence at Fashoda represented a direct threat to the achievement of such control. And while Salisbury was the quintessential phlegmatic Englishman—cool and calculating to the point that he sometimes disturbed even his fellow Conservatives by the apparent cold-bloodedness of his decision making—Salisbury could not help but be affected by the nerve-jangling events of the previous six months. "I know it is foolish to think so," Salisbury confided to Chamberlin shortly after Kitchener's report had been received, "but I cannot help the sensation that we are being probed for a weak spot. Well, France and its allies are about to learn just how dangerous a game that can be." Unfortunately, Salisbury's determination to stand firm in defense of his vision of British vital interests now collided with a French government made belligerent as much by domestic circumstances as by the calculations of international power politics.

For much of the 1890s, French politics had been roiled by a spy scandal that came to be known as the Dreyfus Affair. In 1894, a French Army captain named Alfred Dreyfus was convicted by a court-martial of espionage on behalf of Germany. Because Dreyfus was a Jew, his case had been seized upon by the anti-Semitic press and made much of until Dreyfus's conviction—at which point the matter seemed fated to fade into obscurity. Then, certain liberal elements came into the possession of information they claimed conclusively established Dreyfus had been framed, supposedly to protect another officer whose defenders included members of the General Staff. Sufficient evidence of dubious official conduct was uncovered to force a court-martial of this other officer, Commandant Ferdinand Walsin-Esterhazy. When Esterhazy was acquitted, the French novelist Emile Zola entered the fray (in January 1898) with a public letter accusing an array of Army officers and other officials of conspiring to sustain the conviction of an innocent man. The letter, addressed to the French President Félix Faure and distributed as a pamphlet, reignited the affair. Zola was charged with criminal libel—exactly as he had intended in order to force yet another trial at which the (supposed) evidence of official misconduct would be forced into the open and a revision of the Dreyfus verdict thereby compelled. But unfortunately for the *Dreyfusards*, their literary champion had launched a broadside attack on the Army's integrity just weeks before France would be stirred to a fever-pitch by the prospect of war over someplace called the "Oo-Kahn" in distant North America.

The resulting backlash fed a nationalist frenzy that kept French politics at a near-boil, even after it had become apparent there would be no war over the Yukon. In turn, this environment strengthened the hand of Minister of Colonies Georges Clemenceau, France's most respected—and most feared—politician. Clemenceau had returned to France from a self-imposed exile, just before the fall of the Second Empire of Louis Napoleon. Clemenceau had emigrated to North America, where he lived in the North, and also visited the Confederacy—an experience from which he took away an abiding hostility to *la puissance esclavier*. Clemenceau played a key role in the creation of the Third Republic, then established a power base among anticlerical but chauvinist—and therefore pro-Army—Republicans. (Clemenceau's credibility among Army officers helped the government defuse the challenge of the *Boulangists* in 1889.) Yet, for all his influence, Clemenceau had been deprived of the prize of the premiership. Clemenceau was feared as much as respected for his ruthless leadership abilities, and none of his rivals wanted to take the risk of giving "the Tiger" a chance actually to head a government. But with the onset of the double crisis created by Zola's incendiary attack on the Army's handling of the Dreyfus Affair and the threat of war against the Anglo–German coalition over the Yukon, the political climate in France shifted radically in favor of Clemenceau's brand of strong leadership. At President Faure's suggestion, Premier Freycinet reshuffled his cabinet and invited Clemenceau to take the Colonial Ministry. Clemenceau agreed. He knew matters in Africa could also soon be coming to a head: with Kitchener moving against the Mahdists and word anxiously awaited from Marchand's expeditionary force. In that event, the Colonial Ministry would become one of the country's three most important departments—matched only by the Foreign and War Ministries—and Clemenceau would be one of the four most powerful men in France.

In return for the Colonial Ministry, Clemenceau agreed to turn his potent political artillery against the *Dreyfusards*. Despite roots in the Radical Republican tradition, Clemenceau had never expressed sympathy for the *Dreyfusard* cause. Above all, Clemenceau cared for power; he sensed the Republican infatuation with Dreyfus was a losing political proposition and therefore held himself above the fray, awaiting the chance to bridge the gap between pro- and anti-Dreyfus Republican factions based on some (yet-to-be-identified) common ground. Clemenceau believed that ground would almost certainly be a foreign crisis that would reignite *revanchist* passion against Germany. "Of course," he told a confidant, "in such a crisis, the claims of a single individual such as Dreyfus can no longer be considered of any moment." Did Clemenceau believe Dreyfus guilty of espionage? "Who can say?" Clemenceau replied. "Perhaps Zola is right; perhaps the critical documents against Dreyfus are forgeries. Then again, how are we to judge such matters? In the end, we must rely on our individual experience, and nothing in my own leads me to credit this rather elaborate tale of government fraud." With such a sensibility, Clemenceau probably found it fairly easy finally to weigh in against the *Dreyfusards*, and his intervention constituted a blow from which neither they—nor Zola—ever recovered.

In February, Zola had been found guilty of criminal libel. But the complaint reportedly had been narrowly drawn to minimize the risk of government embarrassment—lest supposedly shadier aspects of the affair be brought to light. Zola had delivered an eloquent statement on behalf of himself and the *Dreyfusard* cause which had received extensive publicity; the end result seemed at best a mixed bag for the government and the Army High Command. Moreover, Zola appealed to the Court of Assizes, where his case was to be heard in April and where the *Dreyfusards* had hopes of a reversal and an order for a new—and more wide-ranging—trial. But by April, war fever induced by the Yukon Crisis had swept into France. Moreover, Premier Freycinet, seeking to strengthen his government before the Assembly elections scheduled for May, chose this moment to ask Clemenceau to become Colonies Minister. Just two weeks before Zola's appeal was to be heard, Clemenceau took to the Assembly tribune and denounced the *Dreyfusards* and Zola by name, accusing them of forgetting their "patriotic duty" at a time of threatened war; *L'Aurore* and *La Justice*, Clemenceau's own newspapers, then continued the attack in print. The anti-Dreyfus forces were invigorated by Clemenceau's declaration of support, while the *Dreyfusards* felt demoralized by the decision of so powerful a *Republicaine* to join their opposition. (Zola had earlier approached Clemenceau about publishing the author's open letter to President Faure in one of Clemenceau's papers, but Clemenceau had declined—and in a clear hint of his ultimate position, asked

Zola how inviting a third trial, i.e., of Zola for criminal libel, could "serve the good interests of France in these increasingly dangerous times?")

Even if Clemenceau's intervention did not constitute the turning point in the course of the Dreyfus Affair (the *Dreyfusard* cause already being on the wane, having suffered a damaging double blow with Esterhazy's acquittal and Zola's conviction), Clemenceau's vigorous joinder of the debate coincided with the opening of the sorry episode's final chapter, and the Tiger's assumption of the leadership of the anti-Dreyfus forces certainly contributed to their ultimate success. At the end of April, Zola lost his appeal and then shocked moderate French opinion by fleeing to England to avoid serving his sentence. Although Zola promptly initiated a vigorous campaign to persuade public opinion of Dreyfus's innocence, it was now May, and the Yukon Crisis had yet to run its course. Hundreds of thousands of soldiers and dozens of warships had been mobilized in Europe and in North America. War with Great Britain, Germany, and their allies loomed. Zola himself doubted the wisdom of going to London in such circumstances, but went in the end because no other city in Europe offered comparable opportunities for organizing a campaign to overturn Dreyfus's conviction. Zola was probably right, but the soundness of that judgment could not change the fact that Clemenceau's ensuing broadsides, against "literarist treason in time of national danger," now inflicted a mortal blow on the already badly wounded *Dreyfusard* cause.

(I pause to note my own agnosticism about the Dreyfus Affair; as a former prosecutor, I prefer to deal in facts. While the *Dreyfusards* did raise serious questions about some of the evidence against Dreyfus, the fact remains that three different courts rejected the essential elements of their case. Of course, the war crisis that began in the spring of 1898 quickly sidetracked the remaining investigations, and then the war saw the death of several key figures—notably the controversial Colonel Picquart—which effectively foreclosed a resumption of investigative efforts after the war's end. Dreyfus died in captivity on Devil's Island in 1901; whether he truly was a spy for Germany will almost certainly forever remain a mystery, and one I doubt will trouble many, if any, in the grim world of humanity's foreseeable future.)

For this narrative, the significance of the last act of the Dreyfus Affair was political. Clemenceau had seemingly brought the matter to an end—

on terms satisfactory to all but the most dedicated Dreyfusard. By midsummer of 1898, the "Tiger" was the most potent political force in France. Clemenceau, the most determined of *revanchists*, had made clear his belief that France must be willing to go to war to undo the results of 1871: to recover the "Lost Provinces" of Alsace and Lorraine and restore France's position as the preeminent power on the European continent. For such a belligerent man to achieve preeminence in France—when the Fashoda crisis burst upon the world that September—immeasurably lengthened the odds against a peaceful resolution of the dispute. When the British government made clear its insistence on a total French evacuation of the Sudan, Clemenceau pushed hard for France to reject such terms—even at the risk of war. "We are ready!" Clemenceau insisted, through the pages of *L'Aurore* (in unsigned editorials everyone knew reflected what the "Tiger" was saying during cabinet meetings). "Our navy is ready, our army's artillery is now second to none, and we have powerful allies in Europe and across the Atlantic. If the English will not accede to the restoration of our shared responsibility for the Nile, then we must be prepared to fight for what is ours." Moreover, Clemenceau was confident that, if war came, France really would not have to fight alone. He had taken steps, shortly after joining the government in April, to ensure that Washington knew France would support the USA in a war over the Yukon. Now, France made clear its expectation that America would reciprocate. And while President McKinley was appalled at the prospect of war over "some miserable mud hut in the middle of an African swamp," he also recognized that a refusal to back France over Fashoda would destroy the Franco–American alliance. "I don't see how we can afford to pay that price—we seem to have gone too far down the road to be able to do an about-face and turn back just because we don't like the looks of what's up ahead," McKinley acknowledged to his Cabinet at the end of September.

By this grim admission, McKinley had put his finger on the real reason why the world faced the increasing likelihood of world war. For as the prospects for a peaceful solution of the Anglo–French dispute over Fashoda faded in the last days of September, each of the members of the two Alliances was discovering how their individual freedom of maneuver had been so drastically curtailed by the iron logic of alliance politics. To be sure, some were actually enthused at the prospect of war. The Confederacy and Japan had just finished secret plans for a joint attack on the Spanish Philippines, and final testing of new long-range Tredegar–Krupp artillery that would bring Washington under direct bombardment—without violating the Arlington Heights demilitarization provisions of the 1863 Treaty of London—had been successfully completed only a few months before. "Frankly, boys," CSA President Benjamin Tillman told his Cabinet, "this looks like a pretty good opportunity to give the damnyanks a licking, and I say we ought to take it." Likewise, Kaiser Wilhelm thrilled like a schoolboy at the prospect of "my first great war"—the restraining advice of the German General Staff notwithstanding. Such attitudes, however, were the exception among those who made the decisions for war or peace. The fundamental problem for world peace was not the belligerency of the individual decision makers, but the dynamic of the alliance system itself: if two opposing powers became engaged in a confrontation and the leaders of those powers could not see a way out other than war, their allies were effectively committed to war as well.

In the end, global war over the Yukon had been avoided only because McKinley and Laurier found a peaceful solution to their border dispute. McKinley and Laurier, however, were men deeply committed to the cause of peace. Salisbury and Clemenceau were not. Salisbury was not prepared to tolerate a French presence along the Nile, because he considered it a threat to Great Britain's most vital African interests. Salisbury was certainly not a belligerent man—in the sense Clemenceau was. But Salisbury also did not flinch from the prospect of going to war to protect his country's vital interests; he considered British control of the Sudan such an interest. And while French Premier Freycinet or Foreign Minister Delcasse might have flinched at making the decision for war in the absence of Clemenceau, the "Tiger's" evident determination—and his newfound position as the fulcrum of French politics—helped steel them to the task. (Personally, I think the importance of Clemenceau's role as a member of the government to be somewhat exaggerated; even if Clemenceau had persuaded Zola to withhold his accusatory open letter and the Dreyfus Affair had faded away with Esterhazy's acquittal—leaving Freycinet free to keep Clemenceau outside the cabinet—"the Tiger" would still have exerted powerful pressure from the outside against any concessions to *Les Anglais*.)

By the first week of October, it had become apparent to Salisbury and his cabinet that the French would not agree to withdraw Marchand; they instead insisted on the reestablishment of an Anglo–French "co-dominium," at least in the Upper Nile Valley. Moreover, although the French expeditions out of Ethiopia had been forced to turn back, the fact Ethiopian Emperor Menelik had allowed them to try raised in the minds of the British leadership the danger of a Franco–Ethiopian alliance that threatened a severance of the connection between Egypt and Uganda. "Sometimes, great conflicts are fought over seemingly infinitesimal stakes," Salisbury wrote to Queen Victoria on October 7, the day Great Britain issued its ultimatum demanding a French assurance that Marchand would be ordered to withdraw from the Sudan. "But, as Your Majesty knows all too well, in this case, the stakes go far beyond who will occupy a small Sudanese island in the midst of the Nile." France rejected the British note on October 9. The following day, Great Britain declared war on France. Within forty-eight hours, Germany, Austria–Hungary, the Confederacy, and Japan had followed suit; by week's end, the USA, Mexico, Spain, and Russia had reciprocated. The First World War had begun.

Perhaps France and Great Britain were fated to confront each other in the Southern Sudan. But I doubt they would have fought a war over Fashoda had France not had the reassurance of a network of powerful allies prepared to support it in a conflict with the British Empire. Clemenceau may have been a belligerent man, and his presence in the government virtually guaranteed the failure of any peace initiative; but Clemenceau was not a foolishly reckless man, and it is far from obvious he would have opted for war had France stood alone. Nor should the effects of the French naval modernization program on French confidence be underestimated—a program initiated as part of the formation of the Franco–American naval convention of 1889, and without which the French navy could not possibly have entertained the notion it was ready to take on the British Mediterranean fleet (a notion that would quickly prove ill founded, as the reader shall soon see). And even if France and Great Britain had gone to war over Fashoda, it is inconceivable that the other powers would have been drawn in. That consequence was entirely the product of the inflexibility of an Alliance System which owed its existence to Lee's triumph over McClellan, thirty-six years before.

The mass of gold-seekers
pouring from the USA through
the Chilkoot Pass into the
Canadian Yukon, who brought
the USA and Canada and their
allies to the brink of war, which
only the determined efforts of
USA President William McKinley
and Canadian Prime Minister
Wilfred Laurier managed
to avoid.

Although the Alliances managed
to avoid war over the Yukon in
the Spring of 1898, they failed
to do so when France and
Great Britain squared off over
Fashoda in the Southern Sudan
that Fall.

(above) a 15" Rodham shore battery.

(below) The C.S.S. Tennessee, a battle ship of the modified "Royal Sovereign" class, built for the Confederacy at the Royal Portsmouth Dockyard.

Emblematic of the massive military buildup by the USA and the Confederacy, which began soon after the Confederacy's successful bid for independence and accelerated following the Western War and which the outbreak of global war in 1898 would transform into instruments of actual destruction.

16

WORLD WAR I: (3) THE WAR'S EARLY STAGES INVOLVING THE USA AND THE CONFEDERACY— THE SACK OF WASHINGTON, THE INVASION OF CANADA, AND THE FALL OF THE PHILIPPINES

———

World War One can best be characterized as a conflict conducted largely within isolated regional theaters by combatants lacking any clear understanding of the implications for warfare of the industrial technology they were about to employ. Bluntly put, the outbreak of war in 1898 caught the Alliance Powers unprepared to fight a modern, global war.

By "unprepared" I do not mean that the Powers had neglected to pursue the technical modernization of their armed forces. To the contrary, and as the opening events of the war in the North American theater in particular all too graphically demonstrated, the military establishments of the Powers almost uniformly showed flexibility in pursuing technological modernization and providing their forces with a wide array of weapons of the latest design. What neither the military nor political leadership of any Power possessed, however, was either the imaginative ability to appreciate the degree to which new technologies would change the nature of alliance warfare or the ability to conduct a truly *global* war in which success in one region could be made to change the fate of operations in another. Although all the Powers had fought (in some cases, several) wars since the War of Secession, none had experience of alliance warfare on a truly global scale since the days of Napoleon, and none anticipated the degree to which the continuing revolution in military technology could affect the nature of such a struggle.

I will begin my narrative of the war's course with the opening events of the war in North America—and particularly with what became known to every citizen of the USA as the "Sack of Washington." If any reader concludes I have dwelt too long over the events of October 14 and 15, 1898, I can only offer this in my defense: First, the Sack of Washington marked a decisive point in the deteriorating relationship between the two unions created by the War of Secession. After the Sack, reconciliation between Yankee and Confederate was a dead letter. The Sack began a sequence of brutal events that, within a year, had transformed rivalry into bitter hatred and thereby insured that North America would be a center of conflict until either—or, as history has tragically unfolded, both—the USA or the Confederacy had been destroyed. Second, I am an American whose life was shaped by the transforming events of October 1898. The readers of this narrative, if only to appreciate its limitations, should understand how the history I chronicle has shaped me and affected my point of view. For although I seek to present the history of the last century in an honest way, I cannot say I do so dispassionately.

Returning to the outbreak of World War One and the opening moves of that conflict between the USA and CSA, I will first discuss how the Confederate leadership came to select as their strategy the "Maryland Option"—an attempt to detach the states of Maryland and Delaware from the North and add them to the territory of the Confederacy. The "Maryland Option" was born of a political fantasy and a technological possibility. The political fantasy was the notion that Maryland remained culturally at one with the Confederacy. Maryland had been a slave state at the outbreak of the War of Secession, and if Union troops had not dispersed the Maryland Legislature's secessionist majority at a particularly volatile moment in September 1861, Maryland might have voted to secede and thereby might have dealt a politically fatal blow to the North's cause a year before Lee dealt the militarily fatal stroke at Gettysburg. Moreover, after Secession, Maryland became a Democratic Party stronghold, and its "Eastern Shore" (which after the Treaty of London included the formerly Virginian counties of Accomac and Northampton) became a center for opposition to the military preparedness program of every Republican administration (leading to some highly publicized prosecutions by federal authorities, concerned about the security of vital fortifications guarding the entrance to Chesapeake Bay and Baltimore Harbor). Even so, Richmond was allowing nostalgic romanticism to substitute for sound political intelligence when Fitzhugh Lee's administration concluded—shortly after the establishment of the Confederate alliance with Great Britain—that there existed in Maryland a "silent Confederate majority" that would rise up in support of a Southern "army of liberation."

To begin, the abolition of slavery, coupled with the integration of Afro–Americans into the political and social life of the North, had broken up the cultural patterns that had once closely linked Maryland to her slaveholding sisters. Moreover, Baltimore had been transformed by the exigencies of Northern defense into a major military and armaments industry center, while Washington City itself had been changed by an ambitious program of public and military works. The close connection established between these two metropolises further contributed to the "Northernization" of the Maryland economy and of Maryland society, which spread east to Annapolis and south to the Union fortifications of Cape Charles, the northern entrance of the Chesapeake. Although Maryland still voted Democratic in 1896, the fact that McKinley nearly won the state against Bryan should have spoken volumes to Richmond.

But it did not: in part, because the Confederacy by then was well along the road to perfecting the "Very Long Range" artillery that would make execution of the Maryland Option a militarily realistic possibility. The Treaty of London had required the demilitarization of the Arlington Heights on the Virginia side of the Potomac River directly across from Washington, to eliminate the danger of Confederate bombardment. Unfortunately for the future denizens of the USA capital, the negotiators of the Secession peace settled on a formula proscribing only the placement of Southern guns within a specified distance of the city. Richmond therefore was left free to develop artillery that could reach Washington—even when placed well outside the "demilitarized zone" established by the treaty.

As to why the North did not insist on a ban against the development of such weapons, the answer should be obvious: it could not have, because the South would never have agreed to such an intrusion on its sovereignty. Of course, the development of such a long-range gun was also unimaginable in 1863, given the state of artillery technology. But by the 1890s, technology had advanced to the point where the fantasies of the most imaginative Confederate artillery captains could now come to pass. Nickel-plated steel and the recoilless gun had made possible the development of a breech-loading rifled artillery piece that could hurl high-explosive shells unheard-of distances. And since the Tredegar–Krupp combine had mastered both techniques (Krupp having invented the process for nickel reinforcement of steel plate at its Essen plants, while the mass-production system was perfected at the great Tredegar–Krupp works in Birmingham), the Confederate General Staff by the mid-1890s could promise to put in the hands of the country's political leadership the technological means for achieving the fantasy of smashing the "Damnyank" capital from outside the DMZ imposed by the Treaty of London.

Moreover, the ensuing chaos would create a chance for the Confederates to overrun the DMZ itself and force a crossing of the Potomac at the one place along the river where the North had not built a full system of fortifications—the capital itself. The Northern General Staff planned that Northern forces would immediately smash through the limited Confederate forces allowed on the opposite side under the Treaty of London and occupy the DMZ—if not, Washington would be exposed to a terrible bombardment by conventional Confederate artillery that was certain to be brought up once war had torn away the constraints of an agreement meant for peacetime. But precisely because Northern war plans seemed to promise a successful move into the DMZ, the War Department could not politically justify the expense of extending the great fortification line to shield Washington, proper. To be sure, Gatling gun nests and field artillery emplacements were established along the river bank, but when the Army proposed to sow the new antipersonnel mines above the tide line, a public outcry over "unnecessary risk" to boaters and wandering children forced cancellation of the project. "After all," as one member of the Senate Committee on Military Affairs rebuked Chief of General Staff Nelson Miles during hearings on the issue, "you boys will be on both sides of the river in any fight, so what's the point of such a scheme?"

By January 1898, Tredegar–Krupp was able to guarantee that two dozen VLR guns—nicknamed the *"Washingtonkannon"* by the Krupp engineers at the Richmond works—would be ready for action by that fall. These guns were a land-based modification of the 28 cm naval rifles developed by Krupp for contemporary Imperial battleships. The 28 cm SK-L (*Schnellakanone–Lange*) had been under development since 1890. Emplacing the gun on a railcar allowed rapid transport of weapon and ammunition to pre-assigned stations in Northern Virginia freight yards. Freed from the confines of a naval turret, the 28 cm rifled cannon could be elevated fifty degrees or more to achieve a maximum range of some thirty thousand yards (more than seventeen miles) and sufficient to inundate official Washington with a rain of fire from the sky—and delivered from outside the DMZ. When war appeared imminent at the end of September, Richmond ordered a "partial" mobilization and closed a zone forty miles deep, extending the length of the DMZ line. Behind that zone were soon concentrated one hundred thousand crack troops (the cream of the CSA's Army of Northern Virginia) along with six VLR batteries of four guns each. War was declared on October 13; at dusk, both infantry and railroad guns advanced, and early the next morning, the citizens of Washington were awakened by a sound never before heard in the history of warfare.

Henry Adams, who for years had lived in one of the fashionable Lafayette Square townhouses just across Pennsylvania Avenue from the White House, described the terror and destruction that ensued:

> I was awakened at 4:00 in the morning by a curious sound and sensation. The sound approximated the distant shriek of an approaching train; the sensation was a dull thud, which shook the depths of our residence. Groggy from the strain of the last twenty-four hours, as all Washington was aquiver at the approach of war and awaited the first blow to be struck across the Potomac against the Johnnies with eager anticipation, it took me, and doubtless virtually every other resident of the city, several moments to clear one's head and deduce that the capital was under bombardment!

"No! This is not possible! The Treaty of London assures that such a thing cannot be." Well, as Washingtonians now learned to their horror and disgust, the value of parchment as protection against cannon fire is an illusion. At least, that is surely so when the cannon are wielded by a people as ruthless as our former compatriots of the Southland. For within a few moments, the escalating noise—the crash of explosions, the screams of people awakened only to be smashed to pulp moments later in their homes, and the overarching shriek of the incoming shells—made painfully obvious that the Confederates were laying down a murderous fire, and our capital was its target.

I rushed from the house as soon as I had dressed. Even at this early hour, the streets were a chaos of people, horses, and wagons (and the very occasional automobile). Nature's dawn had yet to strike the eastern sky, but that was of little account, for the Confederates' bombardment had ushered in a man-made dawn. The awful glow of reflected light from the conflagration already spreading across the city illuminated the streets and permitted one to view distant buildings as if it were already day. Fires already raged out of control in the newly completed Library of Congress building, in the chamber of the House of Representatives, and along Pennsylvania Avenue to the White House and beyond into Georgetown. (My home within the hour would be shattered by an all-too-well-placed shot—fortunately for this narrative, after I had vacated the premises.) We did not know it then, but we would soon see all too clearly that the Johnnies had picked their targets for maximum demoralizing effect—as well as destruction.

With nature's dawn, the even glow cast by the fire's reflection was replaced by a sky obscured by plumes of smoke which, combined with the swirl of debris and the dust raised by the panicked traffic along dirt roads, made it almost as difficult to see as if it were still night. As the shells continued to rain down destruction and the fires spread unchecked despite the desperate efforts of the fire brigades, it became all too clear that, like Nineveh and Tyre, Washington's end had come. Upon the close of this dreadful day, the sun of history would have proven to have forever set upon a city swathed in fire and smoke—just as the sun had similarly set upon countless cities before our own, doomed capital. (H. Adams. *A Personal History of the Great War*, at 12 (Philadelphia, 1903)).

Although American agents had warned of just such an attack, bureaucratic rivalries, combined with a stubborn unwillingness on the part of key leaders to accept the notion that the South would actually choose to destroy "the city of our common heritage," left the capital unprepared for the sudden rain of destruction. By noon on Friday, October 14, fires had consumed—or were in the process of consuming—the Library of Congress along with most of its collection (including all of the remaining books donated by Thomas Jefferson); both Houses of Congress; the Willard Hotel; the Treasury and State Department buildings; and many lesser offices along with hundreds of homes. Just before noon, several shells crashed through the roof of the Old Senate Wing, shattering the Supreme Court's chambers and killing Chief Justice Stephen Fields and Associate Justice Horace Gray of Massachusetts. (Fields, old and ill, had stubbornly insisted on going to the court that morning, and Gray had come along to try and keep the aging "Chief" out of harm's way.) Several members of Congress, including Speaker of the House of Representatives Thomas Reed, were also killed, and many more were wounded. (Both Houses had been called back from the midterm election campaign for an emergency session to declare war, and the bombardment caught most still in the city.) President McKinley ordered the government to evacuate to Philadelphia; the President himself only narrowly escaped injury when shells fell close to the White House. The presidential mansion was not hit, but it burned that afternoon as fire fighters lost control of the conflagrations in the neighboring Treasury and State Department buildings, and showers of sparks ignited the structure and surrounding trees. By nightfall, the four sides of Lafayette Square were bounded by nothing but charred ruins.

The Confederate bombardment had been planned to induce maximum chaos, and the CSA's new guns achieved this aim with appalling effectiveness. Washington presented a scene of bedlam. Most of its population of over 450,000 surged out of the city in a blind panic that jammed the roads north toward Pennsylvania and northeast toward Baltimore. Nor was the CSA's bombardment an exercise in terror war for its own sake. As the Confederate General Staff had correctly estimated, the bombardment completely disrupted the American military along a front extending from above the Chain Bridge, through Georgetown and Anacostia, to old Fort Washington opposite Mount Vernon. Units scheduled to strike across the Potomac and move into the Arlington Heights DMZ were hastily required to turn about and assist with fire fighting, crowd control, evacuation of key personnel and records, and a myriad other tasks. And these unanticipated missions left the capital's Potomac waterfront virtually bereft of troops to respond to the Confederate crossing through the DMZ and over the Potomac into Washington—which now surged ahead. Shortly before midnight on October 14, USA pickets at the Confederate ends of the Aqueduct and Long Bridges were surprised by troops of I Corps of the Army of Northern Virginia. (The Confederates had earlier yielded both bridges intact to Northern forces, but this seeming reverse was actually part of the CSA plan for a lightning strike across the Potomac and into Washington; to disguise this intent, the Confederates made a show of resistance by intentionally abortive attempts at blowing these spans and by actually demolishing the Chain Bridge farther to the north.) Although Northern forces were able to effect the timely demolition of the Aqueduct Bridge from the American side, the Long Bridge fell to Johnny's counterstroke. The Confederates also swarmed across the river in dozens of small boats which had been slipped into the DMZ just before the outbreak of the war and secreted in small creeks such as Spout Run, Hunting Creek, Four Mile Run, and Difficult Run. Resistance at the water's edge was quickly overcome with the aid of smothering light artillery fire from the opposite shore. (As the Northern General Staff had long feared, failure to seize the Heights now exposed Washington to bombardment by Confederate guns brought into the DMZ upon the outbreak of war; but it was the wholly unanticipated employment of artillery that could strike the city from beyond the DMZ which had transformed the threat into a reality.)

By dawn on October 15, the CSA already had over fifteen thousand troops across the river. By that afternoon, the Confederates had forced the fragmented and disorganized Northern opposition out of the city center, and Southern forces were pressing hard into the suburbs to the north and east. This fighting set numerous new fires and reignited many others, and it was this conflagration that finally reduced the heart of the American capital to a smoking ruin. The Confederate plan was simple—cross the Potomac directly into Washington, then fan out *behind* the great fortresses guarding the river crossings to the northwest, thereby taking these obstacles from the rear and allowing the main Confederate force to cross at multiple points: White's Ferry, Monocacy, Point-of-Rocks, and even north toward Sharpsburg. By October 17, the Confederates had triumphed. The line guarding the Potomac banks northwest of Washington had been taken from the rear—their riverine gun emplacements useless. Forces striking southeast from the city forced the evacuation of river defenses at and below Alexandria. Within less than a week of the war's outbreak, the USA had lost its capital and over 150,000 Confederate troops were in Maryland, preparing to drive in three columns: (1) north toward Frederick and the old battlefields of the Maryland–Pennsylvania border; (2) northeast toward Baltimore, with its vital harbor, rail yards, and munitions works; and (3) southeast toward the Chesapeake Bay coast just south of the town of Deale (thereby cutting off Northern forces guarding the approaches to the great Potomac fortress at Point Lookout). Given the brilliance of their success in the first days of fighting—with Washington in hand and the Potomac defenses fully breached—the Confederates can be forgiven a certain degree of cockiness at their prospects. In fact, Northern forces had already recovered from the shock of losing the capital and were preparing to resist with vigor the Confederate attempts to advance out of their lodgment.

The Confederate push toward the Chesapeake moved forward rapidly, and by October 23, CSA forces had captured Deale. Those Northern forces cut off by the Confederate advance now withdrew toward the extensive trench lines guarding the approach to Point Lookout. Elsewhere, however,

Johnny made progress only fitfully—and at a high price in men and material. Although Confederate forces initially occupied Frederick, a Northern counterattack forced the Confederates to withdraw to a line running several blocks south of the town center. Subsequent efforts to turn the Northern left flank were thrown back with heavy losses (principally due to a devastating combination of Gatling gun fire along with effective employment of the new French "75" field artillery, which the Americans had purchased in substantial numbers earlier that year and were also manufacturing under license from Schneider et Cie). In the meantime, the Confederate advance against Baltimore bogged down in the city's southwest suburbs. Frustrated by their inability to capture a prize essential to the success of their Maryland plan, the Confederates resorted to a punishing bombardment. Two battalions of Very Long Range 28 cm guns were run over the rail bridge at Harpers Ferry—seized intact by a *coup de main* at the war's outset—toward Baltimore. Their bombardment set off fires that ran wild and utterly destroyed the city's harbor and business center over the course of several days in mid-November. Over 1,500 buildings in eighty-six city blocks were destroyed, and thousands of people were killed or injured; the ensuing Siege of Baltimore would not be lifted until war's end, and by then, every major public and private building—including the City Hall, Post Office, Custom House, and the great Continental Trust Company tower— had been reduced to rubble.

And still, the most critical factor favored the North. For Maryland did not rise in support of the South's "liberating" forces. Although the failure of the Confederates to capture Baltimore blocked their line of advance into the eastern counties, it also was the case that Richmond had utterly miscalculated the sentiments of the Eastern Shore. Appalled by the seemingly wanton destructiveness of the Confederate campaign, these Marylanders rallied as fiercely to the Northern cause as did any other group of Americans. Thus, by December, although the Confederates had driven the "Yankees" from their capital, reached the western shore of Chesapeake Bay, and placed Baltimore and the fortress of Lookout Point under siege, the Maryland Option had self-evidently failed. Worse, the spectacle of what was already being referred to as the "sack" of Washington had stirred Northern blood to a ferocious boil. "Richmond Delenda Est!" thundered Massachusetts Senator Henry

Cabot Lodge, and the Senate (meeting in temporary quarters in the Bank of the United States Building in Philadelphia) roared its approval—a cry quickly taken up by the popular press across the country. "I fear we have only managed to awaken a sleeping Yankeedom and fill them with a terrible resolve," former CSA President Longstreet warned a select group of leading Confederate industrialists and politicians as stalemate settled onto the "Maryland Front" by year's end.

From the vantage point of our time, looking back over the destruction wrought in recent decades, one must ask why the fall of Washington proved so traumatic. The city was thoroughly wrecked, to be sure. The Library of Congress; the Capitol Building; the White House; the State, Treasury, War and other Department buildings and offices; the Smithsonian Institution— virtually every major public structure was either smashed by the guns or burned out by the ensuing fires. (Miraculously, the Washington Monument survived. George Washington stood at the apex of the Confederate pantheon, and many Southerners dreamed of dismantling the North's monument to the man both countries claimed as "Founding Father" and rebuilding it in Richmond. The Confederates actually planned the trajectory of their bombardment to spare the Monument, although the fact they did not strike the spire was more the product of chance and the thin coverage achievable by the number of VLRs engaged in the assault. Left intact by the withdrawing Confederates at war's end, the Monument was removed to Philadelphia, where it would survive the dirigible raids of World War Two but not World War Three's "Terror Week" raids of October 1939.) Upward of five thousand civilian Washingtonians were killed and thousands more injured—many in the panic that ensued when CSA forces thrust across the Potomac and engaged a disorganized Northern resistance in the very midst of the civilian exodus. The Confederates, however, did not engage in wanton destruction of public buildings and monuments—notwithstanding the lurid claims to the contrary of the North's "yellow press." ("McKinley, despite himself, has at least supplied us a war," William Randolph Hearst reportedly told his staff, "but it is up to us to give our readers the Confederate atrocities that will assure the purchase of our papers.")

In fact, as much as a part of me bridles at saying so, the "sack" of Washington is almost entirely a Northern myth. Once the Confederates were in the city, they behaved with admirable restraint. Shortly after war's end, yellow press claims of deliberate firing of public buildings and dynamiting of monuments were proven to be pure fiction. The only dynamiting was done to stop the spread of the fires and save at least a portion of the city's northwestern neighborhoods. The truth about the "sack" was successfully kept from the Northern public for decades. When the dissident historian Charles Beard attempted to publicize the matter in his 1923 book, *The Tragedy of North–South Relations*, the Hughes administration managed to have the book suppressed as violating the Official Secrets Act of 1919, and Beard and his complicit wife were imprisoned. But in fairness to my countrymen, I must also point out that at the awful moment of Washington's fall, no one—even at the highest levels of the American government—had any reason to believe other than that the great public buildings of the nation's capital had been wrecked due to a deliberate decision taken by people who still claimed the right to call themselves "Americans." The destruction of Washington also marked the first time that the North confronted what would prove a terrible truth of global war in the Alliance Age: that the denizens of North America could expect to suffer its effects in measures equal to the inhabitants of the "Old World," whose ills the American Union had at one time promised to cure by enlightened example.

At the time, however, few if any observers in the USA or the Confederacy appreciated that something comparable to the destruction of Washington was a virtually inevitable consequence of Secession and the dynamic of the global alliance politics unleashed by the South's successful war of independence. To the contrary: precisely because the deeper roots were not perceived, Northerners were virtually compelled—as a psychological matter—to treat the destruction of their capital as an act of wanton vandalism on the part of the Confederacy and therefore to seek revenge at the earliest opportunity.

That revenge, however, would have to await the outcome of events to the north, for while the Confederacy launched its attack into Maryland, the USA had unleashed a far larger effort to conquer Canada. By the mid-1890s, it had become a given for strategic planners in Washington, London, and Ottawa that, in the event of war, the USA would make a bid for Canada. To begin, such a move would satisfy a decades-old urge to absorb the rump

of British North America left when the Colonies seceded—a desire reinforced by the post-Secession conviction that acquiring what soon became
known as the Canadian Confederation would (somehow) counterbalance
the loss of the South. Moreover, once the Spirit of New York had soured
and the USA and Great Britain evolved into rivals and likely enemies in the
next Great Power War, Canada would of necessity become an American
target—even if there had been no tradition of "Northern Manifest Destiny."

Canada was home to the Royal Navy stations of Esquimault (on
the southern tip of Vancouver Island, just west of the provincial capital
Victoria) and Halifax (the capital of Nova Scotia, on the Atlantic coast).
If these bases were not neutralized, the Royal Navy could isolate Alaska,
threaten Hawaii, raid the Pacific and Atlantic coasts with impunity, and—
perhaps most important—disrupt a blockade of the Confederacy. The most
effective way to eliminate the Royal Navy threat would be to capture both
bases from the rear—which would require an invasion of British Columbia
from Washington State and of Nova Scotia from Maine. The assault on
BC would be greatly aided by a thrust into the Great Plains Northwest
Territory districts of Alberta and Assiniboia—as well as into the Province
of Manitoba—to cut the Canadian Pacific Railway and prevent reinforcements reaching the Pacific Coast. Similarly, occupying the heartland of
the original United Canadas (Ontario and Quebec) would protect the left
flank of the attack on Halifax and also mean the capture of the political
and economic center of British North America. And once the North had
triumphed in these efforts, the pressure for annexation of the whole of the
Canadian Confederation would be irresistible—for with the Royal Navy
expelled from its Northern American bases, Great Britain would be powerless to deny the USA the fruits of its victory.

To conquer Canada, the USA committed the bulk of its army, totaling some 450,000 troops, to the northward campaigns. The initial attacks
would be concentrated in the West, the Great Plains, and the East. Separate
columns would move to occupy British Columbia; cut the Canadian Pacific
Railway between the Rocky Mountain Divide and the western edge of the
Great Shield; and strike out from Maine across the rugged woodlands
of New Brunswick toward Nova Scotia and Halifax. By design, the USA
elected to hold back a force of one hundred thousand troops, mobilized to

move rapidly into southwestern Ontario as soon as opportunity warranted. "First we will cut off the West and then so threaten Halifax that Ottawa must commit its reserves," Chief of Staff Miles explained to President McKinley and his cabinet on the eve of war. "At that point, Ontario and Quebec will be naked for the taking—and take them we will." But before the first guns opened up along either the British Columbia–Washington State or New Brunswick–Maine borders, torpedo boats of the USA Navy would launch daring night raids against the Royal Navy squadrons riding at anchor at Esquimault and Halifax.

The audacity of attacking the primary British Western Hemisphere naval bases with some of the smallest ships in the USA navy's inventory is made clear by a brief digression into the changed nature of naval warfare which the last quarter of the nineteenth century spawned. For centuries, naval battles had been decided by encounters between large fleets of ships of the battle line. These wooden "battle line ships"—battleships—were rated according to the number of smoothbore cannons carried broadside: the more numerous the guns, the more powerful the ship. This equilibrium was upset by the introduction of iron, steam power, rifled ordinance firing explosive shells, and eventually steel—all of which became significant in a naval context in the middle of the last century. Great Britain laid down a broadside "ironclad" (essentially an ordinary steam frigate with an iron hull) in 1860. France had launched the first of three wooden-hulled but iron-plated ships a year earlier; the latter two, *Solferino* and *Magenta*, were the only two-decked broadside ironclads ever built. Superimposed on this state of affairs was the battle between USS *Monitor* and CSS *Virginia* in Hampton Roads early in 1862; the heavy plate of each ship proved impervious even at point-blank range, while the innovative turret of *Monitor*, designed by John Ericsson, overcame the inherent limitations on maneuverability in close waters that had plagued navies since the abandonment of the galley after the Battle of Lepanto in 1571.

Accordingly, the navies of the world found themselves, quite literally, at sea as to what constituted a first-rate battle ship during the 1860s—even to the 1880s. A certain innate conservatism existed which was compounded by the imperative not to build a large number of sister ships that would undergo block obsolescence or, worse, be made completely irrelevant by the next round of innovation. The USA Navy kept building larger and larger monitors, convinced that the low-freeboard, armored turret ships would remain impervious to enemy fire. In this, the USA was largely correct, but their monitors—slow and low—proved almost more dangerous to sail in the open seas than to fight. The United Kingdom experimented with various types of broadside ironclads, seeking a balance of protection, seaworthiness, and speed and usually generating a design that was woefully deficient in at least one area. The Confederate navy focused on construction of casemate ironclads similar to *Virginia* for more than a decade after the Secession War ended, as the South's industrial base matured. The Confederate States Navy purchased most of its oceangoing warships abroad during this period, including CSS *Lexington* (an armored ram mounting a three-hundred-pound Armstrong rifle, built in France in 1864) and *Montgomery*-class armored export corvettes, built in the United Kingdom and armed with Tredegar–Krupp breach-loaders—two of which we have already encountered in their happenstance entry into Chilean service during the War of the Pacific. Gradually, by the end of the 1880s, the major powers' shipbuilding programs had coalesced around two basic ship types: a heavily armed and armored "battleship" (with a small number of very large guns in two or more turrets or barbettes), and a fleeter "cruiser" (less heavily armored and bearing smaller guns) for reconnaissance, attacks on merchant shipping, showing the flag on distant stations, and scouting for the battle line. By 1890, the CSA, the USA, the United Kingdom, France, Italy, the recently united German Empire, Japan, the major South American states, and most middle powers were, to varying degrees, building or (more often) purchasing steel-hulled armored battleships and cruisers with increasingly efficient steam engines, increasingly effective rifled guns, and increasingly protective types of steel, compound, and cemented armor plate. Battleships grew in size from the one-thousand-ton *Monitor* and the nine-thousand-ton *Warrior* to seventeen-thousand-ton, 420 foot-long steel behemoths.

Why, then, the American reliance on small, fast, lightly armed and unarmored boats? The strategy was the brainchild of Secretary of the Navy Theodore Roosevelt. Assistant Secretary of the Navy in Schofield's administration, the ambitious TR had demanded the Secretary's office as the price of his vigorous—and invaluable—efforts on McKinley's behalf during the hard-fought 1896 presidential campaign. McKinley resisted, put off by the young New Yorker's bellicosity, but eventually succumbed to the combination of TR's relentless pursuit of the position and a strong lobbying effort on his behalf by key Republican war hawks led by Senator Lodge. Roosevelt had an innovative and daring mind, and his close study of naval warfare had convinced him that modern battleships were vulnerable to torpedo attack: especially at night while at anchor in the seeming security of a battle fleet's own base.

We have already seen how crude experimental torpedo craft rudely surprised the USA bombardment squadron at Santiago de Cuba during the Western War. Modern locomotive torpedo development began a few years after the War of Secession, with the first successful experiments by the English engineer Robert Whitehead at Fiume in 1868. In the remarkably open world of military technology that characterized the nineteenth century, Whitehead promptly made his innovation available to a wide variety of interested parties. The USA Navy began producing Mark II Whitehead torpedoes under a license from the inventor at the Newport, Rhode Island development center as early as 1869; the CSA followed suit at Charleston the next year, under an identical arrangement. By the 1880s, Whitehead torpedoes had been installed on warships worldwide, including on the first "torpedo boats" designed expressly for the purpose of launching torpedoes against other—larger—ships. But although the Whitehead torpedo had claimed its first victim within ten years of its initial development (a Turkish customs boat, sunk by a Russian torpedo boat in 1878), early torpedo designs lacked range, speed, warhead size, and the directional reliability needed to transform them into truly potent weapons against capital ships.

With the onset of the naval arms race triggered by the formation of the Great Alliances, finding a solution to the ineffectiveness of the torpedo became a priority—particularly for the USA and French navies, challenging as they were the Royal Navy. One major improvement—a gyroscope to allow a torpedo to run "true" for an extended distance—was arrived at simultaneously by the Royal and American Navies. Rapid testing followed, and by the outbreak of World War One, both sides had perfected torpedoes that multiplied the weapon's reliable range, increased its speed, and allowed it to mount an effective warhead. Those with the vision to see recognized that the "little boats" now had the capacity to fight on (near) equal terms with their great, armored companions—an innovation particularly welcomed by the French (whose attempts at creating a successful battleship design stalled disastrously after the departure of designer Dupuy de Lôme to the world of politics in 1870).

The Royal Navy inaugurated the era of the modern torpedo gunboat with the launch of HMS *Rattlesnake* in 1886. She was large for the type, displacing 550 tons and being two hundred feet in length. Although quick for her day, her 19-knot top speed would soon be eclipsed by her successors. She mounted four fourteen-inch torpedo tubes as well as one four-inch gun for self-defense. The United States responded by laying down USS *Cushing* at Bristol, Rhode Island. *Cushing* spent most of her career as an adjunct to the Newport Naval Torpedo Station and was the centerpiece platform for the development of the larger eighteen-inch torpedoes that quickly became standard in the US fleet. *Cushing* represented a departure in both style and theory from the *Rattlesnake*. At 140 feet, *Cushing* was a third shorter than *Rattlesnake* and, at only 116 tons' displacement, far fleeter of foot. Her quadruple expansion engines drove her twin screws to make 23 knots. (In a nod—more romantic than practical—to the Battle of Lissa, *Cushing*'s all-steel hull narrowed to a sharp ram, never used.) And *Cushing*'s three eighteen-inch tubes, soon to be virtually standard in the US Navy, gave her a sting equivalent to *Rattlesnake*.

A series of successful experiments with *Cushing* led the North to the rapid construction and deployment of torpedo boat squadrons—ostensibly for coastal defense. On the Atlantic, two basic types were laid down: exemplified by the large *Foote* class and the diminutive *Talbot* class, respectively. The *Foote*s were as long as *Rattlesnake* but, at only 140 tons, were able to reach 25 knots on a regular basis. USS *DuPont*, the evolutionary successor to the *Foote* class, spread her 165 tons over a hull length of 175 feet and could attack at 28 knots or better. The *Blakely* class, built in South Boston, were similar to *DuPont*, if a knot or two slower. And by mid-1898, the Bath Iron Works had deployed the first of the *Dahlgren*-class boats. By reducing the number of torpedo tubes to two and spreading 146 tons over 151 feet of hull, the *Dahlgren* made 30 knots, and her sister, *Craven*, made 32 knots on trials. (Unfortunately for the USA, only these two of the class would be ready in time for service in October 1898.) The *Talbot* class, designed self-consciously for a defensive role, were both smaller and slower. At forty-six tons and under one hundred feet in length, they could make 21 knots (the second-of-class *Gwin* claimed 24 knots on one run). Two feet longer but with similar speed and armament to the Bristol-built *Talbots,* the *MacKenzie* class laid down in Philadelphia supplemented the coast defense force. With a crew of sixteen to operate the two eighteen-inch tubes and two one-pounder quick-firing guns, they were expendable.

The West Coast flotillas were centered around the *Davis*-class boats, built in Portland, Oregon, beginning in 1896. At 155 tons and 148 feet, these 23-knot ships were, in reality, slightly more seaworthy *Foote*-class vessels. The one-off USS *Ericsson*—fabricated in Dubuque of all places—was attached to the Pacific squadron. And in the fall of 1898, two very effective French boats of the *Forban* class were at Everett Naval Station on a training cruise. These excellent sea boats could make 30 knots, although their two tubes were fitted for the lighter fourteen-inch torpedo prevalent in European navies.

By the summer of 1898, the American Navy—"my navy," as TR liked to say—had deployed squadrons of torpedo boats training for a night attack on both Halifax and Esquimault at the very outbreak of war. As tensions heightened through September and into October, Roosevelt ordered the Atlantic squadrons concentrated at Kennebunk and Bar Harbor, Maine. On October 10, President McKinley issued the orders for the country's "Torpedo Task Forces" to move into position. When the hour of twelve midnight (Washington State time) had passed on October 13, the USA would be at war with Great Britain, and the torpedo boat forces were to coordinate their attacks so as to strike simultaneously and before dawn broke over Nova Scotia.

The attack on Esquimault proved a brilliant success and sealed the fate of British Columbia. HMS *Ramillies* was the flagship of the Royal Navy's North Pacific Fleet. A member of the highly successful *Royal Sovereign* class, she had been the largest and fastest battleship in the world when she was commissioned. Her main armament, four 13.5" guns, was placed in barbette rather than turrets to save weight and maximize speed. She was joined on station by HMS *Majestic*—newer, even larger, and yet faster. The namesake of her class, *Majestic* made almost 19 knots on her trials and boasted the newly developed Mk VIII twelve-inch gun, a significant improvement from the 13.5" guns previously deployed with the fleet. They were accompanied by the obsolescent HMS *Superb*, an eighteen-year-old relic (for such was the rate of technological innovation) originally laid down for the Sublime Porte. About half the size of her colleagues, *Superb* was refitted in 1891 to carry a total of sixteen ten-inch rifled guns—the largest number of heavy guns ever fitted on a Royal Navy battleship. Although her main battery consisted of muzzle-loaders and her rate of fire was desultory, she was still thought to be useful for shore bombardment.

At 0200 hours local time, the Americans attacked. The fifteen boats of the "Pacific Torpedo Force"—*Ericsson,* an even dozen of the *Davis* class, plus the two visiting French boats (their commanders and crew eager for the chance to prove their mettle)—had been sheltered at the American naval base at Roche Harbor in the San Juan Islands, a facility that had been wrapped with security truly remarkable for the nineteenth century and admirable even for well into the next. In a daring maneuver, the Americans cut across the entrance to Victoria's harbor and struck Esquimault from the east. Never expecting the Americans would be so "foolish" as to attack from that direction (which risked exposure from the lights of Victoria), the British had failed to picket or set full watches. The few British torpedo boat destroyers rode quietly at anchor, and the crews of the battleships slept. Running flat out at well over 20 knots in restricted waters, the Americans penetrated to the heart of the station. Within moments, the night lights of Victoria were eclipsed by fiery explosions to the west. Surprise was complete; the results, devastating. *Ramillies* was attacked by a dedicated three-boat detail and suffered five hits almost before anyone knew an action was underway. *Ramillies* had been scheduled to take on coal the next day, and her cavernous bunkers—designed as added protection against torpedo attack—were largely empty. At least one of the initial salvo of torpedoes hit a coal bunker and ignited an explosion of coal dust; another found her forward magazine. The explosions blew out her starboard side, and she turned turtle, taking almost seven hundred men down with her. The old *Superb* shook from multiple hits, one of which broke her keel and sent her to the bottom; it was a matter of luck for the British that many of her crew of 650 were on shore leave that night. The armored cruisers *Royal Arthur* and *Grafton* each took two hits. *Grafton* remained afloat and was in the process of refitting when Vancouver Island fell to the Americans. *Royal Arthur* was holed in the engine room and hit in her steering gear; she survived the night only to be towed aground the next day and scrapped.

The real prize for the swift American boats was *Majestic*. Her side belt was nine inches of Harvey steel, sixteen feet wide, but covering only 220 of her 413-foot length. According to pre-arranged assignments, both French boats loosed their lighter torpedoes at *Majestic*'s stern, destroying both screws and her rudder and flooding her steering room. A three-boat section led by *Fox* scored seven additional hits broadside—one of which hit below the armored belt. *Ericsson* added three more hits toward the bow; two of her torpedoes ran deep and exploded on unarmored steel. *Majestic* settled slowly and slipped under, although taking only forty of her crew with her.

As the attackers withdrew at high speed, attention attracted by desultory firing from destroyers HMS *Fervent* and HMS *Zephyr* led to the sinking of the former and the holing of the latter. Against these losses, the British had accounted for only two of the attackers, *Ericsson* and *Forban*, the Americans and French losing a total of only fifty-one dead and twenty captured. Both lost boats, moreover, fell victim not to British destroyers or secondary battleship armament, but to quick-firing 4.7" guns used by quick-witted junior commanders in the old, slow, but not-ineffective *Gossamer*-class torpedo boats *Skipjack* and *Seagull*. In any event, by 0345 on October 13, the Royal Navy threat in the Northern Pacific had ceased to exist. The surviving British detachment—two protected cruisers, one armored cruiser, and a handful of destroyers—could never challenge the American battle line based at the Everett Naval Station on Puget Sound, and they would remain holed up at Esquimault until the fall of Vancouver Island the following year.

The Halifax raid, on the other hand, developed (in the words of TR's report to McKinley) "not necessarily to our advantage." It was, in fact, a disaster. The torpedo boats launched against the Royal Navy's station on the Eastern Canada coast suffered as complete a defeat as the Esquimault raiders achieved a decisive triumph.

From the British point of view, Halifax constituted a far more important station than Esquimault. The North Atlantic Squadron based at Halifax had a triple task in the event of war with the USA. First, it would act as the western anchor for the supply line between Canada and the Home Islands. Second, Halifax would serve as the springboard for raids against the USA's Atlantic coast (thereby bringing the war to the North and forcing Washington to divert naval assets from efforts to interdict supplies to Canada and blockade the CSA). Finally, the Royal Navy's North Atlantic Squadron was assigned directly to support the efforts of the CSA navy (in conjunction with the Royal Navy's Caribbean squadron, operating from the West Indies stations on Jamaica and St. Lucia) to break any Northern blockade. The resulting commitment of vital naval assets naturally prompted increased attention to the quality and quantity of the Halifax station defenses.

By October 1898, Halifax boasted a patrol and searchlight network that left no gap in station defenses. Perhaps most important of all, Halifax benefited from a state of mind. The Admiralty believed (correctly) that while a successful "Yankee" attack on Halifax would probably be fatal to Canada and therefore to British interests in North America, a defeat at Esquimault—while an undoubted blow to Imperial prestige—at most would cost the Empire an already isolated and perhaps indefensible position on the North American Pacific coast. The comparative importance of the two stations was also reflected in the quality of their commanders. And there can be little doubt that the Halifax defenses reflected in vital part the energy and ability brought to bear by Rear Admiral Jackie Fisher, who presided over the Halifax station until his transfer in mid-1898 to command the Mediterranean Fleet—and who would return to Halifax in early 1899 to organize the devastating "Great Raid" of that year against New York City and Boston and then command the fleet in its victory over the Americans in the Battle of Sable Island.

Moreover, with the benefit of hindsight, it appears clear that the geography of the situation made the attack on Halifax impracticable with the technology available in 1898. As part of his "defense in depth" of Halifax, Admiral Fisher had established small-boat observation squadrons at strategic points along the Nova Scotian coast: Lunenberg, Liverpool, Yarmouth, and at Clark's Harbour at the southern tip of the island. To avoid these positions, the USA striking force was obliged to swing widely out into the North Atlantic and come to Halifax from due south. Even from the advanced US base at Bar Harbor, this required a voyage of some five hundred miles each way. Lacking any proven method to coal at sea and with an endurance insufficient for the round trip, the larger torpedo boats—eight members of the *Foote, MacKenzie,* and *Blakeley* classes and the two new *Dahlgrens*—were packed to overflowing with coal. Six smaller *Talbot*-class boats were towed to the scene of operations by two *Helena*-class gunboats: *Dover* and *Helena* herself. To bolster the force on approach—although not intended to take part in the actual assault—the gunboat *Machias* and the new, fast destroyers *Barry* and *Stewart* were seconded to the operation. Unfortunately, the squadron's passage was limited to 8–10 knots, the greatest practical speed of *Dover* and *Helena* while acting as towboats. The plan called for the flotilla to leave under cover of darkness just after midnight on October 11. The little fleet spent the rest of the eleventh swinging wide out to sea to clear the patrols out of southern Nova Scotia, turning north on the twelfth to approach to within thirty miles off Morris Point shortly after dusk.

To that point, the flotilla's luck held. The British patrols, concentrating in-shore along the southern coast of the island, did not detect the approaching threat. Through the evening, the larger torpedo boats were cleared for action, while the smaller boats were cut free. It was almost 0300 on October 13—two hours behind schedule—that the sixteen vessels of the attacking squadron set off toward Halifax harbor at a steady 18 knots, leaving the five larger ships to await their return.

The delay would prove fatal for many. At 0500, when the attack had been scheduled to begin, the boats were still in the outer approaches to the harbor, miles from a passage through the Narrows into Bedford Basin where most of the Royal Navy's big ships lay at berth. At 5:07 a.m., a subaltern ashore received a frantic cable from his counterpart at Esquimault, announcing the attack on the North Pacific Fleet, driving the point home with the highly un-English exclamatory emphasis, "This is no drill!" Well trained, he immediately signaled that all forces should "stand to" to face "likely enemy attack west." And even as word of the attack at Esquimault was being received, alert patrol forces, acutely aware of the expiration of the USA ultimatum as well as the importance of neutralization of Halifax to any American designs, had discovered the attackers moments earlier.

In accordance with Admiral Fisher's standing orders, one cruiser was to keep up steam in the outer roadstead at all times. In the early morning hours of October 13, this task fell to HMCS *Niobe*, a new addition to the *Diadem* class of armoured cruisers that had been seconded to the Royal Canadian Navy. As the American torpedo boats accelerated to their maximum speeds south of McNabb's Island, the eleven-thousand-ton four-stacker opened up with a broadside of eight six-inch guns supplemented by twelve-pounder quick-firers. Searchlights from shore and ship lanced through the night. The destroyer *Electra*, consort to *Niobe* and also under steam, cut into the midst of the attacking force at 30 knots and peppered the boats with six-pounder shot. Searchlight-directed shore batteries from Point Pleasant poured 4.7-inch shells into the attackers (at least one of which overshot the rapid torpedo boats and splintered on *Niobe*'s forward gun shield, wounding several and killing two outright).

Yet the Americans pressed on, for even with the disaster of their early discovery, there was still a great prize to be won. In Bedford Basin—now as seemingly remote from the USA forces as the far side of the moon—lay the battleships *Repulse*, *Empress of India*, and *Royal Oak*, all powerful units of the *Royal Sovereign* class. With them rested *Jupiter*, sister to the ill-fated *Majestic* that was, even at that moment, settling into the Canadian Pacific mud. An attack on these behemoths now appeared entirely out of the question. But the brilliant illumination of the outer harbor disclosed, behind *Niobe*, the hulking shape of HMS *Goliath*—just arrived from the Channel Fleet and one of the newest battleships in the fleet. This *Canopus*-class vessel boasted a primary armament of four twelve-inch guns and a top speed of almost 19 knots—a dangerous opponent indeed for the US battle line. She drew the torpedo boats as moths to a flame. *Rodgers*, *Winslow*, *DuPont*, *DeLong*, and *Tingey* each emptied their tubes at *Goliath*, scoring seven or eight hits—the exact count, we never will know for sure—including one that opened her bow to the sea. None of the five American boats survived the attack, however. *Talbot* and *MacKenzie* swung around the rear of *Goliath*. *Talbot* scored at least one hit on her stern before literally disintegrating under the coordinated fire of *Goliath's* now-active twelve-pounder defensive armament. *MacKenzie* itself rammed into *Goliath*, detonating both of her torpedoes and crushing *Goliath's* hull for some forty feet. (*Goliath* was put out of action for twenty months while she was repaired; that and the sinking of the small destroyer HMS *Bat* balanced—at least in Roosevelt's mind—the loss of fourteen torpedo boats.)

Much faster than their compatriots, *Dahlgren* and *Craven* attempted to divert the attention of *Niobe*, emptying their tubes at her but without success. Both boats made repeated passes between *Niobe* and the remaining American torpedo boats, hammering the cruiser with their quick-firing one-pounders as dawn broke. Although leaving *Niobe* herself unharmed, this volume of small-arms fire and the elusive targets of the two newest US boats distracted the British fire long enough to allow the remaining raiders—*Foote*, *Blakeley*, and the remaining *Talbot*-class small boats—to loose their torpedoes and run back toward the open sea. This parting shot blew the stem off the *Bat*, but it caused no other damage. In the meantime, *Niobe*, accompanied by *Electra*, made rapidly after the fleeing Americans. Outside the entrance to the harbor, a patrol squadron consisting of two destroyers, HMS *Avon* and HMS *Otter*, ran to cut off the torpedo boats, now bereft of torpedoes and running evasive courses at high speed. *Foote* was hit by a torpedo from *Otter* and disappeared in a cloud of smoke. *Blakeley* was holed repeatedly at her waterline near the bow and drove itself under at 25 knots; most of her men escaped to become prisoners. Running at over 33 knots—well above their design speed—*Dahlgren* escaped with minor damage and *Craven* was unscathed. Three of the *Talbot* class were sunk and a fourth was run aground and captured in the brightening daylight.

Two subsidiary tales remain to be told. The daylight pursuit of *Dahlgren* and *Craven* led *Avon*, *Electra*, and *Otter* toward the support ships waiting to rendezvous with the returning torpedo boats; *Niobe* remained in the outer harbor to ward off any further, undiscovered attackers. The single twelve-pounder guns comprising the main armament of the British destroyers were well-matched with the two three-inchers brandished by *Barry* and *Stewart*, but the British did not test their opponents. Mistaking the four-funneled American destroyers for light cruisers, the British destroyers broke off the chase and returned to their base. By the time a cruiser squadron sortied from Halifax, the Americans were gone.

The second story is one every American schoolboy knows (or, at least, did know, until American schools ceased to exist as a transmittal belt of knowledge last October). Joseph M. Reeves, an 1894 Naval Academy graduate (where he excelled in football and was credited with the invention of the football helmet) was the skipper of the *Gwin*. "Bull" Reeves took advantage of the confusion to hide his small craft in one of the many inlets that rim Halifax Harbor. Miraculously escaping detection until nightfall, he worked his way up the Narrows at slow speed and managed to fire two torpedoes at *Royal Oak* at her berth. As planned, he and his fifteen men promptly scuttled their boat and were taken into custody as they reached shore. In point of fact, *Royal Oak*'s armored belt absorbed the hits without substantial damage, and no one was injured in the attack. TR, desperate for a hero to redeem the Halifax fiasco, insisted on awarding the Congressional Medal of Honor to Reeves and the Navy Cross to his crew. It was only by the most narrow of margins—and substantial diplomatic pressure, both from the United States and third-party neutrals—that the captives avoided indictment and trial by a civilian court for attempted murder.

On the whole, the USA could be well satisfied with the results of Secretary Roosevelt's daring torpedo strategy. At Esquimault, the Royal Navy had been dealt its first major defeat of any kind in well over a century. Moreover, with the North Pacific squadron emasculated by the loss of its battleships, the Americans now had control of an area extending as far west as the Marianas and Carolines and bounded on the south by an east–west line running roughly to the Colombian coast of South America. And the losses from the raid on Halifax, while unredeemed by commensurate success, in the larger scheme of things were limited to small combatants.

Canada, however, was not a prize that could be won solely at sea, no matter how decisive the blow struck against its Royal Navy defenders. On October 13, even as the torpedo boats were moving against Esquimault and Halifax, American artillery opened up concentrated barrages at key points from Blaine, Washington to Orient, Maine. In Washington State, a force of fifty thousand moved out along a narrow front between the Puget Sound coast and the town of Sumas. The Americans aimed to overwhelm

Canadian border defenses then move swiftly across the flat country of the Fraser River Delta toward the port of Vancouver, Canada's principal outlet to the Pacific. After some sharp fighting in the suburbs south of the city, Vancouver fell on October 20. Most of the surviving Canadian and British forces retreated up the line of the Canadian Pacific Railway along the Fraser River; some escaped across the Straits of Georgia to Vancouver Island.

With the destruction of its North Pacific squadron, the Royal Navy was powerless to prevent landings on Vancouver Island, and on November 1, the Americans came ashore to the north and west of Victoria. On November 7, after a fierce bombardment that wrecked the new provincial Parliament House and most of the central business district, the city's defenders surrendered. With this victory, the USA now held the North American coast from the Aleutian Islands in Alaska to the California–Tijuana border. As for the rump of the Royal Navy's North Pacific squadron, at the end, the survivors attempted to break out to the open sea—only to be met and smashed by the big guns of the battleships *Nebraska*, *Oregon*, and *Vermont*. The Americans did not pursue their foes up the Fraser River, counting on the advance of forces east of the Rockies to cut the enemy's line of retreat. By mid-November, before heavy snows compelled a suspension of operations, American columns advancing out of Montana, North Dakota, and Minnesota had seized Calgary, Regina, and Winnipeg. The CPR was cut from west of the Great Shield, and while the Americans had been stopped short of Edmonton, that city (and the Yukon to the northwest) now depended on a tenuous supply line across the frozen tundra lands of the central Northwest Territories to Hudson Bay. The winter of 1898–99 would be remembered as the "Hunger Winter" in the Northwest Territories; among the victims were thousands of Klondikers and would-be Klondikers, mostly American citizens, trapped at Dawson or well along the Canadian routes to the Yukon by the outbreak of war and the rapid advance of American forces from Manitoba westward—although, somewhat ironically, not along the disputed Alaska–British Colombia border, where a scratch force of Mounties and Canadian regulars threw back an American attempt to force the passes.

East of the Great Plains, however, the course of the campaign gave the Americans little to crow about. Seventy-five thousand men had been allotted to the drive against Halifax. The main force was charged with pushing down the St. John River, capturing the capital of New Brunswick (Frederickton) and then advancing east to, and across, the narrow peninsula joining Nova Scotia to the mainland. A supporting force was to cross the face of the Bay of Fundy, land between Port Maitland and Yarmouth, then move east against Halifax itself. The first of these efforts—the push down the St. John River to Frederickton—was stopped well short of the New Brunswick capital by a combination of rugged terrain and well-executed defensive warfare (principally by Canadian troops that included many New Brunswickers who knew the ground and fought passionately in defense of their homes, although British Army regulars were also involved). The attempted landings on the Nova Scotia coast fared even worse. Although the Americans managed to get a few thousand troops ashore, interference from a powerful Royal Navy torpedo boat destroyer and patrol boat flotilla based on Grand Manan Island at the mouth of the bay crippled supply efforts. After a belated attempt to capture Grand Manan was beaten off in mid-November, the American high command reluctantly decided to withdraw from their lodgment—lest the troops holding the position against increasingly powerful Anglo–Canadian forces succumb to a combination of starvation and the elements. A daring night evacuation operation in rough seas and blowing snows—masterminded by the Navy's Charles Clark—successfully extricated the survivors just before Christmas.

This brilliantly executed withdrawal could not obscure the virtually complete failure of American arms in eastern Canada. In retrospect, it is difficult to imagine why the American Army pursued the attack on Halifax—especially given the outbreak of war on the eve of the winter season. Although capturing Halifax would have crippled the British position in the North Atlantic and probably doomed the whole of Canada to conquest (the events of 1917 provide at least some, if after-the-fact, evidence in support of both propositions), the American plan was singularly ill suited to its end, even if the attack had been launched at the height of summer. For one thing, the center of gravity of the assault—its *Schwerpunkt*, as the Germans would say—should have been the amphibious attack across the Bay of Fundy. The drive across New Brunswick, even if successful, would only have brought American forces to the narrow spit connecting

Nova Scotia to the mainland. Even if that natural defensive line had been breached, the Americans would have had to push southeast across another narrow waist (between Cobequid Bay on the west and New Glasgow on the east), and then would have had to turn *southwest* and fight through nearly another one hundred miles before reaching the campaign's goal. By contrast, the amphibious assault route at a stroke brought American troops within 150 miles of Halifax. But a successful amphibious assault required complete control of the entrance to the Bay of Fundy—something extraordinarily difficult to achieve because of the naval power the Anglo–Canadians could project from Halifax (the same power that the assault was intended to suppress). In short, General Miles's plan was too ambitious by half.

A tremendous concentration of American naval power might have done the trick (and would do so nineteen years later), but the scope of the concentration required simply was not appreciated by the American high command. Of course, if the Americans had not pursued the Halifax option, they would undoubtedly have moved directly against Ontario and Quebec, immediately committing at the outset the one hundred thousand men reserved for that phase of operations—as well as the seventy-five thousand employed in the Halifax campaign, the bulk of which would probably have been used to launch a drive along the old campaign routes of the Revolutionary War against Montreal and Quebec. If so, the USA might have been unable to prevent the Confederates from overrunning the whole of Maryland. In fact, the counterattacks that threw the Confederates out of Frederick and the defensive line that held Johnny in the Baltimore suburbs were both made possible only by the rapid rail redeployment of a corps originally scheduled to lead the assault into southeastern Ontario. But this fortuity should not obscure the harsh truth of the Halifax fiasco, which showed that the American General Staff had much to learn about the effective deployment of the mass forces of war in the industrial age. The failure of the American army on land in eastern Canada was exceeded only by the Navy's catastrophic performance nearly nine thousand miles to the west in the battle for the Spanish Philippines against a combined Confederate–Japanese fleet.

Even now, some sixty-five years later, I confess to a continuing puzzlement—both at the Confederacy's decision to pursue an empire so far from

Southern shores and the utter failure of the Spanish and their American allies to prevent the Confederates from achieving that aim. The Philippines quickly proved a financial drain on Confederate coffers and eventually a strategic liability as well. The doomed defense against an overwhelming Anglo–American assault in 1942 would cost the CSA tens of thousands of troops and the striking arm of the Confederate navy at a time when Richmond could not afford to expend men and material so far from home. But the fact that a foreign, imperial effort is proven years later to have been a costly mistake does not mean the effort should necessarily have been recognized to have been so at the time of the initial undertaking. Moreover, the tests used at some future point to declare a colonial venture bankrupt often obscure the reasons why a country chooses to pursue the venture in the first place. Certainly this was the case with the Confederacy's pursuit of the Philippines, which was the product of several factors, none of which could fairly be characterized as decisive, yet all of which materially contributed to Richmond's decision to make the acquisition of the Philippines— by military conquest, if need be—a goal of Confederate policy.

The reader will recall how the Confederacy's social and political development in the decades immediately following Secession were characterized by the triumph of the "Big South" party, with its vision of an industrialized and militarized Confederacy based on the primacy of slavery and dedicated to the strengthening of that institution through the acquisition of new territory to which the slave economy could be spread. Initially, the Confederates looked south and southwest: to the islands of the Caribbean Basin, Mexico, and the Central American Isthmus. All these areas had been objects of American desire during the pre-Secession days of "Manifest Destiny," especially on the part of Southern slave expansionists. Once the South had achieved independence, its leaders put in motion policies designed to acquire these territories (or at least parts of them). When Spain refused to sell Cuba, Richmond exploited fears of abolition on the part of island slaveholders to foment a rebellion against Madrid, then it manipulated that rebellion to trigger a war in which the CSA could take by force what it had been refused by voluntary sale. In Mexico, the Confederacy hoped its support for Emperor Maximilian would be rewarded: if not by outright cession of a portion of the northwestern Mexican states of Chihuahua, Coahuila, Neuvo Leon, and Tamaulipas, then at least a modification of Mexican law to permit the establishment on Mexican soil of slave-powered cotton plantations owned and operated by Confederate interests. But Maximilian fell; the CSA had to withdraw its forces from Northwest Mexico; and Richmond's fallback policy of promoting insurrection only produced the fiasco of the Western War—extinguishing any possibility of extending the slave economy into Mexico for the foreseeable future.

As for Central America, Richmond's victory in Cuba galvanized Mexico and Colombia to cooperate with the USA and Spain in a successful effort to prevent the Confederates from gaining a foothold among the squabbling collection of Central American "statelets." Thus, by the mid-1880s, Confederate leaders had to acknowledge the effective "closure" of the Caribbean Basin lands to the further expansion of the slave economy. Cuba represented a valuable addition to the slave system, but slavery's opponents had managed to frustrate the balance of expansionist plans for the region. And since the Caribbean Basin had long been considered the "frontier" of Southern slavery, its closure caused what amounted to a "spiritual crisis" among slaveholders and slavery proponents. The notion that slavery required new territory to sustain its vitality was deeply rooted in Southern slaveholder tradition and had long since been decoupled from that tradition's prosaic roots (i.e., the exhausting effect of cotton on the soil, which had pushed the slave system across the Mississippi early in the nineteenth century). With the loss of slavery's Caribbean frontier, questions began to be raised about the institution's long-term viability—and from quarters that could not easily be dismissed with the charge of abolitionism. While the closure of the Caribbean prompted some to wonder if slavery might prove an economic dead end, many more now called for the identification of new frontiers to which the slave system could be exported.

It was this search for new territory that led Southerners to cast covetous eyes on the Philippine Islands. Even before the "closure crisis" of the mid-1880s, Confederate and Brazilian agents had been scouting the Spanish–held Philippines as a possible place to which the slave plantation system might be exported. Slavery was not abolished throughout the Spanish Empire until 1875. Even then, the caste-based social structure of the Philippines made for an elite social climate receptive to suggestions by Confederate and Brazilian commercial representatives that the islands would be ripe ground for the extension of Confederate–Brazilian plantation methods. Brazilians as a group did not share the Confederate urgency about finding a new frontier. Brazil itself contained vast, undeveloped territory believed suitable for exploitation by slave-based agriculture (the move into coffee in the 1880's being a prime example). But an important segment of Brazilian slaveholders had committed their fortunes to joint ventures with their Confederate *empreendimento conjuntos*, and they now worried that the value of their holdings would decline if the South's slave economy should begin to weaken. These Brazilians provided the enthusiastic ranks from which representatives were recruited to journey to the Philippines and explore the economic and social prospects for transplanting the New World's slave-based plantation system.

The Brazilians proved able to gain quicker entrée into the upper levels of Philippine society: in part because of a common Latin and Catholic outlook and in part because Confederates were looked on with suspicion by the Spanish colonials, who affected a rigid metropolitan loyalty and therefore still resented the loss of Cuba to Richmond in 1870. Spanish snobbishness about dealing with "vulgar Confederates" could be overcome with sufficient financial lubricant, however, and the Confederate–Brazilian promoters had the capital necessary for start-up plantation operations. Of course, these plantations (initially concentrating on sugar production) could not operate on the backs of black slave labor—at least not yet. But the near peonage of the "native" laborers was close enough that glowing reports were soon received in Richmond extolling the "brilliant prospects" in the Philippines for "proper, slave-based" operations. By the 1890s, a powerful lobby group had developed, urging the acquisition of the Philippines by the Confederacy—by purchase, if possible; by force, if necessary.

Still, going into the last decade of the nineteenth century, the odds of a Confederate move to acquire the Philippines remained very long. To most Southerners, including the great majority of the CSA's economic and political leadership, the Philippines seemed ridiculously distant to constitute a realistic opportunity for slavery's expansion. These views, however, underwent a radical change with the political crisis brought on by the Great Depression of 1893. The economic slump that began that spring and continued into 1896 was the most severe of the contractions that plagued the last quarter of the nineteenth century (starting with the so-called "Panic" of 1873). Although the effects were somewhat mitigated by accelerating military outlays on the part of all the Alliance powers, by 1894, there could be no denying the widespread misery that had overtaken a substantial portion of the working-class population of every industrializing society. If the Confederate presidential election had not been held just two years before in 1891, the "Big South" interests might have lost control of the Executive Branch. But as the Confederacy's presidential cycle was fixed to six-year terms, the South's dominant political interests were granted a vital "breathing space" in which to develop a strategy for responding to the pressure for social reform that was soon sweeping the country under the label of "Popular Liberty"—"Populism," for short.

Ultimately, the military-industrial-slavery interests who controlled the dominant Confederate Party opted for the tried-but-true strategies of co-optation and foreign distraction. At the urging of former President Longstreet and other influential Confederate leaders, the party nominated an avowed man of the people, the fiery South Carolinian Senator Benjamin "Pitchfork" Tillman, as the Confederate Party candidate in the presidential election of 1897. Also, at the urging of Longstreet (and with Tillman's enthusiastic support), the party's platform included a call for the Confederacy to fulfill its "Manifest Destiny" by acquiring the Philippine Islands. By 1897, the worst of the economic crisis had passed, and some Confederate Party leaders maintained concessions needed no longer to be made to the social resentments underlying the Populist Movement (which had proven exceptionally effective during midterm elections throughout the South). But Longstreet, joined by fellow former President Fitzhugh Lee and outgoing President Joseph Blackburn, argued successfully for "defusing" still-smoldering Populist passions by co-opting Tillman (whose supporters represented the largest portion of Populist sentiment) and coupling Tillman's nomination with the distracting promise of a Confederate overseas empire. A Tillman Presidency committed to the pursuit of an "Asian Confederate manifest destiny" for slavery would permit the "Big South" establishment to continue its grip on the levers of Confederate power. And as hard-headed military realists like Longstreet recognized, the dream of a Confederate Far Eastern empire was no longer the strategically improbable notion of romantic slavery expansionists.

The decision to embrace a Philippine empire as a realistic aspiration must be attributed to one other factor: the emergence of the Japanese Empire as a prospective partner in a Confederate bid for the archipelago. Japanese interest in the Philippines had developed as part of the Japanese political and social movement calling for a "Southward Advance"—*Nanshin*—into the "South Seas" (*Nan' yo*), a fairly nebulous geographical concept that came during the Meiji Era to focus on the Micronesian Island chains of the Marianas, Carolines, Marshalls, and Gilberts, but *Breck*also encompassed the Philippines in its widest aspirations. By the 1890s, the idea of trade, settlement, and maritime expansion in the tropical Pacific had captured the Japanese popular imagination; even more important, *Nanshin* as national policy had found powerful support in the person of Takeaki Enomoto, a vice admiral in the fledgling Meiji navy who by 1891 had risen to the position of foreign minister. Enomoto was bright, able, and a master of the "behind-the-scenes" style of decision making that characterized Meiji Japan. Directly responsible for promoting the expeditions that led to the discovery (and annexation) of the Bonin Islands in 1887, Enomoto—as early as 1876—showed interest in Japan acquiring the Marianas and Carolines from Spain. Enomoto sponsored trading voyages that led to Japanese commercial settlements on several Micronesian islands then controlled by Spain. Still, these tenuous efforts, involving only a handful of adventurers who braved extraordinarily difficult circumstances with little—or no—profit to show for their pains, probably would have come to naught had Japan not achieved so decisive a triumph over China in the Sino–Japanese War of 1894--95.

The *Nanshin* school had been in a fierce—and losing—competition for influence with the "Northward Advance" (*Hokushin*) group. *Hokushin* proponents urged Japan to move into Korea, Manchuria, and Northwest China, and this policy, with its historic antecedents in the efforts of Hideyoshi in the 1590s and the obvious wealth of Northeast Asia as the promised reward, had received the lion's share of military resources during the 1870s and 1880s. This investment bore rich fruit with the victory over China in 1895; paradoxically, that victory also created a vital opening for *Nanshin* proponents. Under the Treaty of Shimonoseki, Japan's sphere of influence in Korea was recognized, and it received (as the reader will recall) the strategic Liaotung

Peninsula as well as the island of Formosa. These acquisitions temporarily sated *Hokushin* advocates, who privately acknowledged a kind of giddy shock that Japan had forced China to sign so harsh a peace and then managed to retain the fruits of the victory despite intense pressure brought to bear by Russia and France. But these acquisitions also provided new ammunition to *Nanshin* proponents. The problem was the island of Formosa, which Japan had claimed without much thought. Formosa lay hundreds of miles to the south and west of Japan and was exposed to possible attack from several quarters. This concern only increased when Japan joined the Anglo–German alliance system in 1896. All at once, Tokyo had to contemplate how to defend the country's new imperial holdings from a collection of new enemies that included Spain and the USA. Spain controlled the Philippines, the Marianas, and the Carolines, and the USA and Spain maintained powerful navy squadrons based out of Manila Bay (and supported by substantial facilities on the Marianas island of Guam). In the event of war, these forces, especially if they operated in conjunction with the French navy squadron based at Haiphong (in France's Tonkin Protectorate) could easily isolate or even seize Formosa.

Nanshin advocates, however, had a ready answer to these concerns— which also appealed to aggressive Japanese sensibilities. "Instead of waiting passively for our Spanish–American enemies to strike against us," Enomoto urged at a cabinet meeting in late 1896, "we should move first and remove the source of the danger by destroying Spanish and American power in the Philippines, the Marianas, and the Carolines." This, however, was a tall order; as Enomoto himself acknowledged, the Japanese Navy was not strong enough to take on the Spanish, Americans, and French. Japan needed an ally, and the search for that ally quickly led to Richmond. The British were the obvious choice, but London had made clear during negotiations over the Anglo–Japanese alliance that the Royal Navy would not join in any effort to oust the Spanish from the Philippines. When word of Japan's interest in a partner for such a move came to the attention of the Confederate embassy in London, the Blackburn Administration promptly instructed the CSA Minister to the Meiji Court to indicate Richmond's interest. Enomoto and other *Nanshin* leaders responded enthusiastically; so, too, did their normally antagonistic *Hokushin* rivals. The *Nanshin* tended to be concentrated in the ranks of the navy, while the army had provided stalwart support for *Hokushin* goals. Now, the danger to Formosa and the prospect for new lands to conquer by joint Army–Navy operations united the two services in supporting a "confidential memorandum of understanding agreement" with Richmond, under which Japan and the Confederacy would, in the event of war between the two global alliances, launch an immediate attack on the Philippines and the Spanish–American naval forces based there.

With this agreement, Enomoto's tall order had at least acquired a reasonable chance of success. Since 1891, the Confederate Navy had maintained a modest naval presence in the Far East in the form of an "Asia Squadron" consisting of two protected cruisers and associated support vessels. The Asia Squadron had been based at Hong Kong under the reciprocal basing rights provisions of the Anglo–Confederate naval agreements of 1887. Now, at Japan's invitation, an expanded squadron—the battleships CSS *Kentucky* and *Louisiana*, the armored cruisers CSS *Calhoun*, Breckinridge, *Clay*, and *Kershaw*, and a score of *A. P. Hill*-class torpedo boat destroyers joining the protected cruisers CSS *Alexander Stephens* and *Tallahasee*— took up quarters at the new Japanese naval base being developed at Keelung on Formosa. Moreover, the Confederate and Japanese army staffs established a "rotation" agreement by which a full division of Confederate troops came to Japan to train with Japanese troops for a joint assault on the Philippines. Under the agreement, a new Confederate division would "rotate through" every six months; this arrangement permitted the CSA to deny it had established a "permanent" army presence in East Asia; it also permitted the Confederate government to double its ground forces by the simple expedient of delaying the departure of a division at the end of its rotation. Although Richmond and Tokyo disclaimed any aggressive intentions, after the CSA presidential election of 1897, both Washington and Madrid assumed that they would have to repulse a Confederate–Japanese attack on the Philippines (and possibly the Marianas and Carolines) in the event of war. This accurate assessment of enemy intentions makes all the more baffling the utter ineptitude with which the Spanish and Americans met the challenge when it came in October 1898.

The Confederate–Japanese plan was simple and direct. A battle fleet consisting of the CSA's reinforced Asia squadron plus Japan's "First Striking Force" of battleships and armored cruisers would attack the Spanish–American naval forces based at Manila. The destruction of these forces would give the Confederates and Japanese control of the seas around the Philippines archipelago, opening the way to a three-pronged assault: on Luzon, at Lingayen Gulf in the north and Polillo Bight in the east; and on Mindanao, at Sindangan Bay. Once established ashore, these forces (numbering in total well over one hundred thousand troops) would have the Spanish defenders at a terrible disadvantage: Spain having fewer than forty thousand troops committed to the Islands' defense and the USA having made only a token commitment of land forces numbering under five thousand men.

The key would be the outcome of the initial naval clash. The Japanese, having provided the balance of the attacking naval forces, also insisted on developing the plan for the attack. Admiral Togo wanted to catch the defenders at anchor in Manila Bay and proposed a night attack using torpedo boat destroyers to be initiated before the commencement of formal hostilities. The Confederates acceded, albeit reluctantly, to this—flagrant— violation of the established rules of war. Togo, like USA Navy Secretary Theodore Roosevelt, had concluded that a torpedo strike against a fleet at anchor could do great damage; unlike TR, Togo felt unconstrained by the absence of an actual declared state of war. A similar attack had been made against the Chinese, and by mid-1897, Japanese training for such an attack was well advanced. The Japanese had acquired the latest Whitehead torpedo, equipped with gyroscopes, from the Royal Navy (a benefit of the Japanese–British alliance). On their own, the Japanese developed seagoing torpedo boats of the *Kotaka* and new *Hayabusa* classes, built by the score at Kure Arsenal and the Kawasaki Shipyard at Kobe. Originally designed to displace 150 to 200 tons, the Japanese designers departed from their French models to add twenty to thirty tons displacement, accepting a 3 knot diminution in speed in order to carry enough coal for the trip from Formosa to Manila. They were designed, in short, specifically for this attack; how and if they would return if unsuccessful was an issue not included in the design specifications.

Perhaps the shock of this peculiarly Japanese methodology can be offered as an explanation—if not excuse—for why the Spanish and American fleets were taken so badly by surprise on the night of October 12, 1898, when a force of some sixteen Japanese torpedo boats burst into the heart of Manila Bay and made a beeline for the Spanish and American ships riding at anchor near the Cavite naval station. Although Commodore Charles Gridley (the commander of the American fleet) had been warned by Washington just the day before to be on guard against such an attack, Gridley—who had vigorously opposed Roosevelt's "waste" of Navy funds on an American torpedo boat task force—ridiculed the idea that "a bunch of buzz boats" could even reach Manila from Formosa. The small ships sped by the coastal fortifications. Japanese torpedoes crashed into Spanish and American ships unprotected by torpedo nets. Within minutes, the attack had claimed Gridley's flagship *Olympia* as well as USS *Indiana*, a powerful unit with four thirteen-inch guns. Spanish Admiral Patricio Montojo y Pasaron lost the *Pelayo*-class battleship *Hugo Capet* as well as the unarmored cruisers *Vizcaya* and *Almirante Oquendo*. Perhaps more significantly, although Montojo did not appreciate it at the time, Japanese torpedoes had claimed the modern Spanish destroyers *Pluton* and *Terror*, whose absence would be sorely felt at the climactic encounter of Cape Bolinao a few days hence.

Gridley survived the destruction of his flagship, but he would not survive his next—and disastrously final—encounter with the enemy. The torpedo attack had crippled, but not eliminated, Spanish–American naval power in the Philippines. The American squadron still comprised the battleships *Massachusetts* and *Montana* as well as the older protected cruisers USS *Boston* and *Chicago*. The Spanish could still muster an impressive-seeming array of three remaining *Pelayo*-class battleships—*Alfonse XII*, *Infante Alfonso XIII*, and *Pelayo* herself—as well as the one remaining *Regina Christina*-class cruiser (again, the name ship of the class), and the powerful new armored cruiser *Cristobal Colon*, built in Italy. The original *Pelayo* had been built in France in the 1880s, as the lead ship of a three-ship class. Soon after her completion, Spain acceded to both USA requests and French and American subsidies to expand the class to eight. Beginning with *Hugo Capet*, the third-of-class, the ships were built in Spanish yards, with Creusot armor. The subsequent units were armed with four 12.6" guns (as opposed to two 12.6" and two 11" in the original design). The later ships were twenty feet longer and substituted advanced Niclausse boilers to extend their range and augment their speed. (And only *Pelayo* herself was built with sails, which were quickly removed.) *Pelayo* was retrofitted in 1897, although its range and speed remained inferior to its companions. However, to save weight, throughout the class, the two midship batteries were wholly unarmored; even the centerline guns were placed on barbettes rather than in turrets. *Regina Christina* was almost completely unarmored, with a high, unprotected freeboard. And *Colon*, while fleet of foot, had defective main guns; the Spanish navy initially had rejected them, and only under intense political pressure from a government frantic to reinforce the Philippines had they been accepted from their Italian builder. As for the USA squadron, USS *Boston* lacked effective armor and was obsolete by the time she was completed. Much larger, *Chicago* was underpowered and—unbelievably—could still carry a full rig of sail. Her intended main armament—four eight-inch guns ordered from Armstrong in the UK—were impounded by the British government and replaced by American-made six-inchers. *Massachusetts* and *Montana*, sisters of the lost *Indiana*, were badly outmatched. And the state of fleet preparation and crew training may be divined by the fact that Gridley had not cleared his ships of flammable wood and other combustibles, and that they still wore their highly visible peacetime buff-and-white color scheme rather than gray battle paint.

Togo's brilliant opening stroke—every bit the equal of the American *coup de main* against the Royal Navy at Esquimault—had moreover equalized the number of capital ships soon to face off in a battle for control of Philippine waters. There could be little doubt about the necessity of that fight. Gridley recognized that if the Spanish–American forces remained inside Manila Bay, the Confederates and Japanese would effectively have been ceded control of Philippine waters, opening the way to an invasion that almost certainly could not be turned back once the enemy was ashore. Gridley and his Spanish counterpart, Admiral Montojo, agreed that their battered forces must promptly sortie and attempt to smash the Confederate–Japanese battle fleet believed lurking to the northwest.

And that opposing fleet was a powerful force. With six cruisers and two (albeit older) battleships, the CSA squadron by itself might have sufficed. It was commanded by the neigh-ubiquitous Irvine Stephen Bulloch, now a Commodore and a man not known for faint measures. And Togo's fleet was, quite simply, overwhelming: his flagship *Mikasa* and her sister battleship *Fuji* were *Shikishama* class (basically improved versions of the Royal Navy's *Majestic* class). The battleship *Yashima* was similar, although fitted with improved Tredegar–Krupp armor. They were accompanied by the protected cruisers *Tokiwa*, *Chioda*, and *Asama*. As important was the Japanese fleet's use of "Shimosa" in its high explosive and armor-piercing shells. The fruit of industrial espionage against France in the 1880s, the high-powered explosive Shimosa effectively quadrupled the force of Japanese shells. When combined with contact fuses—sowing fire and shell fragments in all directions—Shimosa would prove especially deadly against unprotected ships and Spanish barbettes.

On October 14, the surviving Spanish and American ships weighed anchor. Steaming north, the allies encountered their foes off the Luzon coast: at Cape Bolinao. Togo had withdrawn his forces to this point after recovering the victorious torpedo boats. He knew the enemy would have to follow and therefore picked a position for battle that also put the Confederate–Japanese fleet between the Spanish–American squadron and the troop transports approaching the Lingayen Gulf landing grounds. On the morning of October 15, the opposing forces met in the greatest fleet engagement since Trafalgar. By noon, the Confederates and Japanese had won so complete a victory that the initial reports would be disbelieved in the victors' capitals. The Spanish ships, laden with wooden fixtures their designers had preserved as if in romantic *homage* to ages past, proved extraordinarily vulnerable to fire. Within minutes, the Spanish line lost all semblance of order as blazing ships skewed this way and that. Two of the burning Spaniards plowed into the American line; as the American ships lost order, the enemy—sensing the opportunity—closed around and poured on a disciplined and devastating fire. When the smoke had cleared, observers on the Confederate and Japanese ships beheld a terrible scene. The Spanish and American squadrons had been reduced to a collection of shattered and burning hulks and from across the waters came the cries of literally thousands of sailors, desperately seeking rescue amid the maelstrom of flaming wreckage and exploding powder magazines.

Every major Spanish ship was lost. Among the Americans, only the protected cruiser *Boston* managed to escape; she had been at the rear of the American line and was shielded from the enemy assault by the intervening mass of allied ships. Miraculously, Admiral Montojo survived: thrown clear when an explosion wrecked his flagship *Regina Cristina*. Commodore Gridley was not so fortunate: lost along with the entire complement of the battleship *Montana*, which was literally blown to pieces when enemy fire ignited the ship's powder magazine. In stark contrast, the Confederates and Japanese lost just one capital ship—the Confederate armored cruiser *John C. Calhoun*—to a spread of torpedoes fired by a group of Northern torpedo boats valiantly shielding the retreating *Boston*. Spanish and American dead and wounded exceeded five thousand. Opposing losses were under one hundred. It was a victory on a scale that would make Togo an international hero: to be honored in the capital of every one of Japan's allies. The reader will recall how furious the British were over Togo's role in the sinking of the *Kowshing* during the opening phase of the Sino–Japanese War; all was forgiven in the wake of his Philippine victories, and Togo would be acclaimed "an equal to Nelson" by cheering crowds at a Royal Albert Hall reception commemorating the one-hundredth anniversary of Trafalgar in 1905—an honorific made all the more remarkable by the fact that Jackie Fisher (as commander of the Royal Navy's Mediterranean fleet) won a smashing victory against the French and Spanish at almost the same time as Togo's Far East triumphs.

The Philippines' fate had been sealed by the Battle of Cape Bolinao. On October 16, Confederate and Japanese forces came ashore near Dagupan on the Lingayen Gulf, and the next day, landings (of exclusively Japanese troops) were carried out at Polillo Bight and at Sindangan Bay on Mindanao. Spanish and American defenders managed to contain the enemy at Polillo, but the forces opposing the Lingayen landing were outfought and outmaneuvered by a better-trained and better-equipped enemy. Within a week, Confederate and Japanese columns were marching rapidly south, and Governor General Basilio Augustín Dávila realized that Manila was doomed. Instead of sacrificing the capital and its inhabitants to a futile defense, Dávila declared Manila an "open city" and fled with his family—and the American Minister—by cutter to the island of Mindoro (where they would be rescued by a French cruiser and taken to the comparative safety of Saigon). The surviving American cruiser was not so lucky. Caught by Togo's forces in an attempted night escape from

Manila Bay, *Boston*—damaged but still under power—had to limp back to Cavite, where her captain scuttled the ship to prevent its capture. By the end of November, all the principal islands of the Philippine archipelago were in Confederate and Japanese hands. The surviving Spanish and American troops who surrendered were pleasantly surprised by the generous treatment they received from their Japanese captors, whose soldiers had been derided before the war as "barbarous yellow apes"—sadly, Japanese chivalry would prove a thing of the past by the outbreak of World War Three in September 1939.

Farther east, the Japanese learned a sharp lesson in the consequences of trying to do too much with not enough. Over Togo's protests, the Imperial General Staff detached two armored cruisers and several torpedo boat destroyers from Togo's force, with an eye to capturing the principal Spanish–American base in the Marianas, located on the island of Guam. Poor planning delayed the departure of this "Guam invasion force" until nearly one week after the Battle of Cape Bolinao. By then, word of the disaster to Spanish–American arms had galvanized an effort to stiffen defenses along a new Marianas–Carolines defensive perimeter. Rear Admiral George Dewey, the commander of the USA's Pacific Fleet (a command independent of the unfortunate Gridley's "East Asia" Squadron), ordered an *ad hoc* group made up of the three fastest cruisers available—USS *Minneapolis*, her sister USS *Tacoma*, and the large new *Brooklyn*, with eight-inch guns—to speed from Pearl Harbor and reinforce Spanish and American forces already based at Guam. This small but potent group of one American battleship (the recently commissioned *Michigan*) and three Spanish cruisers (including the unarmored but still powerful *Reina Mercedez*) had already braced to meet the expected Japanese attack. Because of Japanese dithering, the reinforcements from Hawaii arrived before the attackers, who found themselves steaming into battle against a vastly superior force three weeks after Togo had smashed the enemy in the Philippines. This time, it was the Japanese who suffered a crushing defeat, losing the cruisers *Asama* and *Chioda*—as well as a destroyer—to no ships for the Spanish–American force. Moreover, even farther east, the Americans (with French aid from bases in Polynesia) had moved to occupy the principal islands of the German–controlled Marshalls and British–controlled Gilberts. Brushing aside weak resistance, the Americans thereby secured the rear of the Marianas–Caroline perimeter and also positioned themselves for possible moves against the Bismarck Archipelago, the Solomons, and Fiji. Nothing could be done, however, to prevent the loss of French New Caledonia and of American Samoa; these islands lay to the rear of the Anglo–German defense chain in the South Pacific and were no more defensible than the Marshalls and Gilberts. Correlatively, by this time, the Japanese had occupied the strategic island of Hainan in the South China Sea, which contained substantial iron ore deposits. The Imperial Government also announced the annexation of the uninhabited Sinnan, or Spratly Islands; France, whose prior claim to the Spratleys was based on their proximity to French Indochina, could do nothing but protest.

Before moving on to chronicle the War's course on other principal fronts, I will touch on the one place where North and South could have clashed—but did not. After the fiasco of the Western War, the Confederate military was riven by what came to be called the "Mexico Debate." The dispute pitted a faction that wished to renew the push into Mexico, at the earliest opportunity, against a group who argued that the entry into the Anglo–Confederate alliance required a radical reassessment of the Confederacy's war plans. Ultimately, the latter group prevailed. Maryland and the Philippines were to be targeted for offensive efforts, and CSA forces would stand on the defensive elsewhere, including along the Rio Grande. This decision guaranteed quiet along what could have been—and in future would be—a hotly contested "Mexican Front." After the defensive success of Mexican arms in the Western War, President Diaz rejected suggestions that Mexico "take the fight to the enemy" in the next war. "Mexico cannot afford the luxury of an army of conquest or even re-conquest," Diaz told his cabinet in the late 1880's. ("Re-conquest" being a veiled reference to Texas.) "We must rebuild and strengthen our defenses and be prepared to meet and crush the enemy at our borders." For the fourteen years between the end of the Western War and the outbreak of World War One, Mexico did just that, spending tens of millions of dollars on a vast chain of fortifications whose strongest points rivaled such great European fortresses as Liege in Belgium. When war broke out in October of 1898, Mexico braced for the "inevitable" Confederate attack. Only by the end of November did Diaz and his general staff begin to take seriously the notion that—this time, at least—there would be no such attack. Confidence in that conclusion then led the Mexicans to begin planning their own attack across the Rio Grande—to be coordinated with a massive Northern assault down both sides of the Mississippi, with nothing less than the splitting of the Confederacy as its goal. As the reader will see, this Mexican attack would fail disastrously, and the defeat would signal the beginning of the end for the Diaz regime, with grave consequences for Mexican and American security.

(above) Print from "Leslie's Weekly," showing the U.S. Capital building in flames, and the dome beginning to lean just before its collapse onto the Old Senate wing.

(below) Profile of the Tredegar-Krupp *Washingtonkannon*, whose railroad mounting allowed the Confederates to bring it rapidly into range of the USA capitol and then carry out the destructive bombardment that left the city a flaming ruin.

(left) Stephen Field, whose long service on the U.S. Supreme Court ended with his death during the bombardment of Washington, when a shell crashed through the roof of the Old Senate wing and exploded amidst the Supreme Court chambers located immediately below, killing the Chief Justice and Associate Justice Horace Gray.

(right) Oliver Wendell Holmes, Jr., Secession War veteran and Chief Justice of the Massachusetts Judicial Court, who was appointed by USA President McKinley to succeed Field as Chief Justice and whose fierce opposition to sedition in any form would shape the Court's approach to freedom of speech specifically and civil liberties generally.

17

WORLD WAR I: (4) OPENING PHASE OF THE WAR IN EUROPE AND AFRICA—ITALIAN NEUTRALITY, STALEMATE IN ALSACE-LORRAINE, "SITZKRIEG" IN EASTERN EUROPE, POLITICAL CRISIS IN GREAT BRITAIN OVER FOOD SUPPLIES, AND THE STRUGGLE FOR CONTROL OF THE MEDITERRANEAN AND COLONIAL AFRICA

———

I confess to a nagging suspicion that the reader may have read my description of the outbreak of World War One with less than complete satisfaction. After all, saying that the Great Powers proceeded to declare war on each other—and little else—could leave one with the impression that I take a very mechanistic view of such matters. In fact, I do not believe that the outbreak of global war between alliances should be likened, even implicitly, to the fall of dominoes. So, before turning to my narration of the initial course of the war in its European and related theaters (which encompassed the Mediterranean and Colonial Africa), I will discuss the circumstances that led to the honoring of their alliance obligations by Germany and the other European belligerents. I will begin that discussion with an analysis of the reasons why Italy—a member of the Triple Alliance between Germany, Austria–Hungary, and the Kingdom of Italy—chose to repudiate her (seeming) obligation to enter the lists against the Franco–American–Russian *entente.* Italy's renunciation of war in 1898 and determined adherence to neutrality could be taken as tending to discredit my central hypothesis: that the adversarial alliance structure of international relations flowing from the Confederacy's victory in the War of Secession was the chief cause of our century's calamitous history. In fact, and as I shall attempt to demonstrate, Italy's decision to sit out World War One evidences merely another aspect of an international system dominated by hostile power blocs. Far from proving the general capacity of powers to resist the violent antagonisms of such a system, Italy's refusal to honor its Triple Alliance obligations exemplifies how a country will try to exploit the system's dynamic to achieve what that country's leaders consider to be its true vital interests.

The fundamental operative fact that explains Italy's neutrality in World War One is the disjunction between Italy's membership in the Triple Alliance and the Italian elite's perception of the country's true interests. Had war come in 1895 over the attempt by Russia and France to compel Japan to soften the terms of her victory over China, those perceptions might have yielded to the contrary vision of Francesco Crispi. Crispi, born in 1818 in the city of Nice (then a part of the independent Kingdom of Piedmont), was one of the leading figures of the *Risorgimento* movement that produced the United Kingdom of Italy in 1860. A brilliant and talented politician who provided much-needed "realist" ballast for the romantic Garibaldi's successful military and political campaign to win the backward South for the ideal of *"L'Italia,"* Crispi finally became Prime Minister of united Italy in 1887. Galvanized by what he saw as the failure of Italians to develop a sense of loyalty to the new country's institutions, Crispi pursued an aggressive foreign policy in the hope of creating some battlefield opportunity to strengthen the Italian sense of nationhood. Crispi brought to this quest a deep and personal hatred of the French, arising out of the loss of Crispi's home city of Nice to France in 1860. Count Emiliano Cavour, the political leader of the Piedmontese, had yielded Nice and another portion of the Piedmont (the northwestern Savoy, along Lake Geneva) in exchange for Louis Napoleon's support of Cavour's final—and successful—drive to create a united Italy. Although Crispi played a leading role in the unification effort, he bitterly opposed trading away his home city for French aid.

When Crispi came to power, hatred of France for "stealing" Nice helped shape his approach to Italian foreign policy.

In 1882, Italy had been persuaded by Bismarck to join a "Triple Alliance" with Germany and the Austrian Empire. Rechristened Austria–Hungary in 1867 (when Vienna acceded to Hungarian pressure for greater autonomy by establishing a "Dual Monarchy" system), the new Dual Kingdom remained to Italians the hated Habsburg power against which Italian nationalism had struggled for centuries before the triumph of the *Risorgimento*. Even that victory had to be won in part on the battlefield: against Austrian armies sent to frustrate what Vienna perceived as the threat a united Italian state would pose to the stability of the multinational Austro–Hungarian empire. With French help, the Austrians were defeated (at Solferino, in 1859), and Vienna's fears were quickly realized, for the squabbling kingdoms and duchies of the Italian peninsula had no sooner been transformed into a single polity than the new Kingdom of Italy began to press Austria for territorial concessions. In 1866, Italy seized the opportunity of Prussia's attack on Austria to make war on Habsburg power. In a sharp but brief conflict, Italy acquired Venice and the surrounding district of Venezia—although only at the peace conference table and then only because Prussia had crushed the main Austrian army at Königgrätz, the Austrians having defeated the Italians on land (at Custozza) and on sea (at Lissa, the first battle fought between ironclad fleets).

Perhaps if Vienna had exhibited the wisdom to follow up her proven field superiority over the Italians by offering further concessions in the Trentino (the Austrian Tyrol) or the Littoral (the territory east of Venezia, including the Adriatic port cities of Trieste and Fiume), Italian territorial ambitions could have been sated, and a peaceful relationship could have been established between Italy and Austria–Hungary. But the Austrian Empire was convulsed over her defeat by Prussia, which had effectively overthrown the post-Napoleonic order in Germany and set the stage for German unification under Prussian rule. Facing exclusion from the new Germany ruled from Berlin, the Germans of Austria were compelled to reach a constitutional *modus vivendi* with the Magyars of Hungary. Magyar rebellion against Vienna's authority had nearly destroyed the Habsburg empire earlier in the century, and now the Magyars would have to be accommodated because the German-speaking Habsburgs could no longer afford the luxury of behaving like feudal overlords—at least not toward Hungary. But while the ensuing constitutional reforms saved Habsburg rule by establishing the principle of internal equality between Vienna and Budapest under the "Dual Monarchy" (foreign policy remaining a royal, and therefore Austrian, prerogative), the effort exhausted what capacity for imaginative and flexible policy existed among the Austrian and Hungarian elite. If there had been any possibility of a generously creative approach to Italy in the wake of the war of 1866, that chance was lost in the midst of the exhausting process of Habsburg constitutional reform triggered by that same war.

When Prussia followed up her victory in 1866 with the overthrow of Napoleon III at Sedan and the establishment of a German Empire encompassing all the traditional German lands save Austria, Vienna responded by admitting the eclipse of Habsburg authority and accepting Bismarck's invitation to become an ally of the new (and preeminent) German power. It was Bismarck who had persuaded the new Italian state to join Prussia in making war on Austria, and Bismarck continued to cultivate the Italians prior to his master stroke against France (if only to assure that Italy stayed neutral and France was thereby forced to fight alone). In the immediate aftermath of the unification of Germany under Hohenzollern rule, Bismarck no longer valued the Italian alliance. Bismarck was Eager to rebuild even stronger bridges to Vienna, Bismarck was prepared to sacrifice the Italian relationship to that end. By the 1880s, however, Bismarck was ready to reinvigorate the German–Italian link of twenty years before. For Bismarck, isolating France, with her dreams of *revanche* for the humiliation of 1871, remained the touchstone of German foreign policy. When Italy and France fell out over France's seizure of Tunisia in 1881 (Rome had promoted Italian settlement and economic penetration of the area in the hope of acquiring a foothold in North Africa), Bismarck quickly stepped in and offered German friendship to fill the gap created by the rupture with Paris.

Bismarck also made clear, however, that Berlin was not offering a revival of the bilateral ties that preceded the joint war against Austria in 1866. Rome would have to agree to join Berlin and Vienna in a defensive alliance. Although Italy still coveted the Trentino and the Littoral, the Italian leadership was also convinced that the Tunisian "defeat" had been caused by Italy's lack of powerful allies. Reluctantly, Italy acceded to Bismarck's conditions. The "Triplice," as it became known in diplomatic parlance, was a defensive arrangement. Each member pledged to support the others in the event of an attack by a third party. Neither Bismarck nor his Austrian counterpart, Count Gustav Kálnoky, had any illusions about the real value of Italy's alliance membership. For one, Germany and Austria–Hungary could materially benefit from Italian military assistance only in the event of a two-front war with France and Russia, and both the German and Austrian General Staffs believed the Italian armed forces were incapable of rendering such aid. Even more fundamental were doubts about Italian political reliability—if Italy's fidelity should ever be put to the test. Italy's newfound allies both recognized that Italian expansionist ambitions, at Austro–Hungarian expense, had not been extinguished merely because Rome had publicly declared Vienna to be an ally.

Crispi's ascension to power changed these calculations. Crispi allowed his hostility toward France to send Franco–Italian relations into a rapid downward spiral, with the immediate cause a dispute over tariffs on agricultural products. Starting in 1888, a Crispi-inspired "Tariff War" raged between Italy and France, drying up economic exchange and further aggravating Franco–Italian relations, which had already been strained by Tunisia and the formation of the Triplice. Crispi then tried to transform an economic dispute into a shooting war, urging Germany to join Italy in a preventive attack on France. In meetings with Bismarck (with whom Crispi fancied himself to be on intimate terms), the Italian Prime Minister claimed the French were plotting an attack on Germany and Italy. Although the German General Staff was genuinely concerned about France initiating a war to recover the "Lost Provinces" of Alsace and Lorraine, the apparent ease with which the French authorities had overcome the ultra-nationalist *Boulangist* threat in early 1889 eliminated whatever support the German military might have offered to Crispi's proposal. (As for Bismarck, he never took seriously either the notion that France had been on the verge of launching an attack, or that Germany and Italy should upset the now-satisfactory peace of Europe by initiating yet another war with the French.) Rebuffed in his attempts to launch a German–Italian war against France, Crispi tried to use the Triple Alliance as a sword in the pursuit of Italian imperial ambitions outside Europe. In 1890, when the French strengthened their protectorate over Tunisia, Crispi sought German and Austro–Hungarian support for saber-rattling Italian protests. But Berlin and Vienna demurred and did so again when Crispi sought their support for Crispi's plan to develop an Italian colonial empire in East Africa. Despite these setbacks, Crispi doggedly adhered to his evident misapprehension of the Triplice as something more than a defensive alliance. And to the increasing dismay of the Italian intelligentsia and other influential sectors of Italian society, Crispi continued to pursue a policy of *detente* with Austria–Hungary, giving no support to traditional Italian ambitions in the *irredenta* of the Trentino and the Littoral.

Crispi fell from power in February 1891, but his successors were too weak to alter the course of Italian foreign policy set by their imposing predecessor. When Crispi returned to power in November 1893, events leading to the establishment of the rival Anglo–German and Franco–Russian alliances were rapidly coming to a head. That September, the formation of the Anglo–German–Confederate naval convention had been announced. Although Crispi (like his Austrian counterpart) was disappointed that Great Britain had not also been persuaded to join the Triplice, Crispi was nonetheless delighted by what he saw as at least an indirect strengthening of Italy against the hated French. Apparently unaffected by the formation of a rival Franco–American–Russian *entente* the following January (Italian immigration to the USA continued unabated), Crispi again turned his attentions to the pursuit of Italian colonial ambitions in East Africa. The reader will recall that this effort ended disastrously with Italy's defeat by the Ethiopians at Adowa in March 1896. Crispi proved the principal political casualty, and upon Crispi's second—and final—fall from the premiership, Italian foreign policy began to swing back into its natural anti-Austrian course. Crispi's successor, Antonio Di Rudini, presided over the end of the "Tariff War" with France. By the spring of 1898, when the Yukon Crisis brought the Alliances to the brink of war, Italy was prepared to demand substantial concessions from Austria–Hungary as the price for participation in a global war alongside her Triplice allies.

McKinley's and Laurier's exertions brought the Powers back from that brink before the Italians could present their terms. But when the news of Fashoda burst upon Europe's chancelleries and the likelihood of conflict rapidly escalated, the Italian government now made clear that Italy would fight only if Austria–Hungary yielded the Trentino and much of the Istrian portion of the Littoral (including the vital seaport of Trieste). In exchange, Italy pledged her support for "compensatory" territorial adjustments in the Balkans (presumably to come at the expense of the Ottoman Empire). Rome justified these demands on the grounds that Great Britain appeared to be the "aggressor" over Fashoda, and that Italy had no obligation under the Triplice to support such conduct—notwithstanding a decision by Berlin and Vienna to do so. Technically, the Italians had a point. But just as clearly, Italian policy was not being driven by devotion to higher principles of international law. Had Crispi been in power in the fall of 1898, Italy would have gone to war on the side of the British "aggressors" because Crispi would have willingly seized the chance to strike at the hated French and possibly regain Nice in the process. Crispi's successors chose differently—only because their territorial priorities looked east and not west.

Vienna was outraged by this Italian blackmail and received vigorous German support for a blanket rejection of Rome's demands. The Austro–Hungarians, however, were far less enthusiastic than Kaiser Wilhelm II about the prospect of war. While Wilhelm acclaimed his "chance to join the ranks of the Prussian warrior kings," the Habsburg elite (from Emperor Franz–Joseph down) worried about the ability of the rickety multinational structure of the Dual Monarchy to stand the strain of war on a scale not seen in Europe since Napoleon's day. Moreover, despite the tensions created by the establishment of hostile Great Power blocks in the early 1890s, Vienna and St. Petersburg had managed to make real progress on a *modus vivendi* in the Balkans, the principal flash point between the Habsburg and Romanov empires. In 1896, Russia had been persuaded to recognize Ferdinand of Koburg (a former Austrian army officer) as the new prince of Bulgaria, and the Austro–Hungarian foreign minister, Count Agenor Maria Adam Goluchowski, had followed up this agreement by opening negotiations he hoped would lead to an Austro–Russian accord on the Balkans as a whole. Goluchowski, who had become foreign minister in 1895 with the express aim of achieving a reconciliation between Austria–Hungary and Russia, was among those Austrians who had pressed hard for British adherence to the Triplice as a condition for the establishment of an Anglo–German alliance. When Berlin abandoned that requirement, Goluchowski feared that the Dual Monarchy would now be drawn into a disastrous war because of events distant from Europe and of no relevance to Austrian vital interests. "Just because Germany's emperor has chosen to chase the will-o-the-wisp of *Weltmacht* does not mean that the House of Habsburg is bound to follow," Goluchowski said soon after acceding to the post of foreign minister. "Austria–Hungary is a European power and must make every sensible effort to assure that the European powers resolve the differences that could lead to a European war."

Goluchowski had worked diligently toward that end, and by 1896, his work seemed to be bearing fruit. If the disputed status of Alsace–Lorraine was the principal source of European tensions, the Habsburg–Romanov rivalry in the Balkans was a close second. A glance at a map of seventeenth century Europe discloses how the fates of these two great imperial houses became intertwined with that of the Ottoman Turk—their common foe. Starting with the cession to Austria of the Magyar heartlands and neighboring Transylvania in 1699, the Ottomans began the long process of forced withdrawal from Europe—a withdrawal compelled principally by Habsburg and Romanov power. By the 1870s, the Ottomans had lost the Crimea and other Black Sea territories to Russia outright; acceded to the creation of Rumania (nominally under Ottoman suzerainty—but effectively independent of Constantinople); and made further concessions to the Habsburgs in the Balkans.

Then came the Russo–Turkish War of 1877–78. (Rather ironically, this disastrous conflict for the Ottomans also marked the beginning of the long reign of Sultan Abdulhamit II—"Abdulhamit the Great"—who would preside over the reversal of Ottoman territorial fortunes in World Wars One and Two.) The Russo–Turkish war arose out of a series of crises that convulsed the Ottoman Empire: beginning with a drought and famine in Anatolia that by 1875 had left the treasury drained of funds to meet even the most basic of obligations. This triggered an international financial crisis. The Sublime Porte had been deeply in debt to foreign capital since the Crimean War, and by the mid-1870s, debt maintenance had come to absorb an astonishing 80 percent of state revenue. When the Anatolian drought dried up the agricultural sources of tax revenues used to pay the interest owing to foreign bondholders, the Porte had no choice but to default on its obligations.

Brewing international outrage over the reported massacre of Christian peasants in Bulgaria made a bad situation much worse. In 1874, an insurrection by Christian peasants had broken out in neighboring Bosnia–Hercegovina and by the following year had escalated into a series of reprisal massacres whose Christian victims quickly attracted the critical attention of the (Christian) European Powers. Then the violence spread to Bulgaria, where it took on an overt political quality as Bulgarian nationalists attempted to convert peasant grievances into a revolt aiming at the overthrow of Ottoman rule and the establishment of an independent (or at least autonomous) Bulgaria. When this insurrection proved too much for the local regular army garrison to handle, the provincial governor called upon volunteer militias. These irregular forces succeeded in suppressing the rebellion, but the ensuing reports of massacres of Christian peasants on a far greater scale than in neighboring Bosnia–Hercegovina appalled Christian Europe and triggered calls for action to prevent "the Turks" from ever again so indulging their "abominable and bestial lusts" (as Gladstone put the matter in his famous pamphlet, *The Bulgarian Horrors and the Question of the East*). The resulting clamor for a definitive resolution of the "Eastern Question," which had troubled European statesmen ever since the Crimean War, opened the door to a Russian move against the Ottoman position in Bulgaria.

The default on debt obligations had infuriated bondholders (concentrated in Great Britain and France), and they became a powerful lobby for action—no matter how drastic—designed to end the chronic incompetence of the Ottoman financial authorities. The debt crisis alone, however, would probably not have sufficed to give Russia the chance to strike. It was the scandal of the "Bulgarian Horrors" that tipped the scales. The British government was internally divided, and without a united Cabinet behind him, Prime Minister Benjamin Disraeli could not risk a parliamentary confrontation with the Liberal opposition (which had been re-energized by Gladstone's impassioned campaign against Turkish "bestiality"). Great Britain therefore could not firmly confront Russian ambitions at the conference of the Powers, which met at Constantinople from November 1876 until mid-January 1877, to find a solution to the immediate problem of Bulgaria and the more fundamental "Eastern Question" issues underlying the Bulgarian controversy. Although the Porte could not but feel humiliation over serving as host for a gathering at which the dismemberment of the Ottoman Empire was openly discussed, the Turkish authorities actually managed to disarm the proponents of these most extreme of measures by the implementation of a series of dramatic-seeming reforms, culminating in the promulgation of a constitution that the Porte claimed (disingenuously) had transformed the Ottoman realm into a constitutional monarchy. (The establishment of the constitution had actually been made possible by the more traditional Ottoman practice of a series of palace coups: which saw the deposition of two sultans and the elevation of Abdulhamit II to the throne over a space of just three months.)

But while the facade of constitutional reform managed to deflect the danger of a "Polish solution," the Porte proved unable to persuade the Powers that constitutional change had mooted the more immediate Bulgarian question that the conference had been called to resolve. (By "Bulgarian question," I also mean the Bosnian–Hercegovinian violence, which by 1876 had embroiled the Ottomans in a war with neighboring Serbia.) When agreement could not be reached between the Porte and the Powers on these issues, the conference broke up in failure, and the way was cleared for a Russian intervention in support of the Bulgarian Christians. In April 1877, Russia declared war and immediately went on the offensive in Bulgaria and in northeastern Anatolia. Rumania gave Russia permission to move troops through its territory, while Austria–Hungary agreed to remain neutral in exchange for Russian support of Austrian claims to Bosnia–Hercegovina. Most important, the British proved too divided by the "Bulgarian Horrors" debate to threaten to come to Turkey's aid as they had done twenty-four years before, thereby eliminating the danger of a wider war, whose threat might have deterred St. Petersburg.

The details of the ensuing campaigns need not detain the reader. Suffice to say that, by early 1878, the Ottomans had suffered a series of disastrous battlefield defeats that had brought the enemy to the gates of Constantinople. Austria–Hungary belatedly realized the foolishness of giving a green light to the Russian attack, for it was now apparent that Russia intended to create an independent Bulgaria big enough to dominate the Balkans. As the Russians would presumably make sure of their political dominance in the new Bulgaria, St. Petersburg would thereby gain effective control of the region (including Constantinople and the Straits) and also put the Russian Army in a position to strike at Austria–Hungary along a long, encircling line in the event of war between the two powers.

Vienna could not allow such a calamity to come to pass. But preventing it required depriving Russia of the fruits of her victory, thereby creating what would prove an unbreachable rift between the two empires. Just after the turn of the New Year, 1878, Emperor Franz–Joseph sent a personal letter to Tsar Alexander II, warning that the House of Habsburg must oppose the creation of any truly independent Bulgar state and demanding that all the European Powers participate in formulating the terms of any peace. Great Britain unexpectedly followed with a similar warning—the looming prospect of a Russian seizure of Constantinople and control of the Dardanelles having frightened a sufficient number of Conservatives initially distracted from British vital interests by the Bulgarian massacre horrors that Disraeli now felt his parliamentary control restored to take action. But events on the battlefield outpaced the mails of 1878 Europe. By January 31, the Porte had been compelled to ask for an armistice. Despite the ensuing dispatch of a Royal Navy squadron to Constantinople, the Russians successfully pressed the Porte to agree to grant independence to Montenegro and Serbia and "autonomy" to a Bulgaria that would extend from the Danube to the Aegean and into Albania. The Ottomans also agreed to cede the Batum and Kars districts in northeastern Anatolia directly to Russian rule—the Russians claiming the territories by right of conquest. These peace terms, set forth in a treaty entered into at San Stefano, brought Europe to the brink of a war that would have embroiled Russia against the Ottoman and British empires at a minimum and might easily have drawn in Austria–Hungary, Germany, and France as well. (In Great Britain, the national mood had oscillated wildly: from condemnation of Turkish atrocities against Bulgarian Christians to the promises of music hall jingoes pledging the necessary ships, men, and money for a fight on Turkey's side against Russia; by the spring of 1878, the sentiment had shifted decisively against Russia and in favor of Turkey.)

Fortunately for the sake of peace, at the crucial moment, the commander of Russian forces in the Balkans ignored pressure from St. Petersburg to seize Constantinople. Reduced tensions were further eased when Russia acknowledged the right of the Powers to be "consulted"—under prior agreements relating to the status of the Ottoman Empire—on the terms of the San Stefano Treaty. Berlin was selected as the venue, and at the ensuing congress, the Russians were compelled to accept a substantial diminution of her San Stefano gains. Of immediate relevance to this narrative, the "Big Bulgaria" of San Stefano was drastically cut down. An autonomous Bulgaria was recognized, but its territory was confined between the Danube and the Balkan mountains, while the area south of the mountains remained under direct Ottoman rule as the province of East Rumelia (although the Porte was obligated to appoint a Christian as governor). Austria–Hungary, on the other hand, was granted the right to occupy Bosnia–Hercegovina. Thus, although Vienna had stayed out of the war, it received virtually all that Russia had agreed to concede as a *quid pro quo* for Austro–Hungarian support of Russia's claims against the Ottomans—support on which the Habsburgs reneged when the likely extent of Russian gains became clear. The end of the Congress saw Austro–Russian relations in a shambles: with Great Britain and Austria–Hungary reaching an accord on an informal alliance aimed at checking Russian ambitions in the Balkans.

The Congress of Berlin and the Constantinople Conference that preceded it illustrate the early stages of North American–European Great Power interaction arising out of the South's victorious fight for independence. At Constantinople, the high profile role of USA Consul General Eugene Schuler in uncovering and publicizing the extent of Turkish atrocities against the Christians of Bulgaria alarmed Richmond sufficiently to cause the dispatch of Assistant Secretary of State John C. Gordon to monitor the course of the Conference. And at Berlin, *both* the USA and Confederacy dispatched representatives who were granted observer status. The reader will also recall how the crisis in Anglo–Confederate relations triggered by the seizure of the slave trader CSS *Beauregard* caused CSA President Longstreet to send none other than Judah Benjamin to smooth things over with London, and how Benjamin proceeded to Berlin in order to meet with Disraeli and his new Foreign Secretary—and the future Prime Minister—Lord Salisbury, both of whom were then in attendance at the Congress. There, Benjamin renewed his friendship with Disraeli and also made a very favorable impression on Salisbury—which would pay great dividends for the Confederacy only a few years thence. (Disraeli had previously paid Benjamin the compliment of including him in Disraeli's first novel, *Lothair*, in the guise of the brilliant barrister and former CSA Minister to England, Randolph Solomon Smith—a favorably drawn, if altogether cameo, portrait.) The reader will also recall how Benjamin made a favorable impression on Bismarck. And although not even Benjamin could shake Bismarck's determination to avoid entangling Germany in North American affairs, the former Confederate Secretary of State, along with the Confederacy's able observer Lafayette McLaws (who had commanded a division under Longstreet at Gettysburg), reinforced the growing ties between the Confederate and Prussian elite that, after Bismarck's departure from the scene, would blossom into full alliance. At neither of these diplomatic conclaves did the USA or CSA, or their rivalry, have an impact on the outcome of the gathering itself. But the interplay between the principal participants and the representatives of the two rival American Unions did make their own contribution, however subtle and little remarked at the time, to the ever-increasing entanglement of the fates of the Great Powers of Europe with events unfolding to the west of them all.

Although a combination of Bismarck's diligence and Gladstone's fecklessness produced a brief revival of the *Dreikaiserbund* among Germany, Russia, and Austria–Hungary in the early 1880s, the re-establishment of Emperor League ties could not effect a genuine Austro–Russian reconciliation. The conflict between Austria–Hungary and Russia in the Balkans had become a direct clash of interests that each deemed vital and which seemingly could not be resolved on any other than a "zero-sum" basis. Admittedly, the immediate course of that conflict did not take the course expected by either power, because Russia badly overplayed its hand in Bulgaria. Although the unification of Bulgaria and East Rumelia was effected (albeit under continued nominal Ottoman suzerainty) in 1885, Russian political meddling backfired with the rise to power of Stefan Stambulov, a fervent Bulgarian nationalist who had also become a staunch Russophobe. It was

Stambulov who engineered the election of Prince Ferdinand of Colburg as the expanded Bulgaria's new ruler, and together they transformed Bulgaria into an obstacle to—rather than vehicle of—Russian expansionism. For ten years, until Stambulov's death in 1895, Austria–Hungary enjoyed predominant influence in Serbia and Bulgaria and used that influence to extend its commercial and economic penetration of the region (including the opening in 1888 of a direct railroad line between Vienna and Constantinople). But after Stambulov's death, the pendulum began to swing back toward Russia. Sofia re-established diplomatic relations with St. Petersburg. And although Russia's acceptance of Ferdinand legitimately could be claimed by Goluchowski as evidence that a Habsburg–Romanov Balkan *detente* could be achieved, the fact is that the Austro–Hungarian foreign minister's pursuit of a Russo–Austrian rapprochement was driven, in substantial part, by fear of a revival of Russia's active drive for Balkan supremacy.

That Russia and Austria–Hungary remained at loggerheads over Balkan matters, notwithstanding the easing of tensions over Bulgaria, was underscored by their opposing reactions to the Armenian Question and the Greco–Turkish War of 1897. The phrase "Armenian Question" refers to the revival of national consciousness among the Armenian subjects of the Ottoman Sultan and the ensuing cycle of terrorism and reprisal which ended so catastrophically for the Armenians during World War Two. Ancient Armenia, one of the first Christian countries, had fallen under foreign rule long before their territory was conquered by the Ottoman Turks. By the mid-nineteenth century, most Armenians lived within the borders of the Ottoman Empire, where they enjoyed a fair degree of political and social autonomy. But by the 1870s, as the Ottoman Empire stood poised to enter the most perilous period in its six-hundred-year history, Armenian national consciousness had been sufficiently revived by Western Christian missionary and other European influences that prominent members of the Ottoman Armenian community began to demand radical change in their relationship with the Sultan and the Porte. The demands reflected an understandable desire to end a long history of abuse suffered by a Christian minority within a Muslim empire, for, notwithstanding the Sultan's formal devotion to respect for all the "People of the Book" (i.e., Christians and Jews—as well as Muslims), the structure of Ottoman society made abuse of non-Muslim minorities virtually inevitable. Unfortunately, the first Armenian demands for change became linked in the Porte's mind with the increasing danger of outright dismemberment of the empire by the Christian European powers. (The very poor judgment by some Armenians to seek the aid of those powers—by sending representatives to both San Stefano and Berlin—gave credence to the Porte's concerns.)

By the 1890s, the relationship between the Porte and the empire's Armenian subjects had deteriorated to the point where the most extreme Armenian elements felt compelled to turn to force. A cycle of violence, in which Armenian terrorist "outrages" were succeeded by Turkish "massacres," escalated until reports of a particularly vicious exchange (in which thousands of Armenian villagers were killed by Turkish troops on a reprisal raid) captured the attention of Christian European authorities—and perhaps even more important, of the European public. Ignoring the very real problem of Armenian terrorism, Christian Europe treated Ottoman conduct as a vicious "bolt from the blue" against a non-Muslim minority. In truth, the scope of the atrocities against Armenians, which now seemed to surge across Anatolia and into Constantinople itself, was all out of proportion to whatever brutalities had been committed by Armenian nationalist fanatics, and the Porte found itself facing a storm of criticism. Yet the Ottoman leadership also discovered that the division of Christian Europe into rival power blocks had materially changed the diplomatic matrix within which the Porte had been constrained to maneuver at the time of the last great outcry against Turkish brutality. Although Gladstone came out of a nearly decade-long political retirement to thunder once again at Turkish atrocities, the reaction of Lord Salisbury's government showed just how swiftly Alliance *realpolitik* calculations had come to dominate decision making at Whitehall—in a pattern quickly duplicated across Europe. Following the strengthening of the British position in Egypt in 1882, even some conservatives had questioned the continuing necessity of London's commitment to Ottoman integrity as a bulwark against Russian ambitions in the Near East. But the establishment of a hostile Franco–Russian combination reinforced the need for the Straits to remain in friendly hands. "I wish we could cut the cord that binds us to the Sultan," Lord Salisbury confessed to Joseph Chamberlain in the midst of the Armenian Question debate. "But we can no more allow the Russian Black Sea Fleet access to the Mediterranean now than we could forty years ago—especially not when France with its squadrons has gone over to the other side."

The same dynamic put Vienna and St. Petersburg on opposite sides of the Armenian controversy. Among the Christian European powers, only Germany showed genuine enthusiasm for the Porte's defense of its soldiers' conduct. Even under Bismarck, a faction in the German Army and diplomatic corps had pushed for the new German Empire to build up the Ottomans as an ally. While Bismarck could keep this early pursuit of *Weltmacht* in check, he could not entirely quash it: principally because state control of the economy in the late nineteenth century did not approach the pervasiveness achieved in our time. When Krupp sold the Sultan new guns to guard the approaches to Constantinople, Bismarck lacked the authority to block the sale, and these few but symbolically important transactions kept alive the pro–Ottoman enthusiasms of the Pan–Germanists. Moreover, even Bismarck was not entirely immune to the opportunities for expanded German influence that arose when the Sultan approached Berlin and requested assistance in the wake of the souring of Anglo–Ottoman relations over the Egyptian Crisis of 1882, which had left the Porte fearful it might have to confront Russia alone. Bismarck was not about to risk offending either Great Britain or Russia (the latter a German ally under the terms of the *Dreikaiserbund*) by an open embrace of the Porte's proposals. Bismarck agreed, however, to the dispatch of a group of Prussian civil servants to modernize the Ottoman administration and—of far greater significance—a Prussian military mission (under the command of General Kolmar von der Goltz) to modernize the Sultan's large but poorly trained and poorly equipped army.

Both groups had to sever their formal connections with Germany and enter the Sultan's service, thereby permitting Bismarck to downplay their significance in response either to any concerned inquiries from foreign capitals or pressure from the increasingly influential Pan–German movement to claim Turkey as a German protectorate. Moreover, for the duration of his term as Chancellor, Bismarck successfully resisted pressure to increase German aid to the Porte. But with Bismarck's ouster, the one real internal constraint on an overtly Turcophile German policy had been eliminated. Kaiser Wilhelm II was instinctively receptive to the aggressive approach to the "Eastern Question" which the Pan–Germanists had been urging since the founding of the Reich. Now with Bismarck gone, Wilhelm felt free to adopt the policy of "substitution" which Count Paul Hatzfeldt, Germany's veteran ambassador to the Porte, had been urging on Berlin ever since the falling out between London and Constantinople over Egypt. Under the Hatzfeldt approach, Germany would oppose any call for a "Polish solution" to the Eastern Question. Instead, Germany would position itself— by increased military assistance and economic penetration—to replace Great Britain as chief protector of the Ottoman Empire. (The establishment of the Anglo–German alliance did not cause Germany to abandon its aspirations to make the Ottoman Empire a *de facto* German protectorate. As Great Britain would discover even before the conclusion of World War Two in 1918, German ambitions for *Weltmacht* took precedence over any sense of obligation to an ally.)

The eruption of the Armenian question gave Wilhelm his first concrete opportunity to demonstrate Germany's new, "benevolent" intentions to the Sultan and the Porte. In fact, by the time the Armenian issue had captured the attention of European public opinion, Great Britain had already moved to repair the breach with the Porte caused by Egypt. But Salisbury's actions were so discreet that Wilhelm and his advisers may not have realized that the opportunity for Germany to replace Great Britain as Ottoman protector had already passed. This may help to explain why Wilhelm was willing to risk the storm of criticism that followed his sending the Sultan a signed photograph of the Kaiser and his family on the occasion of Abdulhamit II's birthday in September 1896. Coming on the heels of the killing of some five thousand Armenians on the streets of Constantinople the previous month (in reaction to raids on the Ottoman Bank and the Sublime Porte itself, by a gang of Armenian terrorists), this gesture understandably infuriated European liberals—but also earned the heartfelt gratitude of the Sultan (himself a target of an Armenian assassination attempt the month before). With Gladstone denouncing the "unspeakable Turk" and urging that the Ottoman Empire be "rubbed off the map" as a "disgrace to civilization"—and receiving an enthusiastic reception for his efforts—Lord Salisbury's government was in no position to act in a similar fashion so brazenly disdainful of public opinion. London did make quietly clear that it opposed the calls by France and Russia for joint action by the Powers to compel the Porte to provide redress of Armenian grievances. But the uproar over Turkish atrocities whipped up by Gladstone required Salisbury to play a virtual double game that came to the very edge of outright deception of the British public.

In part for that reason, it was principally on Berlin and Vienna that Russia's wrath over the frustration of efforts to help the Armenians fell most heavily. (I don't mean to suggest that Russia acted purely, or even primarily, out of a sense of benevolent protectiveness for fellow Christians—to the contrary, concern over the loyalty to the Tsar of Russian Armenians had prompted St. Petersburg to quash open support for the Turkish Armenians by the end of the 1870s; as in most matters of interstate relations among great powers, Russia supported aid to the Armenians in 1896 in order to weaken a historic foe.) If the Powers had been united in a critical response to the Porte's repressions, Austria–Hungary almost certainly would have backed some kind of punitive action against the Porte. Or, if only Germany had assumed the role of Ottoman defender, Vienna might even have been willing to defy Berlin—so long as London was prepared to use the Royal Navy to back up demands for concessions to the Armenians. But when both Germany and Great Britain made clear their opposition to Franco–Russian calls for action to protect the Armenians, the Austro–Hungarians felt constrained to side with their principal ally (Germany) and their hoped-for ally (Great Britain). As a result, calls for a Powers' conference along the lines of Constantinople and Berlin came to naught. And for this, St. Petersburg blamed Vienna—even more than Berlin. To Russian eyes, Austria–Hungary shared with Russia the unique interest of being a Balkan power, and therefore most immediately concerned with Ottoman mistreatment of non-Muslim minorities—and the resulting opportunities for aggrandizement at the Porte's expense. Moreover, St. Petersburg perceived it had just made a concession to Vienna by recognizing Prince Ferdinand of Bulgaria. Vienna's refusal to support even the calling of a Powers conference to address the Armenian question was taken by the young (and impressionable) Tsar Nicholas II as a betrayal by his senior "cousin," Franz Joseph.

The Greco–Turkish War of 1897 only made a deteriorating situation worse. Since the re-establishment of an independent Greece, its leaders had agitated for expansion beyond the fairly limited boundaries that emerged out of the Greeks' otherwise successful revolt against Ottoman rule during the 1820s. Among the additional territory sought to be "recovered" from the Ottomans was the island of Crete. In 1868, the Porte had made certain concessions (once again, under pressure from the Powers) to the island's Christian majority. But the Sultan suspended these measures in 1889, in the wake of a series of particularly violent provocations by mountain rebels supplied from Athens. Yet repression also failed to bring quiet, and in January of 1897, a group of rebels raised the stakes by declaring Crete's union with Greece. Neither the Sultan nor the Greek king wanted war, but Hellenic nationalist elements forced the issue: war broke out that spring. Within a month, the Greek army had been routed, and the Sultan's forces seemed poised to capture Athens. (In fact, the Porte had no desire to re-incorporate Greece into the Empire.) The Greeks appealed to Christian Europe for aid, hoping to achieve by the intervention of the Powers—effective control over Crete—what could not be won on the battlefield. But the Alliance dynamic again asserted itself, and the Powers proved no more capable of united action over Crete than they had been over the fate of the Armenians. Backed by Great Britain, Germany, and Austria–Hungary, the Porte agreed to a restoration of the 1868 protocols but refused to appoint a Christian governor for the island.

What little chance of a continuing Austro–Russian Balkan *rapprochement* that remained after the Armenian fiasco did not survive the dispute over Crete. Thus, by the time the Yukon crisis broke upon Europe in the spring of 1898, relations between St. Petersburg and Vienna, which had been redolent with the promise of reconciliation only three years before, had completely soured over Balkan matters. Austria–Hungary, faced with the prospect of war between Germany (its principal ally of decades standing) and an alliance of powers including the Russian Empire (Vienna's chief rival in the vital Balkan region bordering the Habsburg Empire's southern frontier), perceived it had little choice but to follow the German lead—even if this meant war with Russia. And while the Yukon Crisis was defused and war avoided, no sooner had the armies and navies of the

Powers stood down than France and Great Britain were confronting each other over Fashoda. For Austria–Hungary, the Yukon and Fashoda crises were effectively indistinguishable; if Germany elected to honor its obligations to Great Britain, then the Dual Monarchy would follow suit.

As for Germany, there was surprisingly little debate over whether to go to war in support of London's claims to the Southern Sudan. In this, the personality—and mood—of the German monarch played an undoubtedly crucial role. Kaiser Wilhelm II had an almost boyish enthusiasm for war, and when combined with his ardent Anglophilia (and particularly his deep and genuine affection for his grandmother, Queen Victoria), there was little doubt that Wilhelm would commit Germany to the English cause unless his advisors united in powerful opposition. But there was no such opposition, as neither the military nor the civilian arm of the German government was opposed to war. The only thing remotely approaching an objection was concern expressed by the General Staff that the time of year would prevent the full commencement of Austro–German operations against Russia for several months until the following spring, to which the Kaiser responded, "The same mud will stick to French boots in the West, so we will all just have to wait awhile before the real fun can begin. "That left Russia, whose government was not at all enthusiastic for the very sound reason that the country was not ready for such a war. Yet, neither Tsar Nicholas II nor his advisors were prepared to press their French ally for an accommodation of British claims in the Sudan. Nor was St. Petersburg willing to repudiate its alliance with France and the USA in order to avoid a fight—even though that struggle would expose Russia to a battle on three fronts: ranging from Poland in the west to Afghanistan in Central Asia to Manchuria in the Far East.

This, then, was the underlying dynamic that caused all but one of the "Christian" Great Powers of Europe to go to war in the fall of 1898—a struggle whose immediate trigger was control of a mud hut grandly called the "fort" of Fashoda, located along the banks of the Nile as it made its languid way through the desolation of the southernmost reaches of the Sudan.

As for the immediate course of the conflict in Europe, the German General Staff and Kaiser Wilhelm were both proven right: the outbreak of war in October of 1898 left too little time before the onset of winter for either the French army in the West or the Austro–German armies in the East to initiate any substantial sort of offensive action. In the West, the French mobilized under longstanding plans to strike along the border with Germany in a concerted effort to retake the lost provinces of Alsace and Lorraine at one blow. In the southeast, French forces managed to penetrate to between Colmar and Mülhausen. But in the center (at the hinge of the provinces lying west of Strasbourg) and in the northwest (facing Diedenhofen and Metz), the French advance immediately bogged down in a grim combination of rain, mud, and tenacious German resistance. Meanwhile in the East, the Germans prevailed upon their Austro–Hungarian allies to postpone major offensive operations until spring. German war planning called for the first blow to be struck—in combination with Austro–Hungarian forces—against Russia. The "Russia First" approach also assumed that operations would not commence until spring—for the very practical reason that the *rasputitsa*, the Russian rainy season that ushered winter in and out, turned roads into impassable channels of mud. By concentrating on the Baltics, Poland and Western Ukraine, Germany and Austria–Hungary aimed to give Russia a sufficiently severe blow so as to persuade St. Petersburg to negotiate a separate peace. But with war erupting in October 1898, that effort could not fully commence until the spring of 1899.

If matters had gone according to plan, an Austro–German assault in Europe would have been coordinated with a British move into Afghanistan, while the Japanese checked an expected Russian attack out of Manchuria against the Liaotung peninsula. The combination of severe reverses on all fronts just might have been enough to persuade Tsar Nicholas II to abandon his father's alliance with "the Republican Powers" of France and the USA. Certainly, Nicholas would have come under strong pressure from several of his key advisors (most notably Finance Minister Count Sergei Witte) to make such a peace—as shown by the pressure those same advisors would bring to bear during the crisis of the peace negotiations in the winter of 1901. But the same bad timing that prevented German and Austrian forces moving east also meant postponing Great Britain's move through the high mountain passes into Afghanistan. And while, as the reader will see, the Japanese easily checked Russia's expected move against the Liaotung, the net effect was to postpone any chance for a political "knockout blow" against Russia until the middle of 1899—at the earliest. This period of inaction became known as the "Sitzkrieg"—the sit-down war—as German and Austrian soldiers dubbed the time between the formal declarations of war in October 1898 and the commencement of the German–Austrian offensive against Russia the following spring.

Germany and her allies thus confronted the prospect of a war that, under the best of circumstances, would drag on against all foes until well into the following year, and this raised the specter of a serious food shortage. By the end of the nineteenth century, the USA and the Russian Empire had become the world's principal agricultural powers—especially in the increasingly vital area of grain production, where American and Russian wheat yields represented a staggering 66 percent of world export output. Anglo–German war planning had assumed a quick restoration of access to Russian grain and other foodstuffs. Now, with operations against Russia postponed until the late spring of 1899, there would be no supplies from that quarter for a substantially longer period than available stocks could sustain peacetime levels of consumption.

Great Britain was by far the most dependent of the Anglo–German alliance members on Russo–American food sources. The ensuing realization that the British Isles faced starvation in a prolonged war gave the opposition Liberals their first real opportunity against the Tory–Unionist alliance since the losing battle over Irish Home Rule in 1886. Despite the Liberals' defeat in that year's general election, Gladstone had remained as party leader, determined to regain power and achieve an Irish reform. (Gladstone also hoped to pursue the franchise reforms that had been shelved during the turbulence created by the twin crises in North America and Ireland in the mid-1880s, but franchise matters had become a decidedly secondary concern in comparison to a resolution of the "Irish Question.") Gladstone continued to receive the support of the Irish leader Charles Parnell, who remained the overwhelmingly dominant figure of Irish politics despite the defeat of Home Rule. Ironically, Parnell reached the apogee of his influence following the publication by the London *Times* of a letter—supposedly authored by Parnell—which expressed sympathy for the political objectives of the Phoenix Park murderers. Parnell initially hesitated to sue for libel, fearing a hostile reception by a propertied London jury. But the Salisbury government's decision to establish a special commission to look into the problem of Irish violence—including the Phoenix Park episode—forced the issue. Parnell retained counsel, and almost two years after the *Times* publication, he won a stunning victory. Under a grueling cross-examination by Parnell's attorneys, an embittered Fenian named Richard Pigott was revealed to have forged the Phoenix Park letter. Pigott fled to Madrid and then shot himself rather than risk extradition to England for criminal fraud. Parnell, in the meantime, received a standing ovation from the Liberal and Irish benches upon his first appearance in the House of Commons following his courtroom vindication.

The drama of the moment, however, could not long obscure that Gladstonian Liberalism had reached a political dead end, and that the continuing pursuit of the Home Rule will-o-the-wisp had led the party to that sorry state. Parnell may have been cheered by Liberals when he was exonerated of the charge that he had expressed sympathy for the political goals of the Phoenix Park murderers, but the harsh reality of Irish politics was the increasing gap between Parnell's commitment to Home Rule (which would keep Ireland within the British Empire) and the Fenian Republican tradition of the IRB. Although the IRB was not prepared to challenge Parnell openly, by the late 1880's, the tactical alliance between Parnell and the Brotherhood had come to an end over the very issue that had brought the two together only a few years before: the land question. In 1886, the Irish countryside had witnessed a resurgence of land-tenure violence. Parnell made clear he opposed reviving the rabble-rousing approach taken by his own Land League during the "Land War" of the early eighties. Parnell could not jeopardize his relationship with the Liberals—above all, with Gladstone—by supporting a reversion to pre–Home Rule tactics while the fate of the reform that Parnell had pledged to support was being decided at the polls. Yet, even after the Liberals lost power to the new Tory–Unionist coalition, Parnell remained convinced that adoption of Home Rule remained a realistic prospect and the best course for the Irish Nation to pursue; he therefore continued to oppose any revival of the insurrectionary violence of the Land War period.

Parnell managed to maintain his hold on Irish public opinion, isolating those who called for a revival of the rent strikes and other Land War measures.

(He was aided by the partial amelioration of rural conditions achieved by the tenancy reform measures adopted in the mid-1880s.) But Parnell lost the support of several important backers who considered further pursuit of Home Rule an exercise in futility. This initial fracture proved the fault line along which the structure of Irish politics shattered when the O'Shea divorce case scandal exploded in late 1889—just a few months after Parnell's triumph in the Phoenix Park letter affair. Parnell and the wife of one Captain O'Shea had been lovers for many years. (She had borne Parnell three children, and in everything but name, they were husband and wife.) Captain O'Shea, after long tolerating the liaison, filed for divorce at the peak of Parnell's popularity. Whether this was a well-timed act of revenge or merely a delayed lunge for money will never be definitively resolved. Mrs. O'Shea had a very wealthy aunt, and some historians suspect the Captain delayed filing until after the aunt died, fearing she would have cut him out of her will had she learned through divorce proceedings of the extent of the captain's tolerance of her niece's misconduct. What matters for this narrative, however, are the political consequences. Within a year, Parnell had been destroyed as a force in British and Irish politics. Although the Irish Nationalist parliamentary caucus initially stood behind him, their support cracked when Gladstone made clear that the Liberal–Irish Nationalist alliance could not continue if Parnell remained the Irish parliamentary leader. Since any hope for Home Rule rested on that alliance and the continuation of the alliance depended upon Gladstone, the Irish caucus members had little choice: in December 1890, they ousted Parnell. Parnell refused to accept their verdict, and the ensuing Irish "civil war"—which involved everything except outright violence and even some of that—effectively destroyed the Irish Nationalist party as a force in British politics.

Parnell died in 1891. He did not die of a broken spirit. To the contrary, Parnell had plunged with renewed vigor into the fight to retain his Irish following, and in the struggle, he inflicted grievous political wounds on his former Liberal allies—especially Gladstone. If anything, it was the recklessness with which Parnell fought that proved his undoing; refusing to make any accommodation, even with the elements, he contracted a fatal pneumonia following a speech in a pouring rain. (His death created a vacuum in Irish politics which the IRB would soon fill—with bloody consequences for Anglo–Irish relations.) Precisely because Parnell's fall meant the undoing of an Irish constituency for an "Intra-Empire" solution to the Irish question, Gladstone's decision to repudiate Parnell seems all the more puzzling. While Gladstone undoubtedly would have faced difficulties from his moralistically rigid Nonconformist Protestant supporters had he refused to repudiate Parnell, Gladstone had been a statesman of sufficient vision and sophistication that one would have expected him to have been willing to ride out whatever intraparty political storm had ensued for the sake of preserving any realistic chance for the adoption of Home Rule. Perhaps Gladstone had convinced himself that the Liberal trend in the by-elections held the two previous years would hold up even without the "Parnell vote" in Ireland. If so, Gladstone proved to have badly misjudged the basic temper of the electorate.

In this regard, the increasingly hostile international environment proved an important factor. Gladstone had vigorously opposed the Anglo–Confederate accords of 1887 and then had fought even more fiercely against the escalating naval estimates required by the worsening arms race with the USA and France. Gladstone's opposition reflected a decades-long hostility to the imperial tendencies of British policy, which he believed had led to a dangerous overextension of British resources even before the commitments represented by what Gladstone had disparagingly called the "Richmond entanglement." (Gladstone's opposition to the alliance with the Confederacy stands in stark contrast to his enthusiasm for the Confederate cause in the fall of 1862; but as Gladstone admitted shortly before his death in 1898, "I had not the vision to see then what any fool should recognize now—the Southern American union has become a force for great mischief, and England will rue the day it chose to betray the tradition of Wilberforce for the sake of claiming a handful of slave-owner ironclads as allies in a North American war we should in any case do all in our power to avoid.") Gladstone's opposition to the Anglo–Confederate alliance and the Salisbury government's naval buildup proved politically damaging to the Liberals. The naval construction program, with its ripple effects through the British economy, proved a popular measure among precisely the skilled laborers whom the Liberals had to win back if they were to defeat the Tory–Unionist alliance in the next general election. Moreover, the unanimity of Irish Catholic opposition to the Anglo–Confederate relationship combined with Gladstone's continued pursuit of Home Rule in tandem with Parnell further alienated an important segment of English Protestant Liberal opinion, which although not yet prepared to follow Joseph Chamberlain out of the Liberal party nonetheless agreed with Unionism's strongly pro–Empire stance and also felt instinctive doubts about the wisdom of granting Home Rule to "Catholic" Ireland.

Perhaps if Captain O'Shea had died before his wife's wealthy aunt or decided not to seek a divorce, Parnell could have held the unruly Irish vote together sufficient for the Liberals to eke out a victory in the 1892 general election. Yet, even given such a result, it seems certain Gladstone could not have pushed through a Home Rule Bill capable of surviving the gauntlet of a hostile House of Lords. Having been defeated twice on the issue, the elderly Gladstone would almost certainly not have stayed on as Prime Minister. And while the Liberals might have lingered on in power a little while longer, the undoubted ensuing collapse of their alliance with Parnell would have meant an early election and the likely return of the Tory–Unionist coalition to office. Gladstone's withdrawal from public life would have signaled the end of the quest for Home Rule, and without that program—and the additional glue of Gladstone's genuine and reciprocated admiration and affection for Parnell—the ties that bound the Liberals to the Irish Nationalist party would have disintegrated. The Anglo–German alliance thus would have been postponed for only a couple of years, and the Powers likely still would have gone to war over Fashoda.

In the event, Captain O'Shea did seek his divorce; Parnell was brought down (and, along with him, the Liberal–Irish Nationalist alliance); and Gladstone led his party to defeat, not victory, in the 1892 elections. Following that defeat, Gladstone retired from public life—leaving a Liberal party in great disarray. Gladstone's two most plausible successors, Lord Rosebery and Sir William Harcourt, rapidly experienced a falling out: rooted in their rivalry for the leadership but exacerbated by incompatible personalities. Harcourt won the battle to lead the Liberals, but the exhausting struggle further weakened the party and contributed to its disastrous performance in the 1897 general election—the "Jubilee Election" called by Salisbury in wake of the triumphant outcome of the South Africa Conference in Berlin, and in which an electorate invigorated by an economic boom and basking in the reflected imperial glory of Queen Victoria's "Diamond Jubilee" celebrations rewarded the Conservatives with their biggest victory of the century. With Rosebery and Harcourt discredited, a shrunken Liberal caucus sought new leaders: in the combination of Sir Henry Campbell-Bannerman ("C-B") and the young Sir Herbert Asquith. It was this team, in which Campbell-Bannerman served as leader but Asquith provided the energy and focus, that found itself, only one year after the Liberals' worst electoral showing of the century, presented with a heaven-sent opportunity to batter the triumphant Conservatives and their Unionist allies with the most fundamental of charges—incompetence in time of war by failing to assure the security of the country's larder.

To understand the circumstances that gave rise to the British "Food Debate" of World War One, one must go back almost a generation: to the early 1870s. With the emergence of the USA as the world's principal agricultural producer, Great Britain responded with a policy of replacing homegrown with imported foodstuffs and farming with trade as a source of national wealth. "Policy" may be too strong a word, suggesting as it does a degree of conscious action that did not actually characterize British conduct between 1870 and 1895. But if Great Britain did not deliberately seek dependence on American wheat, London did choose to maintain the country's commitment to free trade rather than adopt protectionist measures that could have at least slowed the shift from domestic to foreign—and particularly American—supplies. As a result, by the time of the establishment of the rival Alliance systems, the British had abandoned any pretense of agricultural self-sufficiency. In-country food stocks ran no more than a few weeks; Great Britain's granaries had become the wheat and corn fields of foreign lands and the fleet of steamships which carried the grain on which the population of the Home Isles depended for their daily bread.

To be sure, as early as the Second North American Crisis of 1885, questions had begun to be raised about the strategic wisdom of allowing British agricultural capacity to run down while simultaneously permitting dependence on a potentially hostile power—the USA—to increase. But the Tory–Unionist government that established the Anglo–Confederate alliance in 1887 was not about to take on the politically explosive task of reversing the country's commitment to free trade, which dated from the

1846 repeal of the agricultural protection scheme known as the "Corn Laws" ("corn" meaning "wheat" and other grains in British parlance). Although the Tory party's country base might favor a return to agricultural protectionism, urban Conservatives would vigorously oppose such a move. As for Chamberlain's Unionists, while they had broken with Gladstone over the Home Rule and North American questions, as a group, they retained the balance of their Liberal predilections, including a seemingly unshakable abhorrence of protectionism. Even if Chamberlain had then been willing to support some restoration of agricultural protection in the name of national defense, it seems doubtful he could have carried most of his followers with him. In any event, Chamberlain had yet to be convinced of the need for such measures, and without his support there was no possibility that the Salisbury government would push their adoption.

By 1895, circumstances had changed. While British dependence on foreign grain continued to grow, the reliability of that supply in time of war became even more problematic with the establishment of the Franco–American alliance with the Russian Empire. Now both the world's leading grain producers and the chief sources of supply for the British Empire were aligned against it. In the event of war, the British faced the cutoff of her principal grain supplies—not because an enemy fleet would prevent the steamships carrying the wheat and corn from reaching the Home Isles but because the suppliers would refuse to load the grain onto the ships. In his 1897 poem, "The Empty Big Steamers," Rudyard Kipling vividly expressed the essence of the problem:

> Oh, where are you going to, all you Big Steamers,
>> With England's own coal, up and down the salt seas?
> We are going to fetch you your bread and your butter,
>> Your beef, pork and mutton, eggs, apples and cheese!
>
> And where will you fetch it from, all you Big Steamers,
>> And where shall I write you when you are away?
> We fetch most of all from the land of the Yankees,
>> Address us at Boston, New York and the Bay.

And what if you're empty, oh all you Big Steamers,
What if the Yankees refuse food to sell?
Then you'd have no bacon or toast for your breakfast,
Nor muffins or meat your great hunger to quell.

By the time Kipling's poem was published, the question of a wartime grain cutoff had become a subject of discussion and concern. Chamberlain, true to his dynamism and flexibility, had swung around to the belief that "free trade shibboleths must yield to the fundamental imperative of national survival." He urged the adoption of a program to reduce dependence on American grain, including the reimposition of tariffs on "corn" imports. Chamberlain's service as Colonial Secretary had convinced him of the need to reinforce the ties between England and her far-flung imperial possessions, especially the Australian states, Canada, and the new Union of South Africa. Reflecting the connection between the question of food security for the Home Isles and the broader issue of reinforcing the structure of the Empire, Chamberlain dubbed his program "Imperial Preference". Tariffs would be reintroduced on a wide range of products, particularly grains, but these duties would not apply to those products when imported from within the British Empire. "This way," Chamberlain reported to the cabinet, "we can begin the move away from dependence on vulnerable American and Russian supplies, as we will encourage greater production in Australia, Canada, and India—not to mention once again here at home."

Lord Salisbury, however, was not prepared to take the political risk of repudiating a fifty-year commitment to free trade. The Prime Minister was on the verge of calling a general election (the "Jubilee Vote" of 1897) in the wake of the peaceful resolution of the South African question. With the Liberals on the proverbial ropes, why hand them the one campaign issue that might rally their beleaguered troops? The urban classes had benefited from the steady decline in food prices and the improvement in the quality of available food products, directly traceable to the free trade policy of the previous decades. If they believed the Conservatives were planning to reimpose the hated "corn duties," the enfranchised members of the working class might swing to the Liberals. Of course, Salisbury was contemptuous enough of such base political calculations that he was prepared to support Chamberlain if compelled to do so by the Empire's security needs. But Salisbury was persuaded that those needs could be met by an alternative: successful implementation of the German–Austrian plan to knock Russia out of the war in its opening stage, thereby giving Great Britain access to Ukrainian wheat as a substitute for American supplies. "I agree that assuring the food supply of our island is of the utmost importance," Salisbury told Chamberlain in late 1897, "but I am also convinced that we can prudently rely on the power of German and Austrian arms, in combination with those of our Indian Army and our Japanese ally, to force the Tsar to recognize the foolishness of Russia's unnatural relationship with the equalitarian fanatics of France and the United States. And in the meantime, we can initiate measures to begin to wean ourselves from our admittedly dangerous dependence on Yankee corn."

Salisbury was a shrewd man, but this time, his decision to avoid a politically dangerous battle over Chamberlain's proposal to abandon free trade would come uncomfortably close to proving the undoing of Great Britain—and its allies—in the later stages of the First Alliance War. The initial manifestations of the food crisis were principally political, although the ensuing political debate was fueled in part by escalating prices of basic foodstuffs, caused by markups on inventory and a jump in charges imposed by Southern Hemisphere sources all too willing to exploit the drastic change in market conditions. Chamberlain, along with the Conservatives' House Leader, Arthur Balfour, faced withering attacks from Campbell-Bannerman and Asquith for the "government's gross incompetence in plunging the British Empire into a war without regard to the basic needs of the British people" (this, Campbell-Bannerman, in the House of Commons, December 1898). There was little the government could offer to respond substantively to the criticisms beyond giving assurances that all "practicable" steps would be taken to assure a "fair distribution" of food supplies and also making the countercharge that criticism of supply policy was tantamount to a call for repudiation of the alliance with Germany and the Confederacy. In fact, the government was correct on both counts: Steps were being taken to establish a system of rationing to prevent outright starvation, and the Liberal opposition could not point to anything else that might be done short of a separate peace with France, the USA, and Russia.

"That," Lord Salisbury assured the House of Lords just before Christmas 1898, "is something this government shall never do." In fact, although the government undoubtedly suffered erosion of support over escalating food prices (the price of bread in Liverpool doubled in the first four months of the war), the British also had reason to feel encouraged about the performance of British arms—particularly in the Mediterranean and Africa. In the Mediterranean, the maritime dynamic echoed the Franco–British clashes of the Napoleonic Wars—and with a similar outcome. The Spanish, with French support, had placed Gibraltar under siege. It became the task of the Royal Navy's premier squadron, the Mediterranean Fleet under the command of Vice Admiral Sir John Fisher, to "suppress" the Franco–Spanish fleet guarding the approaches to Gibraltar, thereby facilitating the landing of a powerful relief force that could push the enemy out of their siege lines.

Even before the outbreak of war, Fisher—widely known as "Jackie," although never called that to his face—was recognized as Great Britain's ablest fleet commander since Nelson. Born in Ceylon, Fisher was fifty-seven years old and had served in the Royal Navy for four-and-a-half decades. A brilliant eccentric, he is credited both with the invention of the armored train (during a posting to Egypt) and with the first use of "OMG" as shorthand for "Oh My God/Gosh/Goodness/Gracious!" Fisher's Egyptian service gave him a bout of dysentery that laid him low for several years, but by 1886, he had wrangled an appointment as Director of Naval Ordinance, where he pushed for the development of more effective torpedoes and of quick-firing, breach-loading guns to counter the torpedo boat threat. In his capacity as Superintendent of Portsmouth Dockyard, he oversaw the laying down of the first *Royal Sovereign*-class battleships, armed with four 13.5" guns and a powerful secondary battery. He became Third Sea Lord in 1892, was knighted in 1894, and in 1896 was promoted to Vice Admiral and given command of the Royal Navy station at Halifax. I have already mentioned how his methods and motivating force of personality helped that base successfully resist the surprise US attack of 1898.

After the Yukon Crisis had eased, the Admiralty decided to transfer Fisher from command of the North Atlantic squadron to the Mediterranean. "We will need to strike hard at the French," the First Sea Lord informed the

Cabinet in May of 1898, "and only Fisher can assure the fleet is ready for that task." Although the course of events gave Fisher barely four months (from the time of his transfer to the Mediterranean in July to the outbreak of war in October) to whip the Mediterranean squadron into shape, the Admiral's whirlwind style and remarkable attention to detail meant the Royal Navy's "Med" force was ready to—in Fisher's words—"concentrate an overpowering force against the foe five minutes after war is declared." Deeply disappointed with what he found on his arrival, Fisher promptly initiated training based on engaging the enemy from four thousand yards (not the one-thousand-yard range that had been assumed) and gave greater accolades to those captains whose gunnery was effective than to those who kept their ships gleaming and spotless. Fisher quickly transformed the Mediterranean Fleet—as he had Halifax station—and by the time war broke out, his men had been training virtually non-stop against simulated French raids, fleet actions, and torpedo swarms.

Although the combined French and Spanish Mediterranean squadrons outnumbered Fisher's fleet in simple number of battleships, nine Franco-Spanish to seven British, that ratio was hardly meaningful. Before the Secession War, French naval design had led the world, and the French navy launched *Glorie*, the first seagoing ironclad, in 1859. But the four decades since had not been kind to the French fleet or French shipbuilding. For example, the French ship *Friedland* had taken twelve years to build, including three complete changes of sail configuration, but had served for only for a decade before her decommissioning. The French flagship *Hoche* was laid down in 1880 but not commissioned until 1890; by 1892, she had accidentally rammed and sunk a passenger steamer and had killed more than one hundred civilians. Her low freeboard meant that her bow was often awash while underway, while her main armament consisted of two 13.5" guns of a design almost thirty years old. French battleships *Jaureguberry* and *Charles Martel*, albeit newer, also were limited to two main guns each. While *Marceau* and *Magenta* had four large guns each, they were placed in single mounts—fore and aft and port and starboard—so no more than three could possibly bear on any target. Their armored belts were far too short to protect their vitals. Only *Charlemagne* and *St. Louis* were modern ships with modern Harvey armor and modern guns—but again: only two apiece. The thinly spread Spanish fleet had been able to allocate only two battleships to the Mediterranean: *Galicia* and *Diligente*, sisters of the *Pelayo* class. The primary Spanish contribution consisted of a bevy of armored cruisers of the *Emperador Carlos V* and *Princesa de'Asturas* classes as well as a flock of *avisos*, gunboats, and sloops—none of which were equipped with torpedoes. The best that could be said of the Spanish cruisers was that they were new and fast and had a long range. However, they were under-armed for their size and woefully under-armored. Originally designed around superior British machinery and Krupp armor, by the time of their completion in the later part of the 1890s, political circumstances meant that all of their armor and principal weaponry had been supplied by France.

Fisher was acutely, perhaps morbidly, aware of the importance of his role as the British naval commander on the spot. As he wrote to Joseph Chamberlain, the Commander-in-Chief of the British Mediterranean Fleet in the late 1890s, "being the man who will probably preside at the Battle of Armageddon which will probably be fought off Port Mahon in Minorca… has to bear in mind that Admiral Byng was shot…for not getting a victory near that spot." (John Byng, the British Admiral perhaps unfairly held responsible for the loss of Minorca to the French in 1756, was found guilty of dereliction of duty and shot to death by a squad of Royal Marines. Voltaire famously had one of his characters explain, "*Dans ce pays-ci, il est bon de tuer de temps en temps un amiral pour encourager les autres.*") Fisher was no Byng and had no intention of being killed for the encouragement of others. Besides, Fisher intended to fight off Majorca rather than Minorca— no use tempting fate.

Fisher handled his squadron magnificently—and destroyed most of the Franco–Spanish combined fleet—in what was probably the last large-scale fleet engagement fought in the absence of torpedoes and aircraft (or at least the apprehension thereof). Fisher's light cruisers, *Aeolus*, *Brilliant*, and *Iphigenia*, made short work of the gaggle of small Spanish scouts, and the British battle fleet had formed into line before the Franco–Spanish fleet confirmed their bearing. Fisher's flagship HMS *Renown* was actually a light battleship; while leading the line, she focused her attention on Spanish and French cruisers. The remaining British battleships included two *Majestic*-class (*Caesar* and *Mars*), three *Royal Sovereign*-class (*Hood*,

Resolution, and *Revenge*), and the older *Sans Pareil* with her enormous 16.25 guns (and useless ram). All of the *Majestics* and *Royal Sovereigns* had four main guns in dual fore-and-aft barbettes (or in the case of *Hood,* turrets), so despite being outnumbered, the British line could bring to bear more main-battery guns and a greater weight of shell than the combined Franco–Spanish fleet. More importantly, Fisher's drills and emphasis on gunnery practice allowed the British crews to score hits at three thousand and even five thousand yards, while only a miniscule number of French or Spanish shells found their marks. The Spanish lost both battleships, and the French fleet lost six of its seven (*Jaureguberry* alone escaping); the French cruisers *Bruix* and *Amiral Charner,* as well as the Spanish cruisers *Catalina, Fenix,* and *San Ildefonso,* were sunk—the last two in a hopeless charge on the van of the British battle line after every Franco–Spanish battleship had been destroyed or disabled. Fisher's battleships suffered only three hits and fewer than fifty casualties; the protected cruiser *Royal Arthur* and armored cruiser *Terrible* were lost: the former being scuttled after evacuation of most of her crew. It was one of the most complete victories in naval history, and Fisher's "encouragement of the others" would be of a very different sort from that provided by Admiral Byng. And in an amazing fortuity of timing, the victory was won ninety-three years to the very day when Nelson had won his decisive victory at Trafalgar against the same allied enemies.

The Mediterranean was confirmed to be a British lake (and would remain so until the catastrophes of 1940 definitively reversed the verdict of Aboukir Bay). With the French and Spanish naval threat in the Mediterranean neutralized, the British were now in a position to lift the siege of Gibraltar. Landing forces across the bay at Algeciras, the British unhinged the Spanish lines, forcing a withdrawal as far as Barbate in the west and the mouth of the River Guadiaro in the east. Gibraltar was secure, and the passage between the Atlantic and the Mediterranean was firmly in British hands.

Fisher's Mediterranean triumphs were not matched in the struggle for control of Colonial Africa, but the British and their German allies did score gains against the French in this theater as well. In the interior, Marchand quickly withdrew from Fashoda after the British sent formal word of the outbreak of war and notified the French that they could choose "surrender or annihilation." (During the withdrawal, Marchand's plucky band got the better of the much larger blocking force that Kitchener had placed across the Frenchman's line of withdrawal.) On the East Coast, a combined Anglo–German force sailed from Dar-Es-Salaam in German East Africa and effected a landing on the French-held island of Madagascar, whose few defenders quickly capitulated. With that victory, the Indian Ocean was effectively converted into an Anglo–German "lake." The Portuguese, Dutch, and Italians had declared their neutrality, while French holdings in the Seychelles islands—as well as Pondicherry in India—were all occupied before year's end. In West Africa, however, neither side was able to muster the resources for a major push. Dahomey was quickly overrun from Togoland (German) on the West and the territory of the Royal Niger Company and the Lagos Colony (British) to the East. On the other hand, the British were unable to prevent a French occupation of Britain's isolated enclave at the mouth of the Gambia River just south of Cape Verde. The principal African action would have to await the next year's campaigns.

(left) **Royal Navy Admiral Jackie Fisher**
(right) **Imperial Japanese Navy Admiral Heihachiro Togo**

These two men led their fleets to dramatic victories, and gave their navies control of the seas at crucial points during the First Alliance War.

18

WORLD WAR I: (5) 1899—THE AMERICAN AND MEXICAN COUNTERASSAULT ON THE CONFEDERACY, THE NORTH ATLANTIC NAVAL CAMPAIGN AND THE FIRST IRISH INSURRECTION, THE FRENCH FAILURE IN ALSACE-LORRAINE AND THE AUSTRO-GERMAN SUCCESS AGAINST RUSSIA, AND THE ANGLO-RUSSIAN FIGHT FOR AFGHANISTAN

———

By New Year's Day 1899, a deadly quiet had settled across the war fronts that girdled the globe. To those familiar with mid-twentieth century warfare, which respected no holiday or season, this "winter hiatus" observed by the belligerents in 1899 may seem quaint. In fact, their restraint merely reflected the failure of any Power to prepare for winter season operations. The European tradition of the "winter encampment" still controlled general staff planning—if only by default and (as the course of World War Two would reflect) for the last time.

North America had been the scene of the most concentrated fighting, whose destructiveness had appalled most civilian and even many military observers. Now the course of that fighting—particularly the Confederacy's shocking *coup de main* against Washington City—would trigger the first material change in the war plans of a major power. The loss of America's capital and the ensuing besiegement of Baltimore had brought a storm of condemnation down upon the McKinley Administration—which the unfolding Philippines disaster only reinforced and the overall success of Canadian operations did little to mollify. In reality, Americans had reason to be satisfied by the overall outcome of the war's opening phase. Of course, the Confederacy's invasion of Maryland had come as a surprise, and the extent of the destruction wrought in Washington and Baltimore constituted an undeniable blow to morale. (As well as a permanent loss to the country's cultural heritage: Besides the destruction of numerous government archives, little of the Library of Congress collection could be salvaged from the burned-out wreck of the new Library Building—and unlike in 1814 when the British burned Washington, no one managed to save Gilbert Stuart's portrait of the first President from the flames that consumed the White House for a second, and final, time.) But these losses, however painful, should not be allowed to obscure the more important strategic fact: The Confederates had failed to achieve the goal of their Maryland operation. That state's population did not rise in a supportive rebellion against Northern authority, and a superbly efficient long-distance transfer of troops by railroad enabled the North to prevent both the capture of Baltimore and any CSA penetration into Pennsylvania. And while the loss of the Philippines was embarrassing (and an undoubtedly disastrous blow to the fading colonial pretensions of America's Spanish ally), the repulse of the Japanese grab for Guam combined with the occupation of German and British holdings in the Central Pacific actually gave the USA a more defensible strategic position from which to dominate the approaches to Hawaii and the Pacific Coast of North and Central America.

Finally, and perhaps of greatest strategic significance, the conquest of Canada had gotten off to an undeniably good start—especially considering the short time available to advance before the bitter Canadian winter forced a suspension of operations. The Esquimault raid and its aftermath had eliminated any immediate Royal Navy threat in the North Pacific and assured the seizure of British Columbia, while the Canadian Great Plains—the breadbasket lands of Manitoba Province and the Assiniboia and Saskatchewan Districts of the Northwest Territory—had been effectively overrun. In short, although the initial drive on Halifax had failed, the USA was well positioned to concentrate its forces and complete the conquest of Canada by the fall of 1899, for if the Americans launched a full-scale assault against Ontario and Quebec, there was little doubt that the badly outnumbered Canadian and British Army defenders could only delay what would have been an inevitable outcome. (Some readers will recall that the great Canadian fortress and trench-works defensive network, which caused the Americans such terrible difficulties in the opening stages of World War Two in 1914 and 1915, had not yet been completed; nor were Anglo–Canadian forces of sufficient number to man such a system—as they would be fifteen years later.) Why the Americans instead suspended their Canadian operations to launch—in coordination with their Mexican allies—a "counterinvasion" of the Confederacy with the declared goal of splitting that country and overrunning the CSA Trans-Mississippi can only be understood as a manifestation of politics driven by emotionalism.

Washington City was a symbol of the country. It had been burned by the British in the War of 1812, only to be rebuilt and then grow to a wealthy fortified metropolis of over 450,000 by the outbreak of World War One. Now, contrary to every reassurance given by responsible civilian and military authorities, Washington had been quickly overrun and laid waste by *the* enemy: the Confederate States of America. That "Johnny Reb" had captured—and then seemingly wantonly destroyed—what had once been the capital city of a united North and South traumatized every American. The emotional dynamic of the War of Secession, when the Armies of Northern Virginia and the Potomac grappled for advantage during the North's attempt to capture the CSA's capital of Richmond, now reasserted itself. This time, the effect was to inflame the American population with a demand for an avenging strike deep into the vitals of the Confederacy. Senator (and future USA President) Henry Cabot Lodge's cry of "*Richmond delenda est*" struck a responsive chord with many and echoed the Secession War cries of "On to Richmond." And the results of the midterm congressional elections, which left the GOP barely in control of Congress, sent a clear message to the McKinley Administration (in "temporary" quarters in Philadelphia) that the public expected dramatic action directly against the vitals of the South.

Yet such action, if taken at the expense of the looming Canadian conquest, would be contrary to the USA's most vital strategic interests. With

Canada overrun, the chief source of tension in Anglo–American relations would be removed. Although jingoists would undoubtedly bridle at ceding the remaining British position on the mainland of North America to "the Colonials," the realistic statesmen at the helm of the British Empire would just as quickly have recognized that the elimination of Canada as a bone of contention (even by so drastic a means as loss through military conquest) would open the door to a genuine North Atlantic *detente*. (And as the reader will see, this is exactly what transpired in the wake of the American conquest of Canada some twenty years later, during the final stages of the Second Alliance War.) Such an Anglo–American reconciliation, moreover, would render the Anglo–Confederate alliance obsolete. And without the support of the British Empire, the Confederacy would be at a terrible disadvantage in any future conflict with the North. For despite the South's undoubted progress in developing an industrial base capable of supporting a modern army and navy, the North had opened up a tremendous gap compared to the circumstances prevailing at the time of the Western War—during which the South had managed to achieve a draw only by cleverly neutralizing what was already a decided Northern advantage in the material bases of military power in the emerging era of mass warfare.

In short, what the North needed above all was good judgment and patience in the face of the emotionally devastating but strategically secondary setbacks of October 1898: good judgment to recognize where the country's true vital strategic interests lay and patience to see the pursuit of such interests through to the end. Unfortunately, both commodities proved in short supply. After their setbacks in the midterm elections, the Republican congressional leadership made clear their expectation that the war *must* now be taken directly to the South. If that meant postponing further operations in Canada for a year (or even more), so be it. From the point of view of these anxious politicians, the only real issue was whether to launch a counterattack against the CSA positions in Maryland or open up a "second front" by invading the Confederacy itself. Chief of General Staff Nelson Miles was appalled by the idea of suspending the invasion of Canada, but if the country's political leadership insisted on it, Miles urged McKinley to reject a slogging counterattack in Maryland and opt instead for an attack down the Mississippi—with the express goal of splitting the South: isolating and eventually capturing its Trans-Mississippi territory and states to the West. Compelled to suspend Canadian operations, Miles preferred the "big solution" of a Mississippi Valley attack to the "sterile waste" of pushing the Confederates out of Maryland, which would achieve no more than a territorial status quo *ante bellum*. "Once we are moving down the Mississippi, Richmond must withdraw from our soil or risk losing much more—which Johnny will lose, all the same," the Chief of Staff assured President McKinley, in late December 1898.

Miles's assurances rested in part upon the knowledge that Mexico was prepared to throw its army into the balance by launching an offensive across the Rio Grande. But Mexico's participation would come at a price: Northern acquiescence in Mexico's annexation of CSA territory, amounting to over half the area of the state of Texas. The Mexican proposal represented an emotional Rubicon for the American government. By its acceptance, the North was implicitly letting go the dream of reunifying the two halves of the former Union under one (Northern) administration. For precisely that reason and also for fear of the furious Southern reaction that would endanger any chance for a negotiated peace, McKinley required that the agreement be kept secret. (Word of Philadelphia's acceptance was transmitted to Mexico City by encoded telegram addressed to America's Minister, Mr. Robert Lansing; when the Confederacy learned of the existence of the so-called "Lansing Telegram" almost twenty years later, during the penultimate year of World War Two, it produced exactly the political explosion on both sides of the border which McKinley had feared—although without any lasting material effect for relations between the North and South, which by then were already about as embittered as they could get.)

Under the terms of their agreement, Mexico and the USA would coordinate offensives scheduled to commence in April of 1899. The USA would suspend offensive operations against Canada, and two hundred thousand men would be transferred from the Canadian fronts and positioned for the attack down the Mississippi River Valley. In the War of Secession, the North had been able to begin its push on the Confederate side of the Ohio River as Kentucky (although technically "neutral") remained under Northern military control. But Kentucky "went south" under the terms of the Treaty of London. So, too, did the former southeastern "toe" of Missouri. (More familiarly known as the "boot heel," its transfer was a concession made by the North to ease Virginia's relinquishment of the finger of northwestern Virginia that extended above the Mason–Dixon Line as well as its two Eastern Shore counties). Moreover, the Confederacy had fortified its side of the river bank, starting at the Ohio–Virginia border just above New Martin and continuing to a point just below Marston (which marked the boundary between Missouri and its former territory: now a part of Arkansas). The Confederate General Staff remembered how Grant had forced his way past Forts Henry and Donelson, opening up the eastern bank of the Mississippi (from Tennessee south) to a Union invasion. While the former positions of Henry and Donelson were now deep behind the protective barrier of the Ohio River, the CSA leadership still feared a second Northern attempt to split the country along the line of the Mississippi—an effort that might very well have succeeded by the summer of 1863 had not Lee's earlier victory at Gettysburg the previous September triggered the decisive intervention of Great Britain and France.

For that reason, Richmond lavished resources at the point where the Mississippi passed into Southern territory to prevent the North from seizing a passage for troops carried by an invading gunboat fleet. Much of the area consisted of marshy lowlands. These were filled in so as to create artificial "heights" on which fortified gun emplacements could be built, which, when completed, rivaled even the great Belgian fortifications at Liege. Miles, however, had no intention of launching a frontal assault on these formidable defenses. He planned to turn the Confederate flanks by concentrating the initial Northern attack beyond the central zone of the CSA fortifications. The Northern assault would begin on the Confederate left flank, along the Missouri–Arkansas border, with the goal of reaching the Mississippi below the southern terminus of the river-based fortification belt. Once there, the North would cross the Mississippi, west-to-east, into Tennessee. Simultaneously, Miles planned to hazard a crossing into Kentucky just east of the town of Hickman. Although this second assault would confront the guns of the Confederate river line, Miles counted on "Johnny" having been forced to strip the gun emplacements of necessary infantry support. If successful, the great fortress concentration of the New

Madrid Bend would be outflanked. The North could then bring to bear the firepower of new siege guns (the product of a joint Franco–American research effort); although the allies had not yet perfected their 420 mm "supergun" designed to penetrate the strongest CSA armor plate, the new 305 mm would be sufficient to smash the forts at their more vulnerable rear. With the forts in hand, the way to Memphis would be open, for Richmond had elected to adopt a "strong crust" approach rather than a "layered" defense in depth, and once the crust had been smashed in, the vitals of the country would be exposed to a Northern invader able to move down the Mississippi by gunboat.

There was nothing particularly original in the Miles plan. Indeed, the defeat of such an invasion had long been a standard classroom exercise at VMI and the Citadel. But the fact that the Confederacy could anticipate the Northern plan did not necessarily translate into the ability to foil it. To the contrary: Although the CSA had recently begun extending the defensive line west of the Mississippi, the blunt fact was that the North would almost certainly have a clear advantage in men and material, and the fight to prevent the encirclement of the Mississippi fortresses would therefore be a desperate one in the best of circumstances. And the South in the spring of 1899 confronted much less than the best of circumstances. The invasion of Maryland had required committing much of the "national" strategic reserve, and the invasion of the Philippines represented an additional drain. Moreover, the simultaneous commencement of a determined Mexican assault across the Rio Grande with an army of over two hundred thousand would prevent the transfer of forces from the Trans-Mississippi to meet the Northern attack—instead, Richmond would have to divide an already shrunken reserve to meet two invasion threats. Not surprisingly, when the American assault began on April 7, 1899, the clear USA advantage in men and artillery soon asserted itself (despite high initial losses due to the Confederates' effective employment of Maxim gun "nests"). By May, Northern forces had penetrated as far south as Blytheville in Arkansas and taken control of the west bank of the Mississippi from east of Blytheville to as far north as Marston.

Now, the second phase of the offensive began. Northern forces managed to cross into Tennessee at Ridgely, while the "left wing" of the Northern army also effected crossings west of Hickman, Kentucky. By month's end, the vulnerable rearworks of the Confederate fortresses were being smashed by the firepower of the new "Cooper 305s." On June 2, the last of the forts had surrendered, and the way to Memphis lay open to the waiting American gunboat fleet. The Confederates might still have been able to frustrate the American design if they were not also confronting a determined Mexican attack along the Rio Grande. In fact, Mexico's opportunistic decision to launch an offensive war quickly proved a military disaster that marked the beginning of the decline of the *Porfirista* regime—culminating twelve years later with the overthrow of Porfirio Diaz in 1911 and the outbreak of a civil war that would last nearly a decade, opening the door to a devastating Confederate invasion during World War Two. But the repulse of the Mexican invader, however decisive, came only after several weeks of intense fighting that at its height required Richmond to commit over one hundred thousand troops. The Confederate General Staff thus was denied the reinforcements essential to prevent an American penetration farther down the Mississippi. The American gunboat fleet advanced quickly: its pace matched by the forward movement of the forces on either bank. In the fleet's wake came the principal invasion army—carried on self-propelled armored flatboat barges. The aim was to capture Memphis then force a passage through the Mississippi Delta country. Once into Louisiana, Northern forces would be concentrated for a turn southwest into Texas with the goal of reaching the Gulf of Mexico at a point in common with the advancing Mexican armies (e.g., at Galveston).

The unreinforced Confederates were in disarray, and the Americans made good time in their advance on Memphis. By July, the city was threatened by assault from the river and the north. Despite desperate Confederate counterattacks—in which Colonel Thomas Jackson, Jr., second son of "Stonewall" Jackson, distinguished himself for bravery and initiative by personally leading a charge that broke the pace of the Northern assault and delayed the cutting of the last rail line out of the city for a few vital hours—the North could not be denied its prize. On July 14, Memphis fell to cries of "Remember Washington!" Northern forces gave themselves over to what I must acknowledge amounted to a veritable orgy of destruction. Much of a city of over two hundred thousand was reduced to ashes in an emotionally satisfying act of vandalism whose only immediate military consequence proved to be a counterproductive stiffening of Southern resistance. When the North attempted to resume its advance in the first week of July, the initial attacks were stymied just a few miles outside of the Memphis suburbs. Although Northern forces managed to break through this resistance, the American drive soon reached the point of exhaustion well north of the important rail center of Davisville. The combination of the difficult Delta terrain (flooded by the dynamiting of key levees by the retreating Confederates); the breakdown of supply lines (exacerbated by the wanton destruction of the Memphis docks by Northern forces); and the timely arrival of CSA reinforcements (freed up by the South's victory over the principal Mexican army at the Battle of Three Rivers west of Corpus Christi) combined to frustrate American efforts to cut off—and overrun—the Confederate Trans-Mississippi.

By the fall of 1899, after several abortive efforts to resume the offensive, the Americans called a halt to the Mississippi Valley campaign. The failure to achieve the grand goal of splitting the Confederacy was made all the more frustrating because the campaign also did not achieve its indirect goal of forcing a Confederate withdrawal from Maryland—principally because the Mexican attack had been so poorly executed that the Confederates had been able to repulse it without having to transfer substantial forces from the Middle Atlantic front. Thus, although the South had suffered grievous losses to its forces and a deep penetration down the Mississippi Valley, the North had failed to achieve either of the objectives for which Canadian operations had been suspended and the counterinvasion launched.

Worse, these setbacks were reinforced by the course of the North Atlantic naval campaign. The defeat of the assault on Halifax left the British with a powerful squadron to deploy against the American Atlantic fleet and East Coast. When a freshly triumphant Jackie Fisher was dispatched to resume command of the Royal Navy's North Atlantic Squadron, it became a certainty that the British would go on the naval offensive. American concern focused on Chesapeake Bay, where Philadelphia feared the British might attempt to use their powerful battleship guns to destroy the Cape Charles forts and then steam north to silence the batteries of Point Lookout and Fort McHenry, thereby exposing Baltimore and the Eastern shore of Maryland—and perhaps the temporary capital itself—to capture. (The political leadership also fretted over a possible direct assault on Philadelphia launched up the Delaware River estuary, even though Army and Navy staffs considered such an attack to be wholly impracticable—a militarily sensible view, which also failed to take sufficient account of the "once burned, twice shy" state of mind of a government in political hot water for having lost one capital.)

In fact, Richmond was urging precisely the kind of Chesapeake assault whose prevention had become a central preoccupation of American military planners. And these urgings had become well-nigh frantic as Northern forces ground their way down the Mississippi River Valley—*something* needed to be done to force the Yankees to suspend their destructive march into the Confederate heartland. Fisher, however, rejected a Chesapeake operation as superficially appealing but strategically unsound. "We must strike from our Halifax base against the North's vital coastal cities—hard enough that the Yankees will be forced to strike back," Fisher told his Admiralty superiors in a report submitted less than a week after the opening of the Northern assault on the Mississippi Valley. "We then can bring the American fleet to battle on terms of our choosing, and I am confident the superior design of our ships and the training of our crews will prevail. If we win the kind of victory I know we can, Baltimore and Philadelphia may be taken at our leisure." The Admiralty agreed, and Fisher would come perilously close to complete success.

Northern concern over the mouth of the Chesapeake Bay harked back to the Secession War, when for long months, the Union had only the most tenuous of holds on Hampton Roads, anchored on Fort Monroe at Old Point Comfort, the tip of the Virginia "peninsula" between the York and the James Rivers as they flowed to the Chesapeake and the sea. An arguably premature abandonment of Norfolk in 1861—and of the critical Gosport Navy Yard there—left the south side of that enormous sheltered anchorage in Confederate hands. Many still on active service with the US Navy could recall the panic generated by the appearance in 1862 of the re-engineered USS *Merrimack*, including the fear that it would sail up the Potomac River from Hampton Roads and bombard the Union capital at will. Even after the Confederate withdrawal from Norfolk in May of 1862, the Union poured a disproportionate amount of force and treasure into the Hampton Roads area: where John Smith had saved Jamestown, where the French fleet had defeated the British at the Battle of the Virginia Capes, where Cornwallis had been captured at Yorktown, and where the original *Monitor* had saved the wooden US Navy.

After the Secession War, sole Confederate possession of the mouth of the Chesapeake would have been a loaded gun pointed at the Union head: closing the Virginia Capes would have blockaded Washington, D.C. by water and choked off the Port of Baltimore. Conversely, the South could not let the Union retain territory in Hampton Roads on the basis of the *status quo bellum:* Union control of the Capes would blockade Richmond by water, close one of the largest (and most industrialized) Confederate ports at Norfolk, and allow the North to reprise McClellan's Peninsula Campaign at will. Accordingly, the peace treaty split the baby: Neither side would control the Virginia Capes. The two counties comprising the Eastern Shore of Virginia, Northampton and Accomack, would be transferred to Maryland and remain part of the Union (much to the chagrin—occasionally finding violent expression—of the pro-Confederate residents). The remaining Union-occupied parts of Hampton Roads would be returned to Virginia. This permitted the Union to create a large series of coastal defense works anchored on Adams Island and extending throughout Cape Charles on the north side of the Bay entrance. The Confederates built similarly extensive works on Cape Henry to the south. The gap between the two capes is twelve miles, making it impracticable for works on either one side or the other to close the Bay with the technology of the 1860s. The US Army Corps of Engineers built a deep-channel passage between Adams Island and the Northampton mainland to allow Northern vessels to enter the Bay behind the guns of the forts. Fort Monroe sat a comfortable twenty miles farther inside the entrance: able to protect the York, James, and Elizabeth River entrances from Northern attack but unable effectively to interdict traffic up the Bay to the Potomac and Patapsco. A separate convention banned the use of moored mines in the Bay proper, although permitting their use to protect Norfolk harbor and, much farther upstream, allowing a mine barrier at the mouth of the Potomac. In sum, either both sides would be able to use the Bay or neither side would.

Admiral Fisher resolved to take advantage of the US Navy's preoccupation with Chesapeake Bay, a state of mind only heightened by the North's decision to send troops to the Mississippi Valley rather than to the relief of the Cape Charles fort complex. The British and Confederate admiralties encouraged a vociferous press campaign to "redeem Virginia irredentia" and open both capes—particularly now that Washington, D.C. itself was in Southern hands. This hue and cry coincided with the ill-concealed movement of a Confederate squadron slowly up the coast from Charleston, South Carolina, built around the new battleship CSS *Mississippi* (essentially an up-gunned *Canopus* with 13.5" rather than 12" guns, Krupp rather than Harvey armor to save weight, and fewer secondary batteries). Accompanying her, in addition to light cruisers and the obligatory destroyer screen, were the heavy armored cruiser CSS *Mason* and the odd, one-off "monitor" CSS *Kiowa*. This latter ship, with extremely low freeboard, little speed, and two enormous sixteen-inch smoothbore guns, harked back to an earlier generation of coastal defense vessels—but had been maintained in active status for shore bombardment purposes. The supposed mission of this force—carefully leaked to the press—was to attack Cape Charles and take back the Chesapeake.

Accordingly, when Admiral Fisher sailed from Halifax with most of his fleet—evading Northern pickets and disappearing into the vastness of the North Atlantic—it was clear to one and all that a coordinated strike on Chesapeake Bay was imminent. Powerful Union squadrons were assembled from East Coast anchorages and positioned to re-enact the victory of DeGrasse at the Virginia Capes some 118 years earlier. The main USA East Coast fleet at Portsmouth made all possible speed for the Virginia coast. Every effort was made to gather as many ships as could be found for this supreme effort; even those under refit were got underway and joined the southbound exodus. The USA was poised for a great naval victory—talk of which was on everyone's lips throughout the North.

Thus, it was with some consternation that the Navy Department received, at approximately 6:15 a.m. on June 6, 1899, a telegram from the US coast artillery watchtowers at Fishers Island, New York, on the north shore of Long Island Sound: "capital ships heading inbound."

Jackie Fisher had divided his fleet into three squadrons, and the unfortunate artilleryman on Fishers Island had sighted the middle of the three forces. Fishers Island was the site of Fort Wright, one of three coast artillery emplacements intended to close the eastern end of the Long Island Sound to enemy vessels—about ten thousand yards southwest of Fort Wright was Great Gull Island, and some ten thousand yards farther stood Plum Island. Each was the intended recipient of two fourteen-inch disappearing naval rifles to be supplemented by a battery of twelve-inch mortars and assorted six- and five-inch quick-firing guns. When completed, this line would have constituted a major impediment to any naval force seeking to enter the Sound. Unfortunately for the Americans, work had hardly begun on these fortifications as the sun rose on them that June morning. The only artillery in place, two six-inch guns on Fishers Island, were quickly silenced by a rain of fire from the leading units, Imperial German protected cruisers *Kaiserin Augusta* and her sister, *Grand Duchess Luise*, each of which mounted twelve 5.9" guns. Those salvos also silenced the telegraph office—leaving the somewhat cryptic initial message unamplified—and, in a foretaste of what the day would bring, killed over fifty of the civilian residents of Fishers Island, many in their beds.

That initial message was more than sufficient, however, for Admiral Andrew Benham, who had been recalled to duty and given the responsibility of protecting the port of New York. A native of Staten Island, which had only the year before been consolidated into the City of New York, Admiral Bentham's career had been long and varied: among his adventures were having been wounded in a pike attack by Chinese pirates in 1850. He had retired from the Navy in 1894 but had been placed back on the active list upon the outbreak of war. Benham immediately placed all of the harbor's fortifications on alert and ensured that the remaining ships in harbor were ready to sail. Unfortunately, virtually all of the effective units available to Bentham were at that hour cruising off the coast of North Carolina, waiting to intercept a CSS *Mississippi* that had already turned south for home. Bentham had at his disposal only USS *Ohio*, an older "coastal defense" battleship with two ten-inch guns, and two *Annapolis*-class light cruisers: USS *Gary* and USS *Spokane Falls*. Each had been under orders to keep steam up, and by 7:00 a.m., the lonely threesome was heading out the East River to repel the invaders—whoever they might be—in the waters of Long Island Sound. At around 10:00 a.m., the American units sighted the oncoming fleet and signaled its composition to an accompanying dispatch boat.

The Americans had no chance. Just south of Norwalk, Connecticut, in the middle of Long Island Sound, all three US ships were pounded into scrap. Admiral Otto von Diederichs made his flag in the Imperial German battleship SMS *Brandenburg*, accompanied by its companion, SMS *Weissenburg*. Although derided by the British, these seagoing units carried six eleven-inch guns each—in three turrets (one amidships)—and could bring all six guns to bear on a given target. Also under von Diederichs's command were the second-class British battleships *Centurion* and *Barfleur*, each with four ten-inch guns, as well as a screening force of British and Canadian light cruisers. Any one of the four battleships could have taken the small American force without trouble; their combined fire created a massacre. Both US cruisers blew up and went down with all hands before they came into range; torpedoes fired by *Spokane Falls* could not reach the Anglo–German battle line, and one was later found along the Connecticut shore by bathers. The more robust *Ohio*—both main guns dismounted and listing badly—struck her flag, allowing almost 250 of her crew to reach the nearby shores. And the invaders came on.

Another hour's cruising put the big German and British ships in that neck of water where the Long Island Sound becomes New York City's East River. At 16 knots, the fleet again cleared for action: this time to engage the forts protecting the city. As they came around Sands Point, they began to run a gauntlet of coastal batteries. The primary impediment to their passage was Fort Schuyler on Throggs Neck, in the Bronx. Begun in the wake of the War of 1812 and re-imagined and re-armed over the decades, the fort boasted two twelve-inch and two ten-inch disappearing rifled guns. (The "disappearing" gun was a breach-loading, rifled piece that was mounted on a carriage fixed to the fortification. After the gun fired, the recoil forced the gun below the parapet of its emplacement, allowing it to be reloaded in relative safety. General Adelbert Buffington, US Army Chief of Ordinance in 1899, claimed credit for the concept, and by the late 1890s, most new major-caliber rifled guns were on disappearing carriages.) As importantly, Fort Schuyler no longer relied on masonry and brick walls, which had proven so fragile in the face of contemporary naval guns. Rather, the four main pieces were protected by yards of sand, dirt, and reinforced concrete—better able to absorb the force of armor-piercing or high-explosive shell.

In addition to Fort Schuyler, Fort Slocum covered the narrow entrance to the East River. That fort, named for a Union divisional commander at Gettysburg, was located on Davids Island, just off the coast of the Bronx, and close by where Anne Hutchinson had been murdered by Indians so many years earlier. Fort Slocum had two disappearing eight-inch rifled guns and an enormous battery of sixteen twelve-inch mortars. Fort Totten, across the river on Long Island, had two eight-inch rifled guns; plans for larger batteries had not yet been completed. Smaller batteries of concealed six-inch quick-firing guns were found on City Island and on Hart Island—where the width of the Sound narrowed to three thousand yards.

The range from Fort Slocum to East Island across the sound is under thirteen thousand yards, and Slocum's mortars had a nominal range of over fifteen thousand yards; the American mortars fired first. Unfortunately, once the gargantuan first volley of a dozen heavy mortars had been discharged, the lack of room to maneuver in the protective pits interfered with re-loading and aiming. By the time firing solutions could be calculated and adjustments made—and the crews from the nearer weapons cleared out from the path of the rear weapons—the enemy ships had moved out of position. In sum, the mortar batteries made a tremendous noise, unimaginably large splashes, and achieved not a single direct hit. (Leaks caused by damaged joints attributable to near misses did, however, create anxiety, particularly aboard the light cruisers.) The range from Fort Schuyler to Sands Point is under eleven thousand yards, and the fort's twelve-inch guns began firing as soon as the enemy ships presented themselves around the point. These were somewhat more accurate than the mortars. Indeed, the technology of the time ensured that land-based batteries would always be more accurate than those aboard ship—if for no other reason than that the range-finding gear could be placed hundreds of yards apart, rather than just a few yards as on shipboard; it is, after all, a matter of triangulation. First blood went to Fort Schuyler, which scored a direct hit on the bow of the *Grand Duchess Luise*, exploding the ready torpedo in her bow tubes and blowing off the front quarter of the ship almost—but not quite—to the waterline. *Luise* continued to steam and fight.

The British and German battleships continued to pound the forts. As they approached Hart Island, the six-inch batteries camouflaged there and on City Island unmasked and began scoring repeated hits on the escorting light cruisers; HMCS *Algonquin* was hit at least ten times at short range and turned turtle, grounding herself upside down just off Hunter Island. Despite the shallow water and nearness of land, only five men made their way out of the hull. But the light batteries on City Island and Hart Island were overmatched, and it would have been better had they remained silent. Return fire from HMS *Barfleur* took a terrible toll. Her secondary battery of 120 mm (4.7-inch) quick-firing guns shredded the hidden emplacements. The Stepping Stones Light on City Island was destroyed—local legend had it that the "stepping stone" rocks on which it sat were used by the devil when he was chased to City Island and off of the mainland—and the venerable gothic Grace Episcopal Church reduced to ruin. The indiscriminate bombardment of Hart Island was to particularly horrific effect: While the island had no current inhabitants, it had been used as a Potter's Field by the City of New York for decades, and the high-explosive shells from *Barfleur* disinterred the mortal remains of thousands of paupers, throwing them high into the sky from whence they rained down as if part of a macabre Biblical plague.

By noon, the combined large guns of the Anglo–German fleet had begun to take a toll on the defenders. The short-barreled mid-ship turrets of the German battleships proved particularly adept in excavating the American revetments. As importantly, once the ships came abreast of City Island, all of their secondary armament could be brought to bear on the three forts, allowing a veritable rain of high explosive shell. The mortar park at Fort Slocum took an entire volley of a dozen eleven-inch shells from the German battleships at almost point-blank range, which penetrated into the ammunition magazine and destroyed half the island. Fort Totten's eight-inch guns scored a handful of hits before they were dismounted by counter-battery fire; infuriatingly, more than half of those shells did not explode, and most were defeated by armored belts on the big British ships.

At approximately 12:30 p.m., the American forts were reduced to three guns firing from Fort Schuyler (one ten-inch piece having been dismounted; the other, still firing, was running low on ammunition) as well as one gun intermittently from Fort Slocum. The Anglo–German squadron had lost one light cruiser and had taken substantial damage to another; indeed, most of the cruisers had suffered from glancing hits or near misses, and several had taken on water. Yet the core of the squadron—the four battleships—was largely unimpaired. It seemed only a matter of time before they would either silence the remaining shore batteries or simply run their gauntlet. Once past Fort Schuyler, von Diederichs's fleet would have its pick of over a hundred merchantmen in the East River—provided they stayed sufficiently far north of the fortifications protecting the Upper and Lower New York Harbor.

It is at this point that—who else?—Theodore Roosevelt enters the story. No, he was certainly not present. However, as will be discussed in more detail later in this chapter, Roosevelt resigned from McKinley's Cabinet to run for Governor of the State of New York in the 1898 midterm elections. His victory was largely a foregone conclusion. Among the score or more of military projects that continued to engage his fertile mind while governor was the creation of a harbor defense force for the nation's busiest harbor. Thus, in March of 1899, he established the "New York Harbor and Rivers Defense Flotilla," a force of small, fast, and maneuverable boats each armed with one or two torpedoes and a Maxim gun. Roosevelt's conception was that the Defense Flotilla would be manned by gentlemen volunteers, and several *Talbot*-class boats were in fact sponsored by yachting clubs. More, however, were the products of continuing rivalries among volunteer fire companies. Regardless of their provenance, by June 1899, the Defense Flotilla consisted of six squadrons of five fleet boats each, and twenty of these contraptions now came up the East River toward the invaders. Von Diederichs's ships put about and retired back up the Sound, while the cries of celebration rose from the tens of thousands of civilians who had watched the action from the shorelines. In point of fact, German and Canadian light cruisers made short work of Roosevelt's little boats, sinking eighteen of the twenty without sustaining loss. But they had run off the Anglo–Germans!

Actually, nothing could have been further from the truth. It was one o'clock in the afternoon on June 6, 1899, and Admiral Sir Jackie Fisher was leading an even more powerful Anglo–Confederate fleet into Lower New York Harbor—a port now denuded of every defending vessel.

Von Diederichs's small fleet had been designed not to break into the port of New York but rather to divert every last jot and tittle of mobile defense capability out of the harbor, up the East River, and into the Long Island Sound approaches. That, combined with the illusory threat to the Chesapeake Bay, allowed Admiral Fisher to steam into New York utterly unopposed by any enemy ship. The smoke created by his fleet was first sighted from Rockaway Point in Brooklyn. The US Army had planned a substantial fortification there, well outside the Narrows, but work had not yet commenced by that day in 1899. For now, a small signal post, consisting of a telegraph shack and two three-inch rifles, was temporarily sited amid the sand dunes. These small guns withheld their fire and were not noticed by the incoming fleet; by the end of the day, they would be almost the only coastal defense guns remaining in New York.

Fisher had with him by far the major portion of the Halifax fleet. Flying his flag in the light battleship HMS *Renown,* he was accompanied by six modern British battleships: *Empress of India, Royal Oak, Jupiter* and *Goliath* from the Halifax squadron, survivors of the abortive American war-opening attack, as well as *Majestic*-class *Caesar* and *Mars,* transferred from the now-British Mediterranean. A flock of British and Canadian light and armored cruisers scouted for the fleet and kept a sharp watch for torpedo boats; prominent among them was the Canadian protected cruiser HMCS *Niobe.* His Confederate allies were well-represented by the battleships CSS *North Carolina* and *Florida,* both modern units, as well as several light cruisers of the CSS *Samuel Barron* class. Also present was the sole member of the *Galveston* class: a fast, lightly armored cruiser with four ten-inch guns, designed for merchant raiding; her guns would prove just as effective at shore bombardment.

The American defenders had at least a few moments' warning as the Anglo–Confederate fleet rounded Coney Island and headed for the Narrows. The ships first came under fire from the guns of Fort Hancock—at the northern tip of Sandy Hook, New Jersey. Fort Hancock had been designated as the primary long-range coastal position in defense of New York Harbor, but as of 1899, her complement of guns was not yet complete. Her eight heavy mortars were no more nearly accurate—and no more handy to reload or aim—than those which had confronted von Diederichs's squadron off the Bronx earlier in the day; they were ineffective. The primacy of Fort Hancock and its "early modernization" meant that it had been saddled with a couple of "innovative" weapons systems before the technology matured fully. Thus, two of the key batteries at the fort were comprised of fifteen-inch "dynamite guns," a distinctive gun type that had enjoyed a brief popularity in the early part of the decade. In the late 1880s—and Fort Hancock had first been manned in 1885—existing high explosive shells could not take advantage of the even greater explosive power of dynamite: the less-stable dynamite would explode in the barrel if subjected to a substantial propulsive charge. Thus, a series of inventors, including D. M. Medford and Edmund Zalinski, developed a gun that would propel a charge of dynamite toward an enemy position solely by the force of compressed air. The absence of an explosive propulsive charge meant that the gun could use shells filled with dynamite rather than black powder or another conventional explosive. The one eight-inch "pneumatic dynamite gun" at Fort Hancock had been the first in the nation, and the four fifteen-inchers installed in 1893–94 could loft a five-hundred-pound charge of dynamite. Unfortunately, these monsters were difficult to aim, slow to reload, and largely inaccurate. More importantly, they could loft their charges no farther than four miles out; unfortunately, the main channel into New York never approached closer than three-and-a-half miles (and that for only a few hundred yards' steaming). The distance from Fort Hancock to the deep water off Coney Island was almost fourteen thousand yards; the dynamite gun batteries would hit nothing that day.

Fort Hancock did boast two batteries of twelve-inch disappearing rifles, which the Anglo–Confederate fleet did deem a threat. Again, however, the rush to modernize the fort had resulted in the installation of an immature weapons system. The disappearing carriages were not of the kind pioneered by Buffington—which used counterweights to raise the barrels into firing position. Rather, the two two-gun batteries at Fort Hancock were of an earlier design, using a steam hydraulic lift to place the guns into firing position. The difference between the two systems was substantial: a counterweighted system could fire twice a minute; the steam system, only once every two minutes—at best. In effect, the four guns at Fort Hancock were no more effective than a single gun on a disappearing carriage of only slightly more modern design. The US Army had planned to install four batteries of two disappearing twelve-inch guns, of the more modern type, by the end of 1899—but those plans were of little help in June. Fisher's fleet overwhelmed these batteries by sheer weight of fire. None of the weapons on Fort Hancock scored a single hit, and during the afternoon, CSS *Galveston* would stand off Sandy Hook with impunity and pound her defenses into rubble.

The remaining gauntlet for the Anglo–Confederates to run was the twin defenses of Fort Hamilton (on the Brooklyn side of the Narrows) and Fort Tompkins (on Staten Island). As part of a stopgap measure, several batteries of quick-firing, four-inch guns had been placed on two small islands in the lower bay: Swinburne and Hoffman Islands. The troops manning these guns were under no illusions as to the probability of their survival against an enemy battle fleet; their purpose had been to deter merchant raiders and enemy light forces. Both islands were bare rock; the guns were not entrenched and were defended by the bare steel of their splinter shields. The American forces on both islands were wiped out to a man— but not before scoring several hits on Canadian and British light cruisers. The absence of appreciable damage done by these brave men should not obscure their heroic sacrifice.

As Fisher's ships drew closer to the Narrows, the guns of Fort Tompkins and Fort Hamilton opened fire. As with Fort Hancock, both had been scheduled for modernization. Fort Tompkins still mounted two eight-inch Rodman rifles, forty years old, which were ineffective against any form of modern armor. But Tompkins did boast four batteries of two twelve-inch disappearing rifles, with the range to take under fire the whole of Fisher's line. The Confederates were not unfamiliar with Fort Hamilton: Robert E. Lee had served as chief engineer there in the 1840s, and T. J. "Stonewall" Jackson actually was baptized at the fort in 1849. Fort Hamilton's primary weapons were seven modern ten-inch rifles (on disappearing mounts in two separate batteries) as well as an unusually heavy secondary armament of 4.7" rifles, modeled on a British Armstrong design. And to force the

Narrows, Fisher's ships would have to pass between these posts, well in range of even the smallest gun. (Indeed, during the battle, a number of US Marines serving on Fort Tompkins took up rifles and attempted to pick off officers and men visible on deck as the ships passed; at least a handful of them were successful.)

Ultimately, however, the greater weight of shell from the Anglo–Confederate force began to tell. Fort Hamilton, built in the 1830s and slated for modernization in 1900, still relied for defense on a brick-and-mortar curtain wall; her disappearing batteries were not behind sand and concrete embankments but rather raised and lowered behind the type of fortress wall that had proven vulnerable to rifled artillery for over thirty years. After the old walls of the fort were demolished by near-horizontal fire from Fisher's battleships, the re-loading mechanisms and gun carriages were easy targets; all of Hamilton's big guns were dismounted.

The eight modern guns at Fort Tompkins were a tougher nut to crack. The four batteries were well-emplaced in revetments outside the old fort walls: protected by sand, soil, and reinforced concrete. They scored repeated hits on the second-in-line of Fisher's fleet, CSS *Florida*. *Florida*, like her sister *North Carolina*, was essentially modeled on the British *Majestic* class, utilizing an older-model 13.5" gun rather than the newer high-velocity, twelve-inch gun on the British ships. Unfortunately, *Florida* made up for the increased weight of her main battery by, in part, reducing her armor belt; the thinking had been that engagements between battleships would take place at long range, and armoring the deck against plunging fire would take priority. (The Confederate ships also reduced their secondary armament, which was performing hot work during the passage through the Narrows.) *Florida* turned out of line, afire, and ran aground off the coast of Brooklyn—fortunately for Fisher, well out of the main channel he would need for ingress to and egress from the harbor. Her fires were uncontrollable and reached her magazines at about three in the afternoon; by that time, all of her compatriots were well inside the harbor. Fisher also lost the light cruiser HMCS *Iroquois* during passage through the Narrows; she, too, avoided blocking the channel, exiting the gap and eventually sinking off Sandy Hook, where most of her men were rescued by CSS *Galveston*.

Eventually, despite more than a scattering of additional hits on his ships, Fisher's men silenced all of the remaining guns of the Narrows' forts and came into the harbor proper. It was now time for the punitive bombardment to begin—with nary an American ship in sight to contest the battle. From the middle of the harbor, Fisher's big guns could easily reach the nine thousand yards to bombard the financial district of Wall Street as well as the Brooklyn Navy Yard. As his force silenced the small-caliber guns of Governor's Island and other minor emplacements around the harbor, Fisher extended the range of his destruction northward up the island of Manhattan.

For hundreds of years, and through several incarnations, the steeple of Trinity Church at the corner of Wall Street and Broadway had been the tallest structure in Manhattan. Displaced from this first rank as recently as 1890, it still made a prominent aiming point for the British gunners. The church was reduced to rubble, and the mortal remains of such notables as Robert Fulton, Alexander Hamilton, and British nemesis Captain James Lawrence (he of "Don't give up the ship!" fame) were disinterred from the churchyard and scattered about the neighborhood. To the west, British and Confederate gunners were shocked to find Ellis Island already in a state of disrepair. Many in the Confederate government had particularly desired to destroy that symbol of immigration—of "mongrelization" of the race—and were denied their prize by a fire that had taken down the old wooden structure in 1897. The skeletons of the new stone buildings were made a target— albeit with somewhat less satisfaction. To make up for this disappointment, the Captain of CSS *North Carolina* fired upon Castle Garden. That structure, demilitarized since the 1840s, had served as New York's chief immigration receiving station until the opening of Ellis Island. (The famed Jenny Lind also had given a performance there as the "Swedish Nightingale.") But by 1899, no trace of the former immigration station remained at Castle Garden; even its records had been moved to Ellis Island (and lost in the fire of 1897), and all that CSS *North Carolina* managed to do was to effect the utter destruction of the New York Aquarium, quartered at Castle Garden since 1896.

Nothing daunted, the punitive expedition continued. After the neutralization of Governor's Island and the destruction of the Navy Yard had been completed, a specially trained contingent of Canadian marines were landed by HCMS *Athabascan*, which mined the eastern supporting pillars of the great East River Bridge between Manhattan and Brooklyn. While the bridge did not fall that day, the Brooklyn-side supporting tower was so weakened that the largest suspension bridge in the world had to be demolished and replaced over the course of the next five years. Along Park Row in lower Manhattan, the New York World Building (offices of the hated Pulitzer whose editorials so inflamed public opinion) was brought down by naval gunfire; it had been the tallest building in the world in 1890: the first to reach higher than the spire of Trinity Church. The new Potter Building, exemplifying supposedly fireproof "skyscraper" design with iron structure, walls, supports, and cross-braces, proved no more invulnerable than earlier skyscrapers of iron and brick. The roll call of commercial buildings lost that day reads like a poll of modern architecture's tallest and strongest structures: The World Building, the Potter Building, the Home Life Insurance Building, the Metropolitan Life Insurance Building, the American Surety Building, the Washington Life Building, and the just-completed Waldorf–Astoria Hotel were among those shattered by gunfire or gutted by the fires that would sweep as far north as Midtown.

But listing the buildings erased from the map does not do full justice to the scope of the raid. New York City had come to rival London as a commercial center of worldwide import. Fisher's fleet burned out the heart of the city's commercial and financial district as well as the heart of historic old New York in lower Manhattan. Wall Street, Madison Square, Washington Square, and Union Square ended the week of ensuing fires as burned-out districts. Police and fire services could do little; no help for a burning Manhattan could come from Brooklyn, Queens, the Bronx, or the nearby New Jersey cities, for who would venture on a ferry across the "T" of the British fleet? Most of Manhattan south of 34th Street was gutted. Loss of life was shocking to contemporaries. Almost five thousand military had been killed in the bombardment of the forts and destruction of the Navy Yard. Thousands of office workers lost their lives in the financial district. Thousands more longshoremen, stevedores, and workers were killed during the systematic destruction of lower Manhattan's docks (largely accomplished with the multitudes of six-inch quick-firing guns that comprised the secondary armament of the big ships). Perhaps as many as ten thousand—no one will ever know for sure—poor, largely immigrant civilians, died trapped in their dingy tenements that became veritable crematoria. And for the second time in less than a year, the country's cultural heritage suffered grievous loss as numerous and varied collections were consumed by the flames (including the records of the music publishers who clustered around Union Square and the entire collection of the Astor Library). Although he really was not at fault, a distraught American Admiral Benham offered his resignation, which was promptly accepted.

Not surprisingly, the bombardment resurrected many memories of earlier conflicts and commonalities between the Americans, the Confederates, and the British. Fort Hamilton had been a fortified site since 1657, when the New Netherlands colony raised a blockhouse there; it was from that spot that the authority of British King Charles II over the Dutch colonies in America had been proclaimed. It was also Fort Hamilton that fired—on July 4, 1776—the only shots attempting to interdict an earlier British fleet from coming into New York harbor. Aboard CSS *North Carolina*, one ensign was temporarily relieved from his position when he refused to fire on Castle Garden because his grandparents had passed through that portal on their way to settle in Kentucky. Perhaps the most ironic of these events was the participation of the Confederate armored cruiser CSS *Slidell* in the destruction of the Park Row neighborhood of skyscrapers. Along that street rose Fifteen Park Row: an estimated five weeks from completion in June 1899, it was planned to be the tallest building in the world when finished, at 391 feet, and already towered over the island of Manhattan. It was a natural target for enemy shells, and *Slidell's* eight-inch guns were particularly well-positioned to pound the unfinished edifice. The building recently had been purchased by the famously wealthy American financier, August Belmont, Jr., whose parents had emigrated from the Austro–Hungarian Empire at the request of the Rothschilds before the Secession War and whose own independent finance house had prospered mightily in the following years. Belmont was fascinated by horse-racing (and still owned partial interests in a number of Kentucky stud farms) as well as sports (having invented spiked track shoes while competing for Harvard as an undergraduate). There was a particular cachet in owning the world's tallest building which brought

Belmont great satisfaction; that dream now was destroyed by CSS *Slidell*, named after John Slidell, noted Confederate diplomat, at the center of the *Trent* incident in 1861—and August Belmont, Jr.'s great-uncle.

In light of the horrors of the great terror raid on New York City, it is almost anti-climactic to discuss the efforts of Fisher's third squadron that day—the one dispatched to Boston. The two *Centurion*-class coastal battleships HMS *Zealous* and HMS *Caledonia* were accompanied by two *Pelorus*-class light cruisers and the Canadian light cruiser HMCS *Penobscott*. The superannuated American commander of the Port of Boston, Admiral Francis Ramsay, had retired as a full admiral in 1897; his career was sufficiently long for him to have served on board USS *Merrimack* before the Secession War and her conversion to an ironclad. He had only two modern ships at his disposal that day: the *Iowa*-class battleship USS *Illinois*, under the command of Captain Charles Clark, and the armored cruiser USS *St. Paul*, armed with an older model of eight-inch guns. The British commander, Captain Jellicoe, made straight for the defenses of Fort Warren in the center of the harbor, dismounting several of its larger guns and running the remaining batteries at 18 knots into the heart of the harbor. *Zealous* engaged and wounded *Illinois*, which was ultimately sunk by Canadian torpedoes in shallow water; almost all of her crew escaped. *St. Paul* took a salvo of four-inch rounds from the light cruisers and was forced to withdraw. That left HMS *Caledonia* free to bombard the city with her four ten-inch rifles. She scored hits throughout the downtown area, setting fire to Faneuil Hall and the Old Capitol Building as well as landing one shell (thankfully, a dud) in the Old Granary Burying Ground. The degree of destruction did not come close to matching that of New York, although the fear and indignation of the population did. Perhaps the most infamous event of the punitive raid against Boston—it began by one o'clock and was finished by 2:30 p.m.—was Jellicoe's decision to fire upon the third commissioned US warship present in the harbor: USS *Constitution*, known as *Old Ironsides* and an important symbol of Northern national identity. The old frigate took a single hit along the waterline and sank at her moorings (to be raised another day). A schoolchild's poem about one of the midshipmen lost aboard her, while trying to fire her century-old cannon at the invaders, became a rallying point for a generation of Americans.

At the end of the day, the British government made a great deal of noise about Fisher's supposed "restraint." It is clear that the Brooklyn Navy Yard, for example, was a legitimate target of war; so too, of course, with the coastal fortifications. To those of us more accustomed to the economic aspects of international warfare, the destruction of the port facilities, the attempted downing of the East River Bridge, and even the shelling of Wall Street may be justified as legitimate efforts. And, as London correctly noted, Fisher was under specific orders not to fire on the "Statue of Liberty Enlightening the World," gift of the French people to the United States. (That instruction probably owed more to British reluctance to inflame the French than to any concern for American sensibilities.) Yet, Fisher's decision to shell Lower Manhattan indiscriminately shares more in common with the terror tactics of our own time than the Victorian sensibilities of an earlier age. The American "yellow press"—led by an infuriated Pulitzer—howled for vengeance against the "Vandals" who "have no equal this side of Attila." And in the end, Fisher and his superiors at the Admiralty were more than willing to let the Americans believe the worst, since blind American rage would be more likely to bring on the general fleet engagement Fisher sought to clear the North Atlantic of the threat posed by the American fleet.

The American reaction was exactly as Fisher hoped. Fear of additional raids combined with public and Congressional pressure to "do something" soon forced McKinley's hand, and the American Atlantic Fleet was directed to "suppress" the threat posed by Fisher's force. The usually aggressive Theodore Roosevelt registered one of the few strong—if private—dissents to this course of action, and the future president's concerns would prove prescient. TR had resigned as Navy Secretary, following the defusing of the Yukon Crisis. Thinking he had "missed the best chance of this century" to act as steward of the American fleet during war—Roosevelt sneered at the "sob sister pacifism" of McKinley, whom he accused of "throwing away a splendid opportunity to extend our continental dominion"—the ambitious TR moved to position himself to run for President in 1904, by assuming the country's second-most important executive office. As Governor of New York, Roosevelt was politically compelled to publicly champion retaliation for Fisher's raid. Privately, however, Roosevelt lobbied vigorously for the "truly effective course" of resuming the attack on Canada so that Fisher could be deprived of his "Halifax lair" and compelled to "skulk back to England." As a former Navy Secretary and a keen student of naval warfare and technology, Roosevelt recognized that the design of American battle-ships (with their exposed gun barbettes) made them dangerously vulner-able to the precision gunnery of the Royal Navy. By his extended tenure at the Navy Department, TR bore a heavy share of the responsibility for those designs, which emphasized lightly roofed "turrets" for main bat-teries—in effect no more than barbettes—while the side armor of all US main turrets remained flat rather than sloped. But studying the record of the Philippines disaster had persuaded Roosevelt that—whatever his prior views—the American gun turret represented a vulnerability, and war plan-ning had to be modified to take the danger into account until it could be eliminated. (Nor was Roosevelt the kind of man to let his prior convic-tions get in the way when circumstances demanded a radical change of approach.) "If we go ahead with a head-on attack against Fisher, we'll just get a bloody nose—and perhaps much worse," TR cautioned his friend and confidante Senator Henry Cabot Lodge (who, being from Massachusetts, understandably favored an immediate naval counterattack).

Yet the cautionary voices, even from such usually aggressive sources as Roosevelt, were too few to overcome the massive political pressure on McKinley to strike back at the British fleet. The American battle line had been built at extraordinary expense, and in the eyes of the country at large, it represented not only an investment in defense but also the repository of the hopes of the nation. For decades, politicians had rallied support for a modern navy by pointing to the intervention of perfidious Albion in the Secession War and crying, "Never again!" The surprise USA attack in British Columbia had led to American naval supremacy in the Eastern Pacific, preventing the very type of raids on the US West Coast that had ravaged the US East Coast. The Navy had gathered a powerful fleet to oppose Fisher, and there were those in Congress who were demanding Fisher's execution as a war criminal. In these circumstances, it was literally unthinkable that the USA fleet would fail to challenge the Royal Navy in a full-blown fleet action.

And so it came to pass: on July 16, the British fleet sortied to meet the Americans off the coast of Sable Island, Nova Scotia. Given that the

British fleet—for such it was, despite the presence of token Confederate and Imperial German forces—solidly outnumbered the Americans in capital ships, it was providential that the US Navy did not suffer greater loss than it did. The American fleet was built around ten battleships—if one includes the old "sea-going coast line" battleship *Delaware*. The Americans mustered four *Iowa*-class ships (*Iowa*, *Indiana*, *Idaho*, and *Minnesota*) as well as four of the modern *Pennsylvania* class (*West Virginia*, *Maryland*, *Pennsylvania*, and *New Jersey*). The one-off battleship *Kearsarge*, armed as were the *Pennsylvania* class with four thirteen-inch guns, rounded out the American line. To oppose them, Fisher commanded three *Royal Sovereign* class (*Repulse*, *Empress of India*, and *Royal Oak*) as well as the very similar CSS *North Carolina*. Three *Majestics* (*Jupiter*, *Caesar*, and *Mars*) and the *Canopus*-class *Goliath* accompanied them. Four of the six long-range second-class *Centurion* battleships each added their four ten-inch guns (*Centurion*, *Barfleur*, *Zealous*, and *Caledonia*), while the German "coast line" battleships SMS *Brandenburg* and SMS *Weissenburg* each added four eleven-inchers. Fisher flew his flag from HMS *Renown*, a "light battleship" but one for which Fisher had great affection and which he had brought from the Mediterranean after his appointment to Halifax.

The battle began shortly after noon, when Confederate lieutenant (j.g.) Wat Tyler Cluveris, gunnery officer of the Confederate light cruiser *DeBree*, sighted the smoke of the American scouting cruisers *Georgetown* and *Newton*. The initial deployments were cautious on both sides—for fear of torpedoes. Fisher had been an advocate of the "infernal machines" for the Royal Navy, and the American commander Admiral William T. Sampson had served as head of the US Navy Torpedo Station at Newport before becoming Superintendent of the US Naval Academy. Both fleets threw out screening forces of cruisers. From the north came CSS *DeBree* and *Tidball*, accompanied by HMCS *Pegasus*, *Alberta*, *Athabascan*, and *Arcadia*, modeled on the successful *Pelorus* class. From the south, Sampson detached the heavier but slower USS *Trenton* and *Wheeling* (of the *Pittsburgh* class), accompanied by *Harrisburg* and *Albany* of the *Pueblo* class, each with four eight-inch guns (as opposed to eight four-inch guns on most of the Canadian and Confederate light cruisers). By the time the longer-ranged American cruisers had driven off their counterparts—and thus minimized the likelihood of a torpedo attack—the battle lines had formed.

At first, the Americans seemed to have the advantage. Captain Richard Wainwright of USS *West Virginia* opened firing with his thirteen-inch guns from well beyond their extreme range: at seventeen thousand yards. No accuracy was possible at such a distance, but *West Virginia* claimed first blood when a salvo hit the Confederate *J. N. Maffit*-class heavy cruiser CSS *Mallory* at eleven thousand yards, blowing *Mallory* to bits. Admiral Sampson had already signaled to Wainwright to cease firing at such a range—and to be fair, hitting *Mallory* had much more to do with luck than with Wainwright's admitted skill—but Wainwright felt no need to conserve ammunition. Moreover, his family heritage gave him confidence that he could "place his blind eye" (although he did not have one) to the telescope: Wainwright's grandfather had served in the navy of the short-lived Republic of Texas; his great-grandfather had been James Madison's Secretary of the Treasury, and his great-great-grandfather was none other than Benjamin Franklin. (Wainwright's son was also at the battle: a midshipman serving on the light cruiser *Newton*; he would survive the American defeat at Sable Island and go on to win the Medal of Honor in the Second Alliance War.)

As the two lines closed, however, Fisher's dedication to gunnery training began to tell—particularly in ships such as *Caesar* and *Mars,* which he had brought with him from the Mediterranean fleet after crushing French and Spanish sea power there. As the distance separating the two lines fell to ten thousand, then to seven thousand yards, and then still shorter, the weight of secondary eight- and six-inch batteries were brought to bear, with heavy cruisers supplementing the battleships. This found some American vessels at a grave disadvantage: the four *Pennsylvania*-class ships, as well as *Kearsarge,* had their eight-inch guns mounted on turrets atop their thirteen-inch batteries, making it essentially impossible to work the intermediate guns at the same time as the main guns. American secondary and tertiary batteries *en barbette* were dislodged by near misses. But the truth of the matter is that British marksmanship simply proved superior. Sampson's tactical control of the battle—neither innovative nor particularly effective to begin with—was lost completely when his flagship, USS *Pennsylvania,* went down, although the commanding admiral and a majority of the crew survived the sinking. *Pennsylvania* had been holed several times at and below the waterline, lost way, and settled slowly. Less fortunate were *Minnesota* and *Maryland*; each ship suffered catastrophic explosions and took most of their crews with them, including Bowman McCulla, captain of the *Maryland*. *Kearsarge* absorbed no fewer than fourteen large-caliber hits yet somehow survived, albeit badly battered; Lieutenant (j.g.) Reginald Belknap won the Medal of Honor for keeping her aft eight-inch guns firing after the destruction of the thirteen-inch battery below him, sinking the *Diadem*-class protected cruiser HMS *Argonaut*, another of Fisher's Mediterranean veterans.

The only flag officer to be killed during the battle was Admiral von Diederichs, lost when SMS *Brandenburg* was sunk by the combined fire of USS *New Jersey* and USS *Delaware*. (It is emblematic of the rapid change of the era that, when von Diederichs was a Prussian naval cadet, the immediate enemy to be confronted was Denmark.) American shells also accounted for the second-class battleships *Zealous* and her sister *Centurion* (which by rights should have stayed in Halifax) as well as the powerful HMS *Repulse*. Among the smaller ships, Fisher lost HMCS *Alberta*, CSS *Minor*, and CSS *Samuel Barron*, while Simpson lost the heavy cruiser *Trenton*; the superannuated coastal battleship USS *Delaware* made it as far as the approaches to Portsmouth Naval Station before she had to be grounded.

As important as the losses suffered was the damage inflicted on the survivors. Here, Fisher clearly prevailed. Although Fisher did not know it (and the US Navy worked very hard to keep the information secret), every US battleship except for *Idaho* suffered at least one main battery disabled. And while the Americans inflicted severe damage on CSS *North Carolina*, SMS *Weissenburg*, HMS *Goliath*, and HMS *Royal Oak*, Fisher retained a core of powerful and effective units that, for the present at least, could not be challenged by any fleet the USA could assemble in the North Atlantic.

The American gunners did manage to inflict enough damage on the balance of the Anglo–German force to persuade Fisher not to risk additional raids and also to quash yet another suggestion by Richmond for an attempt to force the Chesapeake. Still, the Battle of Sable Island was indisputably Fisher's second great fleet victory in less than a year. The American Atlantic Fleet had been sufficiently damaged so as to compel the Americans to give up any hope of contesting Anglo–German control of the North Atlantic sea-lanes. In the event the Americans resumed their assault on Canada, Ottawa could be confident that supplies and reinforcements would flow from Great Britain without danger of interruption by the USA Navy.

Fisher's victory also had a more immediate effect: It doomed the uprising of the Irish Republican Brotherhood—just as IRB forces were poised to strike against the hated English "occupiers" of "Eire."

After Parnell's death and the Conservative–Unionist alliance victory in the 1892 elections, Irish politics was in a state of transition. The reader will recall how when the Irish Nationalist parliamentary caucus fractured over the Parnell–O'Shea divorce scandal, the majority adhered to the alliance with Gladstone's Liberals in the hope that Gladstone would regain power and pass Home Rule. Whether Gladstone could have done so seems a dubious assumption, because he would have faced an overwhelmingly hostile House of Lords irrespective of the size of any Liberal Commons majority. Yet, however slim the chances for Home Rule may objectively have been, most Nationalist MPs had a powerful personal incentive to seize on that hope—the recognition that the only alternative would be to abandon the prestige of their Westminster seats and return to the "Fenian wilderness." But when the reelected Conservative–Unionist government made clear its utter disinterest in pursuing any form of Home Rule, concerns for personal prestige quickly yielded to the demands of loyalty to the cause of "Free Ireland." Well over half the Irish MPs resigned their seats in protest against what their leader, Tim Healy, called "the futility of Irishmen expecting justice from a conqueror's institution." (Healy had been a principal Parnell lieutenant who turned against his chief over the O'Shea scandal; Healy's repudiation of continued participation in the English parliamentary process exemplified the effective end of Irish hopes for a reform solution to the Irish Question achieved within existing Anglo–Irish political structures.)

The collapse of the reformist alternative opened the door to an IRB resurgence. Although the Brotherhood's trans-Atlantic terror campaign during the Western War nearly succeeded in causing an Anglo–American war, the aftermath proved crippling to the Brotherhood's finances, as the American authorities pursued an aggressive campaign to suppress the

IRB's American fund-raising base. John Devoy, the Brotherhood's North American leader, managed to evade capture, but dozens of IRB operatives were jailed, and the organization's fund-raising effort among the Irish–American community was thrown into disarray. Domestic political imperatives soon caused authorities to relax their efforts (the votes of Irish–Americans helped tip New York to the Democratic ticket in 1884 and put the incoming Cleveland Administration heavily in their debt). But it would take Devoy and his cohorts nearly two years to repair the damage, and the resulting "cash famine" crippled IRB finances and effectively put paid any notion of reviving the terror tactics of the Western War period after Parnell's failure to deliver Home Rule in 1886. In addition, Parnell managed to overcome the disappointment of the Home Rule loss and continued to dominate Ireland with his masterful charismatic style; the IRB leadership correctly sensed that as long as Parnell was in the saddle leading the Home Rule charge, any attempt to pursue a "dynamite alternative" would almost certainly fail—and the organization might be destroyed in the process.

On the other hand, revolutionary movements are difficult to sustain from the sidelines, and by the 1890s, the Brotherhood leadership on both sides of the Atlantic—but especially in Ireland—feared the consequences of further enforced inactivity on the organization's dwindling ranks. Parnell's fall and Gladstone's 1892 defeat therefore could not have come at a better time to revive the IRB's flagging fortunes. The structure of Great Power relations, with the USA and the British Empire already juxtaposed at the head of hostile alliances, seemed to confirm the traditional Fenian view that Ireland's independence would—and could—be won in a war between the USA and England, in which "Eire" would align itself with the Americans against the English. And in John Devoy, the Brotherhood had a dynamic leader on the North American scene ready to press the American government for support of an Irish "war of independence."

Devoy was a young boy when the Great Potato Famine struck Ireland in1845, and the suffering of the time, combined with a family nationalist tradition dating back to the famed—and failed—rebellion of 1798, caused him to embrace the new Fenian movement and join the IRB shortly after its founding in 1858. By then, the Brotherhood had already taken the fateful step of establishing a North American counterpart—the "Fenian Brotherhood"—based in the burgeoning "Irish Diaspora" community of New York City. Devoy's obvious talent for organization and natural leadership skills quickly took him into the IRB's inner circle, where he participated in planning a military uprising against British rule. But that work was cut short by arrest in 1866, and Devoy spent the next five years in prison. In the meantime, the IRB's grand plans for a trans-Atlantic rebellion fizzled ingloriously: Irish-American Fenian raids into Canada proved dismal failures, and the Brotherhood's subsequent efforts in Ireland fared no better.

Had Devoy not been arrested, he probably would have ended his life on a scaffold the following year. Instead, Devoy served five years in prison and then was sent into exile in America. Devoy arrived to find the Fenian Brotherhood a wreck, and as an alternative, he joined the Clan na Gael, an obscure and secretive New York-based organization committed to the Republican cause. However small and insignificant-seeming, Devoy shrewdly recognized in the Clan a conspiratorial outfit that he could use to keep alive the North American Fenian tradition until developments in Ireland created a chance for a restoration of the Brotherhood's Trans-Atlantic effort at Irish liberation. The chance came at the end of the 1870s with the commencement of the "Land War" and Parnell's plunge into the agrarian question. Upon the outbreak of the Western War, Devoy was able to effect a merger of the Clan na Gael into a revitalized "American Wing" of the IRB, which would carry out the North American portion of the Brotherhood's ensuing effort to provoke a war between the British Empire and the USA. Although the Trans-Atlantic terror campaign failed to achieve that goal, Devoy's organization skills had put in place a structure resilient enough to survive the shock of the American government's ensuing suppression efforts. And although the IRB's terrorism during the Western War badly strained the Brotherhood's working relationship with Parnell, the breach was quickly healed, and the organization continued its (behind-the-scenes) support for the adoption of Home Rule. But with Parnell's fall from grace, Gladstone's subsequent defeat and retirement from parliamentary politics, and the resulting death of Home Rule as a realistic goal for the Irish nationalist movement, there remained no compelling reason for the IRB to remain in a state of self-imposed revolutionary inactivity.

Devoy had a keen appreciation for how close the IRB's Western War "dynamite campaign" had come to triggering an Anglo–American conflict. From this, he drew the conclusion that, should Parnell fail to achieve Home Rule, the IRB should resume the pursuit of Irish independence by force of arms: first by provoking an Anglo–American war and second by assuring the Brotherhood of American support for an armed uprising in Ireland in the event of such a war. The emergence of the Anglo–American antagonism in the wake of the British entry into alliance with the Confederacy convinced Devoy that a war between the USA and the British Empire was now only a matter of time, and that the Irish Republican movement should move directly to establishing the status of cobelligerent in the upcoming fight against the hated English. But to open the necessary dialogue with the Executive Branch of the American government required an entrée into Republican party circles, and since their arrival in the wake of the Potato Famine, the Irish had voted solidly Democratic. In New England, there was the bitter social divide between the "Famine Irish" and the Puritan-descended Yankee elite who dominated the local Republican Party organizations. In New York City, a similar social dynamic had quickly driven Irish immigrants into the eager arms of Tammany Hall. In 1888, however, reflexive Democratic opposition to Republican calls for a militantly anti-British response to the Anglo–Confederate alliance (formed the year before) alienated many Irish voters. Democrats had consistently opposed the GOP's "needlessly provocative" policies toward the Confederacy, and when the CSA became an ally of Great Britain, most Democratic politicians reflexively extended to London the indulgence they had historically shown to Richmond. In the process, they placed Democratic President Grover Cleveland in a terrible bind, and when Cleveland tried to straddle the line between the Democratic party base and the country's foreign policy and defense establishment, he only managed to alienate them both. In the election of 1888, the IRB's North American leadership decided to put aside resentment over prior Republican suppression efforts and actively support GOP nominee Schofield. IRB efforts on Schofield's behalf are widely credited with assuring the General's election; in New York, a shift of some thirty thousand Irish–American votes restored that most crucial of states to the Republican column and sent Grover Cleveland home to Buffalo.

In 1892, the Brotherhood vigorously supported President Schofield in his successful rematch with Cleveland, and Devoy found an open door when he traveled to Washington the following spring to present his plan for an "Irish Republican Army" armed by the USA. Devoy argued that this force could throw the English out of Ireland and transform that island into a base from which the Americans could launch an invasion of England. Devoy's proposal was given a polite hearing—but initially, nothing more than that. President Schofield, a former American Chief of General Staff, considered the idea a "fantastical and utterly unrealistic notion." But politics prevented the President from dismissing Devoy outright, and when McKinley succeeded Schofield in January 1897, the new president's lack of a strong professional military bias produced a directive to the General Staff and War Department to see how the IRB might be aided in the event of a war with Great Britain. (McKinley, of course, fervently wished to avoid such a conflict; but the astute politician saw no harm in giving "harmless encouragement" to a valued domestic political ally.) By 1898, "harmless encouragement" had produced a tentative plan clandestinely to land arms in western Ireland sufficient to supply an uprising of twenty-five thousand men. In the meantime, Devoy was working closely with the IRB's "Home Leadership" to organize a force (to be drawn from the Irish Diaspora in America as well as from the native Irish Catholic majority) ready to use the promised American arms to drive the British out of Ireland.

That men with the talent for organization and violence such as John Devoy could take seriously the notion that an irregular band of no more that twenty-five thousand men, armed with weapons no heavier than Gatling guns and light artillery, could drive the British Empire from its centuries-old position in Ireland must be considered a testament to the power of the romantic in the Irish political and military tradition. The myth that only a storm had prevented Wolfe Tone and his French allies from effecting the liberation of Ireland in December of 1796 inspired Devoy and the IRB leadership, and they were not about to let nettlesome details such as a systematic expansion of the British military presence get in the way of the dream of achieving what Tone had failed to accomplish.

By the spring of 1899, the IRB was poised for the assault on British power, awaiting only the arrival of the final shipment of arms from America. Then fate—in the form of Jackie Fisher's powerful Royal Navy North Atlantic squadron—intervened. The IRB's uprising had been set for one week after the delivery of the last shipment of arms from the USA—which was to have included all of the artillery and over half the Gatling guns. But defeat in the Battle of Sable Island had forced the American fleet to seek shelter, and Chief of General Staff Nelson Miles decided to suspend further arms shipments to Ireland until the American Navy could re-establish at least an equality of position with the Royal Navy and its German allies. This decision deprived the IRB of over half its expected arms. Instead of twenty-five thousand men, the Republicans would be able to field less than half that number. Devoy promptly urged a suspension of plans until sufficient munitions could be assured. But the IRB's home leadership had already crossed the psychological Rubicon and had proved unwilling to turn back. (Moreover, the operation had advanced to the point that a "stand-down" without British discovery was likely no longer possible.)

On August 14, 1899, the uprising was launched. The effort was violent but scattered, and the resulting suppression proved even more brutal than that of 1798. The IRB managed to seize control of several western towns but never got off the ground in Dublin (where efforts were crippled by last-minute confusion over redistribution of the suddenly reduced supply of American arms). The failure to seize Dublin or even force a pitched battle for control of the city doomed the uprising at the threshold because it left intact the nerve center of British rule. Dublin Castle could, and did, move quickly to dispatch thousands of well-armed troops to contain the uprising in its locus in the southwest of the island. Cork, the rebellion's effective center, was quickly isolated, while government forces moved to prevent the uprising's spread by suppressing its outbreak in those areas of the countryside considered sympathetic to Republicanism and the Brotherhood.

The British response proved as merciless as it was swift. After a series of dynamite bombings in 1897 (the IRB's self-proclaimed "present" to Queen Victoria on the occasion of her jubilee), London reinstituted the repressive measures of the Land and Western War periods but also combined these "traditional" responses with a program of establishing local

Loyalist militias to supplement the constabulary and regular army garrisons. The militias were to some degree a Unionist program that Salisbury and Chamberlin felt compelled to incorporate into the government's anti-terrorism effort. When Gladstone failed in his final bid to return to the premiership in 1892, the end of the Home Rule "threat" caused the Irish Unionist community (centered on Ulster in the northeast) to stand down from what would have been an impressive political mobilization against a second Home Rule push. The IRB's Jubilee Year campaign thus acted like an electric current shot through a dormant but powerful battery. By petitions and assemblages, "Ulstermen" by the hundreds of thousands demanded the right to organize against the "Republican threat." Seeing a way to calm an agitated population which would also spare an exchequer already strained by the burden of arming against the Franco–American–Russian alliance, Lord Salisbury agreed to the establishment of a "Royal Irish Militia" of fifty thousand men to be called up in the event of an emergency "threatening the safety and security of the United Kingdom in Her Majesty's Irish realm." In other words, Ireland's Unionists, overwhelmingly Protestant, were to be given guns and told that—if called upon—they could use them to maintain Ireland as a part of the British Empire.

Such an implicit appeal to sectarian prejudices risked a horrible bloodletting, since Unionists were bound to view their Catholic neighbors as the source of any threat the militia was called out to suppress. And that is precisely what happened when the "RIM" was called out two years later. With the regular army exercising little or no control, an overwhelmingly Protestant force ran savagely amok. In a repeat of the sectarian violence of a century before, Protestants descended upon Catholic property and persons. Farms (and sometimes whole villages) were laid waste by militia bands who all too frequently treated entire families and communities as "terrorists" to be dealt with by summary measures. Nor could these actions be blamed entirely on "rogue" militia members. As the horrific destruction of Cork by British regular units showed all too clearly, punitive force applied indiscriminately was Dublin Castle's (and by implication Westminster's) chosen instrument for suppressing what the overwhelming majority of Englishmen considered—in Joseph Chamberlin's words—a "loathsome and cowardly stab in the back."

An estimated thirty thousand Irish (men, women, and children) died during the uprising and its suppression. The uprising proved of little strategic or even tactical significance to the course of the First World War, as the British were able to suppress the rebellion with essentially no effect on operations elsewhere—particularly in Canada, from whence the Americans had naively hoped the British would be compelled to withdraw tens of thousands of troops. No such movement proved necessary—while the IRB seemed to have been dealt a mortal blow, given the grievous losses suffered among the leadership as well as the ranks. (Virtually, the entire command structure of the IRB numbered among the dead, including its young field commander James MacBride—who chose death in the flaming ruins of the IRB's headquarters (established in Cork's Victoria Hotel) over the certain punishment of execution by hanging should he have been captured alive.) In fact, the brutality of the British suppression would prove a watershed moment in Anglo–Irish history, converting almost overnight the overwhelming majority of the Irish into fervent opponents of English rule. Within five years, the IRB's home network would be stronger than ever before, and a new group of IRB leaders would already be engaged in discussions with the American military that would lay the foundations for what would prove the far more ambitious reprise of Easter 1916. As the reader will see, that second effort would also fail to achieve the goal of Irish independence—and at a cost even more terrible than the awful price paid seventeen years before.

But those events will be recounted at a later point in this narrative. For now, I must leave Ireland at the point when the IRB's uprising has been utterly crushed and turn my attention to matters across the Irish Sea. The year 1899 saw a clash of armies on the continent of Europe of a scale unprecedented for the size of the forces involved as well as the destructive power those forces employed. The reader will recall that the late fall outbreak of the war caused the Austrian and German General Staffs to postpone offensive operations against Russia until the following spring, while French efforts to mount a liberating offensive into Alsace and Lorraine quickly ground to a muddy halt. Both sides (the French in the west; Austro–German armies in the east) opened their offensives of the following spring at almost exactly the same time: during the first week of May.

For the French, the result proved a bloody fiasco. The Germans had used their winter respite wisely. The intended lines of advance, plainly telegraphed by the initial French attacks the previous October, had been transformed into a defensive network that would channel the enemy into lethal cul-de-sacs. Yet, the French stubbornly insisted on resuming their assault via precisely the corridors pursued the previous fall. Supremely confident that their superb field artillery would reverse the balance that had devastated French armies twenty-nine years before, the French utterly failed to take into account the impact of intervening technological developments—especially the effective integration of machine guns and barbed wire, which had tipped the balance—between fairly equally matched armies, at any rate—in favor of the defensive. All along the Alsace–Lorraine front, the result was the same: French troops cut down by the thousands, unable to make any material progress. (The French even overestimated the value of their famous Schneider "75s"; the guns performed superbly, but their power was checked by Tredegar–Krupp's own recoil cylinder gun—a development that French artillery specialists should, but did not, anticipate.) Although some progress was made in the south toward Mülhausen and in the center toward Saarburg (west of Strasbourg), by August, the French high command was compelled to break off an offensive that cost over one hundred thousand casualties with nothing achieved remotely commensurate to such a bloody effort.

While the Germans frustrated France's attempt to wrest back the "lost provinces" of Alsace and Lorraine, to the east, their armies (in conjunction with those of Austria–Hungary) inflicted a series of sharp reverses on France's and America's Russian ally. By May, the mud-bringing rains had passed, and Austro–German forces (collectively numbering over one million men) prepared to swing into action. As a result, the world would witness industrialized mass warfare on a scale dwarfing any previous armed encounter in the course of history. The Franco–German clashes that same year, as well as the scale of the fighting raging across the North American continent, would otherwise have contested for this dubious title. But the battles that now ensued between the million men of the combined armies of Germany and Austria–Hungary—and the equal numbers put into the field by their Russian opponents—dwarfed the scale of even those savage combats.

While the gross numbers might suggest an equality of juxtaposed forces, in fact, the Russians were at a serious disadvantage. The Russian army lagged behind its rivals across the spectrum of weapons development, including the vital fields of recoilless artillery and machine gun technology. Compounding these basic deficiencies was a woefully inadequate logistical capacity, a function of surprisingly rudimentary development of the railroad net lying behind the Russian border with Germany and Austria-Hungary, and a complete lack of appreciation for the need to assure stockpiles of the supplies necessary to sustain operations on a modern battlefield. Finally, there was the culture of the Russian army itself. While the Russian foot soldier would prove a tenacious foe, the effectiveness of the officer corps was still crippled by a near-feudal advancement process which continued to make obsequious demonstrations of loyalty to the Tsar the overriding test for higher command.

All these factors combined to set the stage for a series of calamitous Russian defeats along a front stretching from the Baltic coast in the north to the Dniester River in the south. In the center, the Russians attempted a withdrawal, recognizing that Russian Poland west of the Vistula and Narew Rivers could not be held against an assault consisting of the main body of the German army. But unwillingness to yield Warsaw introduced a fatal incoherence into Russian plans. To protect the traditional Polish capital, a course insisted on by Tsar Nicholas II, the Russian high command had to keep substantial forces on the west bank of the Vistula. This weakened the flanks, and the Germans and Austrians proved quick to exploit the opportunity. By mid-June, the Russian left flank, pounded by a barrage of Tredegar–Krupp heavy artillery of the like never before seen, collapsed on a line between Kovno and Bialystok. Pivoting on the Bialowizza Forest, the Germans smashed through to Brest–Litovsk, well east of Warsaw. There they met their Austrian allies, whose armies (employing an equally effective artillery advantage: this, courtesy of the great Skoda works outside Prague) had broken through the Russians trying to hold between Lublin and Kholm. Into the resulting bag fell over one hundred thousand Russian troops, as well as the city which Nicholas had refused to yield— an immature and emotional decision, which would be neither the last nor the worst of such choices by the man destined to be the final Romanov to rule Russia. The surrounded Russians fell back on "Fortress Warsaw" and prepared to endure a siege that would end months later with the surrender of a shattered city in which over fifty thousand Polish civilians—as well as half their Russian "defenders"—would perish (most from starvation and disease, although the devastating effect of a relentless bombardment by hundreds of German and Austrian guns also took a dreadful toll).

Only in the south did the Russians manage to blunt their enemies. There, Austro–Hungarian forces proved unable to penetrate into the Ukraine while simultaneously engaged in Poland. This failure, moreover, was of greater strategic significance than a glance at the map would suggest. The reader will recall the dependence of the British Home Islands on American grain imports. The same was true, if to a lesser extent, for Germany and even Austria–Hungary (notwithstanding that Franz-Joseph's Hungarian dominions were net exporters of grain). All of the principal powers of the Anglo–German *Entente* had grown dependent in the last decades of the nineteenth century on grain imports from the very countries (the USA and Russia) with which they were now at war. Yet, the German and Austrian General Staffs showed only the dimmest awareness of the potentially calamitous implications of this logistically fundamental fact. In part, this reflected the lack of appreciation, by military leaders everywhere, that modern industrialized mass warfare blurred previous distinctions between the military and civilian spheres, rendering the striking power of the military dependent on the—literal—health of the civilians who manned the factories from which flowed the armaments of modern warfare. In addition, neither Germany nor Austria–Hungary, with their autocratic political traditions, inculcated in their elites (including the military leadership) any sensitivity to the suffering of the mass population—something their British counterparts had begun to develop by the necessities of a semi-democratic political system. Had the German and Austrian leadership at least developed a partial democratic political sensibility, they might have altered the axis of advance and made an invasion of the Ukrainian breadbasket their principal objective. But they did not, and the weaker right wing of the Austrian armies failed utterly to make any progress in an effort to cross the Dniester River and penetrate into the Northeastern Ukraine. Only as the fall mud brought offensive operations to a sticky halt did Berlin and Vienna begin to awake to the fact that the Russian grain lands would remain beyond their reach until 1900 at the earliest.

Still, one should not exaggerate by implication the immediate consequences of this failure. Especially in the vital area of perceptions, the outcome of the vast battles on the European Eastern front was seen by leaders of all the warring powers as a disastrous setback to Russian arms. And not just by the leaders of the warring powers: for the government of the Ottoman Empire had been watching the course of the struggle between Russia and her enemies with a keen eye, and the extent of Russia's defeats had helped persuade Sultan Abdulhamit II and his counselors that the opportunity had come to begin the reversal of centuries of Ottoman defeats at Russian hands. I say "helped," for 1899 proved a disastrous year for Russian arms on other fronts as well. Because the Russo–Japanese struggle in Northeastern China is inextricably intertwined with the course of the events leading to the Suspension of Hostilities in August of 1900, I will postpone my discussion of that Russian setback to my recounting of the Suspension itself. For now, I will turn to the Anglo–Russian fight in Central Asia, in which the "Great Game" that the British and Russian Empires had played for decades achieved a bloody resolution with a British victory in the chief theaters of Afghanistan and Tibet.

As in Poland, Russia's neglect of her railroad network would make a decisive contribution to defeat. As late as 1890, Russia held a distinct advantage over the Government of India in the ability to concentrate forces for a thrust into Afghanistan in the event of war. The British then moved to redress the imbalance, and the reader will recall how Viceroy Curzon had pushed for an acceleration of that effort—even at the expense of increasing the tax burden during a time of mounting famine. Thus, by the outbreak of war in 1898, the Indian Army had the ability to concentrate forces on the Afghan–India border nearly twice as large as those the Russians could muster on the opposite side. Moreover, due to Curzon's decision to keep much of the army on alert in forward positions even after the immediate war threat of the Yukon crisis had passed, the principal striking force of the Indian Army was positioned to jump off into Afghanistan virtually on a moment's notice. The cost of this forward deployment would have proved intolerable to India's peacetime exchequer if extended for more than a few months. But Curzon's intuitive sense—that the Yukon might be quickly succeeded by another imbroglio leading to a general war in which the constraints on London's purse strings would be removed—proved sound. Fashoda and the outbreak of war, however, came too late in the season for the British to exploit their advantage. Moreover, the storms that proceeded to close the passes from India into Afghanistan represented an opportunity for the Russians to move sufficient troops into position so that when the spring thaws came, the British would have to race in earnest to deprive Russia of effective control of the Afghan interior.

If the Russians had only a war with the British Empire to fight, the ensuing race might have seen a different outcome. But Russia had allowed itself to be dragged into a war in which it had to fight enemies on three, widely separated fronts. And the Russian rail net proved unready to the task. Although some historians have emphasized the literal gaps in the railroad system (especially the hundreds of unbuilt miles along the projected route of the Trans-Siberian Railroad—about which, more later), the root problem was not unlaid track but insufficient rolling stock, as the course of the Central Asian campaign so clearly shows. When the weather frustrated British plans for a fast move north, the effect was more than to afford the Russians the opportunity to equalize forces for the upcoming campaign. For while British access into Afghanistan was blocked at the threshold for so long as the principal passes remained closed by snow, the Russians could begin their advance at once by moving against Herat (the country's second ranking city, located in the northwest and lacking the protection of the formidable mountains guarding the southern approaches from the Indian plain). Yet, the woefully insufficient state of Russia's rolling stock effectively thwarted this chance to steal a march on the British. The demands of the European and Northwest Asian fronts reduced the flow of troops—and more important: arms and other essential supplies—heading to the Central Asian front to a mere trickle. Not until March were Russian forces ready to begin their move on Herat. And by then, such a move was assured to drive the ambivalent Afghani Emir, Abdur Rahman, into the arms of the British.

Rahman had been at the center of the Anglo–Russian struggle in Central Asia since he attained the Emirship in 1880, following the death of the bitterly Anglophobic Sher Ali. Having lived for twelve years in exile in

Samarkand (under Russian protection that extended to a pension granted by Tsar Alexander II), Rahman could have been expected to align his country with Russia against the British. Precisely for that reason, voices had been raised in Calcutta and London urging that British forces—at that very moment engaged in the second Anglo–Afghan war to be fought in less than a generation—should block Rahman's rise to power. But wiser heads, recognizing that Great Britain had no credible alternative to Rahman to put forward, prevailed with a policy of *quid pro quo*: Calcutta and London would not oppose Rahman as Emir if Rahman agreed that Kabul henceforth would speak to the outside world (including St. Petersburg) through the good offices of the British Empire. Rahman recognized the practical sense of accepting the British proposal: his country convulsed by war, British support would assure him control of Kabul and give him the upper hand against those challenging him for the Emirship. Even more important, Rahman was not a Russian tool, as feared by some, but an Afghan nationalist. And as a nationalist, Rahman could see that the Russians— given the chance—would subjugate Afghanistan as they had subjugated the ancient Muslim Khanates along the Silk Road route to the north.

Thus, for eighteen years, Rahman (to the great disappointment of his former Russian hosts) resisted Russia's encroachments on Afghanistan's sovereignty. But Rahman did so in part by making clear that Afghanistan should not be considered a mere appendage of British India. During the Chitral succession crisis, Rahman actually opposed the initial British favorite. Rahman believed that Afghanistan could not preserve its independence unless it maintained a degree of separation from Calcutta and London as well as St. Petersburg. For that reason, the Emir watched the storm clouds gathering during the 1890s with ever-increasing concern. The troop movements during the Yukon Crisis left no doubt in Rahman's mind that, in the event of war, Afghanistan would become an Anglo–Russian battlefield. If so, Rahman had to hope for a Russian defeat, as a victorious Russia would certainly incorporate Afghanistan into the Tsar's dominions. But preventing that outcome just as certainly required allowing the Indian Army to pour hundreds of thousands of troops into the country. And once in, could the British ever be persuaded to leave? "You say Queen Victoria will order her army to withdraw once the Russians have been dealt with," Rahman told the British counsel in September 1898. "But if Viceroy Curzon advises the Queen that it would be better for Afghans as well as the British if they stayed, how can I know that she will not take his advice?"

The question struck home: precisely because Curzon had for months been urging Salisbury and Chamberlin to adopt a policy of annexation of Afghanistan in the event of war with the Franco–American–Russian alliance. And no amount of soothing diplomatic double-talk on the part of British representatives undoubtedly in the know could put off as insightful and shrewd a leader as the Emir. So, Rahman adopted the tactic of delay when the fall snows sealed up the approaches to his country and smothered Russian—as well as British—plans for an advance. But as Rahman put off British pressure to admit an Indian Army advance force, Rahman also risked a rupture with Calcutta by sending a secret emissary to St. Petersburg to negotiate an agreement by which Russia would accept territorial concessions in the Northwest (including a favored status in Herat) in exchange for a public renunciation of any further claims on Afghan territory. By this move—a clear violation of the terms by which Great Britain recognized Rahman as emir eighteen years before—the Afghan leader hoped to avoid the Anglo–Russian battle he feared would end in Afghanistan's outright incorporation into British India. Rahman, however, did not reckon with the extent of Russian arrogance—as well as her longstanding Central Asian ambitions.

Incredibly, St. Petersburg entered the war's first full year brimming with confidence about Russian prospects on every principal front. In fact, the Russians did have one reason to feel moderately good about the upcoming year: the outbreak of war caught Russia in an extraordinarily vulnerable position, and the winter-imposed lull had given the Russian armed forces valuable time to improve that position. But Tsar Nicholas II and his generals confused a chance to strengthen a weak logistical network with a readiness to launch offensives on two fronts, while holding a forward position on the third. Hence, when Rahman's emissary presented the Emir's proposal, he was told that Russia insisted on: the outright annexation of territory amounting to 40 percent of Afghanistan, including Herat in the northwest and the vital Pamir heights in the east; occupation of Kabul; and the balance of the country to be subject to the "Tsar's special protection," with free passage for Russian forces. When Rahman learned of these terms, he must have recognized the futility of attempting to deal with St. Petersburg on any terms except either abject surrender or outright resistance. And if the Emir still had any doubts, they would quickly have been dispelled by news that followed on the heels of Russia's onerous "counteroffer"—the Russian Central Asian army had moved into northwestern Afghanistan, heading for Herat. Whether the Russian move was the product of an overly aggressive local command or was carefully coordinated by St. Petersburg (the former seems more likely, if only because the latter seems beyond the communications capacity of the Russian high command to manage), the effect was the same—Rahman, his choice forced between a Russian or British Afghanistan, moved swiftly in favor of the latter.

There now ensued what has become generally thought of as the "Race for Kabul," principally due to Winston Churchill's famous chronicle of the Central Asian campaign. Churchill himself emerged a hero, his escape from a Russian camp—including an arduous march across mountains in the company of a band of Afghanis loyal to Rahman—propelling him into the House of Commons as a Conservative–Unionist in the "Khaki Election" of 1902. Churchill had been recalled to his regiment after participating in Kitchener's victory at Omdurman—as the subsequent Fashoda crisis began to spin inexorably toward war. I do not doubt either the genuineness of Churchill's heroism in the ensuing campaign (which, among other things, earned him the friendship—and subsequent political sponsorship—of Viceroy Curzon) or that Churchill's ensuing career, both as an enemy and then staunch ally of America, exhibited a brilliant grasp of military grand strategy. Nevertheless, I must dissent from Churchill's characterization of the Central Asian campaign of 1899 as a race for the Afghani capital in which the British barely beat the Russians to the mark. In fact, that race was over before it began, and the Russians were the losers precisely because of their earlier move against Herat. Besides dividing forces too weak to sustain a concerted drive toward two such widely separated targets, the drive on Herat pushed Rahman into issuing an invitation to the British to come to his aid. In a stroke, the great passes were converted from formidable chokepoints into open passageways. And while the late winter snows hampered the British, that natural obstacle proved insufficient, on its own, to prevent advance units of the Indian Army from reaching Kabul by April—beating the nearest Russians by several weeks.

So much for any close-run race for the Afghani capital. But while I may disagree with Churchill's overdramatization of the British drive from the Anglo–Indian border to Kabul, I do agree with the late Prime Minister that Great Britain effectively won the battle for Afghanistan by beating Russia to Kabul. The British did not rest on their laurels but instead pushed columns northwest in relief of Herat and pressed along a separate axis into the disputed Pamirs (where the reader will recall how Russian "mistreatment" of future Field Marshal Younghusband nearly ignited a war five years before). It was outside of Herat that the only pitched engagement of the campaign was fought: a battle involving some fifty thousand Russians against a combined Anglo–Afghan force of about thirty-five thousand. The battle raged for weeks across barren valleys and through unnamed passes. A thoroughly beaten Russian army withdrew in mid-June, having suffered nearly 50 percent casualties. In the Pamirs, the fighting proved even more diffuse, but the outcome was the same: The Russians withdrew, leaving the British in firm control of territory that had for decades been a valued prize in the "Great Game." Thus, by the fall of 1899, the struggle for Afghanistan had ended with a decisive British victory—so decisive, that Viceroy Curzon now felt free to prepare a surprise move into Tibet (to be taken the following year and with none other than Francis Younghusband in command).

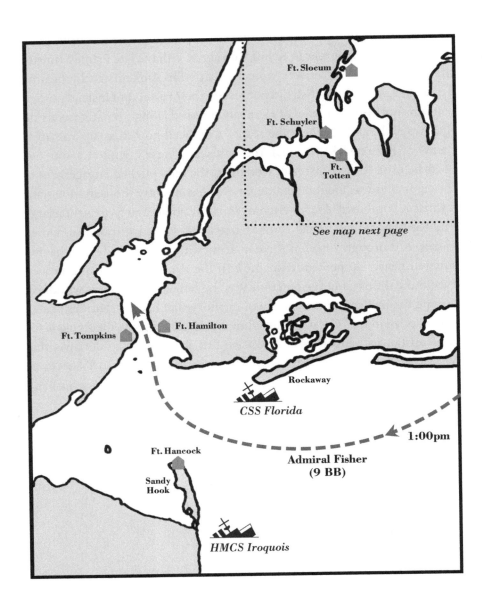

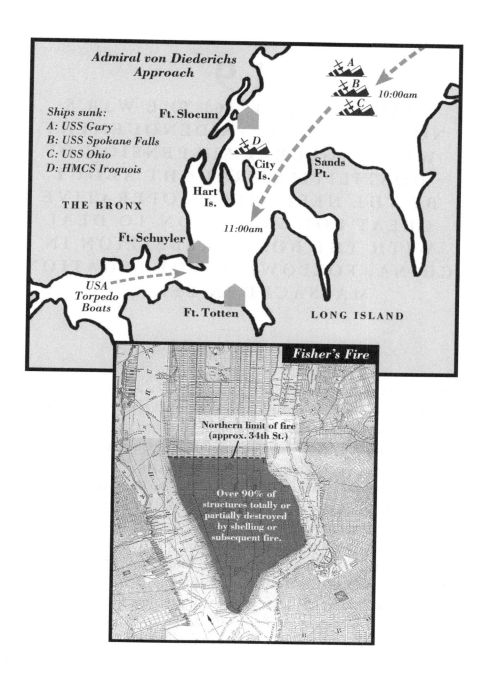

Admiral von Diederichs Approach

Ships sunk:
A: USS Gary
B: USS Spokane Falls
C: USS Ohio
D: HMCS Iroquois

Ft. Slocum

A
B
C

10:00am

D
City Is.

Sands Pt.

Hart Is.

THE BRONX

11:00am

Ft. Schuyler

USA Torpedo Boats

Ft. Totten

LONG ISLAND

Fisher's Fire

Northern limit of fire (approx. 34th St.)

Over 90% of structures totally or partially destroyed by shelling or subsequent fire.

19

WORLD WAR I: (6) THE WAR'S NORTHEAST ASIAN DENOUEMENT, WITH A GLOBAL SUSPENSION OF HOSTILITIES BROUGHT ABOUT BY THE NEED FOR COOPERATIVE GREAT POWER ACTION TO DEAL WITH THE BOXER REBELLION IN CHINA, FOLLOWING THE LEGATION MASSACRE IN PEKING

I have now reached the point in the narrative when the "dramatic center" shifts to Northeast Asia: the Russo–Japanese struggle over the Liaotung Peninsula and southern Manchuria and the near-simultaneous uprising of the indigenous Chinese group that called itself the League of Righteous Fists—or as the world came to know them, the "Boxers."

The reader will recall that, in 1896, the Manchu Court entered into an alliance with the Russian Empire, which committed Russia to defend China against Japan; in return, China would open its ports to Russian warships and allow Russian troops passage across Chinese territory in the event of a Japanese attack on Russia's Far Eastern territories. From May 1896 (when the Sino–Russian alliance treaty was signed) until November 1897, both sides worked together effectively and substantially honored their commitments. The Russians pushed ahead with the accelerated construction of the Trans-Siberian Railway and initiated the building of a rail link across Manchuria to Vladivostok (underwritten by French and Franco–American loans), while the Chinese proceeded with the establishment of an arsenal and other supply centers at the northern border of the Japanese-held Liaotung Peninsula. But starting with the Shantung Crisis of November 1897, relations between Peking and St. Petersburg began to deteriorate.

The Shantung crisis was a specific manifestation of deeper trends in China's relationship with the Great Powers, which would end with the collapse of the Manchu Dynasty and the country's outright partition (the prospect of which would also help mightily to "grease the skids" for a peaceful settlement, bringing the First World War to a—fairly abrupt—close). By the 1890s, the more far-seeing among China's elite recognized that China faced a true *crise de regime*. Without swift and effective reform of the most fundamental kind, the Middle Kingdom would almost certainly be divided and subjugated to Great Power rule—a catastrophe unprecedented in China's long history: combining the chaos of the Warring Kingdoms period with the shame of foreign conquest experienced at the hands of the Mongols and from which not even China's uniquely resilient civilization might recover. But reform efforts, which had been pursued in fits and starts since the Opium War and Taiping Rebellion had made plain the grave weaknesses of the Manchu order, remained stymied by the fierce resistance of the Manchu Court itself—in the person of the Dowager Empress, Tzu Hsi.

No single person bears greater responsibility for China's decline and fall than this concubine-turned-empress. Born in 1835, the daughter of a minor official, Tzu Hsi became a consort to the Emperor Hsien-Feng— and then his favorite upon giving him a son. Undeniably intelligent, Tzu Hsi proved gifted in the manipulative ways of the Manchu Court. Following Hsien-Feng's death in 1861, Tzu Hsi became co-regent for her son, the Emperor Tung-Chih. When he died suddenly in 1875, Tzu Hsi managed to have her nephew, Kuang-Hsu, named as Tung-Chih's successor. The manner in which Tzu Hsi achieved Kuang-Hsu's elevation illustrates how she subordinated everything and everyone to her determination to hold onto the power she had achieved by her relationship with Hsien-Feng. Tzu Hsi hounded Tung-Chih's young pregnant widow to suicide, thereby preventing the birth of a potential successor. She also compelled the bureaucracy to accept Kuang-Hsü as a successor, even though Kuang-Hsu (being of the same generation as Tung-Chih) could not perform the required filial rites to the deceased emperor when Kuang-Hsu reached maturity (a violation of constitutional tradition so serious that at least one prominent bureaucrat committed ritual suicide in protest).

Tzu Hsi's will to power, exercised within the familiar structure of Manchu Court politics, crippled her ability to respond effectively to the Great Power challenge. She feared the loss of power from reforms that threatened to erode the relative importance of the court she dominated. Tzu Hsi did permit a fairly substantial modernization of China's armed forces, including the admission of British and Confederate technical advisors. But the inability of technical change alone to redress the imbalance between China and even the westernized power of Japan—never mind the Western Powers themselves—was all too painfully demonstrated by the Sino–Japanese War. Despite an army and navy that appeared superior on paper, China suffered a disastrous defeat at the hands of another ancient Oriental power—but one that had grasped the need to combine reform of institutions with the acquisition of Western technology. (If the Tokugawa Shogunate had managed to hold onto power in Japan and Tzu Hsi had been frustrated in her effort to replace Tung-Chih with Kuang-Hsu and thereby lost her stultifying stranglehold on the levers of power, the outcome of any Sino–Japanese war might very well have been reversed: with China emerging as the Asian power that combined technical change with the social reform necessary to effectively capitalize on that change.)

After defeat at the hands of the Japanese, the pressure for reform increased several-fold. Tzu Hsi agreed to a program of military reconstruction and endorsed the alliance negotiated by Li Huang-Chang while in Moscow for Tsar Nicholas II's coronation. But she was unwilling to go beyond the purchase of yet more western arms and related strategic measures such as the construction of arms depots immediately north of Japan's new Liaotung holdings. Frustrated by Tzu Hsi's apparently implacable hostility to any sort of fundamental administrative or social change, a new generation of leaders drawn from the Confucian scholar-elite system turned to the Emperor himself. Although a supporter of the alliance with Russia, Kuang-Hsu had grown increasingly concerned that China could be drawn by that connection into a global war for which the country remained woefully unready. He therefore proved receptive to the arguments of men such as K'ang Yu-Wei, who urged the Emperor to assert his authority and push through a broad and radical reform program. Nothing constitutional stood in the way of Kuang-Hsu taking such steps, since Tzu Hsi's regency had ended, and the power she continued to wield was, at least formally, at the Emperor's sufferance. In June 1898, Kuang-Hsu startled the court and the country at large with the announcement of a program that, if carried out, would have represented for China the equivalent of Japan's Meiji reforms of thirty years before.

But after only a hundred days—marked by a flood of edicts touching virtually every vital aspect of society and government—Kuang-Hsu's efforts were cut short by his aunt. Tzu Hsi had ostensibly gone into retirement, putatively ending her regency and moving from the Forbidden City to reside outside Peking at the restored Summer Palace. (Burned by the British during a punitive expedition launched at the close of the Opium War period in 1860, the palace had been lavishly restored at Tzu Hsi's insistence, even though the effort diverted monies needed to replace armaments lost in the Sino-Japanese War; when the Manchu Dynasty fell at the end of 1900, the same joint Great Power force that sacked Peking and the Forbidden City would also burn Tzu Hsi's rebuilt pleasure garden.) Tzu Hsi's formal retirement, however, only masked her determination to maintain the traditional privileges of the court which were at the root of her own power. Seeing the foundation of that power endangered by the actions of her nephew, Tzu Hsi moved swiftly against both the young Emperor and his radical advisers. Returning to the Forbidden City on September 19, Tzu Hsi issued an edict claiming the Emperor had asked her to resume power. The claim was patently false: Tzu Hsi had placed Kuang-Hsu under house arrest, a state from which he would only emerge two years later when he and his aunt fled the flaming ruins of the Forbidden City in a desperate bid to escape capture by the Great Powers' Joint Pacification Force. Nor did Tzu Hsi settle for deposing her nephew. She also had his principal reform advisors arrested and executed without even the most rudimentary of trials—a ruthless move that deprived any potential resistance of leaders around whom to coalesce. (Among the principals of the ill-fated "self-strengthening" movement, only K'ang Yu-Wei managed to escape; making his way from Hong Kong to Japan, K'ang went into exile in Hawaii after

World War One and there wrote the fiery tracts that helped inspire the terrible River Valley Uprising of the 1920s.)

Less than one month later, World War One erupted. When called upon by their Russian ally to open hostilities against the Japanese, the Manchu Court demurred. China declared her neutrality and sent word to Japanese forces approaching Tientsin (the port city that also served as the traditional eastern gateway to Peking) that the Chinese would not look unfavorably on a Japanese occupation of the city if the Japanese would agree to halt their advance at Tientsin. The Japanese readily agreed, as it would permit Japan to concentrate their forces to meet an expected Russian move against Liaotung while simultaneously depriving the Russians of support by their supposed Chinese ally.

To understand why Tzu Hsi and her advisers made this choice in the fall of 1898, one must return to the Shantung Peninsula and the dramatic events that transpired there almost precisely one year before. The Shantung Crisis of November 1897 reflected the deeper stresses in China's relationship with the Great Powers. In this case, German colonial ambition collided with ever-increasing Chinese resentment against the growing—and arrogant—Christian missionary movement. Missionaries had long acted as trailblazers for Western commercial and political influence, and after China's defeat by Great Britain in the Opium War, missionaries associated with every European Power (as well as the USA and CSA) pushed aggressively into a Chinese interior opened up by the "Treaty Port" provisions of the Treaty of Tientsin in 1858. The increasing willingness of missionaries to call upon the military of their country of origin soon created an association in the mind of many Chinese (elite as well as peasant), who increasingly linked Christianity with the most abusive Western practices.

These patterns were reproduced in Shantung, a strategically important coastal province whose mountainous interior had traditionally been the refuge of rebellion and outright banditry and which had suffered a series of devastating economic reverses during the course of the nineteenth century. By the 1890s, the peasantry of Shantung were in a desperate state, and their resentment soon coalesced against the missionaries active in their midst. As it happened, the most visible of the missionaries in the province were associated with a German group known as the Society of the Divine Word (or SVD). The SVD was a Catholic organization whose members combined a typical proselytizing mentality with a near-fanatic commitment to German nationalism—a reflection of the effort by German Catholics to demonstrate their loyalty to the new German Empire in the face of Chancellor Bismarck's openly hostile policy of *kulturkampf*. By 1896, the behavior of SVD missionaries had become so offensive to the local population that they became the targets of the "Big Sword Society," a precursor of the Boxers. The Big Sword Society emerged in Shantung due to a congruence of factors peculiar to the province: its history of banditry, its deteriorating economy, and the need for filling an official vacuum created by the withdrawal of imperial troops during the Sino–Japanese War. The "Big Swords" began as an unofficial militia welcomed by officials nearly overwhelmed by a wave of bandit attacks; within a year, however, the Big Swords had shifted from bandit suppression to anti-Christian violence.

In June 1896, a series of Big Sword attacks on Christians (in this case, primarily French Jesuits) prompted a—somewhat belated—response by the Manchu authorities. But the ensuing suppression only scattered the Big Swords and drove them underground. In November 1897, they resurfaced with a vengeance. This time, their target was a group of particularly obnoxious German SVD missionaries in the Shantung county of Juye. Two SVD members were murdered; one escaped, and his appalling report—for the murder of his colleagues was atrocious: the two men having been literally hacked to death—aroused Kaiser Wilhelm II to a fury. The genuineness of the Kaiser's outrage should not be doubted. But it must also be acknowledged that Germany had long been looking for some excuse to seize a foothold on the Chinese mainland, and the Juye murders provided the needed excuse. Admiral Tirpitz himself had visited China the previous year in search of potential sites for a Germany coaling station and base; he returned recommending the acquisition of the port of Tsingtao along Shantung's southern coast. Now Germany swiftly moved in the wake of the Juye murders, demanding a ninety-nine year lease to the territory surrounding the superb harbor of Kiaochow Bay on which the port of Tsingtao sat. The Manchu Court's only hope was support from her Russian ally. But Wilhelm had (for once) cleverly preempted a potential enemy's move, dispatching a carefully crafted telegram to Tsar Nicholas II, emphasizing the anti-Christian aspect of Chinese conduct and assuring his "cousin" that Germany was acting only to protect the lives and property of Christians everywhere in China. The Tsar's naive and hesitant response—"cannot approve or disapprove"—cut the ground out from under those Russian officials who might otherwise have pressed for open support of their Manchu allies.

Frankly, I doubt whether Russia would have supported the Manchus—even if the Tsar had not sent his telegram. In the fall of 1898, Russia was the most reluctant of the belligerents precisely because Russia's leadership recognized that their country was not yet ready to wage a major war. Russian confidence in the following spring reflected—as much as anything else—genuine surprise at how well the country had fared compared to the gloomy pre-war estimates of the general staff. Be that as it might have been, Russian unwillingness to support their Chinese ally in the fall of 1897 proved a disruptive shock to the Manchu Court. Officials who had urged engagement with at least some of the Western Powers now lost influence to those who believed that China should instead stand aloof and await the opportunity of a war between the Alliances to strike a blow against all the "foreign devils." Although Tzu Hsi declined suggestions that she press Kuang-Hsu for a public break with Russia, there could be little doubt that the Russian failure to support the Manchu Court caused the Empress to re-assess the wisdom of China taking sides in a Great Power war. Indeed, it seems likely that the Sino–Russian alliance would not have lasted much beyond the fall of 1898 even if the Fashoda Crisis had somehow been defused and global war avoided—certainly not as long as Tzu Hsi remained in power. And she might have managed that well into this century if the distraction of a global war had not transformed the Boxer siege of the Peking legations from an annoying episode into a wholesale slaughter, triggering the Great Power intervention that brought an end to Manchu rule and also cost the Empress her own life.

As events actually transpired, the Sino–Russian alliance was terminated by Peking in October 1898, and China's Russian allies were left to battle Japan alone. The ensuing Russo–Japanese conflict was fought over some of the world's harshest terrain and subject to one of the world's harshest climates. Although Russian plans called for an assault against the Japanese-held Liaotung Peninsula, Russian forces proved woefully unready for the task. The troops were principally territorial regiments: badly trained and poorly officered. Nor did the Russian General Staff transfer any but a handful of regular army units to stiffen forces in place. Tsar Nicholas II insisted that almost the entirety of the regular army be retained in Europe (to meet the expected Austro–German assault) and in Central Asia (to launch the long-awaited drive into Afghanistan). Moreover, despite the undeniable acceleration of the rate of construction of the Trans-Siberian Railway, gaps totaling several hundred miles remained. These, combined with the shortage of rolling stock previously discussed, threatened to cripple the Russians' ability to maintain the extraordinary level of fire power—especially the rate of artillery fire—required to sustain either a modern offensive or defensive campaign.

Arrayed against the Russians was a Japanese army that had—since its victory over China three years before—sustained and even accelerated the intensive program of modernization and expansion initiated in the 1870s. The decision to pursue a Philippines invasion with their Confederate ally (to which the cream of the army would be committed at the war's outset) dictated an initially defensive strategy on the Asian mainland. But the historically aggressive Japanese intended to remain on the defensive only as long as absolutely necessary. If the Philippines operation went as planned—the general staff called for effective victory just thirty days after the outbreak of hostilities!—the Japanese would transfer three crack divisions totaling 42,500 men from the Philippines to the mainland. These troops, moreover, would not go to reinforce against the expected joint Sino–Russian assault on the Liaotung Peninsula's defenses. Instead, they would be landed in Korea and promptly moved north to launch an attack across the Yalu River into Manchuria. This bold move would simultaneously threaten Vladivostok and unhinge the left flank of the Russian lines facing the Liaotung.

As on other fronts, the war's outbreak so late in the year frustrated plans on both sides. For the Russians, the combination of the onset of the Manchurian winter and China's abrupt withdrawal of support effectively blocked the planned attack against the Japanese defensive line strung across the north end of the Liaotung. For the Japanese, the opportunity to effect a quick thrust from Korea—created by a brilliant success (in concert with their Confederate allies) in the Philippines—ran afoul of the even harsher Korean winter. The units transferred from the Philippines could not be ready to move from their staging positions until mid-December, by which time northern Korea had been turned into a frozen waste, hopelessly inhospitable to the human supply transport (the Korean "coolies") that the Japanese had to employ. Thus, as in Central Asia and Europe, the principal clash of arms in Northeast Asia was perforce postponed until the following spring.

With one exception: In December, the Russian Far East Fleet based at Vladivostok sortied on a raid, aiming to disrupt Japanese supply lines between the Home Islands and the mainland. The Russian Imperial Navy maintained a squadron of protected cruisers—*Rossia, Gromoboi,* and *Rurik*—at Vladivostok and with great exertion had managed to keep an ice-free channel to the port available until the beginning of December. This force alone would not have concerned the Japanese had the Russians not managed to slip a squadron of its newest battleships into Vladivostok just weeks before war's outbreak. The Yukon Crisis had badly rattled the Russian Admiralty, and with Tsar Nicholas II's consent, the decision was taken that summer to dispatch a group of Russia's newest battleships to the Far East—so new that most of them sailed with fitting-out workers and engineers still aboard. The fleet comprised three small but powerful second-class battleships, *Peresvet, Pobeda,* and *Oslyabya,* and three somewhat larger units, the sisters *Sevastopol, Poltava,* and *Petropavlovich.* This force, especially when combined with the protected cruisers already on station, was of sufficient power to worry the Japanese that it could interfere with the planned invasion of the Philippines. But that bold move caught the Russians unawares, and a hesitant St. Petersburg rejected requests from its Far East commander, the aggressive Rear Admiral S. O. Markov, to steam to the relief of the Americans and their Spanish ally.

Stymied in his efforts to participate in the naval fight for Southeast Asia, Markov decided to try his hand at disrupting the Japanese supply lines from the Home Islands and its forces on the Asian mainland. The first week of December, the Russians sortied but were detected by Japanese pickets, and an alerted Admiral Togo (having transferred the main body of his fleet back to Japan after the destruction of the Spanish and American Far Eastern squadrons) took hold of the opportunity to deal with the

Russian fleet with both hands. Togo again flew his flag in *Mikasa*. With him were three of the four *Fuji*-class battleships, as well as two of the original six *Shikishima*-class ships: *Kongo* and *Tone*. These six battleships were accompanied by armored cruisers *Nissen* and *Kasuga*—built at Kure (from purloined Italian plans, of all things) and quite fast for their size.

On paper, the two fleets looked evenly matched. The main battery of almost every battleship, on both sides, consisted of two two-gun turrets mounting 305 mm (twelve-inch) guns. The Russian fleet outnumbered the Japanese in armored cruisers: eight to four. But in fact, the encounter proved entirely one-sided. On December 7, the Japanese fleet intercepted the Russians as the combined Russian fleet was attempting to move through Tsushima Strait between the Korean peninsula and Japan. The Russian battleships had not had the opportunity for either gunnery practice or for steaming as a fleet—beyond what little that could be done during their hurried cruise to the Far East. The *Peresvet*-class battleships had been designed for commerce raiding and not for standing in a line to slug it out with first-rate battleships; they were perilously lightly armored. And while the Russian commander, Rear Admiral S. O. Makarov, had shown commendable initiative in deciding to concentrate his force and threaten meaningful Japanese supply lines to the mainland, his overly aggressive tactics now allowed Togo to cross the Russian "T" and defeat Makarov's ships in detail.

The result was Togo's second overwhelming victory in three months. The Russians lost all three of the *Peresvet*-class ships as well as *Poltava*; *Sevastopol* ran aground and was captured by Japanese special landing force troops. (She was repaired and promptly commissioned into Japanese service.) Four of the Russian armored cruisers were sunk, and all save *Novik* were damaged severely. In exchange, Togo lost the armored cruiser *Nisshen* and suffered damage to *Kongo* sufficient to lay her up for six months.

The Russian threat to Japanese sea communications had been eliminated. Admiral Makarov did not survive the destruction of his command: going down with more than six hundred others in the sinking of his flagship *Poltava*. The remaining Russian ships scurried back to port, from whence they would not venture for the remainder of the war. In less than one hour's combat, Japan had achieved absolute mastery of the seas between Japan and the Northeast Asian mainland.

As the spring of 1899 approached, Russian General Staff planners stubbornly adhered to their plan for an attack against the Japanese-held Liaotung Peninsula—notwithstanding growing evidence of a Japanese plan to attack across the Yalu, which could at the very least unhinge the Russian left and which raised the even more dreadful specter of the encirclement of the nearly two hundred thousand troops facing the Japanese defenses running across the northern end of the Liaotung. On March 12, the Russians opened their offensive, but the attack quickly bogged down in a deadly network of Maxim gun nests for which the poorly trained "territorials" proved singularly ill prepared. Then, less than a week later, the Japanese launched their own offensive across the Yalu, striking with a force of nearly seventy thousand men. (The delay enforced by the Korean winter also gave the Japanese General Staff the chance to beef up the attack with two more veteran divisions, with the resulting gaps in the Liaotung defenses being filled with new raised troops from the Home Islands.) The Japanese had employed masterful concealment to hide both the main body of their troops as well as supporting artillery—including several powerful 406 mm Tredegar–Krupp howitzers of a type that Russian intelligence insisted Japan did not possess. When the Japanese struck, the result was a rout. The Russian defenders were sent reeling into a disordered retreat; within less than seventy-two hours, the left flank of the Russian position along the Liaotung had been uncovered and lay exposed to an attack from the east.

Had the Russians provided for an adequate strategic reserve, they might have been able to hold their ground. But the only force resembling a reserve was a single under-force division stationed in Mukden—too distant to arrive in time and too weak to affect the course of the battle. Within days, the Russian forces along the Liaotung were engaged in a frantic effort to disengage. The dream of capturing Dairen and Port Arthur was abandoned: replaced by the more immediate goal of preventing a Japanese encirclement. Fortunately for the Russians, the Japanese lacked the capacity to project forces deep behind enemy lines. Japanese cavalry was ineffective to the point of haplessness—a reflection of the country's rudimentary horsemanship tradition. (Among other problems, Japanese horses proved utterly unsuited for the rugged terrain of northern Korea and southern

Manchuria.) In this last major war fought without the benefit of motorized transport, the Japanese deficiency in cavalry meant they could not effectively pursue and harry a retreating foe. And precisely because they so clearly lacked this capacity, the Japanese high command was psychologically unprepared to follow up the stunning completeness of their breakthrough. General Maresuke Nogi, in command of Japanese forces along the Yalu, seemed satisfied to consolidate the initial positions won and then resume only an incremental advance. This decision, however, gave the Russians the vital breathing space they needed to regroup in front of Nogi while effecting an orderly withdrawal from their now outflanked position on the Liaotung.

The fervently anti-Japanese Viceroy for the Far East, Admiral Yevgyeni Alexiev, whom Tsar Nicholas II had appointed at the outbreak of the war to assure a "vigorous prosecution" of offensive plans against Japan, insisted that Russian forces hold their ground and counterattack. But Minister of War General Alexei Kuropatkin sided with the field commanders on the scene and persuaded the Tsar to allow a withdrawal to a defensive position based on the Manchurian city of Liaoyung. This decision probably saved the Russian army from destruction. Alexiev's plan called for the Russians facing the Japanese on the Liaotung to ignore the enemy forces approaching from the east and continue the frontal assaults that to date had achieved few gains while incurring terrible casualties. Alexiev willfully disregarded the extent of the defeat inflicted by Nogi's forces advancing across the Yalu, insisting against all available evidence that the Russians facing Nogi remained capable of repelling what Alexiev denigrated as "nothing more than a raid by little monkeys who know nothing of real war." In fact, Nogi's "monkeys" had utterly smashed the Russians opposing the Yalu crossing, and unless the Russians pulled back from the Liaotung, they would find Nogi's powerful force in their rear. At a minimum, the Russian left would have been destroyed; in the worst case, the Japanese might have rolled up the entire line, and only a fraction would have escaped to fall back in disorder on Liaoyung and Mukden, leaving those cities ripe for capture by the triumphant Japanese.

This disaster did not happen because Kuropatkin was given the authority to bypass the viceroy and issue orders directly to field commanders to effect a withdrawal from the Liaotung. The Russian left pulled back then slipped northeast to occupy a blocking position between Nogi and the intended line of withdrawal. Kuropatkin had as many veteran regular army units concentrated at this point as practicable, with orders to make limited but sharp attacks against Nogi's slowly advancing forces. If the Japanese could be induced to halt their advance—if only for a few days—vital time would be bought to achieve the withdrawal of the Russian center and right. In the event, Kuropatkin's plan worked: partially because the uneven Russian officer corps rose to the occasion and partially because the principal Japanese forces—Nogi's as well as those of General Iwao Oyama, commander of the Liaotung defenders—did not coordinate their operations and thereby forfeited the chance to place pressure on the enemy at the moment of their maximum vulnerability. (Oyama's failure to recognize and exploit the gap that momentarily opened between the Russian left and center—as the left shifted east to block Nogi—was especially inexcusable.) By mid-May, the chance for a Japanese encirclement victory had been lost; the Russians had been forced to abandon their attempt to overrun the Liaotung, but they had made good their withdrawal and had been energetically engaged in constructing defensive positions south of Liaoyung.

The Japanese were now compelled by the very scope of their victory to halt offensive operations. The army, drained of vital supplies and its crack units reduced to an average of 50 percent in strength, was in no state to open an immediate drive against Liaoyung. To the contrary: If the Japanese launched an attack without pausing to restock supplies and rebuild weakened units, they risked a shattering defeat that could expose the Liaotung *and* Korean peninsulas to a counterinvasion by a reinforced Russian army—to which badly needed reinforcements of men and material had finally been dispatched by a St. Petersburg fearful of being driven from Manchuria and then finding Vladivostok placed under siege. Reluctantly, the ever-aggressive Japanese concluded that they would move north into the vacuum left by the retreating Russians, but they could not launch an immediate attack against the Russian positions in front of Liaoyung. Instead, the Japanese would begin construction of a counterline of fortifications to guard against a possible Russian move back toward the Liaotung and Korea. In the meantime, all available resources would be poured into rebuilding the armies of Generals Nogi and Oyama into a force capable of first placing Liaoyung under siege then battering the Russians out of their positions and opening the door to a drive on Mukden—whose capture would signal the effective Japanese conquest of Manchuria.

This process took somewhat longer than the Japanese high command had expected, and not until September did the Japanese consider themselves ready to begin the first stage of placing Liaoyung under siege. By "siege," I do not mean an encirclement in the classic sense: as the Germans and Austrians were doing to Warsaw at almost the very same time. Rather, the Japanese intended to push the Russian lines back sufficient to bring the city under fire from heavy artillery, while also moving west and east of the city to take up positions that *threatened* an encirclement. The Japanese launched their initial assault on September 15, and for a time, the Russians held. Japanese artillery could not reach well-concealed and long-range Russian batteries, and these played havoc with the attacking Japanese infantry, whose diminished ranks could not penetrate the Russian trench lines. But then the Japanese moved to flank the Russians by swinging through forested mountains lying south and east of the city. Wading a river crossing left uncovered by the defense, the Japanese seized a strategic height—known by the felicitously prosaic name of "Rice Cake Hill." Quickly placing several guns, the Japanese unleashed a rain of shells upon the city and its only railroad connection to Mukden. After a series of increasingly desperate counterattacks failed to dislodge the Japanese, the Russian commander (General G. K. Stackelberg) declared Liaoyung no longer tenable and ordered a retreat toward Mukden. Once again, the exhausted Japanese could not muster the resources to organize a quick pursuit; while the Russians, for the second time in less than six months, displayed a knack for the demanding task of an orderly withdrawal under fire. Indeed, the Russian recovery proved so quick that in early November, Stackelberg ordered a counterattack—in the hope that the Russians could smash through weakened and overextended Japanese lines and recapture Liaoyung. But the Japanese managed to withdraw from their immediate forward positions and then hit a confused Russian advance with withering artillery fire. The poorly prepared Russian attack collapsed, and the Russians withdrew even farther north toward Mukden, where they began preparations to resist an expected Japanese assault the following spring.

As the reader will see, the Japanese would not wait until spring—with bloody consequences for themselves, the opposing Russians, and the citizens of Mukden. But at this point, the focus of my narrative will shift from the Russo–Japanese struggle to internal developments within Manchu-controlled China. The insurrection of the "League of Righteous Fists"—the Boxers—which led to the downfall of the Manchus and the partition of China, originated in the Province of Shantung. The name "Boxers" derived from the boxing-like rituals performed by the movement's members and reflected the martial arts tradition of the province. Shantung had long been vulnerable to barbarian incursions from the north, which encouraged the development of self-defense skills among the local peasantry and townspeople. Shantung was also a mountainous peninsula whose valleys suffered from repeated flooding by "China's Sorrow," the great Hwang–Ho (or "Yellow") River. A peasantry thus forced to live on the very knife edge of economic existence—and acculturated to employ force against threatening outsiders—proved a veritable spawning ground for bandits who would take to the nearby mountains. Imperial authority—whether Han, Tang, Sung, Mongol, Ming, or Manchu—found the rooting-out of these bandits a next-to-impossible task. Moreover, as the "Big Sword" episode illustrates, dynastic representatives sometimes encouraged the formation of local militia—only to lose control and see the solution to one problem transformed into yet another challenge to Peking's ever-tenuous hold over the Shantung countryside.

The Boxers must be understood as yet another manifestation of this centuries-old resistance to central authority. What was always bubbling just beneath the surface would usually boil over in times of economic decline—generally brought on by some combination of natural disaster and political turmoil. In the 1890s, Shantung was hit hard by both. Then, from August into September of 1898, the Hwang–Ho burst its banks. A brown tide covered over two thousand villages, driving literally millions from their homes and land. Among the areas worst affected was the county of Ch'in P'ing, which also happened to be the center of the "Spirit Boxer" movement. The Spirit Boxers exemplified the centuries-old connection between the peasant self-defense tradition and the spiritualist movements that periodically emerged to challenge the Confucian orthodox authority of the ruling dynasty. The Spirit Boxers combined training in the martial arts with an egalitarian doctrine of "possession" by the "spirits" of various shamanistic gods, which were believed to render the possessed person invulnerable to mortal dangers. Perhaps it was the "democratic" nature of the doctrine—at a time of widespread suffering and the obvious inability of Manchu institutions to alleviate it—which made the Spirit Boxer movement so attractive. Whatever the precise and immediate causes, the salient fact is that the "Boxers United in Righteousness" (as the Spirit Boxers came to be known) grew rapidly in the immediate wake of the Yellow River floods. At the same time, the Spirit Boxers took on a distinctly anti-Christian and antiforeign character. By mid-1899, attacks on Christians—and other foreigners—were being reported in the provinces bordering Shantung to the west and northwest as well as throughout Shantung.

The initial Manchu reaction was hostile—in part, because Peking was still trying to avoid giving either Alliance an excuse to move deeper into China, and in part because many Manchu officials feared another Taiping or Nian-scale rebellion. But by the winter of 1900, an influential group at court had convinced the Empress Tzu Hsi to take advantage of the Great Power division and use the Boxers to drive all "foreigners" from China. In retrospect, it seems incredible that the Manchu leadership could have deluded themselves into thinking that the Boxers, even in combination with the Imperial army, could defeat the combined forces of the Great Powers—or even just the powerful Japanese garrison occupying the port city of Tientsin. But one must remember the degree to which Manchu decision making was shaped by their remarkable ignorance of the Western technical civilization; this willful disregard of technological advance was the true threat to continued Chinese sovereignty. In the case of the reactionary group at court that came to be known as the "Iron Hats," ignorance was a conscious choice—an aspect of a deeply held conviction that the West represented a threat to Chinese culture that could only be overcome by resisting any form of "contamination." Not that these reactionaries refused to countenance any reliance on Western technology. Although groups like the Iron Hats initially did oppose the importation of any foreign technology—not even the railroad was acceptable to the most slavish devotees of Chinese tradition—the evident inability of the Empire to resist Great Power encroachment, unless the Imperial army and navy were equipped with the barbarian's weaponry, at least allowed for the modernization of the armed forces to proceed. But what should have been the obvious lesson of the Sino–Japanese War—that merely acquiring modern weapons would not give the Manchus an army or navy capable of defeating any of the Great Powers in battle—was lost on the reactionaries at court. Instead, as Japan and Russia grappled for control of the Manchu homeland, the Iron Hats urged Tzu Hsi to seize the supposed resulting opportunity to "unleash" the Boxers and with them "drive the foreign devils" from China.

It was the fiasco of Japan's assault on Mukden which persuaded Tzu Hsi that now was indeed the time to "unleash" the Boxers. The Japanese attacked the last week of January 1900. The Russians were caught off guard; the Japanese drastically overestimated their own readiness; and the result was a bloody disaster all around—particularly for the people of Mukden, who found themselves caught in a ferocious urban battle which, like Memphis half a world away, presaged the horrors of urban warfare to come. By March, it was obvious that the Japanese and Russian armies were caught in a horrific meat grinder from which neither seemed able to escape either by victory or withdrawal. When the Japanese then reduced the garrison holding Tientsin to a single division (attempting to reinforce a deteriorating position on the Mukden front line), Prince Tuan—the leader of the Iron Hats—persuaded Tzu Hsi that the time was ripe to use the Boxers to expel the foreigners from Peking as the first step in effecting their expulsion from all of China.

Boxers had been streaming into Peking by the thousands for several weeks. Initially, the court became fearful at their presence and transferred Muslim troops from Kansu Province in the west to reinforce the local imperial garrison. But when the Empress was persuaded to let the Boxers loose on the foreign community in Peking, these additional forces were moved east to assume a position blocking the Japanese in Tientsin from coming to the rescue. The principal object of the Boxer attack would be the legations representing several of the Western powers and Japan. When China repudiated its treaty with Russia and declared neutrality in October 1898, the expected withdrawal of foreign representatives had not occurred. Even the Russians decided to keep their minister in place to preserve lines of communication with the Manchu authorities. The war, however, crippled the ability of the legations to respond in any coordinated fashion as the Boxer threat began to develop around them. When Sir Claude McDonald, the British ambassador, suggested the presentation of a joint note demanding that each country be allowed to augment their woefully inadequate military guards, the French and Russian ministers refused to sign—claiming that the Japanese would attack any French, Russian, or American forces that tried to move through Tientsin toward Peking. (In a rare display of North–South cooperation, the CSA and USA ministers both strongly endorsed McDonald's proposal.)

On June 8, the Boxers made their first move: burning down the grandstand of the Peking race course—a hated symbol of foreign privilege. The next day, Imperial troops took up threatening positions near the legation compound. McDonald telegraphed to the Japanese at Tientsin for help, claiming to speak for all the ministers at Peking. Whatever the subsequent doubts about McDonald's authorization to make this claim, there can be no disputing that his assertion of Great Power unity in the face of a Chinese threat would later have a profound impact on the Powers—albeit too late for McDonald or any of his ministerial colleagues. The Japanese in Tientsin showed commendable initiative, but the 1,500 troops dispatched toward Peking were thrown back by the overwhelmingly superior force of the Kansu Muslims. In the meantime, conditions in Peking rapidly deteriorated. On June 17, the Boxers overran the Peitang Cathedral two miles north of the legation quarter, slaughtering several dozen Europeans and over three thousand Chinese Christians. Emboldened by this horrific deed, the Empress Tzu Hsi formally declared war on June 21 against *all* foreign powers. This was the signal for a full-scale assault on the legation by Imperial troops as well as the Boxers. A devastating cannonade reduced the legation buildings to rubble, killing and wounding scores of Europeans along with hundreds of Chinese Christians who had sought shelter from marauding Boxers. On June 25, the guns fell silent, and thousands of Boxers and Imperial troops surged through the gaping breaches in the compound walls. The defenders were overwhelmed, and there ensued a ghastly slaughter of men, women, and children—Chinese as well as European and Japanese. (The dead included the French and Russian ministers who had opposed McDonald's demand for the right to reinforce legation defenses.)

Thus the Manchus won their first—and only—"victory" of what would also prove their last war. A small group of refugees, sheltered by Chinese opposed to Prince Tuan, reached Tientsin two weeks after the awful events of June 25. The Japanese commander of the Tientsin garrison had the news of what would come to be known as the "Legation Massacre" passed along to Tokyo as well as local representatives of Japan's German, British, and Confederate allies. By mid-July, the citizens of every Great Power had read with horror of the terrible fate shared by persons from every warring power—as well as citizens of several European neutrals. The uproar that ensued was spontaneous—and universal. A July 17 editorial by William Randolph Hearst aptly captured the sentiments expressed on both sides of the front lines:

> The civilizing powers have allowed their struggle to distract from the danger posed by a revival of Asiatic despotism, in the sinister person of the Chinese Empress and her band of eunuch courtiers. A fearful price, in the blood of men, women and children, has been paid as a consequence of this neglect. No more! Honor demands that the guns firing here, in Europe and the Far East be silenced so that every effort may be made to extirpate, once and for all, the loathsome and savage beast that is the Manchu and subject the Chinese masses to the direct and benevolent influence of a truly civilized rule.

Such sentiment alone probably would not have impelled the warring Powers to implement a "suspension of hostilities." The Legation Massacre, however, came at a time of acute vulnerability for both Alliances. The vulnerabilities were not symmetrical and reflected the new characteristics of mass industrialized war. But they were each sufficiently serious that the political leadership of the belligerents proved willing—in some cases, eager—to seize the chance for a respite created by the terrible events of June 1900 in Peking.

In essence, by the summer of 1900, the Great Power Alliances confronted two distinct and developing crises. The first, on the battlefield, threatened the Franco–American–Russian alliance with a decisive defeat in Europe and Asia. The second, on the home front, threatened the Anglo–German–Austrians with a paralyzing social upheaval due to a disastrous shortfall in grain supplies.

The reader will recall that, by the fall of 1899, the Mexican–American attempt to split the Confederacy had failed. The CSA had suffered a serious penetration of the Mississippi Valley by the North but had managed to stymie the Northern advance while routing Mexico's attack across the Rio Grande. The Mexicans had suffered a disastrous defeat: fifty thousand had been killed or wounded, another fifty thousand captured, and barely half of the attackers made it back across the river. This exhausted and demoralized force was in no state to hold against a determined Confederate counterassault.

Unfortunately for Mexico and its American ally, the Confederacy had resolved to launch just such an attack. A Confederate Mexican slave empire had been a dream of the country's leaders since Secession, and the opportunity to make progress on that goal—by overrunning the Northwestern Mexican states of Coahuila, Nuevo León, and Tamaulipas—now proved irresistible. Moreover, an attack across the Rio Grande would provide the Tillman Administration at least some political cover for what must soon be acknowledged as the bloody failure of its attempt to win Maryland for the Confederacy. To launch an attack across the Rio Grande, the Confederate General Staff would transfer to Texas the bulk of the forces still engaged in besieging Baltimore and holding forward positions along the Maryland–Pennsylvania border; a rump force would then withdraw to fortified lines anchored on the ruins of Washington, D.C. The Confederates expected the North to launch a massive effort to drive "Johnny" from Northern soil; pulling back from what had become an exposed position into a powerful defensive one—and still on the "Yankee" side of the Potomac—would at least retain a "bargaining chip" that might be traded away at a future peace conference.

By December 1899, the Confederates had amassed over three hundred thousand troops for the attack into Mexico. This move had not gone unremarked by the Mexican and American General Staffs, but there was precious little that could be done to shore up Mexican defenses. On December 24, the Confederates struck, concentrating their attack in three columns. The Mexicans still had the benefit of a strong fortified defensive line, and

initial CSA casualties were high. But the weakened Mexican troops holding that line soon gave way. By New Year's Day, the Mexicans were in full
retreat, and Confederate columns were slashing deep into Nuevo León and
Tamaulipas; only in Coahuila did the Mexicans hold. (And even here, the
CSA managed to seize the city of Piedras Negras and establish a threatening lodgment extending some forty miles into the interior.) As Confederate
forces overran Monterrey (the capital of Nuevo León) and approached
Ciudad Victoria (the capital of Tamaulipas), a desperate President Diaz
urged USA President McKinley, as well as Columbian President Reyes, to
send aid—troops, as well as badly needed materiel—lest "the enemy reach
the gates of Mexico City itself."

The unfolding disaster in Mexico knocked American plans into a cocked
hat. Until the Confederates broke through Mexican defenses, the American
General Staff was still planning a push to drive CSA forces back across
the Potomac, followed by a renewal of Canadian operations—particularly,
the long-delayed assault against Ontario. But when the Mexican defenses
crumbled, the Americans recognized that they would have to effect a rapid
transfer of thousands of troops—as well as vast quantities of equipment
and supplies—lest Mexico's resistance collapse and the Confederates literally overrun the country. Once again, the Ontario attack was postponed: as
it turned out, for fourteen years. Moreover, the Confederate withdrawal to
fortified lines anchored on Washington had converted a Northern opportunity (an overextended Southern position, vulnerable to a flanking attack)
into a dangerous challenge (how to crack a tough defensive position and
without suffering terrible casualties in the process). Although Northern
forces followed the withdrawing Confederates back into Maryland and the
beleaguered citizens of Baltimore celebrated the end of over a year of an
unending CSA bombardment—a celebration muted by the fact that over
90 percent of the city had been leveled by enemy guns—there was little
question that the demands of the Mexican crisis would allow the Johnnies
to remain in their entrenchments, still in possession of Washington and its
immediate environs.

There was substantially more controversy over the General Staff's recommendation not to resume offensive operations in the Mississippi Valley.
Many politicians, and virtually every major newspaper editorial page,

called loudly for a renewed thrust toward New Orleans. "The best way to help our brave Mexican ally and also to strike Johnny a blow from which he may never recover would be to march down the Mississippi River Valley to the sea," urged the *New York Times*, in an editorial that aptly captured what were likely the views of an overwhelming majority of the American public. But the professional advice given President McKinley was blunt and left no room for politically impelled fudgery: Unless the USA moved every available resource to Mexico's aid, a vital ally would collapse within six weeks— with calamitous consequences for America's strategic position. McKinley agreed. There would be no resumption of offensive operations anywhere until the Mexican front had been stabilized.

Fortunately for Mexico, once the USA made the decision to help, the Americans proved they had the wherewithal to intervene quickly and decisively. Unlike during the Western War, the Confederacy made no move to disrupt the USA's Southwestern rail network—not even when the Confederate army launched its attack across the Rio Grande into Northwestern Mexico. The Confederate command hoped that a quick victory over Mexico would excuse what in reality was an operational omission compelled by an inability to muster forces sufficient to launch both a full-scale invasion of Mexico and an attack into the USA Southwest. This omission proved a strategic miscalculation of the first order, as the Americans proved able to rush forces "around the bend" of West Texas on Atchison, Topeka & Santa Fe trains. These locomotives could proceed directly onto the lines of the Ferrocarril Mexicano due to the shrewd decision of nearly a generation before to coordinate the development of the Southwestern American and Mexican railway lines so they would be ready to facilitate precisely this kind of maneuver in response to a Confederate invasion of Mexico. Over 250,000 troops were moved from the Midwest and East of the USA in less than six weeks to concentration points centered on Monclova in Coahuila and Ciudad Victoria in Tamaulipas. Ciudad Victoria was already under fire from long-range Confederate artillery, and the Americans found themselves hurried to the front where they went directly into action against the approaching Confederates.

Although the CSA General Staff knew the American troop transfer was underway, the speed of their arrival on the battlefield caught "Johnny" off guard. The advance on Ciudad Victoria ground to a halt as the Mexicans and Americans established an effective defensive line north and east of the city. Meanwhile, to the west (in Coahuila), a second American force launched an attack against the Confederate right flank, hoping to unhinge the enemy line and compel a general CSA withdrawal. This effort, however, did not succeed. The Confederates proved to have anticipated the move in sufficient time to put in place a defensive entrenchment network, and the American attacks were cut down in waves—just as the Confederates trying to batter their way into Ciudad Victoria were slaughtered by Mexican and American Gatling guns and artillery fire. By May, both sides realized that neither could make progress through continued attacks—at least not with the forces immediately available for offensive operations. There ensued a race to build up the reserves of men and supplies required both to check an enemy attack and also to exploit the opportunity for a breakthrough.

This was the battlefield situation in North America when the public clamor arose for a suspension of hostilities and united action against the Manchu. As for Europe, 1900 saw an increasingly isolated France preparing for an Anglo-German invasion, while the Russians suffered a serious strategic reverse with the entry of the Ottoman Empire on the side of Germany and Austria–Hungary, whose armies had renewed offensive operations that May.

By 1900, France's leadership recognized that it could not achieve its principal goal of the restoration of Alsace and Lorraine to French rule. This brought on a political crisis of the first order. Georges Clemenceau now became premier as the leader of an avowed "War Cabinet" that pledged "merciless prosecution" of the struggle with Germany. But Clemenceau, however bellicose in public, recognized privately that France lacked the ability to smash through the ever thickening German defenses blocking further progress anywhere along the Alsace–Lorraine front lines. Worse, France now confronted the need to look to her own defenses against the increasing likelihood that Germany and Austria would shift forces west and try to achieve there the decisive victory that had—so far—eluded them in the east.

In this regard, the real danger did not come from a "role reversal" in Alsace–Lorraine but from the possibility of such an attack combined with landings along the Channel coast. The Battle of Sable Island had given the Anglo–German alliance effective control of the North Atlantic. The French fleet, weakened by its crushing defeat off Majorca at the outset of the war, lacked the ability to repel an invasion—should the British and Germans concentrate their forces in support of such an effort. Because of Sable Island (which had neutralized the American naval threat to Canada), the British could seriously contemplate the possibility of transferring a substantial portion of the Royal Navy's North Atlantic squadron to Home Island waters, where it could support an Austro–German landing (e.g., along the Normandy coast). Thus, instead of concentrating the French army for one more push in Alsace–Lorraine, Clemenceau faced the need to divert resources to begin the preparation of some sort of defensive network along the coast. And Clemenceau was right to begin that effort, for the German and Austro–Hungarian General Staffs had begun discussions with their British counterparts as well as with representatives of the Royal Navy and the *Kaiserliche Marine* about effecting a landing in France—to take place in the spring of 1901.

But first, the Germans and Austrians intended to make one more effort to compel Tsar Nicholas II to "see reason" and withdraw from an alliance that had—so far—brought his empire nothing but trouble. The problem for Germany and Austria–Hungary, however, was Russia's stubborn unwillingness to recognize its seeming best interests. Peace feelers, communicated through the good offices of the King of Denmark, had been peremptorily rebuffed. Still, as Germany and Austro–Hungarian staff planners contemplated the upcoming spring campaign choices, there remained at least some reason to believe they could break Russia's continued adherence to its alliance with France and the USA. Above all else, Berlin and Vienna knew—upon the completion of secret negotiations conducted for reasons of security at the remote Bavarian town of Berchtesgaden, near the German–Austrian border—that the forces of the Ottoman Empire would be unleashed against Russia. Nor was this an inconsiderable point. Since Europe had divided into hostile camps in the mid-1890s, Sultan Abdulhamit II and his ministers had recognized that, in the event of war between the Alliances, Constantinople would probably be unable to remain neutral for the duration of the conflict. But while the centuries-old rivalry with Russia may have argued for open adherence to the Anglo–German–Austrian coalition, the Porte realized that modernization of the Ottoman armed forces lagged dangerously behind those of Russia. Moreover, during the Russo–Turkish War less than twenty years before, the Russians had come perilously close to capturing Constantinople and forcing the Empire's dismemberment. Unless Turkey could be assured that Germany and Austria–Hungary would be able to prevent the Russians from launching an all-out drive to overrun European Turkey and seize the Dardanelles, the Sultan and his ministers did not feel sufficiently secure to take the risk of open adherence to an anti-Russian coalition.

Although both Berlin and Vienna attempted to reassure Constantinople that, indeed, the German and Austrian armies would push the Russians with such vigor that they could not divert forces sufficient to mount a serious threat against the Dardanelles, ultimately, the Sultan concluded that Turkey should not openly adhere to an Austro–German alliance until sufficient progress had been made on modernization of the Ottoman armed forces. In 1896, the Porte had begun implementation of a six-year plan, intended to double the size of the army while also providing the latest in arms and to effect a complete overhaul in training so as to assure the troop's readiness to fight against the Russians on at least fairly equal terms. When war broke out in October 1898, the Porte demurred to importunings by Berlin and Vienna that Turkey come in immediately against the Russians. "Give us another year of preparation, and we shall see," the Ottoman Ambassador told an impatient member of the German General Staff early in November 1898. Of course, what the Porte was also waiting for was a clear indication that the Germans and Austrians would be able to give the Russians sufficient trouble that St. Petersburg would be unable to threaten Constantinople.

By the fall of 1899, the Ottoman General Staff could report to the Sultan that the Austro–German armies had dealt a crushing defeat to the principal Russian forces facing them in Poland. Moreover, the Russians had suffered serious reverses in Central Asia and Northeast Asia—indeed, on every major front, their forces had been defeated and were in retreat. Despite the fact that the Ottoman modernization program was not scheduled to be completed until 1902 (and actually was lagging behind in the vital category of improving the army's logistical support capacity), Abdulhamit II decided it was time for Turkey to enter the fray. "We have been retreating ever since Küchük Kainarji," the Sultan is reputed to have said at the decisive meeting with his ministers in October of 1899. (Abdulhamit was referring to the treaty between the Russian and Ottoman empires in 1774, under which the Porte made the first of what would prove a debilitating series of territorial concessions to St. Petersburg.) "Now, we begin the task of undoing all of that and restoring the glory that was ours under Suleiman the Magnificent." A team of negotiators was dispatched to hammer out the terms of Constantinople's entry into the war. Berchtesgaden was selected as the site for these talks because of lingering concern on the Porte's part that Russian spies in any of the three capitals involved might uncover the ongoing discussions, and that Russia—as weakened as it might be—would make a preemptive strike out of the Caucasus (which Turkey intended to be the focus of her own offensive). By mid-January, the negotiations—to which the British also sent representatives—were effectively complete. Initially, Turkey would concentrate on a land-based thrust out of Anatolia. When the Russians had been fully engaged, a second Ottoman army, supported by a powerful squadron comprised of elements of the Turkish and Austrian navies as well as a battle group on detached service from the Royal Navy's Mediterranean Fleet, would be landed on the Crimea. This latter force would not make the conquest of the Crimean peninsula its primary objective. Instead, the Turks—joined by two divisions of the British Indian Army, which could now be spared in light of Great Britain's triumphant conclusion of the Afghanistan campaign—would leave blocking forces to contain the Russians in Sevastopol and push north and east into the Ukraine. The goal was to link up with Austro–German forces east of Kiev, thereby achieving the occupation of a substantial portion of the Ukrainian grain lands and perhaps bringing relief to the increasingly desperate food situation faced by the urban populations of Germany and Austria–Hungary.

This ambitious plan proved beyond the capabilities of the turn-of-century armies involved. They lacked both the mass and mobility required to achieve what their successors could—and would—accomplish sixteen years later. But while the ultimate strategic goal may have been unrealistic, the weakened state of the Russian armed forces made them vulnerable to local defeats that could further undermine the political base in St. Petersburg for continuing the war.

The Germans and Austrians renewed their offensive in May. Nearly three hundred thousand troops had been transferred to the southern flank of the Austro–German position in Poland as well as even farther south along the border between Russia and Austria–Hungary along a northwest–southeast axis running from just east of Rava Russkaya to Czernowitz (the latter lying at the intersection of Austrian Galicia, the Russian Ukraine, and Rumania). The resulting force of nearly five hundred thousand would strike east out of this corridor and drive in a concentrated front toward Kiev; the balance would hold the line north against a possible Russian counterattack. The attack got off well, and the Austro–German columns made remarkable progress—especially considering that neither the Germans nor the Austro–Hungarians had any motor vehicle transport. By mid-June, however, the advance had become badly overextended, and the Russians were able to concentrate superior forces near the Ukrainian town of Zhitomir. Poor coordination between the Germans and Austrians—aggravated by Berlin's acquiescence in Vienna's insistence that an attack launched out of Austrian territory be commanded by an Austrian—produced a Russian victory that not only stopped the Austro–German advance but actually required the attackers to give up nearly half the territory gained to date. Still, by mid-summer, Austro–German forces remained lodged deep into the Ukraine, and this represented another damaging blow to the prestige of the Tsar's regime.

This blow, moreover, was exacerbated by developments farther south. On the same day, the Germans and Austro–Hungarians struck east, Ottoman armies attacked out of Anatolia, and the Turks truly caught their bitter Russian rivals napping. Bypassing—and isolating—the Black Sea port of Batum, the Ottoman forces swept up into Georgia, while a second column drove northwest toward Kars and a third toward Erivan in Russian Armenia. A combination of difficult terrain, a still-rudimentary supply train, and desperate Russian counterattacks forced the Turks to halt short of their principal goals (although the Russians were compelled to evacuate Kars). But there could be no denying that the Russian Empire had suffered a grievous blow to her prestige: and from an enemy who had known virtually nothing but defeat at Russian hands for over two hundred years. St. Petersburg, however, was spared the planned Anglo–Turkish assault on the Crimea. The Crimean landings had been scheduled for June 15, but the strain of Caucasus operations on the Turkish logistical system caused the Porte to order a thirty-day delay. By then, news of the Legation Massacre had thrown all Great Power capitals into turmoil, and the ensuing decision in favor of a suspension of hostilities would put plans for the Crimean invasion on ice.

This was the state of the principal battlefronts at the time of the Legation Massacre crisis. (I have not discussed the struggle in Africa, because Africa was not a strategically vital area during World War One; I will deal with Africa when I address the terms of the Peace of Rio de Janeiro, which ended the First World War in 1901.) As the reader can surmise, by mid-1900, the battlefield relations of the combatants clearly favored the forces of the Anglo–German Alliance. France's efforts to reclaim Alsace and Lorraine had been frustrated, and the French were girding themselves to repel an Anglo–German attack. Russia had experienced a series of reverses in Europe and Asia: it had been driven from Russian Poland; had suffered an invasion of the Ukraine and the Caucasus; and had been placed on the defensive by Japan in Manchuria. The USA had been unable to prevent a Japanese–Confederate conquest of the Spanish Philippines; had suffered the loss of its capital and devastating raids on two of its principal port cities; and had been forced to divert substantial forces to prevent a potentially decisive defeat of Mexico by Confederate invaders. On the other hand, the Americans and Spanish had held the line in the Marianas, while the Americans had destroyed the Royal Navy's North Pacific squadron; had conquered British Columbia and overrun the Canadian Great Plains; and had driven deep into the Confederate Mississippi Valley. Still, there could be no gainsaying that the Anglo–German coalition held the upper hand on the battlefield as the war had approached the end of its second year.

This battlefield imbalance, however, was at least matched by the increasingly desperate circumstances of the Anglo–German–Austrian home front. The problem, in a word, was grain. The reader will recall that, at the time of the war's outbreak, Great Britain, Germany, and Austria-Hungary were dependent on grain imports, of which a substantial portion came from the USA and Russia—by then, the world's primary grain producers. In fact, World War One coincided with what would prove to be the moment of greatest dependence by the Anglo–German–Austrian coalition on these sources and therefore of maximum vulnerability to the wielding of the "food weapon" by the USA and its allies. After 1900, spurred by the nearly fatal experience of the First Alliance War, Great Britain would take the lead in developing alternative grain supplies. As the reader will see, these efforts—along with other measures (such as improved food-storage systems and encouraging a shift in consumption toward legumes)—would effectively blunt the food weapon when America and Russia attempted to wield it with even greater determination during World War Two. None of these measures, however, were in place at the outbreak of World War One, and by the spring of 1900, the British, Germans, and Austrians—particularly the British—were suffering privation at home nearly proportionate to the success of their arms on the war's far-flung battlefields.

Rationing was introduced by Germany within a month of the war's outbreak, and Austria–Hungary quickly followed suit—although only in the Austrian territory of the Dual Monarchy and then only in Vienna and other principal cities. Incredibly, Great Britain, the alliance member most dependent on foreign grain supplies now cut off by hostilities, delayed instituting any form of rationing until March 1899—nearly six months into the fight. Yet, even when in full operation, rationing alone could not effectively address the fundamental problem: that the diet of the British, German, and Austro–Hungarian urban working and middle class had shifted over a generation to a heavy dependence on products based on grain imports. Wheat bread had replaced rye, and the high-protein strains grown in the USA and Russia were preferred over lower-protein local strains. To the resulting direct dependence on foreign grain sources had to be added the indirect dependence created by increased consumption of fat proteins in the form of meat also raised on foreign grain sources. Crash programs to fill the ensuing protein gap (e.g., developing urban vegetable garden plots by converting Hyde Park in London and the Tiergarten in Berlin) could only go so far. Nor could increased purchases from neutral or secure grain sources (such as Argentina and Australia) make up the difference represented by the complete cutoff of supply from the world's two principal grain producers.

By the fall of 1899, death rates among the most vulnerable populations—the elderly and young children—had begun to rise.

In a constitutional monarchy like the United Kingdom, with a working class at least partially enfranchised for some thirty years, human suffering had direct and destabilizing political consequences. An emboldened Asquith attacked the Unionist government in terms that fell on increasingly receptive ears:

> What have we to show for the privations of our people? How many victories won by our Navy are worth the death by starvation of the most venerable and most vulnerable among us? I see no glory in our course: only the dishonor of a government too stubborn to admit its policy has driven this country into a cul-de-sac of suffering and privation.

Nor did the fact that the opposition was not prepared openly to advocate the only alternative policy that might immediately restore the flow of foreign foodstuffs—a separate peace with the USA and its allies—change the political reality of an erosion in government support by a public whose miserable state bred angry resentment at the expense of dispassionate analysis. Then, in April of 1900, a food riot in London's East End got the better of the Metropolitan Police. For the first time in nearly a century, a British government was compelled to use regular army troops to restore order in the nation's capital. A worried Queen Victoria wrote to her Prime Minister expressing concern that "this terrible war has begun to erode the very foundation of our constitution." To which Salisbury could only respond: "Your Majesty knows the stakes for which we are engaged—and it remains my firm belief that we must, and still can, see this struggle through to a victory whose scope should justify the undeniable sacrifices of your people."

This was the shape of the global struggle at the moment when the news of the Legation Massacre burst like a thunderclap upon every warring capital. The immediate concern was the port city of Tientsin, held by a single understrength Japanese division and now a refuge to which hundreds of European and Japanese civilians—and thousands of Chinese Christians—had fled even before the terrifying news from Peking. The Imperial troops from Kansu Province, which had already given the Japanese a bloody nose when they tried to move toward Peking, were reported to have begun a march on Tientsin. The Japanese garrison, fearing the city would be overrun and a second massacre even more frightful than Peking would be perpetrated, asked for reinforcements. But the Japanese General Staff could send no help without weakening—perhaps fatally—the fighting lines at Mukden. Here was the immediate tactical and strategic genesis of the "suspension of hostilities" that would create the opportunity for a general armistice and peace negotiations that would bring the First World War to a close the following year, for the only way the Japanese could reinforce the Tientsin garrison would be to transfer forces from the Mukden line. But the only way the Japanese could effect such a transfer would be if the Russians agreed to a cease-fire. And if the Russians would not agree, Manchu forces would almost certainly seize Tientsin, and a second massacre would ensue.

Such might have been the case, if not for the presence in Tientsin of a young American mining engineer named Herbert Hoover. Hoover had a knack for organizing scarce resources in desperate times and also for conveying the need for action in language that instantly seized the public imagination. Best remembered for his extraordinary work that saved literally hundreds of thousands of Russian Jews from starving to death in the Turkish and Persian refugee camps to which they fled at the end of World War Two, Hoover's twin talents for humanitarian organization and publicity ("[t]he world lives by phrases," he told the *Saturday Evening Post* years later) were put to their first real test in Tientsin. Without those abilities, Hoover would probably have perished as an unknown mining engineer, and the world would have been denied the services of "the Great Humanitarian." But Hoover had those abilities, and as he set about—aided by his equally dedicated and energetic wife, Lou—to bring order out of the chaos of a city flooded with thousands of refugees, Hoover worked on a report addressed to USA President William McKinley. In that report, Hoover marshaled a powerful case for the "taking of every step necessary, no matter the political cost, to organize a campaign by every representative of the world's great and powerful nations, to restore order in China and prevent the murder of tens of thousands of Christian men, women, and children—White as well as Chinese." Hoover's report closed by urging

McKinley to "take the course of duty and righteousness, even at the cost of victory on some distant battlefield."

Hoover's Quaker-inspired missionary plea reached President McKinley through the fortunate good offices of the British government (who received the report from their Japanese ally). The commander of the beleaguered Tientsin garrison, overwhelmed by the burden of coping with refugees as well as defending against a Manchu assault, accepted Hoover's offer of assistance notwithstanding that the man was an enemy national, and then was completely won over by the American's obvious effectiveness in bringing life-saving order out of death-dealing chaos. Hoover's words struck home with an equally devout American president, who was sickened by the prospect of another "Chinese Horror" and eager to use any excuse to compel at least a suspension of global fighting that had already taken over two million lives. Recognizing that the immediate need was a cease-fire in Manchuria so the Japanese could shift forces south to defend Tientsin, McKinley appealed by a telegrammed letter to Tsar Nicholas II. In his letter, McKinley proposed that a cease-fire should be granted even if limited to the Northeast Asian front. But McKinley went beyond the notion of a local cease-fire, noting that the repulse of the Manchu threat to Tientsin would only "put balm on the wound, when the real need is to lance the underlying abscess":

> The civilized nations must act now to restore order in China.
> If this requires a suspension of the present hostilities in their
> entirety, so much the better.

McKinley's proposal for both a local cease-fire and a general "suspension of hostilities" (as the proposal came to be known) was seized upon by Nicholas as a chance to deliver Russia from a disastrous military *cul-de-sac*. The Tsar promptly notified the Japanese that Russia would honor a local cease-fire in Manchuria "to allow the Imperial Japanese Army the opportunity to stabilize the dangerous conditions in and around the port city of Tientsin." Simultaneously, McKinley and Nicholas issued an open call for a general "suspension of hostilities" for the twin purpose of organizing a "joint effort" by the "civilized world" to "restore order" in China and to use the resulting respite from fighting among some of the members of that civilized world to try to bring global war to a "peaceful and satisfactory resolution."

The combination of Russia's generous gesture of a local cease-fire and the call for a general suspension of hostilities proved an irresistible master stroke. Salisbury and Chamberlain, (confronted by a Liberal minority in the House of Commons demanding acceptance and massive street demonstrations by the middle and working class of London and other cities supporting that demand) agreed that the government would have to say "yes"—or face defeat on a vote of confidence. "If we say 'no' now," Chamberlin advised Lord Salisbury, "I cannot assure you that the Unionist lines in the Commons will hold." "And even if they do," the weary and aging Prime Minister replied, "we cannot be sure that the mob will respect the authority of that decision"—a frank acknowledgment that the government could not count on the police and army to suppress a violent uprising aiming at the overthrow of the government in the name of peace. (McKinley's confidential assurances of a swift resumption of grain shipments to Great Britain—in exchange for Salisbury delivering a Confederate "standstill" along the Mexican front—provided additional impetus.) London informed Berlin, Vienna, Constantinople, Richmond, and Tokyo that Her Majesty's Government would accept the proposal for a general suspension of hostilities and "recommended" that her allies do likewise. Faced with the alternative of a unilateral British withdrawal from the war, those allies had little choice but to follow suit. (The USA's and Russia's allies had already done so, although a suspicious Clemenceau had delayed France's acceptance until the last possible moment.) On August 14, 1900, the Suspension of Hostilities went into effect across the globe. Although no one could then know for sure, the First World War—at least the fighting stage—had come to a close.

(above) **Russian Troops, elements of the Great Power Expeditionary Force, storming the gates of Peking.**

(left) **The Dowager Empress Tzu-Hsi, who encouraged the Boxer attack on the Foreign Legations in Peking, setting in motion the events that would end with the destruction of the city by the Great Power Expeditionary Force, the overthrow of the Manchu Dynasty, and the partition of China.**

20

WORLD WAR I (7): THE SUPPRESSION OF THE MANCHUS BY THE GREAT POWERS' JOINT INTERVENTION FORCE AND THE ENSUING PARTITION OF CHINA—A PRINCIPAL TERM OF THE PEACE OF RIO DE JANEIRO, WHICH BRINGS THE WAR TO ITS FORMAL END

The end of fighting between the Warring Powers by no means meant the end to all conflict directly attributable to the outbreak of the war. In China, the Manchu Court was at war, by its own declaration, with all foreign powers present on Chinese soil. The Empress—and the xenophobic advisers who persuaded her to issue that declaration—had gambled on the Powers being too deeply engaged in their own conflict to resist a concerted Manchu push. Although the notion that the Manchu army could eject the Powers from their Chinese holdings (even with the Powers' local forces reduced to a bare minimum) reflected the impoverished state of Manchu strategic thinking, one must also admit that the plan made some sense—at least as to China north of the Yangtze River. Had the Court exercised greater control over the forces that stormed the Legations and insisted on the delegations being taken alive (perhaps to be expelled in a gesture mixing mercy with firmness), the Manchus just might have acquired a position of some advantage from which to negotiate better terms once the Great Power War came to a close. But the Court did not exercise that control, and the ensuing massacre united the Powers in an angry determination to bring an end to Manchu rule. Even then, if the Kansu Muslim force had moved quickly against the understrength Japanese holding Tientsin, the Manchus might have bought time at least to negotiate a peace under which they would have preserved a semblance of their rule, as the powerful Taku Forts guarding the approach to Tientsin would have presented a formidable challenge to any Great Power force attempting to mount a drive on Peking.

But the Kansu Muslims did not move against Tientsin. Instead, they took up defensive positions almost twenty miles inland, while their commander returned to Peking—apparently for reasons of internal court politics, related to a move by opponents of Prince Tuan to persuade the Empress to abandon the "anti-foreigners" war. For six weeks, the Manchus made no move against Tientsin, and when they finally did, they were easily repulsed by the advance guard of the powerful force that the Powers had by now assembled and which was preparing to move against Peking.

War-induced suspicions prompted the division of this force in two columns: split along alliance lines. The larger, amounting to some sixty thousand troops, represented the Anglo–German alliance; although the Japanese contributed the bulk of the force, the British and Germans insisted on a European general to command. (The Japanese yielded to this piece of racialist insensitivity with surprising good grace, considering their preponderance provided a powerful case for a Japanese commander.) Confederate cavalry and "British" India Army Gurka troops rounded out this first column. The second column of forty thousand men represented Russia and its allies, but in reality, it was an overwhelmingly Russian operation, with only token representation for the USA (a Marine contingent), Spain, and France. General Nikolai Linevich, commander of the First Siberian Army Corps, assumed overall command.

Coordination between the two columns proved fitful at best, but the opposing Manchu forces were incapable of exploiting this potential weakness. It took less than two weeks for the Powers to push past weak Manchu resistance—General Tung Fu-hsiang actually withdrew the bulk of his Kansu army to the *west* of Peking, thereby assuring the city's swift fall but also preserving his force for the civil conflict that would ensue if, as anticipated, the avenging Powers insisted upon the end of Manchu rule. General Guwalgiya Jung-lu, commander of the Wuwei Troop—a modern combined arms force with direct responsibility for guarding the Forbidden City itself—similarly declined to defend the capital. (What these two generals and virtually every other member of the Chinese elite did not anticipate was the determination of the Powers to use the Legation Massacre as an excuse to partition the country outright.) As the columns approached the capital, Tzu Hsi tried to assuage foreign anger by moving against the Iron Hats, whose advice the Empress had followed to such disastrous effect. Prince Tuan and dozens of others were arrested; Tzu Hsi also prevailed upon the aged statesman Li Huang Chang to attempt to open peace negotiations. But Li and his delegation were arrested by the Russians—Li had sought them out, hoping these former allies would prove receptive to a dialogue—and the Powers continued their advance, coming within artillery range of Peking by the first of October. Promptly, the guns opened up, raining down destruction for a forty-eight-hour period. This deliberate echo of the bombardment of the legation quarter, which had immediately preceded the Manchu and Boxer assault, devastated the ancient heart of Peking while throwing the Manchu Court into complete disarray.

(A preliminary note about sources is in order, as what I am about to relate will come as a shock to all but the handful of readers who, like myself, have had access to our government's voluminous "closed" files. Unfortunately, my recounting must be based on the limited notes I made of the "China Expedition" records; I was not able to make any duplicates, and the originals undoubtedly were lost along with the balance of the National Archives when Philadelphia was destroyed by German H-bombs at the outset of the fourth, and final, Alliance War. Nonetheless, I hope those of my readers inclined by national pride to doubt the veracity of what follows will recognize the pain it causes me, a former President of the USA, to disclose the role American forces played in such atrocious and indefensible conduct. I feel compelled to set the record straight—for history's sake if no other. After all, at this point, what do we have left, save our duty to make an honest accounting at history's bar?)

The destruction of Peking which now ensued must be understood as *the* harbinger—*the* warning sign—of the course and quality of twentieth century history. Americans insist that the "sack" of Washington City by the Confederacy or the destruction wrought by the Great Raids of the Royal

Navy against New York City and Boston qualify as *the* precedent-setting "outrages" for our benighted times. Confederates respond by denying there was any sack of Washington and point to the plundering of Memphis one year later. Then there are the Poles, a people deprived of nationhood for centuries, who may argue that the horrific Siege of Warsaw should take "pride of place" at the head of what would prove so long and awful a list. Nor should one forget the suffering of the people of Mukden. But what the Powers' "Joint Chinese Pacification Force" wrought in Peking in October 1900 eclipsed anything done by any Power to that date: both in scope of material destruction and wanton disregard for human life.

The myth of the destruction of Peking holds that the city was sacked by the Boxers and renegade Manchu troops, following the flight of Empress Tzu Hsi and her court, before the forces of the Powers entered through the wreck of the city's ancient gates. Indeed, this widely circulated tale was proffered as "proof" of the need to subject China to the Powers' "protective rule"—in other words, as a justification for suppressing Chinese self-rule and partitioning the country. But while there was undoubted looting and other forms of lawlessness engaged in by the city's criminal elements as the guns of the expeditionary force shattered both Manchu social control along with the palaces of the Forbidden City, the historical record paints a far different picture of the causes for Peking's fate.

First, the guns of the Powers devastated the city. The imperial quarter was wrecked, and fires set within and outside its confines quickly spread out of control. Within twenty-four hours, the city was a sea of fire from which hundreds of thousands sought to flee. Although the Empress, her nephew Emperor Kuang-Hsu, and a handful of her closest courtiers managed to escape the blaze, little or nothing of the artistic treasures built up over the centuries by a succession of dynasties could be saved.

Second, this cultural holocaust was followed by a true sack: as brutal as any carried out by the Mongol hordes of Genghis Khan. Nor was this a case of troops who broke loose from a commander's restraint and could not be brought to heel until after they had their way with a helpless populace. To the contrary, the Powers intended their forces to wreak havoc—an act of policy by terror designed to cow the Chinese into accepting the partition of their country.

Here is how the confidential Report to the Secretary of War on the Conduct of the Joint Expeditionary Force put the matter, just three weeks after the fall of Peking:

> The suppression of the Manchus in Peking has been carried out with a thorough-going brutality. Although we may question the extent to which the Expeditionary Forces have employed techniques more typical of the enemy than of civilized armies, still it must be conceded the undeniable effectiveness of the methods of "the Hun"—as the German Kaiser so aptly characterized such tactics—when it comes to impressing an Oriental population such as the Chinese.

Moreover, that same report discloses how the Powers from the outset conspired to hide the true nature of their forces' actions from publics not yet accustomed to accept the employment of such methods as legitimate tactics of war among Western "civilized" nations:

> Earlier, we referred to Kaiser Wilhelm II's comment about employing the methods of the Huns against the Manchus. It is unfortunate that the Kaiser chose to make his comments in so public a setting as the leave-taking from Bremerhaven of a contingent of German marines being dispatched to join the Expeditionary Forces gathering in Tientsin. Fortunately, conditions in Peking have been sufficiently isolated from the inquiries of the press that it has been possible to divert attention from the actions of the Forces. In this regard, the willingness of the public to believe the worst of the enemy has been of invaluable service.

In short, the widely accepted tale of a city destroyed by the Manchus was just that—a tale put about to help obscure the actual facts, which were that the city was deliberately given over to the Powers' troops to do with as they would.

For over a week, the Chinese inhabitants of Peking suffered theft, beatings, rapine, and worse. At least twenty-five thousand perished in the bombardment and fires; perhaps as many again died at the hands of the Powers' troops. To be sure, anarchic conditions contributed to these casualties, as European troops, whipped into a frenzy over the Boxers, were all too quick to employ gunfire—including Gatling, Maxim, and artillery—against crowds feared to be Boxer mobs readying for the attack. But even these extenuating circumstances cannot fully account for the extent of the pillage and violence visited upon what was, in fact, an unarmed, terrified, and thoroughly cowed population.

By October 15, the commanders of the Powers' forces were satisfied that Peking and the immediate area had been effectively pacified. Initial reports indicated that the Empress and her surviving retinue had fled inland, seeking refuge in the city of Hsi-an. But then came news that the imperial refugees had been waylaid and everyone—including Tzu Hsi and her nephew, the Emperor—murdered. To this day, no one has been able to confirm the identity either of the immediate perpetrators or their sponsors. Be that as it may, the sudden removal of the principal symbols of Manchu authority radically simplified the Powers' task. Once the death of the Dowager Empress and Emperor had been confirmed, representatives of the Powers who had gathered in Tientsin agreed to the issuance of a declaration finding that "legitimate authority" in China had "ceased to function"; proclaiming that the "former Chinese Empire" had "reverted" to the "protective supervision" of the "civilized world"; and directing that the disposition of China should be referred to a "general conference of all interested powers" for the resolution. This declaration was issued on November 1; by that time, the suspension of hostilities had ripened into a *de facto* armistice, and the belligerent powers were in the process of accepting the invitation of the Empire of Brazil to send representatives to a peace conference to be held in the Brazilian capital of Rio de Janeiro.

The reader will recall how the efforts of Brazilian Prime Minister Rio-Branco had avoided war between Argentina and Chile in 1898, and that the good feelings engendered by this process helped to keep South America's "Southern Core" Powers on the sidelines at the outbreak of World War One. By the mid-summer of 1900, however, the strains of global war had substantially dissipated those sentiments. Colombia's decision to close the Panama Canal to "hostile" traffic and search all neutral ships suspected of carrying "contraband" goods destined for enemy destinations had caused an uproar in Chile at the outset of the war. Only the ability to pass along the increased cost of shipping around the Horn may have kept Chile from joining the fray on the Anglo–German side—a decision that could have changed the course of the war, given Chile's near-monopoly position as the world's nitrate source and the rudimentary state of research into synthetic alternatives. Then, as Chile's nitrate industry battened on the orders placed by both sides, the Chilean government decided to invest much of their nitrate tax earnings in an accelerated expansion of the Chilean army and navy—a choice that alarmed Argentina, which accurately saw the move as directed against it.

Argentines began openly debating the merits of joining the USA-led alliance and launching a "preventive" campaign against Chile—possibly recruiting Bolivia and Peru for the effort. To be sure, powerful interests opposed such a move, especially given Argentina's economic dependence on trade with Great Britain (whose purchases of Argentine grain and beef had skyrocketed since the cutoff of supplies from the USA). But the fact of these interests could not stifle a lively and open debate, and this talk in turn alarmed Chilean moderates and stoked the fires for Chilean nationalists. Moreover, Santiago was already alarmed by talk in Philadelphia of moving to cut off the flow of nitrates to the Anglo–German alliance by seizing the mining centers of Antofagasta Province (itself seized by Chile from Bolivia during the War of the Pacific). Members of the Chilean military now approached their Brazilian counterparts to urge that Santiago and Rio de Janeiro strike before Buenos Aires could organize an alliance to attack Chile. "If Argentina, with American aid, is allowed to crush Chile, do you think the Argentines will settle for anything less than total dominance of our continent?"—so the matter was put by newspaper proponents of a Santiago–Rio "axis." Confederate representatives chimed in to urge Brazilians to repudiate "the unnatural neutrality imposed by Rio-Branco" and join their "natural ally," the slaveholding Confederacy, on the field of battle—holding out the prospect of profit to be earned by the extension of slave-based agriculture to a Confederate-ruled Mexico.

Rio-Branco, however, was determined to avoid what he regarded as the "catastrophe" of the war's expansion to South America. He therefore seized upon the Legation Massacre and the ensuing call for a suspension of hostilities as an opportunity to bring the belligerents to the peace table and end the conflict before it engulfed Brazil and her neighbors. With the strong support of Empress Isabel, Rio-Branco approached Argentine President Julio Argention Roca, who shared Rio-Branco's conviction that war would be a disaster for all the countries of the Southern Cone. Roca agreed that Rio-Branco could approach the warring powers in the name of Argentina as well as Brazil and propose a peace conference sponsored by Buenos Aires and Rio de Janeiro. Rio-Branco then used Brazil's close connections with its mother country of Portugal and his personal relationship with the foreign minister of the Netherlands to persuade these two important European neutrals to join as sponsors of a peace conference to be held in Rio de Janeiro. Although the ensuing call has often been described as a surprise public initiative, in fact, Rio-Branco had carefully sounded out the two warring powers he believed most likely to respond positively: the USA and Great Britain. Rio-Branco knew that the American and British populations had grown increasingly war weary (although for somewhat different reasons), and that both the McKinley Administration (facing a difficult reelection challenge) and Lord Salisbury's government (having only just maintained control in the face of food riots in London that April) would both seize a chance to extend the suspension of hostilities in order to try to bring the war to a close. Rio-Branco's judgment proved especially insightful regarding the USA. For although the Americans did not suffer from the food shortages that had reached crisis proportions in Great Britain, ironically, the same circumstances that had brought on the British food shortage threatened President McKinley's reelection chances.

The cutoff of trade with the British Isles, Germany, and Austria–Hungary and the disruption of trade with European neutrals due to loss of control of the North Atlantic trade routes to the Royal Navy and its German ally had by mid-1900 plunged the American agricultural heartland into a depression. The political implications were grave. McKinley had barely defeated William Jennings Bryan four years before—and then only by the employment in the Upper and Industrial Midwestern states of Wisconsin, Illinois, and Indiana of tactics that can only by the most generous of stretches be described as "rough and tumble." Bryan was again the Democratic standard-bearer in 1900, and the economic slump in the heartland threatened to give him the vital edge needed to capture these states and oust McKinley. To be sure, Bryan insisted on making "reconciliation" with the South a chief theme of his campaign, and this stubborn adherence to partisan principle might still have offended enough voters to deprive the Democratic standard-bearer of victory—especially with the dynamic Theodore Roosevelt added to the GOP ticket. No one else in the Republican Party could match Bryan's energy while flailing the Democrats with the emotional charge of "treason while our country is engaged, for the third time in less than a generation, in combat with the vicious and benighted Slave Power that glowers just across our border"—as "TR" put the matter to a crowd of enthusiastic Chicagoans the night of his nomination as the Republican candidate for Vice President.

But the GOP leadership could not count on such an outcome with anything close to comfortable certainty. Perhaps more important, the GOP standard-bearer, President McKinley, had so sickened of the war that he was ready to grasp at any chance to end it. He had done so with Herbert Hoover's report by pressing for a suspension of hostilities, and now he did so again when Rio-Branco's invitation arrived at the temporary White House in Philadelphia. McKinley promptly telegraphed his acceptance (over the vociferous objection, among others, of his running mate from New York) and also dispatched personal letters to the leaders of every warring power urging their acceptance. But as with the Suspension of Hostilities, the key would prove the actions of just one: Great Britain—and the decisions to be taken by the government of Lord Salisbury's Unionist coalition. Again, Rio-Branco correctly judged that the British leadership would not refuse a chance to end a war that had brought the British Empire victories in the field but also threatened her domestic cohesion. Joseph Chamberlain worried about a possible fracture of London's alliances with Richmond and Berlin, but Lord Salisbury shared his monarch's view that now was the time to try to end the war. "Years ago, you wrote me of the pride you would feel when English and German troops marched shoulder to shoulder into battle," Queen Victoria wrote her grandson, Kaiser Wilhelm II. "Now join me in trying to bring those soldiers home, lest more die on distant battlefields and for no good purpose." When Salisbury notified Rio-Branco of London's joinder in McKinley's acceptance of the Brazilian–Argentine invitation, it became a given that the other belligerents would promptly follow suit.

Negotiations informally opened in Rio in mid-October with the arrival of the first delegations. By then, Mother Nature had intervened to change the North American military balance and in a fashion that would ease the way to peace. On September 8, the Texas Gulf Coast was struck by a ferocious hurricane. Galveston bore the brunt of the storm: winds of 145 miles per hour drove a storm surge over fifteen feet, which rolled through and over a harbor crowded with Confederate supply ships, then smashed into the Confederacy's primary staging area for troops scheduled to join a resumption of the CSA drive into Mexico. The result was nothing short of a military catastrophe. Dozens of ships were sunk, and over twenty-five thousand soldiers and civilians drowned by waves that literally wiped the city of Galveston off the map. In less than one day, an act of God had inflicted a setback to Confederate arms more severe than any wrought by American and Mexican forces. And with that hurricane went any realistic hope of the Confederacy achieving even its minimum aims in Mexico— at least not until well into the following year. President Tillman and his cabinet recognized as much, and the moderating effect on what could have been one of the most recalcitrant powers at the peace conference would open the door even wider to those genuinely interested in bringing the war to a swift conclusion.

Indeed, had the Confederacy not suffered the Galveston disaster, a belligerent South combined with a defiant North might very well have wrecked the Rio Conference and reignited the war. As matters transpired, the USA almost managed to do that—all by itself. President McKinley devoutly wished to avoid further fighting, but his party was dominated by "war hawks" like Vice Presidential nominee Theodore Roosevelt and Massachusetts Senator Henry Cabot Lodge. Although Roosevelt could not go to the Peace Conference—the final weeks of a close and bitter election campaign would quickly be followed, assuming a Republican victory, by preparing for the Vice Presidency (an office TR intended to transform from powerless sinecure to power platform)—the influential New York governor managed to have his close friend Lodge named as one of the congressional representatives. Lodge, with his formidable intellect and energy, quickly came to dominate the American delegation, which was headed by the able but aging John Hay (serving his second consecutive President in the office of Secretary of State). Lodge successfully pressed Hay to demand the American acquisition of all of Canada west of the Albany River. The Yukon Territory, the Province of British Columbia, the Districts of Alberta, Assiniboia, Athabaska, Keenwatin, and Saskatchewan, the Province of Manitoba, and the Northwest Territories lying west and north of Hudson's Bay—all would be ceded to the USA, if Lodge had his way.

Under the "Lodge Demands" (as they have become known to history), the Americans would have acquired over 80 percent of Canadian territory along with effective control of Hudson's Bay, as Canada would have had to yield Southampton Island and Cockburn's Land—although retaining Fox Land lying across the Hudson Strait from the portion of the Northwest Territory immediately adjacent to Quebec, which Lodge "generously" proposed to leave in Canadian hands. To this territorial evisceration, Lodge added the demand that the Royal Navy remove its powerful North Atlantic squadron from the Halifax Naval Station and limit any future force to a mix of light cruisers and torpedo boat destroyers. Lodge's proposal thus was tantamount to a *de facto* cession of Canada to the USA. For without an effective Royal Navy presence, the Confederation's surviving eastern rump would have been at America's mercy in any future conflict. Unblushingly, Lodge combined these demands with equally provocative terms for the remainder of North America. The Confederacy was to withdraw from Mexico and Maryland and pay an indemnity of $250 million to cover the cost of rebuilding Washington City. The demilitarized zone on the Virginia side of the Potomac would be restored and expanded, and the USA would have the right to station armed "observers" to assure CSA compliance. In exchange, the USA would withdraw from the Mississippi Valley—but pay nothing toward restoring the damaged levee system.

Tellingly, these terms were not disclosed until after McKinley had defeated Bryan in November of 1900. Had the Democrats learned of Lodge's aggressive proposals before the vote, they could have made electoral hay with the charge that the GOP was engaged in a war of conquest. The Lodge plan, however, did not become public knowledge—in part because its proponents (which included Roosevelt) knew that President

McKinley would have promptly repudiated it. In the event, McKinley was furious when he learned that Lodge's plan had been made the basis for the American negotiating position when the Rio Conference formally opened in mid-November. Perhaps for that reason, Secretary Hay quickly indicated that the American demands constituted only a "basis" for discussions rather than a "definitive statement of essential terms." Hay's retreat infuriated Lodge and like-minded Republican leaders (including the Vice President-elect, whom Lodge kept apprised of conference developments by daily secret reports). Yet, Hay really had no other choice—at least not if the Americans genuinely wanted to avoid a resumption of the fighting. The Canadians and British did recognize that the Americans would have to be made some grant of territory—if only because the destruction of the Royal Navy's North Pacific Squadron made a reconquest of British Columbia utterly impractical. And once the Galveston Hurricane had smashed the Confederates' local strategic reserve, Richmond knew it would have to yield its Mexican lodgments—the Confederate advance had failed to seize sufficient territory to make worthwhile the cost of a renewed and prolonged war.

But London, much less Ontario, was not prepared to cede effective control of British North America to the USA—certainly not when the Americans had failed to win that privilege on the battlefield. Likewise, the Confederacy considered as pure "Yankee effrontery" the demand that Richmond pay for the reconstruction of Washington City while also admitting armed Northern troops onto Virginia soil. The resulting intensity of emotion, particularly on each side of the North–South divide, might have frustrated further negotiations had not the USA's principal allies proved eager to bring the war to an end. France had been strategically isolated. Her Mediterranean fleet had been driven back to port, cutting off the sea route to her North African colonies. Then, the American defeat at Sable Island had ruptured the flow of armaments from the USA at the very moment when French armies had to prepare for an Anglo–German–Austrian invasion. Russia, unlike France, had the asset of a vast area with which to swallow up any invader. But while the Russians may not have been threatened by outright conquest, there could be no denying that Russian arms had suffered serious—even calamitous—defeat. Only along the Manchurian front did Russia seem poised to gain the upper hand when Nicholas II announced the cease-fire that permitted the Japanese to transfer forces south to reinforce Tientsin. The ensuing suspension of hostilities and subsequent Great Power move against the Manchus then had the effect of reconciling Russia to adverse peace terms on some fronts because of the gains it could now make in a "peaceful" partition of China. As for Mexico: Diaz and his advisers wanted a respite from fighting that had begun to undermine the country's social cohesion—almost as much as they wanted the Confederates back across the Rio Grande. Finally, Spanish pride might desire the restoration of the Philippines, but Madrid also recognized the military and diplomatic impracticability of that goal.

Great Britain, Germany, and their allies, on the other hand, recognized an opportunity to bring the war to an end on favorable terms. Great Britain looked to make gains in Asia and Africa that would more than counter-balance any losses in North America. To be sure, British Columbia, and probably the gold-bearing portion of the Yukon, would have to be ceded by Canada to the USA. But American forces would be compelled to evacuate the Great Plains territory seized at the war's outset. Also, there would not be any concessions required in the Caribbean, where neither side had managed to do more than carry out hit-and-run raids against the other's principal naval bases. (A combined Anglo–Confederate raid on the Panama Canal failed when a Colombian and American squadron intercepted the attackers. The USA squadron forced a withdrawal after sinking two troop transports and two cruiser escorts; a retaliatory Spanish–American raid on the Royal Navy's base at Kingston, Jamaica, fared equally badly.) And on the Asian mainland, the British had done very well indeed. The "Great Game" with Russia was over: with Great Britain the decisive victor. Afghanistan would become a protectorate subject to the jurisdiction of the Government of India, and Indian Army troops would take up positions along the Afghan–Russian border. Moreover, despite the Suspension of Hostilities, Viceroy Curzon took no steps to recall Sir Francis Youngblood, whose force of five thousand crack Gurkha and Sikh troopers pressed on into Tibet. On November 8, even as the delegates gathered in Rio de Janeiro, Youngblood—backed by the threat of an artillery bombardment that would have quickly smashed the sacred Potala Palace—forced the Dalai Lama to sign a treaty effectively making Tibet a British protectorate. Finally, the impending Partition of China promised to connect Great Britain's new Tibetan holdings with a great swath of Chinese territory running from the border with Tibet to where the Yangtze River emptied into the East China Sea. As for Africa, the war's immediate *casus belli*—control of the Sudan—had been resolved by Marchand's nimble but undeniable retreat from Fashoda. There was no question but that any peace would ratify the resulting British control of the Sudan, which also would mark the effective achievement of the "Cairo to Cape Town" East Africa corridor, long sought by British imperial strategists. London also would insist on France's cession of the island of Madagascar; seized at the outset of the war, its acquisition, along with France's tiny holdings on the Indian Subcontinent, would expel the French from the Indian Ocean. (Should the French demand some countervailing adjustments in West Africa, Salisbury, for one, was prepared to be generous.)

Like Great Britain, Germany was poised, along with her Austro–Hungarian ally, to profit handsomely from the impending peace. In the West, Germany had repelled a furious French effort to undo the verdict of the Franco–Prussian War and restore Alsace and Lorraine to French rule. In the East, in conjunction with the efforts of their Austro–Hungarian ally, the Germans had dealt the Russians a grievous defeat, driving them from their portion of Congress Poland. Moreover, although the Russian forces managed to blunt the Austro–German drive on Kiev, the cessation of operations still left the German and Austro–Hungarian armies deep in the Russian Ukraine. Berlin was prepared to settle for the *status quo ante bellum* in the West, but Kaiser Wilhelm II—backed by his Chief of Staff, Count Alfred Von Schlieffen—had determined to insist that the Russians withdraw from Poland, with the new border to be set well east of Warsaw (along the River Bug). Germany and Austria–Hungary would divide the evacuated territory, with Warsaw to be jointly occupied and administered as the capital of an Austro–German Poland. In effect, Germany proposed to undo the tripartite partition of Poland effected over a century before, with St. Petersburg compelled to yield its share to Berlin and Vienna—Russia's partners in the eighteenth century dismemberment of the ancient Polish state. In exchange, Germany and Austria–Hungary would withdraw their forces in the Ukraine, which (in combination with any Anglo–Turkish army to be put ashore on the Crimea) could still deprive Russia of her Ukrainian breadbasket should negotiations fail and hostilities resume.

Vienna was generally satisfied with these terms. Reflecting the tension between the Austrian--German and Hungarian–Magyar wings of the Dual Monarchy, Budapest resented a peace that would result in territorial aggrandizements for Austria (the acquisitions in Poland) while abandoning the possibility of conquest that would inure to the benefit of Hungary (the occupied territory of the Russian Ukraine). But the more sober-minded among the Hungarian elite also recognized that the defeat before Zhitomir had effectively foreclosed such gains, unless Budapest was prepared to insist on a resumption of a global war—which simply was not politically practicable. Moreover, many established Magyar landowners were reluctant to wean Austria from dependence on Hungarian foodstuffs by annexing fertile Ukrainian fields. That left the latecomer ally in the Euro–Asian Theater: the Ottoman Empire. The Turks had done well in the field—much better, in fact, than had been expected by either their allies or their principal enemy, Russia. Although logistical difficulties had delayed the Crimean landings until the Suspension of Hostilities rendered the planned operation a moot point, the Ottoman armies attacking out of Anatolia had achieved so much that the Porte could not be expected to settle for anything short of substantial concessions in the Caucasus and along the eastern Black Sea coast—at a minimum, the yielding up by Russia of the port of Batum and the fortress city of Kars.

Finally, there was the Confederacy and Japan. In North America, the CSA confronted the painful fact that it had failed in both principal offensive efforts: the initial drive to "liberate" Maryland and the more improvisational but equally determined effort to bite off a chunk of northwestern Mexico. On the other hand, the daring joint CSA–Japanese operation in the Philippines had succeeded brilliantly, and the Tillman Administration could at least deliver to an increasingly anxious and war-weary population the "success" of a new Confederate Empire in the Far East. As for the Japanese, they shared with the Confederates the victory in the Philippines; their fleet had performed brilliantly against Spanish–American and Russian foes; and their armies had thrown back a Russian threat to the

Liaotung Peninsula in northeastern China. But the grinding struggle around Mukden had srained Japanese resources to the breaking point, and Tokyo was eager to negotiate an end to the conflict before the Russians, with their superior numbers and materiel, broke through the ever-thinning crust of Japanese guarding the approaches to the Liaotung and Korea.

This, then, was the structure of the negotiation dynamic when the Rio negotiations formally opened on November 11. Fairly quickly, the Americans found themselves isolated as China provided the means by which the British were able to divide the USA from its allies—most importantly, from the Russians. Under what came to be known as the "Balfour Plan" for the partition of China (named for Sir Arthur Balfour, the languid but very able head of the British delegation), Russia would receive the northern half of Sinkiang, all of Outer and Inner Mongolia, and the northeastern two thirds of Manchuria. Of course, Balfour's "generosity" also reflected the realities on the ground. Russia had long been engaged in the penetration of Sinkiang and Mongolia, even though these territories remained under Peking's—increasingly tenuous—control, while in Manchuria, Russian forces were on the verge of defeating the exhausted Japanese. If anything, Balfour's proposal, which would give the British an equal share of territory in Sinkiang (which the British were in no position to wrest from Russia's already closing grasp) while preserving for the Japanese gains in southwestern Manchuria (which they probably could not have held against resurgent Russian forces) could have been taken as an affront by the Tsar. But the Balfour Plan represented a sufficient concession to Russian ambitions that Sir Arthur was able to report back to London that his counterpart, Count Sergei Witte, had positively received the British proposal. "While we may have to make certain adjustments, I am fairly confident that Russia will make peace along these lines," Balfour telegraphed to Prime Minister Salisbury.

Balfour was right. Although the Russians did insist on "adjustments," these proved fairly minor. The whole of Sinkiang would go to Russia, but the Russians agreed to post no more forces than necessary to maintain "good order" among the area's nomadic population. In Manchuria, the Russians would receive somewhat more territory, but they also agreed not to exclude British, German, or Japanese commercial interests from the development of

Manchurian natural resources (most importantly, its rich deposits of coal and iron ore). But otherwise, the Balfour Plan was accepted by the Russians as a basis for partitioning China and also as an offset for the concessions Russia had to make in Central Asia, the Caucasus, and Poland. And once the Russian acceptance of the Balfour Plan had become generally known, the delegates quickly recognized that the negotiations had reached the end stage. The Americans soon faced the unpleasant fact that Russia would not support her ally should the USA threaten a resumption of fighting unless the Lodge Demands were met. Moreover, the French also made clear that Russia's determination to make peace would compel France to follow the Russian lead. In short, if the USA was determined to resume the struggle, it would have to do so without any of its European allies. Secretary of State Hay returned to Philadelphia for the Christmas recess to deliver the grim news to President McKinley and his cabinet. "I see no way out," Hay advised the President. "We can probably wrest British Columbia and the Yukon from Canada, but unless we are willing to take on Great Britain and her allies supported only by Mexico and Colombia, we must be prepared to give up our hope for anything beyond these minimal gains."

If the tragic events of September 1901 had already come to pass and Theodore Roosevelt had acceded to the Presidency, the choice might very well have been for war. But McKinley saw the war as a calamity to be ended—not an opportunity to be pursued. Over the vociferous objections of several prominent GOP "war hawks"—including Lodge, who resigned in disgust from the American delegation—McKinley instructed Hay to return to Rio de Janeiro and make peace, even if this required giving up such emotionally important goals as a Confederate-financed reconstruction of Washington City. McKinley's decision effectively removed the last principal obstacle to a comprehensive settlement. On January 22, a delighted Rio-Branco announced to a delirious crowd outside the Catete Palace the news that the representatives of the warring powers gathered within had just signed what would be known as the Treaty of Rio de Janeiro: "I believe it is not only peace in our time, but with the good efforts of peace-loving people everywhere, I believe it can be a lasting peace for ages to come."

Rio-Branco would be proven wrong, of course. In less than fourteen years, the world would be convulsed by an even more terrible conflict, and this time, it would extend to the Southern cone of South America. It would prove an act of historical mercy that Rio-Branco himself, one of the most far-sighted statesmen of the modern age, would be spared the knowledge of the failure of his truly noble efforts: dying two years before the outbreak of the Second Alliance War, in February 1912.

Why this proved to be so—why the Peace and Reconciliation movements of the First Inter-war Period failed so utterly in their undeniably noble tasks—will be taken up later. For now, I will review the terms of the treaty that ended the First Alliance War, beginning with North America, where Hay's gloomy Christmas prediction was fully borne out. The USA received British Columbia and the adjacent Yukon Territory, including the Klondike gold fields. (The Yukon Territory had only been formed shortly before the outbreak of the war to rationalize administration in the portion of the Northwest Territories directly affected by the gold rush; now, the boundary between the Yukon and Northwest Territories would constitute the northernmost border between the USA and Canada.) American troops, however, would be withdrawn from the portions of the Districts of Alberta and Assiniboia and the Province of Manitoba which they had seized two years before. Nor would any limits be placed on Royal Navy forces stationed at Halifax—to the contrary, even as negotiators in Rio de Janeiro were clinking glasses of champagne to celebrate peace, the British Admiralty was preparing a report calling for expansion of the Halifax Station to accommodate a recommended doubling of the striking power of the navy's North Atlantic squadron. Farther south, the USA and the CSA agreed to a peace substantially along *ante bellum* lines. The Confederacy would pay no indemnity toward the reconstruction of Washington City, however, and Richmond's related refusal to permit the posting of Northern monitors in an expanded Arlington Heights demilitarized zone effectively doomed American hopes to restore the country's pre-Secession capital.

A vigorous debate then ensued over whether Philadelphia should be converted to the status of permanent capital or the seat of government moved west to the country's geographic center—with Chicago the favored choice of most "Heartlanders." The matter was definitively resolved in 1905 with the passage of the National Capital Act, formally recognizing Philadelphia as the permanent federal capital and authorizing a massive construction program for new public buildings—Houses of Congress, Presidential and Vice Presidential residences, a Supreme Court, and offices for the principal departments—along with a series of monuments, including a massive pile topped by a two-hundred-foot dome to honor the nation's armed forces. This last effort, a magnificent granite and marble structure filled with statues honoring the General and Service Chiefs of Staff and plaques listing the war dead of every conflict starting with the Revolution (but omitting the names of men from the Seceding States who died in battles preceding the War of Secession), became an instant national shrine upon its completion in 1923. (And like so much of Philadelphia, the "National Monument" would not survive the terrible bombing raids of October 1939.)

Farther south still, the *status quo ante bellum* was fully restored between the Confederacy and Mexico—although the return of all Mexican territory so infuriated Southern war hawks that this peace term nearly undid ratification of the Rio treaty by the Confederate Senate. The *ante bellum* principle was also observed in the Caribbean, where both sides had, in any case, failed to capture the other's island naval bases. Indeed, the only other change of territory in the Northern half of the Western Hemisphere was the transfer by France to Great Britain of the two, tiny islands of St. Pierre and Miquelon, off the coast of Newfoundland. And in the only other area of the globe where the USA was involved in territorial shuffles, the Central Pacific, the peace agreements ratified the changes wrought by force of arms in the war's opening phases. The USA yielded its share of the Samoas, and France relinquished New Caledonia; these transfers were at least offset by the surrender of the Marshall Islands by Germany and of the Gilberts chain by Great Britain.

In Africa, the peace recognized Great Britain's achievement of the long-sought "Cairo to Cape Town" corridor by acknowledging Britain's control of the Sudan. The British also retained the island of Madagascar and a smattering of other French possessions (French Somaliland, the islands of Comoro and Reunion, and French India's coastal enclaves), which made the Indian Ocean an English lake shared only with Germany—whose limited holdings made Berlin a very junior regional partner. Lord Salisbury, however, insisted that France be at least partially compensated by recognizing her occupation of Gambia and Sierra Leone; over Chamberlain's vigorous objection, Salisbury threw in the Ashanti territory located on the southern hinterland of Great Britain's Gold Coast colony. Salisbury believed that the Anglo–French rift had been produced by a failure to resolve the two countries' African rivalries; by conceding French supremacy in West Africa, Salisbury hoped to lay a foundation for the restoration of an Anglo–French *detente*. Any chance of such a reconciliation between London and Paris, however, was almost certainly lost on the same continent when Berlin insisted on the acquisition of Gabon and the French Congo, and London backed up the German demand. Kaiser Wilhelm II spurned British urgings that these territories, occupied by Germany during the war, be returned to France. And Paris, with justification, blamed the British for allowing their German ally to carry out what Clemenceau bitingly described as "equatorial thievery."

In Europe, the peace effected few changes in the West. The Franco–German border remained fixed along the lines set in 1871. The British withdrew from their more advanced positions near Gibraltar but insisted on the transfer of an additional buffer zone. (To try to ease the bitterness of this blow to Spanish pride, the British—over Jackie Fisher's loud protests—evacuated Majorca and also abandoned the notion of demanding that Spain relinquish the strategic Canary Islands off the Northwest African coast.) In the East, however, there were significant territorial adjustments—and all of them at Russia's expense. In Poland, the tripartite partition of the eighteenth century was transformed into a dual division. Russia lost her Polish holdings and was compelled to withdraw east of the River Bug. Germany and Austria–Hungary divided the spoils between them roughly on an east–west line, with Warsaw placed in a separate district in the middle to serve as a joint administrative capital for the now-restored fiction of a semi-independent Poland. The Germans and Austrians, however, withdrew from the Russian Ukraine. In the Caucasus and along the Black Sea's eastern coast, the Ottomans made good the Sultan's goal of beginning the reversal of two centuries of withdrawal in the face of Russian arms: taking back the port of Batum, the fortress city of Kars, and the adjacent territory. In Central Asia, the peace ratified the results achieved by British arms, as Russia recognized the absorption of Afghanistan and Tibet by British India.

In East Asia, the great prize of China was carved up like a melon—with the biggest pieces going to Great Britain and her battlefield rival, Russia. As previously described, Russia received Sinkiang, Outer and Inner Mongolia, and approximately three quarters of Manchuria. Japan was awarded the southernmost portion of Manchuria (parts of Fengten and Kirin provinces), connecting Korea to the Liaotung Peninsula. The Japanese also received: the port of Tientsin; the district surrounding Peking; portions of Chihli, Shansi, Shensi, and Kansu provinces; and Fukien across the Taiwan Strait from the island of Formosa (the latter taken by Japan as part of the spoils of victory over China five years before). Germany extended her holdings westward from the Shantung Peninsula to encompass all of Shantung Province and the northern portions of Honan, Anhwei, and Kiangsu Provinces. The British got the lion's share of China south of the Hwang Ho and east of Sinkiang. The Confederacy received a grant in Chekiang and Kwangtung Provinces, and the French were allowed to acquire a portion of their former sphere of influence in Yunnan and Kwangsi Provinces adjacent to French Indo-China (which Salisbury had directed be restored as part of his—unsuccessful—effort to revive Anglo–French *detente*); otherwise, central and southern China were absorbed into the British Empire. The USA received no piece of the mainland spoils, but it was named to the seven-member Great Power commission that would sit in Peking.

Technically, the Great Powers held their new Chinese territories "in trust." The Manchus having been overthrown, it became necessary for the Powers to "spare" China the "horrors" of "anarchy" and "unrestrained civil unrest"—this from the Prologue to Article III of the Rio treaty, governing the resolution of the "China Question." The fiction that China had not suffered outright dismemberment would be maintained by the device of the "Joint China Administrative Commission," with putative jurisdiction over all "questions relating to the trusteeship now being exercised over the territory and people of the former Manchu-ruled Empire of China." The Commission was empowered to take decisions by majority vote— but as the majority consisted of Great Britain, Germany, Japan, and the Confederacy, it could only be expected that Commission decisions would reproduce the dynamics of the rival Alliances, and that the Anglo–German coalition would have the upper hand in disputes where the two sides might jockey for advantage. (The collapse of that dynamic in the aftermath of World War Two would destabilize Great Power relations in China when Great Britain found itself facing a new, and hostile, Commission majority—a matter addressed later in this narrative.) In the only other territorial change in East Asia, the peace treaty ratified the Confederate–Japanese conquest of the Philippines—leaving the victors to decide how to divide the spoils: a process that would be postponed until the effective defeat of a determined "native" insurrection with the capture and execution in 1903 of the rebel leader, Emilio Aguinaldo. The one guarantee Richmond extracted from Tokyo was to ensure the institution of plantation agriculture and by treaty to recognize "chattel rights" in human property, regardless of the ultimate political disposition of the Islands. The Confederate Congress swiftly passed the "Philippines Property Protection Act" the same day the Confederate Senate ratified the Rio Treaty—providing that slaves, held or born in the Philippines, would be "deemed" Confederate slaves held domestically for purposes of the Confederate Constitution's nominal ban on the international slave trade. In short, slavery had come to the Philippines, and it was there to stay.

As a matter of basic outline, these were the terms of the Treaty of Rio de Janeiro that brought the First Alliance War—World War One—to a close. I think it appropriate to pause at this point and briefly assess the destruction wrought by what would prove only the first of several Great Power Alliance Wars. The cost of the wars fought exclusively in our century—never mind the catastrophe of the nuclear strikes last October, which I am reluctant to categorize as a war, in any classic sense of that term—have tended to overshadow the casualty tolls (human and material) of World War One. Yet to understand the history of our traumatized century, the reader needs to try to grasp the enormity of that war's destructiveness as felt at the time by the populations that experienced it, for the First World War was the most destructive Great Power conflict that the world had yet experienced. In speaking of "Great Power" wars, I exclude the several Chinese civil wars (e.g., the Taiping Rebellion) known to have taken tens of millions of lives as well as such ancient or medieval eruptions as the Mongol devastations of the thirteenth century. The former are not international conflicts, and the course of the latter are too shrouded in mystery—they are more folk memory than history for the areas involved. By contrast, the First World War was an international conflict whose basic facts are all too well known.

In less than two years, the First World War exceeded the death, injury, and destruction wrought by all wars fought by the Great Powers of Europe and Asia for the previous *three hundred years*. At least 2,500,000 men, women, and children were killed—and an even greater number injured. The extent of civilian losses exceeded anything seen in Europe since the catastrophe of the Thirty Years War. Equally shocking was the extent of the physical destruction, whose psychological effect was heightened due to the concentration of the damage in the urban areas of North America and Europe. Moreover, the development of motion picture technology shortly before the war as well as the widespread distribution of "mass" still photography methods (e.g., George Eastman's "Brownie" camera) meant the images of the suffering wrought by the war were widely distributed. The wreckage of Washington and Memphis; the devastation wrought by the fires in Lower Manhattan and Boston; the shelled-out ruins of Warsaw; starving peasants in the Ukraine; the bodies of children in China—these and many other horrors of industrialized mass war became the common visual experience, in still and motion-picture media, for the populations of the "civilized" world.

And then there was the economic waste: represented by the diversion of resources from peaceful productive pursuits to the enterprise of war as well as the loss of wealth due to the outright destruction of capital assets. At the war's height, the conflict has been estimated to have consumed over fifty percent of the economic production of the Great Powers—a productive output that had already suffered a precipitous decline due to the war's suppression of normal economic activity, most notably: international trade. Billions were expended on expanding and sustaining enterprises and institutions whose sole purpose was the generation of machines and the employment of persons in the "business" of killing and destruction. At the same time, civilian populations suffered shortages of a wide variety of vital commodities, both absolutely and relatively (inflation being an affliction common to all, even for belligerents such as the USA that could supply most needs from internal resources).

Finally, there was the coarsening of day-to-day life, accompanied by the rise of what would come to be called the "garrison state" mentality. As will be discussed more fully in the next portion of this narrative, the demands of mass industrialized warfare promoted the extension of military ways of thinking into the social and political spheres. The military model of organization, with its limited tolerance for dissent, could not long be reconciled with a free political tradition—and as the reader will see, in short order, freedom would prove the loser, in the USA and elsewhere. In my view, this would prove *the* tragedy of our century—one that the horrors of October past did not transcend, but only confirmed. For fighting this series of wars caused Americans to throw away that which I have come to believe truly made us the promise of a better future: our commitment as a people and a nation to respecting and protecting the freedom of every American—no matter how fiercely he or she might dissent from the majority's felt necessities of the here and now.

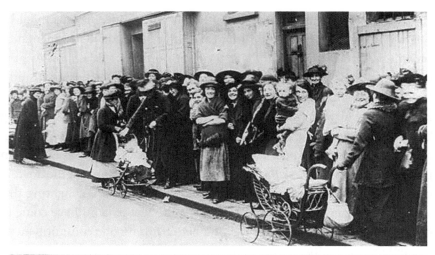

(above) A crowd of English housewives standing in line awaiting the distribution of their weekly ration of flour and meat during the Winter of 1899, the dwindling availability of which would transform these initially cheerful and tolerant women into the food rioters who threatened to topple the British Government.

(below) Confederate Army railroad cars, wrecked by the fury of the hurricane that destroyed the Texas port city of Galveston in September 1900, and in the process ended any remaining Confederate hope for resuming the offensive against Mexico.

MAJOR TERRITORIAL ADJUSTMENTS OF THE PEACE OF RIO, 1901

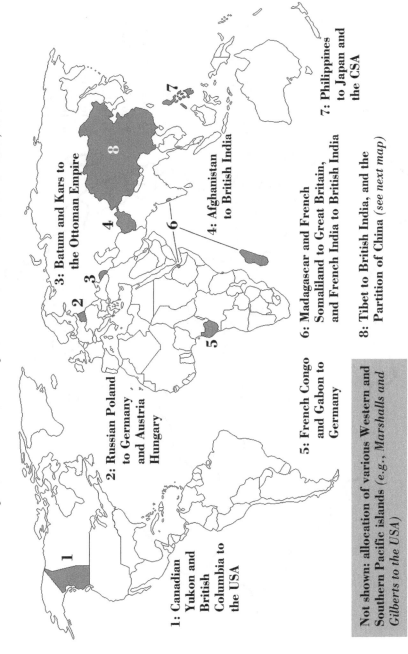

1: Canadian Yukon and British Columbia to the USA

2: Russian Poland to Germany, and Austria Hungary

3: Batum and Kars to the Ottoman Empire

4: Afghanistan to British India

5: French Congo and Gabon to Germany

6: Madagascar and French Somaliland to Great Britain, and French India to British India

7: Philippines to Japan and the CSA

8: Tibet to British India, and the Partition of China (see next map)

Not shown: allocation of various Western and Southern Pacific islands (e.g., Marshalls and Gilberts to the USA)

THE PARTITION OF CHINA

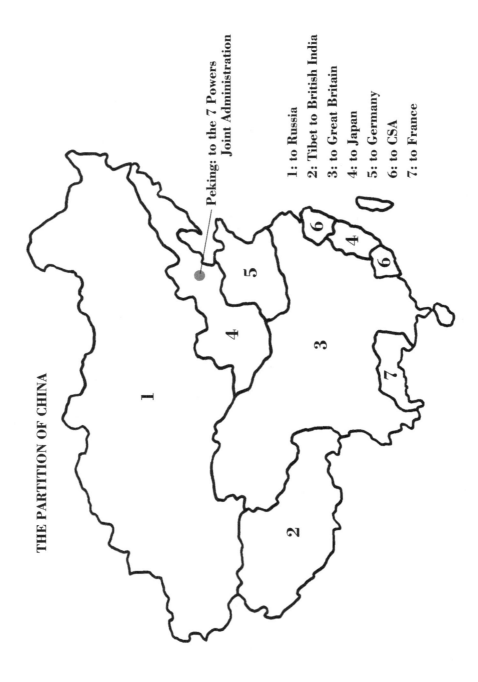

Peking: to the 7 Powers
Joint Administration

1: to Russia
2: Tibet to British India
3: to Great Britain
4: to Japan
5: to Germany
6: to CSA
7: to France

2 1

THE BALEFUL CONSEQUENCES OF THE FIRST GREAT POWER WAR FOR SOCIAL JUSTICE AND PERSONAL LIBERTY, AS DEMONSTRATED BY EVENTS IN THE USA FROM SECESSION THROUGH THE FIRST ALLIANCE WAR

———

Paradoxically, the immediate effect of the Secession War had been to enhance the prospects for racial freedom in the North. The North's Afro–American population, relieved of the incubus of association with their far more numerous cousins held in bondage by the South, had achieved within twenty years a fairly full measure of political and social equality (a process more fully described in previous chapters of this narrative). This liberating act, moreover, reflected the power of the pre-Secession "free soil" and "free labor" movement, which not only became the national ideology in the wake of the South's departure but itself was transformed and further liberalized as the North grappled with the economic and social challenges of accelerating industrialization. Central to this process was the national answer to the "Labor Question," which initially focused on the relationship between capital and labor in the development and operation of the North's burgeoning railroad network.

The reader will recall how the construction of multiple transcontinental rail links became the post-Secession "national mission," leading to the completion of the Union Pacific–Central Pacific link in 1869 and its northern and southern counterparts within ten years thereafter. The railroads, along with the great industries whose development the railroad boom encouraged, posed a fundamental challenge to labor's traditional "guild approach" to salary and work-condition issues. The resulting social tension came to a head with the economic contraction of the mid-1870s. Although the slump proved less severe in the USA than in just about any other industrializing nation (for reasons discussed earlier in this narrative), the downturn that began in the fall of 1873 still brought on a crisis in labor-management relations which opened the door to federal intervention in the form of the Donnelly–Schurz National Labor Relations Act of 1877. The major railroads managed to weather the initial slide, but continuing high international interest rates and the resulting prolonged scarcity of loan capital had by the summer of 1876 brought even such powerhouses as the Northern Pacific to the brink of failure. None of the transcontinental companies were actually forced into receivership, but several important regional lines were compelled to seek court protection from creditors; some of these managed to get orders issued declaring striking employees in contempt of court, and management then used the authority of these declarations to have union leaders arrested by compliant local police.

The public reaction against this abusive practice contributed heavily to the passage of the Donnelly–Schurz Act. Federal loan guarantees authorized in the mid-1860s had established the precedent of government involvement in interstate railroad operations. And while the Railroad Loan Bureau refused union invitations to become involved in wage and working-conditions disputes, by the mid-1870s, the railroads had come to be seen as quasi-public undertakings in whose management the federal government should be able to intervene when necessary to protect the nation's vital interest in railway development. The Republican leadership was willing to support a further extension of public credit, but the party's powerful "free labor" wing would support a "railroad bailout" only if railroads engaged in interstate commerce who received the benefits of this "second round" of federal largesse would agree to renounce the use of injunctions to break strikes, and to negotiate with *bona fide* worker representatives. Although management "hard-liners" (such as Philadelphia and Reading president Franklin Gowen) denounced the proposal, the influential Frederick Billings of the Northern Pacific persuaded the other transcontinental roads of the wisdom of accepting the GOP's conditions. Aided by generous financial support from those railroads expecting to benefit from a second issue of federal credit, incumbent James G. Blaine handily won reelection that November over Democrat Samuel J. Tilden—who, despite his corporate law background, ran on a staunch Jeffersonian platform that condemned any loan program on constitutional grounds. The following spring, a bill embodying the tripartite deal between the government, the railroads, and their unions was introduced by its sponsors Ignatius Donnelly (Republican Representative from Minnesota) and Carl Schurz (Republican Senator from Missouri) and moved quickly through both houses of Congress.

Had Donnelly–Schurz failed to pass, it seems likely that the country would have been convulsed by labor violence. Deprived of public credit, the Northern Pacific—and possibly several other major roads—would probably have been forced into receivership. The ensuing wave of sharp wage cuts would undoubtedly have met staunch resistance from the various railway worker unions, and the virtually certain employment of injunctions under conditions of severe economic duress would have turned the great urban railroad centers into virtual "social tinderboxes" in which the slightest of confrontations could have exploded into a brutal cycle of mob violence and official repression. That Donnelly–Schurz passed must be attributed at least in part to the South's successful pursuit of Secession. If the South had been defeated, and unless a Northern military occupation continued well into the 1870s, a Southern economy based on a nominally emancipated slave population would probably have been dominated by a *de facto* coalition of *ante bellum* cotton interests and a "New South" industrial elite, sharing a common anti-labor outlook. Thus, military defeat of the "Slave Power" could well have had the ironic effect of the South's traditional agrarian and new industrial interests making common cause with the determinedly anti-labor element of Northern industrialism, resulting in a powerful political coalition that might easily have marginalized "free labor" forces and blocked any effort to check the employment of the courts and local constabularies to break the nascent industrial unions. If so, the politics of a re-United States would probably have come to be characterized—at least for a time—by a brutal class conflict that could also have made the country vulnerable to violent revolutionary movements.

Instead, the passage of Donnelly–Schurz insured a period of labor peace while setting the stage for further steps along the road to the development of a genuine social welfare state. By the end of the 1870s, the international economy had recovered from the depressed conditions of mid-decade, and the North enjoyed a period of substantial growth that further eased labor-management tensions. The outbreak of the Western War in 1882, however, led to a renewal of these tensions—this time centered on the steel and armaments industries but also affecting the railroads—and stemming from the strains of war production and logistics demands. The reader will recall that the Confederate attack into New Mexico cut the southwestern trans-continental rail link, placing great strain on the Union Pacific and its badly underdeveloped Omaha east–west transfer point. Although the Union Pacific had agreed to a maximum six-day-/forty-eight-hour-work-week formula in collective bargaining the prior year, railroad management now invoked a *force majeure* clause to suspend work-hour limitations, citing agreements with the government regarding war schedules. Almost simultaneously, principal armament manufacturers and their primary materiel suppliers announced an increase of the work week—with no compensatory increase in wages.

A shutdown in vital war production was averted by the narrowest of margins. Only President Garfield's personal assurance that he would appoint a commission to address hours and other work conditions in industries "vital to any national war effort" avoided a crippling steel strike in March of 1883. But Garfield was defeated for reelection by Grover Cleveland in 1884, and the new president—although owing his election to the votes of disaffected industrial workers—refused to honor his predecessor's pledge. Frustrated by the *laissez faire* Jeffersonianism of what would prove the first (and last) Democratic administration after Secession, labor interests organized a nationwide campaign of assembly and petition in favor of eight-hour-day laws to be adopted at the state as well as the federal level. Cleveland's staunch opposition to what he regarded as "impermissible interference with liberty of contract" contributed mightily to his defeat by General John Schofield in the 1888 presidential vote. But the Schofield Administration failed to get a maximum-hours bill through the Congress, and with the onset of an economic depression in 1893, the issue was seized upon by the radical political movement known as the "Populists." The Democrats, however, proved incapable of exploiting the demand for labor relations reform. Nominating the dynamic but economically unsophisticated William Jennings Bryan, the Democrats instead made the inflationist nostrum of "free silver" the centerpiece of their economic program. GOP nominee William McKinley thus was able to attack the "irresponsibility" of "Bryan's voodoo economics," while simultaneously promising to push both for federal maximum hour legislation and "some form" of unemployment insurance. Despite the Populists' decision to endorse Bryan, McKinley was able to hold onto sufficient industrial working class votes to win a narrow victory.

McKinley proved far more adept than his predecessor in persuading the Congress to enact social welfare measures. The Sherman-Altgeld Act imposed a maximum eight-hour work day for anyone employed on public contracts (e.g., armaments orders placed by the War Department), while companion legislation established a system of unemployment compensation for those employed on the interstate railway network or in other industries engaged in interstate commerce "vital to the national defense." The federal example also inspired similar measures at the state level: several of which went beyond the government contract and interstate commerce limitations of the new federal programs. The outbreak of the First World War, however, gave rise to pressure for "relief" from maximum working hours as well as other "confining" pro-labor working-condition rules. The challenge posed by the First Alliance War was quickly recognized by government, management, and labor alike to be an order of magnitude greater than the problems presented by the Western War of fourteen years before. The government's flight from Washington to Philadelphia delayed for several weeks the convening of a "national war production" conference to which President McKinley invited representatives of management and labor from literally dozens of industries. In the interim, McKinley was able to arrange for "no strike" pledges on the part of workers employed by several such businesses, including the great Cooper armament works in Philadelphia. But when the national conference finally convened in early January 1899, it became readily apparent that labor and capital were at odds over most issues, including the vital symbolic question of whether recently enacted federal hour limitations should be "suspended for the duration of the present conflict."

Under the desperate-seeming circumstances of early 1899, with Confederate troops besieging Baltimore just one hundred miles from the "temporary" capital in Philadelphia, it should come as no surprise that representatives of the McKinley administration proved to have little patience with labor concerns about "exploitive" work conditions. Labor did receive the concession that there would be established by Congressional enactment a "Council of National Defense," a quasi-official national agency with powers to fix wartime work rules (including maximum hours) for "essential" war industries. Moreover, the Council was granted jurisdiction to hear claims of violation of those rules, and labor would be guaranteed representation on the Council during both its rule-making and adjudicative phases. But the Council's tripartite composition assured that labor could be overruled by the combined votes of government and management representatives, and with the singular exception of the *Bath Shipyards* case, labor lost every vote of consequence taken by the Council during its two-year existence.

The effect, over the war's two-year course, was the *de facto* repeal of virtually every pro-labor measure adopted—whether by collective bargaining or statute—during the two decades preceding the outbreak of the war. Moreover, during the course of the war itself, management often used "war rules" disputes as a means of weakening unions (e.g., by engineering criminal prosecutions of particularly effective union leaders on trumped-up charges of "impeding the war effort") in an effort to assure a more compliant—and exploitable—postwar labor force. To be sure, labor was able after the war to restore most pre-war work rules, despite management resistance—a result explained in part by the forceful intervention on labor's side by President Theodore Roosevelt, most notably in the great anthracite coal dispute of 1902. Nonetheless, the war had set a grim precedent: In matters of national defense, labor's needs would be forced to yield to the perceived alignment of national and management interests. Moreover, this precedent in the social arena was matched by an equally anti-libertarian outcome in the political arena as the country struggled to reconcile the rights of free speech, assembly, and association with the perceived requirements of wartime unity.

At the outset, I feel constrained to admit that my views of the mean-ing of "free speech" have changed much in recent years. During my time as a federal prosecutor and then as a state—and later federal—executive, I felt entirely comfortable with the restrictive view of speech and associated rights taken by the state and federal courts. I agreed wholeheartedly with Chief Justice Oliver Wendell Holmes, when he wrote for the United States Supreme Court in the *World War Two Espionage Act* cases, that:

> [t]he most stringent protection of free speech would not protect a man in falsely shouting fire in a theater and causing a panic.... The question in every case is whether the words used are used in such circumstances and are of such a nature as to tend to bring about substantive ends that Congress has a right to prevent. The First Amendment does not mean that the government must stand by powerless to act, until the danger presents itself in such clear and present terms that all but the purblind could see the need for action. Especially in time of war, when the survival of the nation itself is at stake, no reasonable man would wish to see the state's hands tied in so crippling a fashion. (*Schenk v. United States*, 249 US 47, 52, 1919)

But I no longer take this view. To the contrary, I have become con-vinced that one of the tragedies of our history in the post-Secession years is how the circumstances of a continent divided between hostile federations effectively foreclosed the development of a more liberal understanding of those rights that constitute the true foundation of free government. To be sure, the view of speech rights expressed by Holmes in the Espionage Act cases reflected the application of doctrine rooted in authorities as vener-able as Blackstone. But along with the restrictive Blackstonian view (which held that "freedom of speech" meant only freedom from prior restraint), in the years immediately following Secession there existed an influen-tial—if admittedly minority—view that insisted on protection of speech even after publication. Drawing in part on the "free speech" tradition of the pre-Secession abolition movement—which had condemned Southern

suppression of anti-slavery opinion as a violation of free speech rights—
these post-Secession libertarians insisted that the First Amendment to the
federal Constitution as well as the amendment's state counterparts should
be construed to limit the government's power to restrict speech after as
well as prior to publication.

Had the country not been faced by a series of crises, beginning with
the Western War, which seemed to place the very existence of the nation
at risk, the libertarian view might very well have prevailed, for the libertarians recognized a basic truth that became all too plain well before the
middle of this benighted century: that allowing the government to pun-
ish speech after publication, based on nothing more than a "tendency" to
cause untoward effects, gives the state the ability to intimidate potential
critics to remain silent rather than risk the penalty of criminal prosecution. The libertarian view, however, also represented an undeniable break
with what could fairly be characterized as the original understanding of
the Framers of the Bill of Rights. To adopt the libertarian interpretation
of "freedom of speech" would have required an act of judicial imagination
of the sort made doubly difficult when courts are called upon to do *their*
"patriotic duty" in time of war. And beginning with the Western War, that
is precisely what happened: time and again, courts succumbed to the pressure of demands for the punishment of speech grounded in the perceived
needs of the country at war.

Consider the Irish–American Society decision of the Massachusetts
Supreme Court, handed down in 1884 and authored by none other than
then Massachusetts Supreme Court Justice Holmes. The Irish–American
Society was a Boston offshoot of John Devoy's Clan na Gael. The IAS
considered Devoy's organization too moderate, and the IAS paper, *Free
Ireland!*, called for "provocation of a war between America and England,
by any means necessary, no matter the cost, so long as it ends in the establishment of a free and republican Ireland." Several society members were
arrested for distributing issues of *Free Ireland!* containing these "incendiary urgings"—as Holmes's opinion characterized them—on the grounds of
the Boston Common, without a permit authorizing such distribution. (A
city ordinance passed soon after the outbreak of the war, and indisputably
for the express purpose of curbing anti-British agitation by the city's large

Irish population, had imposed such a requirement.) Local authorities had actually granted the IAS such a permit but revoked it prior to a visit by the British consul-general.

The defendants—who included the president of the society, charged with aiding and abetting the conduct of society members—contended that their conduct was protected speech. In affirming the convictions, Holmes embraced the narrow, Blackstonian view of freedom of speech and for reasons openly grounded in what he called the "immediate necessities of our national emergency":

> For the Legislature absolutely or conditionally to forbid pamphleteering in a public park is no more an infringement of the rights of a member of the public than for the owner of a private house to forbid it in his house. To exercise that authority and prevent the distribution of pamphlets whose avowed purpose is the incitement of violence no more infringes on the right of free speech than if the pamphleteer had instead been seized in the act of drawing a bead on the object of his invective. Our nation is already at war with one country, and the Commonwealth is under no constitutional compunction to tolerate speech that could put us in conflict with another, and far more puissant power. (*Commonwealth v. O'Leary*, 138 Mass. 145, 148, 1884)

O'Leary was soon followed by several decisions in other jurisdictions, in all of which the "felt necessities of the times"—to borrow Holmes's famous phrase about the common law, which he himself paraphrased in *O'Leary*—led courts to take a restrictive view of speech rights. And while these decisions (including *O'Leary*) were confined by their facts to persons and groups inhabiting the country's political fringes, their rationale was quickly extended to "mainstream" dissenters under the even more intense hydraulic pressure exerted by the far more desperate circumstances of World War One. Dozens of "antiwar" Democrats, including at least two candidates for the House of Representatives, faced charges of sedition during the bitter "Armistice Election" of 1900. And while the United States

Supreme Court managed, by clever employment of standing and other doctrines, to avoid directly entering into the fray, the Court—speaking through yet another opinion by Holmes—several years later made clear its endorsement of the repressive measures taken that year.

Patterson v. Colorado involved the criminal contempt conviction of Thomas Patterson (a newspaper editor and longtime Colorado Democratic Party politician) for criticizing the Colorado Supreme Court about matters then pending before that court. Patterson had not been allowed to put on evidence supporting the—alleged—truth of his attacks on the court, and his appeal challenged this refusal on free speech grounds. In making short shrift of the contention, Holmes went out of his way to endorse the sedition prosecutions of the recently concluded world war:

> The plaintiff in error [Patterson] also overlooks the vital need for confidence in public institutions, at a time of continuing tension with neighbors with whom we have all too recently grappled on the field of battle. Our country rightly refused to tolerate sedition during that recent conflict. Freedom of speech protects against prior restraint. But once words have been spoken—or printed—the publisher must account for the consequences that may flow from them. A battle over the truth of an attack upon the integrity of a high court is a luxury that state cannot afford and need not indulge in the heat of battle. Nothing in the phrase "freedom of speech" compels this Court to direct the State of Colorado to take that risk. (*Patterson v. Colorado*, 205 U.S. 454, 462, 1907)

It is no accident that Oliver Wendell Holmes played so prominent a role in the development of a free speech doctrine that—as the reader will see—ultimately produced the effective suppression of free speech in America. A genuine legal philosopher who seemed serenely independent of political and social buffetings, Holmes was also very much a product of Secession and its aftermath. He served in the War of Secession and was wounded twice, including a near-fatal neck wound at Gettysburg while serving as an officer of the 20th Massachusetts. His accession to the United States Supreme Court occurred under extraordinary and traumatic circumstances: Chief Justice Field and Associate Justice Horace Gray of Massachusetts died in the Confederate bombardment of Washington at the outset of World War One, and William Howard Taft of Ohio and Holmes were named to take their places (with Holmes assuming the Chief Justiceship). How could Holmes not be affected by the bloody events that directly touched both his personal and professional life? I submit that Holmes's jurisprudence was shaped by those experiences—and specifically, that they helped make Holmes a powerful voice favoring state power over individual liberty precisely because Holmes saw the stakes as a stark struggle for survival between the North and Confederacy.

If the South had been defeated and the Union preserved, one might wonder if Justice Holmes—had he still reached the nation's highest court, which seems at least a fairly possible outcome given his undeniable abilities as an appellate judge—would have felt freer to give greater rein to the doubts about the dogmatic exercise of state power he is known to have expressed in more private moments. Of course, had Lee been defeated at Gettysburg and the war had gone on for several more years until it ended in the South's defeat, Holmes might have been killed in a later battle and his legal acumen lost to posterity. My point, however, does not depend upon the fact of a Chief Justice Holmes but the environment—the *specific* felt necessities of a *particular* time—that shaped American jurisprudence on the vital question of freedom of speech and those rights associated with that freedom.

I will leave this topic for now and resume my primary narrative. Obviously, what I have described does not qualify as the "garrison state" to which I referred at the end of the prior chapter. The events just recounted, however, would provide the vital precedents used to justify far more authoritarian measures in the years ahead. When I return to this subject, I will expand the discussion to encompass those other countries that could claim to enjoy at least a fair modicum of political freedom at the twentieth century's outset. As I will show, well before the catastrophic events of a few months ago, that freedom would everywhere be sacrificed in the name of national survival.

(left) **Winston Churchill, shown in the uniform he wore during the Battle of Omdurman, while serving with Kitchener's expedition to restore British control over the Sudan.**

(right) **Theodore Roosevelt, shown shortly before his election as USA Vice President.**

These two men would play crucial and opposing roles in the years following the Peace of Rio. The next Alliance War that ended that peace would prove to be orders of magnitude more destructive than the war of 1898-1900.

EPILOGUE

So ends the first part of our global alternate history of a world in which the American South won its fight for independence. The Great Powers, including the United States of America and the Confederacy, after two years of unprecedented destructive fighting, have barely managed to extricate themselves from that fight—and only because an act of "Oriental" savagery gave those leaders seeking a way out an opportunity to re-focus the destructive energies of the Powers against a supposed common foe. The reader may already have surmised that the "Suspension of Hostilities" and the subsequent Peace of Rio De Janeiro do not represent a genuine peace but merely an interruption of a fight that will be resumed—to even deadlier and more destructive effect.

One of the principal challenges of alternate history is calculating how the chosen "point of divergence" affects the course of history and, even more to the point, how that "POD" will *not* affect the course of events until the ripples of change interact with those events. We believe strongly that, until there is a specific reason why the change represented by the chosen POD should interact with an event and cause a change in the course of events flowing from that event, then that event should unfold as it did in "real" history.

The fundamental premise of *DMA* is that the division of North America into two rival English-speaking "American" unions would unleash an interaction with the rest of the world whose principal international effect would be the creation of rival Great Power Alliances many years before those alliances emerged in our history. In turn, the earlier emergence of these rival alliances would transform events that in our history passed by without bringing those Powers to the brink of war into true "crises" on a par with those that characterized Great Power relationships in the years immediately preceding our World War One.

Thus, the Fashoda Incident, which has gone down in the history of our timeline as an amusing *opéra bouffe*, becomes the trigger for a world war in the *DMA* timeline. The "fateful alliance" of George Kennan's vision is no longer the *entente* reached between France and the Russian Empire in 1894, but an Anglo–Confederate naval "understanding" entered into seven years before. This is the agreement that sets in motion a process of Great Power alignment that within just a few years has replicated the rigid and combustible structures of our timeline's 1914. By the time Marchand and Kitchener have their encounter at that mud hut on the Nile, the mindset of the leaders of France and Great Britain is that of Powers girding for years for the likelihood of war. Moreover, Paris and London are not free agents able to work out their dispute alone but members of great alliances whose interests are seen to be implicated wherever and whenever members of those alliances come into conflict. This is the "alliance dynamic" of the *DMA* timeline: the same "alliance dynamic" that in our history played out to such terrible effect in the summer of 1914 and which in the *DMA* time-line reaches that critical point of combustion a decade and a half earlier.

As our narrative attempts to demonstrate, the world reaches this point because a Confederate victory sets in motion a process of change in rela-tions among the Great Powers. We do so, however, while also adhering to the rule that, unless there is a particularized reason in our history of post-September 1862 for a Confederate victory to produce a change in the course of that history, *our alternate history should postulate no such change.* Things that happened as they did would still have happened as they did until the ripple effect of Confederate independence intersected with that other course of events. And even then, we postulate that this intersection works only that change proportionate to the degree of the ensuing inter-play between a course of events that was in real history and the course of Confederate history unfolding in the world of *DMA.*

For example: In the *DMA* timeline, the Confederacy sets its eye on acquir-ing Cuba. Ultimately, this ambition produces a "Spanish–Confederate War" in 1870 which unfolds similarly to the Spanish–American War of 1898. There is no reason to conclude, however, that this Confederate ambition would change the course of Spanish internal history preceding such a Spanish–Confederate conflict. Queen Isabella would still be overthrown in 1868, and even with a war between Spain and the Confederacy breaking out in early 1870, the question of the Spanish Succession should still give Bismarck the opportunity to goad France into a war leading to the overthrow of the French Second Empire and the establishment of the German Second Reich. Similarly, that the Confederacy wins its fight for independence in 1862 should make no difference to the course of Sino–Japanese relations which led to the Sino–Japanese War of 1894–95. But if by the mid-1890s the Great Powers of Europe had already divided into alliances comparable to the division between the *Entente Cordiale* and the Triple Alliance of our timeline, the consequent wooing of Japan by both sides, already underway by 1895, would make highly unlikely the anti-Japanese Triple Intervention which in our timeline saw Japan forced to yield to Russia the Liaotung Peninsula and Port Arthur, awarded to her by the Treaty of Shimonoseki.

This process of calculation also requires consideration of how the changed course of history may affect the actions of individuals. For example, in our timeline, Georges Clemenceau was caught up in a scandal relating to the failed French attempt to build a Panama Canal in the 1870s and 1880s. Clemenceau was innocent of the charges of corruption leveled against him; yet, he suffered a terrible political fall because of them which by the mid-1890s left him on the fringe of French politics. Thus, when the Dreyfus Affair unfolded and Emile Zola came to Clemenceau and asked Clemenceau to publish Zola's philippic "J'Accuse!" in Clemenceau's newspaper *L'Aurore*, Clemenceau, personally identifying with another victim of injustice, willingly agreed. But in the *DMA* timeline, the Panama Canal is successfully developed by a Franco–American combine. There is no Panama Canal scandal. Georges Clemenceau never undergoes the searing experience of being the victim of unjust charges. His pugnacious nationalism is never tempered by a commitment to justice for the individual. When Emile Zola comes to him in 1898, pleading for support of Zola's campaign for a revision of the verdict against Dreyfus, Clemenceau, utterly consumed by the politics of *revanche*, not only spurns Zola but instead turns his powerful voice against the *Dreyfusards*, condemning them as unpatriotic as the Crisis Year of 1898 unfolds.

Changes affecting individuals can extend to the lengthening—or short-ening—of their lives. Judah Benjamin, the Confederacy's Secretary of State, in our timeline fled the United States in a small boat to Bermuda, eventually making his way to England (where he became a leading barrister). Benjamin suffered a massive heart attack in 1882, which compelled his retirement from the law; he died the following year. In the *DMA* timeline, Benjamin's body is not subjected to the terrible stresses of three more years of war—ending in the destruction of the Confederacy from which he is compelled to undertake a physically punishing escape. Benjamin's heart attack in 1883 therefore is fairly mild, and he is able to continue to render great service to the Confederate cause for several more years, including the negotiation of the Anglo–Confederate Naval Understanding. George Pickett, on the other hand, suffers an earlier death, leading a charge up San Juan Hill during the Confederate conquest of Cuba in 1870—instead of expiring of Scarlett Fever five years later as he did in our timeline. (One suspects Pickett's shade would not object to the shortening of his mortal span, considering the more glorious nature of his passing in the world of *DMA*.)

Central to the course of the *DMA* timeline is the question of whether an independent South would have emancipated its slaves. We take the view that the South would have maintained its peculiar institution, and that this continuing commitment would also have turned the tide in the global struggle against slavery which was underway when the South made its bid for independence. Recent scholarship (see, e.g., *The Fall of the House of Dixie* by Bruce Levine, published in January of 2013) has underscored the depth of the South's planter elite's commitment to slavery. And that elite, having just won a war of independence in order to preserve slavery, is not likely to give it up unless dire circumstances compel them to do so.

The timing of a Southern victory therefore becomes crucial to the fate of slavery. We agree with those who contend that a Southern victory delayed until late 1864 or early 1865 would have left the Confederacy with a slave system severely damaged by the penetration of Northern armies deep into the country's slavery heartland. Moreover, a Southern victory delayed that late—presumably brought about only because a change in the course of Sherman's campaign costs Lincoln the presidency in 1864—would force Southern national and state governments to focus all of their energies for many years to come on the task of rebuilding a country ravaged by war. There would be little time or energy left over for reaching out and establishing a close relationship with the slave owners of Brazil. The War of the Triple Alliance likely would have remained nothing but something about which Confederates read in the newspapers; the Law of the Womb would have been adopted as it was in our history, and as 1880 approached, the Confederacy would have found itself standing alone as the last "civilized" country still holding people in bondage. In that event, the notion of some sort of "Brazilian Solution," some form of gradual, compensated emancipation, becomes far more plausible. (See, e.g., Roger L. Ransom, *The Confederate States of America: What Might Have Been*—New York and London: W.W. Norton 2005—positing that a Southern victory achieved in late 1864–early 1865 sets the stage for a compensated emancipation in 1880.)

A Confederate victory in the fall of 1862, however, is a very different matter. Union forces had barely begun their disruptive penetration of the Southern slave lands, and the vast majority of slave-based enterprises remained undisturbed by the fighting. The process of dealing with the war's immediate aftermath would have been much less demanding, and by 1865, the government of Jefferson Davis would have been able to turn its attention to making the Western Hemisphere safe for slavery by reaching out to their Brazilian counterparts. Should the kind of "positive socioeconomic feedback loop" we posit have developed between the two countries' slave-based economies, and especially if the South had managed to add to it by the acquisition of Cuba (whether by force of arms or outright purchase), the result could very well have been the reversal of the tide that had been running against slavery since the English announced their intention to suppress the international slave trade in 1808.

As for the future course of Southern economic development: We are firmly of the view that a Southern industrialization, on a scale much greater than that seen in the New South of our timeline, could have been carried out with a mix of slave and free labor. The notion that slavery is economically incompatible with the creation of a modern industrial base ignores, among other things, the extent to which the New South of our timeline built a modern industrial economy on the backs of hundreds of thousands of African–American men who were made the subjects of a system of "neo-slavery" in some ways more terrible than the system ended by the Thirteenth Amendment.

And what of a United States whose political and economic development is no longer subject to the veto of the Slave Power? A common-place in alternate history writing on the question of a Confederate victory in the American Civil War is positing an extended postwar depression in the North. We don't share this view. Secession broke a logjam in the USA Congress, and the Congressional session of 1862 saw a flood of progressive measures passed that would profoundly reshape America and accelerate her economic growth. The effective end of the war by November 1862 would leave the American exchequer in much better shape than it would be in our timeline by the end of 1863 or 1864. Northern dead and wounded number less than a fourth of what they were in our timeline, and the country would be able to turn to the pursuit of peaceful industry and agriculture much more quickly—and without the drag on the economy represented by a devastated and defeated South still within the Union. Moreover, the loss of the heavy industry developing spur represented by the war business of 1863 and 1864 would soon be offset by the need to maintain and even expand armed forces able to at least match, and more likely exceed, those of the new independent South.

As for political and social developments: The removal from the North's political system of the greatest concentration of wealthy Americans—the Southern planter, in terms of the dollar value of his wealth, including his human capital, dominated the One Percent of that day—would significantly weaken resistance to such economically equalitarian measures as making permanent a federal income tax. And the removal from the North's internal economy of the South as an anti-labor counterweight would significantly weaken resistance to the demands of organized labor. Labor and Capital remain at odds, but their struggle now plays out in a political environment that does not allow corporate managers to so freely employ the instruments of state power to crush the nascent industrial union movement by brute force—as was done time and again in the re-United States during the 1870s, 1880s, and 1890s of our timeline. The New Social Covenant of the *DMA* timeline is certainly less complete a Magna Charta for organized labor than that granted by the New Deal, but it represents real and progressive change from a sociopolitical system whose leaders (in 1877) called out federal troops and ordered them to clear the streets of major American cities by shooting down strikers and their families. And by the 1890s, the benefits of this more equalitarian social and political structure are being extended to the North's (much smaller) African–American population. Race prejudice is still very much a commonplace in the North, but without the toxic effect of Southern White Supremacy sharing the national bloodstream, the progressive tendencies of our own timeline's 1870s and 1880s should not wither and die but instead grow and develop—however fitful and uneven the process undoubtedly would have been.

Which brings us to the question of technology: As with other aspects, we have attempted not to depart from real-world technological development unless our point of departure and its sequela would indicate such a change. For example, in the presence of a hostile Confederacy, and one moreover supported in 1862 by the Royal Navy, we believe it unreasonable to posit that the US Navy would have stagnated in the manner it did in the original timeline. At the beginning of our period, this implies a larger building program for monitors; toward the end of the period covered by this volume, it implies an earlier switch to steel and armor, an earlier implementation of the non-coastal-battleship fleet concept, and construction of a larger number of ships of each type. Similarly, the reader will note that Spain, for example, builds many more battleships than it did in the original timeline, while by 1900 there are additional ships of each major British battleship class, and the classes have come online somewhat earlier (perhaps two years by the turn of the century) than otherwise. We have taken similar liberties with items such as coastal fortifications and the occasional artillery piece. On the other hand, there is no reason to believe that the absence of access to Kitty Hawk would have inspired the Wright Brothers to conceive their critical wing-warping experiments any earlier. Hence, there are no airplanes upon the outbreak of World War One in 1898, although as the reader of Volume Two will see, their development would accelerate under the pressures of a political and military climate very different from our timeline's 1901–1914.

A final note: The reader of this volume may come away with the impression that we believe the world of *DMA* would, at least in some ways, have been a better place. And that would be a correct surmise. We do believe that socially, politically, and economically, the United States of America would have developed, at least for a time, along what we would consider better lines. Certainly, the condition of the Northern working class, and also its African–American population, would have been much improved over what either group experienced during the 1870s and 1880s of our timeline. But eating away at this limited progress is the terrible cancer of an independent slaveholding South, whose efforts to make the world safe for the institution of slavery has, even before the end of the nineteenth century, doomed the campaign to suppress the slave trade and extirpate slavery itself from the "civilized" world. In Volume Two, the reader will see how this cancer metastasizes and spreads from its Confederate–Brazilian locus. And even more destructive of hope for a progressive and liberated future for humanity is the cycle of Great Power war. *DMA's* truncated World War One is just the foretaste of even wider and more destructive wars to come. And all this comes to pass because Robert E. Lee and the Army of Northern Virginia *did* win *a* Battle of Gettysburg in September of 1862.

A Partial Bibliography—and Some Related
Thoughts about the Process of Writing *Alternate* History

Set forth below is a partial bibliography for Volume One of *Democracy's Missing Arsenal*.

Of course, at one level, the very idea of having a bibliography for an "alternate" history raises some interesting existential questions. Must a bibliography of an alternate history, especially one written from "within" the alternate postulated timeline, be composed of sources "from" that timeline? The redoubtable Peter Tsouras has excelled at that device in his many alternate history collections. John and I might have taken the same route, but to the extent we have proposed alternate works that might have been in the world of *Democracy's Missing Arsenal*, we have chosen instead to make them part of the narrative (for example, USA Chief Justice W. E. B. DuBois's *Failure of the Suppression of the Slave Trade*). This bibliography is a list of works written in the world of "real" history and which helped shape us to shape the narrative of our alternate history.

Writing an alternate history is, in a way, an intellectual suicide mission. One steps forth into what amounts to a minefield of "real" history. From the starting point of one's chosen "point of divergence" (or "POD"), one moves forward into a future that, step-by-step, diverges increasingly from "known" history. Quite frankly, it is only a matter of time before one steps on a landmine, as the narrative of the alternate history collides with some hard fact that means the change one is postulating just could not have been because of some overlooked fact of "real" history. The trick is to try to detect as many of these mines as one can before one steps on them and, having detected them, to adjust the course of the alternate history's narrative so as to move around the mine and leave it safely behind.

To do that, one must immerse oneself in the chronicles of history as we know it. The bibliography set forth below is an attempt to provide at least a representative list of the many works we consulted to avoid the landmines that can render one's narrative implausible. Crafting a credible alternate history involves identifying the intersection point between the chosen POD and the flow of events elsewhere. A change of course should be predicted in a certain place at a certain point in time only if there is a plausible reason rooted in the course of actual history for believing that at that point the changes set in motion by the POD will come into contact with the flow of actual history and alter its course. To identify that point requires a working knowledge of that actual history, and when the working thesis of the alternate history in question is that the chosen POD will eventually work a radical change in the course of global history, well....

Let's just say that the authors of such an alternate history must be prepared to learn a lot of actual history: about a kaleidoscope of places and peoples and individuals. The bibliography set forth below is a reflection of our effort to learn that history. We are *not* saying that we read every one of these works—cover to cover. In many cases, we only sampled as we moved back and forth from source to source, trying to get a good sense for all of the major moving parts that came together to form the particular history of immediate concern. Nor is the list of works intended to be comprehensive. Besides the works we consulted over the seventeen-year course of creating *Democracy's Missing Arsenal* and now can't recall, there are many other sources—articles in newspapers, newsmagazines, history journals, encyclopedia (including a mint condition set of the 1911 *Encyclopedia Britannica*), and even postings on the web (yes, we *did* rely from time to time on Wikipedia)—which we belatedly recognize we ought to have carefully catalogued but, alas, failed to record. At least the listing set forth below will give the reader an idea of the degree of our effort to avoid as many of those mines as we could!

The bibliography is divided into two parts. The first part lists works dealing with subjects other than the American Civil War; as the reader will quickly surmise, when one is writing an alternate *world* history, one must delve into a wide variety of subjects. The second part lists works dealing with the American Civil War—and particularly the Battles of Antietam and Gettysburg. The course of the Battle of Gettysburg of our alternate history is shaped most fundamentally by the fact that it flows out of the Battle of Antietam that does not happen, because the Lost Order remains lost. Yet, "our" Gettysburg of September 1862 takes place on much the same ground and involves the same two armies as the Gettysburg of July 1863, and as the image of that later battle would be so familiar to many who might read our work, it was essential that we study the "real" Gettysburg with care so that the students of that battle would come to see why we believe a battle of Gettysburg fought in September 1862 would likely have unfolded in the way we have set forth. Works about slavery not specific to the United States are listed in Part One; those focused on the United States are listed in Part Two. Biographies of figures known primarily for their role in the American Civil War are listed in Part Two; others, in Part One. (We have not listed any biographies for Abraham Lincoln or Winston Churchill because it would be a futile exercise to figure out which portions of the voluminous literature on these two gigantic figures were particularly influential in shaping our narrative.)

We have provided the last printing date indicated in the copy of the work available to us. In some cases we had the hardback, in other cases the paperback version of the work. The reader may notice a concentration of titles from the 1990s. This reflects that the primary drafting of what has become Volume One of "DMA" took place in the late 1990s, with the authors returning to finish that portion in late 2012 and early 2013. We also have included the place of publication, per citation convention, when we could figure that out -- which is harder than one might think, especially when it comes to *paperback* printing.

Finally, we again want to acknowledge the formative influence of one work of alternate history: Winston Churchill's remarkable 1931 essay, "If Lee Had Not the Battle of Gettysburg." Part of a truly astonishing collection of alternate history essays published that year under the title, *If History Had Happened Otherwise*, Churchill wrote from the perspective of a 1931 in which Lee *had* won the Battle of Gettysburg in July 1863, and as a result the South won its fight for independence. Churchill describes how the South's victory unleashed an arms race between the two American Unions, which might have produced a terrible war by the early 1900s had not Great Britain stepped in to mediate. The mediation not only prevents a war, but leads to the formation by the three English-speaking powers of a mighty "Anglo–Saxon" confederation, which then wields its power to compel a peaceful resolution of the European Crisis of 1914. At the end of the piece, Churchill suggests that, without a victory by Lee, the South would have been defeated, no Anglo–Saxon confederation would have been formed, and the Crisis of 1914 would have plunged Europe into a ruinous war. We agree with Churchill that the outcome of the American Civil War had a profound impact on the course of European, indeed world history. As the reader of our work realizes, we demur from Churchill's view that a Southern victory could have had anything but a disastrous effect on the course of that history.

Part One—Works of History Other Than the History of the American Civil War

Bain, David H. *Empire Express: Building the First Transcontinental Railroad.* Penguin Books, 2000.

Balfour, Michael. *The Kaiser and His Times.* New York: W.W. Norton & Company, 1972.

Berton, Pierre. *The Great Railway* (abridged by the author from *The National Dream* and *The Last Spike*). Toronto: McClelland & Stewart Inc., 1992.

Berton, Pierre. *Klondike: The Last Great Gold Rush*, rev. ed. Toronto: McClelland & Stewart, Inc., 1993.

Blake, Robert. *Disraeli.* New York: St. Martin's Press, 1967.

Blanning, T. C. W., editor. *The Oxford Illustrated History of Modern Europe.* New York: Oxford University Press, 1996.

Bönker, Dirk. *Militarism in a Global Age: Naval Ambitions in Germany and the United states Before World War I.* Ithaca and London: Cornell University Press, 2012.

Bothwell, Robert. *Canada and Quebec: One Country, Two Histories*, rev.ed. Vancouver: UBC Press, 1999.

Brecher, Jeremy. *Strike!* San Francisco: Straight Arrow Books, 1977.

Bredin, Jean-Denis. *The Affair: The Case of Alfred Dreyfus.* New York: George Braziller, 1986.

Bruce, Robert V. *1877: Year of Violence.* Chicago: Ivan R. Dee, Inc., First Elephant Paperback edition, 1989.

Bryant, Keith L., Jr. *History of the Atchison, Topeka and Santa Fe Railway.* Lincoln and London: University of Nebraska Press, Bison Book Printing, 1982.

Brysac, Shareen Blair, and Karl E. Meyer. *Tournament of Shadows: The Great Game and the Race for Empire in Central Asia.* Washington, D.C.: Perseus Books Group, Counterpoint, 1999.

Burns, E. Bradford. *A History of Brazil*, 3rd ed. New York: Columbia University Press, 1993.

Burr, Lawrence. *US Cruisers 1883–1904: The Birth of the Steel Navy.* New York and Oxford: Osprey Publishing, 2008.

Carr, Raymond. *Spain 1808–1975*, 2nd ed. Oxford: Clarendon Press, 1982.

Coletta, Paolo E., ed. *American Secretaries of the Navy: Vol. I 1775–1913.* Annapolis: Naval Institute Press, 1980.

Collier, Simon, and William F. Sater. *A History of Chile, 1808–1994.* Cambridge University Press, 1996.

Craig, Gordon A. *Germany 1866–1945.* New York: Oxford University Press, 1978.

Crawford, Steve. *Battleships and Carriers.* New York: Barnes & Noble Books, 1999

Dallas, Gregor. *At the Heart of a Tiger: Clemenceau and His World 1841–1929.* New York: Carroll & Graf Publishers, Inc., 1993.

Dangerfield, George. *The Damnable Question: A History of Anglo–Irish Relations.* New York: Barnes & Noble Books, 1976, 1999.

Davenport, T. R. H. *South Africa: A Modern History.* Toronto and Buffalo: University of Toronto Press, 1978.

Davis, David B. *Inhuman Bondage: The Rise and Fall of Slavery in the New World.* New York: Oxford University Press, 2006.

Davis, David B. *Slavery and Human Progress.* New York and Oxford: Oxford University Press, 1984.

Di Scala, Spencer M. *Italy: From Revolution to Republic:1700 to the Present.* Boulder, San Francisco, Oxford: Westview Press, 1995.

Douglas, George H. *All Aboard! The Railroad in American Life.* New York: U.S. Media Holdings, Smithmark Publishers, 1996.

Duggan, Christopher. *A Concise History of Italy.* Cambridge University Press, 1994.

Edgerton, Robert B. *Warriors of the Rising Sun: A History of the Japanese Military.* New York and London: W.W. Norton & Company, 1997.

Esherick, Joseph W. *The Origins of the Boxer Uprising.* Berkeley, Los Angeles, and London: University of California Press, 1987.

Fage, J. D., and Roland Oliver. *A Short History of Africa*, 6th ed. Penguin Books, 1990.

Faulk, Odie B. *Arizona, a Short History.* Norman and London: University of Oklahoma Press: 1988.

Faulk, Odie B. *The Geronimo Campaign.* New York, Oxford: Oxford University Press, 1993.

Fausto, Boris. *A Concise History of Brazil.* Cambridge University Press, 1999.

Foner, Eric. *The Story of American Freedom.* New York, London: W. W. Norton & Company, 1998.

Forczyck, Robert. *Russian Battleship v. Japanese Battleship: Yellow Sea 1904–05.* New York and Oxford: Osprey Publishing, 2009.

Foster, R. F. *Modern Ireland: 1600–1972.* Penguin Books, 1989.

French, Patrick: *Younghusband: The Last Great Imperial Adventure.* London: HarperCollins, Flamingo, 1995.

Friedberg, Aaron L. *The Weary Titan: Britain and the Experience of Relative Decline, 1895–1905.* Princeton University Press, 1988.

Friesen, Geral. *The Canadian Prairies: A History.* Lincoln and London: University of Nebraska Press, 1984.

Fry, Joseph A. *Dixie Looks Abroad: The South and U.S. Foreign Relations 1789–1973.* Baton Rouge: Louisiana State University Press, 2002.

Furet, François. *Revolutionary France 1770–1880.* Oxford UK and Cambridge USA: Blackwell, 1995.

Golway, Terry. *Irish Rebel: John Devoy and America's Fight for Ireland's Freedom.* New York: St. Martin's Press, 1998.

Graham, Richard, ed. *The Idea of Race in Latin America, 1870–1940.* Austin: University of Texas Press, 1996.

Grant, George, Angus Konstam, and Leo Marriott. *Warships: From the Galley to the Present Day.* New York: Random House Value Publishing, Inc., Gramercy Books, 2001.

Gray, Francine Du Plessix. *Hawaii: The Sugar-Coated Fortress.* New York and Toronto: Random House, 1972.

Grove, Eric, and Bernard Ireland. *Jane's War at Sea 1897–1997: 100 Years of Jane's Fighting Ships.* New York and London: HarperCollins, 1997.

Han, Woo-keun. *The History of Korea.* Honolulu: University of Hawaii Press, 1974.

Harries, Meirion, and Susie Harries. *Soldiers of the Sun: The Rise and Fall of the Imperial Japanese Army*. New York: Random House, 1991.

Hill, Richard. *War at Sea in the Ironclad Age*. New York and London: HarperCollins, Smithsonian Books, 2006.

Hochschild, Adam. *King Leopold's Ghost: A Story of Greed, Terror and Heroism in Colonial Africa*. New York: Houghton Mifflin, 1998.

Hogg, Ian. *Twentieth Century Artillery*. New York: Barnes & Noble Books, 2000

Hopkirk, Peter. *The Great Game: The Struggle for Empire in Central Asia*. New York, Tokyo and London: Kodansha International, 1992.

Horne, Alistair. *The Fall of Paris: The Siege and the Commune 1870–71*. Penguin Books, 1987.

Horsman, Reginald. *Race and Manifest Destiny: The Origins of American Racial Anglo–Saxonism*. Harvard University Press, 1981.

Jackson, Robert. *Destroyers, Corvettes and Frigates*. New York: Barnes & Noble Books, 2000

James, Lawrence. *RAJ: The Making and Unmaking of British India*. London: Little, Brown & Company, Abacus, 1998.

Jenkins, Roy. *Gladstone: A Biography*. New York: Random House, 1997.

Kann, Robert A. *A History of Habsburg Empire 1526–1918*. Berkeley, Los Angeles, London: University of California Press, 1980.

Karnow, Stanley. *In Our Image: America's Empire in the Philippines*. New York: Ballantine Books, 1989.

Kaufmann, H. W., and J. E. Kaufmann. *Fortress America: The Forts that Defended America, 1600 to the Present*. Cambridge, Mass: Perseus Book Groups, DaCapo Press, 2004

Kee, Robert. *The Green Flag Volume Two: The Bold Fenian Men.* Penguin Books, 1972.

Keegan, John. *Fields of Battle: The Wars for North America.* New York: Alfred A. Knopf, 1996.

Keller, Julia. *Mr. Gatling's Terrible Marvel: The Gun That Changed Everything and the Misunderstood Genius Who Invented It.* New York: Penguin Group, Viking, 2008.

Kennan, George F. *The Fateful Alliance: France, Russia, and the Coming of the First World War.* New York: Random House, Inc., Pantheon Books, 1984.

Kennedy, Paul M. *The Rise of Anglo-German Antagonism 1860-1914.* London and Atlantic Highlands, NJ: The Ashfield Press, 1994.

Kennedy, Paul M., ed. *The War Plans of the Great Powers 1880-1914.* Boston: Allen & Unwin, 1985.

Kens, Paul. *Justice Stephen Field: Shaping Liberty from the Gold Rush to the Gilded Age.* Lawrence, Kansas: University Press of Kansas, 1997.

Krauze, Enrique. *Mexico: Biography of Power – A History of Modern Mexico, 1810–1996.* New York: HarperCollins Publishers, 1997.

Lapping, Adrian. *Apartheid: A History,* rev. ed. New York: George Braziller, 1989.

LaPierre, Laurier L. *1759: The Battle for Canada.* Toronto, McClelland & Stewart Inc., 1990.

LaPierre, Laurier L. *Québec: A Tale of love.* London: Penguin, Viking, 2001.

Larson, Gustive O. *Prelude to the Kingdom: Mormon Desert Conquest – A Chapter in American Cooperative Experience.* Francestown, New Hampshire: Marshall Jones Company, 1947.

Leech, Margaret. *In the Days of McKinley*. Norwalk, Connecticut: Harper & Row, The Easton Press, 1986.

Loechl, Suzanne K., and Adam Smith. *Fort Hamilton, New York: Historic Landscape Inventory*. U.S. Army Corps of Engineers Engineer Research and Development Center, December 2000

Lerner, Max, ed. *The Mind and Faith of Justice Holmes: His Speeches, Essays, Letters, and Judicial Opinions*. New Brunswick (U.S.A.) and Oxford (U.K.): Transaction Publishers, 1989.

Lewis, David Levering. *W. E. B. Du Bois: Biography of a Race 1868–1919*. New York: Henry Holt and Company, 1993.

Lewis, Emmanuel Raymond. *Seacoast Fortifications of the United States: An Introductory History*. Annapolis: Naval Institute Press, 1992

Lord Kinross. *The Ottoman Centuries: The Rise and Fall of the Turkish Empire*. New York: Morrow Quill Paperbacks, 1977.

Love, Robert W., Jr. *History of the U. S. Navy 1775–1941*. Harrisburg, PA: Stackpole Books, 1992.

Malone, Michael P. *James J. Hill: Empire Builder of the Northwest*. Norman and London: University of Oklahoma Press, 1996.

Manchester, William. *The Arms of Krupp: 1587–1968*. Boston and Toronto: Little, Brown and Company, 1968.

Massie, Robert K. *Castles of Steel: Britain, Germany, and the Winning of the Great War at Sea*. New York: Random House, 2003.

Massie, Robert K. *Dreadnought: Britain, Germany, and the Coming of the Great War*. New York: Ballantine Books, 1992.

McCaffrey, Lawrence J. *Ireland: From Colony to Nation State*. Englewood Cliffs, N.J.: Prentice–Hall, Inc., 1979.

McCullough, David. *The Path Between the Seas: The Creation of the Panama Canal 1870–1914*. New York: Simon and Schuster, 1977.

McFeely, William S. *Frederick Douglas*. New York and London: W. W. Norton & Company, 1991.

McNaught, Kenneth. *The Penguin History of Canada*. Penguin Books, 1988.

McSherry, Patrick. "Wallowin' in a Typhoon Before Morning." U.S. Naval Institute, *Naval History*, Vol. 22, No. 5, October 2008.

Meyer, Michael C., and William L. Sherman. *The Course of Mexican History*, Fifth Edition. New York and Oxford: Oxford University Press, 1995.

Miller, Edward S. *War Plan Orange: The U.S. Strategy to Defeat Japan, 1897–1945*. Annapolis, Maryland: Naval Institute Press, 1991.

Miller, Paul. "The Big Guns of Fort Schuyler," *The Bronx County Historical Society Journal*, Vol. XXIV, No. 1, Spring 1987.

Moore, Christopher. *1867: How the Fathers Made a Deal*. Toronto: McClelland & Stewart Inc., 1997.

Morgan, Murray. *Puget's Sound: A Narrative of Early Tacoma and the Southern Sound*. Seattle and London: University of Washington Press, 1981.

Morris, Donald R. *The Washington of the Spears: A History of the Rise of the Zulu Nation under Shaka and Its Fall in the Zulu War of 1879*. New York: Simon and Schuster, 1965.

Morris, Edmund. *The Rise of Theodore Roosevelt*. New York: Coward, McCann & Geoghegan, Inc., 1979.

Morris, Jan. *Fisher's Face*. Penguin Books, 1995.

Morton, Desmond. *A Military History of Canada*. Toronto: McClelland & Stewart Inc., 1992.

Morton, Desmond. *A Short History of Canada*, Second Revised Edition. Toronto: McClelland & Stewart Inc., 1994.

Morton, W. L. *The Critical Years: The Union of British North America 1857–1873*. Toronto: McClelland and Stewart, 1964.

Murdock, John R., M.A. *Constitutional Development of Arizona*. Tempe, Arizona: 1933.

Newhart, Max. R. *American Battleships: A Pictorial History of BB-1 to BB-71 with Prototypes Maine & Texas*. Missoula: Pictorial Histories Publishing Co., 2007.

O'Toole, G. J. A. *The Spanish War: An American Epic – 1898*. New York and London: W. W. Norton & Company, 1984.

Offer, Avner. *The First World War: An Agrarian Interpretation*. Oxford: Clarendon Press, 1989.

Pakenham, Thomas. *The Boer War*. New York: Random House, 1979.

Pakenham, Thomas. *The Scramble for America: 1876–1912*. New York: Random House, 1991.

Peattie, Mark R. *Nan'yō: The Rise and Fall of the Japanese in Micronesia, 1885–1945*. Honolulu: University of Hawaii Press, 1992.

Pelling, Henry. *America and the British Left: From Bright to Bevan*. New York University Press, 1957.

Pendergrast, Mark. *Uncommon Grounds: The History of Coffee and How It Transformed Our World*. New York: Perseus Books Group, Basic Books, 1999.

Perez-Brignoli, Hector. *A Brief History of Central America*. Berkeley, Los Angeles and London: University of California Press, 1989.

Perry, John Curtis, Peter W. Stanley, and James C. Thomson, Jr. *Sentimental Imperialists: The American Experience in East Asia.* New York: Harper & Row, Harper Colophon Books, 1981.

Pflanze, Otto. *Bismarck and the Development of Germany: Volume I – The Period of Unification, 1815–1871.* Princeton University Press, 1990.

Plummer, Brenda Gayle. *Haiti and the United States: The Psychological Moment.* Athens and London: The University of Georgia Press, 1992.

Preston, Diana. *The Boxer Rebellion: The Dramatic Story of China's War on Foreigners That Shook the World in the Summer of 1900.* New York: Berkley Books, 2001.

Preston, Richard A. *The Defence of the Undefended Border: Planning for War in North America 1867–1939.* Montreal and London: McGill-Queen's University Press, 1977.

Pringle, Henry F. *Theodore Roosevelt: A Biography.* San Diego, New York and London: Harcourt Brace & Company, A Harvest Book, 1984.

Quarsetin, John V. *A History of Ironclads: The Power of Iron over Wood.* Charleston: The History Press, 2006.

Rabban, David M. *Free Speech in Its Forgotten Years.* Cambridge University Press, 1997.

Randall, Stephen J. *Colombia and the United States: Hegemony and Interdependence.* Athens and London: University of Georgia Press, 1996.

Reckner, James R. "The Rebirth of the Fleet." U.S. Naval Institute, *Naval History*, Vol. 21, No. 6, December 2007.

Rock, David, *Argentina 1516–1987: From Spanish Colonization to Alfonsín.* Berkeley and Los Angeles, University of California Press, 1987.

Sater, William F. *Chile and the United States: Empires in Conflict.* Athens and London: The University of Georgia Press, 1990.

Seton-Watson, Hugh. *The Russian Empire: 1801–1917.* Oxford: Clarendon Press, 1967.

Shirer, William L. *The Collapse of the Third Republic: An Inquiry into the Fall of France in 1940.* New York: Da Capo Press, 1994.

Spector, Ronald. *Admiral of the New Empire: The Life and Career of George Dewey.* Columbia, South Carolina: University of South Carolina Press, 1988.

Spector, Ronald. *At War at Sea: Sailors and Naval Combat in the Twentieth Century.* New York: Penguin Group, Viking, 2001.

Speidel, William C. *Sons of the Profits or, There's No Business Like Grow Business! The Seattle Story, 1851–1901.* Seattle, Washington: Nettle Creek Publishing Company, 1967.

Spence, Jonathan D. *The Search for Modern China.* New York, London: W. W. Norton & Company, 1990.

Starrett, Col. W. A. *Skyscrapers and the Men Who Build Them.* New York and London: Charles Scribner's Sons, 1928.

Stürmer, Michael. *The German Empire 1871–1919.* London: Orion Books, Phoenix Press, 2002.

Sugar, Peter F., gen.ed. *A Story of Hungary.* Bloomington and Indianapolis: Indiana University Press, 1994.

Taylor, A. J. P. *The Habsburg Monarchy 1809–1918: A History of the Austrian Empire and Austria–Hungary.* Chicago and London: The University of Chicago Press, 1976.

Thomas, Hugh. *The Slave Trade: The Story of the Atlantic Slave Trade – 1440–1870.* New York: Simon & Schuster, 1997.

Thompson, Leonard. *A History of South Africa,* rev. ed. Newhaven and London: Yale University Press, 1995.

Traxel, David. *1898: The Birth of the American Century.* New York: Alfred A. Knopf, 1998.

Tuchman, Barbara W. *The Proud Tower: A Portrait of the World Before the War 1890–1914.* New York: The Macmillan Company, 1966.

Utley, Robert M. *Frontier Regulars: The United States Army and the Indian, 1866–1891.* New York and London: Macmillan Publishing Co., Inc., 1973.

Whitley, M. J. *Battleships of World War Two: An International Encyclopedia.* Annapolis: Naval Institute Press, 1998.

Winks, Robin W. *Frederick Billings: A Life.* New York, Oxford: Oxford University Press, 1991.

Wolpert, Stanley. *A New History of India,* Fourth Edition. New York, Oxford: Oxford University Press, 1993.

Womack, John, Jr. *Zapata and the Mexican Revolution.* New York: Random House, Vintage Books, 1970.

Wood, Charles R. *The Northern Pacific: Main Street of the Northwest.* New York: Bonanza Books, 1968.

Woodward, C. Vann *Origins of the New South: 1877–1913.* Baton Rouge: Louisiana State University Press, 1951.

Wooster, Robert. *Nelson A. Miles and the Twilight of the Frontier Army.* Lincoln and London: University of Nebraska Press, 1993.

Part Two—Works of History of the American Civil War

Boaz, Thomas. *Guns for Cotton: England Arms the Confederacy*. Shippensburg: Burd Street Press, 1996.

Carhart, Tom. *Lost Triumph: Lee's Real Plan at Gettysburg—And Why It Failed*. New York: Penguin Group, G. P. Putnam & Sons, 2008.

Coddington, Edwin B. *The Gettysburg Campaign: A Study in Command*. New York: Charles Scribner's Sons, Morningside Bookshop hardcover ed., 1979.

Davis, Major George B, Joseph W. Kirkley, and Leslie J. Perry. *The Official Military Atlas of the Civil War*. Washington, D.C.: Government Prtining Office 1891–1895 (reprinted by Barnes & Noble Books, 2003).

Davis, William C. *Breckinridge: Statesman Soldier, Symbol*. Baton Rouge and London: Louisiana State University Press, 1992.

DeRosa, Marshall L. *The Confederate Constitution of 1861: An Inquiry into American Constitutionalism*. Columbia and London: University of Missouri Press, 1991.

Dew, Charles B. *Ironmaker to the Confederacy: Joseph R. Anderson and the Tredegar Iron Works*. Richmond: The Library of Virginia, 1999.

Evans, Eli N. *Judah P. Benjamin: The Jewish Confederate*. New York: MacMillan, Inc., The Free Press, 1989.

Foote, Shelby. *The Civil War: A Narrative* (Volumes One, Two, and Three) (1958, 1963, 1974)

Fuller, Howard J. *Clad in Iron: The American Civil War and the Challenge of British Naval Power*. Westport and London: Greenwood Publishing Group, Prager Publishers, 2008.

Gallagher, Gary W., ed. *The Antietam Campaign*. Chapel Hill and London: University of North Carolina Press, 1999.

Gottfried, Bradley M. *The Maps of Gettysburg: An Atlas of the Gettysburg Campaign, June 3–July 13, 1863*. New York and California: Savas Beatie, 2007.

Heysinger, Captain Isaac W. *Antietam and the Maryland and Virginia Campaigns of 1862*. New York: Neale Publishing Company, 1912 (reprinted by Olde Soldier Books, Gaithersburg, Maryland, 1987)

Jones, Howard. *Union in Peril: The Crisis over British Intervention in the Civil War*. Chapel Hill and London: The University of North Carolina Press, 1992.

Jordan, David M. *Winfield Scott Hancock: A Soldier's Life*. Bloomington and Indianapolis: Indiana University Press, 1996.

Konstam, Angus. *Confederate Submarines and Torpedo Vessels 1861–65*. Oxford: Osprey Publishing, 2004.

Konstam, Angus. *Union Monitor 1861–65*. Oxford: Osprey Publishing, 2002.

Levine, Bruce. *The Fall of the House of Dixie: The Civil War and the Social Revolution that Transformed the South*. New York: Random House, 2013.

Luvas, Jay, and Harold W. Nelson, eds. *The U.S. Army War College Guide to the Battle of Antietam: The Maryland Campaign of 1862*. Carlisle: South Mountain Press, Inc., 1987.

Luvas, Jay, and Harold W. Nelson, eds. *The U.S. Army War College Guide to the Battle of Gettysburg*. Carlisle: South Mountain Press, Inc., 1986

McPherson, James M. *Crossroads of Freedom: Antietam, The Battle That Changed the Course of the Civil War*. New York: Oxford University Press, 2002.

McPherson, James M. *Battle Cry of Freedom: The Civil War Era*. New York and Oxford: Oxford University Press, 1988.

Majewski, John. *Modernizing a Slave Economy: The Economic Vision of the Confederate Nation*. Chapel Hill: University of North Carolina Press, 2009.

Morris, Roy, Jr. *Sheridan: The Life and Wars of General Phil Sheridan*. New York: Vintage Civil War Library, Vintage Books, 1993.

Phelps, W. Chris. *The Bombardment of Charleston 1863–1895*. Gretna: Pelican Publishing Company, Inc., 2002.

Roberts, William H. *Civil War Ironclads: The U.S. Navy and Industrial Mobilization*. Baltimore and London: Johns Hopkins University Press, 2002.

Rosen, Robert N. *Confederate Charleston: An Illustrated History of the City and the People During the Civil War*. Columbia: University of South Carolina Press, 1994.

Sears, Stephen, ed. *The Civil War Papers of George B. McClellan: Selected Correspondence 1860–1865*. New York: Plenum Publishing Corporation, Da Capo Press, 1992.

Sears, Stephen. *Gettysburg*. Boston and New York: Houghton Mifflin Company, 2003.

Sears, Stephen. *Landscape Turned Red: The Battle of Antietam*. New Haven and New York: Ticknor & Fields, 1983.

Stahr, Walter. *Seward: Lincoln's Indispensable Man*. New York: Simon & Schuster, 2012.

Still, William N., Jr. *Iron Afloat: The Story of the Confederate Ironclads*. Columbia: University of South Carolina Press, 1991

Taylor, John M. *William Henry Seward: Lincoln's Right Hand.* Washington and London: Brassey's, 1991.

Witt, John Fabian. *Lincoln's Code: The Laws of War in American History.* New York: Simon & Schuster, Inc., Free Press, 2012.

CPSIA information can be obtained at www.ICGtesting.com
Printed in the USA
LVOW01s1054160414

381941LV00001B/87/P